BackNtime

K. Carson Kirk

PublishAmerica
Baltimore

First printing

At the specific preference of the author, PublishAmerica allowed this work to remain exactly as the author intended, verbatim, without editorial input.

ISBN: 1-4241-1159-5
PUBLISHED BY PUBLISHAMERICA, LLLP
www.publishamerica.com
Baltimore

Printed in the United States of America

BackNtime

*In loving memory of my wife Irma Aleze Kirk and
others that meant so much to me. They left behind
lasting memories, and I dedicate my heart felt thoughts
to them in the words below.*

At first I titled it 'Bits and Pieces" about some stories of mine.
But after looking back at my life and memories I renamed it "BackNtime"
Back in time I go daily searching for footprints where I once trod.
Sorting through shreds of memories and wondering if they have been
pleasing to God.

My future footsteps may be a short journey as I slowly go on my way.
And I give thanks to him for my sanity so I can go back in time each day.
The faces I see are of friends and loved ones from many years past.
With their arms spread wide to greet me I feel my journey is ending at last.

But not before I tell their stories that they left behind.
I pray that God will be present and guide me as I go back in time.
Their memories are like a vase of roses that lost color and were pushed
aside.
But I can still see their beauty, yes faded, but to me they never died.

Acknowledgements

Many thanks to Shane Moad, and his wife Val, in far off Australia for allowing me to use their pictures and all the information they passed on to me over the Internet.

Without the Australian phrases, the Australian part of my journey back in the past would have been rather dull, but thanks to them and the Scottish brogue I tried to mix in I hope will make it a little more readable.

Also want to thank others for permission to use their pictures. And the ones that encouraged me to keep on with my manuscript you'll never know how much that meant to me because I became discouraged and was on the verge of giving up on it several times. You know who you are. So thanks again.

Thanks to Allan Young better known as the "Appalachian Writer" for all the help and advice he has gave me. "A friend indeed to a friend in need."

Prologue

Lee County is in the extreme Southwest part of Virginia nestled up against parts of Tennessee on one side and Kentucky on the other, and as you follow the Daniel Boone trail the three states come together at Cumberland Gap thirty five miles from where I was born and raised in Lee County Virginia, west of Pennington Gap, on Route 421 known as the Harlan Road. Lee and Wise Counties in Virginia, Harlan and Bell Counties in Kentucky are rich in coal along with other counties that join them. But the counties mentioned above are the setting for my journey back in the past starting in the nineteen thirties and into the nineteen fifties when demand for coal hit rock bottom and most of the underground mines shut down forcing thousands of miners to find work in northern states causing a mass exodus of the areas people.

I will try to walk with them from page to page as they move away, and follow one family all the way to far off Australia.

In the sixties and seventies new equipment became available, huge machinery to use in strip mining, plus massive augers for underground mining, now more coal was being mined than ever before but with fewer workers. One piece of new equipment with its components can mine as much coal as perhaps one hundred workers.

My father met my mother in 1925 the year she was assigned to teach at Pine Grove Grammar School on Elys Creek. They were married shortly afterward and that would be her first and last year as a teacher until many years later after most of her children were grown, she started teaching again. I have never been able to find out about that unless maybe I'm the culprit I was born in 1926. I have always thought that the time she spent in college was a waste of time, and maybe with that kind of attitude is why I didn't try to knuckle down and stay in school.

My dad's father owned a little hillside farm with a decent apple orchard, a barn and a house not a fancy one but never the less he had raised most of his children to adulthood in it. There were steep hills on either side that he somehow managed to clear off and raise corn to feed his cows, hogs, and one old workhorse named Dan.

There were a few acres of timber covered with hardwoods and some chestnut trees that had been wiped out by blight before I was born and by the time I was about eight years old the dead chestnut trees were seasoned just right for Lumber or firewood. I would help my father and mother gather firewood for the cook stove and the fireplace even though coal was plentiful I guess money was too short to afford it.

But the thing that has remained a mystery to me over the years is why my grandpa moved away and left his place to my dad. He never owned another place after that but rented and lived in several places.

In the late thirties he divided the land among his children giving my dad the old house and six acres around it. Many times I wanted to ask my grandfather why he would walk away from a home that he had worked so hard on for so many years.

I can see him now as he cuts a chew from a plug of Apple chewing tobacco and puts it in his mouth with crooked arthritic fingers. He has been gone for many years now, but he is still fresh in my thoughts and memories. Thank you grandpa, our family owes you a deep depth of gratitude instead of a fleeting thought now and then.

My dad was a coal miner working long hours entering the darkness of the mine before day-break and often getting home in darkness all for about one dollar a day back in the nineteen thirties.

My mother's workday began early and ended late also. She took care of the garden and many times hoed corn on the old rocky hillsides with help from the children, the ones that were big enough to handle a hoe. In the meantime the children kept coming and by the time I was thirteen in nineteen thirty-nine the number had grown to nine.

I quit school while in the fifth grade and worked for different ones hoeing corn or anything else that a skinny kid could do, one of my schoolmates and I got a job at a sawmill catching heavy green boards as they came from the saw and glided down the steel rollers. We had to carry and stack them some times higher than our heads. We soon found out that we were just kids trying to do a man's job and moved on.

The pay was about fifty cents a day which seems paltry compared to today or even the nineteen forties standard which improved greatly over the thirties.

Hazen Pennington, a good man in Lee County Virginia, opened a truck mine in the Napier hollow off the Elys Creek road. He hired several people, adults and youngsters like myself to grade a road through the woods to the mine. The pay was fifty cents a day to cut down trees, dig out stumps, move rocks and tons of dirt by wheelbarrow.

He finally ran out of money and promised to pay us in coal as soon as the mine became operational. I worked out thirteen tons of coal and he delivered it a ton at a time over the following winter, enough for the cook stove and the fireplace, the first winter that I was free of cutting wood.

Then in the late thirties as I stated earlier my grandfather divided his land between his children, his daughter Onie, got the six acres that joined ours on the left and ran down to the creek. Her husband my uncle Lloyd Martin, decided to build a house on a bank right at creeks edge to rent out. He asked me if I would help my dad grade out a space for the house.

"I'll pay you twenty five cents a day, you keep track of the days and you can trade it out at the store."

Of course I gladly accepted his offer and tore in to the steep bank with pick, shovel, and wheelbarrow.

My dad would work to build a rock wall at creeks edge on his days off from the mine and I would keep filling it in with dirt. I worked at it for most of the summer and finally a space big enough for the house was ready, backed up by a nice looking wall built from fieldstone to protect from the creek waters that could become raging during heavy rains.

The only draw back was the high bank in back where all of the dirt had been removed caused loose dirt to slide down during heavy rains over the years.

My uncle ran a general merchandise store at that time and I traded out my wages for denim overalls, shirt, and a denim inner lined jacket, which was much warmer than the ones I had ever had before.

And of course I splurged some of it on candy, ice cream, etc. before turning the rest over to my family, which I was happy to do.

We later bought the rental house and moved there, leaving the old house standing forlornly in the background. In a way I never moved out because in my mind I often return there and can still hear the grunts and squeals of the hogs in the lot in back. Hear a familiar cowbell ringing, follow the sound and spot the old jersey cow grazing on the hillside.

But the clearest memory of all is the noise and gaiety of eleven children at play unaware of just how poor we were. It's funny that years later I realize it was probably the hardest part of my life, but yet I long to live it all over again.

My dad could do a pretty good job cutting hair and neighbors would show up pretty often to get a haircut. All free of course because the most of them were in the same boat as we were and didn't have enough change in their pockets to go to a barber.

He would always complain about my hair growing around the side of my neck instead of straight down. "It's hard to cut." He would say. I can remember a few times that he'd tell me to be still, and jerk my head even though I was being very careful not to move.

It was during one of these times when I was about thirteen that I decided he would never cut my hair again and he didn't, from then on I managed to hold on to a quarter long enough to go to a barber in the little mining town St. Charles.

As I think back I have doubts that I did the right thing considering the old dull worn-out scissors and hand clippers that he was using and the tiredness that showed in his eyes.

I'm sure he must have been highly frustrated with life at times working hard trying to clothe and feed a gang of kids.

He died in 1969 at the age of 61 after suffering and losing part of a lung to the dreaded black lung disease. I pray God has a special place for long sufferers and combat soldiers because they went through hell here on earth.

In nineteen 1941 at the age of fifteen my uncle gave me a job at his store. A turning point in my life for sure because with the experience and the facts of life I gained while working for him, plus his guidance made up for my lack of education just enough to let me get by in life.

I feel forever indebted to him, he was married to my dad's sister and was not my blood uncle but I will always remember him as one of the finest men that I ever knew.

Twin brothers were born in 1943 at our new home to make a total of thirteen. Eleven were born in the old house. My dad would often laugh and say. We wanted an even dozen but got a bakers-dozen instead.

As of this date 2003 all the children are still living. Mother passed away in 1999.

I have often thought about writing something about that area during the war years of the 1940's and afterward when the coal industry hit rock bottom causing a mass exodus of its people to northern states to find work leaving behind once busy vibrant little mining towns to wilt away, and coal camps that once housed hundreds to be stifled and smothered by weeds and the slate dumps that surround them.

So I have decided to give it a try before time runs out, because at my age the years are flying by.

I might be disappointed with the way it turns out along with the few that might read it, but at least I will know that I tried.

So come along with me and we'll see what the out come will be. It's not about me, after the first thirty to forty pages I will tell you about some of the characters and we will follow the story of their lives throughout the pages. Some ending good and some not so good as stories go.

I will relate them in my own simple way because I simply don't have the ability to tell them any other way. So if you like to read behind a writer who uses big fancy words this is not your book to read and I warn you that you might be offended by some of the language although it pales to what you might hear from someone out in public using a cell phone, or the sleazy programs that are on television daily.

I use it because that's the way it was in that era and during World War Two, which at the time I thought was gutter language that would soon disappear after the war ended but today they have improved on that and taken it to a lower level, the sewer, which is about as low as you can go.

So if you're ready we'll get moving and go 'BackNtime' which is the title of the book.

Thanks for coming along.

In 1941 at the age of fifteen I started to work full time for my uncle Lloyd Martin in his general merchandise store at Stone Creek in Lee County, Virginia.

An alley ran along one side of the store, and a barbed wire fence lined the alley in back of several houses. Along side the fence on the alley side was a space for horseshoe pitching and there, usually late in the day is where you would find several waiting to show their skills at the game.

My uncle had an old Chevrolet pickup truck that was used for delivery and was always parked on that side of the store in the alley. I had only been working there for a short time and he had told me several times that I should learn how to drive.

"Go ahead get in the truck, drive it to the end of the alley and then back it up, back and forth real slow that way you'll get used to shifting gears and a feel of the clutch."

I was reluctant at first, there had never been a car in our family and I had never ridden in one any distance, a few times to St. Charles and Pennington Gap, and maybe once as far as Woodway a distance of about twelve miles from my home on the Harlan road.

But finally one day after I got caught up with my work in the store I slipped out and stood looking up and down the alley to make sure no one was in sight. I crawled in the old truck and with sweaty brow and shaky hands I cranked it up, pushed in the clutch mashed on the gas and let out the clutch, it lurched forward a few feet before the engine died. I had spent a lot of time in the old truck practicing changing gears and easing the clutch out without the motor running, but now with the motor running I realized all the practice did nothing much to help me drive this thing.

I cranked her up again and tried to ease the clutch out, this time she jumped ahead several times and finally leveled off to a low gear crawl, but to me it was no crawl, my hands were gripping the wheel, sweat running down my face, knees shaking but some how I managed to drive it to the end of the alley.

I shut her down and sat there for a while before I could get up enough nerve to try backing up. After several tries I started backing her up and was doing a pretty good job of it until I noticed I was headed for the barbwire fence. I quickly turned the wheel and took care of that but then I could see I was on course to hit the side of a storage building that sat behind the store, I turned the wheel again and headed back for the fence, I managed to avoid the fence again but headed toward the store building, I jerked the wheel again barely missing the wall, by this time I was back at the parking place. I shut her down, sat there and wiped the sweat from my face, held on to my shaking legs till they finally calmed down. Then I thought. 'That's not bad, I'll have another go at it tomorrow, sure am glad no one was watching.'

I got out and swaggered in the store where uncle Lloyd and another one of my uncles that worked there, Wright Kirk were exchanging grins with one another.

Then it hit me they had been peeking out the side door to the alley all the time I was hanging on to the steering wheel of the old truck trying to stay out of the fence on one side and the storage building and store on the other side.

Finally one of them spoke up.

"Drove the old truck yet?"

"Yeah." I answered. "Just got back from St. Charles."

Every day after that I'd jump in the old truck and drive to the end of the alley, back her up and drive down again, back and forth, got a lot of practice clutching and changing gears except for high gear, couldn't get up enough speed in the alley for that. I even got bold enough to do it later in the day while the guys were pitching horseshoes. I could hear them holler out.

"I wish you would get your practice in before we start our game." More than once I would come pretty close when backing up and one of them would hit the side of the truck and yell.

"Watch where you're going, you're gonna run over some body."

It was one of these times they scared the daylights out of me. I heard a loud bang on the back of the truck as I was backing up and some one yelled out. "Hold it you've killed a man."

I jumped out and ran to the back of the truck and there lay one of the horseshoe pitchers with his eyes rolled back in his head still clutching a horseshoe in his hand. As I looked down at him numbness swept over my whole body and I just knew that my world had came to an end. I held on to the truck bed and slid to the ground with tears in my eyes I looked at the guy and thought. 'I want to die too right here and now.'

About that time he could hold it no longer. He jumped to his feet and started laughing, everybody joined in and I took quite a ribbing.

Then about two weeks later someone rode with me, can't recall who it was. I drove up to the Pocket Power Plant a distance of about one mile, one way. Done pretty good and the very next day uncle Lloyd said.

"Take it for a spin, just drive slow and keep your eyes on the road."

So I headed up 421 Harlan road to my home three miles away. I got a good start, shifted all the gears smoothly but then got carried away in excitement. 'God what a feeling.' I thought. 'I hope my cousin Lynn is out in the yard when I go by his house so he can see me driving this truck. But as I passed his house he was nowhere in sight.

I parked in front of my house but not before blowing the horn to bring everybody out on the porch to see me get out of the truck. I spent a few minutes there strutting around and headed back down the road toward the store. I looked ahead and spotted my cousin in his yard, the house was on a hill above the road, the new road had taken some of their property right up in the yard and left a steep bank in front of the house. I started blowing the horn before I got there, wanted to make sure he seen me. Trouble was the house was on my right and I had to lay over in the seat to see him up the steep bank. As I waved I felt the right wheels leave the pavement and when I straightened up I could see I was headed for the ditch and before I knew what was happening the old truck was in the ditch bouncing up and down like a bucking horse. I held on to the steering wheel with all my strength and finally the old truck was back on the pavement. It must have righted itself because I'm sure my driving skills had nothing to do with it.

I drove real slow the rest of the way, never took my eyes off the road, not even when I seen a pretty girl sitting in a porch swing.

"Well how did it go?" My uncle asked.

"Oh fine." I answered. "Nothing to it, nothing to it." '

If he only knew.' I thought. He found out later and I was in for more ribbing.

Some time after that my dad went with me to Jonesville to get a drivers license. He had to sign because I was only fifteen years old.

I remember one of my older cousins Virgil Kirk about the same age as my dad was there to renew his license. I guess he noticed how nervous I was and said.

"Carson honey don't worry you'll pass that test, it's easy."

I did pass it and felt like I had conquered the world. We headed back toward Stone Creek tooting the horn and waving at folks along the way, even had my dad waving and laughing.

Looking back I see my life as a long journey with stopovers in many places, some for short periods of time that meant nothing or changed anything in my life. But I will forever hold the memories of the time I spent working at my uncle's store in Stone Creek, Virginia as the most important.

A time of youth and Innocence, a time of learning, a time of a more simple way of life, a time when the word love meant just that as apposed to the way it's used today which amounts to no more than a "Good morning how are you?"

A time when everyone knew right from wrong even if they didn't practice doing the right thing they certainly knew the difference. Today our youth are exposed to a number of things in schools and every day life that are labeled as gray areas and are no longer considered a sin. If you feel okay doing it, go ahead, is the standard today.

Most television shows are gutter rated and continue to get worse each year.

Hollywood and most of our big cities must be like Sodom and Gomorrah that the bible speaks of.

Some of our past and present elected officials would fit right in there along with a few supreme court judges, that have allowed mass murder of the unborn.

Yes it was a time in my life of coping with all the good natured ribbing that came my way that at the time I considered degrading but as time went on I began to realize my tormentors did it simply because they liked me and lasting friendships formed between us.

She asked me to take a tray of beef roasts from the display case so she could have a better look at them. I sat them on the counter in front of her, she had me turn each one as she made remarks like, "No that one has too much fat, why do you always turn the bad side to the bottom?" "Is this all you have?"

"Got a side of beef in the cooler." I answer. "If you want to take a look I'll bring it out."

"No that's too much trouble, can I go in the cooler and look at it?"

Didn't get many requests like that from a woman, but I thought. Why not?

can't blame her for wanting a good lean beef roast. So I walked to the cooler and opened the door, followed her in and closed the door behind us.

She looked at the side of beef hanging in front of her.

"I don't know about this." She said. "The three roasts you have on display look better than anything that would come from this, but right here looks lean, no there's some gristle, that's no good."

As she moved around and inspected it I couldn't help but notice how shapely she was, not a very beautiful woman in her face but very shapely. Then I thought. I'm only fifteen and she must be in her mid twenties, but when I get old enough to marry she's the kind of woman I want, shapely, friendly, and not at all prissy.

"Oh heck." She said. "I'll pick one from the three out there."

I opened the cooler door and followed her out. My heart sank as soon as I seen who had entered the store while we in the cooler, Walt and Henry, two of my worst tormentors when it came to kidding. And I could tell by the look on their faces that I was in for a hard time as soon as she left the store.

She picked one of the roasts and purchased a few other things. And even before she got out the door Walt and Henry, were exchanging devilish looks between them.

After an interval of silence Henry remarked. "Well ain't you gonna tell us about it?"

"About what." I answered.

Then Walt chimed in. "About what? Don't act so innocent what was you doing with that girl in the cooler? We walk in here and the store is empty and all of a sudden you follow that girl out of the cooler all red in your face and now you want us to believe nothing happened."

"Well by gosh nothing did happen, she wanted a beef roast and wanted to look at the side of beef to see if the meat was any leaner than the ones here in the display_____." They didn't let me finish.

"Hear that Walt?" Henry piped in. "She wants a beef roast, so they go in the cooler and when they come out she buys a beef roast right there out of the display cooler, now does that make any sense?"

"No it don't," Walt answers. Where's Lloyd? I wonder if he knows what all goes on when he leaves you here alone."

"You know that girl's married don't you?" Henry asks.

"Sure I know her husband." I answered.

"You do eh, well what do you think he'll do when he finds out that you had his wife in the meat cooler? Boy I'd hate to be in your shoes right now."

19

Walt and Henry both lived and worked at old Dominion Power Company about a mile away in the Pocket community. They would drive down to the store three or four times a week for groceries. And like a lot of other folks that got their groceries there, they came to visit, talk baseball, pitch horseshoes, and of course to kid me, and they seemed to enjoy that better than anything else.

They would start something and spread it around to some of the older fellows, Roy, Ed, and others and soon it would filter down to the younger fellows. I spent a good deal of my time trying to explain my way out of things. Now as I thought about this one I knew I was in for at least two weeks of explaining maybe longer.

I could hear voices in the alley along side the store and knew the horseshoe gang was gathering. Pretty soon Walt and Henry joined them. But just before closing time they came back in the store to get their groceries. My uncle had returned and I was bracing for what I knew was sure to come.

"Lloyd did he tell you anything?" Walt asked, nodding toward me.

"Tell me what? No he didn't tell me anything." My uncle answered.

"Tell him what we seen Henry."

Henry cleared his throat and hesitated as if he hated to tell my uncle what they had seen. Finally he said.

"Lloyd, I hate to tell you this, but we came in here while you were gone today and there was not a soul in sight. We stood here wondering where ever body was, lo and behold the walk in cooler door opens and there he is with a girl. Now what in the world would he be doing with a girl in the cooler?"

"Don't ask me." My uncle answered. Out of the corner of my eye I could see he was about to burst out in laughter. I could see there had been some nods and winking going on but at the same time I felt that I had to explain things. As I tried to explain they kept up a steady chatter.

"Wonder what her husband is going to say?" Walt asks.

"I hate to think about it." Henry answered. "Maybe we should keep it to ourselves."

Oh sure, I thought. You may not tell him, but everybody else will know about it before the week is over, looks like I'm in for a rough couple of weeks. I can hear it now.

"I heard you got caught in the cooler with a girl, did she warm you up?"

"Been in the cooler with anybody lately? There must be a better place than that."

Then one day about two weeks later the same young lady asked my uncle about linoleum. She wanted size 10+12 and a certain pattern and color. He told her he didn't have what she was looking for but had some on order that should be in by the end of the week. The linoleum came in on Friday and I remember thinking at the time. 'She'll be here tomorrow for sure and I hope I'm not the one that has to get the key and take her back there in the alley to the storage building.'

The beef roast thing had just about played out and I sure would hate to go through something like that again.

Around noontime on Saturday she walked in the store, I was busy with a customer and so were my uncles. I wasn't worried much about it at first thinking that one of them would be finished before me and wait on her.

But as much as I stalled trying not to be available to wait on her I finished before either of them and it was her turn. I nodded toward her and she asked. "Did that linoleum come in yet?"

"Yes." I answered.

"Can I have a look at it?"

As I reached for the key hanging on the wall I glanced at my two uncles, and was sure from the look on their faces that they had been stalling just as much as I had to make sure I waited on her.

I opened the screen door on the side of the store that led to the alley. As I followed her out onto the platform and down three steps I could feel the hush from the horseshoe gang as they watched. I stumbled and almost fell on the bottom step bringing low murmuring and laughter from the gang.

As I fumbled with the padlock I could feel all eyes on me, 'but maybe this won't be as bad as the beef roast caper.' I thought. I had noticed that my two worst tormentors weren't in the crowd. I knew some of these guys would carry it on for a couple of days but nothing compared to Walt and Henry.

Inside I reached for the string that dangled from the light bulb and turned it on. The single bulb didn't light the room up a whole lot because there were no windows in the little building.

She followed me through bags of cow feed, chicken feed, Etc. stacked on pallets on the floor, to the linoleum at the darkest corner of the building.

The linoleum was rolled around a cardboard tube and wrapped in heavy brown paper. I moved them around to find the size she wanted 10+12 then began tearing the heavy paper away on one end to expose the pattern and color.

I felt she would make a quick decision and I would be out of there before the crowd outside could cook up something.

21

As she bent over each roll of carpet I couldn't help but notice how nice she looked. 'Even her face looks much better than it did in the cooler.' I thought.

She finally found two that she liked but was having a hard time making up her mind which one to choose. In the meantime outside I heard a familiar voice from the horseshoe gang.

"How long has he been in there?" Then I heard a laugh from someone that I could recognize anytime. My tormentors had arrived and were eagerly waiting for me to step out in the alley with the beef roast lady. I knew I was in for another two or three weeks of embarrassment.

It seemed to take her forever but finally she said. "Sorry it's took me so long, I'll go home and get my husband, maybe he can help me choose the right one."

I followed her out the door to the alley and as I faced the door locking the padlock I wished I could get in the store without having to walk by that horseshoe gang. As I walked along behind her Walt stood looking at me with his hands on his hips, with that look. 'Oh yeah we caught you again.'

Back in the store I made myself busy, dreading to face what I knew was coming. Pretty soon Walt and Henry came in with that familiar devilish look on their faces.

Walt stared at me and said. "Well looks like we caught you red handed again, what's your excuse this time?"

Then Henry asked. "What was you doing in there all that time?"

"I was only in there for a few minutes." I answered.

"A few minutes is long enough." He said. "What did you go in there for?"

"She was looking at linoleum." I answered.

Then he laughed. "Hear that Walt, she was looking at the linoleum but she didn't buy any, just like the day she went in the cooler to look at the side of beef."

Then I blurted out. "She went home to get her husband to help her

_____

"What! You'd better hope and pray that she don't come back with her husband, ain't you afraid somebody will tip him off as to what's been going on?"

Walt and Henry usually went to town on Saturdays and today was no exception I gave out a sigh of relief as they drove away.

Within ten minutes after they left she returned with her husband to help her choose the linoleum. They made their choice and I watched her drive away with him holding the roll to the side of the car.

Then I thought. 'Durn it! Why couldn't Walt and Henry have stayed a few minutes longer and seen them haul it away?'

'But heck that's not the way they want it they'd rather hang me out to dry for another two weeks.'

I opened the screen door and walked on the platform facing the alley crowd, thinking I may as well get used to it. didn't take long for them to open up. "Boy you sure were in there a long time with that girl, what took so long?"

Then somebody else said. "You're darn lucky no one told her husband, I hope for your sake he never finds out."

'Yep looks like they've got me set up again may as well get used to

Sugar: I had heard lots of talk about her from some of the young men that hang around the store. They called her 'Sugar'. From what I gathered she had disobeyed and defied her parents at an early age. Their hope was that after she finished high school things would turn around for the better.

Her younger sister was just the opposite, straight A's in school, helped out around the house, everything that parent's expect from a daughter.

One fellow told me. "Ol Sugar will run with anyone, makes no difference with her if you take her to the movies or just for a ride and park somewhere along side the road. And hell! If you don't have a car or any money just meet her after dark on her back porch."

"Does her parent's know she meets guys on the back porch?" I asked.

"Sure they know, they gave up on Sugar long ago, they just let her do whatever she wants."

"Have you seen her yet?" He asked.

"No I don't think so, why do they call her Sugar, is that her real name?"

"No that's her nickname, you see from the time she could talk, she would call everybody Sugar, so it just became natural for folks to call her Sugar."

"You mean she ain't been in the store since you started here? He asked.

"I don't think so." I answer.

"Well you'll know it when she comes in cause she'll call you Sugar."

The next day was no different, it seemed that all the young fellows knew a lot about Sugar.

"You seen Sugar lately?"

"Oh yeah! I took her to the movies last night."

"Well I'm broke so I guess I'll have to settle for the back porch." The other guy remarked.

I'm only fifteen and not used to this kind of talk about girls, but she shore

23

sounds interesting. Most of these fellows are eighteen to twenty years of age and seem to know a heck of a lot more about girls than me. But I do look forward to seeing her.

A few days later a young girl comes in the store with a smile on her face that would win over any grouch. As she walked toward me I thought,

'That smile is directed straight at me.' Dang! She's so pretty, looks about sixteen or seventeen, long black hair, can't see the color of her eyes yet, but they must be brown. Blue blouse fits so snug, and one of them wide bottomed skirts, whatever you call them. 'I wonder who she is, then I thought, could this be Sugar? No it can't be, this girl is beautiful, the kind that would be easy to fall in love with.'

I was spellbound as she stopped in front of me. "Hey Sugar, she said. So you're the new guy I've been hearing about, well I have a list of things for you to deliver this afternoon."

As she handed me the list she said. " My Dad has a charge account here so he'll take care of that later."

About that time two young guys entered the store and as she turned away from me, she struck up a conversation with them and it was plain to see that she had called them 'Sugar' many times before. And what a let down, the smile that I thought was so special and directed only toward me was now even more radiant as she charmed these guys.

She went out to a waiting car and hopped in, she leaned over and kissed the driver on the cheek as they headed toward town.

'So that's Sugar, no wonder I've heard so much about her, She's a beauty, I'm surprised that one of these guy's hasn't ask for her hand in marriage, but guess that will never happen, cause Sugar loves them all I'm told. Then I thought I wonder if that includes me.

I finally came back to my senses and looked at the list that she gave me.

One fifty pound bag chicken feed, one hundred pound bag Purina cow feed, one hundred pound bag hog feed, three bails of hay. A note at the bottom read.

Please put everything but the hay in the padlocked room at the end of the barn, it will not be locked. Put the hay at the far end of the barn along side the horse stall.

Marty: Later that day after getting directions to the home I delivered the feed.

As I unloaded the hay I noticed a horse and rider coming toward the barn from a fenced in area. As they came closer I could see the rider was a girl sitting proud and erect in the saddle. I purposely slowed down just to give her time to get there before I left. 'This must be the perfect sister that I was told about.'

She halted the horse near the fence and stared at me, no smile, no howdy, no Sugar, no nothing. I finally nodded, but she didn't nod back.

"Pretty horse, what's his name?" I asked.

"I call him 'Cody', but my sister calls him 'Sugar' he answers to either one."

She looks younger than Sugar, about my age, she's pretty, but not beautiful like Sugar, and not once have I seen her smile.

She kept staring at me and I wondered if she was sizing me up. She looks younger than sugar, maybe about my age, she's pretty but not beautiful like Sugar, and not once have I seen her smile.

But then it hit me, who is it that's doing most of the staring? Here I am with my eyes glued to her face and at the same time trying to accuse her of the same thing. I got in the old truck waved goodbye and said. "See you later."

Then as I drove along I realized I hadn't bothered to ask her name or introduce myself. 'I bet she's irked that I asked the horse's name but not hers, oh well I ain't gonna worry about it I like her sister Sugar better anyway.'

Bud: So you finally seen Sugar" one of the guy's remarked later. "How you like her, ain't she a beauty?"

"Oh well she's not bad, but from all the things I've heard about her she's not for me. What's her sister's name?"

"Her name's Martha but they call her Marty. But I'll tell you this, she will never take over a man's heart like sugar does even if she lives to be a hundred years old."

"Sounds like you like sugar a lot."

"Yes I do. I like her more than I care to, and you will to before it's over just like the rest of us guy's she has a way with you that don't come across very often in women."

"What's that?"

"She makes you feel that you are wanted and that she cares for you. When I first met her she really put a spell on me, and there for a while I was sure that she would choose me and only me if I would just be patient, but she's still running wild, so I've made up my mind that she will never change. I came to the conclusion that I will take what I can get and maybe some day someone will come along that will make me forget Sugar, but in the meantime she still makes me feel good."

I could see by the expressions on his face as he rambled on about Sugar that he really meant what he said. His name was—well we wont mention his name—instead I'll use his nickname, 'Bud.' Many times in the last few weeks I had heard remarks from some of the guys. One said.

"Went skinny dipping with Sugar late yesterday at the upper dam above Old Dominion."

"Oh yeah, better not let Bud find out, it's really getting to him, can't figure how he can care so much for her, heck he knows what she is, and God knows she will never change."

"Well I can understand it." Another replies. I've got feelings for her, and you know damned well you do to, she's gonna break a lot of hearts before she leaves this world. It just happens that Bud is the first one, but he sure as hell won't be the last."

Hoss: One of the guys came in the store one day and asked me in a loud voice so everyone could hear. "Heh! I seen you parked above the Pocket late last Sunday."

"You're craz-crazy" I stammered. I was home all day Sunday."

"Did you take the old truck home with you?" he asked.

"Sure I did." I answered. "I take it home every day."

"Well as shore as I'm standing here, that old truck was parked up there and I recognized Sugar, and I thought it was you, did you let somebody else have the truck Sunday?"

Everybody's looking at me and I know my face is blood red cause it feels like its on fire.

Then instead of saying "No" and let it go at that, I blurted out. "Where was it parked?"

"Right there below the upper dam where everybody parks to smooch, you know where it is, under them oak trees along side the river."

Just like the times before, I could sense that no one really believed it but for some reason I couldn't hold my own with these fellows when it came to kidding.

He was one of the young fellows nineteen or twenty, and when it came to ribbing me he was on a par with the older men.

After that I cringed every time he walked in the store because it seemed he was determined to embarrass me with something about Sugar.

Then one day he took me aside and said. "I've been having a lot of fun with you about Sugar, I hope you don't take it to heart, it's all in fun."

"Oh yeah! But you're having all the fun." I answered.

He slapped me on the shoulder and laughed. "Want me to tell you what's going to happen one of these days? If Sugar ever gets you in the right place, she'll be all over you before you know it, so you may as well get ready for it."

"You're full of shit 'Hoss.' (His nickname) I don't want nothing to do with Sugar, I can pick em better than that."

"Ah come off that B.S. boy, you're only fifteen, you ain't been no where, ain't seen nothing, still wet behind the ears, and much to young to be in the company of the likes of Sugar, but I guarantee you that one of these days Sugar will take you to where you've never been before, and once that happens you'll be right in Sugar's clutches and coming back for more just like me and some others."

As I watched him walk away I had mixed feelings about what he had said despising him for his hateful ways but wondering if what he told me about her would come to pass, 'something to look forward to' I thought.

Then on a Saturday a short time later Sugar's father and mother came in the store. They were on their way to town to take in a movie, they would do that about once or twice a month and leave their Grocery and feed order on the way by.

"Put the groceries on the back porch." Her mother told me. "There's nothing on the list that will spoil, and you know where the feed goes, the feed room is unlocked."

Then I thought, 'Marty must not be home either, and I know Sugar ain't cause I seen her go in the Café across the way just a few minutes ago.'

'Too bad that Marty wont be there, I have seen her several times on my delivery trips and I feel that she's not all that bad.'

Once I mentioned that Cody looked like he would be fun to ride, and she replied. "Yes he is come out here some Sunday and I'll let you ride him."

"Sounds good to me I'll let you know." I answered.

Heck! I thought. Just my luck she won't be home, I intended to tell her I would be there tomorrow afternoon.

I got busy filling the list, put the groceries in the truck and drove past the horseshoe Pitcher's to load the feed. As I was heaving a bag of feed in the truck, someone from the gang remarked.

"Should have seen him the day he came out of there all red faced with that girl he was showing the linoleum to."

27

"Oh yeah!" Someone else remarked. "Wait' till Sugar gets him cornered he'll have more than a red face. And just as sure as today's Saturday she'll corner him one of these days."

I recognized that voice, my young tormentor, 'Hoss.' Unlike the other guy's that ribbed me constantly, I had begun to develop a dislike for this guy. There was something about him that surpassed good-natured kidding.

I pretended I hadn't heard as they laughed.

I hoisted the last bag of feed on the truck and checked the list to make sure I had everything, as I turned to lock the padlock I heard another familiar voice.

"Hey Sugar! You ready?" I'll ride with you, I left the house without my sweater I'll need it at the drive in movie tonight."

I could hear murmur and laughter from the horseshoe gang. They were truly enjoying what they were seeing.

"Yeah I'm ready." I stammered.

As I backed the truck past them I heard 'Hoss' say. "Remember what I told you a few minutes ago, he's in for the ride of his life, can't wait to see him crawl out of that thing after she's through with him."

As we rode along Sugar pulled her skirt up and I could see above her knees. She slid over in the seat almost up against me to look in the rearview mirror on the pretense of smoothing out her hair. Finished with that, she stayed put and rested her left arm on the top of the seat and played her fingers along the back of my neck.

As we passed the 'Pocket' community at Old Dominion Power Company the water was spraying over the lower dam and there were many rainbow's making it a beautiful sight. And I thought. 'Gosh! She's so pretty but I just don't know how to handle something like this.'

I glanced over as she rambled on about how much she enjoyed my company and, "Hey Sugar, lets go to the drive in some Saturday night, you need to get out and enjoy yourself, how old are you Sugar?"

"I'm fifteen," I answered. "And I don't like drive in movies."

"You don't like drive in movies! Have you ever been to one?"

"No I ain't.'

"Well now Sugar, you should go to one before deciding that you don't like it, and there's other things that you might want to try. You might be surprised how well you like it."

By this time she has gotten closer to me and is running her hand over my leg.

I thought. "God I'm going to die, her beauty and teasing is killing me, but I must resist her, I must."

I pressed the gas pedal and sped up so as to get there as soon as possible, as I rounded a curve on the narrow road I had to swerve toward the river to miss a huge coal truck. I hit the loose gravel on the shoulder of the road and darned near lost it.

"Heck fire Sugar! You're gonna wreck this thing what's the big hurry?"

Then she laughed as she dropped her arm around my neck and raised herself to kiss me on the cheek.

We finally rolled down the driveway along side the house leading to the barn.

I got out to put the groceries on the back porch. She grabbed a bag of groceries to help me, laughing and kidding me all the time.

"What's wrong sugar, why are you so nervous?"

"I'm not nervous." I answer. " I gotta get back to the store."

"Calm down, we have lots of time."

Oh yeah I thought. 'Go ahead and torment me but it ain't gonna work, I've got more will power than you think I have.'

As I placed the last bag of groceries on the porch, I was sure that she would go in the house to get her sweater and I would hurry down to the barn and unload the feed.

I rushed back and climbed in the old truck, as I sped toward the barn I heard some one holler from behind me, I looked in the rearview mirror and there she was running and laughing as she hollered. "Wait for me, wait for me."

At that moment I almost felt defeated but I told myself, 'hurry up get that damn feed unloaded, pay no attention to her, don't let her outsmart you.'

I let down the tailgate and reached for a hundred pound bag of feed, as I pulled it to me she grabbed one end of it. "Here sugar, let me give you a hand no use straining yourself."

She helped with each bag and I thought. 'Sure is easier this way, but at what price, I know she has something up her sleeve.'

We tossed the last bag of feed on one of the wooden pallets on the floor and turned for the door. She was leading the way and as we reached the door she reached outside for the open door and pulled it shut. Suddenly we're in total darkness and I thought. 'Oh shit, she thinks she's smarter than me but I'm gonna blow that door open and get out of here.'

As I headed for the door I walked right into her arms. 'Oh God she smells so good, her body's so soft she's kissing me, go on hold her, kiss her, no dammit get the hell outta here.'

I backed toward the door as she hung on to me, as the door opened and the bright sunshine revealed her beauty to go along with the softness and smell I closed my arms around her just for a second. 'Oh God! What can I do.'

I quickly released her and ran for the truck, she followed and was sliding over next to me before I could get the old truck going.

Then I could see a glimmer of hope as I remembered that she hadn't gone in the house for her sweater. 'I'll remind her of that and as soon as she gets out of this thing I'm gone, she can get back to Stone Creek any way she can, she sure as hell ain't gonna torment me anymore.'

As I slowed to a stop I said. " Heh! you forget to get your sweater hurry up I need to get back to the store.

"Oh Sugar, I have to confess I lied to you my sweater's at the Café."

At that moment I felt like pushing her out of the truck, but thought. 'Well maybe the worst is over, surely by now she must know that she can't get anywhere with me.'

She slouched down in the seat, stuck one foot against the windshield and the other one over her head against the top of the truck. The wide bottomed skirt fell down around her arms to reveal her shapely legs and everything right down to her waist.

She twisted around in the seat and laid her head in my lap. She reached up and as she tickled me under my chin she cooed. "Lets stop down by the trees on the way back Sugar."

"What trees? I aint stopping by no trees."

"Ah come on Sugar, you know that spot down by the river there below the upper dam."

"I ain't stopping at no damn dam and I ain't stopping no where else, so come on sit up in the seat before we get to the Pocket, what's people gonna think with your legs up in the air showing everything? I sure don't Walt or Henry to see this, I would never live it down."

She laughed. "Do they give you a hard time Sugar?"

"Yes they do, now come on sit up, if you don't I'm gonna stop and throw you out."

"Oh Sugar, this is so funny. She said as she sat up. Are you mad at me?"

"You bet I am." I lied. Because by now I had begun to realize how much I liked her and her fun loving ways.

She scooted over to the other end of the seat and as I glanced over at her

I thought. 'This whole thing has been a set up between her and 'Hoss', it all comes together now as I think of what he said as we were backing out of the alley.'

"Was Hoss behind this?" I asked.

"Behind what sugar?"

"You know what, all the crap you've put me through today." I replied.

"Oh don't be mad he thought it would be fun." She said.

"Well it ain't funny to me and you can tell him that."

We were nearing the store and I was thinking. 'I got through it all, 'Hoss' will spread it around and kid me for a while but nobody much will believe it anyway.'

All eyes were on the truck as I pulled in the alley and parked. She got out and I couldn't believe what I was seeing. There she stood pulling and straightening up her skirt. She must have unbuttoned her blouse all the way down before getting out of the truck. She buttoned it up as all the horseshoe gang watched even the ones pitching at the time. There they stood horseshoes in hand as they gawked.

Done with that, she started smoothing out her hair.

Hoss was looking at me and grinning that leering grin of his and I heard him say, "I told you so, I told you so, she worked him over he can't even get out of the truck."

All the gang roared with laughter and I thought. 'I shore am glad that my uncles are busy in the store and don't see this.'

Sugar stuck her radiant face in the truck and said.

"Oh Sugar, we must go to the drive in movie sometime, you don't know what you're missing."

As she headed for the Café I got out of the truck and thought. 'If I had a gun I'd shoot you and Hoss both right between the eyes, well maybe not you Sugar, but Hoss for sure.'

As I listened to the horseshoe gang's taunts and laughter I thought.

'Shit he sat me up and I ain't got nothing to show for it, I think it's about time I start dishing it out in his direction, yeah I've got an idea I think I can get his goat.'

Time will tell, time will tell.

The next day Sunday afternoon I sit on the railing that surrounds the flower bed in front of Cooper's Café waiting for some of the fellows to show up. We always meet there on Sunday afternoons.

Most of the time is spent talking about the things that happened the past week including the capers that I have managed to get myself in. but of late the conversation has turned to the war. It's December 1941 just two weeks after Japan attacked Pearl Harbor.

Most of the guys are already of age anywhere from eighteen to twenty one years old. There's talk among them about signing up. As one of them put it, "May as well go in early and get it over with, we'll have to go sooner or later anyway."

Once I remarked. "Yeah I think I'll enlist, no use waiting around for the draft."

That brought a chuckle and one of them said.

"B.S. you're to young to go off to a mans war, just like 'Hoss' said, you're still wet behind the ears. The damn war will be over before you ever grow up."

"That's what you think." I replied. " I'll be sixteen in less that two months."

"You will eh? Shit I wish I was sixteen I wouldn't have to worry about the damn war, and besides I would have Sugar all to myself. But hell you'll have her for the taking after us guys leave, but you won't touch her, but that's alright that way she'll be waiting and ready when I get back."

They all laughed and I could feel my face heating up so I turned away and pretended not to hear.

As I sat there thinking about all this 'Hoss' came to mind again, more than one of the guys had told me. "Don't trust him too much he's overbearing, a bully if there ever was one and always has been."

And I remembered one of them said. "He thinks he's God's gift to women."

From the remarks that they had made I came to the conclusion that none of them liked him but had learned to tolerate him.

I'm still waiting for someone to show up when I see a car pull in and park in front of the Café. I recognize the car. 'Oh heck it's Hoss, I didn't want to confront him this early but he's heading this way.'

"Well by God look who's here. I didn't expect to see you out today after Sugar got through with you yesterday. Boy you don't look good got no color in your face, but you'll be all right in a day or two. Well how'd it go? She took you where you've never been eh?"

"Hell no! I took her where she's never been." I lied.

"Don't gimmie that bull shit baby face, he leered. You ain't got nothing for no woman yet and probably never will."

"That's what you think buddy we hit it off just fine, said she had rather be with me than anybody she's ever been with. She went as far as to mention you, said you weren't worth a damn and that she only put up with you because she was afraid of you."

As I watched the leering grin fade I knew I had hit pay dirt. 'He can dish it out but he sure don't like to be on the receiving end.'

"You're lying like hell and you know it so let me warn you right now you better watch your mouth or you might wind up with it busted all over your face."

He turned and headed for the Café muttering something about, "Damned smart assed kid."

A few minutes later a couple of the guy's showed up and I told them what happened.

They had a good laugh but warned me. "Don't rile him too much he can be mean, real mean."

Two days later he came in the store and I could tell that he had something on his mind. He bought a carton of Camels and on his way out asked me to go with him.

"Something in the car I want to show you."

A lot of things went through my mind as I followed him out.

'What's on his mind? Is he about to beat the shit out of me? What's he got in the car that he wants me to see? A gun? Would this bastard shoot me?

Oh God! I remember what the guy's said. "Don't rile him too much he can be mean, real mean."

He opened the car door and motioned for me to get in, he went around and got under the wheel. I thought. 'Is this guy kidnapping me?' Should I jump out? He's gonna kill me.'

He sat there looking at me for about a minute before he finally said.

"Okay baby face, remember what I told you Sunday about keeping your mouth shut? Well looks like you have to be told again."

"Tell me what? I ain't said anything."

"Oh yeah, then how come everybody knows it.?"

"Knows what?" I answered.

"You know damned well what I'm getting at it's that damned lie you told about what Sugar said about me."

I thought. 'Why in the world would the guy's warn me not to push him too far and then go out and spread the story around?'

"Now I'm telling you again you keep your damned mouth shut, cause if you don't I'll beat the living hell out of you." He grabbed my shoulders and shook me as the leering grin came back to his face.

"Now get the hell out and stay out of my sight till you grow up if it's one thing I hate is a smart ass kid." I got out and went back in the store hoping that my uncle hadn't missed me.

I lay awake that night and wondered what I would do if he ever decided to beat me up. 'Not much of anything I guess, my skinny one hundred fifty pound frame is nothing compared to his two hundred pound plus solid muscled body. So my lips are sealed, I just hope the other guy's will shut up about it, cause if they don't that bastard will kill me.'

Lonnie and Carlie: Right down the road from Sugar's home, about a half-mile away near the community Church lived a coal miner 'Lonnie' and his wife Carlie.

They had met when Lonnie was nineteen and she was seventeen and still in High School. It had been love at first sight for the both of them, and within a year they were married.

Lonnie was born and raised in a mining camp near St. Charles, Va. and she was raised in a coal camp in Harlan, KY.

They both had dreamed of someday leaving the coal camps behind and live some place out away from the mines and all the noise and coal dust.

So they found this little house for rent on the Keokee road. The house was not that much better than the old camp houses but it had a little front porch with a swing and rocking chair. And best of all there was a fenced in plot to one side of the house for a garden.

The first ten years of their marriage was perfect, Lonnie managed to always drive a decent car and have enough money for their needs and do what some of the other miners could afford like going to town on a Saturday night to take in a movie, or just driving to nearby towns, Harlan, Pennington Gap, Big Stone Gap, and sometimes all the way to Knoxville, TN.

Carlie put her whole being into the little house and garden. She would see Lonnie off to the mine early in the morning. Spring time and summer were her most favorite times of the year. By the time the sun started to sparkle over the mountain she would be in the garden tending her peas, tomatoes, potatoes, beans, cucumbers, squash, okra, and all the rose bushes that lined the fence. She had a passion for rose bushes, roses of all colors but more of different shades of red. Passers by would refer to her as 'The Rose lady'

As time passed Lonnie saved for the day that he could put a small down payment on the little place. The owner had told him that he would sell it to him and was asking a reasonable price.

He and Carlie had already made a rough sketch of how to add a couple more rooms on to the small house in expectations of an addition to the family. They had been trying for ten years without success to bring a little one into their little paradise. Carlie had gone through the agony of two miscarriages, but they were determined to keep trying.

If some rain must fall in all our lives as the saying goes, I guess this one thing dampened their first tens years together.

Finally in the eleventh year of their marriage Carlie was in to her ninth month of Pregnancy looking forward to a boy for Lonnie's sake, or a girl would be fine.

They both adored the little seven-year-old girl of their neighbor a half-mile up the road that went by the name of Sugar, and she would call them Sugar as she passed on her way back and forth to grammar School.

She once had asked Carlie if she could pick some roses to take to school. Carlie took her hand and said.

"Sugar, you can have all the roses you want, take some home to your mother, I bet she likes roses."

So it became a common sight to see Sugar picking the roses that hang over the fence next to the road on her way to school and on her way back home.

Carlie noticed that she preferred the red roses, never seen her take a white or pink, so one day she asked her.

"Why don't you take some of the pink and white roses Sugar they're beautiful?"

"No, she answered. I like red roses."

"Well that's alright Sugar take all you want there's plenty of the red ones."

Shortly after Lonnie arrived home from work one day in early spring Carlie started having labor pains. They didn't have a phone so he hurried to his car, sped to Stone Creek and called the Doctor at St. Charles, from Cooper's Café.

About thirty minutes later the Doctor arrived, and one hour later little Lonnie Jr. popped into the lives of Lonnie Sr. and 'the rose lady Carlie.'

Lonnie stayed home from work the next day.

The next morning, the now eight-year old Sugar was at the fence picking her favorite red roses to take to school.

Lonnie had been watching for her, he walked out on the porch and asked her to come in. "Got something to show you," he told her.

She laid her fresh picked roses on the swing and followed him in the house. He showed her to the bed where a smiling Carlie was holding Lonnie Jr. close to her heart.

At first she said nothing and seemed to be confused. But then the radiant look that only Sugar could put forth came over her face as she rushed forward shouting," Oh Sugar! Oh Sugar! When did it come, what's it's name?"

"It's a boy I named him Lonnie after his Dad," Carlie answered.

"Oh Sugar," she said as she rubbed his little hands. " You're so sweet Sugar."

Lonnie and Carlie exchanged knowing looks. He would always be Sugar to her just as was everybody else.

Lonnie had once told Carlie when they were wondering why she called everybody Sugar. "One thing good about it you don't have to remember names, maybe that's why she calls everybody Sugar."

Before leaving she ran to the porch swing and brought back a single red rose and laid it across Lonnie's little arms.

"Here Sugar, a pretty red rose just for you I'll stop in on my way home from school, bye Sugar."

So it would be, as long as the roses were in season, a single red rose delivered to Lonnie Jr. twice daily. "A red rose just for you Sugar."

Lonnie finally saved enough to put a down payment on the little place, and with the help of one of his miner friends found an old house that was ready to be torn down. The owner wanted it out of the way so he could build a better house, so he said. " You tear it down and haul it away it's yours."

Within three months the little house became two rooms larger with a few pieces of new furniture scattered here and there. Outside, the fence got a fresh coat of white paint that brought out the color in the red roses even more.

Things are going well at the little paradise house on the way to Keokee.

Six years later just after Little Lonnie's birthday Sugar stopped in for her daily visit, as she handed Lonnie JR. a fresh picked red rose, Carlie could see that something was wrong. Her radiant smile had been replaced by sadness or fear. Then she noticed bruises on her arms and shoulders and her eyes were red from crying.

When Carlie asked her about it she began to cry and quickly ran from the house. She watched her as she disappeared around the curve on her way home.

Carlie was puzzled and thought about following her home just to see if her parents knew what the trouble was, but thought better of it thinking maybe it could be something that was family related, or could it be she got into a scuffle at school? 'After all she's fourteen years old and kids can get quite rough with one another at that age.' She thought.

Later on when Lonnie came home from work she told him about it. Lonnie listened closely as she described the bruises, and now that she thought about it she remembered that her dress was all soiled and wrinkled.

A scowl came across Lonnie's face. They both had formed a bond with Sugar and thought of her almost as one of their own. She and little Lonnie loved each other like brother and sister.

They talked it over and decided not to confront Sugar's parents until they had a chance to talk with Sugar again about it.

"If she won't tell us then we'll have to go see them." Lonnie stated.

She stopped by every day the rest of the week but Carlie waited till Lonnie was there on Saturday before mentioning it to Sugar.

They watched as she picked a red rose alongside the fence for little Lonnie. As she came up the steps to the porch the bruises were clearly visible and Lonnie thought. 'No school kid did that in a scuffle, the person who done this is a very strong person with a lot of grip.' He could clearly see the bruises came from someone gripping her arms and shoulders, not from slapping or a blow from a fist.

They watched as she handed little Lonnie the red rose. Little Lonnie squealed as they embraced.

They could sense that she was ill at ease and was on the verge of leaving. So Carlie ask her to keep an eye on Lonnie Jr. while her and Lonnie Sr. grilled some Hamburgers.

"No I have to get on home." She said.

"Oh no Sugar, don't go it won't take long you always have hamburgers with us on Saturday, little Lonnie will be disappointed if you go."

"Okay" she answered. "But I can't stay long."

Nothing much was said as they ate the hamburgers. Carlie brought out some apple pie and ice cream and they all laughed as they watched little Lonnie clowning around after he ate all he wanted.

Lonnie Sr. reached across the table and put his finger on one of the bruises and asked.

"Sugar, who did this to you?"

She dropped her head and whispered.

37

"One of the girls at school, we were fighting."

Lonnie looked at her for some time and she would not face him. Finally he said.

"Now Sugar, you're not being truthful, come on tell us what happened, cause if you don't I intend to find out, one thing I do know, no school girl put them bruises on you."

She began to sob as Carlie held her, little Lonnie was troubled he had never seen her cry before.

Carlie whispered. "Will you tell us Sugar? Tell us what happened maybe we can help you." She looked up at Carlie and said. "I'll tell you but I can't tell him."

Lonnie took little Lonnie's hand and headed for the porch so Carlie and Sugar could be alone.

About twenty minutes passed before they came on the porch. Lonnie could see that the crying had never stopped from the redness of her eyes. And as he glanced at Carlie he could see that she was very upset and had been crying also.

Sugar ran over and hugged little Lonnie once more before running down the steps on her way home.

Carlie came over and embraced Lonnie crying uncontrollably. Lonnie knew that something had happened to a sweet young girl just barely fourteen years old that would haunt her the rest of her life.

"Oh God! Oh God Lonnie, She's been raped." She sobbed. "God help her she's been raped"

He tried to wipe away her tears as she told him all that Sugar had told her.

"Who done it, did she know him?" He asked.

"Yes, it's that big strong boy that we see around Stone Creek and St. Charles, you know who I mean, sometimes we see him there at the store in Stone Creek pitching horseshoes.

Muscles showed in Lonnie's face as he clinched his teeth.

"Damn! What's being done about it, did she report it, how about her momma and dad do they know about it? How did it happen Carlie?"

"She was out riding her horse Cody, I think she calls him Sugar. You know how she likes to ride him out on the road even though there's plenty of pasture area. Her dad don't want her riding on the road but you know Sugar, when he's off at work she will do just that.

She was on her way back home after a ride of about four miles up toward Keokee. He drove by her headed toward Keokee, but turned around and came back. She said he stopped and asked where she lived and the horse's name, just small talk. Said he got out of his car and started rubbing the horse's neck. And before she knew what was taking place he led the horse off the road into the woods. Tied the horse to a tree and then pulled her from the saddle. Oh God Lonnie what can we do?"

"We'll report it to the Sheriff Carlie, that's what we'll do, that son of a bitch needs to spend the rest of his life behind bars."

"No Lonnie, we can't do that, he told her if she tells anyone he will harm her family. She's afraid he will kill her father. And you know yourself that he is capable of that, he has a bad reputation from the time he was ten years old."

She went on to tell him that Sugar had told her parents that the horse stumbled and fell throwing her from the saddle and pinned her underneath for a couple minutes. She convinced them that the bruises were a result of that.

" I promised her that we would never tell anyone Lonnie, its bad enough already, I sure would hate to see anything happen to her father."

Lonnie spent a sleepless night trying to decide if he should go to the police the next day. But as his tired eyes watched little Lonnie romp over the bedroom the next morning he could see Carlie's point of view. He shuddered at the thought of something happening to him and leaving Little Lonnie and Carlie behind.

Sugar's father would be leaving a wife and two daughters behind.

So they kept the secret and Sugar came by and picked a red rose for Lonnie Jr. daily.

Soon she was fifteen and they noticed that she had shed some of her moody spells and seemed more like the radiant little girl they had known through her preteen years. But by the time she turned sixteen Carlie was hearing gossip from more than one in the neighborhood about Sugar.

"That girls going bad." As one lady put it. "She's out late at night with different boys, even with that boy from down around Stone Creek, you know the one with the bad reputation, he's at least twenty one and she is just barely sixteen. I hear her mom and dad can't do a thing with her. And she has been such a sweet little girl and still is I don't understand it."

Finally on one of Sugar's visits Carlie confronted her with it.

"Sugar, I've been hearing talk around the neighborhood that you've been staying out late at night and causing your mom and dad a lot of worry and grief, why are you doing that?"

Sugar smiled and said. "I can't tell you why I do it, I guess I'm just trying to have some fun."

"But I hear that you're running around with the one that raped you, why would you want to do that?" Carlie asked.

She dropped her head and the tears started down her cheeks.

" I can't do anything about that he forces me he still says he'll kill daddy if I refuse him. And I have felt so dirty since he did that to me and even more now that he won't leave me alone I just don't care anymore, what else can I do?"

Carlie put her arms around her as she sobbed.

"I tried breaking away from him but he means what he says. Daddy was carrying a small basket of tomatoes from the garden last Saturday when a gunshot came from the woods there behind the barn the bullet tore right through the basket of tomatoes. Daddy thought it was a stray bullet from a hunter's gun he reported it to the sheriff and the sheriff said he thought so to, but I know he did it that's his way of warning me, so what am I going to do?"

Lonnie and Carlie talked about it the next day and came to the conclusion that maybe they should keep it secret.

"I guess we'll have to keep it secret and just hope somebody kills that bastard in one of his Saturday night brawls, I can understand why she's so afraid of him." Lonnie said.

As time went on her reputation became more tainted and she was 'That Girl' or "That girl is giving her parents all kinds of trouble she's throwing her life away."

Little did they know the burden that had been cast on 'That girl' when she was barely fourteen years old.

Finally on a Sunday in January 1942 I sat on the fence listening to Marty lecture me about how wrong I was about quitting school and going to work full time.

"You need to go back and at least finish high school if you don't you'll live to regret it later." She said.

"Heck by the time I went back to grammar school and then on to high school I'd be old and gray before I finished." I answered.

Then I thought. 'This is my first visit with her and all and all it has went very well. Her father and mother seem like every day folks and have treated me real nice.'

Earlier she had saddled Cody and laughed as I attempted to get in the saddle.

"Just relax now." She said. "He's easy to ride, take the path there it goes all the way to the back fence."

I headed out hoping Cody would sense that I was green as a gourd at riding and would go easy for me. It didn't take long to reach the back fence and I was real proud of myself, felt kind of like when I passed the drivers license test. 'Conquered the world again.'

But on the way back he seemed to get fidgety for some reason and broke into a trot. No matter what I tried to do to slow him to a walk he paid no attention. Here I am rolling from one side to the other trying to hang on.

I could see Marty in the distance and wondered if she had whistled for Cody to go into a trot. 'Dang! I hope he don't go any faster than this.'

I managed to hang on and wasted no time getting off once he stopped in front of Marty.

She was laughing as she said. "You did fine, but I thought you were a goner there a couple times, why didn't you slow him to a walk?"

"Heck! I tried but he wouldn't stop, did you whistle for him to come to you?" I asked.

By now she was shaking with laughter and I couldn't help but compare her to Sugar. 'The same devilish nature.' I thought. 'I'm beginning to like her about as much as I like Sugar.'

I climbed back on the fence and reached and took her hand as she climbed up.

I held her hand and listened as she went on about teaching me to ride.

"Come back next Sunday and I'll have you riding in no time." She said.

"I don't know about that I'm afraid you and Cody are plotting against me." I answered. She leaned toward me and rested her head on my chest as she shook with laughter.

I closed my arms around her and thought. 'God I like her.'

"Hey Sugar." Came a voice from behind us. 'No mistaking that voice, that's Sugar, what's she doing here I didn't expect to see her here today. Dang! Why is she butting in?'

She climbed on the fence beside us and asked. "Hey sugar, how'd your ride go?

Did you like it?"

"Oh it went okay I guess but I've got a lot to learn, maybe I'll like it better next time." I said.

"Sure you will Sugar, it's a lot of fun. Looks like you all are finished riding and in to something else now so if you don't mind I'll go for a ride."

I watched as she pulled herself to the saddle with ease and galloped away. She crossed the field in record time and disappeared down the fence line out of sight.

"Does my sister bother you?" Marty asked.

"No, no, not at all, why you ask me that?" I answered.

"Oh I just wondered, she has her ways and some times she gets a little reckless."

Now as I listen to her lecture me again about going back to school again I can't help but wonder. 'What if Sugar hadn't butted in? Heck we were doing fine I had my arms around her and it's no telling what was coming next.'

Across the field we see Sugar on her way back so we climb down from the fence and head for the house.

Before leaving I held her hand and thought once about kissing her on the cheek, but thought better of it when I noticed the expression on her face was still in the lecture mode.

As I drove toward home my thoughts were.

'I sure do like her and can't wait till next Sunday, I hope she forgets about teaching me to ride Cody, cause right now there's more important things than learning to ride a horse.'

The week finally dragged by and Sunday afternoon I sit and listen to Marty's father and mother talk. I'm beginning to feel more at ease around them. Her mother asks my age and the date of my birthday. Turns out that I'm only ten days older than Marty and soon we will be 'sweet sixteen' as her mother put it.

As we put our jackets on getting ready to go outside her dad says.

"So you're learning to ride, she should be a good teacher she started riding when she was six. But be careful you never know what a horse has in mind they can be unpredictable."

"I'm going to show him the picnic area first, we've got plenty of time." Marty said.

Out by the fence Cody stood patiently, she climbed to the top rail and wrapped one arm around his neck and rubbed his nose with her other hand while saying all kinds of sweet things. I thought. 'Heck! 'Cody ain't got it all that bad, good barn, good pasture and two pretty girls to whisper sweet things in his ear what else could a horse ask for.'

As she climbed down she said. "Okay Cody we're going down to the picnic area we'll be back soon."

We used a small gateway at one end of the barn to enter a cleared path through the woods. The path wound around trees and large boulders.

After about a half mile I saw a small clearing up ahead and as we drew nearer I could hear what sounded like water running swiftly over rocks.

As we walked into the clearing she said. "Daddy cleared this out and made us this picnic area, we love it out here especially in the spring and summer it's so nice and cool."

"He sure did a lot of work" I remarked.

"Yes he did." She said. " He worked in here two or three years on weekends clearing out all the trees and underbrush."

The area measured about two hundred feet one way and ran along side the branch about another three hundred feet. The water came from a higher level until it reached the cleared area. From there it plunged about twenty feet straight down over large slippery rocks to the level below and made it's way over smaller rocks until it disappeared on down into the woods out of sight.

A picnic table had been placed near the waterfall sheltered by a huge pine tree.

From another tree above the waterfall a steel cable had been looped over a limb with a large truck tire dangling from the other end.

We went up the embankment above the falls and Marty lifted herself in the tire, backed up the hill above the waterfall and shot forward high in the air above the waterfall as the water rushed over the rocks below. Back and forth, back and forth she sailed several times before she even had to touch her feet to the ground for a kick off on the back swing to keep going.

Finally she stopped. "Try it. She said. Its fun."

And it was fun, of course I had done this many times before at one of the old swimming holes where we held on to the bare cable as we would swing wildly out over the water turn loose and splash down.

When we grew tired of this she brushed back leaves from under one end of the picnic table and picked up some horseshoes. And after finding the stakes covered with leaves we pitched horseshoes.

I'm thinking. 'This is a lot better than trying to hang on to a horse I hope she forgets about that I like it out here better.'

After a while we sat at the picnic table and talked. It was a very nice day for January, warm enough in the sun but started to get a little chilly later in the afternoon. We inched closer together and I held her in my arms on the pretense of keeping her warm but, 'Oh God, I don't know how much longer I can take this, I go for a kiss and she responds.

We slip from the bench to the ground covered with leaves and soft pine needles. I manage to unbutton her jacket and put my arms around her underneath the jacket. Closer, closer we come together.

'Is this passion?' whatever it is I can't stop, I'm in another world, I think we both are.'

Then just as nature was on the verge of taking its course the real world returned.

"Hey Sugar's, what's you doing? Momma said you were out here, come on its getting late and cold lets go home."

As we tagged along behind Sugar I had mixed feelings, embarrassment, guilt, and at the same time mad as hell that she had horned in on us again.

'It's clear to me that she's trying to protect Marty and intends to keep an eye on us.' I thought.

Before going in the house Marty gave me a long warm look and said. "See you next Sunday, stay warm." At that moment I thought that in spite of all that Sugar had managed to deprive me of today I would gain it all back in the end. These thoughts were doused in a hurry when Sugar walked over to the truck before I could pull away and said.

"Look Sugar, I hope you ain't mad at me, but you see I don't want something bad happening to my little sister. You do understand that don't you?" I nodded yes.

As I drove away my thoughts were.

'But I don't understand you Sugar, you are a complete mystery you are bad, but at the same time you are good in a lot of ways and there's no way I can stay mad at you. You put a stop to my ventures into another world this afternoon but I will forgive you cause I know that you meant it when you said.

"I don't want something bad to happen to my little sister."

'That's your good side showing through Sugar, I like that.'

The more I thought about it over the week I could see that Sugar was right in spying on us and protecting her younger sister. Coming around to that way of thinking made me feel much better and I actually looked forward to keeping up my relationship with Marty.

Maybe this is just what I need to start all over on the right track this time.

Then in early February her parents came in the store with their Grocery and feed order.

"Both girls are home, they'll take the groceries in from the back porch, ask them for some of the cookies I made this morning you'll like them, made from my own special recipe."

'Good.' I thought. 'Sugar didn't say anything to them about what she seen last Sunday I didn't think she would, but it's good to know that she didn't for sure.'

As I came to a stop alongside the house I wondered if Marty was here alone. 'Could be because Sugar may have already left to start her weekend of fun.'

But no such luck, the screen door flew open and out popped Sugar on her way to give me a hand.

"How you doing Sugar." She beamed. "Here I'll give you a hand."

She's showing no signs of what happened last Sunday.

'Shucks!' I thought. 'She's not mad at me at all I was worried that she might be, and god she looks pretty today, I wonder if I should tell her that.'

I went back to the truck for the last two bags of groceries and she held the screen door open for me.

"Come on in Sugar, and have a cup of hot coffee and some of momma's cookies."

I sat down at the table and as she poured the coffee I noticed her blouse was unbuttoned at least two buttons more than it should be and wondered if she did that for my benefit.

"Is Marty here?" I asked. "No Sugar she left a few minutes ago she went down the road to visit Carlie, our neighbor. Little Lonnie "Sugar"I call him has been pretty sick for the past week so we've been keeping check on them and helping in any way we can."

"Hey I heard you turned sixteen this week, Momma said she was going to bake a cake for you and my little sister she'll be sixteen in a few days, so make sure you get here tomorrow, Mamma knows how to bake a good cake. I'll be eighteen next month myself and I'll give you a piece of my birthday cake too."

She rambled on saying that this is her last year of high school and. "I'm going to graduate Sugar, but just barely I never liked going to school."

I watched as she darted around putting the groceries away and wondered if she would start her teasing ways with me after she finished. 'If she don't I'm going to be disappointed for sure.' Then it hit me. 'Whoa! What about Marty?' But soon my attention was back to Sugar.

Finished with the groceries she sat down across from me still showing no signs of her old flirty ways.

"Here have some more cookies sugar."

"Yes they are good, tell your mother I said so." I said.

45

As she sat across from me I couldn't take my eyes off the partially open blouse and thought. 'Should I make a move? Maybe that's what she's waiting on.'

I thought better of it and said.

"I better get the feed unloaded and get back to the store."

"Wait till I get my jacket it's a little chilly out there I'll give you a hand." She said.

As we dropped a bag of Purina cow feed on the pallet next to a partially used bag of chicken feed I noticed a small pile of chicken feed on the floor underneath the bag.

"Daddy will have to set the rat trap in here again or find out how that rat gets in here." She said.

As we tossed the last bag of feed on another pallet her head was turned away and I reached out to touch her, but didn't.

"God what a difference the other time I couldn't wait to get out of here but now, oh hell I've got to do something.'

This time I led the way to the open door. And just as she had done the other time, I reached out and pulled the door shut.

I turned in the darkness halfway expecting her to go around me and out the door.

'But no she's there, she's warm, she's responding, it wasn't meant to be last Sunday with Marty, but nothing can stop this.'

Outside I heard Cody snort but no worry there, he always stands at the fence and watches me unload the feed. Guess he sees the two bales of hay still in the truck that I have to unload down by the barn stall.

We wound up on top of the bag of chicken feed and the Purina cow feed, not very comfortable but who cares. And there with the mixture of Sugar's sweet smell and the Aroma of cow feed smelling like molasses, passion took over and nature ran its course. Outside Cody snorted one more time. We lay there for a few minutes longer and I could hear the chicken feed running from the hole in the bag to the floor. Then I thought of what she said a few minutes before about her Dad setting the rattrap and started to laugh.

"What's so funny Sugar?" she asked.

"Oh nothing. I said. I was just thinking I'm glad your Dad didn't have that trap set, would be just my luck to get caught in a trap."

I got myself together and groped toward the door. I pushed it open and turned to see Sugar smoothing out her skirt. As she walked toward me I noticed that she was looking past me outside toward Cody with a frown on her face. As I turned to walk out I could see why. Cody was at the fence as I expected but so was Marty. There she sat in the saddle much like the first time I seen her, no smile, no howdy, no nothing. I was speechless and was glad when Sugar broke the silence.

"Oh Sugar, I thought you were going down to see little Lonnie?"

"I changed my mind I'll go down there later." She replied.

As Sugar headed for the house I cranked up the old truck and drove to the other end of the barn and unloaded the hay.

Marty never took her eyes off me as I drove by on my way out. Reminded me of a statue there in the saddle, no matter which way you move the eyes follow you. I heard a long loud 'Neigh' from Cody just as I left the driveway. Then I thought of the rattrap again. 'But this time its not funny, shit! Marty set this trap and I took the bait and walked right in.' 'May as well forget about the birthday cake tomorrow, how can I explain to her mother why I didn't show up?' 'What caused me to do this, was it Sugar? By this time I'm talking out loud as I pass the pocket community. 'Hell no its me, I could have walked out of that damn feed room just like I did the first time.' But as I thought back I could still feel the warmth of Sugar as we clung to each other atop the chicken and cow feed.

'Nothing could have stopped it. What a way to start sweet sixteen but I've lost Marty.'

Doc: Over a period of three days Lonnie Jr. grew steadily worse, so Lonnie Sr. called the Doctor at St. Charles.

After a brief examination the doctor turned from the bed to the worried faces of Lonnie Sr. and Carlie, standing behind him. He dropped his head and stared at the floor knowing the news that he was about to tell them would break their hearts.

He had seen several cases of this disease for about three years now and the results weren't all that good. They usually died within seven to ten days, and the few that had survived were now struggling through life without being able to talk or hear, loss of limb or handicapped in some way, and in most all cases brain damage.

Finally he looked up and reached out to touch them. "I'm afraid the news is not good." He said. "He has Meningitis and as of now there's no cure. I will tap his spine, that's the only procedure that shows any promise up to now. But I'll have to do that here, because the state law requires that anyone with

Meningitis be quarantined to his or her home. And that means the both of you will be confined here also, I am the only one authorized to come into your home till this is over. I'm sure you have neighbors that will bring you groceries or anything else that you might need and place it on your porch."

"How bad is he Doc, what's his chances?" Lonnie asked.

"Well as I said before there's no cure, I'll do the spinal and all we can do is pray that in the next few days he'll improve."

Lonnie held Carlie as she cried. "Oh God! Oh God! Please let him live, please God don't take him from us."

The doctor went out to his car to get some things needed for the spinal tap procedure. And as in all the other times he had faced situations like this that would most likely end up in death he was saddened. 'Sometimes I wonder if it's worth all the loss of sleep and heart ache I witness as I make my daily rounds among these mining families?' He thought. 'It hurts me too but I can't let them see that.' As he searched for the things he would need among all the medical gear that was strewn through the car, tears began to flow. and he mumbled out loud. 'God please help me, lead me through this procedure and let this boy live, as you know it's breaking their hearts. And Lord let me sleep tonight, I don't know how much longer I can go on without rest.' Then he reached for the pint bottle of Bourbon that lay on the floorboard and took a long swig. He slipped it in his inside coat pocket. 'May as well take it with me.' he muttered. 'I'll be here for a while.'

Four days later Lonnie Jr. lay in his casket in the little neighborhood church surrounded by many flower arrangements, but mostly fresh cut red roses.

The whole neighborhood had turned out and folks from Stone Creek and other communities had come to pay their respects.

The Pastor: The pastor stood and looked out at all the sad faces and wondered what he could say that would bring comfort to them especially Lonnie Sr. and Carlie.

He had noticed Carlie was taking it very hard and wondered if she would ever

recover from it. It had been plain to all the people in the neighborhood that she literally worshiped Lonnie Jr.

Finally he cleared his throat and said. "I want to thank all of you for coming to this celebration today. Yes you heard right, I did say celebration. God has decided to take Lonnie Jr. out of this world of strife. Why? Well maybe he don't want him to face all that's ahead, we have a raging war going on that has already taken some of our young men off to foreign lands, and we all know some of them will never return."

"God's ways are sometimes hard to understand, but you can be assured he does everything for a good reason. He placed Lonnie with Lonnie Sr. and Carlie a little over ten years ago. I remember the first time they carried him in this church and the happiness that showed on their faces."

"So all of us here have parted with Lonnie today, but it's cause for celebration not sadness. God puts us all here for a time and we never know how long he will allow us to stay. In Lonnie's case he let him be among us for just over ten years, then whispered.

"Your time is up Lonnie I'm taking you home. So lets rejoice and sing the Lord's praises for taking Lonnie out of this wicked world to a better place where there's no pain or sorrow. Lets live our lives in a way that will be pleasing in the eyes of our Lord and when he whispers our name we will see Lonnie and all our loved ones again and will be together forever."

As he went on he said a lot more that was consoling but it didn't have much effect on Carlie.

They laid him to rest in the little Cemetery in back of the Church. I heard later that Carlie would not leave his grave site and Lonnie Sr. stayed there with her all night.

Over the next few days Carlie literally went to pieces. Lonnie stayed home from work to be with her. The neighbors, especially Sugar, Marty, and their parents spent a lot of time trying to console her, which wasn't easy for Sugar because she was very close to little Lonnie and was trying to hide a broken heart herself.

After several weeks the bills were piling up and Lonnie needed to get back to work. Folks from the church organized a group to take turns staying with Carlie during the day until he got home from work.

Carlie would hang on to him and beg him not to leave her every morning as he was leaving. And weather permitting she would sit on the porch all day long talking to her self and passers by.

"God took little Lonnie and now Lonnie's left me. He's never coming back.

I don't want to live any more, please God take me."

She was overjoyed to see him when he would come home from work each day and would calm down considerably until the next morning when he started getting ready to leave for work again.

As the days passed she seemed to be getting worse and her condition along with losing little Lonnie was taking its toll on Lonnie.

A man from the Church came to talk with Lonnie and was telling him that Carlie was subject to burning the house down by accident or hurting her self some way.

"Why don't you commit her to the Sanatorium in Marion? She will be well taken care of and it's not that far away, you can visit her often."

"No, I will never do that. Lonnie replied. She'll be with me right here in this house till one of us dies."

Rose bushes still lined the fence out side the little house on the way to Keokee and everything looked the same, but inside there was no joy and laughter.

God reached down and took one of his own from the little house reminding all of us that there is no such thing as paradise here on earth.

Tex: He was raised by his grandparents in one of the hollows off the Pucketts Creek road. His mother died shortly after he was born, his father? Well only two people knew, and up until now both of them had kept the secret from everyone else.

His mother had dated different ones after the age of sixteen, but he looked like none of them. But he did look like his mother, his facial features, expressions, the way he walked and her quiet gentle ways.

Pa and Ma: His grandparents were devastated with the death of their daughter but as time went by he filled a void in their lives.

They were pleased with his grades in grammar school and amazed that he passed all his exams with ease.

They bought him a new Bicycle in his first year of high school at ST. Charles.

And it became a familiar sight to see him riding his shiny bike with all the latest gadgets attached to it on the road between ST. Charles, and Pucketts Creek.

He could have taken the school bus but he preferred his bike.

After he graduated high school he did as so many of the young men before him had done, he went to work in the coal mine. And after about one year working hard at Benidict Coal Company above ST. Charles he had saved enough money to make a down payment on a brand new Chevrolet convertible.

He was pretty much a loner. Monday through Friday he worked and spent his nights at home with his grandparents. But his Saturdays were spent in St. Charles, at the little movie theater watching cowboy movies. Gene, Hoppy, Lash, Ken, Tex, and the other cowboy stars.

After the movie he would head for Shoun's drugstore and buy the latest dime Westerns as they were called at that time. He literally lived the old west through the Saturday cowboy movies and the dime Westerns.

He started wearing cowboy shirts and a wide belt with a huge silver colored belt buckle adorned with TEXAS in big letters.

So it became quite natural that he attained the nickname Tex.

Later he started wearing a small badge like trinket pinned to his shirt that had the head of a Texas longhorn etched on it and his nickname Tex that overlay that.

The Belt and the cowboy shirts that he had in many colors and patterns was all that he ever wore pertaining to the old west. Otherwise his clothing was pretty much the same as the other young men. But he was easy to pick out in a crowd his colorful shirts and the big shiny belt buckle soon became his trademark.

He took a lot of good-natured ribbing from some of the guys except for Hoss.

And it would be no different a Saturday morning here in the poolroom at Stone Creek.

He had came in early and played a couple games of pool and was now getting a shoeshine as Hoss walked in the door.

He sensed what was coming and wondered why he even bothered to stop here on his way to ST. Charles. He had so far managed to evade Hoss much of the time, but other times like this one he tried to ignore him and walk away simply because he didn't want to get into any kind of trouble.

As everyone could see Hoss had consumed a few early beers and was well on his way to another wild and mean Saturday night. He looked the gang over and when he spotted Tex the leering hateful grin marked his face.

"Well Damn! If it aint cowboy, how'd you manage to get away from yore mommy so early on Saturday little doggie? I see you got another new flowery cowboy shirt, why in hell don't you go out and buy some boots, cowboy hat, the whole damn works if'n you gonna play cowboy huh?"

Tex got down from the shoeshine stand and headed for the door.

Hoss steps in front of him and sticks out his right foot and rubs the bottom of his shoe over Tex fresh shined shoes.

"I see you got a shoeshine, going to town are ye, bet ye try to get one of them St. Charles pretties tonight? I know you won't but if you should by accident just holler and I'll take care of her."

Tex backed away and then side stepped toward the door.

Hoss reached out and grabbed his arm. "Whoa cowboy! Where th hell you think you're going? And why don't you talk to me, open yore damn mouth."

Then he reached and grabbed the Tex emblem and jerked it from his shirt tearing a hole in the brand new shirt.

He followed Tex out the door. "Don't you want yore damn trinket back cowboy? Here take it!'

As Tex reached for the emblem Hoss turned and threw it toward the little bridge that crossed the creek on the old road. It sailed over the four feet railing into the rocky creek below.

"Now go get it cowboy and get the hell outta my sight, nothing I hate worse than a damn cowboy that won't even talk."

Tex made his way down to the rocky creek bed and retrieved the shiny piece of metal from the shallow water.

As the guys watched him drive away toward St. Charles most of them understood why he evaded and took so much crap from Hoss because they felt the same way.

'Just trying to stay out of trouble, a run in with Hoss would never end until some one gets hurt.'

'Better to stay healthy and out of Jail he just ain't worth it.'

Bama: The following Saturday night in St. Charles, the sidewalks are crowded, jukeboxes blaring from the beer joints, the air is filled with the smell of popcorn, hot dogs, hamburgers, beer, tobacco smoke.

And smoke from the old steam engine switching coal cars near the depot.

Sweet smelling perfume from the girls and the ever-present foul odor from the sewer system. All of these mixed together turned out to be like a fine recipe blended to taste or smell like St. Charles. A smell and taste all its own long before the Colonel's secret recipe.

Inside one of the joints near the Depot every stool at the counter is taken and all the booths that line the other wall are full.

Some of the young men have made their choice from the girls on the street earlier in the day and are now enjoying their company till closing time.

A small selection box on each booth table, drop a quarter in the slot and five- records will play on the brightly lit up Jukebox at the far end of the room.

Young men and girls out for a night of fun, maybe next Saturday a different partner, a different Juke joint, a different song, a better movie, a better hot dog or a bigger hamburger.

But more than once a young man and a young lady from the street had their night of fun and went their way only to look for each other again the following Saturday, realizing that there had been something special about the night of fun they shared.

Many would turn a new leaf in their lives and vow to uphold the 'do you take this woman?' 'Do you take this man?' 'Through health and sickness,' 'till death you part,' and I do, I do.'

Some were stormy and lasted only a short time usually one or the other couldn't resist the sights and smells of St. Charles, and eventually would return to the call of the wild.

A young couple occupies a booth near the Jukebox in the rear of the room. They have been seeing each other ever since they first met on a typical rowdy St. Charles Saturday night three months ago.

He's a farm boy from Anniston, Alabama. And like many more from that area he came to St. Charles to get a job in one of the mines that surround the town. His older brother had worked at Leona mines for three years and helped him get on there.

Since nicknames were widely used among the miners, I'll call him 'Bama.' Bama was a quiet guy who minded his own business and tried to stay out of trouble, which was no easy feat on a Saturday night in St. Charles.

Gina: Three months earlier he was amazed at the sights and sounds on his first Saturday night in St. Charles.

"You be careful." His brother had warned him. "It's a tough town."

Of course he noticed the girls on the street, one in particular caught his eye and he wondered if he would have a chance with her. So happened the very next Saturday he spotted her in Shouns drugstore sipping on a coke.

He straddled a stool next to her and ordered a coke. Soon they were exchanging glances and pretty soon the small talk followed as it always does between two souls that are looking for someone to brighten their lives even it be for just a Saturday night.

Her name was 'Gina' a pretty girl who lived in the Bonny Blue Coal Camp above town.

Soon they were holding hands watching a movie at the little theater and afterward went for a ride in Bama's old ford car that he had purchased the week before.

Later that night they returned to St. Charles and had a snack at Jake's place.

Bama thought. 'If there is such a thing as love at first sight, then this must be what I'm experiencing. I've never felt this way about a girl before.'

And right from the time he sat down by her in Shouns, Gina knew that she wanted more from him than just a Saturday night of fun.

'I like him a lot' She thought. 'And I hope he likes me'

So in the weeks to follow Bama and Gina were together every weekend.

Today they took a ride all the way to Harlan, KY. Took in a movie, ate at the little café next door and headed back to St. Charles.

The old ford struggled to make it to the top of Black mountain on the way back and they laughed and wondered if one of them would have to get out and push.

Once on the Virginia side they stopped at a dancehall that had a bad reputation. They didn't know this, but soon found out that it was a very unhealthy place to visit on a Saturday night.

Back at St. Charles, Bama parked near the railroad on a little rise with a view of the theater, taxi stand, and juke joints. There as they had done many times in the past three months, they sat and talked oblivious to the noise of the old steam engine in back of them.

They decided to go in the little beer joint right across the street and have a bowl of beef stew before leaving for home.

As they sit there enjoying the stew and coke the owner and another fellow are busy popping caps from the beer bottles and rushing back and forth between the booths and the little opening in the wall behind the counter where the orders of hamburgers, hotdogs, etc. are placed by the cook from the kitchen.

Bama and Gina had decided to stop drinking beer more than a month ago.

"We don't need that to have fun, Gina had said. It's like throwing money away."

Bama had always enjoyed his beer and wondered if he could go along with that.

"Okay if you say so." He said. "You're the boss."

Now as he watched the guzzlers here and could relate with how they were going to feel tomorrow morning he knew that he and Gina had made the right choice.

He reached across and took Gina's hand and said. "What are we doing in here?"

"I don't understand, what do you mean?" She answered.

"We don't belong in a place like this anymore, so from now on lets find somewhere decent to spend our Saturday's, maybe up at Big Stone, or even Bristol, if the old ford will hold out that far."

"Sure," she answered. But she could tell by the way he was looking at her that he had something else on his mind.

He leaned forward and gripped her hand in both of his. "How about, how bout we?"

"How bout we what?" She asked.

"Oh hell! Will you marry me? He stammered. We can drive over to Harlan this coming Friday. I've already made arrangements to take Friday off, I hear it's easier to get a license and get it over with over there. Then we'll drive to Bristol and spend Friday night, Saturday and Saturday night in a nice hotel the arrangements have already been made."

She looked into his eyes as he squeezed her hand even tighter. 'God! What's happening to me? I've never felt like this before, is this a dream? I hope he's not kidding me.'

"Well damn! Say something." He whispered.

"Sure I will, you know I will, I can't wait." Tears trickled down her cheeks, he wiped them away with a napkin and leaned across the table and kissed her.

After a bit she started laughing.

"What's so funny? He asked.

"You made all the arrangements without asking me before hand, suppose I turned you down, then what?"

"Hell I would have went out and picked one from the street." He laughed. "Gina, some things are meant to happen and some folks are destined to meet and spend the rest of their lives together, I knew that the first time I laid my eyes on you there at Shouns drugs. I knew you would say yes because it's meant to be."

"But there's one other thing that I have to do. You have no father or mother, but I think I should ask your aunt and uncle, after all they have raised you since you were ten."

"You have nothing to worry about they'll probably be glad to get rid of me, and especially if you're the one that takes me off their hands, they both think a lot of you and have told me so a number of times, which I took as hints, hints, hints."

55

"Okay let's get out of this joint." He said.

As he reached to open the door it suddenly slammed into him from someone coming in. He and Gina stepped aside to allow the guy to pass.

He stopped and stared down at Bama, he was at least four inches taller and fifty pounds or more heavier. Bama had heard all about him and had steered clear of him in the past.

"Well if it ain't the Alabama boy out on the town tonight. Where ye headed? Taking this pretty girl with you eh? Well don't be in too big of a hurry, cause I think I'll take her off yore hands for tonight and let her get to know what it's like to be around a real man."

"I've had my eye on you and can see that you blow in here from Alabama and think you can take the prettiest girl in this town and call her all yore own, well by god! I'm gonna put a stop to that right here and now."

The owner was serving a booth nearby and immediately knew that he had trouble on his hands. The day had been trouble free except for having to call on some of the beer drinkers to watch their language, and a mild argument with some fellows when he refused to serve them beer when they walked in from some other joint already loaded to the gills.

'Damn! I'm tired.' He thought. 'Why in hell does this bully have to show up, it's only an hour till closing time, wish somebody would beat the living hell out of him, but guess I'll never live long enough to see that happen.'

He whispered to his helper. "Go find the chief, look in the pool room first. Tell him Hoss is here and there's going be trouble, hurry dammit! Before he tears the place up."

Bama knew he was in a losing situation, because he was no match for this guy. 'But I be damned if I'll give in to him even if the bastard kills me.' He thought.

He quickly grabbed Gina by the arm and somehow managed to duck out the door before Hoss could stop him. They ran across the street and up the little rise to where his car was parked.

'I've got a new pick handle in the car.' He thought. 'I've got to get it, that's the only chance I have against this manic.' But Hoss was close behind followed by a half dozen other guys. Some of these fellows had managed to pull Hoss from atop his victims as he pounded them into the ground on other occasions.

Bama reached to open the car door but too late, Hoss grabbed him by the arm and spun him around.

"No by god! Ye fight me fair and square, none of this tire iron or baseball bat shit. Fer all I know you may have a gun in there."

As he stood over Bama and the leering grin started to form on his face he was truly enjoying himself. And just as he did in all the other fights he slowly and deliberately threw both arms behind him to shake off his jacket. Bama took advantage of this and aimed a right to the jaw with every ounce of his hundred and sixty pounds behind it.

The force of the blow sent Hoss reeling backwards, he landed on his back in the sharp cinders close to the railroad track. His arms were only about half way out of his jacket and as he lay on his back he could not free them.

Handcuffed by his own jacket, Bama seen this and pounced on him and began to pound him.

The same bystanders that had pulled Hoss from his victims in the past and no doubt saved some of them from death now stood and watched as Bama landed blow after blow to the face of the Leering bully.

The old steam engine locomotive that had been noisily busy lining up empty coal cars to push into Blue diamond Coal Company now sat along side the fight.

The engineer gazed down from his perch and recognized Hoss as the one that had beat up one of the town character's down at the sand house a while back.

The guy got away or else he may have been killed. He reported it to the town police, but it was his word against Hoss, so nothing was done about it.

Hoss seemed to be able to wiggle free almost every time.

The engineer thought. 'Well this time he's going to have a hard time wiggling free, he's handcuffed and getting the hell beat out of him, and be damned if I'll turn a hand to stop it.'

The Chief: About that time some one said. "Here comes the chief."

They pulled Bama off Hoss and one said. "Get th hell outta here you don't need to go to jail over this bastard."

Bama looked at his car and knew he would never be able to get away because the chief was already crossing the street followed by his deputies just a few yards away. He took Gina by the hand and raced down the track alongside the steam engine. The engineer let off a great burst of steam just as the police came up the little embankment shielding Bama and Gina, they crossed the tracks to the other side of the engine.

There they stood in the darkness and listened to the conversation on the other side.

"Who is it, who done it?" They heard the chief ask.

"It's Hoss we found him here, don't know who done it, but I seen a car leave here like a bat out of hell headed toward Stone Creek, one of them old boys from down there must have worked him over."

"Looks like he finally met his match." Another one added.

The chief looked up at the engineer and asked.

"Did you see anybody Ray?"

"No not a soul Bill, but I was busy lining up coal cars anything could have happened without me knowing about it."

The chief looked at one of his deputies and said.

"Run over there and call Copeland we've got to get him to the hospital in Pennington, Damn! He's bloody all over, nose smashed all over his face I know it's broke, both jaws all out of whack, and hell look at this, three teeth here on th ground."

"I can't believe what I'm seeing it's usually the other guy that ends up beat to a pulp when he tangles with this bird, but by god he sure as hell met his match and more this time."

Then he noticed he was laying on both arms and leaned over to turn him over thinking he might have a broken arm, then he seen his arms were trapped in the sleeves of his half off jacket. Now he knew exactly what happened, he turned away from the bystanders and smiled.

'Hoss got th hell beat out of him all because of his slow and deliberate way of throwing his arms behind his back to remove his jacket before a fight, but this time the other guy has taken advantage of it.' 'I'm glad some one finally worked him over.' He thought.

He stood up and said. "Well if nobody seen anything there's not much I can do, he may tell us when he comes to, but I doubt that. Most likely his story will be that a gang jumped him or something like that."

The ambulance came and Bama and Gina still hiding on the other side of the steam engine listened to what they were saying.

"Man this guy's face is a mess, looks like a broken jaw, nose all out of shape it's broke for sure. Look at the teeth on the ground, we'd better check in his mouth for loose ones, lets see, oh hell! he tried to bite me looks like he's coming around."

"What happened buddy? Looks like you ran into some trouble."

"Yeah some guy's jumped me from behind, had me on the ground and on top of me before I had a chance to do anything."

"Ok here we'll get you on this stretcher, here turn your head this way."

"Damn that hurts be careful."

"Yeah I know buddy, you've been worked over pretty good."

They heard the ambulance pull away and soon the bystanders were all gone.

Ray looked down from the locomotive with a grin on his face and said.

"Okay the coast is clear, head on home and remember you've got to steer clear of that guy from now on he's a mean son of a bitch."

As Bama drove away toward Bonny Blue the engineer put the old locomotive to work again and blew the steam whistle long and loud till they were out of sight. And since there was nothing around the old steam engine but empty coal cars and no reason to blow the whistle it meant only one thing, Ray was celebrating the fact that Hoss had finally got a good dose of the same thing that he had been dosing out for a long time.

Up the street Bill and his deputies listened and smiled. Finally Bill said.

"Old Ray's celebrating boys he feels good about what happened tonight, in fact I feel pretty good about it myself and I've got a feeling the whole town does."

"Reckon we'll ever find out who worked him over?" One deputy asked.

"Sure I already know." Bill replied. "That young man from Alabama that came here a few months ago, he lives with his brother at Leona mines, goes by the nickname Bama."

"Oh yeah I know him he's a quiet guy, I see him a lot with the tall dark haired girl, I think her name is Gina. How'd you find out it was him Bill?"

"Rogers, the owner of the joint that sent for us, he said he wanted to be truthful about it, said he didn't know what happened after they left his place but he was sure that Hoss beat the guy up, but when I went back in his place and told him that Hoss was the one that took a beating, then he worried I would arrest Bama."

"Well are you?'

"No not on your life, but I plan on driving up to see him tomorrow and give him a little advice. I want to warn him about Hoses, to tell you the truth I'd hate to be in his shoes right now, he'll have to watch his back at all times and that will be hard to do with a sneaky one like Hoss at your heels."

Bama and Gina were married the following Saturday by a 'Justice of the peace' in Harlan, KY.

After spending the weekend at Bristol they returned to live temporarily with Bama's brother's family at Leona mines.

Bill had convinced Bama that he would no longer be safe living anywhere in Lee County. So he planned on staying just long enough to earn enough money to move to Jenkins, KY. He had a friend living there and the friend assured him that he would be able to get a job in the mine there.

He made it a point to stay away from ST. Charles, especially on weekends to avoid a chance meeting with Hoss.

He worked two more weeks at Leona mines and planned to load all his and Gina's belongings in the old ford and slip away after midnight on Friday. Other than his brother's family, no one else knew his plans.

His brother said he would put the word out that he went back to Alabama, because Jenkins Kentucky was not that far away, and knowing Hoss he would probably go there looking for Bama if he should find out he was there.

On Thursday night before they were to leave on Friday Bama awoke to voices and the bedroom was lit up from a light or something outside. He jumped from the bed pulling Gina with him. He headed for his brother's bedroom to warn them, but his brother was already up and running through the house gathering up his two children while his wife shooed their old dog out.

His brother had already heard the neighbors shouting 'fire' and responded immediately.

Once outside they could see Bama's old ford in flames and the neighbors pushing it toward the nearby creek to keep the flames from catching the house and his brother's car on fire.

The first thing to cross Bama's mind was. 'This is the work of Hoss.'

He looked toward the road and there on the ground he could see a five gallon gas can in the edge of the road with flames around it's snout, and smoke coming from a trail from where the old ford was parked and the gas can.

Hoss had poured the gas over the old ford and intended to take his gas can, but failed to empty the can completely. When he tossed the match it ignited the gas around the car and the blaze followed him and the dripping can to the edge of the road and there he threw it to the ground.

They left just before midnight on Friday as planned, but in his brother's car.

His brother drove them to Jenkins and returned Saturday morning making sure to stop in ST. Charles, and spread the word that he had just returned from Pennington Gap, Bus station where he had taken Bama and Gina to catch the bus to Alabama.

BACKNTIME

In the weeks that followed Hoss finally started looking and acting like him self again.

Just as before there was no evidence to link him to the car burning although everyone knew he did it.

"Good thing Bama got out of here." The chief told his brother. "The car burning was just a start, he wouldn't have been satisfied until he put a bullet in Bama's back."

So Bama and Gina settled down in Jenkins, KY. Not many miles away living normal lives as Hoss roamed the sidewalks of ST. Charles every Saturday night satisfied that he had ran Bama back to Alabama.

But one thing he learned was to never throw his arms behind his back to take his jacket off anymore. Bama took full advantage of that and with that kind of bully you need an advantage.

Meanwhile the horseshoe gang met every day in the alley alongside the store.

The teasers had let up a bit on me as the topic turned more toward the war.

Several young men had already enlisted and were scattered out over the country in training camps. Some of them had returned on short furlough's looking lean and neat in their uniforms.

But many were sweating it out knowing that the draft would soon catch up with them. Many times I thought about what one of them had told me. "The damn war will be over before you ever grow up."

And another had said. "You'll have Sugar all to yourself, but hell you won't touch her."

Then I thought. 'Maybe the war will end before I'm eighteen, but I've been with Sugar a second time and looking forward to seeing her again, and she has grown on me just like Bud said she would.'

Sugar Graduated High school and started working in a beauty salon in Pennington Gap. The mother of one of Sugar's classmates owned the shop and took Sugar on to teach her the trade.

She rides the bus to work each morning, but Bud picks her up after he completes his day at the mine. Guess ol Bud still has hopes that Sugar will someday choose him from all the rest.

Carlie is steadily getting worse and it shows on Lonnie, the hard work at the mine and her pleading with him every morning not to leave her is sapping

61

his strength and is heartbreaking.

Ladies from the little church are well organized and one of them is there each morning as Lonnie leaves for the mine. They have to listen to Carlie cry and tell them about Lonnie leaving her.

"Now I have nobody, God took little Lonnie and now Lonnie's left me." She'd say.

The words. "Maybe you should commit her, she'll never get any better. She's getting worse day by day." Became more frequent causing Lonnie to yell at one of the ladies.

"As I said before I will never commit her to that hell hole of a place in Marion, so if you don't want to stay with her then go, I'll make out some way. You see I love her and you don't, there's the difference."

At first it hurt the church lady's feelings, but later she apologized to him.

"Yes I understand Lonnie, I do love her, but not as you do, so please forgive me for ever suggesting that you should commit her. And remember this. I talked to the other ladies at church and we have agreed to never mention that to you ever again. And another thing one of us will be with her daily, so don't you worry we understand what you're going through."

I see Marty almost every Saturday when I deliver the groceries and feed for the stock. Usually she's sitting in the saddle like a statue never taking her eyes off me and saying nothing. Cody snorts and paws the ground as if he wants to get at me over the fence. And never fails to give out a loud 'neigh' as I head out the driveway toward the road. Sometimes I feel that he's trying to say.

"Get the hell out and stay away we don't need you around here."

In spite of having to suffer this little discomfort I am pleased at the way things turned out after she caught me in her trap.

Sugar told me later she had explained to her mother that I wouldn't be there to share the birthday cake with Marty because Marty and I had a little spat.

"I lied for you Sugar, Momma won't be mad at you, here she sent you a piece of the birthday cake."

'Damn! I thought. You can have your cake and eat it to.' As the saying goes.

Hoss's mother died after a short illness. Some folks said she was better off.

"Hell she was like a prisoner in her own home." One miner remarked. "She was a slave to Hoss and her old man. She seldom left the house, Jess, their neighbor told me he could hear the old man and Hoss yelling at her every day of the week."

"And by God! They're going to miss her, who in hell's going to cook and keep a clean house after them two slobs? Who you think kept that damned Bully's clothes clean and pressed all the time? Hell she did, Jess said he heard Hoss yell at her many times.

"Hurry up, wash and iron this shirt, this is the one I want to wear tonight. Jess said no doubt he had a half dozen shirts ironed and ready to wear but no, he demanded that she wash and iron that one. That woman's better off rest her soul away from them two bastards."

Saturday's were the same for Tex, wash and polish the black convertible, put on his best cowboy shirt and head for ST. Charles, take in the double feature at the little theater. Go by Shoun's to pick up the latest dime westerns, sit quietly on a stool sipping a coke while listening to the girls giggle.

He knew that some folks thought it odd that he didn't go for girls. With the shiny convertible he could have 'the pick of the litter' as one fellow put it. 'Some day I'll meet the right one.' But right now I'm satisfied just the way I am. I got my car, I save my money, don't throw it away on beer and women like most of the young guys do.'

'And most of all I help my grandparents in return for the way they worked to raise me up and seen that I got through high school.'

All these thoughts would go through his mind as he listened to the giggles and all the noises around him.

But every time without fail he would think of his mother.

'I can't remember her, everybody says I'm a lot like her.'

'And nobody's ever told me who my dad was, somebody must know.'

Then long before anyone else even thought about leaving ST. Charles, on a boisterous Saturday night, Tex would head for his car with a hand full of the latest dime westerns and a heart filled with sadness.

Midday on a Friday in July 1942, everyone in Stone Creek stopped what they were doing when they heard the dreadful sounds of a screaming siren coming from the direction of St. Charles. That usually meant that a miner had been hurt in one of the mines surrounding the town.

Most heads of families in Stone Creek worked in the mines. So it was only natural for them to react as if it were one of their own.

Telephones weren't in every household in Stone Creek, so word traveled from family to family by mouth.

Most always the same questions were asked. "Have you heard who it was?" What mine was it? Was it Benidict? That's where Bob works."

"I'm worried to death that it might be Carl, let me know if you hear anything."

As the ambulance slows to make a left turn on 421 and screams on toward the hospital at Pennington Gap, the questions above are already being asked.

Some of the miners stopped at the store after work about every day. The first to stop that day was a fellow who lived on Elys Creek, in the Pine Grove community. He worked at the Blue Diamond coal company at Bonny Blue above St. Charles.

As soon as he entered the store some one asked. "Do you know who got hurt today? Copeland came through here about twelve in a big hurry somebody must have been hurt bad."

"Yeah it happened at the number nine seam at Bonny Blue, I heard he died before they got him to the hospital. He was a motorman and a good one too I'm told. But he didn't have a chance. He was pulling a trip of coal and was just about to enter daylight toward the tipple when one of the loaded coal cars left the rails for some reason. Then there was a chain reaction as more cars left the track. Finally the Tram motor jumped rail and ran over some timber piled near the tracks. That forced the Tram toward the top and it pinned him between the Tram and the sandstone top, he didn't have a chance, I doubt if he was still alive when they brought him through here."

"Who was it?" someone asked.

"Can't remember his last name, but he went by the name of Lon, lives up on the Keokee road. Lost a boy a while back, they say his wife ain't been right since. I hear he was a good man, but seems that don't make a difference, we all gotta go some day, good and bad."

Lonnie didn't come home that day and two of the church ladies stayed with Carlie all night as she paced the floor crying and calling for Lonnie.

The church members made all the funeral arrangements with a lot of help from Sugar and her family. They decided to keep it from Carlie. One of the ladies said. "She thinks he leaves her every day never to come back anyway, so lets just let her think that he left her. It would be much worse I'm afraid if she found out that he was killed."

So once again the little church was filled with mourners as the Pastor wiped his brow and tried to think of something to say that would sound appropriate.

'A celebration won't work this time.' He thought. 'He leaves behind a wife, and Oh God! That's all she had. Why Lord! Why did you take him from her? Now she'll have to go to that awful place in Marion, as Lonnie called it.'

Carlie's parents had made the trip from Kentucky to attend the funeral. The pastor had noted when they walked in that her mother was very frail and he surmised that her husband had his hands full taking care of her. He had been told there were no other close relatives to help with Carlie.

As he thumbed through his bible pretending to search for something, he thought.

'I've got to start this service and I have to be honest with these people.' 'I don't have a clue as to why God took him, and I'm going to tell them that.'

As he looked out over the crowd he could sense that they were wondering why he didn't get the service started.

"Well as the most of you know we said goodbye to Lonnie Jr. just a short while ago, and here we are today to say farewell to Lonnie Sr."

"If you remember I told you that we were here to celebrate little Lonnie's passing because God wanted him out of this world for some reason."

"But today I have to be honest with you I just cannot understand why God took Lonnie Sr. We all know the condition that Carlie is in, and we all know how much they loved each other."

"Why didn't he take you? Why didn't he take me?' Why did he take Carlie's husband? She needed him so badly, is God fair, does he pick and choose?"

"I know some of you have these same thoughts and you are waiting for the answer from me."

"Well surprise! Surprise!!! I don't have the answer. I don't have the answer, let me stress that. I don't have the answer! To me it seems cruel and I can sense some of you think so to. It's times like this that test my faith. I want to cry out to the heavens. Why Lord! Why!"

"But rest assured God had a reason for calling Lonnie home and leaving Carlie here. He does things his way and we may not understand, but we are not to question his wisdom."

"So lets just say goodbye to Lonnie here today and lay him to rest out there beside Lonnie Jr."

"Lets take a verse from an old church hymn that all of you are familiar with."

"We'll understand it better all bye and bye."

"I'm sorry and feel bad about not being able to explain and give some comfort to you, but like you, I just don't understand God's ways."

"Take that verse and tuck it away somewhere in your mind. 'We'll understand it better all bye and bye'

"Let us pray"

"Lord we trust in your wisdom although there are times when we are prone to question your decisions. Lonnie was all Carlie had, oh well she has her parents but they are in the twilight of their lives and unable to take care of Carlie."

"Take care of her Lord maybe it's your plan to take her soon, if so it will be a blessing to all of us gathered in this room today. Cause they loved each other so much Lord, we pray that you call her soon and put that little family back together again. Let them live in a little house with a little garden spot, with a white picket fence lined with red roses. Let her be known as 'The rose lady' that used to live in a little paradise house on the road to Keokee."

"We leave here today Lord with sad hearts and confused minds. But 'we'll understand it better all bye and bye."

"Amen."

The following week Carlie became worse as expected. One of the ladies called the Doctor at St. Charles

Doc examined her as best he could and prescribed a medication that he hoped would calm her, especially at night so as to allow her to sleep not to mention the person that stayed with her all night listening at her calls for Lonnie to return as she paced the floor.

"Make sure you give her this twice daily and try to get her to eat more, her strength is waning, at this rate she will be bedfast within a week."

"Doctor some of the ladies at our church have been talking about sending her away to the Sanatorium in Marion, do you think they could help her there?"

"To be truthful with you I don't believe they can do anything for her but keep her confined. I never like to send anyone there unless they are a danger to the folks around them. At this time she shows no signs of harming anyone. But if you ladies decide that's what you want to do I will help you commit her."

"If she don't start eating more soon, she won't last long anyway."

" We try to get her to eat Doctor, in fact we beg her but she will not eat."

"Well there's not much we can do to help her if she won't take nourishment, there comes a time in cases like this that they just don't want to live any longer, and literally 'will' themselves to die."

"Let me know if this medication helps, and you ladies at church pray long and hard and ask God to intervene, and if it be his will she can get better, But if his plans are to take her, then so be it, what could be better than this family reunited in heaven?"

As Doc Drove away he could still hear the mournful wails coming from Carlie.

"Where's Lonnie? Lonnie please come back, why did you leave me? I don't want to live anymore."

He reached for the bottle on the seat beside him and took a long drink. Except for being exhausted the day has gone well for him up to this call.

Brought a crying healthy baby girl into the home of a young mining camp couple at four this morning to join it's little two-year-old brother.

About sunrise he returned home and slept no more than two hours, then went to his office in St. Charles.

Removed a splint from a miners leg and was pleased to see that the broken leg had healed and the miner was elated that he would soon be returning to work.

Then a lady came in to tell him that the medication he had prescribed for her a month ago had helped her considerably.

He had smiled as he heard a familiar voice coming from the waiting room.

"He shore is a good doctor, I come in here last week, don't know what in hell was wrong with me, all I know is I was gonna die afore the day was over iff'en sumpin ain't done, and damned fast. He give me some little white pills and said take one in the morning and one afore bedtime, and drink plenty water. And damn! I want you to know I took them pills like he said and I bet I drunk twenty five gallons of water in the last five days, and I'm telling you I feel better than when I was a young man working th mines. And By God! I'm here to get me some more of them little pills and if they keep hepping me like that I'll go back to work at Virginia Lee, betcha I can load more coal right now than some of the younger ones there."

Then he heard someone ask. "What was wrong with you?"

"Hell, I don't know what it wuz, I hurt all over, all I know is I wouldn't be here today iffen he hadn't give me them pills, no sir I would have been laying up there in the Wallen's Cemetery for shore."

As Doc listened he thought.

'That's old Limpy as he his known. Comes in at least once a month, have never been able to find anything wrong with him. I usually prescribe something with no more strength than a baby aspirin, and I can count on him coming back to tell me how I saved his life, but he always has a brand new ailment and needs something done about that.'

'The little white tablets I gave him are some I had made up from baking soda and a little salt. Looks like I have hit on to something that will take care of all his ailments, so this time I'll give him a couple months supply.'

All this time he had been cleaning out an infection from an old wound in a miner's foot. As he put the bandage on the miner said.

"Doc, I want to ask you something. Why in hell did you smile all the time you was gouging around in my foot? Damn! That hurt, ain't nothing funny about that."

"That's not what I was smiling about, didn't you hear old Limpy out in the waiting room spreading the word that I saved his life? Well I know I didn't, but it makes me feel good anyway."

Once finished at his office he headed toward Dryden to see a lady that had been having a hard time recovering from a bad case of Pneumonia.

He was surprised to see her out of bed and sitting in the porch swing. He chatted with her for a few minutes and as he got up to leave she told him how grateful she was for what he had done for her.

"Doctor, I believe you saved my life, I don't believe anyone knows how close I was to death just a few days ago."

"Oh yes." He said. "I knew how bad you were, and don't forget God, he's the one that deserves the credit, I prayed to him to help me heal you as I do for all my patients. Sometimes he does and sometimes he don't, but I never question him if he don't, because he has his reasons for when to take us and when to let us stay, and as far as I'm concerned he is always right."

As he drove along he was thinking. 'Yes the day has went pretty good with Carlie being an exception. I hope she'll start eating something soon, if not she won't be here very much longer.'

'Come to think of it, when did I eat last?'

'Got a long day ahead of me yet, so I'll worry about that later.'

He reaches for the bottle and takes another long drink. Then he realizes he just ran a stop sign.

He runs the back of his hand over his sleepy eyes and said out loud.

"Lord I've tried to stop this old habit like I told you I would, but Lord for some reason I can't stop."

"How much longer can I last? Is it in your plans to take me soon? If so Lord. Please grant me this one thing."

"Allow me some time with my family Lord, my work and this bottle have separated us and we hardly ever get to sit down and talk or share a meal together."

"I would like for my young children and my dear faithful wife to get to know me better. So please give me enough time to make amends and get closer to them, for I love them dearly. And Lord please watch over them."

Then with tears in his eyes he reaches for the bottle and takes another long swig.

"There I go again Lord, I can't stop this habit, so it's in your hands."

One week later on a Wednesday night after prayer meeting the ladies stayed and discussed the plight of Carlie. Each one of them had stayed with Carlie over the past week either in the daytime or at night.

And each had come to the conclusion that Carlie belonged in the hospital, or at the sanatorium in Marion, VA.

She paced the floor day and night and only slept when she could no longer stay on her feet or think. She refused to take the medication that Doc had prescribed and her food intake was just barely enough to keep her alive.

One of the ladies suggested that they call the Doctor the next day and let him make the decision to send her to the hospital or to the sanatorium in Marion.

Tears came to their eyes as each one of them raised their hand in agreement.

"What more can we do?" One of them uttered as she wiped away tears.

"There's nothing else we can do." Another one said. "And we shouldn't feel guilty about it cause God knows we have tried. She has no income and the mining company pays no insurance."

Then the lady that had made the suggestion said. "So be it, tomorrow morning I'll call the Doctor and notify her parents in KY. I'm sure they will take it hard, but we have no other choice and we all know that they are not able to take her in and care for her."

As they stood to leave someone came down the aisle toward them. 'That's that girl.' One of them thought.

"Oh! That's sugar." Another one said out loud.

Sugar's smile lit up her face as she said.

" I heard that you all were meeting to discuss the plight of Carlie. I'm sorry that I'm late. But if you don't mind I would like to say something."

"Sure that's what we're here for." One of them replied. They sat back down and Sugar stood before them.

"As all of you know I have always been close to Carlie. I am here to make a proposal that I think will be of help to her.

I am aware of the worry and stress that you all have went through trying to console and watch over her especially the past week."

"I have no idea as to what you decided to do about her here tonight, you may have already decided that she belongs in the hospital or the sanatorium."

"I work at the beauty parlor in Pennington, and am not free to stay with her in the daytime, but I will stay nights, I mean every night, I will move in with her."

"I know she has no income, I don't make a lot of money but I will share it with her. I heard that the house payments are behind I'm afraid I can't pay them, but one of your members holds the mortgage, and maybe he can be persuaded to defer them for a while."

"So if you all can watch over her during the day from 8 A.M. till 6 P.M. Tuesday's through Saturday's, I can be with her the rest of the time, I have Monday's off and of course the shop is closed on Sunday."

"As I said we have always been close, and I think I can get her to eat more and calm her down."

The ladies began to smile and look at one another and it was plain to see that they were impressed with 'That Girl' as they used to refer to her, and in complete agreement with the proposal that she had just put before them.

One of the ladies rose and asked. " How many hands will I see in favor of this young ladies proposal?"

Without hesitation every hand was raised in agreement. They stayed a little longer and worked out a schedule that would accommodate each of their daily activities.

And as never before they all were so impressed with Sugar.

"Why don't you come to church again like you used to?" One asked.

"Yes I will." Sugar answered. "I'll be here next Sunday and I'll bring Carlie with me."

The ladies exchanged glances and wondered how that would turn out.

Bud came by the next day after work and helped Sugar load all her belongings in his car.

At Carlie's house they could hear the church lady talking softly trying to console her as she sobbed.

They went in and Carlie sprang to her feet and embraced Sugar. "Oh Sugar! Its you, will you stay with me tonight?"

"Of course I will Sugar, I'll stay with you every night from now on, we're going to have fun you and me just like old times."

Carlie's face lit up as the church lady had never seen it before and she wondered if Sugar had a secret place in her heart where she stored all the magic that she seemed to possess.

That night Sugar persuaded Carlie to take her medicine, and she ate more than she had in three days.

But the next morning when another one of the church ladies came so Sugar could go to work the same ritual took place.

She clung to Sugar, begging her not to go. "Please don't leave me little Lonnie died and Lonnie left me, please don't go you're all I have."

"I'm not leaving you Sugar, I have to go to work, but I'll be back before six this evening, this nice lady from the church will be here with you till I get back. You two have fun maybe you'd like to get out and check your roses today they sure are pretty, especially the red ones."

So it went the rest of that week. Bud would be there to take her to work and bring her home after work.

With exception of the mornings when Carlie would cling to her and beg her not to go Carlie improved in every other way. She now was taking her medication and almost back to normal with her eating habits.

Sugar arose early Sunday morning and cooked breakfast while Carlie slept. For two nights in a row she had rested well.

'That's a good sign.' Sugar thought. 'Before you know it she'll be back to her old self again.'

She got Carlie up and coaxed her to eat two eggs bacon and toast. After that she had Carlie take a shower and helped her get dressed.

That done, she said. "Ok Sugar! Look in the mirror and see how pretty you are this morning, today's Sunday we're going to church."

Carlie didn't object, in fact she seemed to be bursting with anticipation.

Sugar thought. 'Every things going to be all right.'

Soon Bud came by and as Carlie got in the car. She asked. "Is this Lonnie's car? I thought he took it with him when he left me."

"No, no! Sugar, this is Bud's car, you remember Bud don't you? He's my steady boyfriend now. My one and only, and just between us three my future husband."

Bud nodded in approval.

How well he remembered the night and the surprise it brought him just a couple of weeks ago. He had asked Sugar if she had ever thought about changing her life for the better.

"Cause if you ever do I want to be a part of it, I have always loved you in spite of knowing how you were and hoping that some day you would change and choose me from all the rest. It's been embarrassing for me and lots of times I called myself a fool like I knew a lot of others were doing."

He took her in his arms and went on. "We could have a good life together, so if you ever think about it let me know."

He felt her shaking in his arms and his thoughts turned to anger.

'Damn! Its no use, this girl has no heart when it comes to this, she's laughing.'

'Does she realize how much she's hurting me? Hell! She just don't give a damn."

Then he felt something wet through his shirt and realized that crying not laughter was why she was shaking.

As he wiped the tears from her eyes he heard the words that he had always hoped to hear from her.

"I love you too, I've known it for a long time, I kept it to myself thinking that we would never make it work because of my past and you knowing about it, but if you're willing to take me, we'll put all of that behind us."

He squeezed her tight and said. "Okay It's a deal, how soon do you want to tie the knot?"

"Lets wait a while Sugar." She answered. "Like maybe two weeks." She laughed.

"And in the meantime lets pretend that either of us has ever been with anyone or each other sexually. In other words lets start going straight right from this moment, don't you think that's a good idea?"

"Oh yes! What ever you say is okay with me." He answered.

As he came to a stop in the church parking lot he thought. 'I wonder if she would like to be married in this church?'

All eyes were directed their way as they entered the church. The ladies that had been caring for Carlie could hardly believe what they were seeing.

Carlie looked pretty much as she used to before little Lonnie died. As one of the ladies looked she thought. 'Sugar, or 'that girl' as some of them still caught themselves calling her is truly a miracle worker.' And you only have to look at her radiant face to see why she has such influence on anyone that she comes in contact with.

Then she whispered to her husband sitting next to her. "God is surly working through that girl Sugar, and she must join this church we need her here."

And yet another member wondered about the young man with her. 'Is he just another one of the ones that chase her, or maybe she's turned a new leaf and this one is for keeps.'

Just before the closing prayer the Minister requested that Sugar, Bud, and Carlie come up front.

As they stood where all could see he pointed to Carlie and said.

"As you know we in this church have been praying for Carlie very hard for some time now. And I must admit that at times I thought God was ignoring us. But it's plain to see that he has performed a miracle, and I believe his tool for the miracle is the young lady standing next to her that we know as Sugar."

"So let me point out to you. Pray, pray, pray! Don't ever let it enter your mind that God don't answer prayers. Take a look at what he has done, He has brought Carlie back to us, and let me say this, I believe in the process he has thrown in the young lady Sugar, and placed her back here in our pews where she belongs. And hopefully the nice looking young man with her will join us in this place of worship."

"Now do you believe in miracles? Do you? If so, make your way up here and shake hands with one."

"Take your time but come on up and shake hands with these folks, God has sent them to us today, he has answered our prayers, this is truly the work of God."

After all the hugging and handshaking was over Bud and Sugar took Carlie to the little cemetery behind the church.

"You do want to visit little Lonnie's grave don't you Sugar?" Sugar had asked.

"Yes I do Sugar, it's been such a long time."

"And Sugar, there's something else I want to show you there. You see after you lost little Lonnie you kind of went to pieces and would think that Lonnie Sr. was leaving you every morning when he left to go to the mines."

"Now what I'm about to tell you is not very pleasant but in a way it should be a relief to you. You see Lonnie didn't leave you, in a sense he did, but not the way you thought. No one wanted to tell you the real truth because of your state of mind at the time."

"Lonnie was in a mine accident, he was pulling a trip of coal, as they say in mining terms, when one of the coal cars left the track causing other cars and the tram motor to leave the track. Lonnie was pinned between the tram and the mine roof."

"He was killed Sugar, he died before they got him to the hospital."

Carlie was listening intently and seemed to be in control until she heard the words, 'he was killed.' She started to cry and leaned into Sugar's arms.

As Sugar held her she thought. 'I knew this would be a blow to her, but at the same time I believe it will be a relief after the initial shock wears off, It has to be better knowing that he was killed in an accident than thinking that he just up and walked out on you.'

Finally she calmed and they walked toward little Lonnie and Lonnie's graves.

Bud had went back to the car to get two huge vases of fresh cut red roses that Sugar had cut early that morning and left on the porch for him to put in the car when he came to pick them up for church.

At the graves Carlie fell to her knees and sobbed. Soon they helped her to her feet and Bud handed her the roses. She placed them on the graves and said a silent prayer.

'God, I miss them so much, when you took little Lonnie it just about killed me." 'Then you took Lonnie, and Lord! Forgive me for thinking that Lonnie walked out on me, he was a good man Lord, please be kind to him.'

'Forgive me Lonnie, I love you both and some day we'll be together again.'

In the days to come Carlie made more progress but not enough to leave her home alone. Because some times she would have a relapse and needed someone there to calm her and bring her back out of her depressive state, and no one performed that better than Sugar.

She insisted on taking red roses to both graves every day, and she wanted to do it alone. Since it was a short walk from her house to the church she was allowed to do that, but if she didn't return in a reasonable amount of time someone would go check on her.

Every Sunday would find Carlie, sugar, and Bud, at the little church.

Some wondered if Sugar and Bud would walk down the aisle and put their lives in God's hands, or maybe they were just trying to take care of Carlie and would never join the little church.

But one Sunday they did walk the aisle and professed their belief in God and asked to be accepted as members of the church.

Of course they were welcomed by all, handshakes and hugs were passed around, and Sugar's radiance seemed to bring new meaning to the little church.

Everyone noticed that Bud and Sugar Stayed huddled with the minister after the handshaking was over and wondered what that was all about. What ever it was it sure put a smile on the minister's face.

And as they stood beside him the minister made this announcement.

"I have more news for you, as you know this fine young couple put their lives in the hands of God here today and chose to join our little congregation."

"They have just whispered to me that they want to be joined as man and wife, so they will be pronounced as man and wife right here in this church at twelve thirty p.m. next Saturday. They would be pleased if you can attend, but please do not bring gifts, they request your presence only."

"Then on Sunday at one p.m. they want to be baptized down at the upper dam."

"I have just been advised by one of our members that the ladies will bring food and we will have a feast in celebration of this wedding right after the ceremony."

"So go home and rejoice for it has been a good day, God has made his presence known again and we have all been blessed."

The news of the wedding spread like wild fire.

"That girl, the one that goes by the name of Sugar, She's getting married Saturday, can you believe that?'

"Tell me who in hell would be crazy enough to marry that gal?"

"Some guy from around Stone Creek goes by the name of Bud."

"Oh yeah I know about him, I've been told he fell for her right from the start and couldn't shake her from his mind even though he knew she was running wild and free."

"Them old boys from down around Stone Creek will be lost without her around to take care of their wants."

"But who knows it could be the best thing that has ever happened in her life, she sure as hell latched on to a man with a lot of patience. We may judge him as being a little foolish for hooking up with her, but in the end he might turn out to have been a hell'va lot smarter than anyone thought. From what I hear she's a charmer and makes you feel good just to be around her, can't say that about many women."

"I wish him luck, I got a feeling he's in for a rough ride, just hope she don't drive him to drink he seems like a nice guy." The other one replied.

"But hell! You ain't heard it all, they joined that little church up on the Keokee road and will be baptized at the upper dam next Sunday."

"Shit! Now I know you're pulling my leg."

"No by God! I'm not, I drove up that way today and somebody has already put up a sign that says. 'A baptismal service will be held here starting at 1 p.m. Sunday. We ask all swimmers to cooperate and stay clear of the area at that time.'

"You don't say! Well by God it shore looks like that gal's turned a new page, old Bud just might be the luckiest man in Lee County right now."

Cam: The church ladies got together and planned the dinner for the reception on Saturday. Happened that the wife of the owner that sold the little house to Lonnie and Carlie was there.

"My husband 'Cam' will come by and tell you what he's willing to do about the back payments on the house, I'm sure all of you will be pleased."

Near the end of their discussion about the dinner plans Cam came in.

"Well ladies I hope you've planned a good dinner for Saturday. No body enjoys your good cooking better than me, can't wait to see all that good food on the table. And please somebody bring some banana pudding. My wife won't make it anymore at our house. She says I make a pig of myself and put on too much weight around the middle here."

"So bring on the pudding, I intend to make up for lost time."

That brought laughter from the ladies and some good-natured kidding was directed at his wife for depriving him of banana pudding.

"Well the reason I broke in here on your meeting is this. One of you had asked my wife what I intended to do about the house and Carlie. As all of you must know the monthly payments are in arrears several months."

"And legally the house is mine once the payment agreements are not met. I know Carlie has no way of making the payments. Lonnie had just went into debt for a better car shortly before his death and of course Jessee Chevrolet had to repossess it."

"So here's my decision. But first let me say this. I have never in my life met any better people than Lonnie and Carlie. Lonnie was a good young man and there's no doubt in my mind that he would have paid the house off and went on to build or buy a better one because he almost had this one paid for."

"Now listen close to what I'm about to tell you. As long as Carlie lives, the house is hers to live in, if something should happen to her the house is mine and then I will decide what I'll do with it."

"And another thing do any of you know what Sugar's plans are after she gets married Saturday, does she plan on staying with Carlie for a while longer? I hope so, she sure has brought Carlie a long ways in just a short time."

"And as far as I'm concerned the young man can live there with her."

One of the ladies spoke up.

"Yes she plans on staying there with Carlie until she thinks Carlie can make it on her own. But her husband Bud will stay with his parents except for Sundays. She said he would spend Saturday nights, Sunday, and Sunday nights with her and Carlie. She don't think it would be right for Bud to move in, said that it would look like they were taking advantage of free rent or whatever."

" Well now look at it this way, she's staying there caring for Carlie and sharing her pay check to keep food on Carlie's table. So I ask you why shouldn't she get something in return?"

"You ladies tell her that I said it is perfectly right and proper for Bud to move in and I expect him to do just that. I guess that about wraps it up I just wanted to come here and tell you, so don't worry about it anymore, we've all got a part to play in helping Carlie, and this is the least I can do, and I am more than glad to do it."

Smiles came across the ladies faces, another problem solved in the life of Carlie, like the minister had said. "Pray, pray, pray! God has answered, he is among us."

I drove by the church on my way to deliver Sugar's family's groceries and feed at twelve fifteen on Saturday.

The parking area was full and a few cars were parked alongside the road.

And it wasn't surprising to me to see a couple of Sugar's ex boy friends cars there. All week long I had heard some of them shed their views on the upcoming marriage.

"Believe it or not I feel good about it," one of them had said. "I'm glad to see her make a change, she's to good a person to go through the rest of her life behaving the way she has since she was fourteen."

"And look at it this way, she couldn't have picked a better person than Bud to share the rest of her life with."

"Shit! I've been with her and so have you and some others, but like I said

I'm happy for them and you can bet that I will respect them and never mention anything about the past in any way."

"I agree one hundred percent." The other one replied. "And I bet you the other guys feel the same with the exception of one, and you know who I mean I'm sure."

"Oh yeah! That bastard I just hope he don't try to stir up something with Bud, if he does I'm going to find it very hard to ignore him like I've done in the past."

"And speaking of him there's a rumor going around that he's about to get married to a young girl from over around Woodway, Did you hear that?"

"No I didn't hear that but I'm not surprised cause he ain't got no one to cook, wash, iron and slave for him and his old man since his mother passed away."

" From what I can gather he and the old man worked his mother to death and yelled at her constantly, I can't figure how she ever put up with it for so many years."

"Well that's funny now that you brought that up, the talk is that the young girl is in a very bad situation living at home and has been wanting to get away from it for a long time. It's said that her father and mother are both heavy into the booze and treat her like dirt. Some that I have talked to tell me that all Hoss wants her for is just what you mentioned, someone to do all the house work for him and his old man."

"I understand she is a very shy and timid person due to the abuse that she has suffered from her parents over the years. Can you imagine a person like that or anyone else for that matter living with a manic like Hoss?"

"No I can't I'm afraid she's in for a lot of heartache before it's over, probably a lot more than she has had to go through at home. Makes me cringe just to think about it. When are they getting married?"

"I don't know but his neighbor says she moved in about a week ago and he never sees her out of the house. But he thinks that Hoss will marry her to protect himself from the law if he ever starts cuffing her around. It's easier to get out of it

if it's your wife, but a different story if you're not married especially a young girl like her."

"Well I'm not a Christian and I doubt if my prayers will go through, but I think I'll say a prayer for her anyway, she's in for a bad time, God help her."

Then the other one said.

"How in hell has that bastard managed to live as long as he has? We'd all be better off if some morning we woke up and learned that somebody put a bullet in his back."

As I took the groceries to the back porch I could see Cody off in the far corner of the pasture and watched as he headed my way.

By the time I reached the feed shed he was already standing at the fence.

As I unloaded the hundred pound bags of feed my thoughts went back to Sugar.

The sweet smell of the Cow feed and the barn odor was always a reminder of the day sugar introduced me to another world. A world that I will have to share with some one else in the future, cause Sugar has stopped sharing with chasers like me. She has finally seen the light and chosen Bud to share her world, and that's the way it should be.

Then I thought.

'Damn! I'm gonna miss her, maybe if I had been a little older she would have chosen me.'

Then Cody snorted as he pawed the ground.

I walked over and rubbed his nose gingerly half expecting him to bite me. To my surprise he seemed to be enjoying it, so I climbed on the fence and put one arm around his neck.

"Looks like you're all by yourself here today boy, They all went to Sugar and Bud's wedding, can you believe that Cody? Did you ever think you'd see the day that Sugar would turn from her wild carefree ways and settle down?"

He shook his head and snorted as if he understood every word I said.

"Okay boy I'm on my way, see you next Saturday."

As I turned on the road from the driveway he gave out his usual loud 'Neigh' but this time it sounded different.

'Maybe he's trying to say that he was never mad at me and was just trying to warn me.' "Stay away from Sugar, she's not right for you, go find some one else." 'Could be, but damn! I'm going to miss her.'

The church came in view and I thought. 'I guess it's over by now and they have been pronounced man and wife. And shit! I didn't even get to kiss the bride, and all that food piled on the tables, heck I'm hungry but ain't no way I'll stop there, can't get her off my mind that way.'

'So go on think about something else like it ain't long till you'll have to register for the draft, go out and find another girl so you'll have some one to come back to when the wars over.'

I tried to get my mind on something else and was doing a pretty good job of it until I looked off to the left at the upper dam.

'No telling how many times Sugar went skinny dipping in that water, but come tomorrow the pastor will dip her under and wash all her sins away.'

'Guess I should give that some thought myself, Lord knows I carry around a bunch of sins.'

I smiled as I neared the Pocket community and remembered the time she had one foot against the windshield and the other one over her head touching the roof of the old truck.

"Come on sit up before we get to the Pocket community, I had said. What in the world will people think with your legs up in the air showing everything?"

I parked the old truck in the alley and someone from the horseshoe gang yelled.

"What took you so long, did you stop for the wedding?"

I didn't answer and thought.

'Forgetting Sugar is going to be impossible, her reminders are everywhere so you may as well get used to it.'

Meantime in Jenkins, Kentucky Bama and Gina have settled in and actually like living there in contrast to the way they felt when they first arrived.

Gina's pregnant and they're happy about that and looking forward to the day the little one arrives.

The war rages on in Europe and in the Pacific. and the draft is claiming more young men around them with each passing day. Gina worries that the draft will catch up to Bama before the baby is born.

Bama is concerned about that to but tries not to let it show. Bama's brother and his family have been to visit several times and have kept them posted on the news around St. Charles and the coal camps in Lee County.

"Everybody thinks you went back to Alabama." His brother tells him.

"Sometimes I wish we had." Bama replied. "I sure do miss momma and dad, and with the war and all it's no telling when I'll see them again."

"Sounds like you're not to happy about leaving there."

"No it's not that, I would never have met Gina if I had stayed there, and I can't imagine going through life without her. It's like, well it's like I'm home sick to see my folks and afraid something will happen to them before I get back there."

"They're not getting any younger you know. I hope to save enough money to visit them after the baby comes, but then there's the draft to worry about, I might get the message in the mail any day now to report for examination."

"Gina's worried about that to. God! It'll break my heart if I have to leave her before the baby comes. That and wanting to see mom and dad is getting to me."

"Ah come on! Snap out of it little brother, every things going to work out for you. Don't let it worry you you're stronger than that. Remember you're the little guy that whupped the shit out of the worst bully in Lee County, Virginia. Not to say that you had to run and hide after you worked him over, but you still beat the hell out of him."

They both laughed and Bama replied.

"I didn't mean to sound like I'm at wits end, but it is worrisome to think that I might have to go off yonder across the seas and maybe never get back to see Gina, the baby, and mom and dad again."

"I know little brother, I know. I know how you feel and I'm proud you feel that way, cause it shows how much you care for your family. There was a time back there in Alabama when I thought you would never grow up and amount to anything, but in the past several months I've seen a complete turn around in your attitude, and I'm proud that you're my brother."

Tex took his grandfather's old twelve-gauge shotgun down from the wall where it hung on two pieces of wood mounted to the wall.

He could remember when his grandfather would go squirrel hunting every year when the season opened.

But squirrel season had come and gone for two years in a row now and his grandfather never mentioned going squirrel hunting anymore.

He had noticed a change in him especially in the past six months, and wondered if his season here on earth was about over.

He had always intended to go with him on one of the hunts, but when the season opened he'd find him self engrossed in something else and put it off till next year.

'I don't want him to leave this world knowing that I promised him that I would go with him some time and never did.'

'So I'm going to ask him if he wants to go maybe in the next three days before the seasons over.' 'I still have a few days to kill before I go back to work.'

'Grandma looks frail too, but she has always looked that way since I can remember, but she's tough as nails as the saying goes.'

'Sure would be a blow for me to lose either of them after all they've done for me.'

'I realize they've treated me like a father and mother, and better than some father's and mother's I'm sure.' 'But at times, I get so down and out when I think about my mother and can't even remember her.'

'But the thing that about drives me over the edge is not knowing who my father is, is he dead? Is he in prison?'

'Why is everybody so tight lipped about him? I have never came right out and asked simply because I thought there was a reason and with time someone would tell me.' 'At times I feel like I ought to get right to the point and demand some answers, but then I have second thoughts. Maybe it would hurt my grandparents, they have a reason for not telling me and it may be a good one.'

As he inspected the old shotgun the past that he never knew about kept racing through his mind.

Then he heard a noise behind him and realized that pa had come in from the porch.

"Going squirrel hunting son? That old gun will sure get them, a squirrel in the top of the tallest hickory in Lee County ain't out of range of that old twelve-gauge. Sure wish I could go again, but I just ain't felt like it for two years in a row now. The season will be over in another three days, why don't you go get us some squirrels? And Speaking of seasons I've had a pretty long one. But I'm afraid my season is about over here on earth."

Tex grimaced when he heard that and didn't look up.

Finally he said.

"I was thinking I might pa, but I had in mind taking you with me."

"You see I've never been squirrel hunting, I need you to show me how it's done."

"Yeah I know son, I tried every year to get you to go with me but you was always half way through one of them dad blamed dime westerns and wouldn't go."

They both laughed and pa said. "I'm not able to go through the woods anymore over all that rough ground and underbrush. But I can direct you to my favorite patch of woods where there's a stand of the tallest hickory trees in this part of the country, and once you get there all you got to do is sit down under one of them trees, be real quiet and wait till the squirrel's start feasting on them hickory nuts."

"Best time to go is early in the morning or just before sunset, that way you get there and get settled down before they come in to feed."

"Where is this patch of woods pa? I think you've talked me into going."

"I'll map it out for you tonight after supper, but right now lets take old Betsy out and waste a few shells and see if she still kicks like a mule. You've got to hold her tight to your shoulder and brace yourself, cause if you don't she'll knock you on your rear end."

By five thirty A.M. the next morning Tex turned off on a little dirt road that pa had told him to take.

Exactly one mile down the road on the right he seen the big tall pine tree that Pa had described to him.

"Th durn thing looks like it's growing right out of that cliff ledge its setting on." He had said. "How it can grow there in that little amount of dirt I'll never know, but heck, it ain't for me to know all of God's mysteries."

He parked off the road under the ledge, got out and headed straight up the steep hill. Once on top he stopped to rest.

'Now I see why pa didn't want to come, he'd never have made it up that hill.'

He looked down on the other side at tops of trees with their leaves turning gold, and no mistake about it he had found the stand of hickory that pa had described to him. There were other kinds of trees under and around them, but the hickory's reached for the sky and dwarfed them all.

Soon all the leaves in the forest would be in full color, red, gold, silvery, brown, all blended with the green of the pines and the cedar that bordered a small clearing far down in the valley.

'I want to come back here next month.' Tex thought. 'When the leaves are in full color, why didn't I come with pa? But like he said I always had a dime western that I had to finish.' 'Anybody that can see this and still say there's no God has to be destined for hell.'

Then further on past the small clearing, he saw something glistening in the sunlight. He made it out as a car moving along a winding road and a small community with a little church down the road a ways. And suddenly it dawned on him.

'That's Keokee road.' Pa had said. "When you get to the top you can see the stand of hickory far below you and you'll see the road beyond that. Go down straight toward the hickory and when you get there you'll be at the back of the Barton place, in fact you'll be on Barton's property, but he don't mind.

He told me years ago that I was welcome to hunt there anytime I wanted to."

"He allows about anybody that wants to, to squirrel hunt on his property. Just asks that you be careful and make sure you are aiming up in the trees, cause his barn and stock are pretty close to the woods there in easy range maybe not a shotgun, but a rifle for sure."

"Barton's a good man, I respect him a lot, he'd give you the shirt off his back if you needed it. So go on over there and bring us some squirrel back, wish I could go with you but I think my hill climbing days are over."

He reached the valley and sat down under one of the tall trees. And the last thing Pa had said was.

"I think my hill climbing days are over." And that kept running through his mind. Pretty soon a tear started down his cheek and he said out loud.

"Pa I'm sorry I always had some lame brained excuse and never came here with you, I now realize how much you mean to me And I'm afraid pa, I'm afraid I'm about to lose you."

He ran the back of his hand across his cheeks to wipe away the tears that were now blurring his vision.

"Ah! Come on son." He could hear Pa say. "I told you to be real quiet, them squirrels will be here shortly raring to get at them hickory nuts."

Pretty soon he could see some small limbs shaking in the tree and the ones around him as the squirrels jumped from tree to tree and limb to limb as if they were putting on an acrobatic show. And soon the air was filled with their chatter, or are they fussing? Only a squirrel would know.

High above he could see one clearly as it sat on a small limb digging in to a hickory nut. Pieces of the hull were falling to the ground right along side him, and two squirrels were playing tag around the trunk of the tree.

He took aim at the one on the limb and remembering what pa had said, braced himself for old Betsy's kick. He squeezed the trigger and the boom from the old twelve-gauge sounded like a cannon.

Then he thought. 'I'm still standing but dang! My jaw hurts.' 'Pa said to hold it tight to the shoulder, I forgot that, Dang! That hurts.'

About ten feet away he spotted the dead squirrel on the ground, about the same time he seen one jump from the tree to a limb in another tree and sit there as if listening and wondering what in the world that loud noise was.

He took aim and fired, this time remembering what pa had said. "Hold the stock hard to your shoulder."

It didn't catch him in the jaw this time, but knocked him flat on his rear.

'Oh shit! He thought. 'I didn't brace my self I wish pa was here he'd get a kick out of this. 'He said old Betsy had quite a kick, now I believe him.'

The squirrels were pretty much scared and in hiding from the two shotgun blasts. But after about ten minutes the activity started all over again.

Three more blasts from old Betsy netted two more squirrels, one missed completely as the squirrel jumped from one limb to another just as he squeezed the trigger.

He picked up the four squirrels and stuffed them in pa's old pouch that was slung over his head and around the neck.

'Four squirrels is enough for today Pa will be proud of me.'

He couldn't see the little clearing from here because of the denseness of the trees but thought it must be near, he could hear a roaring sound like a fast moving stream. 'Think I'll check it out.' He thought.

He walked out into the opening just as some one was coming down a path out of the woods on the opposite side.

'That must be Mister Barton.' Pa said he lived nearby.'

As he got closer Tex recognized him as the man he knew to be Sugar, and Marty's, father.

'So that's his name Barton, I have seen him many times and he seemed to always want to chat and inquire about pa and ma. I never bothered to try to find out his name. And I've never bothered to chase his daughter Sugar, like some of the other guys.'

'He must be under a terrible strain having to put up with Sugar all this time. I hear the other one Marty, gives them no trouble at all.'

"Hey young man! I see you've been squirrel hunting, have any luck?"

"Yes sir, I got four, could have got more but I figure that's enough for one day."

"Where'd you get them, in the hickory stand?"

"Yes sir, and there's plenty of them left in there."

"Yes I know and your grandpa has hunted in there for years, now you must be taking up where he left off, I understand he stopped hunting about two years ago. How's he holding up son? I ain't seen him out and about for a good while."

"Well not so good, I tried to get him to come with me today, but he didn't feel like climbing that hill on the other side of the ridge."

"Well durn! You all could have come in by my house and have no hill to climb. I used to tell him that but he would always come the back way over the ridge."

"When you get back tell him that you all can come in at my place and park down by the barn ."

"Okay I'll tell him and I might get him out here in the next couple of days before the squirrel season ends."

"Any time you're out here feel free to use the table, pitch horseshoes or take a swinging ride in that truck tire hanging in the tree yonder."

" It took me a while to clear this all out, but it's been worth it we've enjoyed it on weekends and holidays. I come out here ever so often to see if every things in place, had a mess out here one time, empty cans, beer bottles and stuff. Most hunters are okay but some don't seem to care how they treat someone else's property, you know how that is."

"Your grandpa and grandma are fine people and they sure are proud of you. You did so well in school, and have kept your nose to the grindstone, saved your money and stayed out of trouble."

"Have you ever thought about leaving the mines and furthering your education?"

"Yes I've decided to postpone it till after the war, I expect to get called up any time now."

"I guess you're doing the right thing son, but let us hope and pray that the war will be over soon."

Finally Tex said. "I better get started back across the ridge, want to get home and have Pa show me how to skin these squirrels."

"Try to get him out here before the season ends, I'd like to sit down with you all and have a cup of coffee, and who knows my wife might put some food on the table for us. Bring your grandmother along, my wife thinks the world of her."

As Tex climbed to the top and down the other side of the hill a lot of things went through his mind.

'I sure like Mister Barton, I'm glad I got to see him there today, I got to know him better.' 'Pa was right he is a fine man, he seems to know Pa and Ma pretty well, I wonder if he knows who my father is.'

'Maybe some day I'll ask him.'

Pa was sitting on the porch as he pulled into the driveway. Tex got out with a big smile on his face and pa knew he had some squirrels in the pouch.

"Do you feel like showing me how to skin them pa?"

" I feel like skinning squirrels anytime son, how many you got in that bag?'

"I got four pa, but I could have got a lot more."

"That's good son, that's good, you're like me I never could see taking more when I already had enough for a meal."

"Pa I went down in that clearing and met mister Barton, he came out to check on his picnic area. I have seen him a lot of times and never knew his name, but I knew he was the father of the girl they call Sugar and the other one Marty."

"He asked about you and ma pa, he bragged about how you all brought me up and things like that, he sure is a nice fellow."

"He wants me to bring you all out there in the next couple of days, said we can go in the hickory stand from his house and we won't have to climb any hills."

"Said he wants to sit down and have a cup of coffee with us. He said his wife might set some food in front of us, but maybe he was kidding about that."

"No he wasn't kidding son, if we go I know we'll see some food on the table."

"Then you want to go pa?"

"Sure I'll go, can't promise you that I'll feel like going squirrel hunting but I'd be glad to visit with Barton."

"Okay pa, we'll go there day after tomorrow, that's the last day of squirrel season. You think ma will want to go?"

"Sure she will, her and ms Barton hit it off just fine."

"Alright son best we stop jabbering and you pay more attention to how to skin and dress a squirrel don't you think?"

He went to bed that night and lay there wondering as he always did if he would ever learn anything about his father.

'If I ever do." He whispered. 'I hope he's like mister Barton, I like him.'

Two days later he and his grandparents sat at the table laden with all the delicious dishes that Mrs. Barton was noted for.

As the older folks talked he and Marty had a conversation about her school and what her plans were when she finished high school. He was surprised to find out that they both were a lot alike. Like him, she was very serious about trying to learn all she could in school.

Just before sunset Tex said. "Okay Pa! You ready to go out yonder and get some squirrel's?"

"No son you go ahead, I just want to sit here and visit with the Barton's, me and your grandma hardly ever get to see them since age has caught up to us and we have a lot to talk about yet."

He thought about asking Marty if she would go with him but changed his mind.

'I've not bothered to ask a girl to go for a ride with me or take in a movie, but now I was about to ask one to go squirrel hunting with me.'

'I do like her but heck! That ain't no way to get to know a girl better.'

These things were still on his mind when he reached the hickory stand.

'I've wasted a lot of time in my life.' He thought. 'It's not that I don't like girls, it's just the thought of not having a father and mother, I guess under that burden I have let it control my life up until now.'

'Well that's all about to change, I'm going to ask Marty if she would like to go for a ride up to Big Stone, or take in a movie at St. Charles on a Saturday.

'Heck! I'll be gone away in the army pretty soon and won't even have a girl to write to. Maybe that's what I need to take away some of this old worry that I carry around all the time.'

He put six squirrels in the bag in record time and was on his way back to the Barton's.

'I'll give them four of them.' He said to himself. 'I know ms Barton knows how to cook wild meat.'

Back at the house Sugar, Bud, and Carlie, had stopped by for a visit and their father and mother insisted that they sit down at the table and eat.

"There's lots of food left, no use letting it go to waste." Sugar's mother had said.

As he sipped on a cup of coffee he noticed how proud the Barton's seemed to be of Sugar and Bud.

'Sure must have lightened their load a great deal when she finally married Bud. I hope it works out for them, I wish them the best.'

Soon Ma said she thought they had better head for home.

"It's been a long day for Pa he tires out easy anymore." She said.

Tex took the bag from the car and handed mister Barton four squirrels.

"Son we don't need that many squirrels for a mess, here take a couple back."

"No I got more in the bag, you keep them."

"Okay, and then he winked as he said.

"Will you help me skin them Bud?"

"Sure will." Bud answered. "If you'll invite me over to help eat them tomorrow."

"You've got yourself a deal, so lets get started." He said.

That night after going to bed Tex lay there and thought about how things had worked out for Sugar and her family in the end.

'I'm happy for her, but most of all for her parents, I wonder if she ever thinks about all the grief she has caused them over the years.' 'I hope she does and will make it up to them some way. She don't know how lucky she is to have parents to love her, she should have to walk a mile in my shoes.'

The shoulders of the road on both sides were jammed with parked cars that were extended a half-mile each way at the upper dam.

Must have been several hundred people there to see Bud and Sugar baptized.

Some were standing on the railroad on higher ground above the road.

A large crowd was expected because of Sugar's notoriety in the past and the good deed that she was performing for Carlie.

I finally found a place to park the old truck quite a ways above the dam. Two other fellows were with me and we walked back towards the dam.

Up ahead I spotted a car that I thought belonged to Hoss, as we got up close he was sitting in the car. He had a better view of the dam than anyone, so he must have gotten there before anyone else.

He was alone and I thought. 'I guess it's like the talk going around, that young girl that moved in with him and his father is nothing more than a slave for them.'

As we passed he growled.

"You all getting yore ass dunked today too?"

"No we're not." One of the fellows answered. "But I got a feeling we ought to."

"What'cha mean ought to? Hell that ain't gonna do any more for you than skinny dipping and that's just what I'll be doing with Sugar in a weeks time, I'll have her down here skinny dipping mark my words."

The leering grin came over his face as we walked away.

After a brief message from the pastor and a song, 'Shall we gather at the river.'

The Pastor waded out in waist deep water.

Two church members one on either side led Sugar out to the Pastor. She had on a long white gown, he immersed her in the water and lifted her to her feet, as she stood there the wet gown clung and revealed the contours of her body and her face lit up with a radiance that surpassed any that I had seen before.

Then they led Bud out and the pastor baptized him. Bud came up smiling too.

Once out of the water the hugs and handshaking took over for the next ten minutes or so.

Pretty soon the crowd started drifting away, everyone seemed pleased with the ceremony and I heard several comments.

"I sure am glad that girl finally came to her senses, she just about destroyed her father and mother with worry."

"Yes I know, she sure put a lot of gray hairs in their head. She'll be a wonderful worker in our church. She has a way with people and she's so likeable."

As I watched them lead her to the car wrapped in a blue blanket to ward off the chill of the September air I could vision her as she once was but now knew that I was seeing a different Sugar.

Then I thought. 'I'm going to miss the old Sugar' and hate to think that I'll never hold her again. But the new Sugar is shining through and like everyone else here today with the exception of Hoss, I'm happy that she made the change and I wish her well."

Bud taught Sugar how to drive and on her Monday's off she would drive him to work and use the car to run errands, or sometimes take Carlie for a ride.

On this Monday she took Carlie to see the Doctor in St. Charles.

Doc seemed to be taken by surprise as he sat down across from Carlie.

'Somebody's been praying again.' He thought. 'The last time I saw her I was sure she would wind up in the sanatorium at Marion.'

"Well what can I do for you today Carlie?" How have you been feeling? You look pretty fit, this young lady with you must be a good cook and giving you the right kind of food, cause you certainly have improved since the last time I saw you."

"Yes doctor she is a good cook and so good in other ways, she's a wonderful person, I credit her and the medicine you prescribed for my improvement."

"Without her I wouldn't be sitting here today. She persuaded me to eat and take my medicine, she's been a God send."

"Yes I've heard a lot about this young lady." He looked over at Sugar and said.

"I hear that you just got married to a fine young man from down at Stone Creek

"I know him and his family well, they're fine people. Congratulations! You made the right choice, and I also heard that you and Bud made another decision, a very important one, I happened to be passing by that way the day you two were being baptized. That may turn out to be the most rewarding decision that you have ever made."

He wrote out a renewal prescription for Carlie. "Keep taking this just as before.

There will be times especially in your waking hours that you will become depressed. I'm sure you've already experienced some of that already." Carlie nodded in agreement.

"When that happens try to stay near someone and talk, anything to get your mind off the way you're feeling. You do have someone near you at all times don't you?"

Sugar spoke up. "Yes, the ladies from church take turns staying with her from the time I leave for work in the morning till I get home about six o'clock in the evenings. I stay with her every night and Sunday's and Monday's, Monday is my day off from work."

"Yes, young lady, I heard about that too. I don't believe you realize how much you mean to Carlie and that little community."

"You're one of a kind, God be with you."

Sugar smiled, and not knowing what else to say, said, "Thank you doctor! And I pray that God will have a special place for you in heaven. You see I've heard and know a lot about you also."

"I know that you never get a full nights sleep and seldom ever get to be with your family for any length of time."

"You mention me and how much I mean to 'that little community. Well let me say this. I don't believe you realize how much you mean to this whole area."

"Folks in this area and especially the mining families are not apt to praise you to your face, but believe me you have already became a legion here in Lee County."

"You are truly a God send, May God bless you."

"Thank you young lady, thank you! I'm not worthy of all that praise but I will ask God to be with me, and I will try to do the very best I can to bring healing and comfort to my patients here in Lee County."

Then Sugar noticed his trembling hand as he handed the prescription renewal to Carlie, and she could plainly see tears in his eyes.

Bud and Sugar continued to live apart except for weekends. Cam had spoken to them again about Bud moving in, but they both thought it best they keep the arrangements they had thinking it might upset Carlie if Bud moved in.

As the weeks went by more of the young men received a greeting in the mail advising them to report to Abington for examination.

One of them being Hoss. He failed the exam. And was classified 4f.

He was elated, and bragged to the others about how he out smarted the doctor's.

"You all go ahead and fight the damn war, you ain't smart enough to know how to get out of it, so go ahead and get your asses shot off, I'll stay here and take care of the women while you're gone."

It was clear that he had ate or taken something to alter his blood pressure and cause his heart rate to change.

But nobody really cared. One of the fellows remarked. "I wouldn't want that bastard in a fox hole with me anyway."

Meanwhile about the same time in Kentucky Bama received his notice to report for exam.

He passed and was asked if he would consider working in a copper mine out west instead of being assigned to the army or navy.

The officer told him to think about it. "If you decide you want to do that give me a call within the next three days. If I don't hear from you, then you will be assigned to either the Army or Navy."

"Actually you'll still be in the service of our country, we have a quota to fill for copper miners because copper is needed for the war effort. And right now there's openings so if you want to take advantage of it let me know."

Bama and Gina talked it over. Gina thought it best he take the mining offer.

"Either way you'll not be here when the baby comes, but at least you won't be overseas and might be allowed to come in after it's born."

Bama thought it over and didn't like the idea of mining copper while his relatives and friends were off in some God forsaken land fighting to keep the country free.

But the officer had said.

"You will still be in the service of our country."

So the next day he called the officer and informed him that he would prefer the copper mine offer over the army or navy.

Within ten days he was assigned to a copper mine in far off Montana.

The induction date allowed him a few more days at home with Gina and time to write his parents in Alabama.

Dear Mom and dad,

I just want to write and tell you how sorry I am about not coming back to see you. I miss you all more than you will ever know, oh! I know what you're thinking I sure didn't act like it when I was home but I guess

> *it took time and a lot of miles between us to make me realize just how much I love and miss you.*

I will be going away to Montana in a couple days to work in a copper

> *mine.I had a choice of going in the Army, Navy, or copper mining, so I chose the copper mine. The officer told me that it is very important to the war effort.*

As I told you in another letter Gina is pregnant and the baby is due in about four months. We are happy and hope that I'll be able to get a furlough when it's born.

I have made arrangements for Gina to go back to Virginia and live with Mike and his family. Actually it was Mike and Vivian's idea. I am grateful to them for their kindness and I hope to repay them some way after the war is over.

I have missed you all so much and had planned on saving money to come there in a few months, but looks like that will have to wait a while. I have been dieing for you to meet Gina she's a wonderful person and I know you'll like her.

Mike says he sees a change in me and I credit that to Gina and the time that I have been away from you all, so maybe it was in God's plans that I leave home and meet Gina, miss you and find myself.

I'll close for this time and write again when I get to Montana.

I dread to think of leaving Gina but it is necessary that I go do my part for our country, so many have already served and some lost their lives. So I feel proud to step up and be a part of the ones that have already served and died so that they may not have died in vain.

I hope to see you all soon. I love you. Carl

P.S. Everybody here calls me Bama, it seems strange to use Carl. HA!

Sugar and the church ladies noticed that Carlie was having her depression spells more frequently as the weeks went by. Sugar talked with the doctor and he advised her to increase her medication whenever she thought she needed to.

"But be careful and don't leave the pills around where she'll be able to get her hands on them, in other words I want you or whoever's with her at the time to control the dosage, an over dose can be fatal."

A few days later Carlie went for her daily visit to Lonnie and little Lonnie's graves. The lady with her that day noticed that she had been gone longer than usual and decided to walk that way to see about her.

Just before she reached the church around the curve she heard loud screaming of tires and several loud noises like a car had hit something or ran off the road. She broke into a run and as she rounded the curve she could see a large coal truck in the deep ditch up ahead near the church. Coal was strewn over the road and in the ditch, the truck was partially lieng on its side up against the bank and

she could see the driver had pushed the passenger side door open and was having some difficulty getting out.

By the time she reached the truck he was out and sitting on the edge of the ditch pale and shaking.

On past the truck near the church she seen Carlie with her hands over her face and thought she must be crying.

"What happened?" She asked the driver. "Are you hurt?"

"No ma'am." He answered. "I'll be okay in a few minutes, don't know how I missed her, she walked right out from the church parking lot right into my path and looked straight at me as she walked toward the truck. She had to be trying to commit suicide. Who is she? She's lucky to be alive, still can't figure how I missed her. God must have been with her and me too I guess."

As she held Carlie, she asked. "What happened? Are you alright?"

"I felt so bad when I left the cemetery, I just wanted to end it all and be with them again." She answered. "Is that man alright? I'm so sorry."

"Yes he's okay except for being unnerved, we'll take him up to the house and fix him some coffee. He'll have to get a wrecker out here to pull the truck out, thank God neither of you was hurt."

Later that day after the truck was pulled from the ditch and the roadway cleared of coal the state patrolman came by.

She had given Carlie a dose of the medicine as soon as they got to the house and told her to go lay down. Checking on her now she could see that she was sleeping soundly.

"That's okay." The patrolman said. "Don't wake her, is she sick?"

"Yes she is." She replied. Then she proceeded to tell him about Carlie's misfortune, about losing little Lonnie, then Lonnie, and how she just went to pieces.

"Does she live here alone?" The patrolman asked.

"No there's someone with her night and day, we allow her to go visit the cemetery daily but guess we'll have to stop that after what happened today."

"Yes you will." He said. "I can understand why you folks want to keep her at home and care for her, but you must understand that she poses a danger to herself and others. So I ask you to try and keep her under control, cause if something like this happens again I'll have to recommend that she be put away in the sanatorium in Marion. Not that I would want to, I just don't have any other choice it's the state law."

Carlie continued to visit the cemetery daily, but now accompanied by one of the church ladies or Sugar.

Sugar showed the ladies where she had hid the medicine and warned them again about what the doctor had said. "An over dose can be fatal."

In mid December Sugar stopped by the flower shop in town after work and purchased a dozen red roses for Carlie. She usually would do this once a week until the roses blossomed again in the spring at Carlie's house.

When she arrived home she was so surprised to see Carlie in such a jolly mood.

"She's been that way all day she seems so happy, a complete turn around from the past few months.' The church lady whispered. "She insisted that she do all the house work today, wouldn't let me do one thing. I sat there in that chair most of the day while she served me coffee. And another thing she didn't even mention going to the cemetery, I'm so happy for her."

That night they stayed up late as Sugar listened to her talk about old times.

"Remember how you used to bring little Lonnie a red rose twice a day?"

"He loved you like a sister, won't it be wonderful that we'll all be together again some day? I was so happy when you and Bud got married, he's a good young man Sugar, and will make a wonderful father."

"Maybe I shouldn't say what I'm about to say, but if you ever think of going back to your old ways, remember how Bud carried the torch for you even though it looked hopeless that you would ever change. Remember that

95

Sugar, he's one in a hundred that would put up with something like that. And he did it because he loved you. And that's the most important thing that will ever happen in our lives Sugar. In the end you may find yourself in the same fix that I'm in, broken hearted and almost out of mind, but it was all because of the love I had for Lonnie and little Lonnie. And it was worth it Sugar, I'd gladly do it all over again."

As tears started to form in Sugar's eyes, she reached for Carlie and held her in her arms.

"I know, Carlie, I know, I always knew how much you and Lonnie loved each other and hoped that one day I would find someone to share my life with, but as you know my life has been a shambles from the time I was fourteen, I was just play acting and trying to look happy and care free on the outside, but on the inside I was going through hell and thinking that no one would ever want me as their own, after all I am tarnished you know, nothing can be done about that."

"Bud had told me many times that he cared for me. I didn't believe him. You see I cared for him right from the start but thought it would never work out."

"A good man deserves a good woman, and that's where I thought I came up short."

"But now I know Bud and I belong with each other and I will put the past behind me as best I can. And that won't be easy, what's that old bible verse?" 'As you sow. So shall you reap.' Or you reap what you sow,' something like that. Well I guess you could say I have a lot of bad crops coming in."

Finally she went to the hidden pills and brought one to Carlie with a glass of water.

"Here take this and lets get to bed, it's getting late."

"Okay Sugar. And let me say again how much I've enjoyed having you around, if not for you I wouldn't be here today. And here take this red rose, it's just for you. And if you don't mind I'll tell you goodbye now, cause I may not be awake when you leave for work in the morning, we've wasted the night away jabbering, but I've enjoyed it."

Sugar put her arms around her and said. "Yes Carlie, I've enjoyed it too every minute of it, and more than that I'm so happy to see you like your old self again."

"Good night and sweet dreams, I'll wake you to say goodbye in the morning."

At six thirty a.m. Sugar opened the door to Carlie's bedroom. As she stood there looking at her, she thought. 'She looks like she's resting so well, maybe I should just let her rest a while longer and let the lady that's coming today get her breakfast.'

But as she started to leave she noticed something in Carlie's right hand. She went closer and seen she was clutching a single red rose. She glanced down at the little table beside the bed and there along with a scribbled note she seen the empty medicine bottle.

She reached to feel Carlie's hand hoping against hope that this is just a dream or a joke.

'But no it's not, her hand is cold, oh God! She's gone.'

She sat down on the bed and ran her hands over Carlie's face and smoothed her hair as she cried.

"You told me goodbye last night because you knew you wouldn't be awake this morning. Oh why didn't I pay more attention, I should have known something like this was on your mind."

The news of Carlie's death spread fast and came as a shock to most everybody.

Everyone knew of her condition and at the same time had heard that her health had improved considerably over a period of time.

That afternoon the pastor called a special meeting at the church at seven p.m. to discuss burial plans.

As he faced the members he had in mind to ask for donations from everyone to help pay for her burial.

"As you know Carlie left behind no bank account, no property, nor any money stashed away in a jar somewhere."

"Her parents in Kentucky have had their share of sickness and expense to the point where they can just barely exist."

"Therefore I believe we here in this church are obligated to see that she gets a decent burial. I have talked to Copeland at the funeral home. He's a decent and fair man. He said he would go ahead and get her ready for burial, and would not use the cheapest Vault, Casket, etc."

"He told me not to worry, just bring me whatever the folks at the church chip in. Now we could just sit back and take advantage and let him bear the burden, but as you know that's not the right thing to do, so I ask all of you to contribute as much as you can toward Carlie's burial."

Cam raised his hand and Asked. "Can I say something? I may have a plan that will be agreeable to all."

"Sure." The pastor replied. "Tell us your plan Cam."

"Well as you all know after Lonnie died Carlie had no income and no way to pay the monthly payments on the mortgage that I hold. The payments are several months in arrears so therefore the property is mine. But I have come to the conclusion that it wouldn't be the right thing for me to take the property back and call it my own, because in less than a year Lonnie would have paid it off if he had lived. So I'm here to tell you that I intend to pay for Carlie's burial, and see that her parent's get what I consider a fair amount of money before I call the property my own again."

Everyone sat there stunned. Finally the pastor stood and said.

"Is there anyone in this room that wants to disagree with this man? If so speak up, so I can expel you from this church as of this minute."

That brought laughter and the buzz of chatter.

"I don't see any hands raised so I guess we're all in agreement."

"God has been with us here tonight, he has been among us many times in the past months. Lets give him praise and glory!"

Two days later the little church was crowded with mourners.

As they walked by the open casket some dabbed their eyes, others paused and closed their eyes in prayer. Sugar placed three fresh cut red roses in Carlie's folded hands, leaned over, kissed her on the forehead and whispered, "A pretty red rose for each of you Sugar, goodbye."

The pastor stood and opened his bible to Psalm 25.

"I would like to read verses fifteen, sixteen, and seventeen, from psalms, chapter 25."

"Please listen closely and I believe you will understand why Carlie went to bed Tuesday night knowing that our Lord would take her before the sun rose on Wednesday morning."

"Verse 15. Mine eyes are ever toward the Lord; for he shall pluck my feet out of the net."

"Versa 16. Turn thee unto me, and have mercy upon me; for I am desolate and afflicted."

"Verse 17. The troubles of my heart are enlarged; O bring thou me" out of my distresses."

"Now lets read the note she left behind and I'm sure you will understand the connection it has with these three verses."

Dear Mom and Dad, and all my dear friends I pray that you will forgive me and try to understand that I prayed and worked this out with our Lord.

My burdens just became unbearable and I went to him for mercy and forgiveness.

This morning I awoke filled with happiness and knew that he had answered my prayers. So before the sun rises Wednesday morning I'll be with Lonnie and little Lonnie again.

Someday I hope to see you all there, so stay the course and our Lord will welcome you and we'll be together again.

All my love until we meet again. Carlie

"Now may I ask you what else can I add to make this any clearer?"

"She went to God and asked him to take her out of this world and all the misery that had became unbearable."

"I'll go as far as to say that it was God's leading hand that led her to the hidden bottle of pills. And of course you know she took them all and went into a deep sleep, never to awake here in this community again, but she did awake and is awake at this moment, because you see, she awoke in the arms of the Lord. Let's bury Carlie out there with Lonnie and little Lonnie today not with a heavy heart, but with gladness and praise to our Lord because he has put them together again, I bet right now he's showing Carlie a little house along side a road some where in heaven that has a white picket fence lined with red roses."

"Let us pray."

"Lord we're going to miss Carlie in this community and in our little church, but we'll leave here today with a smile on our faces knowing that she is now in your care."

"As I have said many times you answer prayers in strange ways at times. But I guess it's not for me to understand, so from this day on I promise never to bring up the subject again."

"Thank you Lord for your patience and all the goodness you bestow on our members in this church. We go from here today knowing that we have just witnessed the closing of the final chapter in the lives of one of our church families."

"But at the same time knowing that they now are in a land free of pain heartaches, and a life made up of chapters, some not so good like Carlie just experienced."

"We ask you to be near us as we walk through this life, for without you our life on earth is nothing more than a book filled with bad chapters."
"AMEN."

Bud and Sugar talked it over and decided they would approach Cam about buying the little house.
"I've saved a little toward a down payment." Bud said. "But if we can't meet the down payment he requires maybe he'll let us rent it with the monthly rent payments going toward the purchase of the place later."
"Yes I would love to have this little place." Sugar said. "I would have somewhere to live if you have to go in the service, I don't want to have to go back home although I know I would be welcome there. I feel that I would be a burden on mom and Dad. God knows I have gave them enough heartaches to last them to their graves already."
"Do you think we can make the payments if I have to go in the service? The allotment you'll get won't be very much."
"Sure we can Sugar." Sugar replied. "I'm doing pretty good at the shop and Betty said she is thinking about making me a partner in the business. She says I have increased her receipts two fold in the last few months and she thinks it's only right that she make me a partner."

Three days later on a Friday Bud came home from work and his mother handed him an envelope that came in the mail that day.
Although she hadn't opened it she knew what it contained for the return address stamped in the upper corner of the envelope was 'Selective service board #2 Pennington Gap, Virginia.
Bud glanced at the envelope and put his arm around his mother, he could see that she had been crying.
"It's okay mom I'm a big boy now! And the country needs big boys right now, so don't worry I'll be alright."
"Yes I know Bud, but I've been so happy that you and Sugar have finally found each other, and now you'll have to leave her. Just don't seem fair."
"That's okay mom, like I said I'm a big boy now and Sugar, Shucks she'll weather the storm she's one of a kind."
He opened the envelope and read the short message with instructions that he be at the selective board parking lot at six a.m. the following Monday to board a special bus to Abingdon, Va. For examination to serve in the United States armed forces.

After prayer meeting on Wednesday night Bud approached Cam about buying the little place.

"Sure I'll think about it." Cam said. "I hear you got your notice from the draft board to report for examination."

"Yes I did but we would like to buy the place anyway. That way Sugar will have a place of her own and won't have to be a burden on her family."

"Tell you what I'll stop by Saturday afternoon and we'll talk about it. I'll bring the wife along if you don't mind. She thinks the world of Sugar, and they need to get to know each other better."

"That's fine." Bud replied. "Don't eat anything before you come and we'll feast on some of Sugar's good cooking."

"Sounds good to me Bud. I'll see you Saturday, and do you think Sugar could whup us up a good banana pudding?"

"Sure she can, she's a good cook she takes that after her mother."

"Oh great! Then you can expect us Saturday afternoon Bud."

Bud was proud of Sugar as she rushed around getting everything in place for the dinner. 'She's a great person.' He thought. 'To bad I have to leave her so soon I'll miss her, God how I'll miss her!"

Cam and his wife came hungry and truly enjoyed the dinner. Cam complemented Sugar on her cooking skills especially the Banana pudding.

"The best I ever ate." He said. "Might put a few inches around the old middle here, but good food was put here for a reason and I intend to enjoy it."

"Well now lets get down to the business that brought us here now that we all have full stomach's and can't think straight." Cam said.

"Sometimes better deals are made when we are in this state, get them over with so we can get our daily nap right after a good dinner."

They all laughed and Bud thought. 'He sure is a jolly cuss, sure would be nice if he would give us a good deal on this place.'

"Now let's get right to the brass tacks of what we're talking about here. Bud, you're going Monday for the exam. And you're most certain to pass cause you look like a healthy specimen to me."

"So where does that put us in regards to you buying this place from me?"

"I'll tell you what it does! It kills the deal that's what it does. The measly amount of the allotment that Sugar would get from you being in the service wouldn't take care of her let alone contribute anything much toward a mortgage payment on this place."

Then Sugar butted in. "Oh yes we can make the payments! We've talked it over. I make a pretty good weekly salary at the shop and expect to make more in the near future. Bud has a little money for a down payment not much but we had hoped that you would consider it."

"Well young lady I have given it considerable thought since I talked to Bud about it last Wednesday and I've made up my mind that it would be to much of a burden on the both of you. So I guess that settles it."

Bud looked at Sugar and thought. 'What a let down, and we had so much faith in Cam, what a disappointment.' 'I wonder if we even have a chance at renting it now.'

Cam seemed to be enjoying the worried look on their faces. Finally he said.

"Now that we've settled that problem let's get down to business."

"As you know I'm much too old for the draft and it bothers me to see our young men go off to war and sacrifice their family life and sometimes their lives while I stay behind and live my life relatively undisturbed."

"So I've come up with this plan that will make me feel that I have done something worth while toward the war effort and most of all for you two."

He reached in his pocket and pulled out some papers. "I went down to the courthouse in Jonesville Thursday and had these papers fixed up."

"Both of you sign right here and right there. Then give me ten dollars, and as you can see you have a clear deed to this property. And may God bless you both."

Tears were running freely down the cheeks of Sugar and Cam's wife faces as they embraced. Bud reached for Cam's hand and said.

"I don't know how to thank you for this, I still don't think it's right that we get this place for just ten dollars."

"Well it is right son, but come to think of it I might want some more of that good banana pudding to close the deal."

When the pastor heard about it in church on Sunday he made this announcement.

"I think all of you have heard about what one of our members did for Bud and Sugar over the past week, but you didn't hear the whole story, he also gave a good sum of money to Carlie's parents in Kentucky that will make their lives a little easier in their old age."

"I want Cam to stand up back there. Stand up Cam! Folks how can we ever repay him for all the good deeds that he has done for our members here?"

Cam's wife stood up smiling, and said.

"Just keep feeding him banana pudding that's the most rewarding thing you can do for him." Cam offered a loud amen and everyone laughed.

They filed out of the little church with smiles on their faces. The pastor had said again.

"God has been amongst us today." Lets give him praise and glory."

Poor Boy: In a matter of days he would be forty-one years old, but with the unkempt beard on his face and wrinkles around his eyes he would pass for fifty.

A pot bellied stove sat in one corner of the shack stoked with coal from the mine nearby.

He sat and stared at the flames through the air slits in the stove door as the coal slowly burned away. Pretty soon more coal will have to be added to keep the fire going.

'Pretty much like me.' He thought. 'I'm slowly burning away only thing is nobody can put more fuel on the flames to keep me going. When I'm burned out the grim reaper comes to call.'

'Just like old 'Rub' damn! I miss him. Just as the saying goes. When your friends forsake you and strangers shun you, your dog will remain at your feet asking nothing more from you than a kind word, a morsel of food from your table or a pat on the head.'

'It's been three weeks today since I woke and felt the coldness of his body at my back. Now that he's gone I have nothing or nobody, pretty much the same shape old Rub found me in ten years ago.'

'Oh I talk with the half dozen miners that work here once in a while and some of the folks in the area that I have known all my life, but when it comes right down to it none of them could care diddly shit about me or what happens to me.'

'And I shore as hell can't blame them, I put my life in the mess it's in. I had help sure, but I'm the one that chose to let it burden me for the rest of my life.'

'Once I had about as much as any young man could expect to have working the coalmines. A father and mother to go home to, decent clothes a good car and a girl that I thought I would marry and live happily ever after. What a crock that turned out to be. I respected and never tried to have sex with her.'

"That can wait till we're married.' We both agreed. But then I went away to Kentucky for three months working as an electrician helping to get a new mine started for Old Dominion.'

'I'll never forget the letter I got from her telling me that she was pregnant, and by a married man at that. 'I'm so sorry.' The letter said. 'Guess you'll never want to marry me, but I want you to know you're the one I love and I hope you'll understand and forgive me.'

'Oh sure I understand, I understand how you have wrecked my life, and hell! How could I ever forgive you?'

'She didn't live long after the baby came. Her parents raised him. I have seen and talked to him several times, seems like a nice young man, I wonder if anybody ever told him who his father is?'

He got up and opened the door to reach outside for another block of coal that was stacked along side the shack.

Just as the door opened a young dog jumped back from where it had been sniffing around the closed door.

He watched as the dog stood there shivering from the unusual December cold winds.

"Oh hell no!" He said. "Get to hell outta here, I ain't never going to get hooked with another dog, so you might as well be on yore way, I know you must be hungry, look at them ribs sticking out. Somebody dropped you off, don't know how in hell people can do that, but you're better off away from them anyway."

"Shit! How can they have a dog around and let it starve?"

"Go on now! You might find somebody down the road there that will take you in."

He started to close the door, but hesitated as he watched the puppy shaking. Then he thought. 'Hell aint nobody that'll take that dog in tonight and it's cold as hell right here before dark, no telling how low it'll get before morning.'

"Well shit you may as well stay here tonight come on in."

The puppy didn't move.

"Well come on dammit! It's cold out here."

With its tail between its legs the puppy moved slowly toward the open door.

Once inside he cowered in a corner of the shack while the stove was being stoked.

"Alright lets get it straight right now, you can stay here tonight but come morning after the sun comes out and warms up a bit you hafta hit th road."

"I meant what I said, when I said I ain't about to get attached to another dog."

"You understand that don't you?"

"Ain't no way you could ever run in old Rub's tracks, I ain't had no true friends in a long time but old Rub made up for all of that."

"So don't get it in yore head that you've found a home, cause come morning you hafta hit th road."

The puppy didn't move from the corner but the shaking had stopped and his gaze wandered to the kettle that sat on top of the old stove.

"Okay I got some beef stew cooking, when it's done I'll give you some. But for now here have a hunk of this balony."

"Dang! You are hungry, here have some more."

He sat down on the bed he had fashioned from material that he had picked up from around the mine.

Two discarded cross ties covered with pieces of scrap lumber kept the bed above the dirt floor.

From the pine trees in the edge of the woods he had cut small pine limbs and laid them over the boards. Then about three inches of pine straw covered the limbs.

A worn army blanket covered the pine straw.

For cover he used another old tattered army blanket and a patchwork cotton filled quilt that had several torn places with the cotton hanging out.

"Well hell! You gonna sit there all night? Come on over here come on. I ain't gonna hurt you."

He reached out and the puppy slowly moved toward him.

"That's it come on I won't hurt you, you've been mistreated, I hate bastards that will take on a dog and then mistreat it."

As he stroked the puppy's head and back he turned it over so he could see its belly and said.

"Let me check and see what you are Oh yeah! There it is backed up by two little peanuts you shore got cheated there."

"I thought for sure you'd be a bitch, that's usually the ones they drop off."

He got up to stir the beef stew and the puppy jumped on the bed. When he seen this he picked him up and looked into his eyes and said.

"You stay off that bed, ain't but one dog that I will ever let sleep on my bed and that was Rub. So you stay away from that bed, hear?"

Soon the beef stew was done and for the next few minutes all was quiet except for the slurping sound of the puppy wolfing down the beef stew from an old iron skillet.

"Okay here's the last of it we shore made short work of that kettle of stew.

Thought I'd have enough for tomorrow, now I'll have to put on a kettle of beans."

He sat back down on the bed rolled a cigarette and lit it with a match, he reached over to an oil lamp that sat on an overturned nail keg near the bed, lifted the globe and lit the lamp.

The puppy sat near the stove never taking his eyes off him.

"Say what's your name, or do you have one?"

"I'll tell you how Rub got his name. I was going down the road there one day back when I was heavy into th booze, not long after I got back from Kentucky and that damn letter was still on my mind. Well shit you don't need to hear about th letter, anyway I was staggering along there about the Pine Grove Church just before you get to the Kentucky Darby Commissary when this small puppy about yore size come up and started leaning against my legs and rubbing himself more like a cat than a dog."

"I yelled at him to get going and mind his own business. Ever time I'd yell he'd drop behind, but in no time he'd be right back rubbing my legs again."

"He followed me all the way home, at that time I rented a little house right there close to the church."

"And By god! Just like you the first thing I knew he had begged his way into my house."

"I fed him something and had a few more drinks, enough to put me to sleep, and when I woke up the next morning there he was laying right up against my back in my bed."

"I raised a little hell and got up and showed him th door, but damned if he'd leave, hung around outside all day and ever time I'd go out he'd come and start rubbing himself around my legs."

"Well by night fall he was still hanging around so I took him in with the understanding that as soon as the sun comes up tomorrow you hit the road."

"But the next day was the same he wouldn't leave, and after about a week of taking him in for just one more night I was hooked on him."

"So one day I said, looks like I'm stuck with you so I better think of a name. I tried to think of a name for two days but couldn't come up with one that suited him, so I said hell! I'll call him Rub."

"Now don't you go getting any ideas that you can work your self in like Rub did cause when th sun comes up in th morning I'll open that door and put you on the road."

He picked up a gunnysack from the floor and placed it near the stove.

"You can sleep on this tonight it's warmer over here near the stove but near morning the coal will be burnt out and it gets pretty nippy in here till I get the fire going in the stove again."

"But remember what I told you stay the hell away from my bed, I better not wake up and find you there."

The puppy wagged his tail and cocked his head to one side as if he was thinking.

'I've got you right where I want you, I'm gonna slip in just where old Rub left off.'

About 5 a.m. he awoke and felt something at his back shaking.

'That must be that damn pup, guess he got cold."

He reached back and lifted the blanket as the pup crawled under it and snuggled up close to his back.

He awoke at 6 a.m. rebuilt the fire in the old potbelly, had bacon and eggs for breakfast. Used about a half loaf of bread to sop up the bacon grease to feed the pup.

"You know you're just like Rub was, running around without a name. It just hit me and the name suits you to a T, them two little things between your legs the size of peanuts, well that's your name from now on you're peanut."

"Ah hell don't look at me like that I didn't mean to upset you they'll get bigger."

He opened the door and stuck his head out.

"Okay Peanut, lets go outside and look around it's warmed up a lot, today's Saturday I don't have to go to work, I may as well show you around."

Bud passed the exam and was inducted into the navy with orders to report in three weeks. Sugar tried to sound upbeat and encourage him cause she could see that he was in turmoil about having to leave her. But at times the worry of losing him would get the best of her and the tears would flow.

Gina settled in with Bama's brother Mike and his wife Vivian back at Leona mine in Virginia.

The letters between them were filled with love and longing.

Wish you were here with me Gina, I've thought about it a hundred times that maybe I could rent something here so we could be together.

But the mine is far away from any city or town with nothing but open land in between. They have erected barrack's like buildings for our quarters I suppose much like the army has.

Copper mining is hard work but no more than coal mining. In fact it might be a little easier, at least I can walk upright. Both the coalmines I worked in I had to bend over because of the small seam of coal and at times crawl.

She would read his letters over and over and though she was dieing inside she tried to be very careful not to let it show in the things she would say in her letters to him.

Don't worry about us being apart I'm well satisfied here with Mike, Vivian and the kids. Vivian says that I have been a godsend to help her with the work around the house, and the kids, I enjoy them so much.

Michael junior will soon be ten and is doing well in school. But you know how quick the folks around here come up with a nickname. Somebody started calling him Jake and it looks like it's caught on. Your brother just laughs about it and sometimes calls him Jake himself. But Vivian is all upset about it and I can't say that I blame her after all she named him after your brother.

Jennifer 'Jennie' turned seven and started to school this year. Right now she hates school but with time she'll be okay I can remember my first year of school I didn't like it either. But as time went on I made new friends and began to look forward to seeing them in school every day.

And Richard, he'll soon be four and getting smarter every day. He asks me almost every day. 'Did you get a letter from uncle Carl today?' 'When you write tell him that when daddy buys me a pony I'm gonna ride out there to Montana and see him.' 'You could too Aunt Gina, buy a horse and come with me.'

He's such a sweet little boy but you know with that name it won't be long till he'll be stuck with 'Dick' as a nickname and Vivian will hit the roof for sure.

Vivian just found out she's pregnant again she says she don't want anymore after this one that four's enough.

We both went to the Doctor in St. Charles yesterday. He said I'm fine and every things on schedule for another little Bama to arrive before too long. He's such a nice person if only he'd quit that booze, but I don't believe he'll ever be able to. He asked about you and wishes you the best.

And like most all letters between lovers they would end in 'I love you' 'I miss you so much.' 'Can't wait to see and hold you again.'

Such a good feeling to know that you were in love but at the same time as I heard a soldier in my platoon once say one time after reading a letter from his wife thousands of miles away in Georgia.

"Ain't nothing like a letter from my wife but after reading it I get so down.

Why in hell did I let myself fall in love and get married before I was called up?"

Damn the Hitler's and Tojo's of the world, I'm so tired of this damned war."

Bud was in boot camp somewhere in California and the letters between him and Sugar were much the same.

He was overjoyed to read in a letter from Sugar in February.

Sugar, I'm so happy to tell you I think I'm pregnant. But after a few days the joy slipped from his mind and was replaced by.

'Will I ever see my baby? Will I ever see Sugar again? Will this war ever end?'

At about the same time Hoss took the young girl to Jonesville where they got a marriage license and they were married by a justice of the piece.

"Pretty much like a business deal." As one fellow put it. "Now he can say she's his wife and treat her pretty much any way he wants to, bastard belongs in jail but guess that will never happen."

"And they say she's pregnant, can you imagine a child growing up under a manic like him?"

Tex expects to get his draft notice any time and is seriously thinking about asking Marty for a date.

'I've been dragging my feet on that and need to get it over with because I think about her more every day. And I believe she's thinking of me to, I can feel it.'

In the meantime peanut has taken over at Poor Boy's Shack. Poor Boy feeds him well and the ribs that once were sticking out right at skins edge are now covered with tissue and solid muscle topped with shiny black hair with distinctive white spots down near the belly line and on one front leg.

"I told you them peanuts would grow." Poor Boy said. They're damn near as big as them muscadine grape's that grow on them vines out there in the woods."

"You're a dog and I guess you don't understand what the hell I'm talking about sometimes. But I'll tell you this anyway."

"I was born red headed and I was told that my mother looked at me and said."

" My goodness, he has red hair but that's alright we love you anyway."

"My mother was great, that's about all the pleasant memories I have left anymore."

"So you see my name Wayne never made it to first base cause ever body called me Red."

"Then some where along the line after I lost my pride and damn near my conscious because of the news that came in th letter I walked these roads in a drunken stupor most of the time."

"Most folks knew what had caused my down fall and felt sorry for me I guess."

"So they would refer to me as "Look at that poor Boy.""

"Well it wasn't long till some smart ass started calling me Poor Boy and it stuck like glue."

"So now when you hear Poor Boy you'll know who they're talking about."

"I'll tell you more about the letter sometime."

Peanut cocked his head to one side and looked at him with what Poor Boy thought was sadness. He reached out pulled him over to him and with his arms around his neck and his face buried on the side of Peanut's big flop ear he cried.

"Damn! I hate to get in these moods but sometimes I can't help it Peanut."

" I believe you understand more than I think you do, but don't you go worrying about me I brought it all on myself.'

February 1943 has passed and I'm seventeen. The time that I have been working here at the store has been the most important thing to happen in my life so far. I have learned to do about anything that is required cutting meat dealing with salesmen, and taking care of reordering when my uncle's are away.

I am the butt of some kidding but not as before. I have great respect for the folks around me especially the older ones and I can sense they respect me.

In a way I think the ongoing joshing I endured caused me to bind closer to the person and get to know them better.

And I think I might have grown up a little in the process. I no longer think of Sugar as I once did and find myself worrying that she might cheat on Bud and break his heart. 'I have great respect for her and I don't believe she will but things like that do happen.' I thought.

In the meantime I met a pretty girl, as hard as I've tried over the years I can't recall when and where I met her. But I do know she was very special to me at that time in my life. I had great respect for her and never tried to take my feelings beyond a passionate kiss.

In that respect I guess you could say I had grown up.

My thoughts were. 'If I have to go off to war a picture of her will always be in my wallet, and if I'm lucky enough to return she's the one I want to spend the rest of my life with.

In September 1943 the war is still raging and I think of what one of the guys had said back when I was fifteen.

"The damn war will be over before you ever grow up."

He was killed last week in some godforsaken place in North Africa. And the parents of one of the young men from Pucketts Creek got the sad news that he died in some far off hospital in the Pacific theater.

Twin brothers from Elys Creek enlisted early on in the war and were in the same division in the Solomon Islands when word came that one of them had been killed in combat.

Thinking of this I wondered if I could stand up and make myself accounted for as these fellows had done.

'Have I grown up? If not I better start thinking about it cause it won't be long till I'm eighteen.'

I had heard one of the fellow's say when he was in on Furlough after taking basic training some where in Texas.

"They try to make a fighting man out of you and the most stand the test but some don't."

Then I thought. 'I sure hope I'm not one of the 'Don't's'

Tex got home from work one day and was told by his grandmother that Pa had been sick most of the day.

"He won't eat anything." She said. "I'm worried son, maybe we should call the Doctor."

Tex sat down by the bed and noticed that Pa seemed to be in deep thought. Even when he turned his head toward Tex his eyes seemed to focus on something way off in the distance.

"You feeling any better Pa? Ma says you've been pretty sick today."

His lips moved but no words came out. Tex got a lump in his throat and had to turn away for a second.

Within an hour Doc drove in the driveway. Tex being one to keep his car clean and shiny noticed the dirt on Doc's car.

'That car ain't been washed in months.' He thought. 'And look at all the dents and the rear bumper, one end's loose, Doc must be a terrible driver.'

"He's had a stroke, see his left leg and arm, he can't move them. Has he said anything?"

"No but his lips moved like he was trying to say something just before you came."

"Well it's affected his speech, I think we better call Copeland and get him to the hospital they can do more for him there and the next few hours are pretty critical."

"The biggest danger right now is he may have another one, so it's best we get him there right away."

At the hospital he was hooked and connected to a few things that were available to the medical profession in the 1940's.

Tex sat beside his bed and rubbed his left arm and leg hoping the circulation might return.

His breathing became more labored as the clock hands moved past midnight.

Then at about four a.m. he was gasping for air. The nurse called the doctor from the other end of the hospital.

The young intern shook his head and said softly. "It's only a matter of hours now, maybe less if he has another stroke." He placed his hand on Tex shoulder and said. "I'm sorry there's nothing else we can do."

Tex sat by the bed and tried not to listen to his gasps for air. His thoughts went back to the times he would sit on the porch with Pa and listen to him relate the stories of his youth and how he met Ma.

"Her parents property joined ours." He said. "One day when I was about fourteen and she was twelve maybe thirteen, her and her older brother about my age, I caught them taking apples from our best apple tree."

"I went for her brother and was giving him a pretty good going over, but the first thing I know I'm on the ground knocked almost out of my senses with something oozing down the back of my neck which I knew had to be blood."

"I rolled over and there she stood over me holding a good sized stick that she had picked up from the ground."

"I guess when she seen the blood coming from the back of my head she got scared, she dropped to the ground and cradled my head in her lap, and the minute I looked up at her face I knew that some day she would be my wife."

"I had seen her many times before and never paid her much attention but that was the day we really met."

"I tease her all the time about it." 'You had to knock me out to get me to pay attention to you, I'll say."

"Then she'll say. Ah go on, you had your eye on me long before that, you just didn't have nerve enough to let it show."

Then he thought. 'I was thinking about asking him about my father some time this weekend but it's too late now, I'll have to work up the nerve to ask ma about it later.'

The nurse came in the room and asked him if he wanted coffee. "It's right down the hall there.' She said.

He got up and started to walk down the hall. Then he heard the nurse say. "No come back!"

He ran back and as he entered the room he could see that the gasping had almost stopped and knew that Pa's season was over.

As he stood over pa seeing him inhale his last breath of air he noticed his eyes were open with that far away look. As he looked into his deep blue eyes he wondered.

'What does he see?' 'Is he looking at the gates of heaven?' "Tell me Pa! What do you see?"

Then as he held Pa's hand and felt it turn cold he looked again into his deep blue eyes and there in the reflection he could see the 'stand of hickory' as Pa called it.

The cool of October had turned the leaves to a rich gold and they glistened in the bright sunshine and blended in with the reds of the oak's, silver and red of the maple, brown of the scattered sycamore, and the different shades of green of the pine and cedar.

And there he could see him and Pa sitting under the trees waiting for the squirrels to come to feed. Could hear Pa say.

"Be real quiet it's about time for them to start coming in, remember hold it tight to your shoulder and brace yourself or else she'll knock you on your rear."

"That old twelve-gauge packs quite a wallop."

Then over come with grief he laid his head on Pa's chest and cried.

"Pa, I'm sorry I never went with you there. I wish I had it to do all over again, we'd go every season Pa, we'd go every season. Mr. Barton said we can park there at his barn and go in that way. Then you wouldn't have to climb that old hill Pa."

As the nurse led him from the room he could still hear Pa the day he said. "I think my season is about over here on earth."

They held the funeral at a little church on Pucketts Creek. A large crowd including the Barton family attended.

Copeland had done a good job everybody remarked how nice Pa looked. "Looks like he's sleeping." Said one lady.

"You have to admire him for the way he brought his grandson up." Said another.

"You'll never know better people than him and his wife." A man remarked. "I have lived right close by them all my life. And Tex, their grandson what a fine young man he turned out to be. Ain't many that could raise a grand child up with so much respect in return."

"I know." Said another. "And he's taking it mighty hard, and it would have to happen here about the time he'll have to go off in the service. Don't look fair at times. But we all have to go, I guess about all we can do about that is stay prepared because we never know the day nor the hour."

The service was short. Ma had informed the pastor that Pa wanted it that way.

"Pa always said makes no difference what's said at your funeral it's how you lived your life that counts in the end."

Tex steadied Ma as they said their last goodbye to pa before Copeland closed the casket.

He tried to stay strong for Ma's sake cause she was shaking with grief.

He conjured up in his mind again the reflection he saw in pa's blue eyes just after he died.

The beauty of the October season there in the hickory stand with their golden leaves blending in and towering above the other trees and their various colors all glistening in the early morning sunrise.

As he and pa stood on the hill. Pa said. "Down there she is son ain't that a beautiful sight?"

While standing there with pa looking down at the beauty he suddenly came back to reality as he held ma who was now sobbing uncontrollably.

Tears filled his eyes and washed away the scene and again he could hear Pa say.

"I think my season is about over here on earth."

The following week ma had to spend four days in the hospital. "It's hit her pretty hard." Doc said. "But other wise she's pretty strong, after she gets over the shock I believe she'll be alright."

"I think I'll get in touch with the draft board and have them give you a deferment until she gets stronger cause she needs someone to watch out for her the next few weeks especially at night."

He had managed to get together with Marty and talk when her family came to the funeral home for Pa's wake.

And now more than ever Tex knew he had to ask Marty for a date cause he could sense that she felt the same way about him as he did for her.

'I'll wait a couple weeks till ma feels better.' He thought. 'Then I'll ask Marty for a date, I've lost enough time thinking about it I know I'm in love with her.'

Poor boy dug a hole measuring four by four and four feet deep along side his shack. He had shoveled two piles of dirt along side the hole and all of a sudden dirt came flying down on him, which contained some small stones some as large as a baseball. And one about that size hit him on his left shoulder.

His first thought was. 'Damn is somebody trying to bury me in here?'

Then he looked up and could see Peanut's rear end hanging over the hole with his hind legs braced right at the edge of the hole. His front paws were busy digging a hole in the fresh dirt and of course all the dirt was being deposited right back where it came from but mostly on Poor Boy.

He yelled out. "Peanut! What the hell you doing? Damn! It's hard work digging this damned hole. What th hell are you trying to do, bury me?"

Peanut stuck his nose in the dirt and sniffed and started the dirt flying again.

Poor boy climbed from the hole and chased him away from the pile of dirt.

"Now dammit you stay right where you are till I get done, you shit ass can't you see I'm tired as hell?"

Then he thought. 'Peanut's been with me nine or ten months and now that I think back on my mental state at the time I believe he's been a God send.'

I'm trying not to break my vow to the boss of the mine here and stay away from the booze, and the lonely nights with nobody to talk to and that damned radio tuned to country music that at times the songs are a story of my life. All of that was just about to send me back to the bottle again.'

'I lost my job at Bonny Blue, and for a while there I was nothing more than a bum.' 'Then one day he came to me and asked if I was about ready to straighten up and start living again.'

'He was once my boss at Bonny Blue till one day he decided to lease this little truck mine here on Elys Creek.'

"If you are." He said. "I'll take you on as a coal loader. I pay by the ton so if you don't load the coal you get no pay. I realize the condition you're in and I know it will take a lot of will power on your part to over come it. You can work whenever you feel like it and if you want to take a day or days off you can do that. To tell you the truth I really don't need any more loaders, the half dozen I have now is about all this little mine can accommodate."

"But it gets at me seeing you walking the roads day after day loaded to the gills trying to forget, Ah hell! I won't use the word forget, cause you're not trying to forget, you're still living it, and let me tell you something ain't no woman on earth worth worrying that much about. You once were a good man and in spite of what you think you still can recover from all the bull shit that you have stored up in that hard head of yours."

"So if you want to give it a try I'll help you all I can. You were a good electrician, but as you know this little mine don't need that, coal loading is all I can offer."

"I have a little shack there close to the mine opening, you can stay there cause I know you have no place to stay. It has a dirt floor but the way I look at it that's a good place for you to start. Hell you've wallowed in dirt so long maybe you'll figure out a way to get above it."

As he thought back on this he could still hear the boss say. "Now there's one thing that I want to get straight with you right now, the first time I catch you back on the booze whether you're working or on an off day, You'll have to vacate that little shack and hit the roads again."

Then he thought. 'I ain't touched the booze since then, I'm still on a dirt floor but it's a hell'va lot better than walking the roads. Yes sir I give a lot of credit to him, old Rub, and Peanut if'n it hadn't been for them no telling where I'd be right now, maybe six foot under.'

He got back down in the hole and scraped all the loose dirt in a pile.

'I'll shovel this out and it's finished, plenty deep enough to keep them taters from freezing this winter.'

As he heaved the last shovel full over his head he glanced over at the pile that peanut had dug in. and on top of that pile sat Peanut with his head cocked to one side looking down at him with that inquisitive look on his face. A look that Poor boy had noticed so many times that seemed to say.

"What's all the fuss about? Shit I'm doing what all dogs do."

He climbed from the hole and sat down by peanut and held him close.

'It's okay boy, it's okay! But what if that damned rock had hit on my head and knocked me out?"

"You'd had me buried in no time. Lets go in and get a bite to eat, we'll go around yonder and dig them taters tomorrow."

As Poor boy came out of the mine entrance he spotted peanut sitting near the coal tipple on a pile of slate and as soon as he seen him he leaped from the slate and ran toward him.

Poor boy dropped to his knees and opened his arms and embraced Peanut as he licked the coal dust from his face.

That was a daily ritual that the other miners liked to witness.

"Hell." Said one. "That dog thinks more of him than my wife does of me, I think I'll get a dog."

"You do by god, and I'll lay you two to one that you'll be the one that winds up in the dog house." Another miner remarked. Then the tipple man added.

"That dog comes out here and climbs on that pile of slate about fifteen minutes before you all are due out. Tell me how in hell does he know it, can he tell time?"

Poor Boy stoked the fire in the old potbelly, filled a five-gallon bucket with water from the mine that ran through a two-inch pipe.

As he sat it on the stove he said. "I'll get us something to eat as soon as this heats and I take a bath Peanut, Then we'll go out yonder and dig them taters."

He reached for a galvanized tub hanging from the wall and sat it in front of the stove and said.

"Hell'va way to have to take a bath after working at Bonny Blue where they had a bath house, but shit I've dropped several notches in every other way since I got that damned letter, so why should this be any different?"

After his bath he warmed up some ham and sweet potatoes that was left over from the day before.

"Damn your soul Peanut you eat more'n I do, you'll wind up eating me out of a 'house and home' as the saying goes."

"And if you look around at what I call house and home it won't take a lot of eating will it peanut?"

"Well let's head around the hill and dig them taters before dark sets in."

His little garden was on mining property. He had asked the boss if he could cut down a couple of trees and clear the under brush.

" I need to raise me some beans and taters." He said.

"Sure go ahead." The boss replied. "But I don't believe you'll get much of a crop from this land, look at all them pine trees, I've heard that they take everything out of the soil."

"I'll try it anyway and see what happens, I've seen my momma raise some pretty good vegetables from the piss poor land we lived on."

"Okay go ahead and clear as much as you want if the price of coal goes any lower I might have to plant something myself, don't know what the hell would grow on that steep part yonder, but you might raise a little something here at the bottom."

Then he added. "If you have any extra tomatoes send them my way."

He cleared and burned the trees and under brush and asked a farmer up the road if he would plow it up for him.

"Sure I'll plow it." The farmer said. "But no use to bring my team, ain't no way to plow this with a turning plow, too many roots, maybe by next year some will have rotted and then I could turn it."

"I'll bring one horse and a bull tongue plow that'll scratch it up pretty good and pull some of the roots."

The potatoes were spaced in hills about two feet apart. He used his hoe to rake the dirt from the top and was being very careful not to cut or bruise them. Peanut sat and watched and pretty soon started digging in one of the hills.

Poor boy watched as peanut uncovered the potatoes and rolled them around with his nose as if waiting for them to come to life.

After a bit he lost interest and sat down again with his head cocked to one side watching Poor Boy.

But soon he was back to the same hole, digging deeper and deeper as he snorted and the dirt flew through the air.

Poor Boy grinned and thought. 'Damned crazy dog, ain't no more taters in there.'

Then he said to Peanut. "You know this little garden fooled ever body including me Peanut, I had lots of tomatoes, beans, but the corn didn't do any good. Had a few peas, lots of onions, lettuce, and the two hills of watermelon, damn! Th vines bout covered the whole garden, had watermelons to give away."

Finally all the potatoes were ready to be loaded in the wheelbarrow. He had to make four trips with the wheelbarrow with as many potatoes as it would hold.

He gathered up some pine straw and lined the bottom of the hole. Then he gently placed the potatoes in so as not to bruise them. He placed the last potato in and used more pine straw to cover them. He covered the pine straw with boards and then covered the boards with dirt, he piled all the dirt on and it made a mound over the potatoes. Then he took three pieces of metal roofing and laid them over the mound of dirt. Then he put four large rocks on top of the metal to hold it in place and keep it from being blown away in the strong winter winds.

"Okay Peanut, all we gotta do is come out here this winter scrape the dirt off, move a board and get some taters and cover the rest up again. They'll go good with them shuck beans I got hanging all over the walls inside."

"Ain't nothing like a good mess of shuck beans on a cold winter day, I've heard them called a lot of different names, string beans, wrinkled beans, and one old feller used to call them leather britches, but I guess the name that fits them best is dried beans."

"Cause that's what they are, you seen me do it Peanut! I picked them green from the garden, then took a needle and long pieces of twine and strung them on it and hung them out in the sun to dry hull and all, and that hull is what makes them so good."

"Well come on let's get in its damn near dark and the chills coming on."

Early in the morning one week later he turned the radio on to listen to a live country music show coming from Knoxville, Tennessee.

Near the end of the show the announcer read the obituaries for east Tennessee and southwest Virginia, as was the custom each morning.

As he put another block of coal on the flames in the stove he heard the name, stunned he watched the flames lick around the block of coal for some time before finally closing the stove door.

"Damn Peanut! He's dead." He said. "Said he died of a heart attack, two three years older than me, I'm coming up on forty two so he can't be more than forty four or forty five."

"Just goes to show you Peanut, look at me th way I abused my health with all that booze and stuff. Hell Clabe never smoked a cigarette let alone drink anything. You'd think he'd live to be ninety years old."

"Well I've got mixed feelings about his death, I hate it for his family but at the same time I don't have any good thoughts about him stored up in my mind."

"Lord knows what he done to me has had me on the ropes for a long, long time."

"I'll give him credit though for providing for his family. Most folks thought of him as a good man, and I guess I'd have to agree with that even after what he done to mess up my life."

"But you know Peanut! The sad part is that boy Tex will never know that he was his father cause me and him was the only ones that knew it and now he's dead. And I sure as hell will never tell him cause like the boss said. 'You're living it instead of trying to forget.'

"Now that he's gone I'm gonna wash my hands of the whole mess. Shit Peanut! We may get off this ground floor any time now."

"Shore would be nice to have a good warm bed to sleep in and a decent place to take a bath, eh Peanut?"

Peanut cocked his head to one side as Poor Boy looked at him.

"Yeah I know what you're thinking, you think I'm about to take you down to the creek and give you a good scrubbing, but I'm not it's to damn cold for that, so don't worry I'll heat some water tonight and put you in that tub and get you as clean as I can. But shit! The way you go around all day digging in the slate dump it won't make a lot of difference anyway."

"I still can't get over him dieing of a heart attack Peanut. The few times I've seen him in the past few years he looked like the picture of health. And like I said I feel sorry for his family. It's gonna be hard on them."

The next three weeks brought bad news for the folks of Lee County.

'Sorry to inform you that your son was wounded some where in Italy. He has been transferred from the field hospital to a hospital in London. As is our policy we will keep you informed as to his progress.'

'Sorry to inform you that your husband was killed in action.' Another said.

And another. 'Your son is missing in action.'

And yet another, 'Sorry to inform you that your son was killed in an accident at the Copper mine.'

He was from Belgum Hollow off the Harlan road on Stone Creek, They shipped him back and he was buried at the Cooper Cemetery on Pucketts Creek.

When Gina heard about it she almost lost her mind worrying about Bama in far off Montana working in the copper mine.

One of my great uncle's lived near the store and would visit every day to talk about the war or tell about a letter that they had received from one of his three sons in the service.

He would pace the floor as he related what Stanley, Chester or Haze had said in a letter.

"When do you think it will end son?" He would ask.

"I think it'll be over in a couple months." I'd reply. Knowing that I didn't have a clue and my eighteenth birthday was getting closer every day.

I could still hear the words. "The damned war will be over before you ever grow up." And I wondered. 'Will it ever end?'

My steady girl friend had grown on me to the point where I would envision the day that I would bid her goodbye maybe never to see her again.

And at times I'd wonder. 'Why did I ever have to meet her? Saying goodbye ain't gonna be easy.'

He took the old dirty wool lined jacket from the wall where it hang on a rusty nail among the dried beans, miners cap, knee pads, the galvanized tub, soiled wash cloth and towel and various other pieces of clothing.

He held the jacket up and asked. "How in hell am I going to get this thing clean Peanut?"

"I'll go ahead and heat some water and put some lye soap in. Got to get some of this dirt off, and damn! It stinks, no wonder you crawled out from under it the other night when I covered you with it Peanut. At the time I thought I was doing you a favor. Thought you needed some extra cover but I can see now why you wanted to get away from this thing."

"I want to spruce myself up a little so I don't look like the bum that I've made of myself since that damn letter screwed up my mind."

"We've got a long walk coming up tomorrow Peanut, me'n old Rub made the same trip one time and he made it better than I did, but I think I'll be okay this time since I've got off the booze, I'm in way better shape than I was back then."

"The boss told me he seen my brother Cliff in town the other day. Said Cliff told him to tell me to get my ass in gear and come spend a week or so with him."

"Oh he told me that many times when I was still on the bottle, and I guess if I had listened to him I would be better off today. But no use looking back on that, that's water over the dam and already poured out in the ocean some where."

"So come morning Peanut, you and me will hit the road for a long walk to Keokee. And I do mean walk, ain't nobody about to give me a ride with you tagging along."

"Once a fellow stopped and gave me and old Rub a ride to town in his truck, he wouldn't let us in the cab so we damn near froze to death before we got there."

"Don't know why I'm telling you this, shit you ain't never rode in a car or truck anyway that I know of, so it ain't no big deal to you."

"You'll be welcome at Cliff and Barbara's house cause they like dogs, no telling how many they have right now, hell they take in every stray mutt that comes along."

"I can hear cliff now. "Hey Barbara Allen! Here comes Wayne and he's brought us another dog. He added the Allen to her name. That's an old folk song brought over from England, Scotland, some where there across the waters."

"Why you looking at me that way for? Hell I didn't mean it, shit you know I wouldn't leave you there."

He searched the pockets of the old jacket before dousing it in the hot lye water. In one pocket he found a partial used book of cigarette papers, a dirty red bandana and a bottle cap from one of the whiskey bottles that he had carried in that pocket so many times.

And of course the letter that had hid in his inside pocket from everyone else but him for so many years. The envelope was wrinkled and so dirty that the address was barely visible but the letter itself was neatly folded and rather clean except for being faded a dull yellow color with dirty finger marks on the edges.

He sat down on the bed and read it again although he knew it word for word from all the times he had read it before.

"I'm gonna read it one more time peanut." He said. "Then I'll never look at it again, it's over, she's dead, he's dead, but I'm still here, for what purpose? I have no idea but I intend to put it all behind me and start all over again. So tomorrow we'll go spend a week or so with Cliff and Barbara, and after that peanut we'll be on our way up again."

He got up and opened the stove door. "Gonna burn this damn thing Peanut, no sense in carrying it around any more."

But as he touched it to the blaze and one corner of the envelope started to burn, he pulled it back and smothered it with his bare fingers.

"Damn! I don't know Peanut, maybe its best I keep this a while, guess it won't hurt anything, seemed like I could hear some body saying, "Don't burn it! Don't burn it!"

He turned and tossed it on an old discarded legless tabletop supported by a half dozen cinder blocks, and laden with assorted cups, plates, pots and pans.

"Shore got a funny feeling when I started to burn it peanut. Guess I better hang on to it for a while."

He wrung out the old jacket and hung it on the wall behind the stove to dry.

"It'll dry out in no time Peanut, I'll put in extra coal and it'll be dry by the time we leave tomorrow."

"All I'd had to do peanut, is go to a phone some where and call Cliff and he'd be glad to come and get us but I want to get there by myself just to show him and Barbara that I'm trying to make a change for the better."

"They ain't had no bed of roses to wallow in, their oldest son got all crippled up from a mine accident there at the Calvin mine below Keokee."

"Good thing he had saved a little money and put it in a small farm down around Jonesville, he can still get around enough to do a little farm work, so he keeps food on the table for his family. You haf'ta give a lot of credit to some one like him Peanut."

"And now their youngest is over there in the Pacific some where fighting them damn Japs."

"Well lets turn it in Peanut it's a long walk from Elys Creek to Keokee and I sure as hell want to get enough sleep, don't want to wake up tired."

"Why th hell you look at me that way peanut? Damn! Sometimes I think you understand every word I say, and again you act like you don't know what th hell I'm talking about, well come on get under the cover here and lay close to my back it's gonna get mighty cold before morning."

The next morning he looked through all his old worn out clothes, put on the best and stuffed the rest in a burlap bag to take along.

"Don't know how long we'll stay Peanut, so I'll take these duds along just in case. The boss said 'stay as long as you want to' he's a good man peanut, weren't for him no telling where I'd be today, probably buried yonder on that hill in the Pine Grove Cemetery."

He put on the old jacket, threw the burlap bag over his shoulder and said. "Okay Peanut, we're on our way."

As he opened the door Peanut rushed out and began leaping and barking as if he knew something exciting was about to happen.

"Oh yeah! You're full of piss and vinegar now but wait till tonight by god, it'll be a different story. This trip will wear yore ass out just like it will mine."

As they headed down toward the road he stopped and said. "Wait a minute

Peanut I'll go back and get that damned letter, don't know what it is but something keeps telling me to take that letter. I reckon after carrying it around for over twenty years it won't hurt to keep it a few more days, but I'm sure as hell never going to read it again."

"Okay, now we're ready, no not that way, lets go across by Pucketts Creek, it's a little closer going that way, and we can stop at Dean's store and get a hunk of bolney and a loaf of bread."

As they neared Dean's store a black shiny convertible pulled in and parked. He recognized Tex and thought.

'Well there he is and I'm the only person still living that can tell him who his daddy is, or was, course he's dead now.'

'But I'll never tell him, not even if he asks.'

"You stay right here peanut, I'll get us some bolney and bread. You stay right there, I'll be right back."

As he paid for the bolney and bread he heard Tex say that he was on his way to Keokee. 'Damn!' He thought, that's where I'm headed but I know damn well he won't let Peanut ride in his car, so I won't even ask him.'

As he and peanut headed down the road he looked back and Tex was getting in his car with a nehi orange drink in his hand.

He heard the hum of the motor as the car approached from behind, he reached down and grabbed Peanut's collar afraid that he might go out in the road.

"Damn Peanut! You're a little skittish of cars, you're gonna haf'ta learn to stay over on the shoulder of th road. Some damn fools won't stop for a dog, hell no they think the road belongs to them.'

The car came to a stop beside them. "Hey! Wanna ride?" Where you going, Stone Creek?"

"No I'm headed for Keokee." Poor Boy replied.

"Okay hop in that's where I'm headed."

"No I better not, you see I've got my dog."

Tex reached across and opened the door. "Well your dog can ride too, I wouldn't think about leaving him here, turn him loose let him hop in."

Poor boy couldn't believe what he was hearing. Peanut was shaking from fear of the car and he knew that he wouldn't get in on his own so he picked him up and sat him on the floor board.

"No, no, put him on the seat between us, it's to cramped down there."

As they passed through Stone Creek, Peanut had calmed down and was taking in the scenery as all dogs do when riding in a black shiny car.

Tex reached over and rubbed Peanut's head. "Must be his first car ride huh?"

"As far as I know it is." Poor Boy replied. "He took up with me a while back."

"Guess somebody dropped him off, he may have been in a car then and maybe that's why he's afraid now."

"Well don't worry boy." Tex said as he leaned over and let his head touch Peanut. "I like dogs."

As they passed the old dominion Power Company at the Pocket community, memories of his youth crept in to Poor Boys thoughts.

He glanced over at Tex and thought. 'I was pretty much like him when I was his age, good job, good car and decent clothes to wear.'

'I hope he don't get off on the wrong track some where like I did and let some woman mess up his life. I like him he's a lot like his mother, makes me wonder if me and her could have had a son that would measure up to him.'

'But her and Clabe messed up my life, don't know which one to blame the most.'

Tex glanced over at Poor Boy and thought. 'He must have went on the wagon, as long as I can remember every time I'd see him on the road he'd be drunk.' I wonder why he fell so low, I've heard that he was a top notch electrician around the mines at one time.'

'I wonder if he'd know who my father is?' 'Maybe I'll ask him some time, but not now, me and Marty have a lot of things to do before my deferment is up, don't want anything to interfere with that.'

'We've grown closer and closer over the past three weeks, and thinking back on the event of her father dieing which was sad, but at the same time brought us closer together in such a short time.'

'I've heard Pa and Ma say many times that all things happen for a reason, so maybe it was God's plan to bring me and Marty together through her father's death.'

Finally he looked over at Poor Boy and said. "That's the Barton place up ahead, that's where I'm headed, but I'll run you on up to Keokee it ain't but a few miles."

"Oh no!" You don't have to do that, me'n and Peanut can walk that little distance."

"No I've got time and it ain't that far. Did You know Clabe Barton?"

"Yeah I knew him." Poor Boy replied. "Never was real acquainted with him, but have knew about him and his family all my life."

"You know he died about three weeks ago, had a massive heart attack."

"Yes I heard about that." Poor Boy replied. "Shore was a surprise he was a picture of health."

"Yes he was." Tex said. " He was a fine man, his family is taking it mighty hard."

"I plan on marrying his youngest daughter Marty before I go in the service. We've only been seeing each other for a short time, but as the saying goes. "The old love bug bit us.' So we decided to go ahead and get hitched before I have to leave."

"I know it must be right cause I can't get her off my mind, did you ever feel that way about a girl when you were my age?"

"Yes I did but it didn't turn out well." Poor Boy replied.

Then he thought. 'Now I know why that damned letter kept bugging me last night, looks like I'll have to let him read it.'

'Too bad cause he's such a nice young man. Dammit! I said I'd never tell him, but I can't stand back and let this happen. Just wouldn't be right, I'd hate to have it on my conscious for the rest of my life."

"Yes sir." Tex went on. "I feel like a new person already, you see I've been pretty much of a loner most of my life and carried around something inside that has caused me a lot of grief. I guess it's like the saying. 'Hidden truth.' I've always known that some one some where had the answer and could have let me in on it but they never stepped forward and I could never work up the nerve to ask afraid that it might hurt me more, or maybe some body else like my grandparents."

"My grandpa died a while back, did you know him?"

"Yes I knew him and your grandmother to, how's she doing?"

"She's not doing well at all, it worries me to have to go off in the service and leave her, but Marty will stay with her while I'm gone. It's a bad situation but like I said I feel better about myself since I've met Marty, and I think I'll be able to discard that old hidden truth and leave it behind."

Poor Boy had been all wrapped up in self-pity for him self for so long that he hardly noticed anyone else's heartaches, but right now he felt like crying. He looked at Peanut and there was that ever-familiar sad look on his face. 'Damnit Peanut.' He thought. 'I'm gonna cry, that damn letter has already brought heartache to me, his mother, and I'm sure Clabe regretted it till the day he died.' 'Last night when I touched it to the fire I had in mind that all involved would be better off without it, but like I said, I had this damn gnawing feeling that it was supposed to stay around for some reason.'

'So now Peanut I'm bound to show it to him, but dammit its gonna break his heart. It'll let out the hidden truth but it sure as hell will store up a lot of grief in this young mans heart. I hope to hell he don't take the same path that I did and wind up on a dirt floor.'

"That brick house on your left there, that's my brother's. Pull off here on the right I got something I want you to read before you go. I'm not looking forward to you reading it, and believe me if there was any other way to get around this I wouldn't think of having you read it. But it's necessary. You'll understand that after it sinks in.'

"You'll find your answer to that hidden truth, but I'm afraid it won't be much comfort."

Tex came to a stop and turned to Poor Boy with a puzzled look on his face. As he watched Poor Boy fumble for the letter in his jacket pocket he thought.

'What is it this guy wants me to read?' 'He mentioned the hidden truth, am I about to find out who my father is? Could it be him?' Why does he look so sad? Dang! 'He looks like he's gonna cry.'

Poor Boy held up the old dirty envelope where Tex could read it.

"See that address? Yeah I know it's pretty hard to read with all that dirt on it."

" See that name Wayne Burke? See the address below, Four Mile, Kentucky? Well that's me, and see your mother's return address there in the corner?" "Bonnie Rathburn, Route one, Pennington Gap, Virginia."

Tex leaned over to have a closer look and noticed Poor Boy's hand was shaking, and wondered why he was so nervous.

Thoughts tumbled through his mind as the excitement of reading his mother's neat handwriting caused him to smile.

'I'm about to find out who my father is and I wonder if it's this man? He sure is nervous, don't know why he would be, seeing that I'm his son. He's not exactly what I had in mind for a father after all the times I've seen him walking the roads, but today he don't come across as all that bad.'

Finally he could hold it no longer as he seen a tear trickling down the face of Poor Boy and come to rest on his chin.

He reached across peanut and drew Poor Boy to him. "Hey! What's so sad about all this? This is a big day for me, I've just found my dad, but I'm beginning to wonder if he wants to admit that I'm his son. You said back there that I'd find the hidden truth, but it wouldn't be much comfort, well I want you to know I'm proud that you're my father"

Now as more tears rolled down Poor Boys face he said.

"Damn! Right now I wish I could tell you that I'm your father, but I'm afraid the news is not good. Sad? Hell yes I'm sad! I've been off the hooch for a long time, but right now I feel like going to St. Charles and hanging one on, but I won't do that cause you and me have something in common and we need each other."

"We've both been carrying around excess baggage called 'Hidden truth' for too long now. So here read this damned letter and it'll lighten our load except in yore case it'll break your heart, but at least you'll know the truth and will be able to go on with your life. But it won't be easy, no it won't be easy."

"Here read the damned thing."

As Tex pulled the letter from the envelope he wondered. 'What's this all about? I was sure I had it figured out, now I don't know what to expect, he said it would break my heart.'

He un-folded the letter and his heart raced as he looked at the words that he knew must have been written by his mother. He touched it to his nose hoping to smell something from a mother that he couldn't remember. But the scent was offensive and stale from nicotine, sweat, cheap whiskey, and without a doubt some of Poor Boys tears mixed in, because his dirty finger prints were clearly visible along the edge of the pages where he had held it over the years to read over and over.

He glanced over at Poor Boy and noticed he had turned his head and was looking out the window but apparently seeing nothing because his body was shaking from crying. He reached across Peanut touched him on his shoulder and said.

"Here take it back I don't think I want to read it if it's that bad, I've been able to cope without knowing who my dad is up until now, it ain't been easy, no sir it ain't, but I have a feeling that whatever it is you want me to read in this letter won't help, so here take it back."

"Hell no I won't take it back you have to read it, so get on with it and lets get this thing settled, ain't no way I could go on with my life knowing that I let you marry that girl without reading that damn letter, so go on read it, trust me you'll be glad you did."

"But you said it would break my heart, tell me why would you want me to read it if it's that bad?"

Poor Boy turned and said.

"Listen son, it's for your own good cause when you marry that girl you're not only messing up your life but hers to. Hell yes it'll break your heart but at the same time you'll thank me for letting you read it. There comes a time in every ones life that they have to do something that's not very pleasant because if they don't they might have to live the rest of their life in misery, and by god I'm telling you now it's best you read that damned letter, or here let me have it and I'll read it to you myself."

"No I'll read it." Tex replied. Once again he studied his mother's neat hand-writing and began to read.

Dec. 10 1922
Dear Wayne.

I have missed you so much in the three months that you have been away, I wish that I could tell you that I can't wait till you get home so we can be together again. But the news that I'm about to tell you will break your heart as it has mine already. I didn't mention it in my other letters because I couldn't bear to.

But now that I know you will be here soon I thought it best that I tell you before you get home.

Shortly after you went away I found out I was pregnant. Please don't ask me why this happened, because I really don't know. I have asked myself over and over, Why, Why, Why? I wish I had the answer.

I have made a mess of my life before you and I ever had a chance to get married and raise a family, and how I looked forward to that, I know you may have a hard time believing that but it's true.

I think of what I've brought on mom and dad. Dad is so proud of the Rathburn name and nothing like this has ever happened in his family, and the same can be said of mom's family.

And you, I feel so sorry for you for what I have done and I want you to know that as long as I live you are the one that will always be in my thoughts and in my heart.

I have told mom and dad. They asked if it was you and didn't seem very worried at first because they knew we were engaged and would be married soon anyway.

129

Of course I told them that you were not the father, I wish with all my heart that you were.

I didn't tell them who it is and don't intend to.

You see not only have I ruined my life and yours and my parents, if I tell I will hurt and lose a dear friend that I have grown up with. It's just unthinkable and I will never tell.

You see it's Laura Barton and as you know we are very close.

A few days after you left for Kentucky Laura had to go in the hospital for three days. She had a miscarriage in her first pregnancy. She was heart broken.

I offered to go over there and cook Clabe's supper and tidy up things in the house while she was away.

Wayne, like I said before I can't imagine how I let this happen to us, but it did and I hope you will understand.

I can't lay all the blame on Clabe because I'm the one that should have stayed strong for my sake and yours not to mention all the other lives that it will touch before it's over.

I want to ask you to never tell anyone and that way Laura will never know, at least one life will be spared. I would never get over it if something should happen to her marriage to Clabe.

I may never get over this anyway Wayne, but I intend to stay strong until the baby comes.

Well that's my story, as sorry as it might seem to you. But I want you to know that I will welcome you home as if nothing ever happened and we can go on with our plans to marry and make a good life together.

I realize that kind of thinking is easy for me, but almost impossible for you, so let me end by saying.

I wish you all the best throughout the remainder of your life because you are truly one of a kind and I will always love you.

And I hope you understand and will forgive me.

All my love always. Bonnie

Near the end he could read no further because of the fury building up in him. He leaned back and closed his eyes.

'Why didn't someone tell me long before now? I would have kept it secret if that's the way they wanted it.'

'Now that I'm about to marry my half sister, I find out. It's not fair. He's right I have found out the hidden truth but this is breaking my heart. I can see why he had to let me read the letter and I owe him for that. But I still can't get over why nobody ever told me.'

'Mr. Barton or my dad I now find out, the day I talked to him in his picnic area and he seemed to have a special interest in me somewhat like a father. Why didn't he tell me, it could have stayed a secret between us and I wouldn't be in the fix I'm in right now.'

'Would have been nice to know that Marty and Sugar were my half sisters and I could have treated them that way.'

'But no! They think it must be kept secret for fear it will hurt someone along the way. Never giving it a thought that maybe that's better than hurting the one that's most involved.'

With these thoughts still running through his mind he straightened up and finished the letter.

He refolded it and placed it in the envelope, once more scanning the address while noting his mother's fluid handwriting. To: Wayne Burke Four Mile, KY. From: Bonnie Rathburn.

He handed it to Poor Boy and said. "Mr. Burke you were right when you said it would expose the hidden truth, but would break my heart. I will forever be grateful to you for what you have done today, not for that and I would have married my half sister in a few days. But I still can't understand why some body didn't tell me, I would have kept it secret and it wouldn't be the mess it's turned out to be."

"No offense to you, it wouldn't be fair to think that you should have told me, God knows you must have suffered since then. No I can't blame you, I guess most of the blame should be on my mother but for some reason I can't direct my feelings to just one person. Right now I'm mad at the world and life itself I guess."

Then as big tears started from his eyes he reached out and held Poor Boy and Peanut one in each arm, and whispered.

"You'll never know the happiness that I was feeling there a few minutes ago when I thought you were my father. There's something about you that's good and decent and I would be proud to walk beside you as my father. Oh yes! I've seen you on the roads and heard the remarks about how you let a woman mess up your life. Well I want you to know that I'm sorry that my mother did this to you. She's the one that's responsible for all your grief. And now look what it's doing to me, there's no end to the damage that 'hidden truths' can do if they're not exposed."

"I know son, I know. Now that you mention it I would have been a hellva lot better off if I had come forward and told you about it years ago, it would have hurt for a while I know, but nothing like it has for the past twenty some years."

"So look at it this way you've finally found out who your father was and now you can move on, hell! There's plenty pretty girls raring to crawl in this shiny black convertible. Don't make the same damned stupid mistake I did and wind up on a dirt floor."

Peanut was busy licking tears away from one to the other and was confused to what it was all about but his instincts told him it was no tail wagging time.

Finally Poor boy opened the door and got out, Peanut looked from one to the other as if trying to figure out which one needed him most.

"Okay Peanut! Come on out, Tex don't want a flea bag like you tagging along."

Tex leaned over and extended his hand to Poor Boy, as they shook hands he said.

"Mr. Burke you're about the only good thing that's happened to me today. Even with all the depressing news you handed me in that letter I feel that I have gained a true friend for the first time in my life."

"And yes I think I can take your advice and not let this put me on a dirt floor as you put it, but you know what I'm about to do? I'm gonna turn around here and head to St. Charles. I'll drive right by the Barton place without stopping. This ain't no day to tell Marty about it, some other time, no use breaking two hearts all on the same day."

"And when I get to St. Charles, I'm gonna head for Jake's place and order up a Falstaff and if it sets right I'll order up several more. And before it's over every soul in St. Charles can say that they seen that boy from Pucketts Creek hang one on in St. Charles on a Saturday night."

"You see Mr. Burke, I have never tasted alcohol in any form and never thought I needed it, but right now I need something to take away this awful feeling so I'm about to find out if it can do anything to take this hurt away."

Poor Boy tossed the letter to the seat of the car and said. "Here hang on to this you might need it later. And do me a favor, I know how you feel right now and I know there's no way in hell that you will listen to me or anybody else, but promise me that you'll stay away from that stuff after tonight, shit look what it did to me, it's set me back and I may never be able to get back to where I can enjoy the rest of my life."

He turned the key and as the motor came to life he said. "I'll promise you that Mr. Burke I don't think alcohol is a good addition to any ones life, but right now I need to sit with the rest of the crowd at St. Charles, and find out if I can handle it for just one night and get up the next day and go on with my life."

"Well now by God you be careful!" Poor Boy replied.

"And do me another favor, stop this Mr. Burke shit, call me Poor Boy, Wayne, anything but Mr. Burke."

Then Tex smiled for the first time since reading the letter and said. "How about dad?"

As he drove away Poor Boy turned to Peanut and said. "This has been one hellva trip Peanut I'm glad it's finally over."

On the porch he could see Cliff keeping two dogs in check as they barked at Peanut, and heard him call out.

"Look who's coming Barbara Allen, It's Wayne and he's bringing us another old flea bitten hound."

Reba: Like all Saturday's, St. Charles was crowded with folks from the coal camps and surrounding areas.

Some there to do their weekend shopping some to take in a movie, some to sit under the sycamore tree and exchange tall tales and others especially, some of the younger ones there for a night of flirting and fun. Then there was always the hard-core bunch crowded in the small joints drinking and feeding the Juke - boxes until the places closed.

One of the nicer and larger ones was Jake's Place there you could get a full coarse meal, a quick hamburger or hotdog along with beer and wine.

The long counter lined with bar stools is where most of the drinkers would gather and on the other side booths lined the wall the full length of the building. In between were nice tables decorated with clean tablecloths napkins and silverware.

And like most Saturdays the place was jammed with diners, drinkers and a scattering of high school kids in the booths nursing a coke after eating a hamburger.

Jake was noted for keeping everything in order in that mixed group of people. The drinkers knew to watch their language and if they did go over the edge, as did happen occasionally he would ask them to leave and if they didn't he would call the police chief to remove them.

In one of the booths near the Juke Box three high school girls sat talking and giggling after eating a hotdog and now were stretching their cokes to the limit in order to occupy the booth as long as possible.

One of them had wavy blond hair that framed a beautiful face with gray-green eyes. Her name was Reba.

Reba was in her last year of high school as were her two companions and their conversation turned to what they intended to do after they graduated.

Neither intended to continue their education but looked ahead to meeting some one to share their lives with.

Reba had often spoke of Tex and how much she admired him for not partaking of the booze like most of the young men around the St. Charles area.

"Wish I knew him better" She once remarked. "I try to flash him my best smile every time I see him but he don't seem to notice me."

"Ah come on Reba be bold" One of the girls had said.

"Like what?" Reba asked.

"Like walk right up in his face and ask him to take you for a ride in that shiny black convertible."

"I might surprise you and do that very thing some time"

"Well go ahead I dare you, and if you don't get the nerve to do it soon I might just try it myself."

As they sit there watching all the activity around them Reba's mind wanders away to Tex and she wonders if he will come in today for his usual hamburger and coke before going to the movie down the street.

"Heh! What's on your mind Reeb?" One of the girls asks. "Must be that cowboy." The other one chimes in. "And speaking of him he's usually here by this time."

"Oh he'll be here." Reba replied. "And today may be the day I ask him to take me for a ride."

Her companions laughed and one said. "That'll be the day Reeb, that'll be the day!"

Ten minutes later Tex walked through the door and found a seat at one of the tables near them.

"Hey! He looks worried about something." One of the girls remarked.

"He lost his grandpa a while back and his grandma is not doing well either I hear." Reba stated.

The waitress came by and took his order, and to the ones that seen it they were in total amazement as they watched her take a bottle of beer and a cold glass to his table.

Some of the drinkers on the stools started elbowing one another not believing what they were about to see.

"Damn! Don't tell me that boy is about to take up this damn drinking habit after shunning it for so long." He muttered to his partner."

"Sure as hell looks that way." The other replied. "I hate to see him do that, Shit he's about the only decent young man around these parts, works hard and don't throw his money away on girls and booze."

"Well shit! If you admire some one like that so much how come you're sitting here downing one after the other?"

"Cause I'm just like you I ain't got no damned sense." He replied.

Reba and her companions sat and watched in shock as Tex picked up the bottle and started to pour it in the cold glass, when the glass was half full he sat the bottle down and stared at the glass, he finally picked the bottle up and filled the glass until the foam ran over the sides.

He raised the glass to almost touch his lips before sitting it back on the table. He sat and looked at it another two minutes and almost everyone in the place were now staring at him.

Finally he picked it up again but hesitated as before when it was almost at his lips.

"Hells fire! Go on and taste it!" Shouted one of the tipsy miners from a bar stool. "Bill" the town police chief had came in right behind Tex and had been standing near the entrance door taking it all in. On hearing this he walked over to the miner and whispered.

"You open your damned mouth one more time and the Calaboose will become your bedroom for the night, now shut up before I decide to take you anyway, looks like you've had a little to much so I'll probably get you before the night is over."

Then Bill walked over and laid his hand on Tex shoulder. "Can't make up your mind son? Well let me give you a little advice, get up and walk away from that stuff, it's never done anything good for nobody and never will."

" Just look around at all the drinkers here and come back next Saturday and you'll see the same ones sitting there wasting their money away while they make fools of them selves and feel bad all day on Sunday."

"You and your ways are respected in this town, look around at the faces in here, can't you see the pleading look on most of them that is saying. "No Tex, please don't give in to that bottle, get up and leave and let us enjoy the way you have always been, clean, decent and free of alcohol."

Then Bill gave him a pat on the shoulder and walked away.

Without hesitation Reba got up and walked to his table. As she had a seat across the table in front of him she smiled and said.

"What's the matter cowboy you look worried?"

At first he said nothing as he stared at the still un-tasted beer in front of him. Finally he looked up at her and said.

"I've had a bad day, the worst one of my life I guess. And I thought this stuff might help, but I'm having a hard time trying to make up my mind."

She reached and laid her hand on his arm and said.

"Could I help you make up your mind?"

He stared at the glass again before answering. "Well you can try, looks like I'm not making much progress on my own."

She let her hand slide down his arm and took his hand and said. "I'll let you in on a little secret. I have always admired you for your clean way of living and I would hate to see you change it just because of one bad day, so I ask you to consider that before you decide to take your first drink of that stuff."

" I know you've lost your grandpa and your grandma is not in very good health I'm told but I believe you are a strong enough person to over come that."

'But if she only knew.' He thought. 'The heartache I've went through since reading the letter today.'

Then he looked her in the eyes for the first time and noticed the pleading expression on her face. 'Darn! She cares.' He thought.

He pushed the glass away and rose from the table thinking. 'I have to get out of here.'

And without thinking said. "How would you and your friends like to take a ride? I feel like that might help and I need some company."

"Sure.' She said as she walked back toward the booth where her two companions had been watching.

"If you all will excuse me he has asked me to go for a ride with him, I'll see you later on tonight."

Astonished, they watched as she walked across to the table and took Tex by the arm and went out the door.

Once out side Tex asked. "Didn't your friends want to come?"

"No," She replied. "They have to be home early."

As they drove toward Stone Creek she couldn't help but notice the worried look on his face and wondered what had taken place in his life today that had almost caused him to taste his first drop of alcohol back at Jake's place.

Near Stone Creek he glanced over and asked. "Do you mind if we just ride for a while? I find driving relaxes me, and God knows I need that after all I've went through today."

"Don't mind at all Tex, but at some point you will turn around and take me back to St. Charles, won't you?"

"Of course I will." He answered. "But to tell you the truth I could just keep going and leave it all behind."

Again she noticed the sadness in his voice and thought about asking him to tell her what happened, but thought it best to wait a while and see if he would open up. 'Might be better that way.' She thought.

"That's okay, I think everyone feels that way once in a while, I know I have." She replied.

They rode in silence until he made a left turn at Pennington Gap and headed toward Big Stone Gap.

"Have you ever been to Bristol?" He asked.

"No I haven't. She answered. But ain't that a long way?"

"No not that far." He replied. Wanna go?"

"Sure why not as long as you get me back home before momma peeks in my bedroom to wake me to get ready for church tomorrow."

"Don't worry I'll have you home long before then, my grandma has a lady friend from Kentucky, with her over the weekend, so she'll be alright but I still want to get home before too late or else she'll be worried about me." He said.

He began to talk more, telling her about his grandparents, how they raised him, and how much he missed his grandpa.

"I miss him a lot. He said. And now I'm worried that grandma won't be around much longer, she's not doing well at all."

By the time they reached Bristol she had learned a lot more about him and in return had told him a lot about herself.

He found a place to park near the bus station. "What would you like to do?" He asked.

"Why don't we just look around and window shop looks like there's more clothing stores than St. Charles and Pennington put together." She laughed.

"Yeah that's true" He replied. "And right here we stand in Virginia, but walk across the street and you're in Tennessee."

For the next hour they walked the streets as she admired all the beautiful dresses in the widow displays.

He watched the expression on her face and could see the excitement building as she gazed at all the pretty clothing that she had never had the privilege of wearing.

He noticed the skirt and blouse she had on was well tailored clean and nice but he wondered if it was the only one she had.

One dress in particular caught her eye and as he watched her, he thought.

'She would look beautiful in that dress.' As they turned to walk away he reached for her arm and turned her toward the store door.

Startled, she gave him a questioning look and said. "Hey I'm just looking I can't afford any of this expensive clothing."

"Never mind.' He said. I want you go in and try that dress on whether you buy it or not."

She was still protesting as he led her through the door. Once inside he asked her to tell the sales lady her size. He insisted, so she reluctantly asked the lady if she had her size in the same color as the one in the window display.

The saleslady found her size in two different colors and he asked her to try them both on. Again she protested but he wouldn't take no for an answer.

They were a perfect fit and he marveled at her beauty as the sales lady had her turn this way and that as she kept up a steady stream of praise.

"Oh you look so pretty, and the color brings out the color of your eyes, you know you're a very pretty girl but either of these dresses makes you a very beautiful girl."

'All sales talk.' Tex thought. 'But in this case its true, now if I can figure out a way to get her to agree to take them.' She went to the dressing room to change back in the skirt and blouse.

When she returned she overheard him telling the sales lady. "Yes we'll take them both."

As she watched the lady ring them up she whispered. "Tex I can't allow you to do this, it isn't right."

"Aw come on I know it ain't." He said. "But not much has went right today for me anyway so don't worry about it."

As they walked along she was embarrassed, feeling guilty, and at the same time a warm glow began to flow over her entire body. 'God what mixed feelings.' She thought. 'Could this be the beginning of something?'

Some one hollered out from the bus station as they went by. "Hey there Pucketts Creek boy! What brings you all the way up here?"

Tex turned to see the smiling face of Roy, the bus driver that drove the Bristol, Pennington Gap, and on to Middlesboro, Kentucky route daily.

They walked over and chatted for a minute.

"How are things around Stone Creek Tex? And say! Where did you find this pretty girl?"

Tex introduced her as Reba and realized he didn't know her last name.

"Then Roy said, Oh yeah! I think I remember you from when you was a little thing, you're Cal Finley's daughter, right?" She nodded yes.

"I thought so." He said. "I used to drive a taxi in St. Charles, took you and your family home from the movies many times, how are your Mom and dad doing? Been a long time since I've seen them."

"Oh they're doing fine." She said. "And now I remember you, I thought I had heard that voice some where when you hollered at Tex."

He glanced at the package that Tex had in his hand and asked. "Hey maybe I'm missing something here, are you two married?"

"No we're not." Tex answered.

"Well you might ought to think about it you shore look good together." He laughed.

They said goodbye and as they walked away. Roy said. "Honey, drive careful on the way back and tell everyone hello for me down there."

As they walked to the car Tex smelled food from a nearby restaurant and suddenly realized that he hadn't ate since morning.

"You hungry?" He asked.

'Not really.' She answered. "I ate a hamburger there at Jake's place."

"Yeah but that's been a while, you need to eat something, here I'll put this package in the car and we'll see what kind of food they have in that restaurant yonder."

They ordered the special of the day, spaghetti and meatballs with a side salad. Tex chose apple pie topped with vanilla ice cream for dessert, while Reba opted for the ice cream only.

During the meal Tex gave some thought to the days events and found that he had calmed down considerably since reading the letter back there on Keokee road earlier in the day.

Now as he looked at her he knew that she had been a Godsend in one of the worst days of his life.

'So calm and understanding' He thought. 'I'll let her read the letter, no sense in keeping it secret any longer.'

He called the waitress over and asked for more coffee. As she poured the coffee he asked. "Would you mind if we stayed a while longer? We've got some things to talk over."

"Not at all honey." She replied. "Stay as long as you want and I'll keep the coffee coming."

He reached across the table and took Reba's hand. "I need to tell you a few things about myself, some you may have heard before but I need to get them off my mind."

"You see I've lived with a hidden truth the most of my life, I can't remember my mother and never knew who my father was until today. Guess you'd think this would be the happiest day of my life after finally finding out who my father was, but to tell you the truth it's been one of the saddest."

"Not sad because I found out who it turned out to be, but sad because of the mess it's turned into."

He pulled the letter from his pocket. "Here read this and you'll understand why I almost went on the booze back there at Jake's place."

As she read she glanced up at him several times with a puzzled look on her face. When she finished she looked at the name on the envelope and asked.

"Was Bonnie your mother and who is Wayne Burke?"

"Yes that's my mother, her and Wayne Burke were engaged to be married but you see what happened she became pregnant by a married man."

"Have you heard of the girl they call Sugar and her sister Marty that live above the Pocket near Keokee?"

"Yes I know of them but never knew them personal." She replied.

"Well the Clabe my mother mentioned in the letter is Clabe Barton, Sugar and Marty's father."

I gave Wayne Burke better known as 'Poor Boy' a ride up to Keokee this morning and he gave me the letter that he has carried around since he received it from my mother. He and Clabe kept the secret for all these years and Clabe died a few weeks ago, guess you heard about that."

"Well what's so bad about that?" She said. "I can understand why you would be sad to find it out after he died but look at this way the burden has finally been lifted and now you can go on with your life."

"And look at it this way, you gained two sisters that you never knew you had."

"Yeah I know but that's where it becomes complicated, for you see me and Marty would have been married in a few days if I hadn't found out today. Marty don't know it yet, I was supposed to pick her up and we were planning on going to a movie here in Bristol today."

"I didn't have the heart to break the news to her, figured it could wait till tomorrow."

"Yes I do understand." She said as she ran her hand over his forehead that had by now became wet with sweat. "Its something you have to face up to and the sooner the better. Is there something I can do to help?"

"You'll never know how much you have helped since we left St. Charles this afternoon and I want you to know that."

"I'll go see Marty tomorrow I know it will break her heart but we both have to get over it and I'm counting on you to put up with me for a while."

"Maybe next Saturday we can ride up here and take in a movie, you can bring your two friends along and that way you won't be bored to death."

"I'll be glad to stick by your side until you overcome this Tex. And sure I'll be looking forward to next Saturday and the movie, but not with my two friends tagging along, you see I didn't ask them to come today I fibbed to you about that. So lets just plan on you and I sharing the movie together."

"Okay Reba I think you're growing on me, we better head back to St. Charles, got to get you home before bed check tonight."

After a few miles she scooted over against him and laid her head on his shoulder and by the time they reached Big Stone Gap her head was in his lap and she was sleeping.

'Gosh I like this girl and feel guilty about it because of Marty.' He thought. 'But time will heal all that and this might be my new beginning for the better.'

Then he smiled as he thought about the dresses and how silly it had been for him to buy them for her. 'I know she must be trying to figure out a way to avoid taking them home with her because its not right, so I'll help her out there.'

She awoke as they passed through Pennington Gap, and soon they were in St. Charles again.

He parked in front of her home and wondered if he should kiss her goodnight or kiss her hand.

"Okay here we are, I hope you enjoyed the trip as much as I enjoyed your company." He said. "And I want to apologize about the dresses, don't know what in the world I was thinking about. It wasn't the right thing to do and I can't expect you to take them with you, so I'll hang on to them for a while Okay?"

"Sure that's fine I was hoping you would come up with something." She answered.

He placed his hands on her shoulders and said. " In spite of the news that made this one of my worst days, I feel that Wayne Burke offered a glimmer of hope this morning when he handed me the letter and I feel he is a true friend."

."And now you come along and light up the darkness in my soul and I feel we can be more than friends."

She leaned forward until her face was touching his and they kissed.
"See you Saturday." She whispered.
He smiled and asked. "Two P.M. okay? It's a long way to Bristol"
"That's fine I'll be ready, see you then."

He awoke Sunday morning and lay in bed for a while listening to the chatter of his grandmother and her visitor from Kentucky and wondered what the day had in store for him.

'Yesterday had to be one of the worst days in my life but meeting Reba helped me get through it and now I think she might be the turning point in my life for the better.'

'But today I have to face Marty and tell her the things that broke my heart yesterday and is sure to break hers today.'

'Will there be some one to ease her pain? Like Reba did for me' God! Please help us through this mess.'

As he turned in the driveway at the Barton place he spotted Marty sitting on the fence out by the barn.

'May as well drive on out there and that way won't have to worry about her mother hearing anything and seeing Marty so upset after I tell her the sad news.'

As he came to a stop Marty glanced at him and then turned away obviously upset about him not showing up or calling yesterday. He leaned across the seat and opened the passenger door. He sat there waiting for her to face him again but she continued to ignore him.

Finally he said almost in a whisper. "Marty, Will you please get in I have something very important to tell you and then you'll understand why I stayed away yesterday."

She turned to face him and after a bit hopped down from the fence but seemed to be undecided about getting in the car. He reached toward her and she slid in beside him.

He placed his hands on her shoulders and held her at a distance being careful about not getting close enough for an embrace that would lead to an impassionate kiss, which he knew she was expecting.

He held her in this fashion and looked into her eyes for a full minute before he said anything. He found it very hard to say anything as he gazed into her eyes but finally managed to whisper. "I have to tell you something I found out yesterday that broke my heart and I'm sure you are going to take it the same way."

"But I want your sister to hear it too so lets ride down to her house."

She looked at him more puzzled and wondered how the news could be that important to the both of them.

As he turned around and headed out he could see Cody rushing toward them from the far corner of the pasture, and at the end of the driveway he heard the loud Neigh that he had heard before, but this time it sounded different and so sad, tears formed in his eyes and he wiped them away as he pretended to blow his nose on a tissue.

Marty slid over closer and ran her fingers over the back of his neck and wondered why he didn't reach out and touch her.

His thoughts were. 'Why should I tell her anything, I could come up with something else.' 'I could say, look Marty I met a girl in St. Charles yesterday and it was love at first sight, I thought I was in love with you but I was mistaken.'

'It would hurt and gnaw at her for a while but she'd get over it.'

'But then she would never know that I'm her half brother and there I would be creating another hidden truth, God knows I never want that again.'

So as soon as we get to Sugar's house I have to let them read 'That damn letter' as Poor Boy calls it, and it will reveal a hidden truth to them but at the same time break their hearts.'

'It might be different with Sugar she may be happy to have a half brother, But Marty will be devastated just as I have been.'

As he rounded the curve Sugar's house came in view and he could vision her greeting them with that sweet smile and saying. "Why what a surprise, come on in Sugars, I was just thinking about you, I hope you can stay a while I have a new meat loaf recipe that's about ready to come out of the oven."

As they came to a stop at the gate Sugar came out on the porch beaming that ever-present smile that always seemed to have some kind of magic and special meaning to any one she made contact with.

Then again he could hear Poor Boy saying. "Here read this Damn letter, it will reveal the hidden truth but it will break your heart."

He sat down and slipped the letter from his shirt pocket as Sugar rambled on about how glad she was to see them. Then she asked. "You all got everything ready for your wedding? I can't wait, you two are the perfect match."

Tex reached for his hankie and trapped the tears that had started down his cheeks as he blew his nose.

143

He handed Sugar the letter and said. "Here read this letter, read it out loud to Marty, it will reveal a hidden truth that you should know about, and with time it might be pleasing and acceptable to all involved but right now it will break your heart."

Still smiling Sugar reached for the letter and said. "My! My! This is an old letter, look at that postmark, can't be nothing but old news in it. So tell me why so much fuss about old news."

He looked away as she unfolded the dirty pages and again thought of the day he had talked with Clabe Barton in the picnic area. 'Why didn't he tell me he was my father that day and we all wouldn't be in this fix today.'

Then his thoughts shifted to the hickory stand and he could hear Pa say. "Down there she is son, ain't that a beautiful sight? Hold it tight to your shoulder and brace yourself, or else you'll wind up on your rear, that old twelve-gauge packs quite a wallop.

As the tears blotted out that scene his thoughts were back at the table in Jake's place in St. Charles and as he watched the foam spill over the sides of the glass trying to make up his mind whether to take that first drink, he could hear Reba say. "Can I help you make that decision?"

As Sugar began to read the letter he thought of Poor Boy and Peanut again and could hear Poor Boy say. "Come on Peanut Tex don't need a flea bag like you tagging along."

By now tears were flowing freely down his face as he listened to Sugar's calm voice as she read the letter and again thought of Jake's place and blurted out. "It ain't fair Lord, ain't nothing fair about this."

He walked out on the porch just as Sugar finished reading the letter thinking, 'I've had enough of this I'm leaving.' But then he could hear Marty sobbing and knew he had to stay.

From inside he heard Sugar say. "I'm so sorry this happened to you little sister but look at it this way, we always wanted a brother and now we have one."

He stood there for another twenty minutes listening to sugar trying to calm Marty.

Finally Sugar came out embraced him and said. "Come on brother lets go in we've got a lot of talking to do, and plans to make for a family get together."

Back inside they embraced each other as Sugar rattled on. "We'll plan a party here at my house this coming Saturday afternoon just for family members, we'll have a celebration and try to make up for all the years that we missed being together as brother and sister's."

Marty had calmed down considerably but was very quiet and obviously still in shock.

They spent the next thirty minutes planning the family party, mostly by Sugar.

When she mentioned she would ask her mother to be there. Tex asked. "Do you think she should know? In the letter my mother said she never wanted her to know about it."

"Don't you worry about that Sugar, that happened a long time ago, momma will be happy that we have gained a brother and her a son, and believe me she will treat you as a son."

"And I want your grandma here also, lets not have any secrets in our family, secrets are not good for the soul, believe me I know because I have harbored one since I was fourteen and it almost destroyed me. So come Saturday we have a lot of things to talk about as we let momma and your grandmother in on our secret, then I will tell what happened to me when I was fourteen and maybe momma will forgive me a tiny bit for giving her so much trouble when I was growing up."

Of course Tex could relate to secrets, 'hidden truths' and knew her thinking was correct. They talked on at length and he told them about all the events from the day before. Seeing the letter for the first time, sitting at the table in Jake's place about to take his first drink of alcohol and if not for Reba he may have gave in.

Through it all Marty said nothing but would nod from time to time.

But as he got up to go she stepped forward and took his hand and said. "That girl Reba, you do like her don't you?"

Tex dropped his head and said. "Well yes but I barely know her yet."

"Well I'm not acquainted with her but have seen her several times, she is very pretty and from what you've told us I would be happy to have her as a sister in law. I want her here with us Saturday because I feel she will be a future family member."

He looked in her eyes and could see the sadness there and knew she must be dieing inside but was glad that she had taken the first step toward recovering from the awful mess they found themselves in.

"Okay little sister I'll ask her to come."

He called Reba the next day and told her about the plans for the family party on Saturday. "Marty would like for you to join us, she said she knows you when she sees you but is not acquainted."

"Oh yes" She replied. "Same here, I know about her and her sister Sugar, but we just went to different schools and never became acquainted."

"Okay I'll pick you up early Saturday afternoon, hope you're not disappointed about not getting to go to Bristol we had that planned you know."

"Yes I know but this is ten times more important, we have the rest of our lives to visit Bristol and other places."

"And another thing, have you noticed your sisters and I are about the same size? Which means you can bring along the two dresses when you pick me up Saturday and we can gift-wrap them. Can't think of a better way for you to start off with your sisters than to give them each a pretty dress."

"Okay I'll see you Saturday and yes I'll bring the dresses."

He could sense the excitement in her voice and thought. 'Darn I like that girl, is this the work of God in my time of heartache? And the dresses, maybe that was why I bought them in the first place I've heard ma and pa talk many times about how God intervenes in our lives and sometimes in strange ways.'

Sugar and Marty had went all out and prepared a delicious meal and the table was set and ready when Tex arrived with Ma, Reba, and their mother.

After the meal and all the dishes were cleared Sugar wasted no time in getting to why they were there.

She started by saying. "Momma we have a secret that we have to share with you and ma, it may be more than you think you can handle, especially you momma but as time goes on I believe you will appreciate learning the secret and it will bind us together as a family even more and I do mean family because last week Marty and I discovered we have a brother and his name is Tex."

"And where does Reba fit in? Well take a look at her and Tex and tell me how you can vision anything else other than them being together the rest of their lives, so that makes her a family member also."

As she talked on Ma and her mother's faces showed nothing but puzzlement and they wondered if it might be some kind of joke.

Finally she unfolded the letter and said. "This is a letter from Bonnie to her boy friend telling him she's pregnant and who the father is. Momma you and Bonnie were best friends and like I said before you will not take this very well but I think its best we share the secret with you. Nothing good seldom comes from keeping secrets, believe me I know because I have harbored one since I was fourteen that I will rid my mind of after we finish with this one."

She started reading the letter and had to stop several times to help Marty console her mother. When she finished tears were on every face as they hugged and tried to calm each other.

After about an hour they found themselves drifting off on other conversations, but nothing seemed to bring much comfort.

Sugar dreaded telling them about her secret of being a rape victim when she was fourteen because she knew her mother would take it very hard.

Choking back tears she told them. " I have a secret that only myself and one other living person know about, Lonnie and Carlie knew about it but as we all know they're resting out yonder in the Cemetery."

She went on to tell them what Hoss did to her when she was fourteen and how it changed her young life. "Now Momma I hope you can understand why I gave you and Daddy so much trouble and heartache all these years. He threatened to kill Daddy if I ever told it to anyone. Now that Daddy's gone I think I'll be safe in sharing it with you, I doubt if he will hurt any other member of our family."

"As far as turning him in to the sheriff I don't care to do that because it would be his word against mine and as you know most of my years in between haven't been lily white. Therefore I'm willing to let it go. I feel better already now that I have shared it with you."

Her mother rushed forward and they embraced and stood there sobbing, she wondered. 'How much can momma take in one day? God help us all.'

Shock and anger showed in every ones faces. Tex thoughts went back to all the times Hoss had intimidated him and thought. 'Why did I let him get away with it?' 'Never again, never again, I'll kill the bastard if he ever crosses me again.'

Late that night they finally said goodbye to each other vowing to bind together as a family, each feeling that the day had taken away something special in their lives, but at the same time replacing it with understanding and love.

And yes Marty's dress was a perfect fit. Sugar's fit a little snug around the waist with the little one inside but she'll size down after the baby comes.

On a warm pleasant evening Sugar got home from work ate her supper, washed the dishes and sat down to write a letter to Bud. She wrote four pages and apologized for repeating some things in the letter about her pregnancy that she had sent in a letter before.

"Please excuse me for going over much the same thing about our little one but I'm so excited and can't wait till his or her arrival."

She ended by saying. "And that goes for you too Sugar, I can't wait till you're home again for good so we can get on with raising our children, I do want more than one and I hope you feel the same, so my prayers are that the war will end soon and let us and all others involved get on with our lives."

"Will end this and get to bed where sweet dreams of you always come while I'm sleeping. Good night my love."

"Your loving wife Sugar."

As she sealed the envelope a loud knock at the door startled her and something told her to be cautious so she picked up a thirty-eight revolver that lay on a table by her bed. Bud had taught her how to use it and urged her to always keep it handy. "Never know when some one will try breaking in on you." He had said. "And never hesitate to use it if you think you are in harms way."

She walked to the door and asked. "Who is it?"

"Come on little lady open the door." Was the reply and she recognized the voice of Hoss.

She took three steps backward and aimed the revolver directly at the center of the door.

"No I won't open the door so be on your way and never bother me again."

"Okay, so you plan on holding out on me eh? Well I can fix that I'm gonna break th damn door down."

Fear gripped her as she retreated a couple more steps but she quickly regained her composure and said.

"I have a gun aimed directly at the door and I know how to use it, so go ahead and try, but remember that may be the last door you break down because I intend to empty this revolver right through the door."

Silence told her that she had been convincing and now she felt she had the upper hand. "Now I'll give you one minute to leave, and I do mean leave never to bother me again, what you did when I was fourteen caused me to live in fear and afraid that you might harm daddy, but now that he's gone I no longer intend to let you bother me again."

She could hear what sounded like shuffling feet, and finally.

"Ye know what yore in for bitch, hear me bitch? Yore ass will pay for this, count on it bitch."

She heard him walk across the porch and down the steps and wondered if he would get something from his car and return maybe even a gun.

But soon she heard the loud sound of the engine as he roared off into the night.

Two weeks later in June I arrived to open my uncle's store at six a.m. for the convenience of the miners to stop and pick up something on their way to work, work gloves, carbide, lunchmeat, etc.

A gray fog hangs above Stone Creek hiding the view of the craggy rocks on Stone Mountain.

My great uncle Robert who lives nearby and is an early riser, more so since three of his boys are in service is one of the first ones to enter the store. I look at his face and wonder if he slept at all last night.

I knew what his first words would be. "Carson, honey, when do you think the war will end?" And I suppose he knew my answer in advance since it never changed from. "Oh I don't know uncle Robert, four months, six months, or maybe in a few weeks."

"I hope you're right son, I hope you're right." Would always be his answer. I think he knew that I didn't have a clue but just liked to hear the prediction anyway.

If he had received a letter from either of the boys the day before he would tell me what they said. The youngest Chester, wrote to me a few times and I would read the letters to him. So he never failed to ask. "Have you heard from Chester lately?"

An hour later I saw a girl coming across the road from the rental cabins that joined the dance hall. As she entered the store I noticed she was very pretty and shapely. She had me slice her two thick slices of cheese. Said she needed to eat something to hold her until the restaurant opened. She added two pints of milk and two five cent cream cakes.

I watched as she walked back across the road and wondered who her companion was. As I looked at the three cars parked at the cabins I recognized one of them belonging to one of the guys home on furlough, and sure enough about an hour later they came out and got in the car.

He came in the store the next day and I jokingly asked him if I sliced the cheese thick enough. "Oh yes." He laughed. "And how'd you like my Kentucky girl?"

" A beauty." I answered. "You sure know how to pick em."

"I just got lucky." He said. "Aint got but a few days before I go back so I can't be too picky."

At the same time a miner who lives in a little rental house a short distance from the store on the old road gets ready to catch his ride to the Benedict mine above St. Charles. He cooked his breakfast, fixed two sandwiches for his lunch and added a moon pie and one banana. All of this went in the top part of the round silver colored dinner bucket, which fit over the bottom that contained drinking water.

He looked at the clock and seen he had at least half an hour before his ride was due so he headed for the porch to sit in the swing. On his way out she was laying on the couch as usual and he had vowed he would walk on out and ignore her but again as usual he stood above her and wondered if he would ever be able to walk away and never look back at all the misery she had caused him since they moved here from Tennessee.

As he looked down at her beautiful face he wondered how much longer they would be together.

'Guess it's been a mismatch right from the start.' He thought. 'Wish my wife was still alive, I needed some body after she died but guess it's my own fault that I let myself fall for this girl. Should have known better after all I was thirty four and she was barely seventeen when we married.'

'Everything worked out well for a while until we moved here so I could get a job in the mines.'

'She took a job helping out in the kitchen at the beer joint and dance hall up yonder across the bridge.'

'First thing I know she's working as a waitress in the bar and dancing with about anybody that cares to hold her, and that led to her dating different ones and staying out till the wee hours of the mornings.'

He reached down to touch her forehead but hesitated, knowing that if he did she would wake up and complain.

'May as well forget it as best I can and hope for a change in her but I suspect I'll get home from work tonight and find my supper cooked but cold, and after I reheat it and eat alone I'll go out on the porch and listen to the music blaring out of the outside speakers from the dance hall where she works and wonder who will hold her tonight and bring her home in the wee hours. And just as I'm doing now I'll stand here wanting to touch her.' 'The same old routine.'

'Each day brings more humiliation and shame but for some reason I don't have the guts to walk away.'

He covered her bare legs with a blanket, and thought again about touching her but turned and walked out just as his ride stopped at the porch.

Across the creek where everyone referred to as 'The Bottom.' The phone rang several times before Doc rolled over and reached for it with shaking hands.

"Doctor, my baby sister is sick and I'm afraid she's about to die, would you please hurry out here? Please hurry, please."

He could sense the urgency in her voice and knew from past experiences that calls of this type usually meant the child was on the verge of dieing.

He asked where she lived. "You go toward Harlan to a logging road at the foot of the mountain. We live two miles up that road near the sawmill. I had to walk out of there to get to a phone. Daddy couldn't get the old logging truck started because the battery is down. He said to tell you that he put the battery on charge and should have the truck waiting for you at the foot of the mountain by the time you get there, said there's no way a car can make it on that road."

"Alright little lady I'll be there shortly.' He answered. He sat up in bed thinking. 'Just got in bed about an hour ago after being out most of the night with a family at Virginia Lee Coal Camp. Took most of the night to deliver their third child. Was hoping that I could eat a late breakfast with my family this morning but guess it's not to be.'

As he reached for his wrinkled shirt and trousers he accidentally knocked the half filled bonded whiskey bottle from the table along side the bed and expressed a sigh of relief when it failed to break.

'Don't know how I could ever make it through the day without this stuff, have to get to the liquor store at Big Stone and stock up or else I'll be lining the pockets of the bootleggers.'

He held the bottle in his shaky hands and took a long drink, slipped it in his pocket and quietly walked out so as not to wake his wife and three children.

He cranked up his old battered car and headed up the Harlan road. As he passed the store some one remarked. "Doc's out early must be some body sick up that way."

"Either that or he's out of bonded whiskey and one his way to get some moonshine." Another added.

He rounded dead mans curve and spotted the logging truck up ahead with the driver standing along side.

He climbed to the ragged seat of the topless cab as the driver fired up the powerful engine he yelled above the noise. "Doc you're in for a rough ride I hope you don't mind, my wife and little girl are just about out of their mind worrying about our baby.'

"How old is the baby and what seems to be wrong?" He asked.

"She's eight months old, started with a mild cold about two weeks ago which all of us had but she never seemed to get over it. We've had her to two Doctors in the past three days and they both said it was a bad cold and she would be okay in a few days. But she got worse last night and to tell you the truth I didn't think she would still be with us come daybreak. We had heard of you before and decided to call. Sorry about this rough ride but there's no way she could ever survive this ride out of there again as sick as she is right now."

Doc bounced up and down, as the truck would rise as it ran over a huge rock and then drop off into a deep rut, up and down, up and down. Then he thought.

'Yeah I'll be lucky if I survive this myself.'

Then he thought about taking the bottle from his coat pocket for a swig, but changed his mind knowing he could never hold it to his lips without spilling it all over.

Finally the sawmill came in view and beyond there he could see a building constructed from unpainted rough lumber and thought that must be where they lived.

As soon as the truck came to a stop he reached in his pocket for the whiskey bottle tilted his head back and with shaky hands held it to his lips. As he screwed the cap back on the bottle he noticed it was almost empty.

'What a place to run out of whiskey.' He thought.' two miles back in Brushy Mountain surrounded by a grieving family as they watch their baby slip away.'

The truck driver showed no surprise as he watched because Doc's drinking habit was common knowledge and some folks refused to use him for that reason, he being one of that group but decided to call him after talking to a worker at the mill. "You get him out here." He had said. "He may be a slave to the bottle but he knows more about his profession than all the other doctors in this area put together."

He followed Doc as they climbed the five steps to the open door where his wife was anciently waiting. On the third step he reeled and would have fallen if not for the truck driver's quick reflexes as he grabbed him by his coattail.

He opened the gown to the baby's tiny chest, placed his stethoscope and listened.

"This baby has pneumonia and we have to get her to the hospital in

Pennington as quick as we can or else she won't last more than twenty four hours. She only has it in one lung so the odds are on her side to recover, but we have to get moving there's not much time left."

"How can you tell it's only in one lung?" The driver asked.

Doc pointed to her left chest and said. " See the color on this side? Pink and natural, now look here on her right side, pale and ashen no color at all, that's the infected lung, lets get moving we don't have a lot of time."

"Doc she'll never survive the ride out of here, damn can you do something?"

"No there's nothing I can do so lets get rolling your wife can hold her and that will cushion her ride a little, once we get to my car we can go the rest of the way in it with you driving cause I need to take a nap, got a long day ahead of me, ain't had no sleep to speak of in the past week."

He wrapped a blanket around the mother's shoulders and fashioned a cradle like shape near her waistline.

"We'll put her in this and it'll help her to swing with the ups and downs instead of the bounces that the rest of us will have to go through, I hate to do this but it's the only chance she has."

They climbed in the truck, the driver his wife and the baby in the topless cab, Doc and the other daughter standing in the bed of the truck behind them holding on to a steel pipe that crossed from one side of the truck to the other right above the cab.

The driver fired the motor up let the clutch out and lurched forward for about a hundred yards and came to a stop alongside a clear unpolluted stream. He jumped from the truck crossed a log that spanned the stream and disappeared among the dense mountain laurel that lined the banks on either side.

Doc was completely puzzled but noticed the driver's wife didn't seem to be concerned at all. In a short time he burst through the laurel with two pint bottles filled with something just as clear as the water in the stream.

He reached them to doc and said.

"Here take these, better'n that bonded stuff you got, go ahead try it."

He slipped one bottle in his pocket and unscrewed the cap from the other, tilted his head back and was surprised how mild the taste was as he let several drams flow down his throat.

And as always he knew what the results would be, restored confidence, new found happiness and all is right in my life, but that soon wears off and the thirst for more takes over.

'No matter if it's beer, wine, bonded whiskey, or stuff as mild and pure looking as the water flowing in that stream it all gives me the same results.' 'Short lived feelings of all is right in my world, but in the end is nothing more than days filled with ups and downs, pretty much like riding this truck over the next four miles.'

He tightened his grip on the steel pipe as the truck lurched forward and as he looked down at the baby swinging gently in the blanket steadied by it's mothers arms tears came to his eyes again not from happiness because the pure stuff hadn't had time to kick in yet, but from sadness as he thought of his family that he loved so very much but never seemed to find any time to spend with them.

'Got no one to blame but myself' He thought. 'I let alcohol take over my life to the point where I can no longer control it, only God has the power to intervene and I pray daily but sometimes I wonder if he hears my prayers.'

Then the truck ran over one of the larger rocks and as it bounced in the air he quickly moved back so the bottles wouldn't come in contact with the truck bed and break.

Pretty much as the mother was doing to protect her baby from the savage bouncing of the truck, a baby that is so much a part of her life, he was also protecting something that was a very large part of his life, the bottle.

Finally the pure stuff began to kick in and the road ahead looked much smoother. 'All is well in my life again' He whispered. 'How long? I have no idea but for now it couldn't be better.'

At the foot of the mountain they transferred to the car and Doc was able to take a short nap on the way to the hospital.

Doctors at the hospital confirmed his diagnosis to be correct, pneumonia in the right lung. Said the baby should stay in the hospital three or four days. After a word with the family, Doc headed toward Stone Creek and home thinking that he would stop and have breakfast with his family before going on to his office in St. Charles.

He pulled off the road and parked at Cold Springs, took a long drink from the bottle, sat there for a few minutes and watched as a man filled several jugs with pure cold water running out of Stone Mountain through a two-inch pipe.

Finally he tilted his head back and held the bottle to his lips until the last drop trickled down his throat.

He pulled away just as the man finished filling his last jug and thought. 'Patients will be waiting at my office I'm already late, so I think I'll skip breakfast with my family this morning, maybe tomorrow.'

He looked across the creek at his house as he drove by and a smile lit up his face as the pure stuff had begun to restore his confidence once again.

'Yeah I'll do it tomorrow for sure.' He thought. 'But I have a lot to do today, I'm not hungry anyway.'

He reached down and felt the other full bottle in his coat pocket and knew that he would get through the day.

A typical day at Stone Creek during the war years most going on with their daily work and routines but never sure of what tomorrow held in store.

But some had already come face to face with tomorrow and it couldn't get much worse.

A father who had spent a sleepless night worrying about his three sons off fighting a war that looked like it would never end, and then pace back and forth watching for the mail man to come hoping he had a letter from one of them.

As his tomorrows piled up before him the lines in his face multiplied and he hastened to old age before his time.

A miner trying to live with a girl of his dreams that he met back in Tennessee.

But the change in her since moving from Tennessee had brought nothing but humiliation and shame to him and for some reason he couldn't bear the thought of ever leaving her.

So his thoughts were. 'Maybe tomorrow will be better, God knows how much I love her.'

Then the young doctor who didn't look young anymore because he let alcohol take over his life and rob him of a family life that he had always dreamed of, but now seemed to be slipping away even more as each tomorrow demanded more of the confidence-builder from the bottle and at the same time taking away his desire to rest and take in nourishment.

His tomorrows had consisted of long days and sleepless nights fueled by spirits from the bottle to get him to the next tomorrow and as they piled up he knew his time was short and soon the time would come when the next one would be out of reach.

The young soldier home on furlough for a few days trying to satisfy his longings to hold a pretty girl as long as he can before going back to camp and getting ready to ship out to some far off land where he is sure to face his tomorrow head on.

That day for me was much like all the others in Stone Creek, I could still hear the fellow say. "The damn war will be over before you ever grow up."
'I'll be eighteen in a few short months and ready for the draft and the war still rages on.' I thought. 'Will it ever end?'

As the weeks went by Marty, Sugar, and their mother had Tex, his grandma, and Reba, visit them almost every weekend. Marty became more at ease around Tex and seemed to become more adapted to having him as a brother day by day.
Tex had about two weeks left on his deferment when he and Reba got married in the little church on Keokee road.
Nothing elaborate but with a large crowd in attendance and as usual lots of food prepared by the church ladies.
He and Reba had talked it over and decided she should move in with his grandmother while he was away in service. "Ma needs someone to look after her.' He said. 'And I can't think of a better person than you.'

On the same day Tex left for induction at Fort George G. Meade in Maryland, Gina gave birth to a baby boy at Monarch. Due to unknown causes he arrived three weeks earlier than was predicted. She was overjoyed and sent a telegram to Bama in far off Montana.
Bama took the telegram to his section foreman at the mine and asked if he could have a few days off to visit his wife and newborn in Virginia.
The section foreman being a dedicated family man himself promised to do everything he could to see that he got to go.
"I'll go right to the top and see what I can do." He promised.

As he approached Bama the following day a big grin was on his face and Bama knew he would soon be on a train headed to Virginia.
The grin spread as he handed Bama a piece of paper stating that he had a twelve- day furlough.
"Okay here you are, you leave here on Sunday two days from now, I tried to get you an earlier start but the big boss wants you to finish out the work week first."
Bama rushed to the telegraph office and fired off a message to Gina.

I got a twelve day leave will be on my way Sunday, Should take about three days by train. Can't wait. Did you name him yet? You didn't say in the telegram." Love always. Bama.

Bama was filled with anticipation as he and the rest of his crew stepped on the mine-shaft elevator early Saturday morning knowing that after this days work he would be riding the rails toward Virginia the next day.

The boss had spread the word about the newborn and some of the crew directed some good-natured kidding Bama's way.

"So I hear your wife gave birth to a son." One fellow remarked. "Well while you're there make sure you fix it so another one will be due some time next year, can't think of a better way for you to get home for a few days."

The elevator dropped several hundred feet down the shaft and came to a halt at the level where they worked.

The doors opened and they began to file off. Then something happened just as Bama and another one of the crew started to step off. A malfunction in the system caused the doors to start closing and the elevator to drop several feet at the same time.

Maintenance workers finally opened the doors and freed one worker that had been caught by the closing doors he walked away with nothing more than a broken finger and bruises.

But thirty-five feet below where the elevator finally stopped the crew could see the lifeless body of Bama where he had fallen landing on his head. The closing doors failed to hold him as it did the other worker releasing him to fall to his death.

Late that day a sheriff's deputy brought the sad news to Gina in Monarch, at about the same time a deputy in Anniston, Alabama knocked on the door of Bama's parents.

His brother Mike started driving toward Alabama with Gina and the baby and his family.

In far off Montana a flag draped casket was rolled on to a passenger train, secured in the baggage car and watched over by an honor guard, began its long journey over the rails not the planned one to Virginia and the joy of a young couple celebrating their first born, but to his final resting place in Alabama deprived of the joy of holding his first born and without ever learning his name.

The funeral was well attended by the patriotic folks in the Anniston area and beyond.

His family took it very hard especially Gina and his mother.

"Why Lord, Why?" Gina wailed. "You didn't let him live long enough to see his baby, don't seem fair."

The haunting sounds of taps fill the air before another body is lowered in the ground leaving behind a grieving family and a baby he will never hear say dada.

No it don't seem fair but war is usually kill or be killed and is never fair.

Through all the grief Gina and his parents formed a bond that made it easy for her to agree to live with them.

"We need each other." His mother said. "He would want you and the baby here with us."

They lived together as a happy family for almost three years when Gina met a young man that had been wounded in the war.

Bama's father and mother knew at Gina's young age she needed to start all over with someone again so with their blessings she married the young man and he embraced her young son as his own.

Twenty years later after the war I heard they were living in Sand Mountain, Alabama near her son who she named Carl Jr. after his father. Carl Jr. gave his first born the name Bama to honor his father's nickname.

Gina never forgot her roots and came back to St. Charles several times over the years still looking much as she had the day she and Bama met at Shoun's drug store, tall dark and beautiful.

When Tex was in basic training at Fort Bliss, Texas. He told one of his buddies about his nickname and from there it caught on and he got permission to wear his Tex emblem.

Reba had settled in with his grandmother and as he read their letters he could sense they were happy together. He spent most of his spare time writing letters and received letters almost daily from some one.

Most of them were informative and upbeat except the ones from Marty that always left him wondering if she had adjusted after the ordeal that they had went through. 'I hope and pray that some one will come in her life like Reba did mine before its too late, I'm worried about her. He would think. 'I now love her as a sister and hope she will love me as her brother and put the past mess behind her, but she needs some one to help, I can't imagine what it would be like for me if not for Reba.'

The level of excitement in letters between Bud and Sugar was building daily with anticipation of the baby coming into their lives.

At the same time she worried about what Hoss might do about her rejection.

She didn't mention it to Bud.

'No sense in telling him he's got enough to worry about, I'll tell him about the rape and all when he comes home on furlough.'

'I worry about that to for fear of what he might do to Hoss, he has always been a calm and level headed person but underneath all that I sense something like this might unleash total revenge.'

She bowed her head and prayed.

"Lord please protect me and my family from the evil ways of Hoss and calm the wrath that is sure to arise in Bud when he learns what Hoss did to me when I was fourteen.'

Marty spent most of her time alone, riding Cody almost every day, and long periods of time out at the picnic area sitting at the table watching the waterfall. Occasionally swinging wildly out over the waterfall in the big truck-tire twenty-five feet above the rocks below.

Her plans for the future that she had so dearly cherished in the past now seemed to be at a stand still.

She had never been the type to call on the Lord but now out of desperation she could vision God's face in the water as it tumbled down with a mighty roar forming many shapes and colors.

So in a weak and troubled voice she would awkwardly ask God for help.

'Please God, can you help me get over this? I never called on you before because I thought I was smart enough to handle anything, but now I can see how much I needed something in my life other than my own ego, help me please.'

'And Lord! Place Tex in my heart as a brother because I still awake at night longing to be in his arms as his wife.'

Poor Boy stirred and tasted the beans mixed with ham that had been simmering in the old black iron kettle for several hours on top of the pot-bellied stove.

"Okay Peanut, we'll eat in a few minutes I'm gonna fry some taters and corn fritters, all that goes good with beans topped off with onion, aw shit don't give me that damned look I know you won't eat onions, but damned if I can think of anything else that you have turned down."

"Guess you're worried about laying at my back all night after I eat beans and onions, well for your information you fart in your sleep to and it sure as hell don't smell like honeysuckle."

" You know something Peanut I miss Cliff and Barbara we had a good three weeks visit with them and I know you miss being around that bunch of dogs especially that young collie female, shit I believe you think more of her than you do me. Do you? Well go ahead sit there and look at me that tells me I'm right you don't care diddly shit about me."

Then Peanut rushed forward and jumped in his arms. As he held him tight he whispered.

"I didn't mean it Peanut, You couldn't get along without me and I sure as hell would be lost without you."

"You know it feels good to be back home again just you and me, and look at all them clothes hanging on the walls. Cliff and Barbara insisted that I go buy some better clothes and hell she burned my old ones. Not only that but she lectured me about my language. "Clean it up." She said. "I get tired of hearing you spit all that garbage out."

All them new duds look out of place hanging over a dirt floor, I sure miss my old stinky jacket that hang there with the letter hid away for so long."

"Speaking of the letter I wonder if Tex carries it around like I did. You notice he likes to call me dad Peanut, and you know something I like that, maybe some day I'll have a son of my own I always wanted one. Yeah I'll settle for that if'n he respects me enough to call me dad I'll be proud to call him son."

"He's off yonder in Texas taking basic training, we had a long talk the day before he left, said he would write and fill me in on army life. Wish I was young again Peanut, I'd join up in a minute and get off this damn dirt floor, aw hell now don't look at me like that you know damn well I wouldn't leave you here, shit I'd take you with me."

"Yeah he's a good boy Peanut, I'm glad he finally got over the mess he was in and found that girl Reba, that was a God send Peanut, no doubt about it you know yourself I'm no bible thumper, but by God I do believe in our master and the way he shows up in peoples lives, sometimes when they're about as low as they can get and living on a dirt floor like you and me, I believe he put us together Peanut, and before its over he'll get us off this damn dirt floor."

"I aint never been one to say prayers and ask for things but tonight when I go to bed I'm gonna try to pray and ask our master to intervene in Marty's life I hear she's having a hard time getting over the mess her and Tex found themselves in after the news in that damn letter, I'll ask him to send some one to her just like he did for Tex.

Okay, here's your bowl every thing mixed in the beans but the onions, you shit ass you don't know what you're missing."

A knock on the door followed by. "Hey, you awake in there? "Open up before I kick this damn shack in." No mistaking that voice. 'That's the Boss and he only talks like that when he's in his best mood, wonder what he has on his mind.'

He opened the door and stood back as his boss squeezed his large frame through the small opening. "Looks like I'm just in time to eat." He said. "What's in that kettle?"

"Ham and beans." Poor Boy answered. "With fried taters onions and corn fritters."

"I'll have a bowl with everything but the onions I like them but they don't like me.'

"Oh shit, you're just like Peanut you don't know what's good with beans."

"Oh yeah, I'll betcha one thing old Peanut has a hard time trying to sleep in these close quarters after you gorge yourself on beans and onions, bet it smells like a shit house on a hot day."

Peanut looked up from his bowl and wagged his tail in agreement.

"See what I mean." The boss laughed. "I'd hate to be in that poor dogs place tonight."

They finished off the whole kettle of beans prompting Poor Boy to say. "Damn I'm glad I don't have to feed you all the time, thought Peanut was bad but hell you eat more'n he does."

The boss lit up a cigarette and eyed the old blackened coffee pot sitting on the pot-bellied stove.

"Got any coffee in that pot?" He asked. "I know it ain't fresh judging by the last cup I had with you a while back, it was as thick as syrup and about two days old but right now I need a cup to go with this cigarette so I'll take my chances."

"Hell yes I got coffee in that pot." Poor Boy answered. "Been aged a few days to bring out th taste."

As he poured the coffee the boss noticed all the new clothes hung from nails on the walls.

"Say! Don't tell me you finally broke down and bought yourself some decent clothes? That visit with your brother must have worked wonders because I've noticed a change in your attitude since you got back, you even look better, still ugly as hell but you have a better skin color."

"Who the hell are you to talk about how I look?" Poor Boy answered. "I ain't seen where you won any beauty contests."

They laughed and the conversation changed to the war.

"I hope its over soon my boy is over there some where, bout worries me and my wife to death especially if we don't hear from him very often."

"Well I come here with news that I think you might like, I sold out my lease to this little operation last week and just got all the papers fixed up yesterday. Didn't want to say anything until the deal was closed."

"Blue Diamond wants me to take over one of their new mining ventures over in Kentucky, for at least a year or until it gets fully operational."

"I will need a top notch electrician and the job is yours if you want to come along. But if you prefer to stay here I talked to the new owner and he agreed to let you stay if you don't want my offer."

"To tell you the truth I had to do a lot of soul searching before I made up my mind to offer you the job."

"The picture of you walking the roads in a drunken stupor for so many years after you let the memory of that woman get the best of you kept appearing before me and I'd have doubts that you could ever be the electrician that you once were there at Bonny Blue."

"But something kept telling me that you had turned the corner and were ready to get back to normal living again. You've kept your word to me since you moved in this shack and stayed away from the booze, and I took that into consideration also. So if you want the job it's yours, the pay is good as you know, top notch electricians are in high demand around the mines."

"Oh yeah, you'll be a little rusty at first because you've been away from the profession for so long but I'll bear with you till you get in the groove again so you don't have to worry about that."

"Blue Diamond will furnish our housing, we'll be close neighbors a two bedroom for my wife and me and a small one bedroom for you right next to ours."

"We'll leave here next Wednesday so today being Saturday you have a few days to make up your mind."

"Remember back there I told you that something kept nagging me to offer you the job even though I had my doubts that you would ever be the electrician that you once were? Well the feeling is still there and I'm having trouble figuring out where it's coming from."

Poor Boy had sat through all this completely shocked and unable to speak, even Peanut sensed something out of the ordinary was taking place and had moved to Poor Boys side holding his head from one side to the other as he took in every word.

With tears in his eyes he got to his feet and embraced the boss.

"I don't need a few days to think about it, I'll be ready Wednesday. And while I'm all mushy I want to tell you how much I appreciate you taking me off the roads, if not for that I wouldn't be here today, as my dad used to say. "Aint many good men in this world if you run into one tell him."

"So I want to tell you this. You are truly a good man to risk taking me back as an electrician after all the years that I've been away from it."

"And about that nagging feeling I know exactly where that's coming from its our Lord working to get me off this dirt floor."

As the boss headed for the door a warm feeling replaced the nagging and he realized that Poor Boy was right, something very special had taken place and had erased all the doubts he had harbored when he first stepped in the shack.

"Okay, get all your things together and I'll pick you up Wednesday morning."

"And hey! Make some fresh coffee that stuff you gave me must be a week old."

Poor Boy said something that was drowned out by peanuts loud barking as he jumped up and down as if he knew a journey lay ahead and he couldn't wait to get started.

Then the memories of Kentucky came rushing back, he could see the old faded letter and envelope that had brought him so much grief but he knew this time would be different.

"This is a new beginning Peanut!" He yelled. "We're on our way up."

Then one day a mighty roar from the skies brought every one in Stone Creek, and St. Charles, outside to gaze upward at a sight that none of them had ever seen before.

A fighter plane darted playfully above the craggy hills visible over Stone Creek, at intervals before darting behind the hills and appearing again above St. Charles. Finally climbing above the fleecy clouds and with a thunderous-earth shaking sound dove straight down toward the tiny town.

It came as a complete surprise and needless to say scared the daylights out of the onlookers. They held their breaths as it fell from the sky at a break neck speed feeling sure it would crash before their eyes.

But at the last moment when only a few hundred feet from the little town it pulled up, leveled off and screeched dangerously close to the towns buildings and power poles.

The fellows gathered under the old sycamore tree watched the trees limbs sway back and forth as it screamed out of sight toward Stone Creek, but reappearing again over Bonny Blue, Benedict, Monarch, and the surrounding area.

Then watch as it climbed higher and higher becoming a tiny dot before turning for another straight down breath taking dive. How many dives? One fellow said he counted. "Two, maybe three, I was too damned scared to count but do know that I peed in my pants at least three times."

Charlie Province once told me. "It shook the ears off the corn stalks."

The playful daring pilot was Hershel Parsons a local boy flying with his unit across the country, they stopped over at Knoxville, Tennessee and he asked permission from his commander to fly over his home town of St. Charles.

Permission was granted but it didn't include any dives or acrobatics that the P-38 fighter plane was noted for.

So when his commander heard about it he disciplined Hershel and warned him to never cross the line again.

He flew the plane throughout World War Two and achieved many honors and decorations. He remained in the Air Force many more years retiring as a Colonel with a spotless distinguished career except for the dive-bombing over St. Charles, Virginia.

I heard of his passing in 2002 or 2003 and the memories became fresh in my mind again as I could feel all the excitement that spread over the area that day as I watched from Stone Creek.

He's finally climbed beyond the fleecy clouds and out of sight, leaving behind a lasting memory to the folks that watched on that day in the nineteen forties. God rest his soul.

A miner who worked at Kemmerer Gem Coal Company decided to spend the rest of an October Saturday afternoon squirrel hunting in the stand of hickory on Clabe Barton's place off Keokee road.

He parked along side another car at the ledge and noticed the heavy bed of needles on the ground from the pine tree sitting atop the cliff.

He climbed the hill to the top of the ridge and stopped to rest.

'Not much use to be in any hurry.' He thought. 'It'll be at least another hour before the squirrels come in to feed.'

'That other car back there, must belong to another hunter I wonder if he's already there and waiting.'

He looked down at the stand of hickory with their leaves glistening a pure gold among all the other colors that surrounded them. Beyond there he could see the little clearing and remembered going there after he had bagged his limit of squirrels one time and while sitting at the picnic table admiring the little water fall he looked up to see Clabe Barton approaching.

"Did you get your limit?" He asked. "Yes I did." He answered. "And they all have heavy bushy tails, guess we're in for a cold winter.'

"Yeah I have always heard that." Clabe had replied. "And the wooly worms are thick as flies this year, all with a heavy coat so we might be in for a rough one."

They had sat and talked for over an hour and he remembered Clabe had told him to come in off the Keokee road and park near his house. "That way you won't have to climb the ridge."

"I just might do that the next time." He replied.

"Well you're welcome any time you want to."

'A good man.' He thought. 'Died a few months ago still a young man in his mid forties.' 'Left behind a wife and two daughters, makes me wonder if I will make it to an old age and enjoy my grand children.'

As he gazed at the beauty below, the crisp autumn breeze was noticeable but the bright sunshine toned it down to almost a perfect temperature.

He made his way down the steep hill at times grabbing a small bush to steady him self when he would slip on the thick bed of leaves that covered the ground. By the time he reached the stand of hickory he could hear the chattering of squirrels as they approached.

He readied his 20-gauge pump and waited. Within minutes the tree above him became a feeding station for a half dozen squirrels and the ground around him was showered as they cracked the large nuts.

One shot from the 20-gauge brought a squirrel tumbling to land in the leaves twenty feet away.

In a span of an hour four squirrels out of five shots, missing one that was near the top and out of range of the 20-gauge.

'That's enough' He thought. 'Think I'll go out in the clearing and sit at the picnic table for a while, something about that water fall that makes me go away feeling better.'

Just as he stepped out in the clearing he noticed someone off to his left enter the woods from the clearing.

'That must be the one that owns the car parked under the ledge.' He thought. 'Guess he's like me probably enjoys sitting out here after getting his limit of squirrels.'

He sat down at the picnic table and noticed the leaves had been disturbed around one of the benches. Bare ground was visible in several spots where the leaves had been pushed away and the ground itself had deep marks that looked like they had been made from some ones shoes.

'Guess some kids have been out here playing.' He thought.

He looked over at the truck tire hanging from the cable on the ledge above the waterfall and noticed it was moving back and forth ever so slightly. 'Not enough wind to cause that.' He thought. 'Some one must have used it in the past few minutes.'

Then his eyes picked up the clear cool water just as it poured over and started its fall downward toward the rocks below and marveled at the different shades of color as it went from shade to bright sunshine and then to a soft green as it poured over the moss covered rocks near the bottom.

His eyes followed it down stream as it wound its way toward two larger stones where it was slowed down and formed a whirlpool. He had often wondered what it would be like to swim in that whirlpool and wondered if anyone had ever tried it.

As he watched the water do its never-ending whirl between the two large boulders he noticed something laying on top of the largest boulder and first thought it was clothing, but as he squinted his eyes from the bright sunshine he could see it was a person.

A person not whiling away the day swimming or sun bathing or even sleeping but a person that had swung out over the rocks in the truck tire and dropped twenty-five feet to the rocks below and was now permanently sleeping.

His first thoughts were to wade out and see if there was anything he could do, but as he moved closer he stopped at waters edge and could make out the lifeless form of a girl with brown hair matted around her blood stained face and mouth.

Then he realized the only way he could help was notify the sheriff.

He followed the path that he was sure would lead him to the Barton place and with each step he dreaded to face the Barton widow knowing that the young girl sprawled atop the boulder must one of hers.

He knocked on the door on the back porch and waited, still not sure how he should break the news.

Mrs. Barton came to the door with a smile on her face as she always did, but it faded quickly as she looked at the face before her, a face that she had no recollection of ever seeing before, a face that showed sadness and worry and she sensed this nameless face carried sad news.

"You Mrs. Barton?" She nodded yes. Do you have a phone?" He asked. " I need to call the sheriff about an accident that's happened out yonder in the woods."

She pointed to the phone hanging on the kitchen wall. " Where in the woods?" She asked. "Is it in the picnic area?"

He nodded yes as he dialed the phone.

She listened as he said. "I'm calling about an accident off the Keokee road in the woods behind the Clabe Barton place. I don't care to tell you anything else right now, I'll wait till you get here."

He hung up the phone just as Mrs. Barton touched his arm and asked.

"My daughter Marty went out there earlier this afternoon, Is it her, did something happen, tell me please is it bad?"

"Yes its bad ma'am, you might ought to call family or friends and get them over here because you all will need each other."

"What happened?" She asked as she headed for the door. "Please tell me something I'm going out there."

He reached out and took her arm. "No Mrs. Barton, I can't let you do that, here sit down at the table I'll get you a cup of coffee. Do you want me to call some one, how about your other daughter?"

She sat down as her whole body shook with grief. "Yes." She sobbed.

"Call my daughter Sugar, she's at work at the beauty shop in Pennington, the number is scribbled on the bottom of that calendar hanging by the phone."

She listened as he said.

"I was squirrel hunting on your mother's property this afternoon and discovered a terrible accident out in the picnic area, you should hurry home she needs you."

"No I'm sorry I can't give you any details, get here as quick as you can, but drive careful."

The sheriff and one of his deputies arrived just ahead of Sugar. He walked to the car just as they got out. And In a low voice he said as he pointed. "There's a dead girl out yonder at the waterfall, looks like she fell from the swing to the rocks below."

"It's Mrs. Barton's daughter Marty, she wants to go out there but I don't think she should, it's a pretty gory sight."

"No we don't want that." The sheriff replied. "Is she alone, who's that coming?"

"Oh, that's her other daughter I called her right after calling you."

"Well I hope she can be strong and be of some comfort to her mother until we get some kind of order out of this."

He looked at his deputy and said. "Drive down to Stone Creek and call Copeland, from Cooper's Café, shore don't care to use the phone here in front of a grieving mother and her daughter."

"And see if you can get a couple of the fellows to come out here, we'll need help getting her out here to the ambulance."

As soon as Sugar seen the sheriff and his deputy and could hear her mother wailing from the porch she knew something bad had happened to Marty.

She hurried toward the sheriff and said. "What happened, is it Marty? Please tell me she's okay."

"Wish I could tell you that but I'm afraid the news is bad, your sister fell from the swing out yonder, she's dead. I'm counting on you to be a brave girl and take care of your mother till we get her body out of there."

She fell forward in his arms and sobbed.

He tried to soothe her with words but the proper words wouldn't come so he said over and over as he stroked her hair.

"I'm sorry honey, I'm sorry, I'm sorry."

Finally she backed away and smiled through her tears. "You can count on me I'll take care of momma. She'll be alright."

As he watched her go up the steps to the porch tears started down his weather beaten face and he turned away so the hunter wouldn't see.

They stepped from one rock to the other to reach the large boulder without getting in the water and climbed to the top, which was no easy task because it was wet and slippery.

As they looked down at the still form the sheriff said. "Well there's one thing for certain she didn't suffer, look at her forehead must have hit the rock head first, and probably broke her neck."

The hunter's face became ashen and he had to look away, he looked down at the whirlpool five feet below and started to reel, the sheriff noticed and took his arm to steady him.

Then the sheriff said. "Look at her neck, do you see what I see? See the marks there just below her chin? And the bruises on each side below her ears."

"I believe this girl was dead before she fell from that swing, some body chocked her and then put her in the swing knowing that she would fall on the rocks."

Then the hunter remembered the person leaving the picnic area just as he entered, also the mussed up leaves around the picnic table and the eerie sight of the swing in motion at the top of the ledge.

"I've got something to tell you sheriff, I didn't give it much thought at first but now I can see where it all fits in since you pointed that out."

He proceeded to tell him the details as the deputy emerged from the path in the woods with Copeland and three of the men from Stone Creek trailing behind.

"Don't go near the picnic table or the swing." The sheriff called out. "We have something more than an accident here, might find something there that will shed some light on this so called accident."

They carefully slid down the rock and made their way to the group.

"Wait right here and don't move around until me and my deputy look around." He said to the group. "Don't want anything disturbed we might find something."

But they found nothing other than the disturbed leaves and fresh marks in the ground around the picnic table.

"This person you seen entering the woods just as you stepped out, did you get a good look at him?"

"No I didn't." The hunter replied. "I thought he was just another hunter on his way back across the ridge to his car, and to be honest if he was carrying a gun I didn't see it, I only got a glimpse of him as he stepped in the woods, can't even remember the color of his clothing."

"And like I said a black car was parked at that overhanging ledge with the pine tree growing on top. I parked right beside it but can't remember if was a Chevy, Ford, Plymouth, or what, all I know it was black."

"Well that ain't much to go on." The sheriff replied. "I guess ninety percent of the cars in Lee County are black."

"But it's as plain as the nose on your face she was choked and killed right here at this table and probably raped to boot."

"But if she was dead how could she have stayed in the swing long enough to fall on them rocks sheriff?" Some one asked.

"Well it's possible that he drug or carried her up there and placed her in the swing and gave it a big push and it carried her out to the highest point before she fell, but I'm thinking he placed her in the tire backed up the hill for a push off and grabbed the cable above the tire and wrapped his legs around her until they sailed out over the big rocks and then let her go."

He looked at the hunter and said. "It happened right before you stepped out of the woods, and the motion you seen from the swing proves it. If you had been two minutes earlier you would have seen them swing out over the rocks."

"Okay lets get her off that rock, be careful and handle her easy I intend to send her for an autopsy."

He looked at the hunter again and said. "Come on out with us and I'll drive you around to your car, that way you won't have to climb that ridge, I want to look around where you seen that parked car."

They put her on the stretcher, covered her body with a blanket, fastened the straps and headed down the narrow pathway through the woods.

As they went through the gate near the barn Cody was standing by the fence snorting and pawing the ground.

"That's her horse Cody." One of the Stone Creek boys remarked. "She spent a lot of time with him, I wonder if he knows?"

"No doubt about it." The deputy answered. "Animals can smell death."

They loaded her in the ambulance as Cody continued to paw the ground.

The sheriff stood and watched the ambulance as it made its way past the porch where Sugar was holding the grieving mother, and as it turned on the road from the driveway Cody reared on his hind legs and gave out a loud lonesome neigh.

170

"Guess my deputy was right that horse knows she's dead. Now I've got to get in there and tell her mother and her sister that it was no accident, sure don't look forward to that. I wont tell them the gory details today, be better to come out tomorrow after they have calmed down a little."

"That's what I hate about this job and some times I wonder if I'm the right person to fill it, but some body has to do it."

He watched Sugar as she tried to keep her mother calm and could see that she herself was dieing inside. 'Brave girl.' He thought. 'But how long will she be able to hold up under this terrible burden?'

"I'll be back tomorrow." He said. A couple of things I want to look in to and I should have more information by then."

Then Sugar said. "If you think it was an accident you're wrong I know she was killed and I know who did it."

The sheriff was taken by surprise and immediately changed his plans about putting it off until tomorrow. He walked out on the porch and told his deputy to take the fellows back to Stone Creek. He nodded toward the hunter and said. "Drive that gentleman to his car and look around where that car was parked can't ever tell you might find something there. Then you can come back looks like I'll be tied up here for a while. Stop at Coopers Café and call my wife, tell her I'll be a little late for supper. Might be a good idea to tell your wife the same thing, women can get all worked up when they put a meal on the table and then sit and watch it get cold."

"Can't say that I blame them, guess I'd feel the same way."

He went back in the house and for the next hour listened to Sugar's story beginning with the rape when she was fourteen.

She would become overwhelmed with grief and have to stop at intervals to embrace her mother.

"Yes I know the no good scoundrel you speak of he has caused trouble all over Lee County but for some reason no one has been able to nail him."

"But now with this information I believe we'll bring him to justice. But it would be a losing cause to try him on what he did to you though, so many years have slipped by since then and it would be his word against yours."

He asked a few more specific questions and made notes.

Soon the deputy returned and he got up to go.

"Give me a little time to tie some things together, I need to see a couple people that might shed some light on this. I'll call the Virginia state police headquarters tomorrow and see if they'll assign some one to help us work this out, they have well trained people and new methods that me and my deputies haven't had the privilege to know about. God knows we need all the help we can get, we're only a four-man force trying to cover the whole county. So I'll be back some time late tomorrow and fill you in on what we have, in the mean time try to get some rest. The autopsy will be over in a few days and you'll be able to go ahead with funeral arrangements."

As he got in the car he whispered. "Details, the worst part of my job but like I said before some body has to do it."

The deputy pointed to a brown knit glove on the seat between them. "Found that half hidden in pine needles where the car was parked, couldn't see any tire marks on the ground because the pine needles have the ground covered."

The sheriff picked it up and examined it. "Takes a big hand to fill this glove and I think I know the fellow that has a hand to fit it."

The deputy looked at him and asked. "Do you know something that I don't?"

"Yeah I found out a lot from Mrs. Barton's daughter, and with a little luck we might nail the bully,you know who' of Lee County."

As they drove along he proceeded to tell his deputy all that he had learned.

The deputy scowled and said.

"I always knew he was a mean one that couldn't be trusted, but I didn't realize he could be this mean. We can't let him get away with this. He belongs behind bars for the rest of his life."

"Well, our work is cut out for us and starting tomorrow morning come to work ready to toil hard and long until we have this evil one behind bars. I know it's Sunday and my day off but we can't afford to let too much time go by I want to question that bird tomorrow."

The deputy nodded in agreement, and then asked. "Sheriff did you ever suspect the hunter might have done it before you got the information from Mrs. Barton's daughter?"

"No I never did and I'll tell you why. First of all he seems like a decent hard workingman and even if he did he wouldn't have came out to report it to Mrs. Barton. Just common sense that I try to make use of in law enforcement."

The next day started with a visit to the home of Hoss. The sheriff knocked on the door and waited. The door opened and a frail young girl stood before them. 'This must be his wife,' He thought. 'I've heard he mistreats her and the baby.'

He tipped his hat and asked. "Is your husband home? we would like to have a word with him."

Her reaction didn't surprise him, fear showed in her face and her hands shook as she tried to speak but words wouldn't come.

'She's living in pure hell.' He thought. 'The bastard has total control over her life.'

"Tell your husband to step outside we have a few questions to ask."

They watched as she walked away toward the rear of the house and soon could hear Hoss yelling.

"I don't give a damn who it is, you know you're not supposed to wake me, now go tell th bastards to get off my property. And here's something to remind you to never wake me again."

Then she screamed followed by a noise of her body falling against the wall.

"The bastard hit her." The deputy said.

"Yes he did and by God we're going in after him." The sheriff said. "Follow me."

They walked in the room to view a heart-breaking scene. He sat on the edge of the bed glaring at her as she cowered in a corner with her little girl clinging to her legs.

The deputy thought. 'I could blow his brains out right now and go home and eat a good meal, wouldn't put a mark on my conscious. In fact it'll bother me more if I don't do it, but that's not the way we do things.'

Blood was running from her mouth and down the front of her dress.

With one swift movement the large body of the sheriff leaped from the bedroom doorway to the bed and with lightening speed pinned his hands behind his back. The deputy snapped the handcuffs as the sheriff jerked him to his feet.

"What the hell you sons of bitches think you're doing? You got no right in my house without a search warrant."

The sheriff shoved him toward the front door and said. "We have a right because we heard and witnessed assault and battery on your wife, now get the hell out of here, you're going to jail."

Once out side he ranted and raved even louder. "You bastards will pay for this mark my words, you'll be sorry you ever set foot in my house."

The sheriff nodded toward his car and said to the deputy. "Look in his car there you might find the mate to that glove ."

"What glove you talking about? Ain't no damn glove in my car."

"I know," The sheriff answered. "I don't expect we'll ever find it because you wasted no time in getting rid of it after you discovered you lost the other one.'

"Lost one? Hell I didn't lose no glove."

The deputy searched the car thoroughly but could find nothing.

"Put him in the front seat and I'll ride in the back so I can keep an eye on him I don't take any chances with his kind."

The deputy put him in the front seat and closed the door just as the sheriff opened the door to get in the back seat.

A loud angry scream came from the porch followed by a shotgun blast that sent the sheriff reeling to the ground along side the car.

Another blast followed with the car taking most of the shot, but the deputy felt a stinging sensation along his side and left shoulder and knew he had been hit.

He aimed his revolver just as the shooter fed another shell in the pump shotgun.

Three rapid shots from the revolver with two finding their mark sent the shooter reeling backwards as the shotgun fell to the floor.

He lay still looking up at the ceiling but seeing nothing, blood trickled down his cheek from where one of the slugs had penetrated his head just above his eye.

The blue denim shirt he wore was now turning red around his heart.

"You killed my dad you bastard, you killed my dad." Hoss screamed. "You'll pay for this, take these damn cuffs off and I'll kill you with my bare hands."

The deputy seen the sheriff holding on to the car to pull himself up and breathed a sigh of relief. He noticed tiny holes in his pant leg and knew some of the buckshot had hit his leg.

"Here, let me check you out." He said as he pulled up his pant leg.

"Nothing but a few buckshot in my leg." The sheriff replied. "You better check yourself out I see blood on your shoulder."

"Yeah I know." The deputy answered. "But it ain't nothing serious, could have been a lot worse."

"You're right," The sheriff answered. "Good thing you drilled him when you did or else both of us would be dead or dieing from blasts from that shotgun. I owe you for saving my life and would like to say more about that, but right now we've got to get Copeland out here to haul him away."

"And at the same time figure out a way to get that poor girl and her child out of this house and in a safe place somewhere before the evil one gets back home from jail. Unless we can pin something else on him assault and battery won't hold him long."

Hoss sat in the car yelling and screaming at them.

"Ought to stuff his mouth with a dirty sock." The deputy remarked.

"Yeah I know how you feel but we're bound by law to treat his kind as human beings even though some of them including this one are several notches below the most savage of animals."

He nodded toward Hoss and said. "Keep an eye on him, I'll go in and check on the girl and her child and call Copeland if they have a phone."

As he walked by the lifeless form on the porch he noticed the flies gathering on his bloody face and thought.

'This could have been me or my deputy or both of us, guess we're lucky makes me wonder how long our luck will hold out, but can't afford to linger on that thought to long cause some body's got to do this job.'

Inside he spotted a phone and called Copeland. "Need you out here at Stone Creek, you know where Hoss lives? "No it's his dad no need to hurry he's dead."

"Me and my deputy took some buckshot, nothing serious we'll go by the hospital later and let them dig them out. Cant talk right now I'll fill you in when you get here."

Through an open door he could see the young girl sitting on the bed holding her little daughter. He walked toward her and noticed the fear on her face. "It's okay." He said. "Do you have some place to go? You need to get away from this place and Hoss."

"I have an aunt in Jonesville, she has been begging me to come live with her but I was afraid to go because of him."

"Well don't be afraid anymore we're taking him to jail, he'll get out on bail but if you get a restraining order he'll have to stay away from you and the child."

"Tell me where your aunt lives and I'll look her up right after we lock him up, If she can't come get you I'll see that you get there."

Soon Copeland arrived and loaded the now cold body in the ambulance as Hoss spat out a steady stream of cuss words toward the sheriff and his deputy.

Some of the folks in Stone Creek, had already heard about the gun fight at Hoss's place and heard that some one was killed, a large crowd stood outside Cooper's Café as Copeland drove by followed by the sheriffs car.

"Must have been the old man." One of them remarked. "I seen Hoss in the sheriffs car."

"That's too bad." Another said. "I was hoping it was Hoss or the both of them would have been better yet."

They locked Hoss up and headed out to find the young girls aunt.

"Sure me and my husband will go get her right now." She said. "Been worried to death about her afraid that maniac would harm her and her baby."

"We'd be glad to have them live with us and see that her little girl gets an education, they sure had no future to look forward to living with him."

"All right don't waste any time she's expecting you and don't forget to go by the court house early Monday morning and get a restraining order to keep him away from your home. "I'll talk to the judge and he might have it ready for you, we want to get all that done before he gets out on bond, would like to hold him without bond but we don't have enough on him at this time."

Later at the hospital the sheriff and deputy sat bravely as the buckshot was removed and small bandages placed over the penetrations.

Then back to the jail and the next hour was spent filling out papers to be sent to the proper officials including the Virginia state police.

"I hope they don't drag their feet about sending some one, we need all the help we can get to nail this bird and rid him from our county for good."

"Yeah I know." The deputy answered. "But did you ever think about it if we don't nail him he'll never be safe in this county again, he's been lucky up to now but he'll never get away with this some body somewhere around St. Charles, or Stone Creek, will put a bullet in him and I for one will not turn a hand to find out who did it.'

"You're right. "The sheriff replied. "I'd say more than one will be laying for him but in the meantime we have to do our job and try to bring him before a jury."

"Now that we've caught up on the paper work and made the call to Richmond for an agent's help we have a long night ahead of us, lets get going I intend to stay awake all night firing questions, who knows he might crack and save us a lot of trouble of digging for clues."

But at the hearing Monday all they had to hold him on was assault and battery with a low bond that was reduced even lower by the judge taking in consideration that he needed to be free to bury his father.

The restraining order was granted with a warning from the judge. "If you go near your wife or daughter or anyone else to cause trouble you'll find yourself right back in jail without bond, so I advise you to tow the line."

A scowl came across Hoss face and he looked like he wanted to rave at the judge but changed his mind.

A call from Norfolk confirmed Marty died from strangulation and examination showed she was raped.

And It was noted that.

A person with very large and strong hands and possibly wearing wool knit gloves the knit pattern clearly was visible on her neck area.

The sheriff scratched his head and said.

"If we could come up with that other glove in his car or on his property we'd have him in a corner. But like I said before, he got rid of it as soon as he discovered he had lost the other one. Who knows he may have burned it."

"He's a hard one to crack, I thought for sure we could wear him down by firing questions at him all night, but in the end he just about wore us out."

On Tuesday morning the sheriff was poring over some notes on his desk when he noticed a young man swagger in.

'Wonder who that is?' He thought. 'Could that be the agent from the Virginia state police?' 'Mighty young and know it all looking, God knows I don't need to be stuck with some one like that, I bet he just graduated I thought for sure they'd send an old and experienced investigator."

"You the sheriff here?" He asked. "I've been assigned from Richmond to take charge of a suspected murder case in your County so lets get all the information on the table here so I can decide where to start."

"Yeah I'm the sheriff and you might notice I'm tired and wore down and so are my deputies, You see there's only four of us to cover this whole county and when there's a murder committed we have no special unit to assign it to. We have to work on it all day and through the night and show up here the following morning all tired and grouchy from lack of sleep."

"So let me tell you where to start, walk out that door and come back in showing a little common courtesy and respect toward this haggard bunch you see sitting around here because By God we deserve it."

He looked from one to the other, clearly he was taken aback but finally said. "I'm sorry sir I didn't mean to offend anyone you have my apologies, I hope you'll work with me on this case."

"Yes sir young man we will work with you, you can count on that but all we ask is for you to get off your high horse and come down to our level because we hate to have some one looking down on us."

Then he awkwardly extended his hand and said. "Consider it done I'm down to your level and ready to get started."

"Okay son, I don't have a lot for you to look at but I'll tell you what we know and then you might want to go over there at the jail and question the suspect. We're holding him on assault and battery charges but he'll be out on bail shortly because he has to bury his father."

"What happened to his father?"

"We were at the suspects home to question him about the murder and he attacked his wife. We arrested him and put him in the car and about that time his father walked out on the porch with a pump shot gun and my deputy there had to put him away."

"You mean he just gunned him down because he was holding a shot gun?"

"He shore did son because you see he had already fired off two shots at us and was ready to pump out some more." He pulled up his pant leg to reveal the bandages covering the buckshot marks. "See here I took a few in my leg and look at him over there, see the tiny holes in his shirt there at the shoulder? Yeah he shot him dead right there on the porch good thing he did because if not for that you would have been here to investigate the killing of two police officers today. Always give that some thought when you're wondering why a police officer gunned some body down."

He rubbed his hands together nervously and said. "Yes sir I'll remember that."

"Okay now that we understand each other I'll show you what we have so far. Just got the report back on the autopsy, the victim was strangled and raped I'll take you out to the site tomorrow."

"The suspect drives a black Chevrolet sedan and a black car was seen parked across a ridge from the murder scene the day of the murder. We found a brown wool knit glove where the car was parked and since have searched the car but couldn't find it's mate."

"See here on the autopsy report it says she was strangled by a very strong person with large hands, which fits our suspect to a T."

"And it goes on to say, possibly wearing wool knit gloves because the knit pattern was visible on her neck. I have a few more things I can let you in on as we go along but you should get over to the jail and grill that bird before he gets out on bail. Tell the jailor who you are and ask to see Hoss that's his nickname. But I warn you he's a mean cagey son of a gun, and he's going to be a hard nut to crack."

The young agent got to his feet and said. "I'll go talk to him before I come to any conclusions along that line, you know some times we jump to conclusions about some one without knowing the facts."

As he headed for the door the sheriff called out.

"Okay, have it your way but a lot of folks in Lee County including town police chiefs will tell you the same thing I've told you about that bird and that's a fact."

He sighed and turned to his deputies. "Looks like they've sent us a Prima Donna this time just when we needed one of the old experienced veterans, something tells me we'll spend most of the next few days defending, why did you do this? And why didn't you do it this way, while all the clues in this case if there is any grow cold and disappear."

"Oh well no use in worrying about it, just take it as it comes and that aint easy to do some times."

Then one of the deputies spoke up. "I know it ain't sheriff but listening to your wisdom prepares us for it and that's half the battle."

Finally the body was brought back from Norfolk and the burial arrangements were finalized.

Bud had completed boot camp training in California and his furlough home had been interrupted when he was assigned to a special training unit but he was now eligible to go home for twelve days before reporting to Norfolk, VA.

Tex was right in the middle of infantry basic training in Texas but was granted a six-day leave to attend the funeral.

A large crowd gathered at the little church on Keokee road long before the black hearse appeared from around the curve rolling slowly through the shadows cast by the road side trees. Not a sound could be heard from the Cadillac motor as it emerged from the gloom into the bright sunshine surrounding the little church.

Strips of chrome glistened from the sun as the door was opened to reveal a gold colored casket.

Under the direction of two well dressed funeral directors pall bearers carried the casket up the steps and down the aisle then sat down in their designated pew in front, mindful of the mourners in back of them and feeling uncomfortable in the quietness penetrated only by whispers, some one clearing their throat, coughing, or the uncontrolled sobbing from a grieving family member.

The Pastor sat slumped facing the crowd pretending to read his well-worn bible and as he listened to the organ played by a young lady dressed in a dark lavender dress his thoughts were.

'I'm growing weary from conducting so many funerals, words seem to get more out of reach especially for the ones that die because of violence. But some one has to step up and do it, and with the Lords help I'll stay the course.'

As he looked out over the mourners he wondered who would be next.

'Lord, I pray and ask you for mercy on our little congregation because we have suffered through a lot over the past few years and I must admit I still question your reasoning for taking them from us even though I promised you a while back that I would never complain about it again.'

'I guess that's a sign of lack of faith and weakness on my part so I ask you to lead me through this service and restore my faith to the point where the words I utter will be of some comfort to the grieving family and our members here in this community.'

These thoughts were still running through his head as he slowly rose to his feet, cleared his throat and said.

"Well here we are again in what's become a far to familiar scene in our little church and it has taken its toll on me over the past three years. It breaks my heart to have to see family members and our community suffer from losing a loved one especially in this case where a young life was snuffed out by someone that must be an agent of the devil himself and is still free to walk among us."

"It's all so sad and at times I feel like lifting my hands toward heaven and calling out, God I'm not your man, I don't fit in with this job, but as always I manage to muster up enough faith to keep going, and I ask you isn't that what faith is all about? We have to strive for it daily, it's not handed to us on a silver platter."

"Things like this often enter my mind and I have to pray about it."

"Am I over the hill, burned out? Or weary from all the times I've stood right here in this same spot and witnessed the pain and suffering of a grieving family. Or could it be God is testing my faith again?"

"That thought came to me as I sat and listened to the organ music. So I've decided to stop searching for the proper words and place my faith in God to get me through this service."

"So I'll read my favorite Verses, Psalms 23. 'A Psalm of David' and trust our Lord to guide me through this service free of worry about finding the correct words, And after this service is over we leave here to have a short grave side service at the Barton family cemetery. Mrs. Barton, and her daughter would like to welcome you to the Barton home right after that service where the table is laden with food brought in by some of our church members and other thoughtful neighbors."

The Service was over in about an hour and fifteen minutes and the black hearse rolled slowly up Keokee road followed by a long line of cars.

Cars pulled over and stopped in respect as the hearse approached.

A gardener near the road removed his hat and stood facing the road as the hearse passed. A young mother stood in her yard holding her baby close to her breast and watched as the hearse disappeared around a curve.

The pall bearers carried the body directly in front of the Barton home out to a knoll, about two hundred yards to one side of the house.

Clabe and his wife had decided to start a family cemetery there the year her father died. And within three years her mother and his father and mother were buried there.

And now just a few short months after they laid Clabe to rest his youngest daughter will take her place near him.

Cody watched from his usual place near the barn as they made their way to the open grave. But before they sat the casket down he broke into a gallop and crossed the pasture and stood at the fence no more than fifty feet away.

He snorted and pawed the ground throughout the short service and when it was over and the crowd drifted away, he watched as the men shoveled the mounds of dirt back in the hole.

They placed the flowers over the fresh grave and started to walk away.

"Look at that horse.' One of them said. "Is that his way of saying goodbye to her?"

As they watched he stood at the fence on his hind legs and stared straight ahead at the grave for at least two minutes without wavering.

Finally he raised his head higher and the long lonesome neigh came again but this time even sadder than the day they carried her from the picnic area.

"I don't know about you but that gives me chills just like when I hear taps." One of them remarked.

"Yeah I know." The other one answered. "Makes me want to cry. Lets get out of here before I do."

Sugar and her mother tried to be sociable with the visitors but inside they both were on the verge of screaming. Sugar because she thought she was to blame for Marty's death and as she looked at her mother she thought.

'Why Marty?' She never gave momma any trouble at all, he should have killed me instead.'

Her mother's thoughts were. 'How much more can I bear I lost Clabe and then learned he bore a son with my best friend. And at the same time found out that my oldest daughter was raped when she was fourteen, and now my youngest is gone.' 'I ask you Lord how much more can you put on me?'

Sugar looked across the room to where Bud and Tex were having a conversation looking so tanned and neat in their uniforms.

'They'll be leaving in a few days.' She thought. 'This should be a happy time for me and Bud with the baby coming but how can I be happy with all this on my mind?' 'And then I have to worry about what Bud might do to Hoss, I never seen him show so much anger when I told him what Hoss did to me when I was fourteen.'

'I told him to let the law handle it and not get himself in trouble, but he said. "That's the trouble the law has never applied to him for some reason and it's time some one did something about it."

'I hope he and Tex stay away from Hoss and let the sheriff do his job, I believe he will bring him to trial this time.'

One by one the visitors said goodbye leaving Bud, Sugar, Tex, Reba, Ma, and Sugar's mother. The mother had asked them to spend the night with her.

They talked way past midnight and it seemed to ease the hurt in all of them especially Sugar and her mother.

Bud and Sugar went outside for a breath of fresh air just before going to bed and in the moonlight could see Cody still standing at the fence near Marty's grave. "Oh God help me.' She cried.

Bud took her in his arms as the anger toward Hoss rose almost to a breaking point and he thought about going looking for him.

Tex had expressed himself to Reba pretty much the same way and like Sugar she advised him to leave it to the sheriff.

"He'll get away with it." He said. "Some body needs to put a stop to it and I would be glad to oblige, I let him walk all over me since I was a kid but them days are over."

Reba held his hand and said. "Remember the day in Jake's place when you needed help? Well I feel that God put us together that day and I would hate to lose you just because you want revenge. He aint worth getting in trouble over, and I guess now is a good time to tell you we have a baby coming and it will need you."

Tex took her in his arms and held her for a long time as he whispered over and over. "You've made my day, you've made my day, can't wait to see it."

The sheriff obtained a search warrant and drove the young agent out to Hoss's place.

"I don't expect we'll find anything, like I told you before he's a cagey one and has been able to stymie law enforcement over the whole county for years."

"But I do feel that he can be cracked under heavy questioning so maybe today we can bombard him from both sides and I do mean bombard, you can't pussy foot around and expect to get anything out of this guy."

"Well we'll see." The young agent replied. "But I'm not much of a believer in strong handed tactics."

"Okay, have it your way but I'm beginning to think that Hoss is on the verge of beating another rap and this time it's murder."

They rode in silence the rest of the way as thoughts ran through the sheriff's mind.

'Why did I ever ask for help from Richmond? I could have asked Bill, the St. Charles Police chief to help me out, he knows a lot about Hoss and is as tough as nails. An all night grilling in that stinking St. Charles calaboose plus a slap in the face now and then might cause him to fess up.'

'Now I'm stuck with this guy that is bent on going by the book even if it means letting a killer go free.'

As they walked up the hill Hoss was standing in the yard glaring at them. "What th hell you doing on my property? Get th hell off while you can still walk."

"Guess by god ye forgot the last time you was here you killed my dad and I ain't about to forget that, and there's hell to pay some where down th road ye jist wait and see."

The sheriff showed him the search warrant and said.

"This is an agent sent down from Richmond to take charge of the Barton girl murder case, we need to look around inside and outside the house and then ask you a few questions."

"Well by god go ahead but don't think you can take yore sweet time at it cause a damn search warrant don't give you the right to camp out on my property."

"And questions, I ain't got no answers to yore so called murder questions, I hear she fell off that damn swing out there over the rocks and killed herself so how'n hell can you say it was murder?"

They searched the inside of the house and could hear him fussing from the porch. They found nothing and as they walked out on the porch he said.

"And another thing you took my wife and kid with no reason and got it fixed where I can't see them, well by god I'm about to look them up and bring them back home."

The sheriff walked over and said. "We arrested you for assault and battery on your wife and she got the restraining order for her and the child's safety. Now if I catch you trying to find them I'll personally work you over so that you'll never walk again, now you can take that as just an empty threat, but go ahead and try it and I guarantee you I'll shoot both legs out from under you."

He glanced at the scowling face of the young agent and knew that he would be lectured on proper law enforcement before the day was over.

They searched a shed alongside the house but found nothing. They headed toward the car and Hoss called out.

"Ye give up eh? Like I said taint no damn murder anyway jist a waste of yore time."

Off to the right the sheriff noticed a blackened hole in the ground that was used to burn refuse.

"Lets take a look over there." He said.

"I don't know what for." The agent answered. " Nothing there but ashes."

Something caught the sheriff's eye at the edge of the ashes. Part of a thumb from a brown wool-knit glove and along side that a tiny piece of cloth covered with blood with a button attached to it, obviously part of a shirt.

He bent over and with a stick carefully raked them on to a hankie.

He looked at Hoss on the porch and asked.

"When's the last time you burned something here?"

"I burned some trash there yesterday why th hell you ask? Ain't nothing there but ashes."

"Got a little more here than ashes. Got part of a thumb from a wool-knit glove and a bloody piece of a shirt bottom, which I think connects you to the murder of the Barton girl. Same color as the glove we found at the parking place under the ledge where the black car was parked. And the blood on the shirt would suggest that came from the rape."

"So ye think you got me eh? Well by god I burned a pair of old wore out gloves and a shirt that had blood on it from skinning squirrels how in hell you figure that ties me to a murder?"

"Well we're going to have to ask you some more questions." The sheriff said as he started up the steps.

"No we don't," The young agent called out. "You seem to forget who's in charge, come on lets go we're done here for today."

The sheriff glared at Hoss and knew this was an opportunity lost. A little arm -twisting might have produced results.

He followed the agent to the car as Hoss's words rang in his ears.

"Bout time the capital sends somebody down here to straighten out these so called law enforcers. Yes sir by god never thought I'd see the day that would happen, guess ye'll think about it th next time you get on yore high horse and think about coming out here."

The sheriff dropped his head in disgust knowing that with this agent in charge there was no hope of ever nailing Hoss.

As they rode along in silence his thoughts were.

'Looks like he's wiggled out again, but from the rumors I've been hearing he'll die with his boots on and when he does damned if I'll even think about investigating it.'

At that moment he glanced over at the young so called learned agent and thought about stopping and 'pistol whip the hell out of him.' 'but, no I'll suppress that he'll find out before too long that you can't always go by the book, but unfortunately not before Hoss and others walk free.'

Two days later the agent informed the sheriff that he would be leaving for Richmond the next day.

"Don't have enough hard evidence to make a case against him." He said. "And I'm not convinced he did it anyway. But let me give you a little warning before I go, if I hear of you using heavy handed tactics on him I'll personally see that you're prosecuted, he has his rights too you know."

"Oh yeah I understand where you're coming from." The sheriff replied. "And if you hang on to that attitude all the sheriffs in the state of Virginia will have their hands tied behind them and crimes solved will come to a standstill."

"Think about that long and hard the next time you're on your way to help some sheriff solve a crime, cause you sure as hell handcuffed me and allowed the criminal to go free."

"Sorry you feel that way but the law must be followed, so don't let me hear of you running rough shod over him. I'm not so sure that you and your deputy done the right thing the day you killed his father, maybe if you had tried to talk to his father he would have listened and gave up the shot gun."

"Will you tell me how in hell you can do that when you hear a yell from out of nowhere followed by two shot gun blasts?"

"You're even dumber than I thought, go ahead and tell your big boss and while you're at it you may as well tell the governor that if I ever ask for help again I shore don't want a dumb ass like you."

"And tell them I'm ready to hand this badge over any time they want it, hell I can't work in handcuffs. Now get the hell out of my sight before I lose my temper."

The young agent walked out slamming the door behind him.

Bud got a telegram from the department of the navy to report to the navy command in Norfolk, Virginia instead of reporting back to California. There he was assigned to a battle ship and joined a large convoy far out in the Atlantic.

He trained as an anti aircraft gunner and was kept too busy to think about Sugar and the coming baby. He and his partners would man the guns for as long as eight hours at a time, be relieved and hit the sack from exhaustion only to be aroused an hour later to participate in a mock attack from German bombers.

In his dreams he would vision Sugar and the baby floating toward him across the never-ending waves of the Atlantic.

They would drift right along side the ship and as he looked down at Sugar's smiling face in waters that had suddenly become calm, but always a giant wave would sweep them out of sight and the leering grin of Hoss would look up at him from the high waves, he would take dead aim at his head and squeeze the trigger and feel the shock of the 45 in his hands as the bullet found its mark and the leering grin was replaced by a face of death and swept out of sight in blood stained waters.

The horror of the dream would awaken him and he would lay there momentarily thinking about Hoss and the evil things he did to Sugar and Marty and wonder how many more times he would kill Hoss only to see him reappear. And just before exhaustion lulled him to sleep again he would recall Sugar's words.

"Don't get yourself in trouble, let the Sheriff handle it, me and the little one will need you."

Tex returned to Texas and finished basic training and was allowed to come home again for a few days en route to Fort Benning, Georgia for more advanced Infantry - training.

Reba, knowing that he was torn with grief from Marty's death at the hand's of Hoss and could sense the hate that he harbored pleaded with him to steer clear of Hoss. "Please Tex, stay away from him I love you too much to have to see you go to prison for killing him, think of me and the coming of our baby and our life together after the war."

"Yes" He would answer. "I do think of that more than anything else but I can't get over him getting away with killing her and what he did to Sugar, they are my half sister's you know."

Both Juke joints in Stone Creek were loaded to capacity, as was the case on any other Saturday night. Juke boxes blaring as the dancers snuggled close to each other on the half lit dance floor. Some couples happy and having fun but others that seemed to be living in an unhappy past and trying to find their way again with a new partner.

Hoss walked in to every ones surprise. "Can you believe that?" A fellow remarked. You'd think he would lay low for a while knowing that he's a marked man and subject to taking a bullet at any time."

"Yeah you're right." Said another. "Wouldn't bother me none if he gets it tonight."

One of Tex friends came by and asked if he would like to go to the poolroom at Stone creek and shoot a game or too. Tex looked uncertain as he glanced at Reba.

"Sure go ahead." She said. " Enjoy yourself."

"I'll take my car too." He told his friend. "Because I might want to come home before you do."

Hoss had a couple of beers as he watched the dancers and noticed that not a soul in the crowded joint would even nod or make eye contact with him.

'To hell with th bastards.' He thought. 'Think I'll go to St. Charles.'

Every eye was on him as he walked out into the darkness surprised that he had came and went so quietly without causing a ruckus.

At nine Sunday morning the sounds of lonesome tunes from the juke boxes was replaced by happy church going families living along the creek and on the hills above the joints as they rushed around getting ready for Sunday school and church.

The pool room owner swept up inside and came out to pick up beer bottles and empty cigarette packs that were strewn in front of his place and off to one side toward the little bridge that crossed the creek on the old road.

He spotted a discarded beer bottle on the bridge and out of his good nature went to pick it up lest some one get a flat tire from running over it.

He glanced over the concrete barrier wall of the bridge at the shallow water making its way through the rocks below, and there laying face down was the body of a rather large man with most of his body on the rocks and out of the water except for his right arm that was extended out to one of the small streams that wound its way through the rocks with minnows nibbling on his fingers.

He pointed it out to a man sitting on his porch and soon a dozen or more stood on the little bridge peering down at the lifeless form.

He went back in the poolroom and called the sheriff.

"Got a man face down in the creek here in Stone Creek. Yeah he's dead. Yeah I think I know who it is but can't be sure because he's face down."

He went back outside and heard the exchanges among the onlookers.

"Yeah that's him alright looks like he met his match this time."

"Maybe he fell off the bridge." Some one remarked.

"Naw some one threw him over and he busted his head against them rocks, or they could have killed him first, maybe up around St. Charles, brought him here and dumped him to make it look like he fell off the bridge."

"Well hell I don't know what to say, I hate to see a lifeless form anywhere especially laying in a creek with fish nibbling at the fingers but can't say I'm moved a whole lot by the one I'm looking at now, shit there'll be a celebration tonight and I plan on being right in the middle of it."

The sheriff and his deputy arrived. "Who is it' anybody recognize him?" He asked.

"Oh yeah that's Hoss." Someone answered. "Looks like some body did him in and dumped him here, I expected it but didn't know it would be this soon you'll have a hard time catching the one that did it sheriff, hell there must have been a whole slew laying for him after the Barton girl was killed."

"We all know he killed her that's no mystery the only mystery is nobody can understand why you didn't nail him for it. There's a lot of talk going around about the next election sheriff if I was you I'd think twice before running again, folks want justice and there sure as hell was no justice done by letting him get away with raping and killing that girl."

"I know, I know." The sheriff answered. "I feel the same way you do, I knew he was guilty but the agent Richmond sent down here to investigate took over and left me powerless to do anything about it."

"Would have been better if you blew his brains out the day your deputy killed his old man sheriff."

"Yeah but that's all hind sight." The sheriff answered. "Looks like justice was finally served anyway."

He nodded to the poolroom owner and said. "How about calling Copeland, tell him we have one face down in the creek. In the meantime me and my deputy will go down and have a look, might be some clues to his death."

As they went down the bank he whispered to his deputy.

"But sure ain't eager to find any, all I care about now is getting him out and sending him for an autopsy. Wouldn't even bother to do that but if I didn't I'd hear from some picky desk bound bastard in Richmond about not performing my duty."

Up close it was pretty obvious that the fall from the bridge onto the jagged rocks had broken his left arm, which was doubled partially under his body with a bone protruding out near his elbow.

The rocks were blood stained around his face and blood had seeped through his trousers on his right leg and flies had already gathered there.

The deputy spoke up. "Pretty gory sight sheriff but you know I can't feel a sorrowful thought no where in my body, God forgive me for what I'm about to say because I mean every word of it. He was a no good son of a bitch and I'd like to pin a badge of honor on whoever did him in."

The sheriff turned laid his hand on his shoulder and said. "I'll sanction that and I don't think you have to worry about what God thinks of your thoughts because I believe he's on our side and hopefully he will forgive whoever put him out of our way here in Lee County."

Then a voice came from the bridge. "Hey sheriff, why even bother with him? Let the next high waters carry him away to the Tennessee river and where ever it goes as a reminder to all the bad things he has caused to our people here in Lee County for so many years."

That was followed by several AMENS and laughter.

189

Copeland arrived and asked some of the onlookers to give him a hand with the stretcher.

The sheriff said. "Handle him easy I'm anxious to see his face and neck, from looking at the back of his neck I think he may have some bruises and swelling on the front of his neck."

They turned him over and placed him on the stretcher. A low moan could be heard from the ones on the bridge.

"Would you look at that." One observed. No way Copeland will ever restore that face."

"Hell who cares." Said another. "Ain't nobody crazy about going to his funeral anyway."

The deputy said. "You were right sheriff look at the bruises and swelling around his neck and his adams apple looks like it's been flattened."

"Yeah I see that." The sheriff replied. "And there's a wood splinter half hid under the skin, see it? There where the blood has dried below his adams apple."

"Alright Copeland I want you to ship him out for an autopsy just as he is, wood splinter and all."

"The last time I hauled this bird was way back yonder one night in St. Charles when some body worked him over pretty good, broke his nose, jaw, and knocked out a half dozen teeth. Had to listen to cussing and abuse all the way to the hospital, said then that I'd never haul this guy in my ambulance again but this is an exception I'll gladly ship him off for the autopsy and haul him to the cemetery and bury him deep and out of our lives here in Lee County. He was a blight on our County, may God have mercy on him."

That brought a chuckle from one of the stretcher-bearers and he said.

"Hells fire, Copeland. You missed your calling. You should have been a preacher instead of an undertaker."

"No thanks," Copeland replied. "How in the world would I ever be able to preach a funeral and say anything good about some body like him?"

"I ask all of you can anyone of you think of anything good to say about him?"

"Oh hell yes." One piped up. He was the best whistler I ever heard."

That brought a roar of laughter as they slid the stretcher in the ambulance and Copeland closed the door.

The sheriff and deputy took another look at the blood stained rocks and a scattering of damp leaves where the body had lay but could find nothing resembling a clue.

"Lets look around for some kind of a piece of wood, I believe some one pressed a baseball bat, pick handle or something to his neck until he died. Or it could have been a piece of raw unfinished lumber judging from the splinter in his neck. I'll go down the creek a ways and you look up that way behind the poolroom. And hey if you find anything don't make it a big deal because I don't intend to follow any clues that we find anyway. I'm just curious and if we should find out who did it I'll let you pin a medal on the guy."

The sheriff placed a call to Richmond and reported the death.

"Okay sheriff, I'll send an agent down there, you seem to have a lot of this kind of thing there in Lee County, tell me is it because of the miners way of life or what? Reminds me of the gold miners of old out west in Virginia City, maybe it's a carry over from back then."

"I can't answer that sir." The sheriff almost bellowed in the phone. "But I can tell you this, me and my three deputies have one hell of a time trying to keep order in this County and I would appreciate it very much if you would send some one down that we can work with this time."

"Alright sheriff, we'll get some one on the way, can't promise you'll like him but I hope you'll see fit to work with him."

He slammed the phone down and said to his deputy. "I hope they don't send that young dumb ass again."

Two days later the sheriff received the report from the autopsy.

Death by strangulation. Possibly from a piece of wood. Two-inch long splinter removed from the neck at the adam's apple. Massive bruises in front part of neck. Classic example of some one holding a piece of wood to the neck while standing behind the victim and exerting great pressure until death.

Also one small splinter removed from right eyebrow suggesting that victim may have suffered a blow to the head from the same piece of wood.

Broken left arm, broken nose and jaw, but death was by strangulation and afore mentioned were caused by the fall from the bridge to the rocks below.

The sheriff looked up just as he finished reading to see the same young agent walk through the door.

"Well look boys here comes Sherlock Holmes again, wish I could say that I'm glad to see you again but by god I have to tell the truth and say that I never wanted to see you again. You see you let Hoss walk after he raped and killed that girl and now some one took it in their own hands to see that justice was done. Now I suppose you're here to find out who done him in and bring him to justice?"

191

"You're exactly right sheriff I'm here to investigate this case and I'll leave no stone unturned until I bring some one to justice for this heinous crime."

"I hope you're ready to cooperate and turn all the evidence that you've collected over to me."

"Oh sure I'll tell you all I know and that ain't a hell'va lot. No telling how many were laying in wait to put him away, all because you let him go, so you've got a lot of suspects to check out, good luck, and here take a look at the autopsy he died from strangulation the same way he killed the Barton girl."

"Yes I'll cooperate with you as much as I can but I'm afraid if you think some one will squeal on who did it you're out of luck, hell people celebrated all over the County after his death."

As the agent scanned over the report he asked. "This girl Marty Barton does she have brothers and sisters?"

"Yes she has an older sister that Hoss raped when she was fourteen. She kept it to herself all these years because Hoss threatened to kill her father if she ever told it. I believe I told you about it the last time you were down here, but hell you let it glide right over your head along with every thing else I told you about that bastard."

The agent looked up from the report but avoided eye contact.

"Does she have brothers?"

"She has a half brother and he is one of our fine young men serving our country, now I suppose you will want to question him."

"No that wouldn't make sense if he's not here."

"Well as bad as I hate to tell you he is here on furlough for a few days and no doubt will be shipped off to fight for the likes of you and me when he gets back to camp."

"Sheriff I have to follow the law by the letter so I ask you to take me to him I'm compelled by law to ask some questions."

The sheriff rose from his desk, reached for his hat and said. "Well by god let's get on with it. Sure as hell makes no sense to talk to an empty head from Richmond. Lets go I want to see how you treat one of our fine fighting soldiers."

As they went up the steps the sheriff noticed a shirt hung up to dry on one of the railings that fronted the porch.

He knocked on the door and waited, Tex came to the door and didn't seem alarmed at all that he was facing two law officers.

'I believe he was expecting us.' The sheriff thought. 'If he's connected in any way to the death of Hoss I hope he has hidden any clues from this eager bastard from Richmond.'

The young agent wasted no time asking questions.

"Were you at Stone Creek the night Hoss was killed?"

"Yes I was at the poolroom for a couple hours." Tex answered.

"Did you see Hoss during that time?" "No I didn't."

"Did you come straight home from the poolroom?"

"Yes I did."

"And what time was it?"

Reba sat off to one side pale and nervous, Tex looked at her and asked. "What time did I get home, do you remember Reba?"

"Yes I think it was around eleven, maybe eleven fifteen, I remember I had just put down a book and went to bed."

The questioning continued on and the sheriff thought. 'The numb skull sure is digging deep but so far Tex has held him at bay.'

But his heart sank when he heard the agent ask. " Were you in civilian clothes or in uniform that night at the poolroom?"

"I was wearing civilian clothes." Tex answered. "My uniform was in the cleaners at St. Charles."

"Did you pick it up from the cleaners? And what date did you put it in the cleaners, was it before the death of Hoss?"

"Yes it was but I can't recall the date." He looked at Reba and she said. "I don't remember either but the cleaners can furnish that because they pick up once a week."

Then he asked to see the uniform. He examined it carefully, handed it back to Reba and said. "I'll check the cleaners for the date they picked it up."

"Now you said you were wearing civilian clothes how about bringing them out trousers, shirt, jacket, socks, anything that you wore that night at the poolroom."

The sheriff squirmed remembering that he had noticed that the left pocket on the shirt hanging out to dry on the porch was torn at the exact spot where Tex wore his Tex nameplate. 'Damn I hope that ain't the shirt he was wearing, although this dummie don't know about the emblem, I'm afraid he might find out.'

Reba brought out the pants he wore that night along with a light jacket. She handed them to the agent and said."I have no way of showing you the socks because I put them with his other socks after I washed them and most of them are the same color, but you're welcome to look at all of them, they're in a drawer in the bedroom."

He raised his voice as he asked. "Where's the shirt?"

"Oh it's hanging on the porch." She answered. "I wanted it to dry out a little more."

"Well bring it in I need to look at it. And how about the belt can you show me that?"

"This belt I'm wearing is the same belt I wore that night."

"You wear that belt all the time? Umm nice buckle, Texas longhorns overlaid with your nick name Tex, You must be a cowboy fan."

"I guess you could say that." Tex answered.

"Well take it off I want to look it over."

Satisfied with the belt he handed it back to Tex and then held the shirt up and looked it over even checked all the buttons. He handed it to the sheriff and asked. "I see one of the pockets is torn, how did that happen?"

Tex pointed to a door that would swing down from the attic and said.

"Went up in the attic to get something and got it hung on a nail." He reached up and pulled the door down which revealed built in steps that led to the attic.

"See that nail sticking out there above the top step? That's what done it, was gonna finish driving that nail in but forgot to."

The agent looked up at an overhead light bulb and asked Tex to turn it on.

He sat down in a chair under the light.

"Now sheriff you're a tall man I want you to hold that shirt up starting with the back so I can see if there's stains in it. The light might show me something that otherwise might not show up in ordinary light."

"Well if you insist." Growled the sheriff. "But this shirt looks as clean as a pin to me."

"Now hold the front up one side at a time."

As the sheriff held up the button side of the shirt he felt a slight prick on his arm from a sleeve of the shirt, he looked and seen a small piece of wood splinter protruding from the shirt sleeve. He closed his hand over it and slowly worked it into the palm of his hand.

The agent seemed satisfied with his examination and rose to his feet.

"Mind if we look around out side and in your car? "He asked.

"Not at all help yourself." Tex answered.

He searched the car but found nothing. Finally he said.

"Sheriff, look around real good here in the front and out there in that garden spot for a piece of wood of some kind that he may have gotten rid of and I'll look in back of the house. I'll call and have them send the splinter from his neck tomorrow and who knows we might find the piece of wood it came from."

The sheriff waited until the agent disappeared behind the house and slipped the splinter from the palm of his hand to his shirt pocket.

The agent found nothing except a piece of rotten wood minus splinters, and the sheriff found nothing and even if he had he would have kicked leaves over it.

At noon the next day they stood on the little bridge as curious onlookers gathered outside the poolroom and the lonesome sounds of the song "Don't Let your Sweet Love Die" poured out of the huge outside speakers at the dance hall.

The sheriff pointed out the spot where the body lay among the small rocks and pebbles now covered with more leaves. It hadn't rained since and the shallow water trickled slowly around the rocks.

The leaves had dried and something caught the sheriff's eye as the breeze lifted one of the larger leaves, something shiny that glistened in the sun light each time the leaf lifted ever so slightly from the gentle breeze.

"Damn! I hope he don't see that.' He thought.

"May as well go down and get a closer look sheriff."

He picked up a stick and stirred the leaves around but the sheriff had already planted his right foot and size twelve-boot on the leaf with the shiny object that hid underneath, being careful not to put too much weight on it.

He looked up and down the creek then asked. "Sheriff did you look around here for a piece of wood?"

"Yes me and my deputy went over this creek with a fine toothed comb, down that way and up there behind the poolroom and found nary a thing."

Finally, he said. "I want to talk with the poolroom owner and some of that gang yonder, never know when you'll run on to some one that can shed some light on what you're looking for."

'Oh yeah.' The sheriff thought. 'No one there will shed any light, nor anyone else in Lee County that knew about Hoss and his doings, so I'm afraid you'll stay in the dark.'

He waited till the agent turned away to climb the bank then quickly bent over and plucked the piece of shiny metal from under the leaf and slipped it in his coat pocket.

The young agent hung around for another two days firing questions to at least a dozen other people before he finally realized it would be next to impossible to get any information pertaining to Hoss's death.

He filled out his report as the sheriff sat across from him in silence. Finally he shuffled the papers and asked. "Sheriff would you like to have a copy?"

"No not in particular." The sheriff growled.

"I thought you might because I've wrote you in as a good man and a well qualified sheriff. My time spent with you this time has taught me a lot about you and the people you represent, you folks have instincts that help you sort out good from bad. Something I never learned in school, but I hope to take it away with me today because when you sort it all out it's common sense pure and simple and that's something I didn't have until I spent time with you over the past few days."

He rose to his feet, walked over and extended his hand. The sheriff, taken aback, rose from his desk and mumbled awkwardly.

"Well son I thank you for the kind words, and yes it is common sense and you'll find it works well in law enforcement."

"Yes I know it will sheriff, now I better hit the road it's a long way to Richmond, I do grow weary of all the travel and being away from my wife and kids. At times I think about dropping out of law enforcement but I guess somebody's got to do it."

The sheriff followed him out to his car. "Sheriff, can't say that I blame Tex for putting Hoss away because I'm sure I would have did the same if he had raped and killed my sister or half sister."

"Now hold on young man how come you're so sure Tex did it?"

"Instinct sheriff, Instinct and common sense learned from you and the folks here in Lee County. Like I said before, you don't learn that in school."

They stood there smiling in admiration of one another just as one of the sheriff's deputies parked along side.

The deputy looked in disbelief as they embraced in a big hug just before the agent got in his car.

"Damn what in hells happened to the sheriff? Never thought I'd see the day he'd put his arms around that know it all college stiff."

The sheriff and deputy watched as the young man drove away. Just a hundred feet away before making a right turn on route 58 headed toward Richmond he stopped and stuck his head out the window.

"Hey Sheriff! Forgot to tell you, I saw you take that wood splinter out of Tex's shirt."

He laughed and waved goodbye again as the sheriff stood there completely baffled.

Then the deputy asked. "Tell me what went on between you two if I hadn't seen it with my own eyes nobody could ever make me believe that you would hug up on that bird. And what's this about the wood splinter?"

The sheriff shrugged and answered. "I'll tell you all about it later, but right now I just want to find a place to sit down and mull over in my mind the thoughts I had about that young man and ask our maker to forgive me because I sure as hell turned out to be wrong about him, dead wrong."

About a dozen people showed up for Hoss's graveside funeral. It was a drizzly cloudy day and the wind blew sharp on Red Hill as the preacher from the little Keokee church hurriedly read some verses of scripture. He said a few words, which were meaningless and seemed to be searching for something good to say about Hoss. He finally thought of something and raised his voice a few syllables so that all could hear.

"I want you all to know that I am at a complete loss and can't find words to praise this soul that we are about to lay to rest here today. I have talked to several people and not a single one knew of any good deeds or talents he left behind so I'll do a little speculation and say that there must have been something good in his past but today we don't know of any. May god rest his soul."

Then came a voice out of the small gathering. "Preacher he shore could whistle."

Copeland smiled sheepishly and thought. 'At least some one thought of something but he's the same guy that said it the day we brought him out of the creek so I guess that's about all he was good for.'

The preacher closed with prayer and two men started shoveling dirt over the wooden vault. Copeland whispered to one of them. "Make sure you get all the dirt on and tamp it down we don't want that bird back with us ever again."

They followed the black hearse back to Stone Creek and watched it disappear toward St. Charles. They all smiled and one of the fellows said. "Can't say I've ever enjoyed being at a funeral but by god this has been an exception because I sure enjoyed this one."

"Yeah me to." Remarked another. "Lets go in and drink a few beers and see if we can remember anything else good about him. We all know he could whistle a fine tune, but hell a man should leave more than that behind."

Two days later Tex left for Fort Benning, Georgia. And like all goodbyes during the war when it is so uncertain whether you will ever see each other again, he and Reba Clung to each other as she cried. "I hope you can come home when the baby's born." She sobbed.

"Yeah me to." He said. "And remember if it's a boy name him Wayne, after Wayne Burke, you know him as Poor Boy, he means a lot to me, glad I got to see him while I was here. He's doing well there in Kentucky, got a good job as an electrician and has met a good looking woman that he likes a lot she has three children by a former marriage. But I think he'll go along with that because he has no children of his own. He's about five years older than her but that shouldn't matter he should be able to persuade her to let him father at least one child every decent man deserves to have a child he can call his own.

"I told him to stop in and see you if he's ever over this way. I promised to write him, yeah he means a lot to me."

He stepped on the bus and she held on until the bus driver said. "Sorry but we have to go I'm behind on schedule already."

As she watched the bus pull away she could see his face pressed against the window and had the strangest feeling that she would never see him again.

'Yes I'll name him Wayne but he'll end up with the name Tex.' She whispered. She got in the car and drove toward home knowing that her life would seem so empty without him but thankful that his grandmother would be there because they had grown close since her marriage to Tex.

One month later sugar gave birth to a healthy baby girl and named her Marty.

She wrote a glowing letter to Bud describing her, eight pounds, twenty inches long, lots of brown hair. "And she has your eyes and forehead Sugar, I declare she looks just like you, I can't wait till you get home."

Bud was some where in the north Atlantic and had already seen battle and it's aftermath aboard the huge battle ship. One month later the letter caught up with him and as he read it joy flowed through his body as he read the words. "I declare she looks just like you."

But ten minutes later while manning the anti Aircraft gun he was hit twice by machine gun fire from a low flying German fighter plane. His wounds were not life threatening but it was obvious that his shattered left arm would have to be amputated.

About a year later after being transferred from hospital to hospital and several surgeries he finally came home to Sugar and the baby, and the little house on the Keokee road became a happy home again surrounded by the sweet aroma of red roses and much love.

I turned eighteen on February 7 -1944 and went to the draft board to register. My friend Clarence Napier's birthday fell on February 13 six days later so he came along with me intending to register. "So we can leave here together." He said.

But the lady at the draft board told him he would have to come back on the 13th. "Can't let you register before you're eighteen young man, so come back six days from now."

Turns out we were inducted on the same date anyway. And on a sun lit morning May 9-1944 we along with several other young men waited for a bus to take us to Bristol, Virginia. There we took a train to Fort George G. Meade Maryland and after a few days there being issued clothing, shots, short arm inspections, orientations, and forever being hollered at we boarded a train to Camp Blanding Florida.

We went through four months of Infantry basic training in the hot Florida sunshine. The days were long and hard and exhaustion took you to bed early and didn't allow you much time to think or worry about home. But my thoughts were always back home in Virginia just before falling to sleep and dreams followed to fill my night. I would dream of Saturday nights with my girlfriend at St. Charles to see a movie at the little theater. My uncle would loan me his old Chevrolet and we would take a ride to the next town. A kiss in the dark, which was always better for me, that way she couldn't see my face turn red.

I cared for her more than she knew and could see us together in the future but never told her that simply because I never could get up the nerve. And maybe that was meant to be considering what happened in my world some months later, something that I prefer not to reveal at this time but perhaps some time later I will.

Her beauty, sweet smile, and personality were always in my dreams and I can still see her waving as the bus pulled away that day in May.

A letter from her at mail call made my day and filled my night with more dreams. She sent me a picture that I proudly showed to my buddies.

"Where's she from?" One asked.

"Virginia." I answered.

"Oh a Virginia girl eh, boy she's pretty."

After that almost every day he would ask. "Hey Kirk did you get a letter from your Virginia girl today?"

I finished Basic training in September and went home on a nine-day furlough.

I was assigned to the 66TH. Infantry Division in Camp Rucker, Alabama. From there we were sent to Camp Shanks New York, crossed the Atlantic to England.

Stayed in England for twenty three days and boarded a troop ship to cross the English Channel. At six p.m. Christmas Eve 1944 our ship was torpedoed by a German UBOAT and eight hundred soldiers from the 66th. Lost their lives.

We lost all of our equipment but were quickly re-supplied with rifles, machine guns, grenades, etc. and were on line in northern France by January first.

Replacements trickled in along with other necessary equipment and we were successful in holding forty thousand German troops against the sea at Lorient and St. Nazire. A huge success considering we were a crippled division at first and supported only by a single division of French infantry on our right.

I could go on and on about my experiences in the hedge row country of northern France, suffering through the snow and cold of winter with only a field jacket to ward off the cold winds. Some of us that lost heavy clothing when the ship went down were never re-supplied with heavy coats etc. until after the war in warm weather and were forced by regulations to lug them every where we went afterward. It's no wonder a soldier was forever bitching.

As I said I won't go into details but would like to mention some of the more memorable events.

My company was on line one ninety-day stretch sleeping in dug out rat-infested holes in the hedgerows under fire from the deadly German 88 artillery guns. We never had a hot meal we ate mostly C rations except for cabbage that was covered with snow on an abandoned French farm behind us. To our surprise the cabbage heads weren't frozen I guess the snow protected them. We would make some kind of fire in the daytime and cook them in some kind of discarded pot that had been salvaged from the war zone. Had to be careful about too much smoke that could be detected by the Germans.

More than once they zeroed in on a whiff of smoke and fired the deadly 88's at will.

I remember going without cigarettes for over a month because of a shortage so they told us, but our first Sergeant had saved chewing tobacco that had been sent up on line and had a pretty good supply because hardly anyone chewed.

I remember the day he passed it out and some of the guys got dog sick from their first chew. I had chewed before and it didn't bother me.

Later we would find out that the Quartermaster unit that supplied us on line had been caught at putting cigarettes on the black market and made a lot of money selling them to the French population. Cigarettes and soap were highly prized in Europe during the war years.

I can still hear the cursing directed toward the quarter master unit and a few fights erupted because of it after we went back to the rest area and would come in contact with them occasionally.

I was in a machine gun position with two other guys. We also had a Bazooka. I remember the day Company B relieved us. Calvin Parsons, another one of my Lee County friends whom I hadn't seen since we were being re-supplied on a cold windy December day back in Cherbourg France.

I looked up the hill and could see three guys coming toward us in the typical crouched war zone position.

"Well here they come." One of my buddies remarked. "I sure as hell am happy to see them, maybe now we can get a bath and find a decent place to sleep, wonder what it would be like to sleep in a bed again or even a damn army cot?"

"I wouldn't count on getting a bed to sleep in or even a cot if I were you." Our other buddy answered. "Betcha ten dollars they'll have us digging holes to sleep in back in that so called rest area that we're supposed to go to."

As they came closer I noticed something about the little guy in the group that looked familiar. 'No it couldn't be.' I thought. But soon they were close enough that I could make out the face of Calvin Parsons. The odds of that happening were great.

I was with my Virginia girl during that September furlough but that would be the last time I ever spoke to her again. After returning home in 1946 I seen her several times, at times close enough to say hello or make eye contact but did neither.

I remember one time about twelve of us were going on a battle patrol and were in single file for a few hundred feet picking our way through booby traps and flares that we had placed in front of our lines. After we made our way through we would then spread out.

The guy in front watched for the trip wires and would say to the guy in back of him.

"Watch this wire, pass it back." And that one would repeat it to the guy in back of him. "Watch the wire, pass it back." That would be repeated till it reached the guy bringing up the rear.

This particular time some one failed to pass it back to the one behind him and the one behind tripped a flare that unfortunately lifted off right under his left arm.

He was rushed to the field hospital in the rear and the last we heard of him he lost his arm and was returned to his home in Texas.

Some said the guy that failed to pass the word was one of the sergeants in the group.

Then the time we were relieved they trucked us back several miles and put us up in three man tents, and yes they did have cots.

I sat down on my cot and cleared my rifle as was ordered. "When we reach the rest area, clear your rifles." A captain ordered. "No use having them loaded this far back."

I lay down on the cot on my right side resting my head on my hand with my right elbow touching the cot.

A rifle shot rang out from one of the tents across the muddy street from our tent. The bullet tore through our tent four inches above my head and only missed the guy that lay on the cot in back of the tent by about eight inches.

We ran outside yelling, "What the hells going on." And there in the tent across from us a pair of combat boots was visible and one of them jerked a couple of times and then was still.

A sergeant had sat down on his bunk and proceeded to clear his rifle. He removed the clip but failed to eject the round from the chamber and as he pulled the trigger he failed to point the rifle upward as a safety precaution.

One of his squad members was standing near the flap opening inside the tent and took the bullet through his body.

His name was Nick Palumbo, Pennsylvania, was his home state.

His parents were notified that he was killed in action.

At that time I was a PFC. And I began to wonder about sergeants and became vocal about it.

"Why are sergeants so dumb?" I would ask about anybody excluding the sergeants of course.

One day one of my buddies asked me. "Damn you must hate sergeants."

"Well shit." I said. "They are dumb remember the one that helped us lay booby traps in front of our position there on line and I kept telling him to watch out for that wire? And in spite of that he tripped a grenade that we had just wired to a tree and if we hadn't hit the ground we would have been killed or injured."

"Yeah I remember that and you cussed him out, never figured how you got away with that."

"And how about the time we were laying low at the outpost at the abandoned French farm house trying to pinpoint a German artillery position in the woods ahead. We heard a noise and found out the damn sergeant in charge was tossing grenades in a well behind the house."

Later on after the war while stationed in Austria guarding a prison camp a sergeant came in the middle of the night to wake some of us to go on guard duty. He walked by the cots shaking each soldier. "Come on get up we gotta relieve them guys its cold out there."

When he got to me he shook me and repeated the same thing, but just as he passed the end of my bunk his 45 went off from the holster on his side and missed my foot by inches.

Yes I cussed him out and asked why he carried the pistol around cocked. Of course I know he didn't do it intentionally because it shook him up and I took advantage of that and asked him. "How come sergeants are so dumb? Damn I got through the war without a scratch but looks like some dumb sergeant will kill me before I get out of this damned army."

A short time later I was promoted to sergeant and took some ribbing about dumb sergeants from my buddies.

"You have always hated dumb sergeants and now you are one." They would say.

It was a rule that when we returned to our quarters after being on duty at the prison camps that we clear our weapons of ammunition

The first time I pulled sergeant of the guard I took two young replacements fresh from the states to a tower that was armed with a 30 caliber air cooled machine gun pointed toward the rear of a wooden building at the rear of the prisoners quarters that housed hot water tanks, laundry room, etc.

I explained that the machine gun was at half load and that if anything happened all they had to do was pull the bolt handle back one more time and pull the trigger.

"You guys did fire a machine gun in training?" I asked and they nodded yes.

"Okay just remember don't pull the lever to fully load it unless you need to."

I went back to the command shack and about an hour later the silence was broken by machine gun fire.

It caused bedlam all around the huge camp that covered several acres.

The first thing that came to mind was we had a prison break taking place some where along the high double wire fences. But when all was sorted out it turned out that the two young replacements had fooled around with the machine gun and it went off and fired several holes through the building and punctured one of the hot water tanks. Of course the captain in charge chewed them out but saved his worst for me.

By the time he got through with me I was furious and chewed them out unmercifully.

"How dumb can you get?" I asked. "Hell I explained everything to you but you go ahead and act like babies with a toy, you belong back home with your momma. I'm glad you weren't old enough when the war was going on, sure as hell wouldn't want you in a fox hole with me."

I went off duty feeling pretty low but at the same time satisfied that I had made my point with the two soldiers.

At that time we were housed in a huge sprawling two-story apartment building but that didn't last long because soon we were back in tents.

I walked to the room that I shared with one other soldier and sat down on my bed. I pointed the 45 toward the ceiling and thought I had cleared the chamber but when I pulled the trigger it fired right through the ceiling barely missing a soldier in the room above.

Well needless to say I had to endure a lot of ribbing plus a good cussing out from the soldier that I almost killed.

For a long time after that some one was always saying. "How come sergeants are so dumb?" Directed at me of course.

Poor Boy met a tall dark beauty in the strangest way in Harlan County Kentucky. She rolled to a stop along side his car just as he opened the door to get in.

"Excuse me." She said. "Aren't you the electrician at the mine?"

"Yes I am." He answered. Noting that she was accompanied by three children, two girls and a boy, ranging in age from five to ten he surmised.

"I was wondering if you could wire my house?" She said sweetly.

"Well I guess I could but I put in a lot of time at the mine, never gave a thought to hire out to wire somebody's house. Do you live close by?" He asked.

"Yes about a mile down the road, would you follow me down there and see what you think?"

"Okay I'll have a look." He answered. "But can't promise you I'll have the time to do it."

As he followed the well-worn pick up she was driving he wondered about her husband and if she even had one. 'Can't imagine a young lady that attractive not belonging to some one.' He thought. 'But she must be unattached or else her husband would be the one taking care of business like having the house wired.'

She turned off on a tree lined dirt driveway that led to a clearing of perhaps two acres. And there on a slight rise sat what looked like a half finished house.

'Hell.' He thought. 'That damned house needs to be finished before it can be wired.'

He watched her get out followed by the children who seemed to be curious and uneasy by his presence.

She smiled again as she asked. "There it is what do you think?"

"Well hell it ain't much of a house, could be wired but most of the damn wiring would be exposed, looks like you need to finish building the house first."

Then he realized he was using language that he shouldn't in front of her and the children and thought about apologizing but noted that she seemed not to mind.

"I do need to get it wired." She said. "Then maybe I can find a way to finish the house."

"Just you and the kids live here?" He asked.

Knowing that he was about to give in to this beauty caused his thoughts to remind him of his past experiences that began in Kentucky some twenty years earlier, the letter and the pain it caused him, the roads that he walked in a drunken stupor, the old mining shack with a dirt floor, and finally with the help of his former boss rising above it all to live again.

'Could it be that this time in Kentucky will be a repeat and put me back on a dirt floor again?' 'Is it worth taking a chance?' 'About all I've had in the past twenty years that I could love and call my own was old Rub and Peanut.' 'And by god the way I feel right now I want something more than a dog in my life.' 'Shit she's younger than me and I'd be saddled with three kids that belong to some one else which I know the kids would rather have around than me.'

She jarred him out of his thoughts with. "Well would you be willing to tackle it? I have no money to pay you, just barely get by keeping food on the table for the kids and it worries me that they don't have enough to eat at times."

"Well guess I could give it a try, but it'll have to be in my spare time and it may take a while."

"Oh that's alright I understand, would you come in and have a cup of coffee with me, and who knows we might get to know each other better."

'Damn.' He thought. 'She sure as hell is straight forward, don't see many like that.' 'Never thought I'd fall for that type but shit she's wrapping me right around her finger.'

Within six months the house was wired and began to look like a finished house.

Dog tired from his days work at the mine he would hurry to get there and finish something that he had started the day before. And some times to his surprise she finished it herself and would have plans for the next project.

She could place a board and drive a nail as good as most men and better than some.

He thought back on the first time he met her and she asked if he would wire her house. Remembered the questions she had asked him over that first cup of coffee.

"Are you married? Have you ever been married? How old are you? You mean to tell me you've lived alone all your life, that's no way to live."

He looked forward to talking to her every evening as they worked to well past dark some times, then having coffee before he finally left for home and get in bed exhausted but would awake in the mornings with her on his mind and looking forward to another evening in her company.

And he especially remembered one night when he got up to go.

"Why don't you stay here tonight?" She said. "It's getting late and you can sleep on the couch there."

She made it easy for him to say "Okay." Because she made it sound more like an order than a request.

Since then he had followed her instructions and moved all his belongings from his house to hers, vacated the couch for closer contact and settled in, even Peanut seemed to like his new surroundings, especially her large French poodle that she called Rene.

One day she said.

" I like Peanut even though he's the most ugly hound that I have ever seen, but I don't want him near my Rene when she comes in heat, can you imagine the looks of puppies that would come from that?"

"Oh hell I don't know." He answered. "You might be surprised at the results."

Rene paid no attention, but Peanut as always seemed to sense that he was being singled out for something. He came and curled up at Poor Boy's feet.

"See there you hurt his feelings, hell he can't help it if he's ugly."

She fell to her knees and took peanut in her arms. "Did I hurt your feelings Peanut?" She held him for a long time cooing in his ear, and soon Peanut melted like falling snow to her charms.

As he watched he thought. 'Shit wont be long till Peanut thinks more of her than he does me.'

'This has to be the most unusual woman I have ever met and for the life of me I can't understand how the husband of her children ever let her go.'

'She says she despises him and tells me he's stupid but has never pinpointed what caused their divorce.'

'Oh shit why worry about that, whatever caused it, it's his loss and my gain.'

'I have grown closer to the children and they seem to respect me but I get the feeling that they are confused and hurt about the breakup and no doubt miss their father.'

Eight months later the house had became two rooms larger with a large screened in porch in back. She would work at it during the day and he would toil into the night after working all day at the mine.

She hired a man with a bull dozier to clear three more acres out of the dense woods. She owned a total of twelve acres and had often talked about buying another fifteen acres that joined her property.

She haggled with a well digger till she got him down to a price that suited her before finally giving him the job to drill a deep well.

Poor Boy earned an above average salary as an electrician and had saved a good sum of money before he met her, but that was all long gone and his earnings were being spent on the house and various other improvements that she would think of from week to week.

She was always saying. "I'll have this done, I want to get this done." Never we will, or what do you think?

Then one day he took a path through the woods to look at the adjoining land that she was interested in.

"Take Peanut and have a look I think you'll like it, most of the fifteen acres is cleared just right for horses which I plan on having some day."

He looked at the very desirable piece of land and decided it was well worth the asking price. On his way back he sat down on a log in the dense woods.

"Hold up Peanut, I need to sit here and clear my head, this fast pace with Pocahontas has got me all fuzzed up inside."

"Oh hell I guess you don't know what I mean by that. Pocahontas was a beautiful Indian princess. And she's tall, dark, and beautiful just like Pocahontas."

"Shit Peanut, all my savings went in that house and my paycheck goes through her hands to pay all the bills that she ran up since I moved in, and now she wants to go deeper in debt for another fifteen acres just so she can have horses. Didn't ask me if I wanted horses, you ever notice peanut? She never asks me about anything, but is constantly telling me what she intends to do."

"Hell she even decided that we would get married. Yeah right out of the blue one night she said. Next Saturday we'll go to Harlan and get married I've got your best shirt and jacket cleaned and ironed. Acted like I had nothing to say about it, I had thought about it myself and planned on asking her, but shit she didn't even let me propose."

"I feel like I'm digging us a hole that we won't be able to get out of Peanut. Hell she still owes for the land the house sits on, and shit it's all in her name. And now she's expecting me to buy her another fifteen acres. What if one day when she thinks I no longer fit in her plans and she shows us the door Peanut? Hell just like that we'd wind up on a dirt floor again because I know I would go back on the booze from a jolt like that."

"Yeah I've got to figure out something Peanut or else we'll be back in a damned shack some where again. Well let's go Peanut I'm craving her company, can't figure what it is about that woman that I'll let her make all the decisions and treat me as one of her children. I should set my foot down but her charm keeps me at bay."

"Well what do you think?" I could run as many as six horses on that fifteen acres after it's fenced in."

"Yeah the land lays well should be no trouble to take a tractor over every foot of it." He answered.

"Okay I'll get the ball rolling Monday morning. I think I can swing the deal with a small down payment, I have enough in my checking account to take care of that."

He looked at peanut and thought.

'Hear that Peanut?' I'll do this and I'll do that with nary a mention of me.' 'My checking account she says, shit it's my money but it's in her name.' 'Gonna have to figure out some way to get my name on something before I dig any deeper.'

Later that night he said. "I've been thinking about our situation, we need to go down to the bank and the mortgage company and have my name put on all the papers, and that way you'll have no problem buying the land."

"Oh shit." She said. "What problem you talking about? I can handle the guy at the bank, I've done business with him before, and I know some one at the mortgage company, it'll be no problem what so ever."

'You sure as hell know a lot of folks.' He thought.

He looked at Peanut and could see the old shack, smell the dampness and the cold winter winds blowing through the cracks. 'Now's the time to stand up and be counted, be damned if I'll let her take all I have and later throw me out.'

"Okay princess, I've went along with you on everything else since we've been together, but by god this is where I draw the line, if you want that piece of property my name will have to be on this property here and on the checking account, bout time you recognize my presence here and how it benefits you."

One of the kids peeked around the corner from a bedroom alarmed at him raising his voice for the first time since he had taken up residence.

She looked at him long and hard. "So you don't trust me?"

"No it's not that, I just happen to think we're in this together and the language should include 'We' once in a while."

She got up and headed for the bedroom, turned and yelled a few choice words before slamming the door.

He looked at peanut and said. "Guess I'm back on the couch again."

She pouted for several days and kept him locked out of the bedroom.

One night he said. "Peanut I think she believes I'll go begging for her to unlock that damn door, but by god as bad as I want to hold her in my arms I be damned if I'll give in, I'll wear this damned couch out first. If she thinks I'll give in and help her buy that land without my name on anything she's got a long wait."

Then one day when he got home from work she greeted him with a smile.

"Alright." She said. "If you can get off work one day this week we'll go down and have your name put on the papers. Then we'll see about buying the land if you still want to."

'Damn.' He thought. 'She used we twice and is leaving it up to me to decide if we should buy the land.' 'I feel like I've won a major victory and best of all the bedroom door won't be locked tonight, I hope supper's ready because I want to get to bed early.' 'Damn! she sure looks good.'

He reached out and she came into his arms, they clung to each other for a long time. Then he thought. 'Who waited who out.' Nobody won at this game, shit supper can wait.'

They headed for the bedroom and closed the door behind them.

Tex was shipped overseas and assigned to an Infantry division that had already suffered heavy losses.

His no nonsense simple ways of looking at things even at their worst and his demeanor soon captured attention and respect from all that made contact with him. In no time he was promoted to Sergeant followed closely by Staff Sergeant after he single handily saved his squad from certain death or capture as they were pinned down by two German machine guns that had them in a crossfire. He managed to crawl close enough to one of them to lob a grenade and that allowed his squad to quickly eliminate the other one.

Luckily the only wounds he suffered after the hail of gunfire he crawled through was a lost earlobe and a superficial wound to one thigh where he was grazed by a 30-caliber machine gun bullet.

The medic sprinkled Sulfa powder and covered the wounds with gauze as Tex talked to his squad members telling them his plans on how to advance forward to the hillside in the distance.

He fought through the cold of Belgium and at one point in time the losses suffered brought his company down to less than half strength, and after one particular battle his squad suffered six killed and two wounded.

Replacements trickled in from the states. Some were assigned to his squad that only fought and lived one or two days not long enough for him to get to know them by name.

In early December 1944 his division and the whole front was slowed by fierce winds and snow and visibility was at a minimum.

It was during this time a truck had finally managed to get through with the mail. He clutched her letter and held it close to his face in order to see through the falling snow as some of his squad members tried to take advantage of the lull in fighting to catch some sleep in the near freezing weather.

He noticed the mailing date was in November.

"Dear Tex." It began.

I have great news the baby came yesterday. He's big and healthy, weighs ten pounds, and you should see the head of hair and his big brown eyes, he's so cute, I named him Wayne like you wanted but I call him Tex. He looks just like you, I would give anything if you could be here with us, I can't begin to explain my feelings when I hold him.

Your grand mother is so thrilled about it and says to tell you to hurry home. She is failing pretty fast and it worries me that she might not be with us much longer. I worry about you so much but I know that some day and I hope soon you will walk in the door and we can get on with living our lives together and raising our family. I have been thinking about having another one, a girl. What do you think? Well I'll cut this short and write more later, little Tex has just aroused from his sleep and started crying, that means he's hungry I breast feed him, Doc says that's the best way as long as I produce enough milk.

And by the way Doc asked about you and said to tell you hello and hurry home.

He still hits the bottle pretty heavy and it has begun to show in his face he looks much older than he did just a short year ago. I feel sorry for him and wish that he would quit that stuff but I guess it has too much of a hold on him.

And Wayne Burke, 'Poor Boy' stopped by two weeks before the baby was born asking about you, said he hadn't heard from you in a while, he seemed worried and said you was almost like a son to him. I told him that you wanted our baby if it was a boy named after him and he seemed so pleased.

Well honey I'll stop and feed our baby, I pray for your safety each day and ask God to bring you and all our fighting men home soon.

You know something that I think about a lot is our trips to Bristol, when you get home maybe we can do that again for old times sake and look in the store windows at all the pretty dresses and you can buy me one, only this time I will gladly accept it.

I better stop here, Tex is getting louder he must be real hungry. Your grandmother sends her love.

My hugs and kisses go out to you wherever you are and you are in my heart and dreams. I love and miss you so much. Reba

He folded the letter and placed it back in the envelope noting again the date. Which would make the baby about a month old.

The sights and sounds of war, death and dieing, had hardened his thoughts and numbed his conscious to a degree, but thoughts of Reba, the baby, and his grandmother softened his heart right to the links to his soul and he cried, but only for a minute because as he looked around at his buddies, some reading a late letter from home while others tried to sleep, he knew that soon they would be on the move again toward the Ardennes and would come face to face with some of Germany's most battle hardened troops.

He slipped the letter into his field jacket pocket next to the old faded letter that Poor Boy had gave him written by his mother.

The weather cleared the next day and the sun came out at intervals, prompting the commander's all up and down the line to get their troops organized as much as possible for the move that was sure to come.

Just before dark that day Tex seen the platoon guide coming, followed by another soldier which he knew was a replacement because the clean clothing he was wearing hadn't yet been exposed to the mud, snow, and stench of combat.

"Got a replacement for you Tex, he's from Virginia, your state so you should hit it off good. I know you need three more but only fifteen showed up today and we spread them around, maybe we'll get some more in a few days."

The guy stood before him weighted down by all his equipment and the heavy pack strapped to his back.

"Make yourself to home." Tex said. "Pick out a hole and shovel the snow out, no take that one over there and you want have to shovel. You can buddy up with Crawford and help him out with his BAR, you did fire the browning automatic rifle in training didn't you?" He nodded yes.

"Well good." Tex went on. "Crawford needs you he lost his buddy last week."

"We'll be on the move again in a couple of days if the bad weather clears out and it looks like it will. And oh yeah, I forgot to ask your name, the guy that brought you didn't bother to introduce us, you see we're not very formal up here and clean either because we just don't have the facilities. See that hole out yonder? If you need to take a crap we'd appreciate it if you use that so the stink don't settle in our beards, but if you want to piss don't bother to go that far, you can tell that by all the piss holes in the snow here."

The replacement managed a grin and spoke for the first time. "My names Larry Witt."

"Okay Larry Witt, but you can forget the Larry part because from now on you're Witt. You can call me Tex. And by the way what part of Virginia are you from?"

"A little community just south of Richmond, you wouldn't recognize the name it's so small." He answered. "But I think I know where you live in Virginia."

"How would you know that?" Tex asked as he studied his face for the first time.

He removed his helmet. And said. "Because I worked a couple of cases with your sheriff there in Lee County."

Tex recognized him immediately without the helmet and said.

"Holy cow this is a small world, never thought I'd have a crime investigator in my squad, especially one from Virginia that tried to nail me."

They shook hands and went on with small talk.

'How'd you wind up here?' Tex asked.

"I had a deferment when I attended school and when I finished I was hired by the state of Virginia and was protected from the draft for a while and having a wife and two children helped keep me out, but that all changed a few months ago, I was notified to report for examination, passed it, took seventeen weeks of Basic training in Texas and here I am."

"Well I have to say I'm glad to have you because we're short of men, but at the same time I feel for you having to be away from your wife and family. I just got a letter that my wife gave birth to a baby boy and I miss not being there to see him something awful, and can imagine how much you must miss yours after holding and watching them grow. Well make yourself at home as best you can, may as well make up your mind that it won't get any better than this until this thing is over, in fact brace yourself and get ready for all hell to break loose as soon as we get to the Ardennes. I pray that we both make it and can return to Virginia together and maybe you and your family could come down to Lee County and visit us, this time under different circumstances. I sure didn't enjoy you questioning me about a murder."

He stuck out his hand and as they squeezed hands he said.

"I promise I'll do that and never worry about me questioning you about something like that again. Guess you don't know it but I decided just after I questioned you that I didn't care to find out who put Hoss away, he had it coming and Lee County and the state of Virginia is better off without him."

"Remember your shirt I had the sheriff hold to the light so I could inspect it? Well I spotted a wood splinter on one sleeve that I surmised came from the piece of wood that was pressed to Hoss's neck. The sheriff tried to hide it from my view and I let it slide."

"And another thing the day I inspected the creek where the body was found I saw a shiny piece of metal with something engraved on it and partially hidden under the leaves. But before I could get a better look the sheriff planted his number twelve- boot on it. As I climbed the bank to leave I glanced back and saw him pick it up and drop it in his pocket."

"Then that night at your house I noticed the torn pocket in the shirt. I couldn't make head or tails from that until I spotted a picture of you and your wife hanging on the wall. And pinned to the shirt pocket was a shiny piece of metal with your name Tex."

"Like I said I had already made up my mind to close the case and never bothered to look into it any further."

'My thinking is that in the struggle Hoss tore the Tex emblem from your shirt and held on to it as he fell from the bridge, is that correct?"

"Yes it is. Tex answered. "And to set the record straight I didn't get him from behind. I watched as he started across the bridge toward his car. I challenged him and rushed forward pushing him against the bridge railing, then I pressed the two foot piece of wood to his adams apple until he stopped breathing."

"Then I hoisted him over the railing, I went home relieved that he was gone, but at the same time sorry that I couldn't have him around longer to torment him for what he did to my sisters."

Witt laid his hand on Tex shoulder and said.

"Like I said before he had it coming. Too bad we don't have the cowardly bastard here I'd like to watch him tremble with fear and in the end die a slow death in a frozen foxhole some where in the Ardennes."

He turned to leave but hesitated. "Hey I bet the sheriff has that Tex emblem all shined up and ready to pin on you if we ever get back there."

Tex watched as he walked away and heard him say to Crawford. "Hi, my names Witt, you must be Crawford, Tex says you need help with your BAR so I'm your man, green when it comes to combat and scared as hell already, but I guess I'll get the hang of it."

"And damned soon I'm afraid." Crawford answered.

Tex grinned and whispered. "He'll make a good soldier, I just hope he'll get through this mess and get back to his wife and kids again."

The weather cleared for two days and they pushed on toward the Ardennes.

By the third day the weather turned bad again with blustery cold winds and heavy snow that drifted up in furrows across the forest. Visibility was at a minimum and they were ordered to dig in near the town of Elsenborn until the weather cleared again.

Seventy five thousand troops that formed a line across Belgium would soon face two hundred and seventy five thousand German troops.

Hitler ordered his commanders to stop the allies in the Ardennes at all costs. The bad weather served to their advantage as it shielded their movement of troops and thousands of tanks in preparation for the push toward the allies that were in a holding position across the wide expanse of the forest waiting for the weather to clear.

Near mid December the German hordes pushed off, an awesome sight to see, tanks pushing ahead through the snow followed by trucks loaded with supplies and soldiers. And some distance behind heavy artillery pieces including the deadly 88's being towed by half-tracks followed the path that the tanks had carved through the snow.

Meanwhile the seventy five thousand allied troops stayed their holding position unaware of the great hordes pressing onward through the Ardennes toward them.

They had faced little resistance on their three day push to the Ardennes encountering scattered pockets of German soldiers which was designed to slow them and buy time for the thousands that were being assembled for the final push to break the allies back and change the out come of the war in their favor.

Tex squad was still short three men with little hope of replacements in the ongoing blizzard. His division was strung out in some of the most-dense part of the Ardennes affording them more shelter from the fierce winds and snow. They shoveled through the snow to the frozen ground leaving great mounds of snow around the hole that kept the cold wind out to a certain extent.

Witt and Crawford cut some tree branches to completely cover their hole from the falling snow, then cut out a hole in the snow bank to the front for the purpose of getting in and out and observing no mans land. That made for a warmer position and started a chain reaction all up and down the line that made life a little more comfortable for the foot weary soldiers.

Some times when the wind died down for a few minutes the silence in the forest was welcomed but if it continued for any length of time the battle hardened soldiers became nervous.

At intervals a rifle shot could be heard in the distance most likely from a German out post that had spotted a patrol from the allied side. Then there were sounds of snow laden tree limbs crashing to the ground.

Witt and Crawford hadn't had a lot of time to get acquainted until now.

"Where you hail from Crawford?" Crawford finished his can of C-rations before answering, prompting Witt to say. "That's okay if you don't care to tell me, but I'm guessing you're from Tennessee."

He tossed the empty C-ration can through the hole and lit a cigarette before answering.

"Nope, but you're close I'm from Kentucky, ever hear of Harlan County, Kentucky?"

"Oh yeah bloody Harlan, I've heard a lot about that County." Witt replied.

"Well it's in eastern Kentucky in the coal country I worked in a mine there near Cumberland in a seam of coal about like it is in this damn hole, had to bend over to get around in it and some times crawl, hard work for sure but not as bad as this mans army, at least you could go home at night to a hot meal and warm bed."

Then Witt asked. "You got family back there?" Crawford took two long draws from the cigarette before flipping it through the hole to the snow out side.

"Well yes and no, I did have but that all ended a few years ago, got three children that I will never be able to call my own and have any kind of relation ship with ever again. The damned crooked lawyer took care of that in divorce court. Had twelve acres and worked my ass off trying to build a house on it, almost had it finished when she decided she wanted a divorce. Biggest mistake I've made was marrying her up until now because joining the damn army may beat it."

"Sorry to hear that Crawford, maybe you'll be able to work something out when you get back home."

"No chance of that ever happening, like I say the lawyer and a couple of lying witnesses fixed it so I can never have contact with my kids again."

"She was a pusher if you know what I mean, never satisfied with the amount of the weekly pay check. Can't you get a better paying job at the mine? Work more over time. Made no difference that I was working some over time at the mine and a hellava lot trying to get the house together enough to live in."

"She got it all, the land and house, an old beat up pick up truck, my kids and damned near my life because I sure as hell almost pulled the trigger a couple of times, but decided I'd join up and help fight this damned war and lose it that way. Been pretty lucky so far, been hit in the calf of my leg here and had some close calls, but I've got a feeling I'll meet my waterloo right here in this damn forest with a name I never heard of before. In a way it'll be a relief from all the hell that I suffer through grieving about my kids."

"Don't guess it bothers her none though, hell I loved her more than anything and looked forward to raising the kids in that little house. She was

216

a moody person at times I knew that when I married her, mean as hell some times for no good reason, then she would come out of it and be the nicest person in Kentucky for a time only to blow up again about something, I felt sorry for the kids and it worries me now thinking about it and if they are still going through the same thing. No doubt she has latched on to some one by now, she has a way with men including that damned lawyer. But I pity the poor bastard that will risk the rest of his life living with her, I only hope he'll be good to my kids."

He reached and pulled the wool nit cap that covered his forehead beneath the steel helmet and rubbed his eyes.

"Got to get some fresh air." He said, as he crawled through the hole to the snow outside.

Witt watched him as he pranced in the snow and thought he must be going through hell.

'How can a man stand up to something like that?' He thought. He took the picture of his wife and two children from his shirt pocket and thought about the sadness it caused him to think about them being so far away and may never see them again. 'But that's nothing compared to Crawford's situation.' He whispered. 'At least I have them to return home to if I get through this war alive, but he has nothing to look forward to and I can see why he must be looking forward to the day he will leave it all behind.'

At daybreak the next day a noise penetrated the snow covered forest ahead of them. It became a steady drone as it drew nearer and soldiers prepared for battle all up and down the line. Visibility was still limited due to the blowing snow.

Then they could hear small saplings falling and being crushed by the on coming tanks. Soon they were visiable each belching out machine gun fire as they roared even closer. The tanks rolled over their snow covered positions, forcing them to abandon them and take up positions behind trees, the element of surprise had truly worked for the Germans as they broke through the lines in several places and encircled entire battalions.

Tex positioned his men as best he could in the on going confusion. A tank bore down on them no more than four hundred feet away with a dozen or more German infantry soldiers following behind to mop up anything that the speeding tank might leave behind.

Crawford had dropped to one knee and was firing his BAR in the direction of the tank and the German soldier's. Witt was close by handing him fresh clips of ammo. And at the same time firing his M1 rifle.

Tex could see that the tank was sure to go right through their positions if it wasn't stopped. He leaped to his feet with a grenade in hand intending to rush forward and try to drop it down the turret, but off to his left he could see Crawford running toward the tank with a bazooka that he had taken from a fallen soldier. He watched as he weaved back and forth from tree to tree as the German Infantry following the tank tried to stop him with small arms fire.

Then he seen Crawford reel and fall to his knees and knew he had been hit from machine gun fire from the tank or a rifle bullet from the soldiers following the tank. But as the tank came along side he pulled himself to his knees and fired the Bazooka directly at the side disabling the track it rolled forward another fifty feet and came to a stop. Crawford slowly sank back to the ground and lay still beside the Bazooka. The tank driver started climbing from the hatch but didn't make it and slumped back out of sight. Tex had raked him with rifle fire and followed up with tossing a grenade through the open hatch.

Witt had taken over the BAR from Crawford and was now mowing down the German soldiers that followed the tank.

But close behind another tank came straight at them and in spite of the valiant battle they put forth the tank made it through followed by several Infantry soldiers armed with mortars that they turned on them after they penetrated the line.

Now they were surrounded, as was much of the division up and down the line. The Germans kept up the mortar fire and called for artillery fire after a few rounds were fired and adjustments were made on the targets the artillery fire was deadly. Tree top level bursts from the 88's sent tree limbs and in some cases small trees crashing to the ground on top of the allied troops.

Some commanders all up and down the line waved white flags of surrender rather than see their unit wiped out completely.

The Germans took prisoners by the thousands but in spite of that they failed to get complete surrender although they had many thousands more surrounded.

Nightfall gave the allies time to regroup and live to fight another day.

The artillery and mortar fire finally ceased after taking many lives and moans from the wounded could be heard through the night.

Tex checked his squad positions and found that he and Witt were the only survivors. Crawford's body lay in the snow near the tank. Tex and Witt checked it out, he had taken one bullet to his left thigh, one to his right arm and another in his chest near his heart. Tex checked his pockets and found a picture of

Crawford, his three children and a tall dark beautiful woman that he surmised must be his wife.

"I'll hang on to this and see that his wife gets it, that is if I stay lucky enough to make it through this war, if not I'll leave it to you Witt, make sure she gets this picture it might make her feel better knowing that he carried it close to his heart."

" I don't know about that." Witt replied. "They were divorced and he lost all rights to ever see his children again, he told me all about it yesterday."

"Is that right? I didn't know about that, Crawford never talked much and seemed to have something on his mind that was bothersome, now I can see why, ain't nothing on earth worse than losing your right to be with your own children that is if there was no legitimate reason for it."

"Well from what he told me he lost everything to his wife, house, truck, and children in divorce court. Said she used a couple of witnesses that lied and swore that he mistreated her and the children, plus a crooked lawyer that she knew that represented her, said he never had a chance and thought about committing suicide. But said he decided to enlist and help fight the war and lose his life that way."

"Well he was one of the best men I've had in my squad so far and I intend to see that he gets the credit he is worthy of, I'll ask the company commander to put him in for a silver star for taking this tank out, not for that you and me would have been killed too. Hey look at this, must be a letter he wrote to mail home."

"Yeah I saw him writing a letter yesterday." Witt replied.

Tex held it up and scrawled across the front was this.

If I fall in battle please see that my kids get this letter, they live in Harlan County Kentucky. I have a brother living there, his name is Burl Crawford, he'll see that they get it.

The envelope was sealed.

"Okay, I'll put this picture in another envelope and keep it

with the letter then I'll give them to the company commander. He'll see that they get filed away for later use. I'll tell him either you or I would like to present them to Crawford's brother after the wars over. And if we don't make it to be sure some one gets it to him."

"Well lets get busy we expect an assault from them before the day is over, from front and rear. I've been ordered to take over the platoon what's left of it."

"I hate to see Crawford and the rest of these guys lay here in the snow, but we're partially surrounded and there's no way our guys can get through to pick them up right now. You hang on to that BAR, you did quite a job on that gang of German Infantry."

He pointed to the dead German soldiers and said. "Look at the faces there, some look fifty to sixty and others like kids, I thought we had a lot of young guys but at least they're eighteen. Look at that one there that's a face of a fifteen-year old, Hitler must be running out of men and is now calling up the young as well as the old."

At two in the afternoon heavy mortar fire rained down on them from the front.

At the same time the break through troops from the rear closed in. The fight went on till near dark. Losses were great on both sides.

Witt fired his BAR till it was red hot, laid it aside and picked up another one that he had taken from a dead comrade in another platoon. Tex noticed and thought. 'He sure shaped up as a good soldier in a hurry on a par with Crawford.'

In spite of heavy losses they still held their ground as darkness closed in the Germans withdrew to their positions but the mortar fire continued. Near midnight a 60-millimeter mortar shell exploded to the right of Tex.

He felt a sharp sting in his right elbow about the same time a heavier shell fragment caught him just under his rib cage taking his breath away momentarily.

As he lay there in the darkness he could feel the warm blood oozing from his elbow and rib cage. He called out but the din of the mortar fire drowned out all human voices. He became terribly cold and weak from loss of blood. His thoughts were of Reba, Ma, and his baby back home on Pucketts Creek. 'Guess

I'm about to die here in this god awful place, I hope it's not in vain and we go on to win, can't imagine my little boy growing up under the likes of

Hitler. 'As he listened to the mortars being fired in the distance and bursting all around him he thought of St. Charles, Jakes place, Reba, and the bottle of beer with the foam running down the sides of the glass, and Bill the police chief.

"Get up and Walk away from that stuff Tex. Take a good look at the boozers in here and come back next Saturday you'll see the same ones making fools of them selves only to feel bad all day on Sunday."

"Okay Peanut, come on out Tex don't need a flea bag like you tagging along."

"I know there's no way in hell I can stop you from what you're about to do, but promise me after tonight you'll never touch that stuff again. Don't wind up on a damn dirt floor like me."

"And that mister Burke shit, call me Wayne, Poor Boy, anything but that." Then he smiled as he remembered the look on Poor Boy's face when he said.

"Well how about dad?"

'All of that seems so far away in time but yet so close to me in a way.'

As the warm blood slowly ran down his side turning the white snow to a strawberry color he became colder and memories caused tears to flow and freeze on his face.

About an hour later his whole body became warm all over and he actually felt at peace even with the noises of battle all around him. As he lay there looking up at the tall tree tops of the Ardennes through the falling snow and darkness a smile marked his face.

"Hold her tight to your shoulder and brace yourself that old twelve-gauge packs quite a wallop."

Hypothermia took away his pain and gave him a sense of well being, even though death was near from freezing he could vision Pa, himself, and his son Wayne there on the ridge above the stand of hickory. Could hear him self say. "Look down there Wayne, ain't that a beautiful site? See that clearing? That once belonged to your Grandpa Barton, he cleared all that out, there's a waterfall down there, and on beyond there that's the Keokee road."

Could see Pa's smiling blue eyes as he said. "Can you imagine your dad never coming here with me Wayne? Never could get him away from them dad blamed dime westerns long enough to go squirrel hunting with me."

Then as hypothermia ran its course he became more comfortable and numbness covered his whole body. Over and over he could hear Pa say.

" I think my season is about over here on earth, I think my season is about over here on earth. I can't climb that old hill anymore."

Slowly the vision and the treetops in the Ardennes faded from his sight and he lay still.

At daybreak two half-tracks pulling long flat beds had managed to get through. As they loaded the bodies one on top of the other like cordwood,

Witt stood over Tex with tears in his eyes. 'How cruel can it get?' He thought.

'Yesterday it was Crawford leaving this world with his three children on

221

his mind. A broken hearted man if there ever was one, and today its Tex gone without ever holding his new born son, don't seem fair Lord, I pray that you have some kind of special arrangements set up for combat soldiers because they have already lived right through hell here on earth.'

He watched as they placed Tex among the other frozen contorted bodies, and noticed that he lay next to Crawford.

With tears flowing freely he watched the halftracks pull away making their way around shell holes until they were out of sight.

As he looked at the tree limbs and blood stained snow he wondered if he would make it through the day. 'Pretty quiet right now.' He thought. But hell will break loose before the days over.'

He slowly walked back to his position and went to work trying to dig a deeper hole in the frozen ground. Preparing as best he could for more of hell on earth that was sure to come.

News of General George Patton's 3rd. Armored Divisions arrival gave new hope to the battle weary troops. And a few days later the weather Improved enough for the air force to put planes in the air again. Within a short time thousands of German troops were in retreat failing to stop the allies in what would become known as 'The Battle Of The Bulge' and a turning point in the war.

Witt fought on into Germany earning many decorations and a battlefield Commission. to 1st. lieutenant without a scratch until the last day of the war when he stepped on a booby trap and lost all the toes on his left foot.

Ma had died shortly after the baby was born. Reba wrote Tex about it but the letter didn't arrive on the front until after his death.

The news of his death was more than Reba could bear living alone so she went to live with her parents.

Crawford's brother Burl, was notified about his death in Kentucky.

He and his brother had always been close and it hit him pretty hard. He had been upset ever since watching what happened to his brother in divorce court.

"I'll do every thing in my power to bring Brad back here for burial." He said.

"He needs to be here for his kids sake, they know he never abused them and I'm sure they miss him."'I try to keep in touch with the kids but she is very restrictive and don't allow them a lot of freedom when it comes to me.'

'Makes my blood boil thinking about it, she latched on to the mine electrician a decent fellow I hear, but I'm afraid he's in for a rough ride.' 'They bought some adjoining land, running three or four horses on it I hear.' 'Built a barn that's better than most houses in this area.'

'Some body said she's never told him about Brad being in the service.'

'Well that's about to come out in the open I intend to spread his accomplishments all over this state, 'I'm told he was a very good and brave soldier and I want his kids to know and never forget it.'

Poor Boy got home from work one day and found the kids alone.

"Where's Momma?" He asked.

"Went out to the barn a little while ago."

The boy answered. "Said she'd be back shortly."

"Come on Peanut, lets take a ride out there she might need some help with something."

The open top jeep sat near the end of the porch. Peanut started barking and didn't bother to use the steps, just barreled to the end of the porch leaped the railing and landed in the passenger seat.

"Damn yore soul Peanut, how many times have I told you to start acting civil, you're the craziest damn dog I've ever seen."

She had the dozer man cut a road through the woods about where the foot path was shortly after they purchased the fifteen acres.

"This ain't a bad road Peanut, might need some repair now and then during the rainy season."

"Yeah there she is guess she just came out to ride, whoa! Who is that other rider? Looks like the dozer man, I'm not too comfortable with that Peanut, shit I never ride with her simply because I don't care to ride horses but by god I know damn well that don't give her the right to pick a riding partner, if it's a woman that's different but come to think of it she don't have many women friends and don't seem to want any."

He pulled up to the gate and she rode over followed by the dozer man.

She smiled sweetly and said. "Hey! I thought you would be working over time Jesse wanted me to teach him to ride we were just getting ready to come to the house.

He noticed Jesse's pick up parked near the fence and surmised he had used the entrance road that ran out to the main road from the barn. That way the kids never knew any one else was out here. Her old pick up was parked near the fence with Rene sitting in the cab.

"Okay I'll see you back at the house." He said. He hollered at Peanut who had went over to the dozer mans pick up and raised his leg to wet the rear wheel.

"Lets go Peanut. As they rode along he looked at Peanut and said. "Bout the same way I feel Peanut, only thing is I would have pissed in his seat."

"So she's teaching Jesse how to ride, ain't that nice, wonder what Jesse's wife would think about that?"

"Wonder what she'd think if Jesse's wife was teaching me to ride?"

"I've got a strange feeling Peanut that things are about to get rough for us and the kids after I question her about this. Yeah she's been in a pretty good mood for a while but she likes to have her way. "I might wind up on the couch again."

"So she's teaching Jesse to ride, how nice eh Peanut."

After eating supper she poured him another cup of coffee. "Want some apple pie and ice cream?" She asked.

"Naw I'm too full for that right now." He answered.

She sat across from him in silence.

'She's waiting for me to say something about Jesse.' He thought. 'I'll let her sweat it out for a while maybe tomorrow I'll bring it up, don't care to get locked out of the bedroom tonight.'

Finally she rose and planted a kiss on his cheek. "Does it bother you that I'm teaching Jesse to ride?"

"How long will it take? How many more lessons do you plan on?"

"Oh no more than two maybe three he's catching on pretty good and I've only gave him three." She looked away realizing that she had slipped up revealing more than she intended to.

"Oh I see and there's the heart of the problem." He said. "What do you mean by that?" She asked.

"Well hell bring me a pencil and a piece of paper and I'll draw you a picture of you slipping out to the barn to meet Jesse without me or the kids knowing anything about it. You see that's the heart of the problem you didn't tell us about it."

She grabbed the coffee cups and tossed them in the sink splashing water on the floor.

"Okay if that's the way you want to look at it, then go ahead god dammit, just shows that you don't trust me."

She headed for the bedroom and closed the door behind her.

He sat there thinking. 'This is all about to come to a head but I'm gonna cut her some slack and see how far she'll go. I'll keep my mouth shut tonight and maybe avoid having to sleep on that damned couch.

He went out on the porch and watched the children playing in the yard.

They had took to him well over the past year and would often stop their playing to sit with him in the swing. They called him Wayne and some times would fire questions at him.

"Was you married before you met Momma? Did you have children? Will you take us to the movie Saturday? Will you take us for a ride?"

It had become a common sight to see them all piled in the jeep on their way to Harlan to see a movie.

'I've been on the verge of asking them about their father many times but changed my mind afraid it might stir up bad memories or something.' 'Can't get a whole lot of information from her. Just yesterday I asked if her ex husband still lived in this area.'

"I don't know where the son of a bitch is." She said. "I heard he enlisted in the army, stupid bastard will probably get his ass shot off."

'A hellva thing to say about a man that's off in some - god forsaken land fighting to keep her ass free.' 'I tried to enlist but was turned down.'

As he sat there thinking the youngest girl came and sat down beside him. He noticed the other two had stopped what they were doing and stood watching him from the yard.

She laid her hand on his arm and said. "Wayne they want me to ask you something."

"Sure honey go ahead what is it they want to know?" She turned away and dropped her head to stare at the floor. He reached and turned her head and looked in her face. "What is it honey, do they want to go for a ride?"

"No it ain't that." She said. "If you and mommy break up we would like to go live with you."

He took her in his arms and turned away so the two in the yard couldn't see his face because he knew by the feeling boiling up inside he was about to cry.

Then Peanut jumped in the swing and started searching for the tears that he knew were sure to come.

'Can't fool peanut,' He thought. 'He knows something ain't right.'

'I don't know how in hell I can answer that question, kids belong with their real momma or dad instead of going off with some one else. But shit I have to tell her something.'

Then he realized that the kids sensed something was about to happen between him and their mother. 'Guess they're getting tired of her temper tantrums for no reason about as much as I am.'

He squeezed her tight and said. "Honey if me and your momma ever decide to go our separate ways I'll do what's right for you kids, you can count on it, now go tell them. She hugged his neck before running to her brother and sister. He watched as she relayed his message.

They all turned toward him smiling from ear to ear. He reached for peanut and thought. 'Damn I'm about to cry again Peanut.' He sat in the swing until after dark thinking about the children and how unhappy they must be.

'Wish I had a better answer than that.' He thought. 'Shit no telling what will happen to these kids.'

Finally he said. "Okay Peanut lets hit the sack, ain't gonna bother to check that damned bedroom door to see if it's locked I'll sleep on the couch tonight.'

Just after midnight he wakened from something touching his face. "Are you coming to bed?" She whispered. "I'm cold."

"No I'm comfortable here." He answered.

"Are you mad at me?" she asked.

"Naw I'm not mad, don't make sense to let a little wrinkle like that tear us apart. Good night, see you in the morning."

"Oh I'm so happy that you're not mad at me." She cooed. "If you get cold the bedroom door is open." As she walked away he thought. 'Yeah I know, and you have left yourself wide open and I'm about to give you enough rope to hang yourself.'

Then one day when he got home from work the dozer man was sitting on the Porch with her.

"Jesse stopped by to see if I would go to Lexington with him tomorrow, he's thinking about buying a horse and wants me to help him pick one."

"What kind of a horse a race horse?"

"No just a horse to ride." She answered.

"I would think buying a horse around Lexington would be kind of expensive that's race horse country."

"I heard there's one farm that has riding horses pretty reasonable." Jesse remarked.

"If we get an early start we should be back home late tomorrow night, the kids will be in school and only here alone a short time before you get home from work." She said.

"Sure go ahead that's okay with me," He said. 'Damn she's taking the rope faster than I thought she would.'

Jesse came by early the next morning to pick her up just as he was leaving for work. He noticed he was driving a big newer model black Buick with lots of chrome and could see a piece of chrome missing over the rear fender on the passenger side.

226

He came home from work and asked the kids if they would like to take a ride to Harlan. "We'll have hamburgers for supper." He said. The kids squealed with joy and that sat off peanut to barking as he leaped in the old jeep.

He drove to Harlan where they had hamburgers topped off with double dipper ice cream cones at a drive in restaurant.

"No Peanut, I ain't buying you no ice cream, you had your hamburger. "Ah hell, here have a lick from mine." The kids laughed and let him take one lick from theirs.

"Okay kids, lets head for home we should get there before dark."

Right out of the city limits he just happened to look over to the right of the road at a small motel and connecting restaurant.

'Oh hell it can't be.' He thought. 'But by god it is.'

There sat the dozer mans big Buick with the piece of chrome missing right in front of room number eight.

Just ahead he pulled into a service station. "Have to make a phone call, I'll be right back, no Peanut, you stay here, hold on to him."

He took a piece of paper from his wallet and dialed the number.

"Hello is this the agency? Let me speak to Brock. Yeah this is Wayne Burke."

"Remember what we talked about a while back? Well don't look like you'll have to tail them anymore, they're right here in your back yard. Big black Buick parked in front of room number eight, if you hurry you can get some pictures before dark. Okay talk to you later."

She got home well after midnight, complaining about all the road work that slowed them down on the way back from Lexington. He lay there pretending to be asleep and caught the smell of whiskey on her breath when she crawled in bed.

The next morning he asked. "Did you find a horse?"

"No' She answered. "You were right they want a fortune for one around Lexington, we'll have to look some where else."

Brock called him at the mine office. "Got some good shots of them coming out of the restaurant and going straight to room number eight."

"Then they spent some time at a dance hall on highway 421. Couldn't take any pictures there without being noticed, but I think we have enough anyway, sent them off to be developed, I'll holler when I get them."

Two days later Brock came in the mine office. '"Here take a look." He said.

"They turned out good."

"Sure as hell did." Poor boy replied. "But I want more than this, I want to be sure I've got her in the cross hairs of justice when we go to court because from what a couple people have told me in the past few days she has connections with a crooked lawyer and got everything including the children when she divorced her first husband. I hear he was a good man to her and the children but the lawyer got two low life's to swear that he was abusing his family, poor guy is off yonder fighting a damn war with no hopes of ever getting to see his children again. So I want you to watch my house for a few days to check the coming and goings.

"You can come in at the barn entrance and cut across the fresh made dirt road to the house. Plenty of places to hide your car there in the woods near the house."

That night the phone woke him, she answered. "Just trying to get some sleep."

He heard her say. " Alright talk to you later." She said, and hung up.

He looked at the clock and seen it was 1 a.m. "Who was that?" He asked.

"That stupid Bernie wanting to know if he could stop by tomorrow for a cup of coffee, said he needed to tell me about a friend of mine that I haven't seen in a long time. Said she has had some bad luck and thought I might be able to help her."

'Oh yeah,' He thought. 'I know this guy, comes around pretty often, uses all kinds of language in front of the kids, thought I was bad but hell he's downright vulgar. Found out he and his wife were into moonshine whiskey and drugs big time, got caught and the big brave lad cut a deal and let his wife take the fall, now she's sitting up there in the big house.'

'Bernie she calls him, damn! she sure as hell has a lot of old friends, I bet the one he told her about has a checkered past. Shit I don't believe she would want to associate with a law abiding citizen.'

Just as he left the mine office the next day headed for home Brock pulled along side his Jeep and parked.

"Well Burke I did as you told me, hid my car there in the woods, found a good place to hide in the bushes near the front porch. And in no time at all a big red Lincoln pulls in. Tall sandy headed guy gets out, about six feet tall, two hundred lbs. He went on the porch and handed her a plain brown grocery bag. They disappeared in the house. About thirty minutes later they came back out, stood on the porch slobbering all over each other, then he left.

'Yeah that's Bernie.' Poor Boy thought. 'That explains the call last night only it sure as hell had nothing to with an old friend of hers. Hell he's using our place for a drug drop off.'

Then Brock went on.

"Said something that sounded like, be sure you count the money. She sat down in the swing on the porch and I decided to hang around a while."

"That bag got my attention. Didn't have to wait long before a black Caddie comes rolling in. Short heavy guy wearing horn rims gets out, he stands in the yard and she hands him the brown bag, he hands her a wad of bills and turns to toward his car."

"Hold on." I heard her say. "I have to count the money."

"It's all there, beautiful."

She finished counting and said. "Don't go out the way you came in, damn county sheriff might be out there watching, take that dirt road there through the woods, brings you out at the barn, take the road from the barn back to the highway."

"No mistake about it she's acting as a go between to keep law enforcement confused. In other words she's in on the deal and making money."

"I got good shots of the whole thing, can't wait to get them developed I figure we have enough to put some people away because it's pretty clear to me that we have stumbled on to a drug ring. But of course it's up to you if you want to go that route."

"I'll let you know after you get the pictures, sure as hell turned out to be a bigger mess than I bargained for. But go ahead and watch the house a few more days, I want all I can get on her."

His thoughts were of the children as he pulled up at the porch. Peanut came flying over the railing and cleared the windshield to made a perfect landing on the seat beside him.

"Damn yore soul Peanut you're gonna hang your balls in that wind shield if you keep doing that."

She jumped up from the swing and planted a kiss square on his lips.

"Give me the keys to the Jeep." She said. " I need to go to the store."

Before she got back the phone rang.

"Hello is this mister Burke?"

"Yes it is, who is this?

"My names Burl Crawford, my brother Brad, was your wife's first husband. I have just been notified that he was killed in action some where in Belgium. I would like to meet with his children and break the news to them preferably at my house. Do you think that could be arranged for Sunday morning? And maybe they could spend the day with me and my family, they will take this pretty hard and I feel that we should be together."

"Yes I'm sure that can be arranged. I hate to hear that about your brother and you have my sympathy. Do you think I should tell the children? Or maybe it would be better if we wait and you tell them."

"Yes I think we should wait till Sunday."

"Well give me your address and I'll have them there by 9 a.m. Sunday."

He was writing down the address as she came in the door. He went in the Kitchen and was watching her put the groceries away.

"Who was that?" She asked.

"Burl Crawford, he said your first husband was his brother."

"What did he want?"

"Some bad news about his brother, then he looked around to make sure none of the children were in earshot, he just got word that he was killed in combat some where in Belgium."

She was reaching to put something on a top shelf and froze in that position.

Finally she brought her arm to her side, dropped her head and stared at the floor.

"He wants the kids at his house Sunday so he can break the news to them."

She kept her eyes on the floor and he thought. 'His death has really shook her up what a strange person she is.' 'At times so humble and emotional but always returning to her old mean conniving ways.

She finally looked up and said.

"You can take them over there Sunday, I don't care to be around that bastard."

'Didn't take long for her emotions to wear off. She's right back to her old self again, she can have the bedroom all to her self tonight, come to think of it I guess I'll be on the couch for the rest of my stay here.' don't hanker for her company anymore.'

He took the kids to their uncle's house on Sunday morning. "Your uncle Burl called and wants me to bring you over and spend the day with them Sunday."

Excitement showed in their faces and he wondered if she had allowed them to go there since her and her first husband's divorce.

He drove up a tree shaded drive to a neat little brick home surrounded by a white picket fence. Three children a boy and two girls, the oldest a girl looked to be about twelve years old and the boy the youngest maybe seven leaving the other girl in between maybe nine or ten years old, hurried out to the jeep from the back yard where they had been playing.

Joy showed in all the children's faces and he could tell it had been some time since they had seen each other. A man and woman came out and walked to the fence. He assumed it was Burl and his wife.

"Good morning Burl said as he extended his hand across the fence, would you like to come in for a cup of coffee?"

"No thanks, I drank two cups before I left the house, I'm trying to cut down on coffee, been drinking it all day long and the caffeine keeps me wound up too tight."

The kids had already scampered off and happy noises from children at play penetrated the sereneness of a peaceful Sunday morning.

"Sorry to hear about your brother I know you must dread having to tell the children."

"Yes I do." He said. "Ours don't know about it yet either, I thought it best to wait until tonight and tell them, no sense in spoiling their day, it's been a while since they've been together. Do you think you could let them stay until about ten tonight?"

"Sure you keep them as long as you want, just give me a call when you're ready and I'll pick them up."

He said goodbye, noting the friendly look on their faces and thought. 'Probably surprised them that I seem to want to cooperate with them after trying to deal with the kids mother.'

Back at the house he seen a car sitting next to her pick up. 'Wonder who that is?' 'Damn she's getting bolder and bolder since I started feeding her the rope, all of her old men friends come around more often. 'Yeah I recognize him, that's the well driller.' They were sitting on the porch drinking coffee and as he went up the steps he said.

"What brings you out this way on a Sunday morning?' She butted in before he could answer. "He stopped by to see you, I told him you'd be right back."

He sat down and asked. "What's on your mind Alvin?"

"Aw nothing in particular." He answered. "Just wanted to stop in and say hello."

'Oh sure.' He thought. 'Trouble is I'm not here half the time when her friends stop in to say hello.'

Alvin stayed another half hour and said he had to move on.

"What time you picking the kids up?" She asked.

"About ten or whenever their uncle calls, I told him to call when they were ready."

"What! You told him that, so you've got the right to tell him to keep my kids as long as he wants?"

"Well I can't see anything wrong with that, he said he would tell them about their father after their day of being together is over, he and his wife seem like nice folks to me."

"Oh yeah." She said. "He's mister nice guy himself and she comes across as so nice, clean, and perfect. I can't stand being around the bastards."

'Sure.' He thought. 'You don't care for folks that try to live their lives with some kind of discipline and direction.'

The telephone rang and she answered. The conversation went on for half an hour, he could hear nothing she said. She hung up and ten minutes later it rang again.

"Shit Peanut, lets ride out to the barn, hell, she'll be on the phone all day while I sit here looking like the fool that I am."

Peanut had headed for the jeep as soon as he said, Lets go, cleared the railing, sailed over the windshield and made a perfect landing in the seat before he finished the sentence.

He stopped at the gate, got out and opened it. "Think I'll drive around out behind the barn Peanut, never had the old jeep over any of the property back there."

He could clearly see the imprint of tire tracks in the grass and followed them behind the barn and could see where the vehicle had turned around and then backed up to the edge of the woods.

'Maybe she had the old pick up in here.' He thought. 'But what the hell for?'

He got out and walked to the tall grass at the edge of the woods and could see that it had been disturbed. 'Some body's been going in and out of there, I wonder what the hell for.'

Peanut had ran past him into the woods and stopped no more than fifty feet ahead. He began to snort and he could see leaves flying through the air.

"Peanut what in hell you doing, you find something? You shore as hell did, damn would you look at that."

There before him he could see several half gallon mason jars that Peanut had uncovered sitting side by side and filled with a clear liquid that he knew was moonshine whiskey. He picked up a long stick and began to rake the leaves away. A trench just a couple inches deeper than a half gallon jar sitting upright had been dug.

"Damn Peanut, has to be at least hundred gallons of this stuff here. Some years ago when I was still on the hooch I would have been happy with this kind of find."

"Stop uncovering them, stop it dammit, I want to cover them back up just like we found them and get Brock out here tomorrow. "I have to believe some one else is in on this besides the big brave lad."

As he raked the leaves back over the jars he glanced down in the woods where dirt was pilled near a tree.

"Yeah that dirt came from here Peanut, they must have wheel barrowed it down there."

"Well come on lets get the hell out of here, no telling when some one will roll in here to pick this up, I doubt they would on Sunday knowing that I'm home but you never can tell, sure as hell don't want to spoil it before finding out who the pick up man is. I've got a feeling this stuff is going off in several directions and no telling how many are involved, shit, this is a big operation Peanut."

"So they're using my place to distribute drugs and moonshine, well by god we're about to upset their apple cart Peanut."

Burl called at ten p.m. she answered the phone and handed it to him.

"I'll be right there." He said. "You want to ride out there with me?" He asked.

"No I'll stay here, don't care to even go around them, and don't waste any time talking to them, I want the kids back here where they belong."

He watched as they walked the kids out to the jeep and could see that the information Burl gave about their father had been devastating to them. Burl and his wife had their arms wrapped around them.

At the jeep Burl, his wife, their kids, and the others, all clung to each other for a long time, finally the one that had ask him the question in the swing about living with him if there was a split up motioned for him to join them.

233

He stood there awkwardly not knowing if he should.

Burl's wife reached out her hand, he took it and as they all stood there embracing and consoling each other. He thought. 'Good thing Peanut ain't here, he'd never find all these falling tears.'

They finally said goodbye and piled in the old jeep. "I'll keep in touch." Burl called out. "Bring the kids back anytime you want to."

He nodded and drove away.

The kids were quiet on the way home. As they got out at the porch he said. "It's getting late I think it's best we go to bed" One by one they stepped forward and hugged his neck. They went on to bed, and he could see she had already went to bed and closed the door behind her.

He sat on the couch for a long time with Peanut laying at his feet thinking about the children.

'I've got to do the right thing for these kids and it won't be easy with her ranting and raving.'

Finally he kicked off his boots and lay down on the couch.

"Pretty much like it was before I moved in here Peanut." He whispered. "Spent some time on this damned couch on the way in, and now I'm spending some time on it on my way out."

For the next three days he noticed the children were coming even closer to him. They would all squeeze in the swing beside him and if she weren't around they would talk about their father and how much they missed him.

"He was good to us just like you are." The oldest one once remarked. "He never did the things that they said he did, that was all lies. Wayne, uncle Burl said he will bring him back here for burial, will you go with us to the memorial? Uncle Burl says he wants to honor him the way he deserves to be."

"Sure I'll go with you honey and be honored to stand along side you because your daddy was truly a hero. His spirit will always be present in my life and especially in yours. You kids can walk straight and proud just like the soldier your father turned out to be."

He noticed she had become more withdrawn and spent even more time on the phone. The house was a mess and she showed no signs of trying to get it back together.

Brock came in the mine office one day and said.

"We need to get together and make plans to wrap this thing up, I have more pictures of activity around the barn, we ought to turn everything over to the sheriff and give him a chance to nail these birds before they change their drop off point. They do that you know to keep law enforcement confused. Your place is perfect for a drop off point because law enforcement has no reason to think you would be involved in anything of this nature, but they will find another place simply because they know they can't stay in one place too long for fear of a neighbor, mail carrier, etc. becoming suspicious of the comings and goings of vehicles that they don't ordinarily see in the neighborhood."

"Right now they're using horse trailers pulled by pickups to transport the whiskey marked BAR Rail Ranch. I watched them unload, had the half-gallon jars in mason jar cases, dozen per case. They take them out of the case and line them up in the hole, then cover with leaves."

"Then the ones that make the pickup put them back in cases and load them in trailers that have the same markings, BAR RAIL Ranch."

" No telling how many city's and town's they are supplying here in Kentucky and maybe even Tennessee and Virginia."

"I have a copy of all the pictures in a sealed envelope back at the office, plus another copy with a lawyer friend of mine in case something should happen to you and me. Because if they should find out that we know something they wouldn't hesitate to rub us off."

"Yeah I know." Poor Boy replied. "This damn thing has got way out of hand and my biggest worry is what will happen to the kids, can't see where they come out a winner which ever way it goes."

"If it's alright with you I'll go see the sheriff tomorrow and give him a chance to get the dead wood on them before they decide to find another place for their transactions."

Poor Boy nodded and said. "Alright go ahead, I dread what lies ahead but guess it don't make any sense to delay it, hell it ain't gonna get any better."

The sheriff and two deputies observed for a week and noted that the drug transaction always took place on a Tuesday and the Moonshine was delivered on Wednesday and picked up on Friday just as Brock had said.

So he decided to arrest the drug drop off person plus the pick up man on Tuesday and keep it secret until after he arrested the ones that made the pick up on the moonshine on Friday.

"I'm more interested in who's behind the distribution of the shine than I am the supplier right now." He said. "We can work on him later, that is if some one in the distribution gang might give us that information."

235

The sheriff and deputies watched as the big brave lad got from his car and went up the steps to the porch carrying the brown bag, she was waiting with open arms he walked into them and they sashayed through the door and closed it behind them.

One deputy crept from the woods and took up a position at the rear of the house. Peanut barked at him from the porch but at the same time wagged his tail running toward him with a greeting. Evidently more important things were taking place in the house than trying to find out what Peanut was barking at.

"It's okay." She whispered. 'Damn stupid dog is always barking at the cat."

The other deputy took a position at the far end of the porch. The sheriff moved out of the woods closer to the end of the porch near the Lincoln.

After about thirty minutes they came on the porch and stood there embraced for a few seconds.

"Alright Bernie, just hold on to her and don't move we've got you covered real good."

She backed away from Bernie and started toward the door.

"Oh no don't try that stay right where you are, that's it stay right there."

By that time the deputies were on the porch getting them in hand cuffs.

"Looks like you're about to be heading for the big house to join your wife, unless you decide to try for a plea deal and send this lady up instead. Either way you're in a heap of trouble. You druggie guys never learn do you?"

One deputy went in the house and retrieved the brown bag. The other one drove the Lincoln out the dirt road and hid it in the woods.

"Now we know that the pick up man will be here shortly." The sheriff said. "Take him out in the woods out of sight, and if you know what's good for you you'll keep your mouth shut."

"Now lady try to regain your composure as if nothing ever happened because we want you to sit there in the swing with the brown bag till the Cadillac shows up and make the transaction as usual. You cooperate and things might go better for you, think about that."

"I'll tell you who it is." She said. "Okay, you can verify that after we get him in custody we want to get him dead to wood passing you the money and taking the bag."

They removed the handcuffs and she nervously sat down in the swing. "What do you plan on doing with me after this is over?" She asked.

"We have to take you in lady after all you've been caught red handed dealing in drugs."

"You can't do that." She said. I have three kids in school, they'll need me here when they get home."

"Should have thought of that before ever getting mixed up in drugs lady." He said. "Now you cross your legs and sit there till the Caddie shows up, we'll be in hiding but close enough to hear whatever you say, so don't think about warning him that he's in a trap. Like I said before cooperate and it might work in your favor."

Soon the Caddie could be seen coming down the driveway. It rolled to a stop and short and heavy got out with a smile on his face. He handed her the wad of money and she handed him the brown bag. He stood there smiling and thought. 'I'd like to spend a little time with her, looks like she'd be fun.'

"Ain't you gonna count it beautiful? Maybe we could have a cup of coffee and I can help you count it. Been thinking I'd like to spend some time with you."

Then the booming voice of the sheriff from behind caused him to wheel around.

"Hold it right there city boy you're about to get your wish because you're going to jail with her, and don't bother we'll count the money."

They put him in handcuffs and brought Bernie, the brave lad out of the woods.

"I assume that you two need no introduction since you must know each other pretty well already. Okay, take them away, I'll let the lady ride along with me."

She spent the night in jail. Poor Boy bailed her out the next day.

Turns out the sheriff got enough information from them to arrest six more participants including the crooked lawyer, he turned out to be the biggest fish in the pond since he was the ringleader.

"No use going through with the moonshine thing we'll go out there and destroy it. We have enough to put them away already."

She got home from jail and went straight to the bedroom and closed the door behind her.

Poor Boy fixed salmon patties with macaroni cheese for the kid's supper. They ate in silence but he knew that questions were bound to come his way before bedtime because they only had heard pieces of the story.

'But I be dammed if I'll tell them the whole story.' He thought. 'I realize me and Tex suffered because we didn't let out our hidden truths but by god these kid's don't need to know all these gory details all at once, better that they find out a little at a time.'

He went out and sat in the swing, Peanut jumped up beside him with that anticipating look on his face that something was not right and tears were about to start. Soon one by one the kid's came out on the porch and squeezed in the swing with him.

"Wayne what happened?" Dale, the oldest asked. "Why did they take mommy to jail?"

"Oh honey it's a long story, she kinda got mixed up with some folks that she shouldn't have. I think it best we don't discuss it right now. Wait a few days until she can tell her side of the story."

"But I assure you kid's that however it turns out you will be alright, now why don't you go out and play a while before bedtime, you need to digest my bad cooking." They smiled and headed for the yard and soon were tossing a baseball to each other.

He looked at Peanut and said. "Damn Peanut! That was close, I was sure that we were ready for the tears to start again."

Later the kid's said good night and went to bed. He sat there thinking. 'How in hell am I going to do what's right for the kid's? Shit they lose no matter what.'

Peanut stirred and he looked up to see her coming toward him. She sat down and was quiet for some time.

Finally she said in her most appealing quiet voice. "Do you believe everything you've heard?"

He didn't answer. So she laid her hand on his leg and said. "Well do you?"

"Hell yes I believe it." He said. "Not that I want to, do you realize what you've done to your children?"

"I haven't done anything to hurt my children." She said softly. "You yourself know I love them dearly."

'Oh sure.' He thought. 'You're putting on your best act to try and sway me, well by god you're not about to win me over.'

"Everybody makes mistakes." She went on. 'No ones perfect."

"Yeah I know." He answered. "But by god the things you've done are down right below human decency, and is a disgrace to you and your children."

"Now wait a minute." She said. "Where is all this coming from?" I make one little mistake and now you try to stretch it into mistakes. Why don't you wait till the trial starts and you'll find out I was suckered in on the whole thing."

"Oh sure you were suckered in all because of greed."

"What you mean by that?" She asked. 'I'm not greedy."

"Then pray tell me is there another name for it?" "Let me go over some of the things that you've done in your past and the pattern continues right up through my relationship with you. You divorced your husband for no good reason according to all I've heard. You and a certain crooked lawyer hired two people to lie that he mistreated you and the children. You literally destroyed the man's desire to live and now he gave his life on the battlefield, and you have the nerve to sit here and tell me that you've only made one little mistake. As far as I'm concerned you and that damned lawyer are directly responsible for your first husbands death. And I hope the bastard has to spend the rest of his life in prison."

"And greed, lets look at that some more, remember how you were never satisfied with my salary? You were always hounding me. You need to move up and make more money, why don't you work more over time? Money is your god and you've always had your hands out for it no matter the source, I just wonder if there's anything on god's earth that you wouldn't do for money."

"Guess you thought you had me fooled, I decided to cut you some slack a while back and see how far you would go. Shit, you went even farther than I thought you would."

"So now you've been digging in my past, I'm beginning to think that I'm in this fix because of you nosing around."

"No it's not that way at all beautiful, you're in the fix you're in because of you and your slipping around with that bunch that you chose to throw in with. You see I decided a while back that I had to get something on you before leaving you, I sure as hell didn't look forward to facing you and that damned lawyer in court and walking out with nothing like your first husband did. I've got enough on you to take the whole damned place if I want to, but I won't do that simply because of the kids, I'll do the right thing by them."

"Okay, so you can go to court and swear to all that bull shit, damn jury will laugh you out of court if that's all you can come up with."

"Oh no that's not the whole story, when I get on the stand I'll tell them about all the men friends you had that were forever dropping in supposedly for a cup of coffee. And how I decided I'd better get everything in line for a divorce that was sure to come."

She jumped to her feet and said. "You want to know something you're the stupidest bastard I have ever come across. The men friends you speak of are just acquaintances from before I knew you and they are nothing more than old friends that want to keep in touch."

239

"Oh sure." He said. "And how about the ones that you didn't know until they did some work for you and keep coming back."

"The bull dozer man, the landscaper, the lawyer, the banker, even the well driller, what the hell does he come by for, to check the water? One thing for sure they don't come to see the kids, or me and yes you're right in a way, the electrician was the only one that chose to move in. Yes you're right, I am a stupid bastard. But not as stupid as you thought, you see I was born at night but it wasn't last night."

She stood above him with a grin on her face. "None of that will sway a jury because it'll be my word against yours. And speaking of greed, you ass hole you know yourself that I've spent the money well in property and still managed to save some."

"Sure I agree with that, in fact there were times when I thought that you must have been getting money from some place else the way the bank account grew.

So now lets get back to what the jury may or may not believe. Will they believe me when I tell them about Jesse coming by to take you to Lexington to help him pick out a horse, and later on in the day I spotted his car parked in front of motel room number eight in Harlan. And how about your druggie friend 'the big brave lad' that let his wife take the fall and now enjoys your company. And how you gonna explain your name on the deed of another man friends property after he divorced his wife? You see, I hired a private investigator to look into all of this and we have documented evidence, plus a slew of pictures. Hell, you don't have a chance, like I said I could walk out of that court room with everything but I'll see that the kids get what's coming to them."

"You son of a bitch." She yelled. You nosey meddling son of a bitch, don't you dare come near the bedroom while you're still in this house."

"Don't worry yourself about that because you haven't appealed to me for some time anyway." He said.

"What do you mean by that?"

"I mean just what I said, you're beginning to look like what you are. Go take a long look in the mirror and you'll see what I mean."

She headed for the bedroom but turned back.

"I shut Rene up in the laundry room because she's in heat, that damned ugly dog of yours is laying at the door wanting to get at her. You keep him away from her, I sure as hell would hate to see anything that he fathered, the ugly bastard."

He heard her slam the bedroom door and thought.

'Yeah I know you don't want your Rene to get tied up with Peanut but I don't intend to honor your wishes. That's about like not wanting a child by me.

I wanted a child of my own but every time I mentioned it she would become all unglued and tell me that the three she had was enough.'

'Am I glad she felt that way, can't imagine what it would be like to go through this divorce with that added burden. Hell, I have time to meet some good woman and have a child of my own, I still have lead in my pencil.'

'I told her more than I intended but it won't make a difference if she knows about it before we go to court because I have enough on her to sway any jury in my favor.'

He went in, kicked off his boots at the couch and crept to the laundry room door where Peanut lay looking up at him with pleading eyes. He opened the door and whispered. "Go on in peanut have a good time tonight, you deserve it."

The next day after work he entered the mine office and was told by the superintendent that he should call Reba Barton, in Lee County, Virginia.

"The lady sounded very upset." He said. "I told her I'd have you call as soon as you came out of the mine."

He dialed the number and wondered what the news would be. 'Must be bad news.' He thought. 'Damn, seems that's about all that comes my way anymore.'

He listened to the sobbing voice of Reba. "I just got word that Tex was killed in action in Belgium."

"Oh honey I'm sorry, I'm so sorry." Was about all that he could manage to say as he listened to her say.

"It just ain't fair." She said. "That he never got to see and hold his son, God knows he had to live most of his life not knowing who his father was, and now he took him away before he ever got to know his son. I want you to know how much he respected you, he mentioned you often and as you know wanted our son named after you." She went on and on and as he listened tears started down his cheeks.

Finally he said. "Honey I'm so sorry because he was almost like a son to me, I'll be over there this weekend, so don't try to give me any details over the phone, wait till we can sit down and talk. Be strong now for the baby's sake, Tex would want it that way, okay bye, I'll see you some time Saturday morning."

241

He hung up the phone and turned away from the office personnel. Finally he turned to the superintendent and said. "Young man I knew over in Lee County, Virginia, got killed in combat, leaves behind his wife and their first born, hell, he never had a chance to see him let alone watch him grow up. I'm not a church going man, but I do believe in our maker, but sometimes I do wonder about his decisions when it comes to taking a daddy or mother from their little ones. Hell, seems like bad news is about all I've had for the past few months, been having nightmares of being on the bottle again, and to tell you the truth it's tempting as all hell sometimes, don't know how much more I can take."

The superintendent stepped forward and laid his hands on his shoulders.

"Yes I know you've been going through hell with all the things that have happened in your family recently, but I want you to know we here at the mine and all over the neighborhood are pulling for you. So if you need some time off you have my permission, take as long as you want and when you come back I intend to promote you to my position because I've been hankering to retire and I can't think of a better man to replace me, folks in the Blue Diamond Company feel the same way because like me they see more in you than just an electrician."

Now go on home and take off as long as it takes to get all your troubles out of the way, then come back with the title."

"Superintendent Wayne Burke, Blue Diamond Mining Company, Harlan, Kentucky."

With tears still visible Poor Boy reached out and shook his hand. "Don't know how in hell you can have that kind of confidence in me but if you feel that way I'll try to come back here and do the best I can with the job but doubt if I will ever fill your shoes." He turned to leave and listened to these words. "Sure you'll fill my shoes, might take a while but after you get the hang of it you'll go on to make new tracks that I never thought of before. Good luck, and hey! Get that bottle off your mind, you're a better man than that, we're all pulling for you."

The powerful diesel engine drowned out the sounds of traffic carrying miners to work as it roared through Stone Creek before day break on it's way to St. Charles, pulling a string of empty coal cars.

Also drowned out the sad country music tune that he was listening to coming from a radio station in Knoxville, Tennessee. As the noise from the diesel faded in the distance the disk jockey had filled a request for another number.

242

And as he tossed his clothing into an old beat up suitcase he listened to. "Candy kisses wrapped in paper mean more to you than any of mine." Followed by another requested number. 'This world is not my home, I'm just passing through, if heaven's not my home, oh lord what can I do?"

Finished with the clothing he squeezed in his personnel things, an old alarm clock, razor, and other things including a bible that was left to him by his mother when she died, the back cover was partially torn away. He turned the front cover and as he read his mother and father's names and his below theirs, his thoughts were. 'Been trying to find the answer in this book to guide me to the right decision but never found it, so I hope and pray I'm making the right one.'

He folded a faded blue bath towel placed it on top and closed the lid on the suitcase. He had to press the lid down before the latches engaged. He reached for an old belt hanging on a chair wrapped it around the suitcase and buckled it tight.

Then he noticed one corner of the towel was hanging out. "Heck.' He thought. 'Ain't gonna worry about that, wish all my worries were little things like that.'

He glanced over to where she lay on the couch and thought. 'I was hoping she wouldn't be there when I left, thought it might be easier to walk out. But after being gone for three days she would have to pick this day to come home again.' 'Came like a thief in the night and plopped down on the couch.'

He picked up the note that he had laboriously written and read it again, hoping that she could read his poor handwriting.

Dear Geneva, I have a few words to say and I will put them down here in this letter. And I reckon it is a letter because we ain't talked and spent much time together since we left Tennessee. You seem so far away and I have tried to figure some way to get us back together like we once was back in Tennessee. But as time has gone by I just run out of hope. I can't lay all the blame on you because I reckon I was foolish for asking you to marry me when I was thirty-four and you was only seventeen.

A friend at the mine decided he was going to Detroit to get a job with General Motors, said his brother worked there and could get him on. He asked me if I would go with him, said his brother said he would help me get a job also.

But I want you to know in spite of the way you have treated me I still love you and this is going to be one of the hardest things that I have faced in my life to walk out of here this morning knowing that I will never see you again.

The old saying is, 'Time and distance will heal a lot of heartache.' 'But I can't see that anywhere in my future, and what makes it worse is knowing that you don't care for me and probably never did.

I paid the rent on the house for another month. Then you'll have to make your own arrangements. The man said he wanted you out when the month is up, said he was afraid that you would start having parties and destroy the furniture.

Well I guess that's about all I can say, ain't no good at setting down something on paper. Would have a lot to say if we was to set down and talk like we used to when we first got married but them days have been gone a long time.

My friend will be here shortly and I guess by the time you wake up and read this we will be riding on highway 25w some where in Kentucky, maybe near Corbin. I would hope that as you read this, your mind will go back to when we got married and all the happiness that we shared together.

Let me say again, I love you and always will. Goodbye, Worley

He placed the letter on the end table, took a twenty-dollar bill from his wallet and laid it along side the letter.

He stood over her noting her beauty but at the same time seeing the tiredness around her face and eyes from all the drinking and so called fun that she had pursued for the better part of three years.

'Looks much older.' He thought. 'And if she don't slow down soon her beauty will vanish like a falling star.'

He reached down to touch her but drew back. 'I've resisted doing that many times before and this sure ain't no good time to do it.'

He heard a car motor out by the porch and knew his friend had arrived. He picked up the old blanket and covered her bare legs just as he had done so many times before.

He took the suitcase in one hand and reached for the aluminum miner's dinner bucket – lunch pail- with the other. 'Just like going to the mine.' He thought. 'Only this time I'm not coming back to eat alone and listen to the jukebox music blaring from the dance hall yonder across the bridge.'

He walked to the door, stopped and turned for one last look at her sleeping on the couch, and wondered what her reaction would be to the letter. Finally he whispered 'I love you, goodbye.' And walked out the door.

"Hey! Where you going with that dinner bucket?" his friend asked. "I don't believe you'll need that working at General Motors."

Old Steam Engine, St. Charles, VA. early 1920s

Left to right: Dewey Parks, Richard Carter, Johnson Jesse, other men unknown.

Picture used with permission from Ronnie Carter.

Natural Rock Formation near the town of Pennington Gap, in Lee County, VA.

Was once called "Nigger Head Rock," now known as "Stone Face Rock."

Permission to use picture from Gene Robbins, Woodway, VA.

George Wright, a successful coal mine operator in Lee County, VA.
Picture used with his permission.

"Yeah I know." He answered. "I made us a half dozen Bacon, egg, lettuce and tomato sandwiches, we can stop at the cold springs and fill the bottom with water, sure am gonna miss that good water."

He got out at the cold spring and filled the bottom half of the dinner bucket with the ice-cold water that came right out of Stone Mountain through a two-inch pipe.

He started to get back in the car but hesitated as he peered through the semi-darkness at the road behind them. 'Could be that I'm making a mistake.' He thought. 'Don't know if I want to leave her this way, might just get my suitcase and tell my friend that I've changed my mind, aint but a quarter mile back there, sure would be better to do it now than it would after I'm six hundred miles away in Detroit.'

"Hey! What's the hold up?" His friend asked. "It's a long way to Detroit, I want to cover some miles while it's still cool, ain't got no air conditioning in this trap, it'll get hot as the day wears on. The way you was looking back I thought you might have forgot something."

"Naw." He answered. "Wish I could forget it."

He got in, and around the next curve it loomed above them. "Take a good look at 'Nigger Head Rock." His friend said. "Might be a long time before we see it again."

They rode in silence until they drove through Jonesville. His friend looked over and said. "I think I know what's on your mind, and I hope you'll snap out of it and get on with your life. She treated you bad the same way I treated my wife, she stuck with me, why? I'll never know, maybe because of the two kids, but in the end she made up her mind to put distance between us and start a new life. The last I heard she remarried and is living in California, her and the kids have a much better life ahead of them than they would ever had with me. So come on cheer up, by night fall we should be near six hundred miles away from her and you'll start feeling like a new man, say, lets enjoy one of them good sandwiches you brought along, I feel a hunger pain."

Just as they drove through Ewing the sun came out and lit up the White Rocks atop Stone Mountain.

His friend slapped him on his leg and said. "See what I mean we ain't but a few miles away but things have already begun to brighten up."

'Yeah.' He thought. 'Maybe for you, but my mind is too crowded with the thoughts of her and the dark shadows it casts around me to notice the sunshine.'

As they crossed the Ohio River in Louisville his friend remarked. "A big lot of the trip is behind us, we've made good time, so we can slow it down and coast the rest of the way."

'Sure.' He thought. 'Maybe for you we've made good time, but to me time has stood still and I'm still standing there looking at her on the couch. The long miles between us have done nothing to ease my pain, oh god how I'd like to be close enough to touch her.'

About two months later he lay in a sleeping room with her on his mind unable to sleep. The lonesome sounds of the foghorns from the cargo boats pierced the walls of the rooming house and made him home sick for the little rental house in Virginia and the image of her there on the couch.

'I've got a good job.' He thought. 'And should be happy about that, but I think I would be satisfied more back there with her even though she treated me like dirt.' 'One thing about it some things have to change, ain't no way I can live out the rest of my life like this.'

Her thoughts were in rhythm with the purring of the powerful diesel engine as it powered the Greyhound bus through the night. As it crossed the Ohio River in Louisville she glanced around at the people, some sleeping, others in whispered conversation, a baby's whimper just before it's mother opened her blouse and touched her nipple to it's lips, the never ending giggling of three teenagers near the back of the bus.

'All a part of every day life.' She thought. 'People on the move, some going, some coming, some confident and knowing exactly where they are going and why.' 'And others that seem not to care one way or the other and mostly go with the flow.' 'I wonder if there's another person on this bus like me, dreading to face some one at the end of their destination, but at the same time can't wait to get there.'

Then her thoughts went back to Lee County, Virginia approximately two months ago. She could remember the morning and the heartache it caused her but in the end may have saved her life.

'I didn't realize how low I had dropped.' She thought. 'I almost destroyed myself, but the sad part is I may have destroyed him already.'

She remembered waking on the couch and as usual the blanket covered her legs and she thought. 'Why does he keep doing that?' 'I guess the answer is love, but I can't understand how he could still love me the way I've treated him.'

She went to the kitchen and reached for a dose of Stanback head ache powder and washed it down with a glass of water. Feeling nauseated she headed for the couch and lay back down. Ten minutes later she sat up, something caught her eye on the coffee table, a sheet of paper with a twenty-dollar bill lying beside it.

As she read the letter her head started throbbing and nausea drove her to the bathroom.

She lay on the couch sobbing until the late afternoon when finally the headache lessened and her stomach settled. She went in the kitchen and ate a hard-boiled egg that he had boiled that morning, just as he had done many other times. But now she realized he did these little things just for her.

The realization opened her mind and for the first time she began to understand why he had stayed with her in spite of the disrespect that she had shown him.

She lay back down on the couch and cried until darkness set in. She could hear the juke box blaring from the dance hall and thought.

'Ordinarily by this time I would be there right in the thick of things but right now I feel that I'll never go there again.'

The phone rang and the voice on the other end asked.

"Hey Geneva! What's the hold up? I thought you would be here by now, remember we're supposed to be at 'The Cedar Grove Inn' to meet with our regular gang tonight, that should be a lot of fun."

"No thanks." She answered. "Count me out, and as of today leave me out of any future plans of that nature, I'm turning over a new leaf before it's too late if it ain't already."

She heard laughter followed by these words. "Ah come on Neve, stop pulling my leg you're beginning to sound like a Sunday school teacher."

She hung up and refused to answer several more times as the phone rang throughout the night.

Early the next morning she caught the bus to St. Charles.

'I don't have a lot of work experience.' She thought. 'But I feel I can do a decent job of cooking in the juke joints.' 'So I'll try to get a job in St. Charles, that way I will be busy in the kitchen and out of sight of the drinking crowd, sure don't care to ever work in the dance hall again here in Stone Creek.'

She landed a job at one of the many joints in St. Charles, and after a week on the job many compliments were passed her way as to the improvement of the food.

"You know." One fellow remarked to the waitress. "This place used to be noted for the grease in the food, and we called it the 'greasy spoon' but now you have the best food in town, which can only mean one thing you must have fired the cook and hired one that knows how to cook. So who ever it is, he or she, tell them the whole town is talking about the delicious food."

At the end of her first month on the job the lady owner gave her a substantial raise and suggested she stay at her house rent-free. "That way you won't have to ride the bus back and forth every day." She said.

A smile crossed her face as she thought. 'You must be my special angel because tomorrow is my last day at the rental house in Stone Creek.'

In the following days of month two she was able to get Worley's address and phone number in Detroit from relatives of the fellow that took him there.

She saved her money and near the end of the month confided her intentions to the lady she worked for.

"Now you've heard my story. She went on. "I hope that you will understand and forgive me for walking away from the job, I know it must leave you in a bind, and I'm real sorry about that, but I must go to him, I must, you see I feel it's a turning point in my life, the difference in living a happy life again or just existing from day to day with no hope at all for the future."

The lady shook her head and frowned looking very uncomfortable for a minute or so, but soon the frown was replaced by a smile and she reached out and took her in her arms, and tears flowed freely as she said.

"Honey, I do understand and I wish you all the best, sure it leaves me in a bind but not near as much as you find yourself in. I can always find another cook, maybe not a good one but I'll find one. There's no comparison to your situation because you're trying to salvage your life from hell right here on earth, not to mention his. You have my blessings and may god protect and reward you."

As the Greyhound drew closer to Detroit she smiled as she remembered the lady pressing a fifty-dollar bill in her hand and saying.

"Honey here's something extra you might need it. Now be careful, that's a long way to have to travel alone on a bus especially for a woman. And remember I'll be praying for you and hope the Lord will get you two back together, but if it don't work out, remember you can always come back here your job will be waiting."

The low murmur of conversation increased as more aroused from sleep and knew Detroit was only minutes away.

The baby cried out for momma's nipple, she smiled and unbuttoned her blouse to reveal a smooth white breast filled with nourishment for the little tummy that craved it. Just one thing of many that makes a mother so special and to deserve the known truth, 'mother's love.'

Laughter from the teenagers was drowned out when the driver announced.

"This is the city limit's of Detroit, Michigan. We will arrive at the station on schedule fifteen minutes from now, please stay seated, and thank you for making my trip a pleasant one."

She nervously approached the ticket agent.

"Sir will you please dial this number and ask for Worley? Tell him that some one from Virginia just arrived and would like to see him."

The agent took the piece of paper and scolded.

"Yes lady I'll dial the number but you tell him yourself, I know you can do that better than I can."

"No sir will you please? I want you to do it because if he knows it's me he may not come."

He dialed the number and as she watched she became more nervous as he held the phone to his ear while staring at her, finally he said.

"Some one from Virginia just arrived here at the Greyhound bus station and would like to see Worley, okay can you rouse him? After a short wait he said.

"You Worley? The reason I called is some one from Virginia wants you to come down here at the Greyhound bus station, yeah they want to see you, no I don't know who it is and don't have the time to find out, I've got folks lined up to buy tickets. You're coming down? Okay thanks."

As he hung up the phone he gave her a knowing look and said. "'Good luck lady he's on his way."

He carefully made his way through Detroit's city streets thankful that traffic was sparse because of the late hour. He had made a down payment on an old Chevrolet from savings after his first month working at General motors.

Who could this be? Kept running through his mind.

'Maybe one of the miner's I worked with.'

'Sure is a late hour to roust a person out of bed, I had just fell asleep.'

Then he remembered the loud knocking on his door and another roomer calling out. "Hey Worley! You're wanted on the phone."

Remembered walking down the hallway half asleep to the phone attached to the wall and listening to a strange voice.

"Some one from Virginia here at the Greyhound bus station wants to see you." 'Said he didn't know who it was and didn't have time to find out, I wonder why whoever it was didn't do the calling.'

He walked in the bus station somewhat excited but at the same time apprehensive not knowing the person he was about to see.

He scanned the travelers, some slumped in the waiting room seats half asleep obviously waiting for another bus to extend their trip while others talked excitedly about the trip they were about to start on.

He scanned the seats again and noticed an old beat up suitcase on the floor, and at about the same time she rose to face him.

The ticket agent stopped what he was doing to stare at them causing others to do the same and wonder what was taking place.

He looked at her, completely in shock. He was facing a person weary from a six hundred mile journey riding a Greyhound bus. A person that had aged far beyond her twenty years, a person pale of face and obviously scared, a person that he had once known and thought that she loved him, but watched it all vanish within three short years, but to him it was the longest and saddest three years of his life.

The image of her sleeping on the couch after a wild night out passed before him.

Coming home from work after a hard days work at the mine to eat alone. Sitting on the porch listening to the jukebox from the dance hall knowing that she was probably clinging to some other man as they glided across the half lit dance floor.

They stood facing each other, each waiting for the other to say something but words would not come.

Her thoughts were. 'Oh God! Please help me I don't know how to explain my actions, all I can say is I love him and want him back.'

As the images filled his vision with all the unpleasant things that she brought on him and herself in Virginia, they shaped a perfect picture of a broken and shameful person standing before him, but through it all he looked into her eyes and there he could see love.

They walked slowly toward each other and embraced without uttering one word. Still in silence they clung to each other as tears ran down their cheeks.

Every one in the station rose to their feet knowing that they had just witnessed a performance that was real and unrehearsed.

Several tried to hold back tears but in the end became overwhelmed with emotion.

The ticket agent whispered. 'I've seen lots of strange things around this bus station, some good, some bad, and some down right weird, but I will always remember this one as the greatest act of true love that I have ever seen, too bad an artist ain't here to put it on canvas.'

Finally without a word he released her and picked up the old beat up suitcase.

As they walked toward the door to leave the ticket agent called out.

"I hope it works out for you this time and I'm sure it will, good luck."

He clapped his hands in applause and everyone joined in.

At the door they turned and bowed, and with a smile on their face they walked to the car and drove away.

They climbed the steps to the second floor of the rooming house. They sat on the bed holding hands for the longest time, both tried to start a conversation but words wouldn't come. I guess love is like that, quiet, tender, mysterious, and sometimes speechless. A few weeks later color returned to her face and beauty graced her body once again.

Two years later twin daughters came into their lives and pushed the unpleasant memories of their three years in Lee County, Virginia further into the past. They made their home in Garden City, Michigan and over the years visited their home state of Tennessee often.

After a long illness he died in her arms at the age of seventy-seven, leaving her many sweet memories to cherish and share with their twin daughter's.

But memories of her wayward ways in Virginia were always present causing her much sadness that would be followed by tears.

Tears of regret, tears of redemption and yes tears of sadness. But thank God love is made up of all these things and more, and will cause that.

Poor Boy, and Peanut, sat in the swing long after the kids went to bed. He reached over and scratched Peanuts head.

"Damn! Peanut, my minds been in a mess for so long, don't know how in hell to ever get it straight enough to get through this damned divorce. My biggest worry is the kids, little by little they are understanding that their mother is in big trouble and have been asking questions. Will mommy go to prison? Are you leaving after the divorce? Can we go with you?"

"Shit, Peanut, The only question I can answer is, yes I will be leaving here. But I have no way of knowing if she will go to prison and for how long, the trial date is still six months away and it could be postponed for another six months after that unless there's a plea agreement."

"I'm hoping that the kids will be put in the custody of their uncle Burl and his wife, they would be perfectly happy there. Burl called and said he and his wife were ready to do anything necessary to have them come live with them."

"The divorce shouldn't be much of a problem, she has already agreed to my terms, rather than take it to a trial that she knows would reveal her sorry record of being a wife and mother to her children."

"She argued like hell to my terms and tried to finagle more than I offered, but I held my ground."

"You know that's not fair," She said. "You're taking the whole fifteen acres for your part and leaving me with this house and the twelve acres it sits on, shit that barn on the fifteen acres is worth more than this house. And on top of that you want two of my horses you don't even ride, so tell me why you want the horses?"

"And another thing, there's not enough cleared land to pasture my two horses, so come on give me six acres from the fifteen."

"She really came apart Peanut, when I replied to that, well shit you've been hearing all her yelling and screaming I don't need to get into that. That's just her way she's greedy even in the face of maybe having to pull some time in prison."

"Yes I want the fifteen acres and the barn." I told her. "And yes I want two of the horses for the kids to ride, you sure as hell never offered to teach them to ride, I'm sure they would enjoy it. And who paid for the horses? I did, they belong to me, so look at it this way, I'm giving you two of the horses. As for the cleared land, you can always have the dozer man clear you a few more acres."

"But what really pissed her off Peanut, is when I told her that all three kids and their uncle Burl's names had to be on the deed."

"Hell no." She said. "I'll never agree to that bastard's name on any of my property."

"Have it your way Princess. " I answered. "So we'll go to court and you'll be left out in the cold with nothing."

"You son of a bitch." She yelled. "Call me by my name, get off that Princess stuff, I'm no Princess."

"You know what I almost said Peanut?" "Yeah I know you look more like a squaw."

"But I lost my nerve."

Peanut sat there in the swing looking at him and waiting for more, but when nothing came he lay down, rested his head on Poor Boy's lap and fell asleep.

As he scratched Peanut's head, thoughts of the past month ran through his mind.

His visit to Lee County, Virginia to visit a grieving mother as she held little Wayne "Tex" close to her broken heart and sobbed.

"It just ain't fair that Tex had to die without ever getting to see his baby. I can't understand how God can do a thing like that. Can some one tell me why? Please, please, I need to know before I go out of my mind."

'I tried to console her.' He thought. 'But hell I'm no preacher and don't have the right words to say, and I doubt if a preacher has the answer to her question either.'

'She handed me little Tex and said something about it being an honor that he was named after me, I didn't hear it all because as I held him all I could think of was, I want a son of my own, and by god I intend to get started in that direction as soon as this mess has cleared out of my life.'

'There has to be some one out there that will share their life with me, could be that young lady my boss's secretary at the mining office that I have so much respect for. 'She goes about her work with a smile on her face and not saying much but I've noticed that she looks at me with concern about the problems I find myself in.' 'I don't know much about her background except that she's single but I'll find out more pretty soon, because I think she will be my secretary when I take the job over. I called the boss yesterday and told him I was ready to come back to work.'

"Okay." He said. "Come on in Monday and we'll get you started on my job, I intend to stick around with you for a month or so until you get the hang of it."

'Damn!' He thought. 'That's only four days away, I hate to start off with all this other stuff on my mind, but in a way it could be a god send and take my mind off some of this crap.'

"I've been wondering if Tex and Brad Crawford were together there in Belgium Peanut. They both were killed about the same time but guess we'll never find out eh Peanut? Aw shit I forgot you're asleep. Well let's go to bed Peanut it's late."

He walked to the darkened doorway just as she was coming out.

"Oh you're going to bed." She said. "I thought we might talk things over, I need to tell you how I feel. It's not too late to make our marriage work I am perfectly willing to try if you are."

Reluctantly he turned and sat back down in the swing, she sat beside him with Peanut lying at their feet.

She laid her hand on his leg and said. "We need to talk this over without all the insane yelling at each other."

'Oh hell.' He thought. 'She's the one that does all the yelling, but she don't mind including me and use the word 'we' there.'

"You know yourself." She went on. "That it's better for the kids if we stay together and keep this property as it is, we have both worked hard to make it our home and it's a shame to think about getting a divorce and dividing it up. We don't know what will happen to me, but if I do have to go away for a while you could take care of the kids until I get back."

He was silent as he looked into the darkness.

"And after I get back we can start all over again, I hear there's another ten acres for sale that joins our fifteen acres, we can buy that with the extra money that comes with your promotion."

'Sure.' He thought. 'I see exactly where you're coming from, you're no different than you ever were, wanting to use me to take care of the kids, work my ass off and save to buy another ten acres.'

'Still the same old conniving person that you have always been and not likely to change even after a prison sentence.'

"Well what do you think?" She asked. "We should talk it over and work something out I'm getting tired of living like this, I miss you in the bedroom and want you with me tonight so if you wake during the night and decide to leave that old couch, come on in I won't bite you."

As she rubbed his leg he said.

"No I'm sorry I intend to see this divorce through and go out and start all over again. You had a good hard working husband and in the end denied him the right to ever see his children again which is about as cold hearted a thing that you could have done to him in my estimation. He died over there in Belgium in the cold of winter no doubt a bitter and broken man. Well by god you can go find some one else to take my place, it took me a while to catch on to your intentions because I have to admit you are a charmer and have a way with men and that's where the problem is, it will always be men because you want it that way it's a way of life with you."

He rose from the swing and said.

"Come on Peanut, lets turn it in it's getting late."

As he went through the door he expected a stream of cuss words from her but instead thought he heard sobbing which was very unusual.

Some time later she passed the couch on her way to the bedroom and he could hear her crying and it went on through the night tempting him to go to her and take her in his arms, but thoughts of his time with her and her deceitful greedy ways told him that she would never change.

Finally he fell off to sleep and had a fitful night filled with dreams of Tex and Brad dieing in a far off land, one that never got to see his baby and the other denied the right to ever see his children again even if he had got back alive from the war.

He slept late and was awakened by a kiss on his lips, she was on her knees at the couch. She had one arm around Peanut's neck as he snuggled close to her completely taken by her charms.

She kissed him again on his cheek, smiled and said.

"Come on get up me and Peanut went to the store and got some steak, I've fixed you steak and eggs for breakfast."

He sat up and pulled his boots on and watched her walk toward the kitchen.

'Damn! She sure looks inviting.' He thought. But I'm having none of that but steak and eggs sounds good I'm hungry.'

'I guess she'll never give up trying to hold us together but it'll take more than steak and eggs and twisting of her tail as she parades before me to change my mind.'

He walked from his jeep to the mine office as thoughts went through his mind.

'Damn! Why in hell did I agree to this promotion, I'm scared as hell that I might not be qualified for the job, shit I make good money as an electrician, I think I'll tell the boss I changed my mind.'

As he opened the door a dozen voices all in unison called out. "Welcome back."

The boss's nameplate had been replaced with his that read.

Wayne 'Poor Boy' Burke
Mine Superintendent

'Oh shit.' He thought. 'To damn late to back out now.'

"Okay." The boss said. "Since you know every body in here you need no Introduction. My secretary Ann, baked a cake for you in celebration of your return so lets make some fresh coffee and enjoy it."

"And by the way Ann is now officially your secretary and I might warn you, she will not tolerate bad language in any form around the office, knowing you that might be hard for you to get used to but I've seen you overcome much larger things than that."

They all laughed. She handed him a piece of cake and their eyes met.

'Damn!' He thought. 'I've got a feeling that some where down the line I'll be spending a lot of time with Ann and by god she can have her way with me because I can tell she comes from good stock a hellva lot better than mine, but maybe with time I'll measure up to it.'

Later on the boss was showing him maps of the mine. "Not much use in wasting a lot of time on these." He said. "You being the electrician you know every foot of this mine. And speaking of electricians do you want to promote your assistant to your job? Is he qualified? If not we will hire some body."

"Oh hell yes." He said. "He's a damned good electrician, shit he could teach me a few things."

The office became deathly quiet and as he glanced at Ann she was trying to Give him her most solemn look but he could see merriment in her eyes.

Soon everyone burst into laughter.

The boss slapped him on the shoulder and said. "I knew it wouldn't take long for you to break Ann's rule. Like I said that will probably be the hardest part of the job for you to get used to. She's laughing now but mark my word she'll hold you to it, so you may as well make up your mind to clean your language up a bit."

As the laughing continued he thought.

'Shit, why in hell did I ever agree to this promotion won't ever be able to talk natural around this damned office.'

He looked toward Ann and as they made eye contact again he knew that he would try his best to clean up his language.

'Shit, she's worth it.' He thought. 'Or should I say, mercy, she's worth it?'

'Anyway like the boss said, it's gonna be hard but I managed to stay away from the booze and get off that damned dirt floor so I should be able to talk a little more civil.' 'With Ann's help I know I can.' I know I can.'

Within three months the divorce and property settlement was finalized not to Princess, liking of course, but she realized if she contested it she might wind up with none of the property and most of all lose her children. And depending on the outcome of her trial on the drug charges she could still lose her children.

She would lay sleepless night after night thinking about the on coming trial and the possibility of losing them.

Once at three a.m. she went to the couch and woke him. "Sorry to wake you."

She said. "But I'm almost out of my mind worrying about my kids, I want to ask you something."

He sat up and rubbed his eyes. "Hellva time to talk about that." He said. "Shit, You could have brought it up before bed time."

"I know." She said. "But I have to tell you something even though you may not believe me. After all the things that have happened to me in the last few months I'm beginning to realize what a rotten person I have made out of myself. Believe It or not I have great respect for you, only wish I had felt that way from the start"

"Now I want to ask you a question, if I have to go away after the trial will you continue to live here and take care of the children until I get back?"

"No I only agreed to stay until after the trial, remember?" He replied. "Then the children will go live with their uncle Burl until you return, but the trial could change that."

"Yes I know and I agreed to that." She said. "But I'm afraid they will get attached to Burl and his family and will never want to live with me again. can't you see my point? They're all I have left, everything else is gone, decency, respect, pride of family, and self respect, which probably accounts for all the troubles that I have brought on myself and others."

She began to cry and sat down on the couch beside him. She leaned forward and rested her head on his shoulder.

"I know you'll never believe how sorry I am about Brad, he loved me and the children more than anything and I am sure he must have welcomed death rather than live out the rest of his life knowing that he would never have the opportunity to enjoy his children again.

And the way I treated you is shameful, what I'm trying to tell you is I'm a different person, I've been praying daily asking God to forgive me and I feel that he has, now I ask your forgiveness. Will you forgive me?"

He took her in his arms and held her tight as she cried uncontrollably.

'Damn.' He thought. 'She does seem like a different person."

He held her for a long time and thought about saying. 'Yes I forgive you, and I love you, we can start all over again.' But changed his mind when he thought of her mean and deceitful ways.

"Yes I'll forgive you." He said. "Now lets get back to sleep I have a long day ahead of me tomorrow."

He led her to the bedroom door. She stood close as they held hands, pulling him ever so slightly toward the bed.

He released his grip on her hands and whispered. "Good night."

He walked out closed the bedroom door behind him and slumped on the couch. Tears welled in his eyes and sleep wouldn't come.

'Damn! how in hell will I ever get this woman off my mind?' 'I know I'm a damned fool for letting her upset me like this, but dammit I can't help it, I know it's a sin to lust after her, guess I'll have to do some praying, shit! if God can forgive her I'm sure he'll forgive me.'

He put in long hours at the mine taking advantage of all the information that his boss passed on to him.

"You're coming along fine." The boss said. "I'm surprised, I knew you had some knowledge about coal mining but never dreamed you had this much. The mine foreman and all the section bosses that I have talked to already have great respect for you, and your assistant electrician that you promoted to your job, they tell me he's doing a top notch job."

"Hell I knew he would." Poor boy replied. "Shit he's a better electrician than I will ever be, damned if I can figure out how he does it, has no education and not a hell'va lot of experience, but by god he can get the job done. Only thing I can think of is God handed him a natural talent, but he sure as hell left me out I can't think of one thing that I'm really good at."

The boss grinned and said. "Well I don't know if God gave you the talent or not maybe he passed it out by mistake, but you have the most natural talent for cussing that I have ever ran across, and it's a good thing we're not in the office right now because Ann would be all over your case. And speaking of Ann, I have noticed some heavenly looks between you two, just want you to know you couldn't make a better choice, her husband was killed in a slate fall about three years ago and about the same time she had a miscarriage. Talk was that she said she would never marry again, but from what I've seen she has her sights set on you, personally I'd love to see you two team up and raise a family, something to think about before all the lead is gone from your pencil you're not getting any younger you know."

"Yeah you're right I do have feelings toward her and intend to get closer after the trial, I promised to stay right where I'm at until after the trial mostly for the kids sake. Gonna build a house on my fifteen acres, already got a contractor lined up construction will start in about two weeks. I can already vision Ann in the house with three or four little ones running and playing, shit, who knows we may wind up with ten or twelve."

"Oh yeah I can vision that.' The boss said. "But a vision is all it is because she'll never agree to that, maybe two or three but never as many as you want because the chances would be better that one of them would take after you and turn out to be a champion curser. And speaking of cussing if you have any more coming you better get it done now because we're headed back to the office you know Ann's rules."

"Yeah I know." He said. "That's the hardest part of this job not being allowed to talk natural around that damned office."

"Well its best you work on it because I can't imagine Ann allowing you to do that after the wedding and you move in that new house."

"Well shit, you would have to bring that up because I've thought about it before and know damned well I'll have to break th habit, but today is no time to start lets get back to that damned office."

"Did you notice that Rene has gained a lot of weight over the past few months? Could it be that she's pregnant? Remember the night I told you I shut her up in the laundry room and asked you to keep Peanut away from her because she was in heat?"

"No I don't recall any of that." He answered.

"Now come on be honest, did you put him with her after I went to bed that night?"

"Can't remember that either, shit with all that's been going on around here I'm lucky to remember how to get home from work some times."

"You know what I think, you're lying right through your tobacco stained teeth and I expect Rene to give birth to a litter of ugly pups any day now."

"Well shit!" He answered. What else can you expect, I know peanut is ugly as hell but you know yourself he's smart and loyal to all of us especially you, shit he'd go through hell for you even though he knows you make fun of him. And hell, I ain't seen you entering Rene in any dog shows, she looks just like any other French poodle they're all ugly to me except she's a little bigger than most and therefore more ugly. So tell me what can you expect from two ugly dogs?"

Hell I wouldn't trade Peanut for any blue ribbon winner because he's been loyal through thick and thin and I don't expect him to change."

Peanut was curled up in the doorway with his head cocked to one side Listening. He came and lay down at Poor Boy's feet.

"See what I mean he understands the word loyal, shit, he understands every thing we say."

"Okay let's see if he does." Then she asked. "Peanut, did he let you in to Rene that night? Did you get Rene pregnant?"

Peanut got up and walked toward her with his tail between his legs. She Scratched his head and said. "Its okay boy, can't blame you for fulfilling the call of nature."

Then she looked at Poor Boy. "You're right he does understand and he just made you out a liar."

"Oh shit." He said. "Telling a lie in this household ain't no big deal, why don't we just wait till they're born before we pass judgment I know they'll be ugly as hell but lets wait and see, and damn you Peanut, you shore as hell ain't very loyal when it comes to covering up for me, just remember that the next time you're laying outside a door begging to get on the other side for a night of lovemaking, damned if I'll open it for you."

She had to turn away to keep him from seeing the smile on her face. She headed for the kitchen and thought.

'He's a very unusual man and a lot of fun, too bad I didn't recognize that right from the start.' 'Thinking back I've never recognized anything much that was good and decent until now.' 'And I guess it came too late.'

She stood at the sink and cried.

Peanut landed in the seat beside him even before the old jeep came to a complete stop at the end of the porch. He was always excited to see him get home from work, but now he bounded up the steps and stood barking and wagging his tail.

"Damn Peanut! Why in hell are you so excited, you act like you ain't seen me in months."

As he followed Peanut through the door he could hear the children's excited voices coming from her bedroom.

'What in hells going on in there.' He thought. 'Ordinarily the kids are out on the porch or in the yard playing when I come home from work.'

He followed peanut to the open bedroom door and there they sat in a semicircle on the floor.

"Come on in." She said. "Our family has increased since you left for work this morning, three boys and a girl."

Rene lay on her side and four little creatures were tugging at her nipples.

Peanut kept jumping and barking as if waiting for his approval and praise.

"Ah hell Peanut." He said. "Cut out the noise, and congratulations to you for what ever that is that you're responsible for gnawing on them tits. Bout the ugliest pups I have ever laid my eyes on and believe me I have seen some ugly litters in my life time."

She looked away and smiled as the kids giggled.

She picked up one and reached it toward him. "Here." She said. "look at that face and ears."

He gently turned it in his hands obviously pleased with its features.

"Still say this is the ugliest litter that's ever been born." He said.

"Yeah I know." She replied. "ugly yes, but cute, the kids want that one, that is if their uncle Burl will allow them to bring it with them if they go there to stay while I'm away. You said you would keep Rene while I'm away, I was wondering if you would mind keeping one for me?"

"Well hell I reckon so, damn! Peanut and Rene are a handful now I'll be saddled with four."

"How do you come up with four?" She asked. "It's only three."

"Hell no it's four, cause I want to keep one of the ugly things for myself."

She turned her head to hide the smile as the kids roared with laughter. Finally she said.

"Well that leaves one that we'll have to find a home for."

As she watched him stroke the puppy remorse spread over her whole body thinking about how she had treated him and the father of her children before him. He handed her the puppy and walked out.

'Wish there was some way I could erase it all and start all over again.' She thought. 'But since that's impossible I'll do the best I can and try to hang on to my children, they're all I have left.'

Tears trickled down her cheeks, the children noticed and threw their arms around her.

'In spite of it all.' She thought. 'They still love me, they can see the change in me, I just wish that others could be that forgiving.'

She sat in silence looking out the sheriff's car window as it rolled across the Blue Grass country near Lexington. Horse farms lined both sides of the highway. One In particular caught her eye since it resembled her life long dream of some day owning a horse farm.

A white fence ran parallel to the highway, the deep rich color of the blue grass, a huge barn and a plantation style mansion beyond that formed a perfect background for the horses of many colors and markings as some stood looking over the fence while others munched on the blue grass.

Two colts were tugging at their mother's breasts while three older ones were racing down the fence line in what looked like each was hell bent on winning the race to the corner of the pasture. Their coats glistened in the early morning sun.

She became lost in her thoughts as the farms unfolded before her, each one different but all bore the same resemblance of being aristocratic and affluent.

She could picture herself and her children in that mansion and thought.

'That has been my life long dream to own a horse farm and be wealthy, guess that's what drove me to think I could make a lot of money in the drug ring and some day own one.'

As the miles ticked off and they neared Louisville, the picture of the mansion was replaced by the little house as Brad, her first husband worked to finish it.

She well remembered the joy that would show in his face as he backed off to admire a certain phase that he had just finished. 'That's where I was wrong.' She thought.

'I only thought of myself, and the kids, and was never satisfied. Wayne is right I am greedy.'

As the farms faded behind them replaced by the urban sprawl of Louisville, the vision of him dieing in far off Belgium and being denied to see his children grow up haunted her, and as they crossed the Ohio River on the way to a women's prison in Indiana, she cried.

The deputy sitting beside her removed her handcuffs and handed her a tissue.

"Give your wrists a rest." He said. "In fact I'll leave them off the rest of the way I'm a pretty good judge of people and I trust you."

"I'm sorry I'm such a baby." She said. "But the memories and regrets of what could have been overwhelmed me, I feel like this is the end of everything."

"That's okay." He said. "I've made this trip many times and most hold their tears through Louisville, but can't ever remember anyone crossing the Ohio River with dry eyes, I was beginning to wonder if you would be the first, and now that I see remorse I have hopes that you will serve your time and come out a different person. I understand you were sentenced to five years but will serve two and the other three under probation, is that right?"

"Yes." She said. "But it will seem like a life time away from my kids."

"Yes I know but try to keep a level head and think positive and the two years will go by before you know it."

"I hope you're right." She said. "I can't wait to get back home again even though I feel that I've had my chance in life and have made a mess of it."

The deputy took her hand and said. "You can still make something of your life, give me a call when you get out." He wrote his phone number down.

"You can bring your kids and visit us, we have three rowdy ones that they can be with, and my wife likes to help folks that need a lift." He squeezed her hand and asked. "Is it a deal?"

"Sure," She answered. "You are very kind and I do appreciate it very much."

The deputy driving looked back and said. "Lady you can take him at his word he and his wife have helped many like yourself get back on the straight and narrow."

Two hours later the driver turned the wheel to the right and a gray dismal building appeared before them.

"Well here it is." He said. I wish you luck just obey the rules and do as they tell you and you'll be surprised how much more pleasant your stay will be here."

As she stared at the huge building surrounded by a high metal fence tears started down her face again.

The deputy handed her a tissue and said. "Sorry but I'll have to put the cuffs back on they have strict rules here, might cost me my job if I didn't."

A guard looked at the papers and waved them through the gate. Once inside the building, papers were again presented signed and exchanged by both sides.

The deputies watched them escort her down a long hallway and listened to the familiar loud clang of the iron-gate that led to another long hallway with cells on both sides.

"Lets get out of here." The driver said. "I can never get used to this experience."

"Yeah I know." His buddy replied. "Makes me want to cry."

The kids went to live with their uncle Burl and his family and fit in right from the start. They were assigned chores to do daily around the house after getting home from school. "It's only fair that they help out around the house just like our own." He and his wife agreed.

"As rules apply lets treat them just as we do our own." His wife stated.

"Makes no sense to have two different set of rules that would only cause jealousy among them."

"Yes I agree." Burl replied. "I want them to be happy here and if we treat them as our own they will feel contented and wanted."

266

The kids had brought their pup along with the one that hadn't been claimed until Burl and his family laid eyes on him.

"We have to find a home for that one." Poor Boy had said. Burl looked at the pleading faces of his wife and children and knew that he was about to take on one of the ugliest puppies he had ever seen. "Can we have him?" he asked.

Poor Boy looked over at Julie who sat on the other end of the porch refusing to take part in the conversation. "Is it okay for them to take this homeless ugly mutt?" He asked. She smiled and answered. "Yes, its okay with me just make sure you feed him and treat him well."

"I promise we'll treat him well, and our dog will be happy to have him around to run and play with." The kids jumped with joy and she smiled again knowing that the puppy had found a good home.

Now six months later as they watched them playing hide and seek among the shrubbery Burl said.

"They sure have grown, only thing is they haven't improved any in their looks only difference is their size, now we have more ugly to look at."

"I know." His wife Laura answered. "But they are so cute I wouldn't take nothing for them and I bet you wouldn't either."

"Yes you're right." He replied. "They have grown on me and the ugly devils have a home here as long as they want to stay. But I guess the kids will take theirs along with them when she returns from prison."

"Yes that's what worries me." His wife replied. "I hate to see the kids go back to her, but in a way it might be best after all she is their mother and they care for her and she cares for them that's plain to see the way she clung to them the day they took her away, I felt so sorry for her being a mother myself I can feel the hurt she must be going through."

"Yes I know." He said. "Who knows she may come out all together a different person, I sure hope so for the kids sake. She'll have to tow the line or she'll lose them for good the judge made that plain."

"You can have your children back after you serve your sentence but you must live within the law or else I will put them with the Burl Crawford family for good." The judge had stated.

"You know I pray that she will take her children and do the right thing by them because that's where they belong, and I have a feeling she will because I seen a change in her in the months before they took her away, and at times I felt like taking her in my arms and having an old fashioned cry that only two women can understand. I can sense why you may not feel that way toward her after the way she treated your brother Brad, but I believe she has changed and became the person she could have been long ago because deep down she is a good person."

"Well I guess this will surprise you." He answered. "I feel the same way and at times find myself pulling for her."

She put her arms around his neck and said. "I'm so glad you feel that way because everyone deserves another chance especially her with three children about the only thing that she has left worth living for."

"And you have to admire Wayne 'Poor Boy' for agreeing to take care of her horses and dogs while she's away, ain't many that would do that he is a very special person."

"Yes he is." She answered. "I'll be glad when he and Ann get married and move in that new house, I hear its about finished."

"Yeah, I ran into him yesterday. "He replied. " He wants us to come over there this weekend, said, "I'll give you a tour of that damned house that's taking every penny that I can scrape up, shit I'll be bankrupt before the thing is finished."

"But that's all talk because he's bringing in good money from the superintendents job there at the mine. He had just got back from Harlan driving a brand new Buick station wagon, said he needed it to haul Julie's kids around and take them to a movie once in a while, That's the first time I've ever heard him call her by her name he has always called her Princess. He asked if it would be okay to take our kids along. I told him I'd ask you."

"Sure its okay with me. " She said. "Its better that they all go and be together."

"He agreed to stay where he is until the house is finished, said his electrician at the mine is getting married and wants to rent Julie's house."

"I'll look after it and bank the rent money for her, guess that's the least I can do." He said. "Don't know why in hell I should after the way she treated me, but shit she's paying for it and hell who knows she might come back a new person, latch on to some one and live out the rest of her life at peace with herself."

"Burl why do you have to use all his cuss words when you tell me what he said, can't you tell it without using them?"

"Well shit I don't know." He answered. "Hell it wouldn't sound like him without using the damned cuss words."

Shock showed on her face as she stared at him.

"Do you realize that's the first time I've heard you utter curse words since we've been married? I sure am glad the kids are out of earshot, you keep that up and you'll find yourself under my orders to quit the habit just like Ann has told Wayne."

"Aw come on." He said. I was just kidding, wanted to see your reaction and now that I have I'm about to have a good laugh."

As he roared with laughter he reached out and pulled her to him. I promise you'll never hear them words again from me even though it would be worth it just to see your face change colors."

She squeezed him tight and the words slipped out before she could even think.

"You shit ass." She said. "I thought you were serious, hell don't worry me like that."

As he gazed into her eyes she dropped her head in shame. Finally she said. "Now believe me that slipped out, we're even I promise never to do it again."

"Yeah I know." He said. "You put on a good act and I get the point, it don't sound good coming from either of us its best we leave the cussing to Wayne."

She squeezed him even tighter and said. "Aw you, shut up before I cry."

It became a common sight on weekends to see Ann and Poor Boy tooling along in the new Buick accompanied by four dogs and sometimes the kids including Burl's.

Rene and Peanut were no problem but the two ugly pups were forever chewing on the upholstery, leaping from the back seat to the front, keeping Ann busy as she tried to calm them down before he went into a cussing fit. So far he had kept it in check at the office. But a few times she had seen him on the verge and could almost hear the words that she knew he was trying to keep from spilling out.

Then one day he said. "What say we go over in Lee County, Virginia this weekend just you and me?"

"Okay." She answered. "I would love to I've never been there. But what about the dogs?"

"Oh hel—heck they can come along, we'll stay one night with my brother Cliff and his wife Barbara shi—shucks they keep a house full of dogs they won't mind."

She noticed he looked embarrassed and said.

"That's okay I like the words you're replacing them with, I know it's hard to do but you'll be able to control it soon now."

"Oh shi—shucks I don't know some times I wonder if I'll ever be able to stop the damn—durned cuss words, I'm lost without them."

She reached out and they came together, as he held her he thought.

269

'Damn! I have to try, I can't afford to lose this woman shit, she's the third one and I sure as hell may never have another chance.' 'So from now on I'm gonna give it all I got to overcome this Damned cussing habit.' 'Be a damned crazy fool to let that stand between me and her, so right now by god I'm about to turn a new leaf no more of this cussing shit, hell I feel better already.'

As she looked at him she wondered what he was thinking. She asked. "What's on your mind? You look so serious."

"Well by go—george it is serious." He said.

"I was just thinking how hard it is for me to try not to say these damn—durned cuss words around you, believe me I've tried but it ain't easy sure as hel—heck don't want to lose you because of it, shi—shucks I like your company."

"Oh hell I guess what I'm trying to say is I love you and the damned house is finished and I need you there to make it a happy home for me."

"Are you proposing to me?" She asked. "Because if you are we've got wedding plans to make, and the words you just used in your proposal I'll let them slide this time but watch your mouth from here on if you don't want it washed out with lye soap."

"Oh hel—help me God I didn't realize I said them forgive me and I'll never utter the damn—durned things again."

"Okay." She said. "It's going to take a while but with a little more time I feel that you will conquer it, don't you?"

"Hell yes I know I can." He answered.

She turned away to hide the laughter in her eyes and said. Well lets get going we have a lot of planning to do." 'Oh hell.' He thought. 'But Damn! She's worth it.'

"Here we are at the state line. A fellow by the name of Roop lives right there just barely on the Kentucky side. He's lived there for as long as I can remember."

"Now we're in Lee County, Virginia, I was born and raised in this county and it holds a lot of memories, some good and some bad."

"Gonna make a left here on the Elys Creek road, a couple of places I want to see and then we'll drive on over to Pucketts Creek and head for Keokee. We have plenty of time I told Cliff that we wouldn't get there till late this afternoon."

"See that little Church? That's Pine Grove Baptist Church I staggered in there one night during prayer meeting dam—durn near got religion guess I would have if I hadn't been loaded to the gills, I can still hear the song they were singing can't think of the title but had a verse that said something like, 'Come home, Come home, Ye who are weary come home."

"Rented that little house there for a short time got two months rent behind and had to move out."

Ann looked at him in surprise. "You mean to tell me you walked in that church drunk? You should have known better than that."

"I shore did Ann not only that church but I walked every foot of this road drunk almost every day. I lived a hard life for a long time all because of that damn—darn letter."

"What letter?" She asked.

"I'll tell you all about it some time Ann, it's a long sad story that you need to know about, no sense in me trying to hide it, me and Tex found out long ago that hidden truths never serve any purpose but to hurt people."

He came to a stop at an old abandoned truck mine. "Well there it is Peanut, look it's ready to fall down and the weeds about to take over."

Peanut's ears stood straight up and he began to whimper and scratch on the upholstery to get out.

"Me and peanut will have a look first and then you can get out with the other dogs, we'll have to watch them dam—durn ugly pups around that slate dump shi—shucks they might start a land slide."

As soon as he opened the car door Peanut hit the ground running headed toward the old shack and disappeared inside. He followed peanut through the open door that hang on one hinge. The musty smell and the picture before him stirred his memories of another time in his life and tears began to trickle down his cheeks.

Old rusty nails still protruded from the now bare walls where once he had hung strings of shuck beans, an old galvanized tub, frying pan, and pieces of worn out clothing including the old smelly jacket that carried that damned letter for so many years.

One of the cross ties that kept his make shift bed off the dirt floor lay there half buried with leaves that had blown through the half open door.

The legs on the old potbelly stove had settled into the dirt floor pulling free of the stovepipe that dangled above it.

He could hear Peanut whimpering in a dark corner. "What th hell Peanut, why are you back there crying? Shit, I need you here with me."

As his eyes adjusted to the darkness he could see Peanut nuzzling something and as he moved closer he could make out three little furry creatures in the leaves obviously hungry and trying to nurse from Peanut thinking that he was their mother.

"Damn! Peanut, what have we here? Here let me see." He picked one up. "Shit, can't be no more than a week or two old, wonder where th momma is?"

He walked out and hollered to Ann. "Bring the dogs and come up here got something for you to see."

The ugly pups were the first ones there, trying to get at the litter but Peanut stood guard snapping and growling to hold them at bay.

"Come on in." he said. "Look back there in that dark corner, be careful of that stove pipe hanging there."

"See that litter of pups? Can't be more than a week or two week old, their momma must be out scrounging for food, some bastard must have dropped her off I hate bastards that'll do that. They can't have any damn conscious at all, their ass belongs in jail." Then he realized he had got caught up in his emotions and broken Ann's rule big time.

He moved closer and laid his hand on her shoulder.

"I'm sorry Ann, forgive me I got carried away."

"I know." She said. "To tell you the truth I think I'd feel better if I could express myself like that some times especially right now looking at that starving litter. Do you think the mother will be back?"

"I think she will." He answered. "Guess she has to roam around every day to find something to eat. We'll go back to the car and wait a few minutes, we'll have to keep the dogs in the car she'll tear them up to protect her pups."

They sat in the car as peanut whined. "Yeah I know Peanut you're worried about the little devils, well you're not alone we are too."

"Tell me something Wayne, why did you stop at this shack in the first place?"

"Me and Peanut used to live there, you notice how bad he wanted out and ran straight inside?"

"You mean to tell me you lived in that place?"

"Yes I did and loaded coal in the mine, see that slate dump? Peanut used to go sit there every day and wait for me to come out of the mine."

"See yonder where the dirt has slid down and sealed the entrance? My guess is that it's worked out, either that or the demand for that kind of coal hit rock bottom."

"Like I said I have some things that I need to tell you about myself, won't be easy because some of it is shameful and dam—darned unpleasant but its better out than hidden inside me."

They had sat there for about fifteen minutes when she said.

"Wayne, can you make out what that is alongside the road up ahead? I hope it's not what I think it is."

"Oh yeah." He answered. " I think it's what you think it is, lets roll up there and have a look."

There she lay with flies feeding from dried blood around her head from where she had been hit by a car. Without a word he backed the car to the shack, got out and brought the litter to the car.

Ann placed the litter on the floor at her feet, Peanut sat in between them keeping the other dogs in the back seat.

Then he drove alongside the lifeless body stopped and dug a hole just off the shoulder of the road with an old rusty shovel that he found near the slate dump.

He lowered the frail body gently in the hole and covered it with the red clay dirt mixed with small pieces of slate and coal.

When finished he stood with his back to the car looking toward the hillside before him.

Ann sat in the car with the little ones nudging at her feet trying to find nourishment for their hungry tummies. And as she watched him she knew exactly why he was lingering and gazing at the hillside, because she was crying too.

Finally he got in and said.

"Cliff and Barbara will be glad to get them and they'll figure out some way to give them milk."

As they drove through the Pucketts Creek community he said. "Hey look Peanut, there's the old Dean store building, looks like its out of business, too bad it ain't open I'd get some bread and bolney. Remember the time we stopped there on our way to Keokee Peanut? Tex came along and let us ride in that shiny black convertible, never forget that day and how it broke his heart when he read the letter."

He glanced over at Ann and noticed the puzzled look on her face. "I'll tell you all about it some time, like I said it's a long story."

At Stone Creek, he stopped at a grocery store and came out with a small cardboard box. "Here Ann put em in this box, I see they're trying to feed off your toes, bet you wish you hadn't wore sandals today. Here I got a pint of milk, maybe you can dip your finger in and put it to their mouth, but not much because it's cold, might do them more harm than good. Won't take long to get to Cliff and Barbara's and we can warm the milk, they'll know what to do,

Barbara should have been a Veterinarian she really knows how to take care of their pets."

"Right there on the left is the Clabe Barton place, remember that name Ann because its a big part of the story more than I care to talk about, but like I said its better to let out old hidden truths."

She laid her hand on his leg and said. "You know something you haven't uttered or even slipped a curse word since we left that shack and I'm proud of you."

"Well I'm trying." He replied. "The last time I visited Cliff and Barbara she threatened to throw me out. Clean up your language." She said. "I'm sick and tired of listening to it."

"So I figure it best to start practicing right now sure would hate to spoil things, one woman on your case is bad enough, but by god two is more than a man can bear, shit, its better to go along with whatever they want."

She leaned over and looked in his face, startled he realized what he had said. "Oh hell Ann, them words slipped out honest they did I didn't mean to say a damn one of them."

She turned away and smiled. 'This man is impossible I don't believe he'll ever overcome that habit, it's going to be fun watching him squirm when we both get on his case.'

"Okay we're here, that's Cliff in the swing on the porch wonder what he's going to say when he sees four dogs headed that way plus three more in that box."

Cliff rose from the swing trying to quiet the half dozen dogs on the porch as they reared to the top of the railings wanting to get at the four dogs that were invading their territory.

Barbara came to the door to see what all the commotion was about.

In a loud kidding voice he said. "Look Barbara Allen there comes Wayne again with a passel of dogs, they'll eat us out of house and home unless they brought their own food in that box she's carrying, and speaking of her, she's the only good looking one in the bunch, look at them ugly dogs and Wayne has always been ugly."

The dogs rubbed noses through the gate at the top of the steps and he let them in.

Pretty soon they settled down and other than a growl here and there they started getting acquainted.

Wayne introduced them to Ann.

"Here let me take that box." Barbara said. I'll put it in the house."

"Oh no." Cliff said. "Do you see what's in that box? A litter of pups, my lord lets total up here, thirteen dogs right here on this porch and two more in the house."

They proceeded to tell them about the puppies as Barbara examined each one and held them to her cheek.

She looked at Cliff and said. "Are you thinking the same thing I am?"

"I think so." He answered. "And I believe she'll let them nurse."

"Come on follow me." He said. "I believe Susie will feed these starving puppies."

They followed him to the laundry room closing the front door behind them to keep the other dogs on the porch.

There on the floor lay a sad faced mixed breed mostly hound and God only knows what else with a lone puppy tugging at her nipples.

"Took her in two days ago, she only had the one pup, some body must have dropped her off I know she had more than one, no telling what happened to the others. Don't know her name or even if she has one, we call her Susie."

"Gimmie one and I'll hold it to her nose, here Susie look what we brought you." He held each one to her face as she licked them as if they were her own.

Then he said. "Put them to her nipples I'll hold her head just in case she won't accept them."

Each one found a nipple and began to feed she showed no signs of refusal so he turned her head loose.

Excitement showed in their faces as they watched the little balls of fur tugging at her nipples along side her puppy, which was twice their size.

Poor Boy's face lit up with total joy and he couldn't contain himself

"Beats all I ever seen." He said. "Damned if I can believe it, here we find a motherless litter and bring them to a mother that has lost most of her litter, Shit, it's hard to believe that things like this happen.'

It got deathly quiet and he realized he had slipped up and headed for the door.

Ann and Barbara exchanged knowing glances and smiled.

They talked till near midnight. "I want you all to come over and look at our new house some weekend."

"You mean to tell me you all went out and tied the knot without letting us know. Cliff asked. "We didn't even know you were engaged."

"Well hel—shi—cripes sake Cliff I guess we were never engaged but we both knew that it was bound to happen, at least I did. And we're not married yet but will be in a few days."

"Okay, so tell us when the wedding is taking place and we'll come for that and that way we can see the house all in one trip."

Poor Boy looked at Ann. "When is it Ann?"

She began to squirm and finally said. "I don't know we didn't discuss that."

Then Cliff, seen an opening for some good-natured joshing.

"Ann did he propose to you at all? I've got a feeling this is his way of proposing."

"Oh yes he proposed."

"Did he get on his knees? tell me about it."

"Aw come on Cliff." Poor Boy said. "You're going to stir up all them damn bad words inside me again." Then he thought 'There I go again.' They all roared with laughter, he couldn't see the fun in it but he joined in anyway.

At bedtime Cliff took Poor Boy aside and asked. "What kind of sleeping arrangements are you two used to?"

"Hell what you mean by that?" He replied. "Shit we're not married yet and I've never tried to take advantage of her, I respect her too much to try and rush things. Damn! You remember how I used to walk the roads in a drunken stupor and lived on a dirt floor, but I'm not there anymore, shit, I see a better life ahead with Ann and by god I intend to live it."

"Yeah I know Wayne, Barbara and I talk about it a lot, just yesterday she said. "He had to be a good person right from the start to finally overcome what Bonnie did to him. All kidding aside we're pulling for you, God knows you deserve it after all you've went through since then with princess, by the way what is her name? You never told us."

"Julia, I understand she went by Julie until I married her and started calling her Princess. She was a very unusual unpredictable woman and that's too bad because I feel that deep down inside she's a good person if she can ever overcome greed. I just hope she'll find herself and come back a different person for the kids sake, she does love them, you can't take that away from her."

The next day Sunday they left in the early afternoon but not before having another look at the litter of pups.

Their little tummies were filled out and strength had replaced weakness in their wobbly legs to the point where Susie's pup was growing tired of them ganging up on him in play. He would tire out and roll on his back with his feet stuck up to fend them off. His strength and size allowed him to send them sprawling with just one slap of a paw or kick of a leg.

They laughed as they watched the puppies roll from his swats only to come back for more.

"Old Buster has his hands full with that bunch." Barbara remarked.

Poor Boy laughed and said. "Is that what you call him?" I never heard a dog called that before."

"Yes you're looking at Buster fighting off two of his adopted brother's and one sister." She answered.

"You thought up any names for the little devils yet?" He asked.

"Sure have." She answered. "I would like to name them after you and Ann if you don't mind, and seeing that Cliff and I agreed to keep them I think we should have the right to name them what ever we want to."

"Oh hel—god help me! Wayne ain't no name for a dog, shi—shucks couldn't be much worse unless it was George."

"No it wont be Wayne, tell him Cliff."

"We want to call one of them Poor Boy, we was talking last night about how you lived in that shack for so long and we wondered if you would ever rise above it. And of course you have gone far beyond any of our expectations and we are proud of you."

"So we thought it would be fitting to name one of them Poor boy. Think about it, do you think it coincidence, or was it providence that caused you to go by that old shack that holds so many unpleasant memories of your past?"

"And there you found three starving puppies waiting for their mother that would never return and you brought them straight here to another mother that has lost all her litter but one, its all too perfect Wayne, no one else can design something like that, has to be Providence, truly the work of God."

He shuffled his feet and they could see he was clearly touched. "Then go ahead." He said. "I guess you're right because something kept nagging me to go by that old shack even though I didn't care for Ann to see it, I was ashamed for her to know I ever lived like that, and at the same time I knew I had to tell her about my past cause me and Tex found out that hidden truths never benefit anyone."

"So go ahead, hang any name you want to on them because I think that might be a part of the plan also and who am I to question God's work?"

Barbara dropped to her knees and picked one up. "This little girl will be called Ann." She said. "And this one is Poor Boy, and this one will answer to Providence. We'll find homes for them with the understanding they keep the names."

Ann came to Poor Boy's side and slipped one arm around his waist. "Yes

I truly believe in providence." She said. "Because my life went to pieces to the point where I could no longer vision ever having some one to love and be loved but that all changed when I met this kind gentle man."

"Aw come on." He said, as they embraced. "I can be mean as he—all git out sometimes."

Finally he said. "Well we better get rolling, got to go by St. Charles and see Reba and Wayne my namesake, I know that name Wayne won't be used much though because he will always be Tex Jr. which is only fitting."

Cliff and Barbara watched them cross the yard to the car with Peanut all excited knowing he was about to go on another adventure with Poor Boy and anything could happen, while Rene tagged along in her own demure way not expecting any thing out of the ordinary to happen, but the two ugly pups romped and threw their bodies against each other in play not caring one way or the other.

Ann waved as they pulled away and when the din from the barking dogs on the porch finally stopped. Cliff looked at Barbara, shook his head and said. "Whew! That's quite a bunch Barbara Allen, quite a bunch, but a good bunch."

"Yes it is." She answered. "And I've got a feeling that there will be additions and it will be a happy bunch for many years to come."

"I hope so." He said. "They deserve it and I pray that God will model them after us because he truly knew what he was doing when he put us together."

"I know." She said. "That's why I so strongly believe in providence."

They held each other for a long time, both with the same thoughts of love and understanding.

Poor Boy held little Tex as he flailed his arms wanting to play with the dogs.

"Oh yes." Reba said. "He loves dogs, begs to pet our neighbor's dog every time he sees him outside. Mom and dad want to get him one, dad says every little boy should have a dog and momma grew up with dogs, she said I shouldn't deprive him of having one, but I never cared that much for dogs maybe because I never was around them very much when I was small."

"So far I have held out and said no but its times like this when I see the joy on his face as he begs to pet and hold a dog that if someone came along and offered me one I would take it."

Poor boy lowered little Tex to the floor and Peanut came wagging his tail and licked his hand, a wide grin lit up his joyful face and he wrapped his arms around Peanut's neck. They all watched a thing of love and beauty as he rested his cheek against Peanut's ear.

Poor Boy and Ann exchanged knowing glances.

"Well by go—gosh you're about to become the owner of a dog." He said. "We know where you can get the pick of a litter and it will be available as soon as the mother weans them, ain't no Pedigree, will grow into a medium size dog.

Looks like a mixture of Fox hound, Blue Tick, Beagle, and god knows what else, might even be some dog in th mixture."

Reba listened dumbfounded knowing that she had put herself in an indefensible position, but as she looked at little Tex still holding Peanut tight her field of defense melted like butter.

"Okay." She stammered. "I guess Tex is about to become a dog owner." Her mother and father smiled. "You won't be sorry." Her mother said.

"He'll be a perfect master." Her father stated. "Just look at the devotion he shows toward a strange dog, wait till he gets his own, yes sir ain't nothing like a boy and his dog."

They proceeded to tell them about finding the pups at the old shack and taking them to a strange mother that accepted them to her supply of life saving nourishment.

"We'll call and tell Cliff and Barbara that you want one." Ann said.

"But you might ought to run up there in the next couple of weeks and pick the one you want, that way you'll get the pick of the litter. We've already named them, the female Ann, and the other two, one Poor Boy, and the other Providence."

Reba smiled and asked. "You mean you gave them your names?"

"No Cliff and Barbara insisted on the names and we don't mind." Ann replied.

"How about the other name Providence how does that name apply to a dog?"

"Well, we all agreed that it was something more than coincidence that caused us to go by the old shack and find a starving litter of pups and proceed to take them to a mother that had lost all her litter but one and took them as her own."

"So Cliff and Barbara thought it only fitting that one should be honored with the name Providence."

Then Poor Boy spoke up. "And that ain't where the story ends, we drive in here today and hear you say. Its times like this that if someone came along and offered me one I would take it. No telling how far it will go shi—shucks ain't none of us here that knows what God can do, all I know is this providence has opened my eyes."

"Well I can't see any reason to go pick out one." Reba said. "Tell them we want Poor Boy." They all laughed."

Then they told her about their wedding plans. "We'll let you know as soon as we decide on the date." Ann said. "Bring your father and mother with you, and little Poor Boy if his mother has weaned him by then."

"How old is little Tex here?" Poor Boy asked as he held him close.

"Soon be two." Reba replied. "Fifteenth of next month."

"Oh good." Poor Boy replied. "Maybe our wedding will be about the same time, Hell—heck if it is we'll put them together and have a jolly old time."

They waved goodbye and headed home. "Why don't you tell me the long story about yourself on the way home." Ann said. "That will help the miles go by."

"Okay.' He said. "May as well, been wanting to get it off my chest, no better time than now I guess."

As they drove along he told in great detail the way he had lived most of his life. About the letter he got from Bonnie and how it broke his heart and he eventually wound up in the old shack listening to country music that seemed to have been written just for him and his troubled mind.

About Tex and how he almost married his half sister. "I swore I would never tell him who his dad was Ann, but in the end I had to show him that damned letter, it broke his heart, hell I could have stood back and watched him marry his half sister but I didn't want to go on living the rest of my life with that on my conscious. In the end he got over it and found happiness with Reba but only for a short time. Don't seem right that he had to die without ever seeing his baby, sometimes I wonder if life is fair Ann."

"Well I guess I about covered it all you know the rest, my last marriage and how it about put me back on the roads again, believe me the temptation of the bottle almost got the best of me a few times. But now I see my future with you and can vision a happy home with little ones running around at our feet, and watching them grow."

"I can see that too, how many you want?" She asked.

"Oh hell I don't know." He answered. "Maybe ten, would twelve be too many?"

She leaned over and rested her head on his shoulder. "You know something I'll be happy with you no matter what if it's six, seven, ten, a dozen or even one, I feel that we belong together."

He leaned over and kissed her cheek. "Yeah I know." He said. "I guess it's meant for some souls to suffer through much of their lives but in the end find peace and happiness, maybe it's providence, whatever it is I'll take it." They rode in silence the rest of the way day dreaming about their future together.

One year and three months later on a warm spring morning Ann sits peacefully on the front part of the wrap around porch of the sprawling house nestled against dense woods at the back of the fifteen acres.

Five hundred yards away to her right the metal roof on the barn glistens in the morning sun and she can see her father busy taking care of the horses needs, while the two ugly pups now one and a half years old and somewhat maturing out of their puppy ways but still very bold and frisky especially around the horses running along the fence line.

Her mother passed away shortly after her and Wayne married and her father asked if he could work with the horses. "I could drive over every day." He had said. "I love to work with horses my dad always had horses when I was growing up, he taught me to ride and I'm sure I could teach the children that you two have spoken about how to ride. I need to keep myself busy or else I'll just sit around all day thinking about your mother, God knows I will never forget her but I should try and get on with my life."

She remembered Wayne saying. "Oh hel—I mean oh yeah, you come over and work with them horses anytime you want to, in fact why don't you move in with us, don't know what in hel—oh shi—what I was thinking about when I had this house built, who in hel—why would anybody want a six bedroom house?"

"So we have plenty of room and I was hoping you'd take over the horses, lord knows I'm too busy, besides I know nothing about horses anyway, shit, I don't know which side to get on one. Would be my luck to be on one and Peanut would spook him and he'd throw me off and break my neck."

She remembered her father saying. "No I'd rather stay where I'm at, it ain't that far to drive over here. And I can teach you to ride too Wayne."

"Oh hell no, I ain't that keen on learning to ride but you can teach Princess kids and Burl and Laura's kids if they don't mind."

A clean white washed fence enclosed the fifteen acres with a cross fence running from just behind the barn and in front of the house to the fence on the other side, about two acres around the house free of horses and the mess they can make.

She smiled as she thought of Wayne and his never ending, "Why in hel—did I fence off two acres for the house? Shi—hel—oh well what I mean is I should have left it all open for the horses that way you could sit here on th porch and feed them, two acres is too dam—too durn much grass to mow."

Her father had done a great job teaching the kids to ride especially Princess's (Julie) kids they picked it up right away.

"It seems so natural for them." her father had said. "I guess they get that from their mother I hear she is good with horses and a darn good rider."

Burl and Laura agreed to let their children participate also. And they were learning more every day about the horses and riding. The whole gang showed up about twice a week. She smiled again as she thought about what her and Wayne had talked about just before they were married she could hear him now. "How many do you want ten, would twelve be too many?"

Thinking back she knew he was kidding but now realized how much he loved kids or else he wouldn't tolerate the noisy gang that swarmed over their house at least twice a week.

She looked down at little two-month old Alvin Wayne his mouth had finally gone lax from her nipple and was now sleeping. She smiled as she admired his facial features that looked so much like his father.

"We've got a start she whispered. "Maybe two more, at least one, a girl would be fine."

His performance at the mine surpassed all expectations and soon he was more than just the superintendent he sat in on board meetings and became a roving ambassador to other Blue Diamond operations throughout Kentucky and Virginia helping solve sluggish problems that had slowed their daily production of coal. His salary increased at a fast rate and soon the house was free of mortgage and the bank account grew.

He purchased an adjoining farm consisting of twenty-seven acres complete with tractor, plows, hay baler, a small barn and a silo.

"We can use most of that land to help feed the horses Ann. Shit buying hay for them will break you up, bout time we start growing our own."

He tore down the dividing fence and combined the two farms. He would hop on the tractor with little Alvin cradled in one arm while Peanut found a seat on a fender and drive all over the fifteen acres in front of the house.

One day he said."Ann you can drive this thing."

"I don't know." She said. That thing looks scary to me."

"Aw come on." He said. "You drive everything else, if you can drive that old two ton truck there you sure as hel—can drive this thing."

Soon she mastered it and about anything else that pertained to the farm. She found it relaxing unlike being confined to her past office job.

She remembered the day before they were wed when he said with authority.

"Now by go—gosh Ann, you won't be going back to your job, no sir I want you to stay home and take care of the young-ins."

"We don't have any to take care of." She replied.

"Well it won't take long to get started." He said. "And look at it this way, I won't have to worry about using them words around the office that come so natural for me."

"I wouldn't bet on that." She said. "My replacement might come down on you harder than I have."

Meanwhile many miles away in Indiana, the stark gray building looked cold and foreboding in the morning fog. In side she had been assigned to the laundry room and was busy folding fresh bleached bed sheets making sure to get them folded and stacked just as she had been told. No in between would be tolerated, they had to be folded and stacked as to the prison rules and regulations.

So far she had obeyed and put up with more than she should have at times, all for the sake of her kids that were constantly on her mind all day and deep into each night.

Burl's family had encouraged them to write to her often and she cherished every letter she received from them. She only had six months left to serve and each letter seemed to put her closer to them.

Words and sentences like this appeared in every letter.

"Momma we miss you so much and can't wait till you get home. We all are making good grades in school. Wayne takes us to Harlan to see the movies almost every week. Uncle Burl took us fishing yesterday, we had a lot of fun he said he'd take us again soon."

"Ann's dad taught us how to ride, you should see your horses mom, they're so sleek and healthy looking. Rene is the same I know she misses you. And your ugly pup, what can I say he has grown a lot but like Wayne says, the only difference is there's more ugly to look at. Ha."

"Well bye for now mom, we all love you and want you home again."

As she folded and stacked the mountain of sheets the letters ran through her mind causing her whole body to warm and glow with pride but at the same time cause her to wonder if because of love and kindness toward them from others that maybe they were slowly slipping away from her. And without fail tears would start and continue for as long as her thoughts dwelled on that subject.

'I lived my life in a reckless way never giving much thought to doing the right thing for myself or others.' She would think. 'And now when I see how wrong I was I have already lost about everything that makes up a family and a happy life.' 'I never thought it would come down to having to worry about losing my kids the only thing I can think of that has kept me from ending it all.'

'Of course I have no one to blame but myself it all started when I treated Brad the way I did, I doubt if God will ever forgive me for that, I pray daily and ask his forgiveness but it is constantly on my conscious.'

'I went down the same path with Wayne, he's a good man and deserved something better than me and my mean and deceitful ways.'

'It hurt me when we divorced and he later married Ann, but now I feel happy for him, maybe now he can get on with his life and father a child of his own.' 'Ann will be a good mother and wife unlike myself greed was my first priority. '

A few months later she walked down the hall escorted by a uniformed security officer to the prison office. And as the familiar sound of the iron-gate closed behind them she felt a sense of freedom for the first time in two years.

After signing several papers and answering numerous questions she was given a bus ticket home.

"Your stay here has been complimentary and free of any kind of resentment of authority on your part, and we here at this institution would hope that when you leave here you continue that in your every day life and we hope to never see you here again."

"Thank you." She said. "I never intend to walk through that door again, and I must admit that you have treated me well and I thank you for that."

The big bus windows gave a clear view of the flat lands of Indiana as it rolled toward Kentucky.

'Two wasted years.' She thought. 'Two years away from my children, two years that could well be the difference between whether they will want to live with me or in the end prefer to stay with Burl and Laura.'

'But I guess the truth is the most of my life has been wasted, and I have no one to share the blame with because I am the sole owner of the way I chose to live.'

'If only I could get over the way I treated Brad I believe I could go on but the wrongness of what I did to him has to surpass all the other bad things I am guilty of, God only knows how sorry I am about that and I have asked for his forgiveness and mercy but I feel it will forever haunt me and maybe that's the Lords way of punishment, if so I have it coming.'

Soon a tall building appeared ahead partially obscured by patchy fog, but then became more visible along with other buildings of various sizes revealing the skyline of Louisville, as the bus drew closer.

As it crossed the Ohio River she began to cry just as she had when she crossed it going the other direction two years ago.

An elderly man sitting next to her said. "Pardon me for asking lady are you crying because you're happy or is it because you're sad? That way I'll know the right words to say to make you feel better."

"Oh I guess it's a little of both sir. I'm happy that we are now in Kentucky because I feel closer to home, but the years behind me especially the last two in Indiana cause me nothing but sadness."

"I'm sorry to hear that and I have no idea what you have done in your past and intend to do in the future but from my own experiences in life I know that you can overcome all of it and live out the rest of your life in a way that will over shadow the bad and make you feel like a new person. It's relatively simple, all you have to do is go to our Lord and ask forgiveness. And don't just walk away and wait for his results, go to him daily until you have formed your own special relationship with him and you'll soon get results."

"I tell you this because what he has done for me, twenty years ago my whole sorry rotten life caught up to me, I lost my wife and two children due to alcohol, gambling, and neglect, topped off with dealing in stolen property."

"I served a term in prison and came out confused as to how I should try to overcome my past. I listened and tried different things from honorable law abiding citizens but nothing seemed to heal the feelings I had of my checkered past, so one day I fell to my knees and literally gave up, I said Lord, I have tried to rid myself of all the sins in my past but it looks impossible. So I ask you to take me out of this world I can no longer stand to awaken each morning looking forward to a day of sadness and regret."

"And you know as I waited for some kind of signal that he might grant my wish I could feel a change taking place in my life. I rose to my feet and looked out the window and for the first time in a long time I could see the beauty of the big oak tree across the street and the sweet musical sounds of two mocking birds as they darted about gathering twigs and grass to build a nest."

I watched a mother reading to her little girl there on a bench under the tree, and later an old man feeding the pigeons. All little things that I had never took the time to notice throughout my life, but now I felt like I had been transformed to blend in, and I think that's what it's all about once we blend in with the joys of life around us we will never go back to the shady ungodly things that should never be in any ones life in the first place."

"What I told you is true." He said. "But here is the rest of the story, I walked to the bathroom and dropped the overdose that I had planned on taking in the toilet and as I watched the mocking birds building a new nest in the old oak tree I knew I was on my way to building a new life and I've never looked back."

"Take an old mans advice and try it young lady you won't be sorry."

He got up and gathered up his jacket and travel bag as the bus pulled in to the Louisville, bus station. "Well this is where I get off, good luck young lady and God bless you."

She watched as he made his way among passengers and parked buses to disappear in the station.

'I have no reason to doubt his story.' She thought. 'But for some reason I can't see that ever happening to me, I feel like I'm an isolated case unlike any others and will never experience a change in my life.'

Soon horses, white fences, and rolling blue grass acres dotted with Barns and mansions unfolded before her as the bus hummed through horse country near Lexington. And just as before when going the other way to prison two years ago the scenery and the vision of the farms fascinated her. 'But there is something different.' She thought. 'This time I see them just as another house or home and I have no desire to live there because my home is waiting up ahead, not as elaborate but it's home and I long to be there.' 'I've never had this feeling before, I always longed for something better, could it be that I have finally turned the corner and found myself?'

The miles flew by and before she knew it the bus pulled into the station at Corbin, Kentucky. Through the window she could see Laura and her three children patiently waiting for her to step off the bus.

She rose from her seat and for a moment felt that her legs would give way but renewed strength returned as she stepped from the bus into the arms of her children. They held on to her without a word and the only sounds were muffled sobs and soft loving sounds of momma, momma, I love you momma I love you.

After a bit she reached out to Laura and they embraced.

As they held each other she thought. 'I have never felt this way about Laura I only showed contempt toward her and Burl, could it be that my life is being transformed and I have a future ahead that I can look forward to?'

Laura squeezed her tight and said. "They have missed you so much more than you will ever know, they cried almost every night, I told them to keep that from you in their letters, I thought it best that you not know about it. Now come on lets go home."

She was surprised how well the house had been taken care of by the electrician and his wife. They had bought a house and moved out a few days before she returned.

Her children had brought all their belongings from Burl and Laura's the day before she came home.

"They made it plain." Laura said. 'That they enjoyed their stay with us but couldn't wait for you to get home so they could be with you."

Happiness showed in her face as she sat in the porch swing watching them romp with the two ugly pups. Rene lay at her feet just as she had since her return from prison and seemed worried that she might leave again.

As she sat there she tried to sort everything out and her thoughts dwelled on her financial situation. 'Wayne deposited the rent money for me, I better go to the bank tomorrow and see how much I have.' 'I need to start looking for a job with three kids three dogs and two horses to feed.' 'Thank God my place is free of mortgage thanks to Wayne.'

'I still have the old wore out pickup but would be afraid to drive it to Harlan so I have to figure out a way to get a used car, maybe after I get a job, and that worries me because some folks don't won't some body like me working for them."

"It's going to be awkward living here next to my ex and his wife because I realize they will want to keep their distance from me, although I am sure they will keep in contact with the children.' 'Would love to see their baby and their home but guess all of that is off limits to me.'

She heard the sound of a motor and looked toward the driveway to see a light blue four door chevy approaching.

'Who could this be?' She thought. 'I hope it's not one of my old so called friends, if it is they'll have a short stay because I never intend to associate with that kind of crowd ever again.'

It came to a stop and a lady got out, then she recognized it was Ann. Ann smiled and asked. "Mind if I join you? You look mighty comfortable there in the swing."

Dumfounded she nodded yes and watched Ann open the passenger side door and pick up little Wayne.

She sat down beside her holding Wayne as he flailed his arms at the dogs and children that had suddenly brought their yard play to a halt and followed her on the porch.

"Just wanted to drop over and tell you we're glad to see you home and have you as a neighbor."

As she sat staring at the baby, Ann Asked. "Here, you want to hold him."

As he lay in her lap looking up at her smiling face she was amazed at how much he looked like his daddy and listened to him jabber as slobbers appeared on his chin, it was all she could do not to laugh as she thought he might be trying to get a curse word out.

She handed him back to Ann and thought about saying how much he looked like Wayne but the awkwardness of mentioning his daddy's name stopped her and instead she said.

"He sure is a cute little fellow and seems so lively."

"Yes he is." Ann replied. "And yes, he's quite a handful and lively especially when he's around kids and dogs."

"Here, Wayne wanted me to give you this, it's your bank book where he deposited your rent money.'

She took it and looked at the total and seen it was much more than rent money could have been. "I don't understand." She said. "The rent money wouldn't have brought it to this total."

"I know." Ann replied. "Wayne put in a little extra every month, said it would help out when you got back home with the kids."

She dropped her head as tears clouded her vision. "I don't know what to say except to thank you but it means a lot more than that, can't understand how I deserve all the kindness you show me."

"Well you do deserve it and we want you to know that we will be neighborly although it may seem awkward to you. Both Wayne and I think the world of your children and they have spent a lot of time at our place with Burl and Laura's kids since you've been gone. And we want that to continue."

"And another thing all you have to get around in is that old wore out pickup, Wayne tried to get it fixed up while you were away but the mechanic said. "It ain't worth working on, it's falling apart."

"So last week Wayne seen an ad in the paper about that Chevrolet and one day came home with it. "Here I bought this for you he said."

"For me? I don't understand." I told him. "I have a car that's almost new and all the other vehicles we have here, Buick station wagon, jeep, new pickup, and a two ton international for hauling hay, this place is beginning to look like a used car lot and here you go out and buy another one. Well you know how he talks."

"Well shi—er hel—aw come on it's yours dammit, do whatever you want with it, maybe you'll find some one that needs a good car."

"So I would like you and the kids to go home with me for a while and I'll show you our house and we can have a snack, we can do all this before Wayne gets home from work if that's a worry for you. Then when you're ready to leave you can take the car because I've decided to give it to you, I'll have the title changed in a few days."

She leaned toward Ann and began to sob as she tried to say words that just wouldn't come.

Ann held her for a long time as the children stood watching and the only other noise was the ugly pups chasing each other from one end of the porch to the other.

She looked at the huge six-bed room home and thought. 'Any other time in my past I would be gritting my teeth with jealousy, but now my feelings are I have a home that is very dear to me and I long for nothing more than to live out the rest of my life there and watch my children grow up and if I live long enough maybe there'll be grandchildren to enjoy.' Then she thought of the old gentleman on the bus.' He said. "I think that's what it's all about once we blend in with all the joys of life around us we will never go back to the shady ungodly things that should never be in any ones life." 'I wonder if the joys of life are slowly transforming me? I certainly hope so and I'll do as he said starting tonight before I go to bed. I'll ask God again to lead me out of my wretched past, I believe it is already happening from what I've experienced the past few days.'

Ann showed her the house inside and they had a snack and after chatting for a while Ann suggested they ride over to the other property. "Wayne had a road cut through there it's a bit bumpy but we'll take the station wagon, that way there's plenty of room for the kids and dogs. They toured the old farm and she noticed the old home place.

Time and weather had taken it's toll some of the tin roof had been blown loose to expose rotting wood, the wooden steps to the screen porch at the rear had rotted away and the screen had holes and was hanging in strips. A picture of total neglect to a home that once housed a happy farm family filled with the joys of life.

"Wayne says he will eventually tear it down." Ann said. "But says he wants to repair the barn for hay storage and farm equipment."

Soon they returned to the house. As they stood in the yard talking Ann handed her the keys to the Blue Chevrolet. "Ok it's all yours." She said. "I'll have your title in a few days, in the meantime enjoy, it's a good car."

She was speechless in spite of giving it some thought and hoping she could express herself for the gift all she could say was. "Well I don't know how to thank you, and intended to add something else but instead broke down and cried.

As they held each other she thought. 'I guess this will qualify as one of the joys of life just to be able to express your feelings of love and being wanted, something that has been missing in my life.'

As they piled in the car Ann pointed and said. "You can go back on the road that you had cut through it's a short cut and the road is in pretty good shape Wayne dozed it off with the tractor on a regular basis all the way to your house."

"But it's fenced off now." She replied.

"Yeah I know but Wayne had them put a gate there, it's not locked just make sure you close it or else you'll wind up with extra horses on your side."

They laughed as she drove away.

'That was nice of him to put a gate there.' She thought. 'He certainly didn't have to but I guess they still want to be good neighbors.'

As she drove through the woods amid the noise of dogs and children for the first time in her life she noticed the beauty of the trees, the animals and birds that darted among them, the sweet fragrance of wild honeysuckle, and thick patches of fern and moss along side the dirt road.

'Yes a thing of beauty.' She thought. 'My life is becoming a thing of beauty and is slowly but certainly joining the joys of life.'

They got out of the car and she backed off to admire it as the children played noisily behind her she said.

"This is almost a new car I can't believe that they are doing this for me how can I ever repay them?" Tears filled her eyes again and she whispered.

'But these are not tears of sadness, like the gentleman said on the bus. 'Blend in with the good things in life and you will shed tears of joy.'

Two weeks later she got a job in a dry cleaning shop in Harlan. It didn't pay much but enough to keep her family going. Both Laura and Ann told her they would watch her kids after school till she got home and would welcome them in their homes if she had to work on Saturday's.

She made plans to fence off four acres of her land from the horses for the purpose of growing corn and hay to feed them.

Then later she planned on setting up a riding school that she would operate after work, a meager operation with only two horses but it would bring in a few dollars and help pay the bills.

Meanwhile Burl and Laura have noticed the change in her and have vowed to help her in any way they can.

Laura called and asked her and the children to dinner one Sunday. To her surprise she accepted, a far cry from two years ago when she didn't care to be near them. They all had a great day together and before long she invited them to her house.

One day working at the cleaners she got to thinking about it and said out loud.

"It's the blending of joy, that's what it is."

One of her startled coworkers asked. "Tell me Julie what prompted that and what does it mean?'

"Oh." She said. "It means if you recognize the beauty of God's nature and associate with joyful people you will blend in with and become a part of all God's creations. And I ask you can you think of a better way to spend your time here on earth?"

She smoothed out the crumpled piece of paper to where she could make out the phone number.

'Don't know if I should call or not.' She thought. 'I believe I have things in my life pretty well under control, but I did promise I'd call him after my sentence was over.'

She dialed the number and waited. No mistaking the voice on the other end as that of the kind deputy. "Hello! Deputy Curt Boyd, what can I do for you?"

"My names Julie, I doubt if you remember me, you transported me to Indiana about two years ago. You gave me your phone number and asked me to call you when I returned home. Said you and your wife worked to help folks after they returned from prison, but I just called to inform you that I feel like I have everything under control and will not need your service, but I want to thank you for your offer and the kindness you showed toward me on the way to Indiana, I will never forget that."

"Oh yes I remember, I took the cuffs off you as we crossed the Ohio River so you could wipe tears from your eyes. And I did look at the report from prison concerning you. The warden gave you good marks throughout the report and summed up your stay as a good obedient person, always willing to work to quell uprisings among other inmates and do the right thing. And I have been hearing more good things about you since your return and wondered if you'd call. It's good to hear from you and know that your life is coming together again."

I haven't been working with things of that nature for over a year now simply because I don't have the time since I lost my wife, she was killed in an auto accident and the burden of trying to work my job and take care of my four children leaves me with little time to contribute to it. My wife was the backbone of the program anyway."

"I'm so sorry to hear about your wife is there anything I can do to help with your children?"

"Well to tell you the truth no, because I heard you're working six days a week and my children would be a burden on you, but I wonder if I could drop them off on a Saturday or Sunday now and then to be with your children? Because all children need to associate with other children it helps to mold and shape their lives."

"Sure I'll be glad to have them over just give me a call any time you want to bring them. How about this coming Sunday?"

"Well okay if you don't care to get your feet wet, I can't promise they'll behave but I'll discipline them if they don't."

"Ah don't let that worry you they can't be any worse than mine and I manage to get through the day with them although it's trying at times."

They both laughed.

"Okay, what time can you check them in? Because I'm on patrol this Sunday and have to start at eight in the morning."

"Bring them by about seven and we can get the proper introductions between the group before you have to go on duty."

"That's fine with me are you sure that's not too early for you?"

"No we're early risers bring them on."

"Okay, I'll see you at seven, and thanks for calling it's been good talking to you."

"Same here." She said. "See you Sunday, Bye."

That was the beginning of complete joy and bedlam, as Poor Boy later would label it.

Not only those two families children coming together but within weeks Burl and Laura's three joined the fray. Every Saturday and Sunday would find them either at Julie's, Burl's, or Poor Boy and Ann's homes creating all the horseplay and noise that a group of children are capable of.

Poor Boy and Ann packed them in the Buick station wagon to go see a movie at Harlan one Saturday. Seems that one or more of the boys had eaten beans or onions or maybe both the night before and was wound up tight with gas. Gasping from the back of the station wagon caused Poor Boy to look back at the laughing bunch as some of the girls held their hands tight over their noses while others tried to get close to the open windows for fresh air. The awful scent quickly spread throughout the vehicle.

Ann pinched her nose and looked back. "Now who ever did that should be ashamed of themselves." She said. But the laughter went on so she added. "Now that's not nice, tell me why do you think its funny?"

That only caused more laughter and obviously more gas letting because by now the smell was almost unbearable.

Poor Boy pulled off and parked in a wide place near the woods. Everyone immediately piled out and the merriment grew louder as some of them rolled in the leaves from laughter.

Finally he got their attention and said. "Now by go-gosh I want who ever it is that's spreading that scent around that smells like sh—scrap to go out there in the woods and get rid of it, ain't no way I'll pay your way in the movies if all you're gonna do is sit and fart and laugh at it."

That did little to quell the noise of laughter, as one of the boys said mockingly. "Fart and laugh at it."

He looked at Ann and could see she was trying hard to hold a straight face and would be more comfortable laughing along with the kids.

"Well shi—shucks Ann I guess it is funny to them but hel—llo its that dam—durn stink that I can't stomach."

As they piled back in the station wagon he said. "Now let me warn you if you do that in the theater so help me I'll drag you out of there and we'll all go home even if its right in the middle of the movie."

"Now by go—sh you remember that as sure as hel—llo I'll do what I said."

"Don't make no dam—urn sense for some body to get in amongst a bunch of people and let off gas that way."

That started the laughter again, frustrated he said. "Now listen up dammi—arnet I mean what I say, no more farting and laughing at it cause if you do I'll turn this damne—arned thing around and head back home."

That did little to stop the merriment he looked at Ann again and could sense that she was about to join them.

"Shit Ann." He said. "I'm getting mighty damned tired of trying to stutter around my cuss words especially when I'm around this bunch of kids, hell its nothing but bedlam."

Finally they quieted down and one of the older boys said. "Okay we've made an agreement that if one of us does it again who ever it is will be expelled from the group for the next three months."

Near town Poor Boy had the urge and let it quietly slip out. As he detected the odor one of the boys piped up. "Hey I smell something and it's coming from up there."

Ann looked over at him and said. "Wayne did you do that? You should be ashamed of your self." She whispered.

"Ann you know I wouldn't do anything like that its one of them back there."

"I don't know." She said. "It does smell different."

That caused the noise and laughter to start all over again. "Well shit." He said.

"May as well join in and laugh along with them, like I said this bunch ain't nothing but complete joy and bedlam."

One week later he came home from work. "Ann I got something I want to tell you. I put in an order for a bus."

"A bus." She frowned. "What on earth for, why do we need a bus?"

"Well shi-ucks Ann to haul that noisy farting bunch around in, you know yourself that the Buick ain't big enough."

"Well if you say so I guess we could use more room, how big is the bus?"

"Like one of the big school buses Ann, in fact I ordered it from the same company that makes the school buses, only thing it will be a different color I told them to paint it a dark green."

"You mean to tell me you bought a bus that big, what on earth for? one half that size would have been fine."

"It's like this, I figure other kids in the neighborhood will want to join the gang and cause even more bedlam and I would hate to have to refuse them just because we don't have room for them in the station wagon. And another thing the church down yonder can find use for it once in a while I'm sure."

"And while I'm at it I may as well tell you that any Sunday you want to get started we'll go to Sunday school and church. I know it's been on your mind about getting our little one headed in the right direction and maybe Julie would like for her kids to go and they could bring along Curt Boyd's gang, Burl and Laura already belong to that church. The way I look at it the whole gang would be there and who could think of a better place for us to gather?"

She walked over and put her arms around him.

"You know something." She said. "You truly amaze me the way you do things."

"What you mean by that?" He asked.

"Well it seems every thing you do has a direct effect on some one other than yourself, take the bus no telling how many folks will benefit from that, might even get some to join the church that other wise would not have."

"Yes you are amazing and I love you."

"Aw shit Ann." He said. "hel—p me I just try to do the right thing, ain't nothing special about me."

Soon the green bus could be seen transporting children and church groups to this and that almost every weekend with several different drivers.

"Shi—ucks Ann th dam—urn thing won't last with all the mileage they're putting on it."

"Hel—lo I'm glad they furnish the gas and oil else I'd be broke in no time."

Of course she listened to his complaining and took it with a grain of salt knowing that inside he was secretly enjoying seeing the bus serve so many and the results that it had already produced in the church and the bedlam gang that had now doubled.

Then one day he said. "Shi-ucks Ann looks like one bus wont be enough, dam—urn It might take two, three, more if this keeps up."

She was careful not to agree for fear he would order another one.

Over a period of six months he and Ann, Curt Boyd, Julie and her oldest son, all joined the church.

And there was a visible change in each life. Ann's because she now knew that she, her husband and their child were on the right track, not to speak of Julie and Curt Boyd's family. Burl and Laura had long before taken on the task of introducing their children to church and Sunday school and dividends were noticeable in their children especially their mannerisms.

Curt was known as the gentle no nonsense deputy sheriff and showed no marked change but it was plain to see the happiness in his face as he watched his children frolic with other families and their children at church.

Julie seemed to become more of a gentle person and didn't hesitate to step forward and offer her assistance in on going church affairs. Soon she became a Sunday school teacher, which led to bible reading and her search for scripture that would help her understand how God would ever forgive her for the way she did her children's father.

As time went on she noticed how much she depended on Curt for assurance in her every day life. And how much she looked forward to chatting with him over a cup of coffee, and at times felt like asking him if he would ever consider marriage again, but would quickly try to rid it from her mind, remembering her old ways and how bold she was to a point of embarrassment as she now thought about it. 'Maybe its wrong for me to think of him this way I know I don't deserve another try at marriage but for some reason I can't get him off my mind.'

He drove the patrol car down the shaded dirt road toward the public park, which was occupied mostly by the church group. The green bus sat with doors and windows open as children and adults busied themselves around the picnic tables. 'Looks like I'm just in time for some food.' He thought. 'Nothing better than a grilled hamburger and all that good food stacked on them tables.'

She seen him get out of the patrol car and watched as he walked toward them. 'I was hoping he'd find time to stop by.' She thought. 'Too bad he has to be on duty so many weekends.'

'I wonder if he'll sit at this table? I sure hope so.'

He stopped and chatted with the ones at the first table before moving on to the next one near the water tap. There a group of small children gathered around him asking questions about the patrol car and his uniform. "Would you blow the siren?" One asked.

"Yes maybe before I leave honey, but right now I need something to eat."

As she watched she was sure that he was about to take a seat at that table but then noticed him looking around as if trying to spot some one, finally he looked toward her table and headed that way.

Laura was sitting beside her on the long bench with Ann sitting directly across the table from her. She noticed they exchanged glances and Laura immediately got up and said. "Can you make room for me on that side Ann? Here Curt you can sit here!"

He laid his hand on her shoulder and asked. "Do you mind if I sit here?"

"No not at all." She replied. "It's an honor, I feel safe and secure sitting next to a deputy sheriff." She looked across at Laura and Ann and knew by their looks that she hadn't did a very good job of concealing her feelings for Curt, because women's instinct was written all over their faces.

'Well if it's been so obvious to them why hasn't he noticed?' She thought. 'Maybe I'll find out soon, because I'm sure he was looking for me and came to this table.'

At that moment he reached for her hand and said. "Yes its an honor for me too, I thought you might like to go fix my hamburger."

She rose from the table with a mixture of feelings, a little embarrassed, happiness, and yes, sadness tried to make its way in as the thoughts of Brad, Poor Boy, and her past appeared before her.

"What would you like on it?" She stammered. "Oh just throw some stuff on, it'll be okay and finish filling the plate with all that other good stuff on the table there."

She returned with his plate and as she handed it to him their eyes met and at that moment she knew he had finally let his feelings be known and she was about to get another chance toward a happy life whether she deserved it or not. She took her seat beside him and swallowed hard trying to hold back the tears, but as her cheeks dampened Laura and Ann looked away pretending not to see.

But Curt had noticed. "Here take this." He whispered as he handed her a tissue.

At that time Laura and Ann got up and walked away knowing that Curt and Julie needed time together.

"Seems I remember having to take the cuffs off and hand you a tissue as we crossed the Ohio River about three years ago, but this time its different, no cuffs or prison up ahead to worry about. Unless you might think sharing your life with me would be like serving a prison term."

She finally regained her composure enough to say.

"I will gladly serve a term with you for as long as you want." She whispered. "And yes it is different this time except for one thing."

"What's that?" He asked.

"The handcuffs." She replied. "They were still there wrapped around my heart and you just removed them."

Soon others at the table drifted away to participate in games etc. Leaving them alone in their world of newfound happiness as they squeezed hands and tried to relay their feelings that had been suppressed for too long.

Four months later she was known as Julie Boyd. Plans were in the works to build three more rooms and an additional bath on her house because as she put it.

"I know yours is a much nicer house but I prefer to live in this one because it seems more like home to me, I hope you understand Curt, but if you don't agree please tell me and I will do what ever you want."

"I do understand Julie and I guess we better get some plans together for extra bedrooms and a bath to accommodate that gang of mine. And speaking of them, have you noticed the excitement that's building in our children?"

"Yes I have." She answered. "And I'm so happy about it because I half expected rebellion from one or more of my children or yours."

One night three months later they were sitting in the swing and noticed how quiet it had become just after the children went to bed.

'Well this is a good time to tell him.' She thought, but before she had time to say anything he spoke up.

"Whew! They sure are a loud bunch, good thing there's only seven I don't believe we could handle any more than that."

"Yes I know." She said. "But you might as well get ready to try because soon there will be eight."

At first he said nothing and she began to worry that he may not be pleased with the news. But he finally took her in his arms and whispered.

"Yes Julie, we can manage eight and I can't tell you how happy and surprised I am about it because I never thought we could have one at our age, after all I'm forty seven and you're forty."

They sat there to past midnight discussing plans for the children and their future together.

"I must admit I had my doubts that we could ever make it together Julie, that's why I stood back for so long even though I wanted to reach out and bring you to me. We both have a past to live with but I think we can go on and finish out our stay here on earth together, love is what matters Julie, and I do love you."

"I love you too." She whispered. "I love you too."

They fell silent and listened to the night noises. 'The joys of life.' She thought. 'This is the end result of the truths that the old man on the bus related to me.'

Finally he arose and said.

"Come on momma, lets get to bed old folks like me need a lot of rest especially after hearing that they are about to become a father again."

"Aw come on Curt." She teased. "Look at it this way, we're starting a brand new life together and its only in its infancy, we may not stack up as youngsters but we can be young at heart."

"Yeah I know Julie, yeah I know, and I hope we have a long life together."

The following year was filled with hard work, excitement, hectic, and at times disappointments would pop up among the children. But shared reasoning with them around the supper table would usually fix the problem.

Julie continued working in Harlan and managed to bring in a few dollars from her riding school after work hours.

Poor Boy told Curt that he could use any of his equipment. "If you need to plow up that field there, don't go out and hire some body, Shi—ucks come get my tractor and plow it yourself. And if you want to haul something come get my old hay truck, anything I got you can use."

Then one day Curt came home and said. "Julie I'm thinking about running for sheriff, sheriff Wolfe don't plan on running and has asked me to run. He says I have a lot of support over the county and thinks I can win."

"Okay Curt, what ever you decide to do I will stand beside you." She said.

"And another thing Julie I would like to ask what you think about taking over where my wife left off and help me with the folks that return from prison.

Seems about every other day some one asks me about it and wants to know if I will start it up again. I know you don't have a lot of time but I think you should give up that job in Harlan and put more effort in what you love to do with your horses. We can go out and shop around for a couple more horses. That way you'll be at home with the little one and have more time to develop your riding school. You could set your own hours, say no more than four hours in the evenings for riding lessons and that way you'd have some time left over for the poor souls that have done their time and need guidance, and I might add that you would be the perfect person for that job."

"Now not all of them will seek help but a few will if they know the service is available. It's an honorable job and what does it pay? Well as you know nothing unless you want to count the troubled ones that it might help and watch them live out the rest of their lives at peace with themselves."

He pulled her to him and said.

"Now don't get me wrong, I'm not suggesting you do this to please me I want you to make up your own mind, and if you decide you would rather not tackle it just say so and nothing will change because life will go on with us regardless. No hurry Julie, take a few days to think it over."

"I can give you the answer right now." She replied. "I would love to work with the poor souls as you call them because I can relate to them and know their needs. If not for some that went out of their way to help me regain my confidence back, and that includes you its no telling what the rest of my life would have turned out to be."

"You know something Julie? I'm glad you showed some remorse and cried as we crossed the Ohio River because if you hadn't I wouldn't have offered you my phone number and asked you to call."

He squeezed her tight and whispered. "I can't imagine living the rest of my life without you, and I want you to know that."

His words left her speechless but as she snuggled in his arms her thoughts were of the old man on the bus and his words of wisdom.

'That's what it's all about, if you blend in with Gods creations and the good things you will experience the joys of life.'

Finally she broke the silence. "I love you Curt, I love you."

He left his home south of Richmond and drove west to spend a night with his father and mother in the Shenandoah Valley. He told them he was leaving the next morning. "Going down to Lee County to take a letter to a widow of one of my fellow soldiers that didn't make it back from the war and then I'll go over in Kentucky and deliver a letter that another one wrote to his kids in case something happened to him. I know it won't be a pleasant experience but I feel it's a duty that I'm bound to fulfill."

Then he answered all their questions about his wife and kids. "I want you to bring them over for a week or so." His mother said. He promised her he would. They sat up late, as is usually the case when family members get together. He awoke early to smell bacon frying, he had told his mother that he would be leaving early and not bother with breakfast because he would eat later on down the road somewhere. He went in the kitchen "Mom don't go to all that trouble I told you I would be leaving early you don't need to be up this early." But in spite of his protests the table was soon filled with bacon, eggs, biscuits, jams and jellies. His father joined them and he wasted more time than he intended to but truly enjoyed having breakfast with them. They followed him to the car and his mother handed him a thermos of hot coffee. "Now you be careful." She said. "I heard on the radio that we might get snow." Yeah." His dad said. "Drive careful son and don't forget to bring your family over when you get back and like your momma said, leave the kids with us for a while." He waved goodbye and noted the tall dark beauty of his mother as she stood close to his father. 'She don't look much different than she did twenty years ago.' He thought.

As he drove through the Virginia landscape his thoughts drifted back to Belgium and the Ardennes Forest. The war ended six years ago and some memories still lingered right down to the smallest details, while others seemed fuzzy and you are never sure if the way you remember them is part of your imagination or maybe it was just a bad dream and never happened at all. War is like that sometimes so horrifying that your memory bank will not hold all the bad things and at the same time nightmares might be added as a fact because they seemed so real.

As the miles ticked off the scenery changed from gentle rolling hills to the higher Blue Ridge mountain chain. That soon changed to the more raw ruggedness of Brushy Mountain in the Jefferson national Forest as he came closer to Lee County.

Near Big Stone Gap, the darkness of the day was suddenly filled with wet snowflakes, and as the worn wiper blades screeched as they cleared the windshield his thoughts were back in Belgium and the snow covered Ardennes forest.

He could see the puzzlement on Tex face when he told him. "But I think I can tell you where you're from in Virginia."

He smiled as he thought of what Tex said about the toilet facilities. "See that hole out there? We'd appreciate it if you go there to take a crap so the stink don't settle in our beards, but its okay to piss right here, you can tell by all the piss holes in the snow."

Remembered telling Crawford. "Hi, my names Witt, you must be Crawford, Tex says you need help with your BAR so I'm your man, green when it comes to combat and scared as hell already, but I guess I'll get the hang of it."

Crawford's answer was. "And damned soon I'm afraid."

Then a few days later Crawford opened up and told him about his failed marriage that cost him everything including his kids. "Damn near pulled the trigger a few times." He said. "But decided to join up and help fight this damned war and lose my life that way."

He could still see him as if it was just yesterday as he pulled the wool knit cap that hang underneath his steel helmet to wipe his eyes and finally crawling out the hole to prance back and forth in the snow. And days later met the onrushing Germans head on fighting without signs of fear but only to die there in the snow covered Ardennes.

And as he and Tex searched his pockets they found a sealed envelope that contained a letter to his children, and a picture of him and his wife and kids.

"We'll see that his wife gets this picture." Tex had said. "Might make her feel better knowing that he carried it close to his heart." Then he remembered telling Tex of Crawford's divorce and losing everything including his children.

He looked over at the picture and letter on the passenger seat, and the message on the envelope written by Crawford's cold and battle stained hands the night before he died. 'If I should fall in battle please see that my kids get this letter, they live in Harlan County, Kentucky. I have a brother living there his name is Burl Crawford, he'll see that they get it.'

'Guess I'll give the picture to his brother along with the letter.' He thought. 'No use trying to find his ex wife she probably wouldn't want it anyway.'

Along side the letter and picture was a letter that Tex had written to his wife in answer to the one he received from her informing him that a little one had came into their lives.

'I'll look her up tomorrow and give her the letter, then I'll get on to Kentucky, and take care of Crawford's request.'

Just as he drove through Pennington Gap, the wind picked up and the swirling snow became almost blinding as he strained his eyes to stay in the fresh plowed lane as he followed closely behind the ghostly slow moving snowplow ahead.

As he strained to stay in the lane the snow plow reminded him of the half track there in the Ardennes as the vision of the contorted frozen bodies, some with out stretched arms as if reaching for something that stirred the imagination, was it a plea for help? A mother's face that had suddenly came in view, or were they reaching for the hand of God?

Then tears streamed down his face as he looked at Tex and Crawford as they lay side by side among the other frozen bodies.

'Together in death.' He thought. 'Two soldiers who hardly had time to get to know one another, but formed a bond that cannot easily be explained,'

A secret that belongs to combat veterans that even they don't know the answer, how one week, one day, or one hour can form a lasting bond between them.

As he followed the plow around the curve into Jonesville, he could vision the half-track bobbing and weaving around the shell holes and fallen tree limbs and finally out of sight, but not before leaving the sight of the stiff outreaching arms frozen in his mind, that caused nightmares as he fought across Belgium and on into Germany hoping that when it was all over it would thaw from his memory but six years later the picture is just as vivid as the day it happened there in the Ardennes Forest.

He pulled off and parked at the courthouse. He sat there for some time until visions, of the Ardennes were replaced by the features of the sheriff's face.

'I wonder if he's still the sheriff here.' He thought. 'If not I can find out where he lives and see him tomorrow.' 'I want him to go with me to see Tex's Widow and son.'

As he entered the office he could hear the bellowing voice of the sheriff as he related something to his deputies.

'Yeah that's him.' He thought. 'I'd know that voice anywhere.'

"Hey! Are you the sheriff of this county? Richmond sent me down here to take over a murder case, and I expect your corporation, so lay all the evidence out on the desk there, we need to get going on it right away."

The sheriff looked up with a scowl on his face and obviously surprised.

"Well danged if it ain't that Prima Donna from the capital boys, what brings you here?"

After a few minutes of shaking hands and good-natured kidding they sat down and he told them why he was there.

"I came down to see Tex widow, I have a letter he wrote to her a few days before his death but never got to mail it." He noticed the puzzled look on the sheriff's face and said.

"Guess I better back up here and explain how I come by the letter, you see I was drafted in the service and after infantry basic training in Texas was sent to Europe as a replacement and assigned to an Infantry division on line in Belgium."

"And as unbelievable as it may seem I wound up in Tex's squad. We pushed on toward the Ardennes Forest and in a matter of days reached the forest but got bogged down by bad weather. We knew the Germans were planning on launching an offensive against us but never dreamed of the enormity of the force, and that along with the surprise element cost us dearly. One morning their tanks and infantry over whelmed our division as well as others up and down the line. They broke through our lines and had us surrounded taking many prisoners up and down the line. Some units managed to survive, including our company. Only two remained alive in Tex's squad,

303

Tex and myself, my fox hole buddy whom I'd only known for a few days a fellow by the name of Brad Crawford from Kentucky lost his life that morning, in fact our platoon took heavy losses including our platoon sergeant, Tex was ordered to take charge of the platoon. "

Some time after the break through they held their fire until late in the day, then launched a mortar and artillery attack that lasted into the night."

"Tex was hit by shrapnel from a mortar round some time during the night and probably could have been saved but no one could move or hear calls for help amidst the artillery and mortar fire."

"And he like some others died from loss of blood and freezing weather, thank God I've been told at a certain point you become warm and comfortable just before death from freezing."

"We managed to hold our own for a few more days until the weather cleared and our planes were in the air again. And about the same time one of General Patton's armored divisions arrived. Within a few days we had the Germans on the run."

"Now back to the letter I took it from Tex field jacket pocket and carried it through the war with intentions of looking his widow up and giving it to her. I intended to do it right away but I lost all my toes on one foot and have been in and out of hospitals since my discharge, so finally here I am, can you tell me if she's still in this area sheriff?"

The sheriff and his deputies had been listening intently while he related his story and knew that he was speaking of the battle of the bulge.

The sheriff glanced at the deputy's and rose slowly from his chair and in unison the deputy's rose to face him.

"Well young man I had a contact in Richmond that I talked to on a regular basis during the war and he kept me up to date on you. He told me all about your heroics during the war, the battle stars, purple heart, silver star, and the battle field commission that you earned. You see I know all this and can say that I'm not surprised about any of it because I knew you had it in you right after your last trip down here in the Hoss investigation."

"So I would like to thank you and all our soldiers for the way they performed for our country, and may God bless the ones that will never return."

"But I didn't know about you being with Tex when he died, that is a coincidence and it hits close to home."

He reached out his hand and said. "Welcome back son we're proud of you."

As each deputy stepped forward to shake his hand he looked at old glory near the wall behind the sheriff's desk and tried hard to hold back tears of pride and joy, but at the same time the vision of Tex and Crawford's frozen bodies being hauled away through the snow covered Ardennes over shadowed all of that and he broke down and cried. The next few minutes were awkward as they always are when tears are shed among men.

Finally the sheriff said. "Yes she's still here. She went back to live with her parents after Tex was killed, I hear the little boy is a spitting image of Tex, some one told me she dresses him in cowboy shirts and he wears a belt with a big buckle with the letters Texas across it."

"Okay I'll go see her tomorrow morning." Witt remarked. "Then the next day I'll head for Kentucky I have a letter that Crawford wrote to his children the night before he was killed."

The sheriff spoke up. "I hope you didn't make any sleeping arrangements yet because I want you to stay at my house while you're here."

"You sure you want me after all the trouble I gave you during the investigations sheriff?"

"Aw don't you worry about that son you know yourself that was a learning experience for you and me too I suppose. You learned to use a little common sense along with the rule book, and I learned to never snap judge a man before he's had time to grow out of his young and some times foolish ways of thinking."

He reached for his hat and said.

"Boys I think I'll go home a little early today if you need me call. Come on son, we have a lot to talk about."

The deputy's watched them walk out and one remarked.

"No way in hell I'd ever thought that bird would have turned out the way he has." They all nodded in agreement.

The sheriff's wife prepared a delicious meal and afterwards she joined them in conversation around the fireplace. She wanted to know about his family which allowed him to talk about his favorite subject his wife and two kids.

Soon she excused herself. "I think I'll go to bed, I know you two have lots to talk about."

The sheriff got up to put another log on the fire and as they watched the flames lick around it causing the bark to pop and crack as sparks darted in all directions the sheriff said.

"Thought about giving it up after I finish this term but decided to try for another four years, at times I think I'm out of place and not suited for this job, but then I look at the ones that want it and know that I can do a better job than they can."

"Glad to hear that sheriff, you may think you come up short on some things pertaining to being sheriff but you have a natural instinct as to when justice should be applied or when its time to move on and accept the consequences."

"Don't know if I see where you're coming from young man, what you just said is all Greek to me, would you sort it out and make it more simple for me because after all I'm not an educated man."

Witt smiled and said. "Well let me go back about seven years when you and I stood on the little bridge looking down at the spot where Hoss died, and as the breeze ruffled the leaves I could see a shiny piece of metal hidden underneath and intended to have a look at it when we went down there, but the first thing you did was plant your foot on the leaves. Then as I was climbing the bank to leave I looked back and saw you pick it up and put it in your coat pocket."

The sheriff went silent as he watched the flames play around the logs in the fireplace. Finally he looked up and said. "You know something Larry Witt, at one time I thought you were one of the most stupid people that I had ever met, and if you remember I told you that, but since then I have been amazed at you. So now I think I'm about to hear what the piece of metal was and how it related to Hoss's murder."

"Yes sheriff, the piece of metal was the nameplate that Tex always wore pinned to his left shirt pocket, and I surmised that Hoss grabbed and tore it from the shirt during the altercation with Tex, and therefore still had it in his hand when Tex lifted him over the bridge railing to fall to the creek below."

"You're right again young man, but tell me how you figured out about the nameplate since you had never met Tex and knew nothing about him wearing it?'

"The day we went there to question him sheriff, I saw the shirt that he said he was wearing the night Hoss was killed and as you know the left pocket was torn. He said he tore it on a nail that stuck out over the attic ladder, of course I didn't believe that and my thinking was confirmed when I noticed a picture of him and his wife hanging on the wall and the nameplate was attached to his shirt pocket."

"Well son you've got me again, because all these years I have carried that piece of metal in my pocket wrapped in a hankie and was sure that I was the only one to know about it, but here you come along and tell me you knew about it all along, like I said you truly amaze me, now I suppose you're about to tell me what I should do with it?"

"Well yes I have a suggestion, I was telling Tex about it and made this remark. "I bet the sheriff will shine the nameplate up and pin it on you when you get back home. And now I'm wondering if you will go with me tomorrow and pin it on Tex junior."

"Well by god you seem to be able to read my mind, you see I once told my deputy if we find who put Hoss away I'll let you pin a metal on him, and that's exactly what I intended to do if Tex made it back home. And now that you mention it, its only fitting that we pass it on to Tex junior, yes we'll do that tomorrow."

They went by the sheriff's office the next morning. The sheriff looked at the deputy and said. "Do you remember the time I told you if we ever found out who put Hoss away I'd let you pin a metal on him?"

"Yes I remember." The deputy answered.

"Well come with us and I'll keep my promise."

The deputy looked confused and said. "Sheriff that ain't possible because the one that did it died in the war."

"I know that." He answered. "But we can do the next best thing and pin it on his son who is a spitting image of him, so grab your hat and lets go."

As they drove toward St. Charles, the sheriff told him about the town and the coal camps that surrounded it. "The coal industry has gone to pot in the past five or six years." He said. "Folks have been leaving by the dozens to places like Ohio, Indiana, Michigan, and Illinois, to find work, looks like the town will go by the wayside pretty much as the old boom towns out west that now are known as ghost towns. Too bad it has to be that way because this little town and its people have been an asset to Lee County in spite of its reputation of being labeled rough and rowdy."

"Yeah, Lee County lost a lot of its youth in the war and now losing more due to lack of work, makes you wonder what it will be like ten, twenty, years from now."

Reba watched as they got out of the car and thought. 'What brings the sheriff and his deputy to see us?' 'And who is that fellow with them?' Then she recognized him. 'Why that's the agent from Richmond, what on earth can this be about?'

She opened the door and the large smiling face of the sheriff towered above her.

"Would you mind if we come in ma'am? It won't take long, just want to visit for a few minutes."

Tex junior stood behind her looking up at the huge brawny sheriff and noted the wood grain handles of the revolver that hang in the holster at his side. He reached for his holster and cap gun on a chair behind him and buckled it around his trim waist. 'Maybe the sheriff is out looking for another deputy.' He thought. 'He might hire me.'

"You must remember me and my deputy." The sheriff beamed. "And this young man here is Larry Witt, you might remember him coming with me to see you and your husband back in 1944."

She nodded yes, because she did recognize him and now was more confused as to why they were there.

"Larry has something he wants to pass on to you and your son. Tell them about it Larry."

Witt took the letter from his pocket and sat staring down at it momentarily not knowing what to say. Finally he looked up and cleared his throat.

"Well ma'am, you see I was sent over seas in 1944 as a replacement and was assigned to your husband's Infantry squad in December 1944. I only served with him for a very short time but I want you and your son to know that he was a very brave soldier." He reached the letter toward her and said. "I took this from his pocket after he was err-er." There he stopped because the word he was about to end the sentence with just would not come. "I thought you might want to read this ma'am, he wrote it right after the letter he received from you telling him about the birth of your son, but he never got it in the mail. And here is a picture of you and him that he carried in his shirt pocket throughout the war."

With shaky hands she reached out and took them and held them close to her heart. Little Tex stood behind her looking at the solemn faces of the men before him.

She was trying hard to control her emotions but suddenly slumped forward in her chair as she began to sob. Little Tex put his arms around her neck and whispered. "It's okay momma, it's okay."

Finally she regained her composure, looked over at Witt and said. "Would you read it please? I don't believe I could ever get through it."

"Yes ma'am I'll read it, but maybe you'd rather wait till later and read it yourself.'

"No I'd prefer you read it." She replied. "Because I want Tex junior to remember this occasion, and especially you, a soldier that served with his daddy and delivered something to us from the battle fields of Europe. It's something he should never forget, and coming from you it will help him to understand the comradeship that is formed between soldiers on the battlefield."

He unfolded the letter and began to read.

Dear Reba,

I don't know how to tell you how happy I am about the news of our son's birth, so I'll just say I feel so proud to be a father and now I have even more to look forward to after this war is over.

And the way you described his features and his resemblance to me makes cold chills run up and down my spine.

You mentioned about having another one and I agree with you, so we'll get to work on that as soon as I get home. HA!

About the trip to Bristol that you mentioned, yes I can't wait to do that again.

Honey I'd like to tell you where I'm at but as you know its against regulations and would only be censored out of my letter, so I'll just say I'm some where in Europe where its snowing and very cold. We have been slowed down by bad weather for a few days but I expect we will be on the move soon because the weather has began to clear.

Well there's not a lot to write about from here so I guess I'll hang up for this time. Hold little Wayne close and kiss him for me, and tell Ma I love her I hope she's feeling well.

Reba I know I have said it over and over but I want to say it again. I love and miss you so much and look forward to getting back home so we can get on with raising a family. But if anything should happen to me, and it often does in war, please remember me as a good and faithful husband, but don't let that stop you from finding some one else to share your life with, because you're still young with many happy years ahead of you, you should choose that instead of spending the rest of your life grieving over me. Well I'll close on that and pray that this war will be over soon so we can be together again. I love you. Tex

With her arms around Tex junior and her head buried on his chest, she sobbed as he caressed her blond wavy hair.

Finally she rose to her feet with a smile of gratitude on her face she hugged each one of the men and thanked them for the respect that they had shown.

"And I have here another very old letter that I took from his pocket." Witt said. "Don't know if it will mean anything to you, it's dated 1922."

Reba held it close to her heart as it brought back memories of that day in St. Charles, when she went to Bristol, with Tex.

"Yes." She finally said. "This old letter meant a lot to him, even though the day some one gave it to him it broke his heart, because you see his mother died when he was a baby and he never knew who his father was until he read this letter. And if you read the letter you see where she revealed who his father was and it should have been one of the happiest days of his life even though his father had died a few months earlier, but it turned out to be one of the saddest because his father turned out to be the father of the girl he fell in love with and would have married her if not for the letter."

Witt looked puzzled so she said. "Yes that's right he was about to marry his half sister. You see Tex lived a very lonely life up until then and I must say I believe the day I came into his life it all turned around for him, I know it did for me and we were on our way to raising a family, it don't seem right that he had to die there in Belgium, in fact it seems cruel that he be denied a little happiness after all the unhappiness that he experienced most of his life."

"Sorry to hear that." Witt replied. "Yes I can see why he carried the letter because I guess it was a way of relating to a mother he never knew."

The sheriff took a neatly folded hankie from his pocket and said.

"One more thing before we leave ma'am, I have something here that I want my deputy to pin on your little boys shirt pocket."

He handed the shiny nameplate to his deputy and said. "I have here something that belonged to Tex and I have carried it around for a while waiting for the chance to pin it back on his shirt, but fate would have it that we will never see him again here on earth so it's only fitting that we pin it on his son, now who could be more deserving?"

The deputy dropped to one knee in front of Tex junior. As he pinned the well-polished nameplate to his bright colored cowboy shirt, the almost seven year old seemed to age well beyond that as he looked down at the nameplate and back up at them.

"That was my daddy's." Then he rubbed his fingers across the letters Tex and said. "Now it's mine.'

And at that instant it was as if a bolt of lighting had surged through their bodies melting all things foreign and trivial and leaving behind kindness, understanding, forgiveness, and yes sadness for the little fellow standing before them knowing that the war had deprived him of ever knowing his father.

Everyone was speechless as they tried to control their emotions. Finally the sheriff, a giant of a man with a big booming voice was barely able to talk above a whisper as he said.

"Yes my little man it's yours and you can treasure and wear it proudly just as your daddy did. He would want it that way."

He looked over to the side against the wall at a trunk filled with paperback books.

Reba noticed his gaze and said. "That's dime westerns that he read and kept over the years." Hearing this little Tex ran to the trunk and said. "My daddy used to read about cowboys in these books, he saved them for me, mommy says when I learn to read I can read them."

By now the sheriff had regained his composure, he reached for little Tex and lifted him high over his head as his big booming voice vibrated through the house. "Yeah I know you'll grow up to be a cowboy some day son, but how would you like to be one of my honoree Deputy's? I betcha with that gun on your hip you can keep law and order here in St. Charles. I have some extra badges down at the office, I'll have one of my deputy's bring one out and swear you in one day this week."

A big smile lit up his face as he said. "Hear that momma? I'm the sheriff of St. Charles, I'm the sheriff of St. Charles."

Then the sheriff said. "Boys I guess we better go now."

"Oh no not yet!" Reba replied. "Let me fix some fresh coffee to go with the pile of doughnuts on the kitchen table. Maybe by then momma and dad will be back, they went down to Stone Creek, they should be back any time now."

Merriment spread around the table as they enjoyed the doughnuts and coffee.

Reba's mom and dad walked in taken by complete surprise, they stood looking at the gang around the table.

"What on earth's going on here?" Her father Cal stammered. "I know there's things in my past that I should have been arrested for, but never dreamed they'd catch up to me in my old age. What brings you here sheriff?"

The sheriff rose from the table and introduced the other two. "The main reason we're here is Larry Witt, he brought something to present to your daughter and grandson that he has carried since the war. Your daughter will tell you about it later, but another reason is I wanted to ask your grandson if he would like to be one of my deputies and he accepted, so some time this week he'll be sworn in and I will trust him to keep law and order here in St. Charles."

Little Tex tugged at his grandfather's sleeve pointed to the nameplate and said. "Look grandpa, this was my daddy's and now its mine." Which had the same effect on his grandparents as it did on the others a little while ago. They both dropped to their knees and embraced him.

They talked on for a while and finally the sheriff rose to his feet. "I guess we better be on our way, thanks for the coffee and doughnuts we've enjoyed our visit."

Handshakes and best wishes were exchanged. Reba thanked and hugged each one of them lingering longer with Witt expressing her appreciation for the trouble he went through to bring her the letters and picture.

"It was no trouble ma'am, more like a duty from one soldier to another, your husband would have did the same for me."

He stepped over to little Tex, laid his hand on his shoulder and said. "Okay little man, it's been a pleasure meeting you, you look like your daddy and he would be pleased with that. I look forward to seeing you again one of these days, but in the meantime take care of your momma and bring some law and order to the town of St. Charles."

Little Tex reached out his hand to shake hands and asked. "Sir, did you see my daddy's grave? Mommy said she will take me there some day."

He dropped to his knee, took him by the hand and said. "No little man I didn't have the chance to visit his grave, but I've heard it's a beautiful cemetery there in Belgium."

"When you talked to my daddy did he tell you about me."

"Yes he did son, he said your mother told him in the letter that you were a spitting image of him and he was so happy about that. And I'll tell you another thing he would be proud of is to see you wearing a cowboy shirt with his nameplate pinned to the pocket."

"Some day I'll be a cowboy like my daddy was."

"Yes I know you will son, because you're a determined little fellow, you take that from your daddy."

They finally waved goodbye and drove away. The sheriff looked over at Witt and said. "Larry, you sure have lots of memories stored up to tell your children and grandchildren."

"Yeah I know." He answered. "Memories are precious but the trouble is you can't forget the bad parts."

Early the next morning he headed for Kentucky. "You plan on coming back this way on your way back home?" The sheriff asked. "If you do, stop and spend the night with us again."

"Wish I could sheriff but I'm anxious to get home to my wife and kids, by the way how about you and your wife paying us a visit some time, you know yourself you need a vacation."

"Guess you're right Witt I'll think about it."

"Well hurry up and make up your mind and give me a call, we have an extra bedroom that you can call all your own, and we will show you and your wife around Richmond."

The sheriff's last words were. "Might just take you up on that young feller, I have always hankered to meet some of them Richmond bureaucrats just to satisfy my mind that I'm not as dumb as they made me out to be in the past."

Witt was smiling as he drove away.

He paid for his gas and asked the station attendant if he could use his phone.

He dialed the number and waited. "Hello is this Burl Crawford? Okay, you don't know me, my names Larry Witt I served with your brother Brad in the war. I have a sealed envelope that he wanted you to have. Can you give me some directions I'm at Burkhart's shell service station?" Then the station attendant interjected. "I can give you directions."

"Okay, Mr. Burkhart said he can direct me there, I'll be there in a few minutes."

As he hung up the phone Al Burkhart, the station owner asked. "Was you with Brad Crawford when he was killed?"

"Yes I was." He answered. "I have a letter he wrote to his kids he requested that the letter go to his brother Burl."

"Yeah the kids are back living with their mother again, she pulled a term in the federal pen you know."

"No I didn't know that."

"Yeah she got mixed up with a dope dealing gang, but she came out a different person, married a deputy sheriff that's well thought of, in fact he's running for sheriff. It's a well known fact that she did Brad wrong when they got the divorce, lying about him mistreating her and the kids he never got over it, finally joined the army and no one ever heard from him until Burl got the notice that he was killed in Belgium."

"Then she married the electrician at the mine, one of the nicest guys you'll ever meet but that didn't last long, they got a divorce just before she went to prison."

"But like I said she's a completely different person now. Are you staying for the memorial service Saturday?"

"You've got me there, what memorial service?"

"Oh I'm sorry, I figured you knew about it, It's for Brad, Burl had him brought back from Belgium he'll be buried at the cemetery right beside the road there, you can see it on that knoll yonder. From what I hear it will be a pretty big thing, expect folks to come from all over the state."

"Well thank you for the information I might change my plans and stay for that. Now tell me how to get to his brother's place."

"That's easy, see the cemetery? Turn right the first road you come to after passing the cemetery and go about two miles you'll see a brick house on the left surrounded by a white picket fence and you're there." Burkhart watched as he walked to his car and thought.

'He reminds me of someone, but I can't recall who.'

"Come on in you must be Larry Witt that called a few minutes ago, here sit here and I'll see if Laura will brew us a fresh pot of coffee."

He soon returned and sat down. "Laura will bring us some coffee shortly. So you served with my brother, did you get to know him well?"

"Well yes and no, I only served with him for a short time and I guess you could say that you really need to be with a person longer than that to really know them, but serving side by side in combat even if it is for a short time brings out the flaws in a man and I can say that your brother had none that I could detect and he died a hero. Here's a letter he wrote to his children the night before he was killed, as you can see he wanted it delivered to you, sorry that it has taken me so long but I was in and out of hospitals off and on after the war and just now able to bring it to you."

"Hey! Don't worry about that I'm just glad you brought it to me."

He turned the envelope in his hands and said. "I guess I'm not supposed to open this until it's in the kids presence, so I'll have to wait till I get them all together."

"And here, I also brought this picture of him and his family, he carried it in his shirt pocket."

Burl looked at the picture and handed it back to him. "I think it best you give this to his former wife yourself, it would mean more to her coming from you."

"I don't know about that." Witt replied. "You see your brother told me about the divorce."

"Yeah I know what you're thinking, because I used to feel the same way, but she has made a complete change in her life and I assure you she will appreciate you bringing her the picture."

Laura came with the coffee and he introduced her. "This is my wife Laura, Laura this is Larry Witt, he brought a letter from Brad to his children."

"How nice of you sir, were you in the war with Brad?"

"Yes ma'am I was." He answered. "And he was a very good soldier."

"We owe a lot to him and others like you who served and risked their lives." She said. "And the loyalty that you have shown to him after death is commendable and worthy of our praise."

"Aw I don't know ma'am, it's just the right thing to do, it don't deserve no special praise."

"Oh yes it does." She replied. "You are very special to us in this household and we owe you a deep debt of gratitude. So we'll start trying to show you that by asking you to eat with us, all the food is on the table and waiting, so when you and Burl wrap up your conversation let me know and I'll heat the rolls."

She walked away as Witt stammered something about he had to go.

Burl smiled and said. "She won't take no for an answer so you may as well get ready to sample her cooking."

"Will you be staying for Brad's memorial Saturday? I had him brought back from Belgium, his body will arrive in Lexington by train on Friday morning and will be brought here Saturday for burial."

"Yes I plan on staying the man at the service station told me about it."

"Okay we have an extra bedroom so you can stay with us."

"Oh I don't know if I should do that I can get a motel room."

"No, no, it makes no sense to do that with an empty bedroom here, and we would be honored for you to spend some time with us."

Witt shrugged his shoulders, smiled and said. "Well I guess I could, but don't want to put you and your family to any extra trouble."

"Don't worry about that, it's an honor to have you as a house guest. Brad would be happy to know that we feel that way."

Laura called from the kitchen. "Dinners ready."

At the dinner table he was introduced to their children and noted their good mannerisms.

"Sir momma says you served with uncle Brad, can you tell us about your experiences there in the Ardennes in Belgium?"

Taken by surprise, he searched for an answer, finally he said. "There's not a lot that I can tell you except that there was snow on the ground much like it is here but a lot more of it, and it was very cold. The Germans secretly amassed a large force that out numbered us three to one and were upon us before we knew what was happening. They broke through our lines in several places and took hundreds of prisoners but we managed to hold on until the weather cleared to where our planes could get in the air and start wiping out their supply lines, that along with the arrival of Patton's third armored division allowed us to put the Germans on the defense and finally they were in disarray and in retreat."

"Your uncle lost his life trying to stop them, I won't get into details but I can tell you that he was a very brave man. I lived to fight with other brave soldiers on in to Germany, but I can truthfully say, that he along with a young man from over in Virginia who went by the name of Tex were two of the bravest soldiers I ever served with. So when you hear the words of praise and appreciation there at the cemetery Saturday, remember not near enough has been said, because hero's are special and beyond explaining. And as you listen to the haunting strains of taps which stirs our emotions but is fleeting much like a flake of snow that evaporates when touched by warm sun rays, then remember your uncle as another unexplainable hero that loved his family and country enough to enlist and risk being brought back home still and cold in a flag draped coffin."

"Yes remember that and store the haunting sounds of taps somewhere in your mind to always remind you of your uncle, because he gave his life for you and me and deserves more than fleeting moments of remembrance. Yes you can be proud of your uncle."

He stood and the solemn faces around the table changed to awe because they knew the words they were hearing were coming from a living hero.

He got out of the car as a horse and rider came toward him from across the pasture that ran back to the woods and barn. 'That must be her.' He thought.

'I should have called before I came, but for some reason I thought it might be best this way.'

As she stopped at the fence he noticed her dark complexion, her beauty and perfect posture in the saddle. The scowl on her face told him that she was uneasy about a complete stranger that would enter her driveway unannounced.

"Ma'am, my names Larry Witt, I served with Brad Crawford in the army, his brother Burl told me how to get to your place, I hope you don't mind that I didn't bother to call but I am a little pressed for time?"

"Oh that's alright." She smiled seeming to be relieved that he didn't represent some unknown bad news of some kind, maybe about her past prison term.

She hitched the horse to the fence, patted him on his rump and climbed across the fence.

"Lets go sit on the porch and I'll get us a cup of coffee." She said.

As he walked along side her and slightly behind he noticed she was almost as tall as he was.

"Here sit in this chair and I'll get us a cup of coffee, would you like some cookies with it? I just made them this morning."

"Yes ma'am, I have never been known to turn down home made cookies."

She brought the coffee and cookies and sat them on a small table that sat at one end of the porch surrounded by four chairs.

"Come sit here." She said. "We use this often, some times when my husband gets home late we eat our meals out here and listen to all the night noises, he's a deputy sheriff and works all kinds of schedules."

"Yes Burl told me about that and said your husband was running for sheriff and was sure to win."

"Well I sure hope so." She replied. "Maybe that way he'll have more time to spend at home."

They sat and talked for about thirty minutes and he began to wonder if he should just get up and go and forget about giving her the picture.

"Do you want more coffee? And here have some more cookies."

"No ma'am." He answered. "I've had enough coffee for today and as for your cookies I could sit here and gorge myself because they are delicious, but I need to control my appetite for sweets."

"So you served with Brad, were you with him when he was killed?"

"Yes I was and he was a very brave man. Here I brought you this picture he carried it in his shirt pocket over his heart."

She took the picture and held it without looking. "Maybe you should give this to his brother Burl." She said.

"I offered it to him but he said I should give it to you. Brad wrote a letter to his children with instructions that it go to Burl, I gave him that."

"Did Brad tell you about us, the divorce and the way I treated him?"

He nodded yes and said. "Yes he did tell me, and Burl told me how much

317

he once hated you for what you did to his brother, but said you have changed and that you are a completely different person now."

She dropped her head and stared at the back of the picture before finally turning it slowly in her hand to reveal the happy family that she once knew but only to fall apart because of her.

Images of Brad working on the little house, romping with the children and holding her close as he whispered "I love you" filled her vision like soap bubbles that look as if they will float on forever in their clear shiny colors, but inevitably burst and disappear in the end. She began to cry as she clutched the picture and finally buried her face in her arms on the table.

Not knowing what to do he reached across and laid his hand on her arm and said. "I'm sorry that I've upset you this way, guess I shouldn't have bothered you."

'No it's alright." She answered. "I'm glad you brought me the picture, God only knows how I've suffered over the way I did him. But I intend to keep his memory alive in my heart because he was a good family man and there will never be a person more deserving."

He stood to leave and she reached for his hand and said. "Thank you for all the time and trouble, you are a very kind man. Will you be at Brad's funeral Saturday? Burl had him brought back you know."

"Yes Burl told me about it, I'll be there."

Then she said. "The letter to the kids, tell Burl he can read it to them here or at his house, tell him to call when he's ready and I'll get them together."

As he drove away she smiled and waved while holding the picture close to her heart.

'What a sad situation.' He thought. 'A woman that wronged the father of her children causing him to will himself to die rather than face the rest of his life without them.' 'But now as you observe her actions and words you can plainly see that she is a changed person, but too late to matter in Brad's life because he died not knowing that she would ever be any different.'

Then he thought. 'I wonder who's the better off, him or her?' 'Guess I'd have to say he is because she's a very sad and broken person having to get up every day with him on her mind remembering the sorry way she treated him.'

'I'm glad she didn't ask a lot of questions about him, I would hate to have to tell her about the tears he shed the night he told me about the divorce, and the way he died there in the Ardennes.'

As he drove on toward Burl's home he noticed workers busy digging a grave at the Cemetery.

'Well he'll finally be closer to her and his children.' He thought. ' 'But what a price to pay, he gave his life, I wonder if she'll be at his funeral.'

She dropped the kids off at Burl's late the next day with this explanation. "Your uncle Burl has something that he wants to read to you."

"What is it?" Her son Dale asked.

"I don't know." She answered. "But I do know it is something very important and you need to hear it."

On her way back home thoughts ran through her mind. 'I hope and pray that what ever is in the letter won't turn my kids against me. But if he did say something about the way I treated him I can't blame him because it is true.'

Burl took them into the room and closed the door. They sat before him as he moved the envelope nervously in his hands.

He looked at them and wondered if there was anything in the letter that would upset them or worse yet turn them against their mother.

Finally he held the envelope so they could read it. "Larry Witt brought me this letter from your father, he wrote it the night before he died. And as you can see he wanted it delivered to me to read to you. I have no idea as to what might be in it as you can see it's sealed."

He could see great excitement and anticipation in their faces as he opened it and prayed that there would be nothing to cause bad feelings toward their mother. As he unfolded the one page letter he could see that it had been hastily and crudely written perhaps in semi darkness with hands that were numb from the cold and without doubt a mind that knew death was near and in a way welcomed it because of the awful thoughts of trying to go on in life without his children.

Then he began to read.

Dear Dale, Connie, and Becky

As you know we have not been in contact for a while I joined the army after your mother and I had a disagreement and got a divorce. Got to thinking about you today as I do every day and decided to write this note that will go to your uncle Burl if something should happen to me.

I want you to know that I'm sorry the way things turned out and wish that your mother and I could have another chance at trying to make our marriage work, but I guess that's out of the question.

You'll never know just how much I have missed you and the happy times we spent together. I hope that you will remember that and cherish it through out your life. Don't let mine and your mothers parting become a dividing factor in your lives I want you to always respect and stick by her side because there's nothing like a mothers love no matter what. She loves you dearly so please honor her always.

Well I guess that's about it, not a lot to write about from here except that it's cold and a lot of snow on the ground here in the Ardennes Forest of Belgium. We have been at a standstill because of the weather but will be on the move again as soon as it breaks. I just wanted to write this in case something should happen to me before this war is over. I will end by saying again how much I have missed you and pray that we will be together again some day. Always remember that I loved you dearly. Bye for now your father.

P.S. Dale you're the oldest and I expect you to honor your mother and help hold the family together.

They had sat quietly as he read but now were sobbing as they embraced each other. As he watched them he thought.

'Why is it that children have to suffer the consequences of divorce and loneliness more than the father and mother?'

He handed the letter to Dale and said. "Here hang on to this and always remember what he said about honoring your mother, you might start by having her read it."

Later when she came to pick them up he watched as each one hugged her neck and was thankful that his brother had written a letter of love and understanding to his children instead of trashing their mother which would have only added to their already troubled young lives.

She stared at the message on the envelope and started reading but stopped and looked away when she read the part that said. 'If anything should happen to me.'

She burst into tears as she handed it back to Dale. "No honey I can't read it." She said.

Dale refused to take it back and said. "Momma I want you to read it because the things he said you need to know about. He wants us to stay with you and always honor you as our mother."

"Okay, I'll read it later Dale, but right now I just want to be alone for a while."

That night she sat in the porch swing wrapped in a blanket waiting for Curt to come home. As she watched him get out of the police car she thought. 'I hope I'm doing the right thing, he might resent my feelings toward Brad.'

"Why are you sitting out here in the cold?" He asked.

"Waiting for you Curt." Was her reply as she stood and they embraced. They went in and she got his supper on the table.

"You know something Julie, I look forward to becoming sheriff and being home at a decent hour to have my evening meals with you and the children."

She laughed and said. "I don't know about that you might get tired of the antics they create around this table, it seems to be increasing as they get older and is pretty noisy at times."

"Yeah I know Julie but I must say I'm surprised how well they get along, oh I know there has been fussing and disagreements among them but nothing that hasn't blown over in a day or two."

"Yes Curt, I know what you mean, at first I was worried that our kids wouldn't get along at all and would eventually cause a breakup between us, but it looks as if they have settled in and want to stay together as much as we do."

"Yes Julie, they seem to be committed to making this family work and I thank God for that."

"And Julie, I want to ask you about the funeral Saturday, I know you said you couldn't bear to be there, but I want you to think about it this way. You belong there with your children and every one expects you to receive the flag. Now if you feel in some way that you shouldn't because of me I want you to get that idea out of your head because I understand and want you to be there. And another thing we have never talked about is when I die I want to be buried beside the wife of my children and I expect you to feel the same way and choose your final resting place with the father of your children."

"We both have cherished memories in our past that need to be preserved, its all a part of our lives Julie, we can't afford to toss them away."

He reached and took her in his arms knowing that he hadn't convinced her but with the funeral still two days ahead maybe she'll come around.

"I guess you're right Curt, but I can't convince myself that I'm worthy of being there after the way I did him. You see its in my thoughts constantly, God only knows how much I regret it and I have prayed to him for forgiveness and I feel that he has but it hasn't erased the awful feeling of guilt that I have suffered through for so long."

"That fellow Larry Witt brought a letter that Brad wrote instructing Burl to read it to the children. I dropped them off over there today and after I picked them up and brought them home Dale asked me to read it but I can't bring myself to even try."

"Yes Burl told me about the letter Julie, and you must read it. Look at it this way you have lived with your feelings about what happened and the pain that it has caused you for so long that you have given up hope, but after reading you might find some words of comfort in it."

He squeezed her tight and asked. "Now will you read it, promise?"

She nodded yes and snuggled closer in his arms.

The next morning she read it, and his words to the children about holding the family together and honoring her as their mother sent chills over her body and joy in her heart but for a short time only, soon the old well worn memories of him working to finish building the house, romping with the children, holding her close as he whispered I love you caused tears to flow again and she knew she would never muster enough courage to be at the funeral and receive the flag that he had so bravely died for.

The service station owner hung the scrawled sign in his window.

'CLOSED FOR FUNERAL' walked out and locked the door behind him.

Before getting in his car he stood for a minute and looked off to the knoll and the crowd that had already began to gather there. The knoll was draped in sunshine warming the crisp December air. Clothing of many different colors stood out against a backdrop of tombstones and the greenery of the tent and artificial grass around the fresh dug grave that the funeral director had prepared in advance.

Below the cemetery at the road he could see two parked police cars and their drivers busy directing cars to parking spaces. All the snow had melted except for a patch on the shaded hillside to the north reminding him of the ominous darkness that the war had cast on some families who lost loved ones that left behind fathers mothers, wives and children.

As Curt directed him to a parking spot he noticed a license plate engraved with the number one, which meant the governor had already arrived.

He climbed the ten stone steps to the cemetery entrance and after an exchange of greetings with some of the familiar faces he walked away to the rear of the gathering crowd, dropped to his knees at his wife's grave, said a silent prayer and whispered "I love you." Finally he stood and looked off toward his station to see a ghostly looking vehicle, long, low, and the color of gray followed by a long line of cars.

The hearse parked near the steps in one of four reserved spaces followed by two other cars that he assumed one was Brad's wife and children, one Burl's family, and the other a small bus that was used to transport the honor guard.

He watched the clean cut neatly dressed soldiers carry the flag draped casket up the steps followed by Brad's three children and Burl and his family.

'I guess she won't be here.' He thought. 'Ever body wondered if she would.'

Then he looked toward the car that the children had gotten out of and noticed some one still sitting in it. 'That must be her.' He thought. 'I guess she'll just sit there till it's over, I was hoping she'd take a part in this.'

Soon the local minister said a few words of introduction to the governor and a state senator who each took a few minutes to honor and express words of praise for fallen service men. "We must never forget the sacrifices these young men and their loved ones made to keep our country free." The governor said. "My heart goes out to Brad's relatives, because I know they are deeply saddened that he will never walk among them anymore, at least here on earth but they can take pride in knowing that he died to keep us all free and I'm sure God has already welcomed him home."

The station owner looked toward the car again as the governor rambled on and could see Curt leaning in the window talking to her. 'I heard he wanted her to be with her children and receive the flag.' He thought. 'Maybe he'll persuade her to join them.'

Then just as the governor finished speaking and the pastor took over Curt opened the car door and she got out. Some one noticed and whispered to the pastor, and all eyes followed his gaze to Curt holding her hand as they made their way up the steps. The pastor turned to face them, as did everyone else as they walked slowly up the gravel pathway her tall dark beauty overshadowed the sadness that showed in her face and eyes.

A seat was made available in the midst of her children and Curt stood behind her straight and assuring along side Ann, Wayne 'Poor Boy' Burke and others and not bothered at all by her paying respects to her former husband.

The pastor cleared his throat and introduced a small singing group from church and as they sang accompanied by a young talented guitar player the station owner never took his eyes off her. He finally dropped his head and whispered. 'I should have told her years ago and it might have prevented some of the misery that she has suffered in her life.'

Then he broke down and cried, some noticed and wondered why.

The command words from the honor guard sergeant 'Fire' followed by rifle shots that echoed off the shadowed snow capped north ridge, and the playing of taps echoed off every ones thoughts, stirring memories of brave soldiers throughout history that sacrificed all. Two members of the honor guard folded the flag neatly and presented it to her.

Burl got up and talked about he and his brother's childhood and how close they were over the years, but he finally gave way to his emotions before he said all that he had planned to and said. "I'm sorry I can't go on." and sat down.

The pastor delivered the sermon and the closing prayer as sobs from her and her children caused others to sniff and wipe away tears.

Some noticed the wide stone that had room for two names that his brother Burl had put there months in advance that had the inscription on one side.

Pfc. Brad Crawford

World War Two

US Army

France Belgium.

They wondered if she would be buried along side him because it was plain to see that Burl had that in mind when he bought the stone.

Then the crowd began to slowly move away, some trying to think of something to say to Brad's family members that might ease the pain of their loss while others talked among themselves, and as always a number of them flocked around the senator and governor unmindful of anyone else around them.

The filling station owner stayed behind and continued to cry and everybody wondered why. Later that day after he reopened for business he took the phone from the wall and dialed his son Jett. "Jett would you come down and take over for the rest of the day? No Jett, I feel fine there's nothing wrong. I just want to go have a talk with my daughter."

Jett drove hurriedly fearing that something was terribly wrong with his father mentally because he was the only child and didn't have a sister.

He parked and ran inside the station not knowing what to expect but found his father sitting calmly in his old familiar easy chair.

"Pop you okay?" He asked. "Yeah I'm fine Jett."

"Well tell me about the daughter you're going to see, what's that all about you know I'm your only child, you don't have a daughter."

"Oh yes I do have a daughter and I intend to let her know who her father is today. It's been on my mind way too long, I kept it to myself because of your mother. I knew it would break her heart if she ever found out, but now that she's gone I have to claim my daughter she's had a hard life and I blame myself for it. You see when she was born her mother left her to her relatives to raise and she never had a mother or father to guide her in life."

"She has made some bad decisions in the way she has treated her husbands and even pulled a prison sentence for dealing in dope. I have watched her actions and died inside a thousand times. But her last marriage seems to be working, in fact she's made a complete turn around for the better and I feel that I'm obligated to go to her now before something happens to me I'm not getting any younger you know."

Jett sat with his mouth open refusing to believe any of what he had heard. "Pop, are you feeling well, or are you poking fun at me? If you are I'll tell you right now ain't nothing funny about it."

"No Jett, I'm leveling with you, the lady Julie, that comes here regular she's your half sister, I had a fling with her mother about six years after you were born. Got her pregnant and it messed up her mind so much that when she had the baby she just up and walked away. Said she couldn't stand to stay here any more and endure the shame. She never came back the last I heard she was working at the shipyards in Baltimore, Maryland during the war years. And you see I have had her on my mind all these years thinking that I was responsible for destroying her life. So today I decided to come clean and claim my daughter because I think she needs me as much as I need her."

"Jett I'm sorry I have to tell you this but now that your mother rests yonder on the knoll and will know nothing about it I think you can handle it."

Jett looked at the floor before answering. Finally he said. "Yes Pop, I understand and wish you the best, no use for you to carry that around with you the rest of your life."

He reached for his felt hat and with car keys in hand walked out and got in his car. Jett stood outside watching and called out as he drove away.

"Hey Pop! Tell her I'm proud to learn she's my sister and I would like to drop by and get acquainted some time."

"Okay Jett, I'll tell her, might be that we can arrange a reunion that would be better yet."

As he drove down the driveway he could see her car and Curt's patrol car parked near the porch but off to the side he recognized the car with the Virginia license plate to be that of Larry Witt. 'Guess I'll have to make it some other time.' He thought. 'They have company.'

He turned and started back down the driveway toward the road. Then he heard someone holler. "Hey Al! where you going?" He looked in his side mirror to see Curt standing on the porch. He backed up and answered. "Thought I'd drop in and chat a while Curt, but it can wait I see you have company."

"Oh no, get out and come in Larry Witt just stopped in to say goodbye he's on his way back home in Virginia."

As he went up the steps Larry came out followed by her. She smiled and said. "Larry, this is Al Burkhart, he runs a shell station down the highway there, he has been a great help to me over the years keeping some of my old clunkers running and other little things he has done for my kids, he's a very kind and gentle man almost like a father to me."

"Yeah I met Mr. Burkhart the first day I rolled in here." He said as he stuck out his hand. "Good to see you again wish I could sit down and chat a while but it's a long drive back home so I better get going toward Virginia."

"Well now you drive careful son and come back and see us sometime."

"I might just do that Mr. Burkhart, been wanting to bring my wife and kids to see the scenery in Southwest Virginia, If we decide to take the trip I'll drive on over here ain't but a few miles from there."

He shook hands with Curt and turned to Julie. "It's been a pleasure ma'am, and I want to wish you all the best in life."

She came forward embraced him and said. "I want to thank you again for your kindness and the things you did for us I will forever be grateful to you. And do bring your wife and kids some time we would be happy to have them."

"Okay ma'am, I promise if we come to Southwest Virginia I'll bring them over here."

He waved as he drove away, Curt called out. "Drive careful over the mountains might be some snow and ice in the shaded spots."

"Yeah I know I'll take it easy." He said.

Al, the station owner had watched him get in the car and thought again. 'He reminds me of someone but it won't come to me.'

Curt turned to Al and said. "Come on in we have a lot of food left on the table that Julie would like for you to sample."

She smiled and said. "Sure Al, come on in and I'll brew some fresh coffee."

He followed them to a table still laden with food, which made his mouth water but remembered what he came there for and decided to go on with that and refuse the food. "No I'm not hungry." He lied. "I just stopped in to tell you something that's been on my mind for way too long and I need to get it off my chest."

"Okay." She said. "But have a seat there and eat something first, Lord knows I owe you something in return for the things you did for me all the years that I was struggling, the flats you fixed for me free and the cold drinks and candy you handed out to my kids on their way to and from school, it must have cut into your profits, I won't take no for an answer so sit down there and dig in while I get some fresh coffee."

As she headed toward the kitchen Curt grinned and said. "May as well go ahead and eat Al, she means what she says and can be pretty stubborn at times."

As he loaded his plate with roast beef, mashed potatoes, and gravy. He thought. 'Yeah I guess she gets that from me.'

He sat and exchanged small talk with them after eating and tried to figure out a way to break the news to her hoping she wouldn't be upset. Finally he came to the conclusion that there was no easy simple way to explain why he had kept a secret like that from his daughter for so long.

"Well what I came for is very important and I hope it will turn out to be a good thing in your life Julie, I know it is in mine. The only thing is I have kept it a secret from you and you might resent that, if you do I'll understand."

"You see I met your mother after my son Jett was born he was six years old. She was a beautiful lady you look just like her Julie. Well we had an affair and she went away after the baby was born, she couldn't bear to stay here amongst her family and friends she couldn't face the shame. It marked my conscious for sure but what could I do, here I have a wife and son, and believe it or not I loved my wife dearly. So I kept it secret, but today while standing at her headstone there on the knoll I decided to share my secret with you because you are my daughter."

She sat dumbfounded for the longest time finally looking at Curt for assurance which came instantly as he moved to her side.

"What great news Julie." He said. "You have a wonderful father."

Al rose and reached out and she melted into his arms with feelings she had never experienced before. A feeling of her fathers arms around her in times of need and understanding. A feeling of never having a mother to talk to, a feeling of guilt because she had never given much thought to anything pertaining to her mother or father and had spent most of her life not caring a lot about anyone including herself with the children being the only exception. And a feeling of resentment toward him because he had kept it from her for so long, but now that he has finally told me I can be forgiving. As she snuggled close to him with tears flowing freely she could hear the old man on the bus as plain as day saying. "That's what its all about blend in with all Gods creatures and the good things around you and you'll find that leads to the joys of life."

Then she thought. 'This has been a wonderful memorable day in my life because at the cemetery I could feel Brad's forgiveness and I came away feeling much better. And now I have something else, a man that I have known all my life to be a kind and sometimes over generous man, now I know why he did it because he was my father. Makes me wonder if my mother is still living and ever thinks of me because starting with today I know I'll always long to hold her in my arms.'

As Curt watched he could sense the happiness they were feeling.

He drove through Middlesboro, Kentucky and within minutes passed the opening to Cudjo's Cave on the bank above the road at Cumberland Gap. As he entered Virginia his thoughts were of the folks he had met back in Kentucky.

The hospitality shown to him by all of them, Burl's love for his brother and his determination to bring him back home for burial. And how he must have despised Julie for how she treated his brother but when he realized she had made a change in her life and was truly regretful for her actions he also changed and treated her as one of the family again. 'A mark of a real man.' He thought.

Then he smiled as Wayne 'Poor Boy' came to mind and he remembered his conversations with him. 'I'm sure he was stuttering over cuss words.' He thought. 'Because a couple times they slipped out anyway.'

'And the way they said Julie treated him while he was married to her, you'd think he would move away and never want to see her again but just like Burl he does the right thing by her now that she has changed, another good man, the world would be a better place if we had more like that.'

'And Al Burkhart, the station owner he was very helpful and friendly, but has a sad forlornness about him that makes you wonder what's on his mind. I wondered why he broke down and cried there at the cemetery, and still do, he was standing by his wife's grave but there seemed to be more to it than that.'

'Curt Flood, the soon to be sheriff, another good man if there ever was one, lost his wife and needed some one, so he winds up marrying a woman that he had helped transport to prison, ain't many that would do that especially a deputy sheriff.'

'And Julie, it's hard for me to see her as they say she once was because she is so nice to be around now. Her and Curt are good for each other and their children, and their love for each other is plain to see. Julie reminds me of my mother, tall, dark, with high cheekbones. My mother was from Kentucky but won't talk about it much. She told me once that she left there as a young girl and had never been back.'

'And Reba, Tex's widow, a nice young lady living with her parents but I'm sure she'll meet up with some one to spend the rest of her life with, she's too young to make a complete commitment to ruling out marriage again.'

He smiled as he could vision little Tex with the cap gun holstered on his waist. But the smile faded when he thought of what he said about the nameplate 'TEX' that the deputy pinned to his shirt pocket. "This used to be my daddy's but now it's mine."

And remembered as he looked around tears were in the eyes of everyone including a giant of a man the sheriff. 'Another good man.' He thought. 'Lot's of good people down in this area, can't wait to bring my wife and kids down here to meet them.'

He turned the radio on and listened to a weather report. Snow was for cast for higher elevations it said. He tuned to another station and listened to a medley of Hank Williams tunes including 'So lonesome I could cry,' which took his thoughts back to the Ardennes Forest to relive the horrors of death and dieing again.

"And damned soon I'm afraid." He could hear Crawford say. And Tex. "It's okay to piss here, see all the piss holes in the snow."

And crackling of snow-laden tree limbs falling to the ground. The dreadful sound of hundreds of tanks as they plowed their way through the heavy snow to overrun their positions. The sounds of the dieing and later watched as their frozen bodies were loaded like cordwood, some with outstretched arms as if reaching for something.

But a few miles south of Lynchburg, his thoughts turned to his family and how nice it was going to be to get home to them. 'Life is too unpredictable.' He thought. 'Anything can happen at anytime that's why I want to make my family the number one priority in my life.'

Then he thought of his mother and father again and the guidance they gave him in his childhood. The way his father dealt with him for misbehavior stern but fair. His mother's gaiety, understanding and gentleness, but underneath all that he could detect a sadness about her that caused him to wonder about her past that she never talked about.

The disk jockey announced that there had been two accidents caused by ice on the road. "It's called black ice folks, the color of the pavement and you can't see it so please drive careful."

He slowed down and as he approached a slight curve a semi was coming from the other direction. At about the middle of the curve it went out of control jackknifed and the trailer came sliding toward him pulling the cab with it. The trailer came sideways covering both lanes of the two lane road hitting him head on sending his mangled car over a ten foot embankment to the railroad below.

The tractor-trailer finally came to a stop with the trailer still blocking the road and the tractor still connected to the trailer hanging partially over a culvert on the other side of the road.

The driver was not hurt and ran to the car that sat upright on the railroad tracks. He became distraught as he looked at the front of the car smashed and pushed up even with the windshield and knew that the driver could not have survived. He ran to the passenger side door that had been forced open from the crash. As he looked at the lifeless body inside the radio was still playing a Hank Williams song. "I saw the light, I saw the light, no more darkness no more night. Praise the Lord I saw the light."

Larry Witt, a young man that did his duty defending our country as a soldier died as a result of extending that duty to his fallen comrades.

A few minutes later a trooper reached in and turned the radio off and recognized the still form as a lifelong friend of his. He watched as they loaded him in the ambulance then walked to his cruiser to fill out the report but had to wait until the tears stopped flowing.

Deputy Curt Boyd, heard about the accident through police channels and brought it up at the Sunday church service. "I managed to get his phone number and called his wife this morning." He said. "She said he would be buried in the Shenandoah Valley at Harrisburg near his father and mother's home. The funeral will be Wednesday 2 P.M. at the Harrisburg First Baptist Church."

"Julie and I plan on going and I have room for a couple more if you want to go."

Burl spoke up. "Laura and I would like to go."

"Okay, we'll get an early start Wednesday morning and should be there in plenty of time." Curt replied. Then everyone noticed Al Burkhart, had tears in his eyes and wondered if he wanted to go.

Poor Boy spoke up. "I wish I could go but I have a meeting scheduled with Blue Diamond for Wednesday. Why don't you take the bus shit—shucks you'd have more room and more could go along."

"That sounds good to me." Curt answered. "If anyone else decides to go let me know before Wednesday, and in the meantime I'll call the sheriff of Lee County, Virginia, Larry was telling me about him, said they were good friends I'm sure he'd like to go, and some one else from there might want to go, we go right through there and can pick them up."

Early Wednesday morning Burl Crawford, his wife and their oldest daughter got on the bus along with Al Burkhart, Curt, Julie, and her oldest son Dale.

Poor boy and Ann assured them they would check on their other children while they were gone. "Don't worry we'll keep them in line." Poor Boy said. "Ann knows how to handle them." They all laughed knowing that he would let them get away with anything but depended on Ann to keep them in line.

Al got his Son Jett to keep the station open.

They stopped at the Jonesville, Virginia courthouse where the sheriff, Reba and Tex junior were waiting. The sheriff had thought it proper that Reba and Tex should attend the funeral also. Little Tex was decked out in his best cowboy shirt, the TEX nameplate pinned to his shirt pocket and the deputy sheriff badge above that.

During the introductions the sheriff said. "This is Tex junior, I'm sure Larry Witt told you folks about him, I just swore him in as one of my deputies a few days ago." Little Tex grinned from ear to ear.

As the miles ticked off the conversation was mostly about Larry Witt. "I've known him for a long time." The sheriff stated. "Never been a finer young man."

"Yeah, I only knew him for a few days." Burl answered. "But long enough to see that he was a good man and a dedicated family man, it's sad that he leaves a wife and two young children behind."

"Just goes to show how little we know about when the Lord will call us away." Laura said. "We all seen and talked to him Saturday and little did we know that we would be attending his funeral today."

They were ushered to seats to the left and toward the front in the large church building noting that most of the pews were taken.

As strains of 'Amazing Grace' from the organ drifted softly over the crowd they watched the casket roll down the aisle followed by his wife, children, and his mother and father.

Curt looked at the tall dark beauty of the older woman and was stunned at how much she looked like Julie. He looked over at Burl and Laura and could see they too were dumfounded at the resemblance.

Unnoticed was Al, as he had turned his head away not believing what he was seeing. 'That's her.' He thought. 'What have I got myself in to, wish now I hadn't come, how can I face her? Now I know who Larry reminded me of.'

Several people got up and made short talks about Larry before the pastor took over, including his life long friend the State Trooper.

The audience was filled with emotion as mournful sounds of grieving came from his family as the service went along.

At the end of the service several came forward to shake hands with the family and give words of encouragement. The sheriff led their group except for Al Burkhart' who sat rigidly gazing at the floor. As Julie placed her hand on the tall dark lady's arm she looked up and to each it was like looking in a mirror. To Julie she was looking at herself in older age, and to the lady it was like looking in a mirror when she was the age of Julie. Neither spoke a word, but stared at each other as if in disbelief. Finally Julie moved on to the next family member and as Curt took the lady's hand and said something of encouragement he noticed her gaze followed Julie and knew she didn't hear a word he uttered.

The crowd watched as the pallbearers put the casket in the hearse. The tall dark lady's group stood near the hearse and Curt noticed again that she and Julie had locked eyes. He sidled over to where Al Burkhart stood looking down at the ground and asked. "Al, is that Julie's mother?" "Yes it is." Al answered. "And right now I could die." Curt patted him on his shoulder and said. "That's okay Al, every things going to turn out fine."

He walked back to Julie and whispered. "Go ahead and do what ever you feel like doing Julie, every things going to be alright."

As Curt steered the bus behind the long line of cars on the way to the cemetery he noticed the silence among the group and could sense that they knew the lady must be Julie's mother. 'I hope Julie will acknowledge it.' He thought. 'But its something she has do herself, if she chooses not to then so be it, she knows her feelings and it's not for me to judge.'

After the short graveside service the two groups were about thirty feet apart and all watched as Julie and the lady stared at each other. And to the ones that had figured it out they wondered if there would be a great joyful climax or would they simply turn and walk away from each other.

Finally they started walking slowly toward each other but the last few steps quickened and as they embraced Julie sobbed. "I've found my mother." To which her mother replied. "And I have found my daughter."

A sad occasion for the lady as she said goodbye to her son, but now had welcomed a daughter into her life, a daughter that she walked away from as a baby because of the shame it caused her but now looked forward to sharing the rest of her life with.

To Julie it was a very good feeling to find her mother just days after learning who her father was, but at the same time sad that she didn't know Larry was her half brother until after his death.

Some of the crowd left without knowing what had taken place, but to the few that knew, tears welled up in their eyes. Off to himself Al Burkhart was sobbing and everybody wondered why, except Curt and the tall dark lady, she glanced his way and wondered if Julie knew he was her father. 'If not I'll tell her.' She thought. 'No use keeping it a secret any longer.'

Earl Witt was pleased that his wife had finally accepted her daughter, she had told him the secret before they were married and he tried to talk her into finding her daughter many times because he could sense the guilt and shame she was feeling about abandoning her at birth.

That day was the beginning of something very special in Julie's life. There were many visits back and forth and a noticeable change could be seen in her children as they became more acquainted with their grandmother and looked forward to seeing her often. They had grown closer to their grandfather Al Burkhart, and could be seen hanging around his filling station almost daily. But when their grandmother would come for a visit Al would not be invited to join them for obvious reasons, and everyone understood that.

Curt was elected sheriff of Harlan County, by a landslide and with all the years he served as a deputy and the experience in his background he settled in to the job easily.

Julie kept working with women that had done their time in prison with a great amount of success. The prison warden in Indiana noticed and asked if she would come there twice a year to talk to the women. "I believe you can help them to prepare for their release." He said. "If they can see that there's hope for them once they've served their time that is the first step toward them never coming back here again." She gladly accepted and as time passed she found that the riding classes took too much of her time so she gave it up and turned the horses over to the children.

As she crossed the Ohio river on her drives to and from the prison in Indiana tears would flow as the image of the old man on the bus would pass before her and she could hear his words. "Blend in with God's creations and the good things and you'll experience the joys of life." 'My life has come full circle.' She'd think. 'If only I could go back and get the kinks out and make it a perfect circle.'

Meanwhile the demand for coal dropped to an all time low in the coal fields of Kentucky and Virginia causing more of the big mining companies to cease operations, leaving many out of work. The small mining towns like St. Charles, Virginia once booming and packed to the brim on weekends now became empty as one by one the café's, juke joints, poolrooms, barbershops, grocery stores, hardware stores, and any other sideline business including bootlegging closed down.

And from that time into the nineteen sixties the exodus of it's people became complete, leaving behind empty buildings that once were a proof of progress but now stood as unattended monuments to the past only to rot away or be torn down years later.

Some of its people toughed it out and waited for the change that was surely to come, it took a while but they have benefited from it greatly. Although the ghostly mining towns and coal camps never recovered other enterprises have flourished and the ones that stuck it out are happy they stayed.

Same goes for the ones that went away to Michigan, Illinois, Indiana, Ohio, or other states to rekindle their dreams, most did well while others managed to get by as is the case in any group of people.

But they all have one thing in common, a yearning for the hills of Lee and Wise Counties in Virginia. Harlan and Bell Counties in Kentucky, and they go back often to see relatives or just stand and gaze at where a juke joint, drugstore, or movie theater, once stood that meant so much to them at that time in their lives.

Many that went away have died and were brought back there for burial at their request a small consolation I suppose to their never ending yearning and the memories they held of their childhood.

The long lines of coal-laden cars pulled by the mighty diesel engines became less frequent out of the coalmining hollows, including St. Charles, Virginia.

But one morning the rumble of the Diesel and the tonnage that followed it rolled through the little community of Maness approaching Stone Creek. The lonesome whistle blew as it approached the long curve that went through Stone Creek and eventually ended at the Pocket community at old Dominion Power Company.

The walls of the houses in the bottom near the railroad vibrated as the long line came closer.

His face was ashen and crusted with matter from his eyes and mouth as he lay there amidst the clutter of his room a small table with a telephone, a flashlight, dirty hankies and a half filled pint bottle of bonded whiskey. A room that he had chosen to sleep in alone so the late night calls and his comings and goings wouldn't disturb his wife and kids. A room that he had begun to recognize as a fort that shut out the outside world and its troubles, a place to lie down for short periods of time knowing the phone would ring with some one requesting they needed him to come see a sick family member. But in the end the room had literally became a room of torture as he would lay there thinking about his past and what it might have been if only he hadn't let the deadly spirits that came out of the bottle take over his life.

Just as the diesel engine passed the whistle blew again and he tried to raise his head from the frothy pillow but could not. He reached out his hand and with a pleading look on his face said something that was drowned out by the noise from the train.

Was he asking for a drink from the bottle that he could no longer hold because of weakness in his dieing body, or was he pleading to see his family, or perhaps asking the Lord to put him on that train and take him away from all the miseries that he had brought on him self. Or could it be that he seen the face of God and was reaching for his hand? The clack clacking sound from a loose connection on the rails as each wheel ran over it was much like a giant clock ticking and then just as the caboose passed and the last wheel ran over it the lonesome whistle sounded again as the diesel passed through the Pocket community. He shuddered once and then his body relaxed as the expression on his face changed from agony to peaceful rest he closed his eyes and left behind all the miseries that had tormented his life here on earth.

And just as many others left Lee County to pursue a better life that their beloved County could no longer offer he also left, but in a different way and

I pray that our Lord welcomed him to heaven, because he put him self through hell here on earth.—So long Doc God bless you.

To some memories of you will only stir visions of you and the bottle that you became a slave to, and at the same time overlooking all the times you struggled through long days and into the night administering to the sick some times knowing, that the family was just getting by from day to day and you would never see a penny for your service.

But I will always remember you as a man that succumbed to one of the every day pit falls that we humans face here on earth. But in spite of the load it put on your shoulders you never gave up and trudged on doing as much as you could for your fellow man.

I will not dwell on the reeling way you walked, the redness of your eyes or the lack of color in your face, I'll look beyond all that to the goodness of your heart and see a man that deserves to be in the presence of our Lord.

Again let me say, So long Doc and God bless your Soul.

As more big mining companies sealed the entrances to the cold damp darkness of underground mining that required a large work force, new equipment began to emerge that would forever change the way to mine coal. Huge Auger like contraptions that can bore right through a seam of coal and deposit it on to a conveyer belt that transports it to a grading tipple outside where its washed and graded before finally being loaded on to railroad cars for shipment to power plants and other facilities over the United States.

And along about the same time strip mining emerged with monster dozers, trucks, etc. that could move tons of dirt and rocks to uncover all the coal on the fringes of the closed mines, including smaller seams that had never been mined before. As the demand increased from power plants in Georgia and Florida more sought leases to strip mine including a few ex-miners and some were successful and became millionaires during the nineteen sixties and seventies.

The mine in Kentucky that Wayne 'Poor Boy' Burke, had kept profitable for so many years finally closed due to the changing times. But with his ties to Blue Diamond he was able to attain some leases that would launch him into becoming a very rich man. Besides his own operation he sub-leased tracts to several others, including two of his close friends Burl Crawford, and Curt Boyd. He used his old adjoining farm to store equipment that was in need of repair along with equipment sent there by Burl and Curt for repair, the place was filled with monster machines, some to never be used again as they were replaced and left to rust away as the weeds grew up around them.

Al Burkhart sold his filling station and was put in charge of keeping the machinery in operating condition he hired his son Jett, and three other mechanics and they all were paid well.

Curt resigned from the County sheriff's position and he and his partner Burl an ex-miner went on to be successful in strip mining.

But the massive removal of trees and dirt to uncover the coal left the landscape desolate looking prompting many complaints from its citizens. It would be years and much damage later before the proper regulations were finally put in place that would protect the landscape from erosion.

More coal was now riding the rails than ever before but it didn't bring back any ex-miners from Detroit, Cleveland, Chicago, or where ever they had reluctantly moved away to because far less men were needed to mine the coal. One piece of equipment plus other components could produce as much coal as perhaps one hundred miners.

Progress yes, but a sad commentary to the coal camps and other communities that housed so many families that were entrenched and happy with their way of life only to be uprooted and forced to go elsewhere to find work and as a result ended up scattered all over the country leaving behind ever lasting memories of a time in their lives that to this day some still hold close to their hearts.

A way of life disrupted by changing times and the power of new inventions in the name of progress, but left behind no apologizes for all the families that had to watch as it slowly but surely forced them to leave, some with large families that had trouble adapting to their new surroundings and homesickness became a daily companion in their lives.

Then there's the miners that were killed in mining accidents and are resting in the cemeteries, some overgrown, unattended, out of the way, with fading markings that are sure to vanish as time goes on, and that's sad because they deserve to be remembered in history much like a soldier that is aware of the dangers that he faces might cost him his life but unselfishly performs his duty anyway. So is the miner that entered the darkness each day knowing that he may never see the light of day or his family again but did it anyway.

Here are just a few of many that I know about.

My great uncle by marriage, Andrew Napier, they lived across the hill from us and he loved to kid me when I was a young boy. He was killed in a

slate fall at the Crummies Creek coalmine in Kentucky in the 1930's. He and
Aunt Lizzie had nine children, the three youngest never really getting to know
him. The oldest Woodrow worked and held the family together and as each
one became old enough they would help support the family. Aunt Lizzie
never remarried.

Joe Baker lost his life in a mine that went by the name of 'Rattling Jar' on
Pucketts Creek in Lee County in the 30's rats had eaten away much of his face
before he was found.

Earl Sprinkle brother of Otis Sprinkle was electrocuted in the Leanrue
mine in Kentucky in 1936. Then Otis was killed at the Bonny Blue mine in
Lee County, Virginia in 1949.

Bill Byrd was killed at the Bonny Blue mine in 1949 also leaving behind
his wife Nancy Harber (She was my second cousin) and three children. He is
buried in a little cemetery on a knoll near the Admant Baptist Church at Stone
Creek, in Lee County. I well remember the day of his funeral I was one of the
pallbearers and there was snow on the ground and it was a struggle to carry
the casket up the hill without falling. As I looked at his grieving wife and
small children I couldn't help but question why God took him away. Nancy
never remarried.

Sam Derossett's uncle Harold Bennett was killed at the High Splint mine
in Harlan County Kentucky in 1952.

M.A. Edens from Ben Hur was killed in the Blue Diamond Coal Company
Mayflower Mine in Lee County, VA, in 1947.

Actually he was in the Kentucky side of the mountain when the accident
happened. Most of the mines in that area of Lee County were mined through
the mountains toward KY. And eventually the coal was being mined in KY.
And brought back through the mountain to be processed in VA. Therefore a
number of accidents took place in KY.

Raymond Baker son of Charlie Baker from Lee County was killed in a
shaft mine in IL. In the1980's.

L.A. 'Fate' Baker was killed at the Bonny Blue mine in 1951 leaving
behind seven children one of them being Kidel a friend of mine. Fate's wife
never remarried.

Brothers Earl and Otis Sprinkle were Kidel's uncles. Also Joe Baker was Kidel's great uncle and Raymond Baker was his cousin.

Brothers John and Virgil Robbins distant cousins of mine from the Belgium Hollow community in Lee County were killed in mining accidents. John at the Mary Helen mine in Harlan county Kentucky and Virgil at a mine on Elys Creek in Lee County Virginia. Then later Richie 'Red' Burgan from the same community was killed in a mine near St. Charles, Virginia.

One of my cousins R.T. Kirk was killed in a coal tipple accident in Holmes Mill Kentucky leaving behind a wife and two children.

Another cousin Alvis Kirk was killed while operating a tram motor in a mine operated by Steve Middleton in Harlan County, KY.

Harold Dowell married my first cousin Agnes Doss, Harold was killed in a mine on Pucketts Creek in Lee County VA. Leaving behind Agnes and four children.
Three other young men were killed in the same rock fall. They were Floyd Buddy Varble, Danny Roberts, and, Wayne Mosley. It took a few days to retrieve their bodies from the massive rock fall.

Another cousin of mine Charles L. Kirk was killed in the L&M mine on Puckets Creek Feb. 24 1975 in Lee County, VA. The same rock fall also took the life of Ronald "Zeke" Britt.

In the late sixties or early seventies a man with the last name Burgin was killed at the bonny Blue mine.

Killed in an explosion in the P & P mine at St. Charles, VA. were four young men from that area.
Harold Johnson, Roger Tester, Randall Wells, and Billy Perkins.

John Thomas, Fay Mayes grandfather, was killed at Monarch # 5 seam in 1953.
Henry Willis lost his life at monarch # 5 seam in 1960.
Clint Hughes once a town policeman in St. Charles, VA. Lost his life at the Kemmer Gem # 5 seam above St. Charles in 1960.

Danny Martin the son of Wilber and Loda Martin and Clint Hughes nephew was killed in the Westmorland mine in the Big Stone Gap, VA. Area on Sept. 29 1979.

Anthony Rogers was killed at the Virginia Lee mine in Lee County, VA. In the late 1920's.

Ewell West lost his life in a little mine on Elys Creek in Lee County.

Eugene Farmer was killed in a mine at Cranks Creek, KY.

Jeff Miller lost his life at the Glenbrook mine in KY.
Vessie "Alabama" Henton and Garrett Bruce both were killed in the Crummies Creek mine in Harlan County, KY.

Tim Shackelford was accidentally electrocuted at the Glenbrook mine in KY.

Also a man by the name of Smithson first name unknown died in the Glenbrook mine.

Richard "Rich' Carter died in the Benedict coal mine in Lee County, VA. In 1951 leaving behind ten children, the two oldest had already left home leaving eight at home, Mrs. Carter raised them and never married again.

Walter Skidmore, a friend of mine from Harlan County, KY. Furnished me these names just from his memory.
Luther Skidmore, Walter's brother was killed in the 'Three Point Mine' in Harlan County KY. In the 1930's.
Henry Pennington, in the Crummies Mine, Harlan County, KY. in 1942.
Bert Jordan's, brother was killed in the Crummies Creek mine in 1942.
Lige Allen, was killed in the Crummies Creek mine in the mid thirties and later his son Lige Jr., was killed in the same mine in the early 40's.
Andy Jackson was killed in the Crummies Creek mine in 1942.
Hobert Johnson was killed in the Leanrue mine in the mid thirties.
John Meadows, and Ken Owens, were killed in the Mary Helen mine in Harlan County, KY. In the early 60's.
Gene Hopkins, and Cris Pennington, both killed at the Mary Helen mine in the 1980's.

Shane Moad, a stockman or cowboy standing in front of his quarters on the Earaheedy Station or Cattle Ranch in Western Australia in 1986. He's holding a 303-25 rifle used for shooting roos or camels.

Picture used with his permission.

Reg Blackman, Shane Moad's great uncle, a stockman or cowboy on a family station or ranch in New South Wales in the 1950s.
Picture used with Shane Moad's permission.

Troy Rogers was killed in the Ben Sergeant mine on Cranks Creek, in Harlan County, KY. In the late 80's.

Morris Davenport, Walter Skidmore's brother in law was killed in the Lacy Miles mine on Cranks Creek in 1958.

Elbert Thompson, and his son Bill, both killed in a truck mine on Cranks Creek in the 1960's.

Luther Young was killed from an explosion in a mine on Mill Creek, in Harlan County, KY. Clarence Woodsby, died some months later from the same explosion.

Twelve men were killed in an explosion at the Three Point Mine in Harlan County, KY. In 1942.

Another explosion from the early thirties claimed the lives of at least seventeen at the Yancy mine in Harlan County, KY. Six of them were brothers. Can you imagine their father and mother at the funeral staring at six caskets? Reminds me of the song, "Nobody knows the trouble I've seen."

Allan Young, better known as "The Appalachian Writer" remembers these men that were killed in the mines around St. Charles, VA. Some were at Kemmerer Gem Coal Company.

Jerry Harbor, Clarence Freels. Clarence left behind his wife three sons and three daughters. Lloyd Fultz, also Allan's father Ab Young lost his twelve-year old brother to a slate fall.

Will Neff, Kathy Conner's great grandfather, lost his life in a massive rock fall in the Bonny Blue mine in Lee County VA. In September 1908.

As I said this is but a few of many that lost their lives while working in the mines in that area.

And during World War Two, Carl Cooper, son of Tom and Alice Cooper, from Belgium Hollow was assigned to work in a Copper or Iron Ore mine in one of the western states and lost his life, he is buried at the Cooper Cemetery on Pucketts Creek in Lee County.

Also killed in a copper mine out west was Bascom White who was living with his brother N.B. in Lee County when he joined the service and chose to work in the copper mine. He is buried in his home state Alabama.

For us, that remember that Era in Lee County, Virginia, and Harlan County, Kentucky. the memories are permanently stored in our hearts, but as our ranks thin we take the memories with us and they will slowly fade away and that's sad.

Thanks to Clarence Napier, Kidel Baker, J.P. Kirk, Sam Derossett, Ronnie Carter, Allan Young, Walter Skidmore, Barbara 'Sturgill' Allison, Fay Mayes, and Kathy Conner for furnishing some of the names above.

Another baby, a girl was born into the lives of Poor Boy and Ann, prompting Poor Boy to say. "Ann this is just a start, hel—lo two ain't enough we need at least a dozen to fill this big house."

"Oh yeah." She answered with a smile on her face knowing that he like her knew this would be the last due to their age. "But at our age we would be more like grandparents to them."

"Yeah I know Ann, we better stop right where we're at before things get out of hand."

More wealth came their way as his mining operations continued to move forward. The church and other organizations along with many individuals were to share in his wealth because sharing was his nature which a few took as a weakness and tried to take advantage but soon found out he had a keen instinct for gold diggers and would drop them like a hot potato. After one such incident he said. "Shit, Ann, there's lots of good people in the world, only thing is you have to sift through so many bad ones to find them."

Curt and Burl's strip mining operations went beyond all expectations affording their families all the good things in life including the best schools and an individual bank account for each child.

Curt and Julie, adored their son that they named Larry after her half brother, but tried to treat him the same as the other children. Of course all things in life are never perfect theirs being no different, bumps in the road tested their faith and many times upset the family stability.

Burl and Laura, were devastated to learn that their oldest daughter was pregnant at a very young age and wondered where they had gone wrong bringing her up. It became a trying time in their lives bringing much heartache but worked out well in the end when the young father came forward and eagerly took her as his bride.

Curt and Julie suffered the ills of jealousy among their children even though they had been very careful to treat them all the same. Same schools and bank accounts, and equal attention, but in spite of it all Julie's son Dale, drifted off to a world of his own as he called it and became a hippy. He dropped out of college and rambled from state to state. His phone calls home were never pleasant, as he would relate his troubles that he blamed on others never on himself. He always needed money to supply the habits that he had acquired in his newfound world, which they never refused for fear of him dropping even lower they supplied and he went through large sums of money.

Julie worried night and day and wondered why her world had suddenly turned sour. She often thought of the old man on the bus and the advice he gave her that had literally put joy back in her life and now to see it disappear was getting more than she could bear. If not for Curt's love and understanding she felt she would surely go completely insane.

"Try not to worry Julie, he'll be okay he's just kind of lost his way and one thing about it we can't give up on him. One day he'll find himself and walk in that door full of remorse asking forgiveness."

"I hope you're right Curt and you usually are." She said. "Oh how I'd love to see him walk through that door again."

Reba's father and mother took her and Tex junior to France for two weeks, the main reason being to visit Tex senior's grave in Belgium.

Reba's mother had served as a nurse in a hospital in England in 1918 and 1919 during World War One and knew the horrors of war and was not surprised at the thousands of crosses that covered several acres at the cemetery.

As they stood at his grave in the midst of a sea of white crosses watching Tex Jr. run his fingers over his father's name Reba had mixed feelings, one of happiness although solemn, and at the same time sadness filled her very soul as she relived her memories with him and the way he died without ever seeing his son.

Back at the hotel they met a young man from Australia who had came there to visit his brother's grave at the same Cemetery who lost his life in the war also.

He was about the same age as Reba and right from the start he and Tex Jr. hit it off.

His family owned a huge cattle ranch in Australia and he was a true working cowboy. Questions from Tex about the ranch never ceased. His name was Lance Kirk and as Reba listened to him and Tex she knew that a bond was building between them that would eventually include her because he had tried to make eye contact with her several times and in spite of her refusal he showed no signs of discouragement. Her father and mother noticed and her mother once remarked. "Reba I don't know if you know it but that nice young man is interested in you."

"Ah momma! He's just being nice because he likes Tex."

"Oh yes he likes Tex, but he also likes his mother, I'm a pretty good judge of young men Reba and this one is special."

They ferried across the English Channel to visit Dorchester England where Reba's mother served as a nurse in a hospital near Dorchester during World War One. There she got to see several people that she had been acquainted with during that war.

After they returned they took several side trips by train over France, Belgium, and Germany and invited the young Australian to come along. The bond between he and Tex grew to the point to where she knew it was only a matter of time before the ties that bind would include her.

So one day she relented and looked into his blue eyes framed by leathery Sun tanned skin with squint wrinkles that had come from long days in the sun but now had became a part of his smiling personality.

He returned her gaze and then she became lost in her thoughts as she relived her life and times with Tex. As it unfolded before her she began to feel guilt and turned away. From behind he laid his hand on her shoulder and said softly.

"I understand Reba, I understand."

The day before they were to board the plane for home they went to visit Tex grave for the third time. Lance took them to his brother's grave first, and afterward joined them at Tex grave. He watched Tex Jr. hold on to the white cross as his mother wiped away tears.

'Too bad.' He thought. 'He had to lose his father that way, and his mother, she must feel terrible that her husband had to die and will never see him grow up.'

'Wish I could console her but I guess it's too early, maybe with time she will decide to move on with her life and I want to be around when it happens.'

They walked away from the grave and out of the cemetery.

Outside Tex Jr. turned and looked back at the rows of crosses for the longest time as if waiting for his dad to appear and wave goodbye.

The next day Lance went to the airport with them and for the first time asked Reba for her address. "Hope you don't mind if I post you a letter."

He drew Tex to him and said. "I'm gonna miss this bloke here, I was hoping you would let him stay with me, he wants to be a cowboy you know. No seriously I would love for him to visit me and my family, and that includes you and your parents we have plenty of room there at the homestead."

Her father and mother had been watching and quickly stepped forward to say their goodbyes to him knowing that he and Reba needed some time together.

"Come on Tex." Her father said. "Lets get in line before we lose our seat on that plane."

Tex looked at his mother and asked. "Momma, can I go to Australia with Lance? He said he'd teach me how to ride, I want to be a cowboy momma."

"Yes I know son, but not now we have to get back home and get you back in school, maybe after schools out, we'll see."

He scowled as he shook hands with Lance and said. "Okay, I guess it'll have to be later but don't forget to send me a picture of that horse you said I could have."

"Oh sure mate he's yours, and I'll take good care of him till you show up, now run along your grandpa's waiting."

As Reba watched them get in the long line she turned to Lance and said. "So you've promised him a horse, makes me wonder what else might be running through your mind."

He reached and drew her to him. "Might shock you Reba so I'll keep it to myself right now, I'll tell you about it in the letter."

In his eyes she could still see the smiling face of Tex giving her permission to look beyond their life together and start over with some one new.

Then as her parents and Tex watched from the long line that had now begun to move toward the plane they embraced and clung to each other for the longest time prompting her mother to remark. "She better get a move on or else she'll miss this flight."

"Right now I don't believe she'd care if she did because she's finally found someone to start all over with again." Her father replied.

She turned and walked away he stood and watched as she joined the long line. Then he could see Tex waving and heard him say. "See you soon Lance, take care of my horse."

"Yeah don't worry mate he'll be in good shape and raring to go when you get to the homestead." He watched as they went to board the plane and later looked up as the plane lifted above the clouds and out of sight. 'Hope the bloody thing stays in the air.' He thought. 'Because it's carrying a part of me, a part I want to have around the rest of my life.'

The Big Brave Lad's wife did her time in prison and was out before he was, she filed for divorce while taking counseling from Julie. She was determined to pick up the pieces of her life and go on but this time without him because it opened her eyes as to the kind of person he was when he let her take the fall for a drug operation that he directed and was wholly responsible for.

Julie did all she could for her although it seemed awkward seeing that she herself had had an affair with him. She helped her find a job in Harlan at a new car dealership. She did well and became a respected citizen and an asset to the company. She finally left there and became involved in real estate as an agent in Bell County at Middlesboro, KY. Along the way she met a fellow agent that had a past much like her own and was struggling to right him self again.

They spent a lot of time together and as time went on they would share their past. Which wasn't all that pleasant but to them it became a way to release pent up feelings and instilled a trust between them that grew into a lasting relationship.

They were married in the early 1950's and shortly afterward set up an agency of their own that struggled to survive for a couple of years but gradually improved to the point where they had to hire more agents to take care of the growing business that had now extended into neighboring Tennessee and Virginia Counties.

The Big Brave Lad finally got his release from a long prison term and chose to live in Bell County near Middlesboro it seemed for two reasons. Number one because he intended to continue making his living on the shady side and that would be easier in Bell rather than Harlan County where he realized he would be watched closely. The other being that he wanted to be close to his ex wife if for nothing else to harass her which he did until she finally told her story to the Bell County sheriff who quickly put a stop to it. The sheriff contacted the Harlan County sheriff and got a complete list of his past crimes in that county including the prison sentence.

The sheriff of Harlan County relayed this message. "Best you keep an eye on him. He likes the drug business and will do almost anything to make it big time. In other words he'll kill if necessary to get what he wants, he's a no good SOB."

And how true the words were as the Bell County sheriff would learn later as he tried to entrap him in what he considered a growing drug ring that had produced three murders over a span of two years in what looked like rival drug dealers that he wanted out so he could take over their turf. But seemed he always stayed a step ahead of law enforcement which was highly frustrating as they watched him tool around in his always new red Lincoln automobile which he traded in yearly. He had put enough fear in his underlings that it was almost impossible to get any of them to talk. So he had free rein and sat back in the comforts of his lavish apartment or the Lincoln while others peddled his drugs over Bell County and into adjoining counties in Tennessee and Virginia.

Back in St. Charles, Virginia Reba and her family were busy telling their neighbors about their trip to Europe.

Tex Jr. would go down the street and join the usual bunch under the sycamore tree daily to relate his experiences about the trip. There he would find a mixed crowd to listen to his stories, some off from work for the day for one reason or another and others that were out of work and came every day to sit in the shade just to talk and listen to some one else's problems or stories that pretty much resembled their own.

"Did you notice." One of them mentioned one day. "Our crowd is getting smaller all the time?"

"Yeah," Another one answered. "Yeah, th mines are laying off every week now and folks are heading off to Michigan and Ohio to find work. Now I hear V.I.C. is about to shut down and think of how many more will be leaving, and on top of that Bonny Blue is down to about a third of what they used to have working there."

Then another spoke up. "I tell you what's happening the coal industry is on it's way out and in another two or three years this town will be almost empty."

"Oh I don't know about that." Another one said as he whittled on a piece of cedar. "This town has went through tough times before and managed to survive."

"Yeah, but this time it's different how is a town going to survive without people?" Hell, ain't nobody much left now and I'm leaving for Ohio next week myself, and the way I figure it that means the town is finished, tell me how in hell can it go on without me?"

The guy whittling looked up and said. "Shit, ain't nobody gonna miss you, I'd say that'll be a good riddance, ain't that right George?"

George 'Washington' Reynolds, one of the town character's had been listening intensely and waiting to get his two cents worth in answered. "Hell yes if'n he thinks he's that damn smart we don't need him here anyway."

That started them to laughing and that was the main reason some of them came daily to try to break the worry and Monotony of already being without a job or would soon be.

Then some one said. "Well here comes Tex to tell us some more about his trip. I hear his mother and her parents are thinking about leaving for Illinois, so there goes another family, sure will miss Tex."

"Yeah I will too, he's such a nice boy and a spitting image of his dad."

He sauntered in lifted his back side to the bridge railing and sat down'

"How's it going cowboy, you put any one in the calaboose today? I hear you might be moving to Illinois."

"My mom says we might but I don't want to go, I want to go live in Australia."

"Australia! why lord that's way off yonder across the waters and down under the rest of th world, about as fer away as you can get from St. Charles."

"Taint no such thing." George Washington piped in. "I been there before."

"Now George, tell me when you went to Australia, shit you ain't been out of the country and not much of any where else except maybe to Georgia with Cowboy Barker to get a load of peaches."

"You're crazy as hell." George retorted. "I flew over there lots of times during th war."

"Now tell me George, who in hell flew you over there and what did you do after you got there?"

"I ain't about to tell you that but I will tell you that I was with the FBI and it was a guverment plane and it was guverment business by god, and that's all you'll get out of me." That brought another roar of laughter that sat George off on one of his cussing fits.

Finally Tex spoke up. "The reason I want to go live in Australia is I have a horse there."

One of the men murmured to another. "Damn don't tell me that boy is going to out do George, shit you know he ain't got no horse over there."

They watched as he fished an envelope from his pocket and removed some pictures. "See here." He said. "That's my horse and there's the man that gave him to me his name is Lance Kirk."

"His name is what? "One asked. "His name is Lance Kirk we seen him in France and he said he'd give me a horse and that's him and my horse."

Then the whittling man spoke up. "Well son if he's a Kirk and anything like the Kirk's we have around here, he'll tell you anything." Which brought another roar of laughter.

"What do you make of it George, do you think Tex has a horse in Australia?"

"Hell yes. "George answered. "I know he does you damn fools are making fun of him just like you do me when I tell you the truth."

"And this is the house Lance lives in." Tex went on. "And here is some of his cattle."

"Damn look at that." One remarked. "Looks like the big rambling ranch houses out west that we see in them westerns there at the theater. And hell, look at that, a white horse just like Ken Maynard's."

"Well son do you think you'll ever get over there to ride this horse?"

"I might, my grandpa says we might go over there to visit if he can get enough money together. It's a long way there and it takes a lot of money to buy plane tickets."

"Yeah I know son I hope you'll be able to get there, don't make much sense to own a good riding horse if'n you can't ride him."

The conversations went on for a while on various subjects but soon the crowd dwindled as one by one they began to drift away.

Back home, Tex asked his mother again if maybe they would go. "Will I ever see my horse mom?"

"Well yes you might son, dad says he's pretty sure he can work something out, he wants to buy the plane tickets. Said he don't feel right about them sending us money and would rather pay our own way but don't get your hopes up too much because anything can happen to spoil his plans."

Then she picked up the letter that Lance had sent along with the pictures and read it for the third time.

Dear Reba, Tex, and your parents.

Well I'm finally back home again, as you know I had three days left before my scheduled flight after you folks left but I couldn't see much sense in staying any longer and asked them for an earlier flight. As luck would have it they found an empty seat the next day. The bloody thing flew through some bad weather and about took my breath away but it managed to stay in the air."

Enclosing some pictures, one of the chap's horse and one of the homestead and some of the cattle.

I have told my parents about you folks and they insist that you visit us soon. My dad said to tell you to make flight arrangements and he will send you the plane fare. Please don't take that the wrong way because he is looking forward to meeting you folks and so is my mum.

And as for me I will just say I miss you and wish you were here, so please let us know as soon as possible. Mum says to tell you to plan on staying a while or as long as you want, said it don't make any bloody sense to travel all that distance just for a short visit.

Tell the chap his horse is waiting and raring to trot him over the ranch. So hurry and post me an answer I miss you. Lance

She folded it and slipped it back in the envelope mindful of the excitement that was racing through her body.

Her days had been long and dreams interrupted her sleep since they returned. Dreams of the cemetery and Tex resting there among some of his fellow comrades not far from the Ardennes where they played a part in history by defeating the Germans as they tried desperately to over run the allied forces and change the out come of the war.

Many times she had asked herself if it was worth all the lives it claimed and the answer was always 'yes' because she knew in her heart that Tex would want it that way. And now her thoughts were the same, since her return home from France the Aussie with smiling blue eyes had become a constant reminder that something was about to change in her life. And each time she asked herself, is it right that I take him into my life' the answer was always 'yes' because in her mind she knew Tex would want it that way. She sighed and slumped to the couch. "What you thinking mom?" Tex asked.

"Oh, lots of things honey." She answered. "But mostly about Australia."

One month later Reba's father sold their home and all it's furnishings in St. Charles, and on a bright sunny morning packed their clothing, pictures, memorabilia, etc. into the well worn Buick sedan but ran out of room and wound up putting some boxes on top of the car covering them with a mildewed tarp and lashing it down with clothes line rope.

They drove through town in silence each with mixed feelings. Sadness showed in the faces of the father and mother as they glanced at familiar buildings that had become so much a part of their-every day lives, across the creek on the left a cluster of homes known as Kirk Town where they once lived when they were first married and a little further down on the right Poe's furniture and appliance.

Then on the left the old brick building that housed the bank with the adjoining pool room and barber shop that Cal had spent many hours in chatting and joking with friends.

Then on the right another poolroom and café sided by a two story building that served as a hotel, and just beyond there a clothing store that had flourished through the years but was now closed.

Then on the left Shoun's drugstore once busy and filled with young folks but now like all other places of business slowly dieing from lack of customers and it would only be a matter of time before it's doors closed sealing forever the faces and laughter of youngsters from St. Charles high school who had gathered there over the years, to some a place to meet and talk over a bubbling fountain coke, and to many it was a place to meet new friends and flirt which led to turning points in some young lives when they chose a mate and said "I do." Some that didn't work out but many others that did and they went on to raise a family together.

And on the right 'Jake's Place.' that catered to a mixed group of people, diners, drinkers, bootleggers, cab drivers, church members and preachers, all walks of life seemed to blend together in harmony as Jake ruled his domain with authority staring down the drinkers if they got out of line.

He came to a stop on the little bridge under the sycamore tree where a half dozen or more had already gathered to while away the day. He leaned over and looked past his wife through the open window and said.

"Well boys we're on our way to Chicago, we hate to leave but looks like this place is done for with all the mines shutting down."

"Yeah I know." One answered. "I'm leaving myself in a few days, I was just telling the fellows the other day that when I leave the town will close down."

The cedar whittler looked up and scowled. "Yeah he told us that but he ain't going no place, ain't got no car or bus fare so tell me how he's gonna make it to Ohio? Betcha ten dollars when you come back on a visit he'll be sitting right here under this tree like the rest of us."

Over the laughter he said. "Can't say that we'll ever be back, sure would like to but we never know, may not live that long, you know how that is, so if we never see you again I want you to know we're gonna miss you and all the folks we've had the pleasure of knowing and living amongst here in St. Charles."

"You plan on staying in Chicago?" One asked. "Yeah I think we will my brother lives there." He answered.

"Don't believe I'd want to live in a big city like Chicago." Another one piped up.

"Then one spotted Tex and asked. "Heh Tex, you still going to that fer off country to see yore horse?"

"Yep, as soon as we get to Chicago and get our plane tickets." Tex answered.

"You mean you're all going where was it, Australia? Shucks you might get over there and never come back."

"Well fellows we better get moving it's a long five hundred miles to

Chicago, I hope every thing works out for you all, and take care of old George Washington there, looks like before it's over he'll be about the only one left in this town."

"Hell no." George replied. "You might see me in Chicago any time, hell I've been there lots of times."

They waved goodbye and drove away. Tex stared at the little theater where he had spent so much time watching cowboy movies and wondered if he would ever be back to see another.

Reba looked at the high school building on the left while trying to hold back tears that had already wet her cheeks.

On the right her father and mother's eyes were glued to the old ballpark and memories of some of the baseball players.

Cowboy Barker, Hobart 'Lefty' Scott, Roy Rutherford, Virgil Wacks, Con Holman, and others.

As they crossed the little bridge the view of Mutt Williams places of business on both sides, along with Copeland's funeral home on the right, Reba thought how strange it was that she was thinking this might be the last time she would see the town ever again and as she gazed at the funeral home that represents death she felt like she was leaving behind a big part of her life and wanted to die instead.

By the time they passed Wagner Town along side the slow moving creek tears were on all cheeks except for Tex, his mind was filled with the strange places he was about to see, Chicago, and beyond to Australia, where Lance and his white horse were waiting.

Back under the sycamore tree the men had grew silent realizing that with each family that left, and they were leaving daily, meant the end was coming for a place that they had grew up and raised their families in would soon be empty.

The cedar whittler looked up and said. "I guess you're right it's going fast and to tell you the truth I ain't able to make a move to some northern state and even if I had the money to take me there I wouldn't want to go, so shit, I think I'll just stay here with George me'n him can keep this damn town going, how about it George?"

A big grin lit up George's face as the importance of the statement sunk in.

"Hell yes." He said. "You can be mayor and I'll be police chief."

That brought a roar of laughter, which caused George to go into one of his cussing fits again.

Just another typical day under the old sycamore tree but slowly coming to an end as the months went by another regular would fail to join the gathering, even the cedar whittler for the sake of his family moved to Indiana but left his memories and heart in St. Charles. He lived out his life without ever returning and when his time came to die he had no fear because he felt his death took place the day he left St. Charles, Virginia.

After arriving in Chicago, and in spite of the warm welcome by Reba's father's brother and his family, surrounded by hordes of people and the strangeness of big-city life painted a gloomy picture for their future happiness and homesickness set in.

His brother was a supervisor at Motorola and said he would get them a job there.

"After your trip to Australia I'll get you on, and don't worry about a place to live you can live here with us until you find a place. And speaking of Australia, I can't figure why you have to visit there in the first place. It costs a lot of money to go there not to speak of the return trip."

Reba turned her head away and thought. 'It does seem foolhardy but inside I feel I must go and the sooner the better.'

Her father and mother looked at each other knowing that there was truth in what he said but at the same time knew they were right in going because it meant a new start for Reba and her restless twelve year old son Tex.

Finally Tex broke the silence with. "I have to go there."

"Why." His great uncle asked.

"Because I have a horse there and I want to learn to ride and be a cowboy some day."

His uncle replied. "Aw come on Tex, you've been watching too many westerns at the theater in St. Charles, you mean to tell me you have to go all the way to Australia to learn to ride a horse, what about your dog I guess you'll have to leave him here with us."

"Well I guess so but I'll come back and get him someday."

So it would be in the days to come, good-natured kidding directed at Tex but never dimming his hopes of getting to Australia.

Two weeks later while looking through brochures about Australia, Reba discovered one about transportation that offered reasonable rates on an Australian freighter. They could fly to New York and board it but the only draw back was it zigzagged and took on freight at several ports including one in Africa, taking two months to get to their destination.

After talking it over they agreed that it was their best bet because of the savings they could save on the fare. "Look at it this way." Her father said.

"We'll get to see some of the world, like going on a long vacation."

Excitement ruled the next few days as they called New York and made arrangements, then shopping around the airlines for the best rates from Chicago to New York.

"We'll leave the car and some other things here with you." He told his brother.

"Sure." His brother answered. "And when you get back I'll get you and Reba on at Motorola and Alice might want to take up nursing again, nurses are in demand here in Chicago. Don't worry you'll get used to Chicago."

As the plane climbed higher and finally leveled off they took in the panoramic view of Chicago, amazed at the vastness of the city, but looking forward to the freighter in New York that would dock at several ports of interest before arriving in Perth, Australia and from there to their final destination the sprawling "Twisted Track" cattle ranch a days ride on a utility truck from Wiluna, a small town northeast of Perth in Western Australia.

The fast paced hustle and bustle of New York City, frayed their nerves during the time it took to cut through all the red tape to board the freighter. Once aboard they discovered there was nothing fancy about their sleeping quarters which they knew in advance because the brochure had stated that, but the food was excellent and the Australian ships crew sprinkled with a few black French Moroccan's were very friendly and helpful.

Two weeks into the journey they were on a first name basis with some of the Australian crew with exceptions being the Moroccan's of course who didn't speak English. One of the crew took great pleasure in ribbing Tex about coming all the way from Virginia to ride a horse in Australia.

"Say Mate! Do you plan on bringing that bloody horse back with you? He might not want to leave Australia you know."

"No I'm gonna stay in Australia, I want to be a cowboy on a cattle ranch."

"Oh I see, we call them Stations but the same thing chap, you'll get a lot of riding experience there but it will leave a big impression on your behind. Tell me chap, are you related to the station owners?"

"No we met Lance Kirk when we went to Belgium to see my daddy's grave, he was killed in the war. Lance lives on a big ranch with his parents and wanted us to come to Australia to see them, and he gave me a horse."

"Is this Lance Kirk married mate?"

"No he's not, he's about the same age as my mother."

"Oh I see mate." He said as he looked at Reba standing at the rail staring at the never ending waves with a far away look in her eyes that meant only one thing. 'Lance Kirk.'

"Oh I see, you know something chap you might just stay in Australia after all, yeah I reckon you will." He smiled and walked away.

He sat in the station hands quarters alone except for his large aging sheep dog he called 'Rogue.'

The other workers had saddled up early that morning and headed for Wiluna to have a little fun, they had a few days off before going out to muster cattle for a shipment to England.

He had learned long before that a trip there for a little fun always turned out to be a wild drinking fling that most always led to fights and hangovers that lasted for days in the hot Australian sun. But he could understand why the fellows couldn't wait to get there because the most of them were much younger than he and he remembered he was much the same way at their age.

His thoughts wandered back over the years stopping to examine events in his life some trivial and not worth wasting time on while others deserved to be remembered.

As he fingered and rolled the ends of his graying handlebar moustache around his long crooked finger stopping momentarily to smile about some distant memory of his childhood growing up in the Highlands of Scotland he strained to find something that would justify his ever being born into mankind.

Born in Scotland in 1902 in the worst part of town to a kind and loving mother but to a father who adored his wife and son at first only to drift away as whiskey and the lure of the wild side finally put him out of their reach and eventually out of their lives.

His mother had heard of a farm family in need of someone to cook and do the housework while the farm mother recuperated from a serious surgery. She got the job and they joined the family on a very large and successful stock farm.

Within six months the farm lady had improved greatly giving he and his mother worries about having to leave at any time. They had settled in and enjoyed their stay with the family of three girls and four boys the oldest boy being his age. Although the wages his mother got didn't go much further than clothing for them but the food was excellent and outside of a few misunderstandings between he and the boys that were quickly forgotten everything went smoothly.

The last Sunday in the seventh month his mother prepared a delicious meal and as they all sat down at the table she wondered if this would be the day the farmer would tell them the bad news because she had noticed something different about his usually jolly make up and was sure that's what he had in mind. Except for the boys and girls joshing back and forth the adults were quiet during the meal.

After everyone finished she started to rise and get busy clearing the table. The farmer cleared his throat and said.

"No sit back down will you please, I av something to talk to you about."

She slumped down in the chair as the blood drained from her face knowing that she and her young son would soon be right back where they started not knowing where their next meal would come from.

"Me and th missus av been talking it over and we both think you and th lad belong here on th farm with us because you both av chiseled yore way right in and we don't want to see you go and that includes th children."

"Th lad can go to school and get his learning right with our bunch. He's a good hand with th stock and helps out a lot an goldang he deserves a shilling here and there and I plan on handing him some change now and again, and I can increase yore measly pay by a few pence for all the housework and cooking you do to help th missus, and give you some time off to get out to yoreself once now and again."

So he and his mother became a part of the farm family in every way bringing much happiness to a mother that had feared the worst for her son but now could see a great promise for his future as the farmer acted a father figure and guided him through a difficult time in his life.

He pulled his finger from one end of his mustache leaving a neat hole from where he had wound it around his finger and smiled remembering the relieved look on his mothers face as she stared at him across the table, in her eyes he could see her thoughts. 'Son we've found a home, thank God!'

And at the time he had looked around the table at the faces nervously waiting for an answer from his mother.

Finally she said. "Yes sir we'll be glad to stay if you want us."

"Well bygol we do so make ye self to home."

Then he remembered sitting at the table laughing and talking for a long time as families often do. This one memory lingered longer than any other because he considered it the happiest day of his life.

From there his thoughts raced through the years of their time on the farm and the knowledge he gained from the man that treated him just like he was his own son. He remembered his persistence. "You av a way with th cattle and sheep lad, better'n any bloke a've ever seen in me life time, and bygol it's best you stick to it."

But tragedy struck a blow to his young life when his mother died from cancer the day after his sixteenth birthday.

Feeling devastated and alone even with the loving comfort from the farm family he decided to go to England and join up to fight the Germans in World War One.

"Goldang it lad you ain't fit to fight no war at yore age you belong here wit us till you finish school." The farmer shouted.

"Yes I know you're right but I must go, don't worry I'll be back."

Thinking of it now he knew he was only running from a place that he and his mother had shared together and did the same thing later when he fell in love with a pretty nurse from America in a hospital in England as he was recuperating from a wound he suffered in the war fighting against the Germans in France.

He lay in the hospital for seven months with a shattered leg from shell fragments and after several operations and kind help from the American nurse he finally was able to walk again but minus most of the flesh on his right thigh.

He was shocked the day the nurse told him her tour of duty was over and she was going home. The war had ended three months earlier and they had made plans to get married and make their home in England.

"No you can't do that." He begged. "Please stay, our plans, what happened? You know I love you, why are you doing this to me? I don't understand."

"I know William." She answered. "Believe me I love you dearly and I have lost sleep over it but I must go back home to my family. Maybe at a later date I will contact you and we'll go through with our plans but right now I must go."

The day she left he held her tight still hoping she would change her mind but stood and watched her go up the gangplank knowing it might be the last time he would ever see her.

She stood leaning over the railing looking down at him and just before the crew loosened the moorings, he opened his wallet and fished out his mother's worn ring and shouted. "Here take this and keep it safe till we meet again."

He started to throw it but she shouted. "No don't I can't catch it and it might fall in the water."

One of the American sailors seeing his uniform and thinking he was an Englishman hollered out. "Come on Limy fling it up here we'll catch it."

He threw it upward and watched three sailors with open hands waiting, it landed in a hand and the sailor yelled down. "Do you want me to put it on her finger?" He nodded yes and watched as they staged a little ceremony, but all in fun.

She stayed at the rail waving as the ship slipped out in the channel and slowly disappeared toward the misty expanses of the Atlantic Ocean.

One month later they gave him his release from the hospital along with an honorable discharge. He made his way back to Scotland only to find the farm family in grief as the deadly flu epidemic had taken both father and mother. He helped the grieving children as much as he could even though he wanted to leave, where? He had no idea but felt he had to get away from it all.

One month later found him in London doing manual labor. The pay was meager but enough to pay for room and board at a make shift boarding house.

He had her address in the states and wrote letters almost daily but never got a reply. It got to the point to where he could no longer get a good nights rest and he knew he had to do something to get away so he hired on an English freighter headed for Australia, with stops in Africa, on the way.

The ship docked in Perth, Australia, unloaded its freight and had a four-day wait for cattle that was bound for Africa and England.

He drew his pay and went ashore, got a haircut and another change of clothes. Then wound up in a bar with a noisy bunch hell bent to get to Wiluna, a small town northeast of Perth.

"Come along mate." One said. "Lots of open country there, just waiting for us, a haven for cattle and sheep, can't lose mate, because the world needs food especially beef."

He touched the other end of his moustache and began to twist it around his finger as memories of his fifty-six years, more than half of it lived in Australia, unfolded before him.

He had arrived in Wiluna, with the wild bunch intent on hanging on to his meager savings but it soon disappeared as whiskey, beer, and his longing for companionship with a sultry blonde-headed beauty almost cost him his life.

A young ringer (cowboy) from one of the stations came to town for a day of fun and after a few drinks challenged him for her attention.

Saying. "That's a good looking Shiela mate, what do you reckon? I believe she likes me better than you mate."

Crazed with drink and lust for the blond he lashed out at the young ringer knocking him to the floor, pinned him down and proceeded to land blow after blow to his face and head and would have killed him but the stock hand carried a concealed pistol that he managed some way to fish from under his shirt.

The bullet tore through his rib cage just above his heart. He rolled off the young ringer and looked at the crowd around him knowing that he was about to die. The stock hand ran for the door obviously in shock, mounted his horse and rode away.

A doctor hurriedly appeared and stopped the bleeding fortunately the bullet went clean through his body without touching any vital arteries and with help and care from some of the town folks in a few days he along with two from the wild bunch hitched a wagon ride to one of the distant stations.

He worked there six months before moving on to another one only to leave there after a short time also.

He thought about giving it up and making his way back to Perth and sign on to a freighter again, but thought better of it as he remembered all the water around him that seemed to serve as a prison.

He had become accustomed to the wide and wild expanses of Western Australia, and saw it as an escape from his past thinking that one day if it got to the point to where he could no longer bear reliving his life over and over he'd stash some staples on his horse and ride off once again to get away from it all, but this time on the Canning Stock Route, the longest and toughest in the world, the famed Chisholm Trail that stretches from San Antonia, Texas to Abiline, Kansas in America would be like a walk in the pasture as compared to the Canning Stock Route.

He knew it was foolhardy to think he would survive but thought it would be a fitting way to leave behind all the miseries he had suffered in his life.

But one day while riding across the expanses after parting ways with his long time friend Shane, who was intent on getting to Queensland, he came upon a Paddock that penned up several thousand head of sheep and cattle.

Out of desperation and hunger he sought out the owner and to his surprise found he was a decent man that offered him food and assistance even if he decided to turn down his offer to work on his station and ride away.

He stopped twirling his moustache for a moment and smiled as he remembered what the station owner said.

"I'll take you on chap, and without asking you for any background cause if you're like most you've got a past that I wouldn't care to know about anyway."

"Jist do th job that I expect you to and your past will never matter to me."

"Well bygol I think I'll sign on not because I'm weary and hungry but I think you be a fair and decent man."

Then he remembered the firm handshake as he said. "Well I try my best chap, I try my best, because out here in this wild country we all need each other."

"My names Thomas Kirk, my grandfather Ward Kirk. selected here way back in the 1800's and handed it down to my father, my father passed on a while back and left it to me, and I will hand it over to my son Lance, some day that is if I can bring him up the right way and he wants to take it on. After that me and th missus plan on living out th rest of our stay here on earth on the coast overlooking th ocean."

"About a million acres some good, some bad, but all of it dangerous and unforgiving, it's known as "The Twisted Track" don't know how long you've roamed over this land cobber but in case you don't know it's a right hard life."

"Yeah I know and my names William 'Warp' Broderick I sprung up in Scotland, joined up with Briton and fought the Germans, took some fragments to me leg but managed to overcome that but had a bad experience with th love o my life and have been on th run ever since, and bygol I reckon ye can get pretty fer away from anything here in this vast land as you know."

"Yeah I reckon you can chap, so you're from Scotland, well that's where my roots are, my grandfather sprung up there and he never talked about it much maybe like you chap he was on the run. But remember I told you I don't have to know about your past and here you have already told me."

"Oh no, I just told you a smidgen, and about all that I care for you to know."

He resumed twisting his moustache around his finger as memories of the years he had put in working on the Twisted Track passed before him. Memories of hard work and the miseries that seemed to be forever present in his life but at the same time it was a change for the better when one day Thomas handed him his pay and said. "A little extra there cobber you've earned it and some because you're about the best I've seen in me lifetime when it comes to working with th stock and from now on I'll look to you as my head stockman."

With each year peace and serenity became his companion as the memory of the war and the pretty nurse faded somewhat. Even though he had met a nice lady that owned the hotel in Wiluna, and could count on her to fulfill his yearnings each time he visited there he had made up his mind long ago that he would never be satisfied married to anyone after having loved the pretty nurse.

He smiled again as he remembered Thomas Kirk's son Lance, as a little boy and how he would hang around him in spite of the kidding he directed his way.

Thomas said one day. "Warp You not only have a way with th stock but you seem to be able to wrap that son of mine right around yore finger and get him to do th things he should in spite of all th joshing you send his way, don't know yore secret but keep it up, that way he stays out o my hair."

He pulled his finger from his moustache leaving a clean hole to match the other side but promptly pulled his fingers through them making them disappear.

He arose opened the door and stood there, Rogue his huge Blue sheep dog stood behind waiting for him to move and when he didn't he walked right through his long bowed legs without touching him and went outside.

He leaned forward so his head would clear and followed Rogue. Once outside he straightened his six foot eight inch frame and noticed a cloud of dust approaching leading back toward the homestead a thousand yards away and could see it was Lance approaching in the old beat up Land Rover.

He came to a stop and called out. "How ye doing Warp?"

"I'm as flat out as a lizard drinking. What brings you over here cobber?"

"Just want to gab a bit Warp, ain't seen a lot of you lately since I got back from France."

"Yeah I know cobber, and what's this I hear about a family coming here from America? You must have chiseled in pretty close to them there in France."

"Well I reckon I did Warp, especially the young twelve year old Tex, you'll like him Warp he's quite a chap."

"Well I reckon you did because I hear you give him Buddy the best riding horse on th station."

"That's what I want to talk to you about Warp, I was wondering if you'll take him on just like you did me when I was that age and teach him to ride and other things that he will have to get the hang of here at the station?"

"Well I reckon I can, but it don't make no bloody sense seeing that he will be leaving after a while."

"Oh no Warp, he'll be staying so do all you can to get him straight."

"Alright cobber, but can't promise you any results, never know about these young folks anymore especially the ones from America, bygol he might try to tell me what to do."

"Okay thanks Warp, you'll like him just like I do."

He turned the key and started to drive away, over the roar of the motor Warp called out.

"Don't worry I'll take care of the little bloke, and how about his mother cobber, is she staying and will I like her as much as you do?"

Lance shook his head and smiled. He had learned long ago that you couldn't stay ahead of Warp.

He stood and watched the dust rising from behind the Land Rover until it reached the homestead. Then turned to Rogue and said. "That bloke's got a good life ahead of him Rogue, wish mine had showed that much promise when I was his age. But we av to make out with what our maker deals us Rogue, and he never deals a pat hand, leaves it to us to figure it out, and bygol I reckon I misplayed mine early on when I met that nurse from America."

He turned and gazed west at the setting sun, watched it disappear as a red glow hovered around and over it signaling dry hot days ahead. Then he turned and slowly walked back to his quarters as Rogue followed close behind immediately going through his legs and on in the quarters.

At the door he turned toward the sunset again and said.

"Yep, it's gone Rogue, but bygol come tomorrow it'll show up again, jist like that nurse from America, I see her standing at th rail every day o me life but when I reach out to touch her she disappears in the foggy English Channel, but jist like old sol she's back the next day."

"I reckon I'm still holding a card that our Lord dealt me Rogue, and unable to discard it out o me mind."

At Perth, they said goodbye to the friendly Aussie crew and as they went down the gangplank one of them yelled. "Now you be careful when you mount that bloody Aussie horse cobber they can be crook to Americans at times."

And another joined in. "And watch out for the Roo's, I reckon they might stick you in their pockets."

Weary from two months on the freighter they rested two days in a hotel before hitching a ride on a supply utility to Wiluna, a long tiresome journey over a dry rutted road that meandered off in many directions, the driver would follow the more shallow ruts that would always lead back to the main track.

Tex being the young one didn't seem to mind the violent lurching of the utility as he became lost in his thoughts as the Australian countryside unfolded before him.

Reba's father much like Tex let his mind absorb the never ending tableland and the color of the soil reminded him of the hard red clay of some parts of Virginia and other parts of America. He rolled with the ups and downs of the utility and imagined he and his family were leaving Oklahoma during the great dust bowl days just like he had seen in the movies.

Tex trained his eyes on the horizon almost expecting to see a band of Indians riding toward them, but that image vanished when his grandfather pointed out a kangaroo in the distance, after that he could vision all kinds of creatures that he had heard about crocodile's, alligator's, wallaby's', colorful lizards and huge snakes. He remembered one of the Aussie crew telling him that a baby wallaby made a good house pet up until it became an adult but then would venture back into the wild, and he wondered if Lance had one.

Reba and her mother were enjoying the scenery also but were tired and wet from perspiration and secretly longed for the journey to end soon but knew another long stretch awaited them from Wiluna, to the homestead.

At Wiluna, Lance was waiting having been posted by the wire service (Ham Radio) as to the time of their arrival, which had been listened to by most of the citizen's on the homesteads and in Wiluna.

A rather large crowd curious about an American family that would travel all that distance, watched as they stepped off the utility. It had been the talk of the town for weeks and some had come to the conclusion that this was something more than a causal visit.

"I hear th boys mother is about Lance's age." Said one. "So I reckon she and th boy will be staying."

"Yep, I think so too." Another remarked. "One o the ringers from Twisted Track told me young Lance is behind it all and seems hell bent on taking her as his life mate."

As they looked at the rather haggard tired looking lot standing in the hot Australian sun, whispers could be heard throughout the crowd.

"She's a beauty she is."

"Yep, she is that." Another whispered. "Young Lance did himself proud."

"I hope it goes well." Stated another. "But it's a crook place for a woman, we all know that."

"Yep, she might change her mind and leave th chap with only her memories for the rest of his life pretty much like old Warp after he was jilted by that American nurse back there after World War One."

Lance stepped forward with hand extended and after a handshake and brief words with each one he laid his hands on Reba's shoulders and as they looked into each other's eyes the crowd waited with anticipation.

Finally they kissed and embraced for the longest time prompting one of the ringers to remark. "Oh my word would you look at that we're about to have a wedding in a few days here in Wiluna, which means a heap o free grog."

They climbed the steps to the hotel veranda where Lance had arraigned for sandwiches and a choice of tea or coca cola.

Some of the town's people began to drift away while others chose to stay and ask questions about America. To some it was surprising to hear that they came from a small coalmining town with a name like St. Charles in the state of Virginia and their lives had never been a bed of roses. Hard work and skimping to make ends meet were nothing new to them and in a way they were suited for the trials and dangers that faced them here on the fringes of the outback in Australia.

The townspeople watched as they rode away in the land rover with one remarking. "Yep she's a beauty I reckon, and oh my word her mother is right flash too."

Then another. "Lance knows how to pick em but I wonder if she'll stick it out at the Twisted Track, I still say this land is a pretty crook place for a woman."

Kate the hotel owner stood with her hands on her hips staring at him and said.

"Aw come on it's you men that talk like that, you never hear us women complaining, now go on you old bugger and sink some more grog."

Then she turned and stormed back into the hotel.

They were welcomed at the homestead with great fanfare and after bathing and a change of clothes they sat down to a table laden with huge juicy steaks surrounded by all kinds of other foods some that were foreign to the Americans but were delicious to their taste buds.

Tex was in awe of the rambling homestead that reminded him so much of the ranch houses in the movies.

The ringers returned from their merry making obviously tired and light headed but only to hear Warp say. "Okay fella's, lets get the plant ready we move out tomorrow morning."

The day was spent loading supplies in the utilities and early the next morning they loaded their saddle horses along with four pack horses in the trucks.

Lance brought Tex down and introduced him to Warp. and the other ringers.

Warp got a glint in his eyes as he took the measure of Tex thinking that. 'This Jackaroo will be a lot of fun I hope he can take my joshing like Lance did when he was that age. I'll get to work on him as soon as this mustering is over.'

Tex was puzzled as to why they loaded the horses in trucks and asked Lance.

"Why do they put the horses in trucks? In America the cowboys ride off on the horses when they go on a roundup."

"This station is over one hundred miles square chap and they have to go eighty miles north to muster and bring the cattle back this way. Makes no bloody sense to ride the horses all that distance because they need them rested and fresh for the mustering and return of the cattle to the paddock where they will be held until the shipping date. And all the poddy's have to be branded, that's all done from horseback a lot of work for the horses chap, so we cart them out there."

"What's a poddy" Tex asked. "Oh, that's young calves I think they're called doggie's on your ranches in America."

"And you brand them just like in America, do you have rustlers here that steal them and put their brand on them?"

"Oh my word we do cobber, we call them poddy dodgers same as your rustlers."

"Aren't you going with them Lance?"

"No not this time chap I decided to stay here and ride out to the paddock and give them a hand when they get the cattle there."

From nearby Warp winked at Tex and grinned causing his long handle barred moustache to lengthen across his suntanned cheeks. "Yep after all th bloody hard work is done he'll ride out and help us bygol I reckon that's it." That brought smiles from the other ringers but they all knew Lance was a hard worker and was staying behind because of his houseguests.

Then Tex asked. "Can I ride out to the Paddock with you Lance? I would like to see the herd."

"I don't know chap it's pretty crook out there you might ought to get used to the heat and all before that."

"Aw bring him along." Warp growled. "That way he'll get used to riding Buddy."

"I'll ask his mother and if it's alright with her I'll bring him along." Lance replied.

"Warp, when the mustering is finished mum wants you and the ringers to come over to the homestead to meet our guests she said to tell you she'll spread the table with tucker and I'll see that there's plenty of grog to wet ya whistles."

"Well bygol that sounds right I reckon." Warp beamed.

They stood and watched the small caravan as it bounced over a deep rutted track leading to the north. Almost out of sight Warp turned and waved as old Rogue sat at his feet content to be with his master whether it be at the station where he could while away his time in the shade and cool of the stockman's quarters never expecting anything out of the ordinary to happen or out in the wilds of the outback where nothing was predictable and danger always lurked. A man and his dog, a dog and his master each committed to each other.

Lance and Tex, walked slowly back to the homestead each lost in his own thoughts.

Lance and Reba, had found some time to themselves since her arrival and spent time sitting on the veranda at night listening to strange animal sounds that were foreign to her ears, but Lance took great pains to explain them to her.

But the subject of their future together always came up and soon it became easy for them to plan it.

"We'll get married in Wiluna." He said. "Mum and pop like to attend events in Wiluna, when all the stockmen and their families come for the races. My word it's exciting to see so many people in town, out here you 're lucky to see them once a year."

"Will they come for our wedding?" She asked.

"Oh my word they will, and lots of them, not as many as to the races mind you and not as flash but a good many will come. "They expect free grog of course and pop will tend to that in fact he can sink more grog than any two ringers."

In the meantime her mother and father chiseled right in with mum and pop, as Warp would say. And Tex followed Lance from morning until night with an unending amount of questions. And a lot of time standing admiring buddy.

'One morning he asked Lance. "Can I ride buddy today?"'

"Sure can mate, I guess you two have to get acquainted before we ride out to the paddock."

Then he thought. 'I wanted to leave th bloody job to Warp he's the best when it comes to teaching riding techniques but I'll do the best I can with th chap.'

'And oh my word I dread it because buddy can be frisky at times and Warp knows how to handle him much better than me.'

'Like pop says,' 'Warp is th best when it comes to stock they seem to understand and respect him, I believe he could meet up with a wild horse and be riding him th next day.'

Then he smiled as his thoughts went back to when he was twelve years old and under Warp's care. 'Yep, Tex is in for some surprises from Warp, but it will shape his future just as it has mine, Warp is strange in a way but a good man he is.'

Lance and Tex, spent a lot of time in the saddle over a period of time and Lance was pleasantly surprised at the progress Tex was making, he and buddy had been wary of each other at first but now seemed to be bonding.

"Yep mate, you and buddy will make a good pair, Warp once said a good ringer deserves a good horse and I think we have a match here. You're doing good."

"Do you think I'm ready to ride out to the paddock with you Lance?"

"Sure mate, and we may not have to wait long before one of the utilities returns with news that the herd has been mustered in the paddock."

A big grin came across Tex face as he thought of he and Lance riding off toward the paddock as his mother and grandparents waved from the veranda.

And in far away St. Charles, Virginia he could vision the group sitting under the sycamore tree and possibly laughing and making jokes about him going all the way to Australia to learn how to ride a horse. 'I wonder what they'd think if they could see me now.' He thought.

Then Lance broke in on his thoughts with. "Now it wont be easy out there chap because Warp will give you plenty to do and teach you how to herd cattle and some of the other things that will qualify you for a ringer, he's set in his ways and you might think he's a little too hard at times but believe me chap he knows how to bring out the best in you. And out there th table won't be spread with th tucker that you might be accustomed to."

"What kind of food do ringers eat on a roundup Lance?"

"Well sometimes beef mate, but mostly bloody tin dog because there's not much time for cooking meals even if we had the facilities which we don't have out there."

"What's tin dog Lance is that dog food?"

Lance toyed with the idea of saying yes, and watch Tex reactions but decided to leave that kind of thing to Warp knowing that Tex was in for some hard times before Warp declared him a true ringer.

"Oh no chap, it's Spam about five pounds compressed in to a long tin that's why we call it tin dog."

"That ain't bad we have that in the states."

"I know mate but when you have to eat it every day for a long period of time it gets pretty bloody hard to swallow."

"I can eat anything if I'm hungry." Tex replied. "Maybe even that stew you told me about that's made from kangaroo tail."

"You may not have to wait long to try that mate, mum said she plans on having that today." He smiled as he seen Tex wince and look away.

'Pretty much like me when I was his age.' He thought. 'Willing to try anything as long as it will help to fulfill a life long ambition to become a ringer, or in his case a cowboy.'

He laid his hand on Tex shoulder and said. "You're on your way to becoming a cowboy chap, oh my word you are."

Tex watched as the ringers branded the calves. Warp moved among the stock with ease. Once as he stood in front of two calves with his crooked bowed legs spread wide much like an open gate to freedom two calves must have thought so and quickly ran through his legs only to have Rogue head them off and drive them back through.

He looked at Lance and smiled careful not to let Warp see because he had already learned that Warp was a mystery in his ways and you never knew what to say or do in any given situation, but was pleasantly surprised when Warp looked straight at him with a big grin on his face.

But ten minutes later Warp was teaching him all the phases of branding as Lance and the other ringers quietly watched knowing that Warp wanted it that way as he went about teaching the skills he had attained from years in the hot Australian sun, but they knew before it was over he would have them all laughing at Tex expense just as he had done to them some time in the past, Lance more than the others.

The grin was now replaced by a face that, expressed determination as he growled out his commands. "No not there cobber, I want th bloody brand here."

"Hold him chap, hold him, now tie him, tie him."

"Watch how you handle that bloody thing it's hot, bygol you almost branded me."

This went on for some time as Tex strained and wrestled with the calves not having time to look or even think about the by standers around them, just he and Warp, Warp determined that he do it Warp's way, the right way. And he just as determined to do it Warp's way because he knew Warp's way was the only way he would ever qualify to be a ringer on the Twisted Track ranch.

As Warp watched him he noticed his agile easy way with the calves and thought. 'Yep bygol, he's on his way to becoming a first class ringer, that he is.'

Then his thoughts drifted back in time to the stock farm in Scotland and he could hear the old Scotchman say.

'You av a way wit th stock lad bout the best I ever seen in me lifetime, and bygol I think ye better stick to it.'

A sense of pride filled his thoughts knowing that he now had met someone much like himself that would eventually go on to become a master with the stock. He felt like repeating the old Scotchman's words to Tex but instead whispered.

'Th chaps a natural, he is, jist like me, but bygol I wish him a better future than I av had.'

Finally he set the stage for the fun part that the by standers had been patiently waiting for. He caught a large rangy calf on the pretense of examining one of its legs. He threw it to the ground and ordered Tex to straddle it.

"Now you hold em cobber whilst I see about this leg."

Tex settled down astraddle the calf as Warp held its head to the ground. He waited for Tex to get settled and released his grip from the calf's head and rose to his feet, in a flash the calf sprang up and went into a run with Tex hanging on for dear life, Rouge took up the chase barking and nipping at the calf's heels.

Lance and the group of ringers were now laughing and shouting instructions.

"Hold on Chap, hold on."

"Don't let em throw you chap."

"Ride em cowboy, You'll make a bull rider some day cobber, hold on."

A smile returned to Warp's face once again as the feeling of accomplishment mixed with a little fun made him feel a little better about himself and his troubled past. He walked over to where the calf had dumped Tex on the ground, helped him to his feet and solemnly said. "That was crook chap, that was crook."

"What do you mean by that?" Tex asked.

"That Poddy's a mean one cobber, once in a while we run on to that kind I reckon."

Smiles had now been replaced by solemn looks on the by standers faces because they knew that was the way Warp wanted it, and Tex never knew the difference. To him it was just as Warp had said. "A mean Poddy." Then he thought using some of Warp's words.

'Yep bygol he is that, and I reckon I did a pretty good job of riding him.' He looked up at Warp's smiling face and felt a sense of pride thinking it was a smile of approval.

One week later they started their long journey back toward the stockman's quarters. As they rode along Warp noticed Tex shifting himself in the saddle from one side to the other and smiled.

'Sore arse I reckon.' He thought. 'Th sun has burned him to th bone and he's shedding his skin like a snake. But bygol, nary a whimper from him, reminds me of Lance, when he was that age and determined to become a ringer he wouldn't admit to pain no matter what.'

A few days later they arrived at the quarters as the sun was sinking in the west awash with the glorious red colors that only a sunset can paint in the heavens.

As they moved around stiffly unsaddling and getting things in order Lance was surprised at Tex question.

"Lance can I sleep here in the bunk house with the ringers tonight?"

"Don't know about that cobber, might have to ask your mother first."

"It'll be okay with her, tell her I want to stay one night to see how the ringers live and what they eat in their quarters."

"Okay chap, I'll tell her but if she don't like the idea you can count on me coming for you. And as for tucker the ringers have a good cook and you'll have a hot meal tonight maybe steak and eggs I reckon."

Lance got the okay from Warp and soon the news had spread to the other ringers.

"I reckon old Warp will give him th works tonight." Said one. "Yep I reckon so." Said another. "Bout time we have a little fun I reckon."

Reba reluctantly agreed to let him stay one night after Lance assured her he would be safe under Warp's wing.

"You can count on Warp." He said. "He's a crook for joshing but oh my word he'll stick by you no matter what."

Tex sat down to a long table laden with thick juicy steaks topped with eggs.

'Never seen this much steak in my life.' He thought. 'Hamburgers is about the only beef we ate back in St. Charles.'

He watched the ringers as they ate and directed good-natured banter back and forth toward each other, but being careful not to go too far and suffer the wrath that Warp was capable of dosing out.

Later Warp assigned him a bunk out of a long line separated by a single thin piece of ply board that afforded a little privacy but only from the sides.

He undressed and went to bed making sure to remove all his clothes after one of the ringers told him.

"It's best you shed all yore duds on th floor and sleep in yore birthday suit chap it gets mighty steamy in here at night I reckon."

He let his clothes fall to the floor in a pile much like he had become accustomed to at home in spite of his mother's nagging. Then he dropped his tired body to the bunk and lay there naked thinking about the past few weeks and all the hard work and training that Warp had put him through.

And using Warp's favorite word he whispered. 'Bygol' I'm a cowboy, if only the gang under the sycamore tree could see me now.'

But that thought vanished in a hurry when he realized he was naked. Then his thoughts drifted to his horse buddy and he could hear the Aussie freight hand saying. "Now you be careful of that bloody Aussie horse chap they can be crook I reckon. 'If only he could see me and buddy—' Peaceful sleep grabbed his senses before he could finish that thought.

A short time later a shadowy slowly moving four-legged critter made several trips between his bunk and Warp's each time dragging a part of his clothing.

He piled them in a neat pile beside Warp's bunk and lay down beside them.

Warp rose from his bunk fully dressed, stepped out of his cubicle and coughed, a signal to the other ringers that the stage was set. They all came from their cubicles fully dressed, and at Warp's signal started running and yelling. "Fire! Fire! Hurry chap th bloody place is on fire!"

He jumped to his feet and several seconds went by while he searched for his clothes on the floor. In the meantime the yelling increased as the ringers darted about the quarters that was now half lit by an oil lamp, just enough to expose his nakedness.

"Come on cobber, out wit ye th bloody thing is burning down."

They all headed for the door and he was close behind.

Once outside the moonlight revealed more of his nakedness than the oil lamp inside. He cupped his hands over his private parts and stared at the building, seeing no signs of flame or smoke he turned his gaze toward Warp and the ringers all in a tight little group with amusement written all over their faces.

He stood there puzzled not knowing what else to do but hide his private parts with his hands and wait for what ever else there was to come in this very bizarre incident.

Finally, Warp walked over and handed him a blanket.

"Here cobber, now you know to hang up yore clothes from now on out o reach of old Rogue, I reckon th old bugger will take anything that ain't nailed down and bring it to me."

By now the night was filled with the ringer's laughter carrying to the homestead a thousand yards away where Lance and Reba sat in a passionate embrace on the veranda.

"What's that noise?" Reba asked. "That's th fella's at th stockman's quarters having a little fun." Lance replied.

"Do you think Tex is okay Lance?" She asked.

"Ah yes Reba, oh my word they like to have fun and I'd say Tex is right in th middle of it." Inside he was laughing right along with the ringers knowing that Tex was probably a brunt of one of Warp's pranks.

Tex wrapped himself in the blanket and headed back inside followed by Warp and the ringer's they were somewhat quieter now patiently awaiting his reaction to the prank.

He stood looking at the pegs and nails above his bunk bed and knew that Warp had taught him another lesson, one that his mother had tried to teach him through out his childhood without results, but Warp had been successful with the help of a thieving dog and a handful of tired ringers.

Warp handed him his clothes and he carefully hung them over the pegs tying his boots together with the laces he hung them over a nail.

He turned ever careful to grip the edges of the blanket to hide his body. He bent over and rubbed Rogue's head as he sat looking up at him with a dog's inquisitive look. 'Rogue's the only one not in on the prank.' He thought.

He turned to the ringers that were watching intently, waiting to see if he would laugh at them or with them.

It came slowly at first but suddenly bubbled to the top as a feeling of belonging and comradeship with Warp and the ringer's filled his twelve-year old body. He took two paces toward Warp and extended his hand and as they gripped hands he said.

"Bygol I reckon you got me Warp, but you taught me a lessen ye did, oh my word ye did."

Then he turned to shake hands with the other ringer's. Warp watched as the good fellowship unfolded before him and whispered.

'Th chaps a winner he is, and jist like Lance before him he has a good future ahead. He's mixing some o me jargon in his speech which makes me proud, bygol, it does.'

After a period of backslapping and more laughter they finally hit the bunks. Tex lay still for some time thinking about the prank and the lesson he learned from it, and wondered what else Warp had stored up for him. What ever it be he thought most likely it will be beneficial.

A smile crossed his face as he could make out a shadowy figure at his side and felt a cold nose nudge him before it slipped out of sight toward it's master's bunk but this time empty handed. The smile remained as he drifted off to sleep hearing these words.

"Now you know to hang up yore clothes out o reach of old Rouge, I reckon th old bugger will take anything that ain't nailed down and bring it to me."

Reba watched her mother clean and polish her best pair of dress shoes as they sat in the cool shade of the vine-covered veranda. They talked about the upcoming get together with the stock hands over the coming weekend.

"I'm anxious to meet them momma, Lance says we'll like them, he said they're a lot of fun."

"Yes Reba I look forward to meeting them to so I can size them up, because I must admit I've been worried about Tex since he decided to stay there at the bunk house with them. You might be making a mistake by allowing him to do that."

"Well as you know momma he asked to stay the one night but then he came to me and asked to let him stay there permantley. I was undecided what to do but Lance assures me it will work out okay, he said Tex is totally dedicated to learning all he can about cattle ranching, he said the head stockman Warp, has taken him under his wing just as he did him when he was at that age. He said he stayed at the bunkhouse until he was eighteen and finally at the nagging of his mother came back here to the homestead to sleep."

"Well I sure hope it works out well Reba but I won't be satisfied until I meet the ringers and this Warp whoever he is, he seems to carry a lot of weight and respect around here."

"Yes momma Lance says he's a top notch stockman, said they don't know a lot about his past except that he was jilted by the love of his life and left Scotland trying to get away from it all."

"Well Reba, I guess you couldn't pick a better place to leave your past behind and start all over again. I must admit I'm beginning to feel overwhelmed by the vast unpopulated nothingness that stretches in all directions, but at the same time it makes me feel happy secure and closer to God."

Finally they got up to go inside leaving the shoes sitting on the floor to air out.

Later she went to get the shoes and discovered they were not there. "Reba did you bring my shoes in?" She asked.

"No momma, I didn't."

"Well tell me what on earth happened to them? I left them right here by this chair."

Lance was approaching the steps to the Veranda and heard the conversation. He smiled as he said.

"That will be old Rogue, he comes every day and takes what ain't nailed down, he takes it to Warp, been doing it since he's a puppy that's where he got the name Rogue. Mum puts things there now and again that she wants Warp and the ringers to have but once in a while he'll take something else, then Warp will bring it back, don't worry about your shoes Warp will bring them back."

The next morning she sat on the veranda watching colorful birds flitter about in a nearby gum tree, and at the same time listening to Reba and mum as they discussed ways to rearrange the homestead. Mum had insisted that Reba change things around to her liking.

"After it's all said and done you and Lance will have it all to yourselves so get busy and fix it to your liking, because me and Thomas plan on living out the rest of our stay on the beach up at Broome. Oh my word, we'll come back to visit and spoil th grandkids as often as we can. So it's best you and Lance get married soon and get a head start on that."

Then as they broke out in laughter she smiled and thought. 'I'm so happy that they have hit it off so well at first I thought we might have been wrong about coming here but now I think it is a great start for Reba and Tex after all the heartache of losing Tex Sr. in the war.' 'And Lance what a fine young man he is, Reba could never have found one like him if she searched the world over.'

She glanced toward a small building about five hundred feet away to see her husband Cal and Thomas examining a piece of equipment. They had become close to each other as they spent a lot of time at the building each day on the pretense of making repairs to various pieces of equipment but she suspected just as mum had said. "Thomas be a bad influence on yore husband, oh my word, he is they're over there sinking grog every day."

"Don't worry about that." She had answered. "He used the poolroom for the same excuse back in St. Charles, he'd sit and drink falstaff beer all day long, so he's right at home with Thomas furnishing all the grog he can drink."

As all this ran through her mind she trained her eyes on the stockman's quarters a thousand yards away. She could make out a group around a utility. 'Perhaps making some repairs to it.' She thought. 'I guess Reba might be right, Tex is getting valuable training that he would never have gotten back in St. Charles.'

As she watched the group a lone figure walked away from it followed by what looked like a large dog. As they came down the dusty track toward the homestead she smiled and thought.

'That must be Warp and his dog Rogue returning my shoes, good I'll finally get to meet the man that seems to have so much influence on everyone here at the Twisted Track.' As they drew closer she could see the dust rise from each step they took and first thought it would take them a long time to get there but changed her mind when she noticed the long legs of Warp as they made great strides through the stifling dust and was suddenly struck by the familiarity it brought to her senses of another time during World War One and a person it reminded her of.

'But no it couldn't be.' She thought. 'If it is I'll die.'

As they came ever closer she noticed his legs were bowed just as she remembered William Broderick so many years ago in England.

'No it can't be.' She thought. 'Please God I know I did him wrong and not a day passes without it coming to mind but I don't deserve to face him after all these years.'

Now two hundred feet away she noticed the tall lean body sway back and forth with the unmistakable walk and a slight limp that she remembered he was left with after his war wounds, and her heart began to pound.

Presently she could make out the features on his leathery tanned face as that of William, she breathed a sigh of relief when she noticed the long slightly graying handlebar moustache that stretched across each cheek knowing that William was ever clean-shaven when she knew him. But that soon vanished as he drew closer with her shoes dangling carelessly from his right hand.

'That's him.' She moaned. She rose and turned toward the door but before she could walk away he said.

"I av here a pair of shoes that me old dog Rogue pilfered, he's a bugger he is and will take anything that ain't nailed to th floor. A bloody habit since he chiseled in on me life about twelve years ago, that's how he got his name Rogue."

For a moment she froze knowing that all she had to do was walk through the door and out of his sight, but for how long? 'I can't hide.' She thought.

She slowly turned to face him. As she stood slightly above him on the veranda looking down at his dusty boots on the lawn grass he handed her the shoes.

'I cleaned em up a bit where th bugger slobbered on them." He said. " And bygol I told him never to do it again."

"You must be th young chaps grandma." He went on. "He's a fine chap he is and about th best a've ever seen when it comes to working wit th stock."

Finally she raised her sight from his dusty boots to his face and with a forced smile thanked him. Their eyes met and she immediately noticed the light in his eyes as he recognized her.

As they locked eyes she could still see him standing on the dock waving as the ship slipped out toward the Atlantic, at the time thinking that after going home to see her family she would some day again join him and honor their engagement. But it didn't work out that way.

Finally she whispered. "I'm so sorry William, I truly am what else can I say."

Then she noticed the expression on his face had changed to sadness and hurt filled his eyes, without a word he turned and walked away with Rogue close behind.

A short distance away he slowly turned and said. "I forgot to tell you me name, it's Warp it is and I must tell you it's a pleasure meeting you and I hope you av a good visit in this vast land that I thought I could get lost in and leave all my unpleasant past behind, but bygol it found me for sure, bygol it did."

She watched as he and Rogue walked slowly toward the stockman's quarters and seen him pause at the door as he turned to look back at her.

"Yep Rogue." He said slowly. "I found a little peace here in this land, oh yeah, she was on me mind about every day but now she's here and I guess about all that's left for me and you is to ride away on th Canning Stock Route. It's a crook it is th Canning Stock Route, many have died from wild animals, hot weather, and thirst trying to conquer her, but bygol we'll give it a try, yep I reckon we won't make it but we'll go out together Rogue, some place out there on the longest stock route in th world we'll find a place to get away from me past for good bygol."

She sat on the veranda late listening to the night noises and wondering what William was thinking in the darkness of the stockman's quarters.

Finally she went to bed knowing that sleep would not come. She tossed and turned most of the night disturbing her husband prompting him to ask the next morning.

"Tell me Alice are you home sick? I was under the impression that you were getting accustomed to this land, I know I am, but if you'd rather we leave just say so because as I have told you many times in the past your happiness is all that matters to me and if you're happy so am I no matter where it might be."

"Oh no Cal I'm okay, I have no idea why I had such a restless night, probably the excitement of events to come, Reba's wedding and all."

She reached out and ran her fingers over his face wishing she could come clean and share her problem with him but knew it would only make things worse if she did.

'The whole thing seems so much like a dream that you awake and realize it could never have happened in the first place.' She thought. 'But this one is real and I have to deal with it no matter what.'

Meantime at the stockman's quarters men were moving about getting ready for the days chores that never seemed to end. Only something was very different on this particular morning, Warp hadn't made his presence known and everyone wondered if he might not be feeling well but at the same time reluctant to go ask him because of his unpredictability about inquires about himself. Afraid that he might bellow out, "Go on mind yore own business you bloody bloke, don't worry about me."

He lay there looking up at the rough hewn boards of the ceiling following the wood grains as they ran straight as an arrow for a few inches only to curve off in several directions to form images that very much resembled animals, a cat, a dog, a snake, a croc, or a cut that came from a large knot where the grains were formed in a circle that reminded him of a raging storm with strong tornado winds spinning counter clock wise causing destruction to everything in its path.

His eyes finally rested on one that he had gazed at many times before, a perfectly shaped heart with an arrow piercing the center. "Yep that's me bygol, she broke me heart th day she left me there on the dock and now she comes and puts a dagger in it."

"Can't make up me mind right now what to do about it so it's best I get out there and get th fella's going in th right direction, a lot of work to be done and it won't get done unless I see to it." Rogue had been listening and now stood and stretched then poked his cold nose to Warp's cheek.

"Yeah you old bugger, we'll go on for a while jist like before but some where down th line th Twisted Track will become a memory jist like Scotland where I lost me mother, then England where Alice jilted me. I loved them both dearly and felt completely empty when I lost them causing me to run away from it all not wanting to stay in a place where me good memories had gone bad. I finally ended up in this vast land that offered a smidgen of solace to me soul, and seems like a long enjoyable cattle drive that ends up with tiredness and a sense of accomplishment, only to be replaced by a stampede, which is what happened to you and me Rogue, and the only way out is out there on the Canning Stock Route, yep that'll be my last run." He pulled his boots on and headed for the door.

"Well come on lets get th chaps started, work never ends here on th Twisted Track, no bygol it don't but it will soon be over for you and me."

Outside his eyes lit up at the sight of Tex going about his chores without being told. 'A good chap he is.' He thought. 'Some day he'll be a head stockman jist like me maybe right here on The Twisted Track, and if he does bygol I av had a hand in it and jist maybe he'll recall old Warp's advice and pass it on to others and that way after all my running from me past I left behind something in spite of me self.'

Tex looked toward him and smiled and then Warp could see why he thought he resembled some one from his past, he had the forehead of his grandmother Alice.

Alice and Reba made themselves busy cleaning the house as mum baked cookies and protested. "My word you're my house guests and I don't expect you to clean the house." She said.

"Never mind." Reba replied. "I've always heard if you spend more than two days on a visit you have overstayed and need to contribute something toward your upkeep."

Alice had been unusually quiet all morning prompting mum to ask. "Alice, are you feeling well? I reckon you might be homesick you be quiet as a mouse all morning."

Alice smiled and said. "I feel fine, and no, I'm not homesick I guess I've been lost in my thoughts most of the morning about things that happened in my younger days which I don't care to discuss."

Mum laughed and replied. "Oh my word, I reckon we all have things from our youth that's better not discussed."

Reba gave her mother a puzzled look and thought. 'I hope she's okay because I noticed it myself, I have never known her to be this quiet.'

Then she said. "Momma why don't you go sit on the veranda a spell the cleaning will be over when we finish here in the kitchen."

"No Reba." She answered. "I'm alright so lets get on with the cleaning."

Mum sat another pan of hot cookies on the table to cool, reached for a small brown paper bag at the end of the table and began to fill it with cookies.

"Speaking of the veranda reminds me to put this bag out for old Rogue. He'll be out there nosing around for something to take to Warp and these are Warp's favorite cookies. I'll set them out there after they cool a bit."

"You mean to tell me that dog will take them to Warp without sampling them himself?" Reba asked.

"Oh my word, he will I reckon, he takes everything to Warp and won't eat it till Warp tells him. He's faithful to Warp he is, Rogue and Warp understand each other." She closed and folded the top of the bag and said. "Yep I reckon the Twisted Track owes a lot to Warp, Thomas says he's the best he's ever seen with th stock, and he took Lance under his wing early on, he can be harsh at times but he seems to have the knack for instilling the right thoughts in young minds, and I'm sure he will shape Tex to become someone that you will be proud of, We call it Warp's way and I reckon it must be the right way."

Now with the cleaning finished and the cookies cooling Alice went to her room. She searched the bottom of her purse until she felt a small wadded ball of silk, as she unfolded it her thoughts were.

'I should have answered his letters and told him about having to take care of my father and mother after I returned from the war. They died two days apart after weeks of suffering from the deadly flu epidemic that took thousands.'

'Then later I met Cal when he returned after many surgeries and months in different hospitals from wounds he suffered in the war. I wish I could some how set it all straight but the more I think about it I can see where I did him a great wrong by not answering his letters and explaining my position.'

Now the old unfolded faded blue silk hankie lay before her revealing a sparkling gold ring that immediately took her back in time, as she looked down at him waving from the dock she could hear the sailor.

"Come on Limy fling it up here we'll catch it." And amid the laughter and banter, "Do you want me to put it on her finger?"

She picked it up and while gently rubbing it with the hankie she began to cry and whispered. "No it's not fair to him I should have at least returned his mother's ring and told Cal about it, but instead I have kept it hidden all these years, oh well I guess the best I can do is return it to him now, what a mess I have made of things."

She picked up a pen and quickly scrawled a letter, folded it neatly, placed it with the ring and enclosed them in the hankie.

Out on the veranda she seen that mum had placed the bag of cookies at the top of the steps. She looked off toward the utility building where Thomas and her husband were busy tinkering with the motor from an aging land rover unaware of anything around them.

She bent over and unfolded the turned down creases of the cookie bag, dropped the hankie in and refolded the top of the bag.

She sat down in one of the rocking chairs and waited.

At the stockman's quarters she could see men darting about some working on the trucks and one group off to the side at a smaller building that to her looked like a black smith shop and they were busy with re-shoeing the horses.

She could make out a group of dogs darting around and knew the larger one was old Rogue soon he emerged out of the group and headed toward her. A group of cackling chooks scattered all over the yard as he neared them.

He climbed the steps hardly noticing her and gently took the bag in his mouth. She watched as he ran briskly over the dusty path in a hurry to deliver the cookies to his master. She watched him enter the group of men near the black smith shop and immediately Warp strode from the group carrying the bag in his right hand with Rogue following close behind.

As they disappeared in the stockman's quarters she breathed a sigh of relief knowing that he would find the ring and note without anyone else knowing about it.

She rose and slowly walked back to her room to spend the rest of the day alone filled with worry about how the nightmare she was experiencing would finally turn out.

He reached in the bag feeling the silk hankie but groping on past it he took two cookies, one for him and one for Rogue.

"Here ye go old bugger, some of th missus good sweets and my favorite flavor." He took two more from the bag again feeling the silk hankie and wondered why it was in there.

He opened the top of the bag and peered in noting the faded blue color of the hankie that had the corners tied together and something inside. He took it from the bag and said. "I reckon th missus has put something else in here Rogue."

He untied the corners and as the ring came in view he said. "Oh my word me mother's ring has finally got back to me."

He turned it over and over in his hand admiring it's luster and remembering his mother and the hard life she lived.

He held it out to Rogue and said. "Me mother's ring Rogue, bout all she ever had and she left it for me to keep and cherish, but I gave it away to some one that didn't care nothing bout me at all bygol."

"So now after all these years she shows up here in my part of God's earth and returns it to me."

Then he glanced down and noticed the folded sheets of paper. As he unfolded it he scowled. "What av we here Rogue?"

He took a hard case from his shirt pocket that contained his reading glasses.

He adjusted the glasses and began to read.

Dearest William,

I wouldn't know where to start or end if I had to tell you how sorry I am about how I treated you, and there's no way I can undo it so I will try to give you some idea of what I went through after I returned home from England after the war.

First of all you were in my thoughts and dreams constantly after my return and I could see you waving from the dock as my ship sailed toward the Atlantic. But it all seemed a lost cause that I would ever see you again, you see my father and mother were very sick and I sat and cared for them night and day at their home because hospitals were few and far between at that time, they died two days apart, the flu epidemic was in full swing and most families lost some one or in some cases it took entire families.

I know that is no excuse for not answering your letters or sending your mother's ring back that's the one thing that bothers me most, because it has never been anything of value to me except knowing that it was a treasure to you. I have kept it hidden from my husband Cal all these years knowing in my heart that you would be overjoyed to get it back.

I met Cal after he returned from the war and just like you he suffered injures that kept him in the hospital for a long time. And what a coincidence I found out he was in the same hospital as the one I cared for you in England but in a different ward and we never seen each other.

William I must tell you I found I was pregnant shortly after I got home, and Reba is your daughter.

I met Cal and not having the courage to tell him the truth I have lived a lie through out our marriage.

Cal has been a good husband and a good father to Reba and it would break my heart if he should ever find out the truth.

I have no doubts that you and I could have shared a life of happiness together because believe it or not I did care for you and intended to stay in touch and keep our relationship alive but the circumstances I found myself in at home seemed so hopeless, and you and I were separated by a vast ocean, so when Cal came along it seemed like a way out of my misery and from then on I tried to block you from my mind. But I guess our Lord has a way of punishment for the likes of me or else how can you explain me coming here to have to meet you again face to face.

William I love Cal dearly and pray that you understand that and keep this secret of our past between just you and me, because it would break Cal's heart if he should find out Reba is not his daughter.

Again let me say how sorry I am about my actions .as I said I won't even try to explain because I can't.

In my short time here I have found out that you are highly respected by all on this station and throughout the territory. Everyone knows Warp and his ways and states that Warp's way is the right way. I have no idea where you got that name but I like it.

So Warp let me end this by saying, never in my life did I ever think I would ever see you again and it has been very upsetting to me but at the same time I feel better now that it has happened.

I will end by saying. I wish you all the best because you deserve it. And please forgive me. Alice

He reached in the bag of cookies but this time only one for Rogue because all of a sudden his taste buds only craved alcohol. "Tis upsetting to me too Rogue, yes bygol it is." He reached for the full gallon bottle of Yellowtail wine that had went untouched under his bunk for many months, popped the cork and drank a third of it before taking a breath. He finished off the wine just as the sun set in the west and as he reeled in the open door he could see the red glow above the sunset and it reminded him again of The Canning Stock Route and the hot arid desert lands that it crossed in spots.

He turned and staggered to his bunk muttering something about his mother's ring. He fell into a deep sleep and Rogue lay faithfully by his bunk with the bag of cookies within easy reach but he didn't touch them knowing that his master would share them with him later. A man and his dog a dog and his master, sharing their lives together through the good and the bad no matter what.

The sun was high and hot before he awoke stirring thoughts among the ringers once again.

"I reckon it ain't like Warp to sleep this late, he don't look sick so he must have something on his mind that's keeping him awake at night."

"Oh my word it ain't Warp, it ain't, could be the memories of that nurse that jilted him is back on his mind." Said another.

About that time he walked out in the sunlight rubbing his eyes, they went about what they were doing afraid to ask him if he was alright knowing that was not Warp's way if he wanted you to know he would tell you.

Mum's long table which she had brought in an additional one and placed them end to end, was laden with food as Warp and the ringers had arrived and were sitting on the veranda, two of the ringers had brought along their guitars and another his accordion the guitar players were strumming along attempting to play different tunes including two American songs, "Tumbling Tumble Weeds" by the sons of the Pioneers was one of the accordion players favorites he could play it quite well, then they practiced on the haunting sad song "Mansion On The Hill" by country music singer Hank Williams.

Mum made a last minute check to make sure everything was in order, then had Alice and Reba stand near the door where she could introduce them to Warp and the other ringers.

"Now you'll like this rowdy looking bunch, you will." She said. "Especially Warp, he might seem strange at first but believe me he's a very special one that Warp is, and don't get alarmed if th ringers sit and stare at you, and they will for sure because it ain't often they get to see two beautiful women like you out here in this wild country."

As they filed by she would introduce each one as she rambled on with, "Seth I want you to meet Alice and her daughter Reba from America, Warp this is Alice and her daughter Reba and its best you keep yore bunch in check because as you know Alice belongs to Cal who you have already met and Reba belongs to Lance or soon will be."

They all laughed except for Warp and Alice who were far from being amused knowing they would have to hide their feelings during the meal and the party to follow that had all the promises of becoming a gala event.

For the next few minutes Mum was busy seating each one making sure she had a complete mix and the ringers were not segregated to a certain part of the table.

"Here Warp rest yore self right here between Lance and Reba, that way you'll be sitting right next to Lance's pretty future wife and right across from you is her beautiful mother Alice."

When all were seated except for her husband and herself she looked at him and said.

"You sit there at the head of the table Thomas, you're still the head of the house." Then with a sly look at her guests she added. "At least he thinks he is."

They all laughed with merriment except for Warp and Alice as they tried hard not to make eye contact as they sat across from each other.

She asked Thomas to give thanks knowing that he had already sank a few pints of grog and should be at his best with words as he earnestly talked to God and thanked him for the abundance of food and asked his blessings on their guests."

All heads were bowed as they listened to his deep bass voice. "Lord, I call on you as we sit around this table as a family blessed with an abundance of food that we are about to partake of, I pray that all here will feel yore presence and enjoy th meal and our family get together for the remainder of this day. I say family because bygol it is family to me and th missus, we know all th ringers and call them by their first names, they have all been loyal and work hard to make this station successful, and Warp he's a big influence in th lives of all our family gathered here. He can be strange at times bygol for sure, I'll never forget th first time I seen him way back some years ago, at that time he had no sense of direction and told me so. Said he had been jilted by a young woman jist after World War One and hired on to a freighter and sailed to our land to get away from it all, Outside of that he's never told anyone much else about his life except he hails from Scotland which is where my roots are giving us something in common. He's a strange cuss at times Lord and we call it Warp's way which has proven to be the right way, we thank you Lord for sending him to this family because I can't imagine ever living here without Warp's presence among us. He's a jewel amongst us he is, and bygol we thank ye."

"And now to our newest members from America, thank ye for sending them. One to become our son Lance's wife in a few weeks, she brings a fine son with her and we have already taken him as our grandson and look forward to him growing up under the watchful eye of Warp that served Lance so well, every young boy needs a Warp in their lives. And then there's Cal and his beautiful wife Alice they have hinted about going back to America, but I ask you Lord to intervene because we need them here as an addition to this family, Cal has grown on me and seems like me brother bygol he does.

Well I have asked these things in my own humble way and if it be your will my master I look forward to ye blessings. Amen!"

Then with a beaming happy face Mum called out. "Now that all th fancy formalities have been followed its time to "bog In" I reckon we have a heaping supply of tucker on th table."

Everyone enjoyed the delicious food and conversation throughout the meal that seemed like forever to Warp and Alice as they tried to hide their true feelings and join in with the fun and laughter.

Alice's thoughts were of Cal and Reba, Cal not knowing that he was not Reba's father and Reba sitting by Warp, her real father, then Tex in between two suntanned ringers eying Warp his Idol, not knowing that he was his real grandfather. As these thoughts raced through her mind she chanced a look at the now sad face of Warp and felt like she was about to burst out crying.

Warp had sat through Thomas's prayer and felt a sense of pride and amusement at his fellow Scotsman's words of praise toward him but only momentarily as he glanced at Alice and reality took over again stripping away any false cover that all the years since

their relationship had afforded him. Knowing that he was sitting next to his daughter and could not now or ever be able to hold and tell her that, seemed more than he could bear, and as he turned toward his grandson sitting so confident and proudly between the two ringers he suddenly had the urge to rise and reveal the truth but changed his mind knowing it would only break Reba's heart to know about it after loving Cal as her father all of her life and Tex who seemed to worship him as his grandfather. The consequences were too great and as he listened to Mum praising Cal for the way he had brought his family up in the right way he could vision Cal going berserk if he should ever find out the truth.

'No bygol taint worth it.' He thought. 'Best I keep th bloody secret and ride off on th Canning Stock Route.'

After the meal the men went to the veranda to talk and sink some more grog while the ladies cleaned off the table and washed the dishes.

Mum came out with a large platter of food for old Rogue who had been patiently waiting on the veranda. "Here Rogue you old bugger." She said. "Eat this and don't share it with Warp he's had enough for today."

Rogue sniffed and finally got a hold on the platter and started pulling it to Warp.One of the ringers remarked. 'Yep that be old Rogue faithful to Warp no matter that he might be starving him self."

He stood over the food looking up at Warp. "It's alright I reckon." Warp said softly. "Go on eat it up you old Bugger." Soon the platter was empty.

More grog was consumed and soon the two guitar players were strumming away and after several starts without success they finally found the right notes to "Mansion On The Hill" and when the ladies joined them they had mastered it very well.

Cal looked at his daughter Reba and asked her to sing it. "No dad." She answered. "I'm a terrible singer."

"Don't you believe her." Cal remarked. "She sings like a song bird." And with a little more urging she moved in between the guitar players and sang the song without missing a beat.

Then they started playing Tumbling Tumble Weeds and everyone joined in with the lyrics that they could remember including the two black ringers as they hummed along in harmony. The merriment went on late in the evening until finally Thomas stopped bringing on the grog and one by one the ringers including Warp drifted away toward the stockman's quarters.

Warp went to bed depressed as ever and mumbling something about the Canning Stock Route.He lay there for some time thinking about his daughter and grandson and how much he enjoyed being around them. He finally said.

"Bygol it ain't right Rogue that I can't claim my daughter and grandson, but it will have to stay that way, so I reckon you and me will be heading up toward Halls Creek on the Canning Stock Route in a few days, I doubt if we'll make it Rogue but I've made up me mind." He finally drifted off to sleep dreaming of Alice waving as the ship sailed away that day toward the Atlantic.

Cal went to bed and fell asleep instantly from all the grog he had consumed and was unaware of Alice laying next to him most of the night filled with worry and shame from her past and sorry that she had kept it from him.

Her thoughts were. 'I did Cal wrong but what can I do about it now? I should tell him but I know he would be devastated, it would literally destroy him, I just can't bring myself to tell him, he deserves better than that.'

Lance and Reba sat nestled closely on the veranda listening to night noises until the early morning hours. Their wedding plans were complete and in two more weeks they would be man and wife. "I feel so happy Lance." She whispered. "Today has turned out to be a perfect day getting to know Warp and the ringers they are all so nice, but momma worries me she just ain't herself I'm afraid something's wrong."

He squeezed her tightly and said. "I wouldn't let it worry me if I were you, she's probably homesick and that will pass."

Another week went by and everyone noticed the change in Warp. He consumed more yellowtail daily. One of the ringers became concerned and mentioned it to Lance. "I reckon Warp ain't right and I think he needs you or your dad to talk to him, he's lost all interest about th work here on th station, gets his dander up for no reason and yells at th ringers, taint like Warp to be that way."

Lance mentioned it to his dad. "The ringers are worried about Warp he's on edge with them for no reason, I've noticed a change in him myself for the past month or so."

"Yeah Lance, bygol there be a change in Warp that I notice and it's puzzling, I think we better go over to th quarters and talk with him."

Rogue rose from beside the bunk and stretched as they walked in. Through the semi-darkness they could make out the form of Warp curled up on the bunk, his quarters were hot and humid and the smell of cheap wine penetrated their nostrils.

Thomas dropped to one knee beside the bunk and as he cuddled and rubbed Rogue who had nosed his way to his side sensing that all was not right with his master, his deep bass voice penetrated the quietness with, "Warp wake up and lets visit a spell."

He rose to a sitting position with arms flailing and a wild look on his face, but recognized them and said. "Well bygol I reckon we can but it must be pretty important to wake me from me sleep." He rose to his feet and said. "Best we go out and watch old sol go down, I reckon it's steaming in here."

They followed him and watched for several seconds as he squinted at the last rays of sunshine as it disappeared to leave behind blood red clouds that resembled a giant forest fire. Finally he turned to Thomas and said. "I think I know what ye be thinking that I not be me self for a spell and bygol ye hit th mark. Remember th day you hired me and I told you about me past and how I came to this vast land to forget it? Well I did rid me self of some of it here on th Twisted Track but not all of it, jist like old sol it would disappear and let me sleep restless through the night but with each morning it would come back to muddle my mind through th day."

"I owe you for taking me on and bygol ye be a decent man through it all and I will never forget it, but now my past has won th battle and a defeated man in mind ain't worth much to anyone, so I must move on, give me a few days to sweat and rid me self of th bloody yellowtail and bygol I'll be on me way."

There was a full minute of silence as Thomas and Lance stood stunned and speechless.

Finally Thomas spoke but his deep bass voice sounded hollow as he said.

"Warp you bloody devil don't talk like that, me and th boy is here to talk and want to help, so forget about ever leaving th Twisted Track cause ye helped make her what she is, because of you Warp this station has been more successful than any other in the territory, bygol I told you before, that ye be the best I have ever known wit th stock and th same goes for th way you have wit th ringers, and my boy Lance here, he took to you and your ways and you pointed him in th right direction, bygol you can't walk away and leave all that behind."

Then he laid his hand on Warp's shoulder and said." Now go sleep on that and we'll talk more about it tomorrow, and that boy Tex he idolizes you and needs yore guidance jist like Lance did at his age, think about that you'll be letting him down right when he needs you."

Warp turned and looked away thinking. 'Yea bygol I need him to because he's my grandson he is, but I have to walk away without him ever knowing it.'

He turned toward the open door and Rogue followed as they entered the rank smelling steamy darkness of the room.

Still in shock Thomas and Lance stood there wondering if they should follow him and talk some more but finally walked away toward the homestead.

The next day as Thomas approached he spotted Warp at the black smiths shop shoeing his horse. He was giving Tex instructions on the proper way to trim the horse's hoof before nailing the shoe on. He stood watching as Warp turned it over to Tex and let him nail the shoe on. "Bygol you got it.' He beamed. "Now get to work on Th other one, trim it off good, here I'll show you how." When the last shoe was nailed on to his satisfaction he said. "Good job lad bygol it is, now ride old Gunner around a little he needs th stiffness worked out o his legs." He watched Tex get in the saddle with ease and gallop away he turned to Thomas and said. "That lads a natural he is, some day he'll have a station o his own."

" I know he will Warp," Thomas replied, "and I want you around to take some credit for it when it happens. Makes no bloody sense for you to leave here after all the years you helped to shape this station, bygol you managed to live with your past up until now, so explain to me why all of a sudden you want to give up and ride off to God knows where?"

"Yep, I suffered with me past and managed to live with it but it's finally caught up to me."

Thomas got a puzzled look on his face, "Now what does that mean, that makes no bloody sense to me, are you telling me you're still leaving?"

"Yea Jist as soon as I get over th shakes from th yellowtail I'll hit th track to Wiluna and take a little from me savings then take the Canning Stock Route to Halls Creek."

"You old fool you'll never make it to Halls Creek over the Canning Route, some of the wells have dried up along the way, you'll die from thirst for sure."

"I av to try, Bygol I do av to try but if I fail to make it I want you to check wit th bank in Wiluna about my savings, I'll leave instructions about what I want done with it."

"And I reckon you plan on taking Rogue with you, you know yourself he's too old to walk all that distance to Halls Creek."

" Oh yeah old Rogue will be wit me bygol, when he tuckers out I will let him ride behind me on old Gunner jist like he did when he was a pup."

Thomas could see that he was determined to leave and was saddened. "Well Warp you bloody fool I guess I'm wasting my breath trying to talk you out of it so take anything you need to get you there, but I still say you'll never make it."

"I'll need one pack horse and some of th missus canned jellies, I can get the rest from the supplies here at th quarters."

"Go ahead and take a pack horse and anything else that you might need, in fact you should take two pack horses."

"One will be enough, and I thank ye for yore offerings," he stuck out his hand and as they gripped he said, "One morning soon I'll be riding out, it's best no one knows but you and me until I get out of sight, and bygol lets you and me bid farewell right now and get that out o the way."

Thomas embraced him and whispered. "You old bloody fool you're like a brother to me and I feel like I'll never see you again after you leave here."

He backed off a few steps and they stood looking at each other, finally Warp turned and walked toward his quarters with old Rogue at his heels, a dog and his master soon to be on the Canning Stock Route, destination Halls Creek, across arid desert country, almost impossible, but a mans past will drive him to try foolish reckless things sometimes out of pride but in Warp's case for the sake of others.

Alice awoke early and lay there thinking about her family worried that things would never be normal again, but she had made up her mind to keep the secret of her and Warp's long ago relationship hidden deep inside although she knew she would feel better if she could sit down with some one like mum and let it all out. But the chances of it spreading to others including her family made it impossible so she decided to suffer in silence.

She rose and sat on the side of the bed for a while listening to Cal's breathing which she noticed seemed more laborious of late, probably from the advancing stage of black lung disease, a malady due to years of working in the coal mines. Finally she slipped her feet in her house slippers, leaned over and kissed his cheek and went out to sit on the verando.

Like many times before she took solace in the still darkness of the early morning that seemed to have a soothing effect on her many worries just before daybreak.

As first light started revealing her surroundings she spotted a horse and rider with another horse following behind coming from the direction of the stockman's quarters. As they drew closer she could see old Rogue running ahead and could make out the silhouette of Warp as he sat tall in the saddle.

She thought about going back in the house but sat transfixed instead and now they were close enough she could hear the soft thud of the horse's feet in the early morning silence. He sat rigid in the saddle looking straight ahead and she wondered if he would even glimpse toward her as he rode by. He rode by but must have spotted her at the last second, he pulled the reins and old Gunner came to a halt. He turned in the saddle bowed graciously, tipped his hat and seemed to be searching for words but when he opened his mouth they refused to come.

She raised her hand and waved feebly, he smiled and gently tapped his knee to Gunner's side and moved on. Two hundred yards from the homestead he turned left on the track to Wiluna. She watched as old Rogue ran ahead but would stop often to let the walking horses catch up.

The breaking light of day afforded her a better view as they went down the long track.

Finally when they were almost out of sight he turned Gunner toward her and waved, she wondered if it was meant for a last goodbye to her or maybe to the homestead that had been such a big part of his troubled life, not knowing which she stood up and waved back and watched as distance reduced his figure to a bobbing dot as he bounced in the saddle, and finally even that disappeared leaving her with the thought, 'Out of sight but not out of mind.' And as the sun peeped over tall trees to the east bringing another glorious day to the Twisted Track she could vision the sad face of Warp as he rode toward Wiluna. It overwhelmed her senses so she sat down and cried.

Warp had moved stealthily when he got up to leave the quarters trying not to awaken any of the ringers, but one of the light sleeping black ringers roused and wondered why he was up so early, he lay and listened to him make several trips to the outside obviously taking something from the quarters. Then when he went out and didn't return right away the ringer slipped outside. He took a position at one end of the building and watched as Warp strapped his provisions to the packhorse. Then watched him ride away in the direction of the Wiluna track.

He hurriedly returned to his quarters and roused the other black ringer. "Warp he go on walk about, he take pack horse loaded with supplies he did, he go on walk about."

His excited jabber woke the other ringers and soon the quarters came alive with speculation.

"Ah hell, he might be going to Wiluna to see that feisty hotel manager, she's always had a crush on him." One said. "Yea," said another. "She'll put him up in a room and keep him supplied with grog and her affections, but he'll soon get burned out on that and return to th station."

393

"Wrong you be," chimed in another, "Warp's a strange cobber he is, and has minor flaws that he manages to overcome but for the past month I see a different Warp, a very troubled man and I don't think we will ever see him on the Twisted Track again."

Tex was troubled by the news and was upset about all the rumors, just after sunrise he headed for the homestead, he could see his grandmother sitting on the veranda with her face buried in her hands. As he went up the steps she removed her hands and he could see she had been crying, 'maybe homesick,' he thought.

"Warp's gone," he said, "Left at daybreak with a packhorse and supplies headed toward Wiluna, some of the ringers said he won't be back."

"Oh I don't know about that," she said, "he may have went on business."

"No grandma," he answered, "He's been on cheap wine for a time and the ringers tell me that ain't like Warp."

Lance was up and came out. "Lance Warp's gone, left at daybreak, one of the black ringers said he went on a walk about, but some of the ringers think he's gone for good. What's a walk about Lance?"

"Walk about, is a term used by the black ringers when they decide to take some time off, mind you out of the blue they'll tell the head stockman that they are leaving for a while. And they might stay away as long as a year but most always return, It's a crook for the head stockman but he usually goes along with it because it's hard to get ringers that will stay loyal. But Warp ain't that kind, my word, he might leave once in a while but not for a walk about, he may have went to Wiluna to take care of business he has an account there at the bank, if so he'll be back in a few days." He said all this knowing that the chances of Warp returning were slim but felt he had to come up with something to soothe Tex worries.

Early the next morning as he rode by the hotel on his way to the livery stable down the street he was spotted by Maxine the cleaning girl at the hotel. A smile lit up her face as
she remembered all the other times he had come to town on the pretext of having some business to take care of at the bank, but in the end he always wound up at the hotel for a couple of days enjoying all the pampering that Kate the hotel owner showered on him.

She made sure he was served all his favorite foods, including longings of his youth back in Scotland for his mother's apple cobbler.

She remembered the first time Kate served him cobbler that she painstakingly had tried to duplicate like his mother's. And remembered the anxiety that marked Kate's face as she watched him take the first bite and the complete joy that lit up her whole body when he said.

"Bygol Kate, ye hit th jackpot fer sure, this cobbler is jist like me mother's it is, now I know who to call on when I get th hunger pains fer me mother's cooking, bygol I do and I'll be back for more."

"Ah go on you old walrus," Kate had replied, "sugar coating will get you nowhere you know yourself you have been lucky to stay welcome here at my hotel after all the times you was supposed to come spend a few days in my company and didn't. I remember once you stayed away a whole year, so don't get your hopes up when you get a hankering for apple cobbler and ride in here with that hungry look on your face."

Then she remembered him rising from the table and taking Kate in his arms and saying.

"Yep bygol yer right Kate and I will make amends fer sure, th day that Thomas Kirk tells me he's ready to hand over th Twisted Track to his son Lance is th day I'll ride in here for good, and not because I'm craving some o me mother's apple cobbler, no because it's you I crave Kate, bygol it is."

As she rushed to the hotel desk where Kate was busy with some paper work she was thinking. 'I wonder if she'll welcome him this time? It's been a long time, maybe a year since he was last here.' And why is he bringing a pack horse and old Rogue with him?' Could it be Thomas Kirk has handed the Twisted Track over to his son Lance, and Warp feels free to leave now that he has fulfilled his obligation to stay until Lance took over?'

"Miz Wampler Warp's in town he is, he's down at the livery stable, and this time he has a pack horse and his old dog Rogue in tow, could it be he's finally calling it quits at the Twisted Track?"

"Now how would I know Maxine? You can come up with the most ridiculous questions, you know yourself he hasn't showed up here for well over a year so how would I know? And I wish you would forget about addressing me with that Miz Wampler stuff and just call me Kate can't you see how irritating it is for me to have to listen to that day after day?"

"Yes but I was just trying to be respectful."

" I know you are Maxine, but I am no less or better than you so lets forget all that formal stuff and know each other on a first name basis, after all we do discuss our most closely held secrets with each other as most women do, now what was that about Warp, did you say he had his dog Rogue with him?"

395

"Yes miz—er Kate and also a pack horse."

"Well he must be up to something and I'm afraid it ain't apple cobbler or me that he has on his mind, we'll find out soon I reckon."

She sat shuffling papers at her desk as he walked in the lobby not bothering to jump to her feet and embrace him as she had in the past. He noticed and stared down at her. "Kate I need to rest me self up a bit, jist two days and bygol I'll be on my way outta yore life fer good."

"So now Warp, I find out what I've thought all along, you never had any intentions of fulfilling all the things you told me in the past. I can hear all your promises over and over, promises like this, "Kate we'll marry up as soon as Thomas sees fit to turn th station over to th lad, we will, Bygol av been happy working at th station but I reckon you and me can enjoy a happy life together right here at this hotel."

Her voice became shrill as she rose to face him, "All that and more you promised Warp, and now after staying away more than a year you walk in here and have the nerve to ask for a room to rest up a few days, and I suppose you'll want some apple cobbler like your mother used to make, and lets not forget while you're here you'll want to cuddle up with me and ride off with a promise that you'll return in a little while to claim me as your life mate, well this time will be different, no special meals, no apple cobbler, and sure as hell you won't feel the warmth of my body close to you as before, and you'll pay for the bloody room this time."

"Kate bygol you be right, I reckon I did say them things but I promise."

"No," she yelled, "I never want to hear another bloody promise from you."

He reached in his pocket and retrieved a well-worn billfold. "I need th room Kate me old bones are weary from th ride from th station."

Then for the first time she noticed the tiredness that showed in his face and his eyes he resembled an animal that had been hemmed off with no way to escape. At that moment she felt like taking him in her arms and telling him to forget all she had said but instead she assigned him a room, as he took the key and walked away she called after him. "Yes you can let old Rogue in the room."

He turned and said, "Well I reckon th old bugger can sleep on th veranda.'

"No," she replied. "He belongs close to you because he's about all you got left."

She watched as he made his way down the hallway toward his room, Maxine passed by followed by old Rogue, down the hall she heard Maxine say, "Hiya Warp, here's your old friend Rogue."

"Ah yeah he is that, th old bugger, and like Kate said, about all I have left."

As Maxine came back down the hallway and passed the desk Kate turned her head away to hide the tears that were now flowing freely.

He bathed and dried off using the same towel to wipe the dust from Rogue's thick coat.

When Maxine made her rounds with a supply of clean towels, he, not wanting to face Kate at dinner asked her to bring his food to his room.

"Kate she be a fair and wise lady, she is, and what you heard her say is true, bygol it is true and I feel like hiding me face. I reckon I av lost her and we will never be close again not even as a friend in need."

"Oh my word Warp, what makes you think that way? You only heard her frustration coming out, she has deep feelings for you and always has you're the only man she has ever wanted since she lost her husband there in France in World War One. She has counted on you to keep your promises and take her as your wife, believe me Warp she cares for you I reckon."

On her way out she paused at the door, turned and said, "Give that some thought Warp, it's not too late, Kate loves you."

He lay down in the bed between clean smelling sheets and relaxed, Rogue curled up on the floor and was soon sleeping peacefully. He tried to sort out the things that Kate had said and wondered if she cared for him as much as Maxine claimed she did.

He knew she was right about the promises he had made because he had more or less taken her for granted, used her and seldom kept a promise.

He stared at the ceiling and as tired as he was sleep would not claim him.

Then sometime in the wee hours of the morning he realized he cared for Kate enough to marry her and hoped she would knock on his door just like old times.

"I think I could have got over Alice a long time ago," he whispered, "And bygol with Kate's help it would have went away cause now I can see it was nothing but bruised pride." He sat up in bed causing Rogue to rouse and look around.

"I should go to her now Rogue, and let out my feelings but I'm afraid she might reject me Rogue, so I reckon the Canning Stock Route is still calling us."

He lay back down and finally sleep overcame his thoughts.

397

She tossed and turned most of the night in a way glad that she had finally stood up to Warp, but at the same time sorry she had been so abrupt without trying to find out if he had a problem that maybe she could be of help.

'The bloody bloke has been unhappy most of his life,' she thought, 'He has let that nurse who jilted him rule his life when all he had to do was marry me to get her off his mind.' 'I wish now I could take back the things I said to him we might have a chance to work it out.'

Just before daybreak she slipped down the hall and paused at his door, inside she could hear him snoring and Rogue was on the other side of the door sniffing aware that some one was at his master's door. She raised her hand to knock softly just as she had done many times before but instead she stiffened and backed away. She turned and headed back down the hallway thinking if there was ever to be any chance that they would mend fences and join together it was up to him. She went back to bed and finally went in to a deep sleep.

Maxine woke her at ten in the morning and wondered if her and Warp had patched things up. But before the day ended she knew they hadn't because she could see the strain in their faces as they went through the day trying to avoid each other.

Warp spent some time at the bank signing proper papers that would dispose of his account the way he wanted it if he didn't make it to Halls Creek.

"You have a fair amount of savings Warp," Herbert the banker said, "Are you sure you want it all to go to the young lad? You have only known him for a short time and don't forget he's from America, he might just up and go back there after he gets his hands on this money."

"Naw th lads a good un he is and bygol I want him to get th benefit o me savings."

"So be it Warp, sign right here, he must be a special person to you I reckon."

"I reckon he is that, bygol he is."

He went out of his way to avoid the places that served grog or any kind of alcoholic beverages knowing the first drink would start him off again. 'Me strength is coming back,' he thought, 'and bygol I be needing it out there on th Canning Stock Route.'

He went to bed that night and thought about Kate and the way he had treated her. "Bygol Rogue, I care about that woman I do, I reckon I av all along but let the memories of Alice blot out me feelings." Rogue cocked his head to one side as if he understood and stood there waiting for his next sentence.

"I reckon I could go tell Kate Rogue and we could live out th rest o our time here at this hotel, th Canning Stock Route is crook and even if we make it to Halls Creek I av to face me troubles all over again. But I reckon she might reject me Rogue, and that would put me back on the yellowtail again."

Rogue stood waiting for another sentence that would maybe have some finality to it but it never came. Then he heard Warp sigh and shortly after heard him snoring, he went to the bed and nosed his master's cheek before curling up on the hotel carpet.

Down the hall Kate tossed and turned just as she had the night before.

At the bank that day the banker knowing of her and Warp's past relationship as most everyone else did approached her. "Ms. Wampler, tell me what's come over Warp? He came in here today to take care of some business and told me he's through at The Twisted Track and seems hell bent on taking the Canning Stock Route all the way to Halls Creek, I reckon you know as well as I do that he'll never make it in this hot weather. Did he tell you anything? I'm worried about him, he's been a fixture at The Twisted Track and means so much to so many people here in Waluna and all over the territory, I'd hate to get word that he died from thirst out there on the Canning Stock Route."

Irritated that he had the nerve to ask her such questions that to her seemed personal, she shot back.

"I have no idea what's going on with the bloody fool and won't lose any sleep about him when he's out there on the Canning Stock Route thirsting his way to Halls Creek if he ever makes it, and I reckon he won't, it's his life and if he sees fit to ride off and die a hellish death only to be eaten by wild animals of the Outback so be it."

She turned and stormed out of the bank leaving the banker stunned and sorry that he had ever mentioned it.

As she thought about it she realized she should have answered the banker in a more civil way because she could sense he was genuinely worried about Warp.

After a while she again got the urge to go to his room and try reasoning with him.

She slipped down the hallway and stopped at his door. She stood there listening to his soft snoring that caused her to wonder if he really cared, if so how could he sleep so well? Soon she detected Rogue at the door sniffing. She turned and walked back down the hallway to her room and after another night of worry and little sleep she faced another day filled with mixed emotions ranging from, 'I need to get a hold on myself, he needs me as bad as I need him,' I reckon he will never make the first move because of his bloody pride,' 'and I reckon it's left up to me, but I have my pride too.'

The day dragged by and late in the evening she seen him walk out and take a seat on the veranda and wondered if she should go and join him, then watched as he sat there looking at the sunset until well after dark twisting the ends of his handlebar mustache as he quietly conveyed his feelings to Rogue.

As she watched she thought about going to him and apologizing for her harsh words, or I reckon I could just take him in my arms and tell him 'I'm ready to cast my lot with you and settle down to a life together.' But after giving it some thought she did neither. 'I still have my pride she whispered.' She rose and made her way to her room.

Finally he rose from the rocking chair and said. "It's time to rest up a bit Rogue and be fresh for our journey on th Canning Stock Route come morning."

As he passed the hotel clerk's office he thought about scribbling a note to leave on Kate's desk telling her how sorry he felt about the way he had treated her, but now realized he cared for her and would like for her to forgive him and consider becoming his wife. He searched for a pencil and paper and began to write.

"Kate you are on me mind, and bygol I be wrong for sure when I made promise after promise and broke them one after the other. I care for you Kate and always have, I jist let me past get in th way and forgot what was important, but now I can see me mistakes and ask of your heart to forgive me. I ask fer yore hand in marriage Kate, well bygol I ain't no good at posting letters or writing love notes, I reckon what I'm trying to say is, I love you Kate, and it would warm me soul if you can see fit to spend the rest of yore life wit me and me bloody old dog Rogue. Think about it Kate and give me a signal of some kind before I head out for Halls Creek." Love ye, Warp.

He laid it on her desk under a paperweight and went to his room.

He lay there for a long time thinking about it and wondering if he did the right thing. "Bygol Rogue I do mean it, but it sounds silly coming from me and she might be amused by th likes o it. I changed me mind Rogue, no way can them words be coming from Warp cause that's not Warp's way. I reckon me pride still rules Rogue, come early morning we be leaving."

He got out of bed pulled his pants on and stole down the hallway to the desk, wadded the note into a tight ball and threw it in the wastebasket.

He slept better than usual now that his nerves had calmed down considerably as the yellowtail slowly left his system. He awoke at daybreak and went to the dining area for coffee knowing that the jack of all trades around the hotel, cleaner, painter, plumber, and some times cook Chung, the Chinaman would be there early as always fussing about all the work he had to do to keep the hotel operating.

"Warp wanna coffee? Chung maka fresh coffee, Warp wanna eggs? Chung hava eggs, no hava ham, ham all gone, Chung hava steak, Warp wanna steak?"

"Give me steak Chung and pile some eggs on I reckon I got a long ride ahead today."

"Why you go Warp? You crazy lika Chinaman t go horseyback on Cannon Route, you neva maka t Hells Cheek, no, no, you die Warp, hot an dry, no water, water all gone."

"Why you no come here to Kate Warp? Kate happy when Warp come and wanna cook, when Warp gone Chung hafta do all cooking. Kate not happy this time I tink Warp stay away too long, why you no come? Chung no understand, Kate happy when you here but notta dis time."

"Chung it be my fault but bygol me pride is in th way and refuses to budge so I reckon I have to ride away from it and hope th next place I land will give me some solace to me soul."

"You die Warp, lissen to Chung, you die out on t Cannon Route, and maka Kate sad, Kate no happy, she happy wi Warp and Chung no havta cook."

"Kate wanna coffee? Chung maka fresh coffee, Kate wanna steak wi eggs on top? No hava ham, ham all gone. Chung wi fix but have other tings to do."

"No thanks Chung I'll just have coffee, and I wish you would stop complaining so much you know yourself that I pay you well and give you room and board."

"Chung know Kate, Chung lika fuss, but Chung worka hard and sava money, some day send for pretty Chinese girl, she can live here wi me atta hotel, she be my wife, okay Kate?"

"Sure Chung, send for her anytime, better you bring her here before she gets old and cranky like you."

401

"Chung no cranky Kate, Chung good Chinaman, Chung work hard an sava money."

For the first time in two days she smiled. "You are a good Chinaman Chung and I'm lucky to have you working for me."

He smiled with pride knowing she meant what she said.

"Warp hava steak an pile eggs on top, he take old dog and go to stable to get hoss, he ride to Halls Cheek onna Cannon Route, he die Kate, he die on Cannon Route, no hava water in wells, water all gone, Chung tell him he die, he belong here wi you Kate, Chung tell him that, he stay here Chung no havta cook."

"I know Chung I know, but Warp is a man of his own, he is, and it's called Warp's way and there's never going to come a time when he'll change."

She finished her coffee and walked away as Chung's sentences came at breakneck speed and followed her down the hallway.

"Chung say he crazy, Warp he crazy lika Chinaman, go horsey riding onna Cannon Route where no hava water, water all gone, he die and big bad birds eat him, why he no stay wi Kate? Chung say he crazy, Kate hava hotel, Kate pretty woman, Warp crazy lika Chinaman."

She went and stood in the doorway looking out on the veranda and beyond to the track, soon she seen him coming from the livery stable sitting tall in the saddle swaying in rhythm to Gunner's easy gait, the pack horse followed tethered to Gunner by a rope tied to Gunner's saddle gear. Old Rogue trotted briskly along in front and seemed happy to be back out on the road again. As they drew even with the veranda she stepped back a little in the shadow of the entrance out of sight. She noticed he looked toward the veranda but didn't stop. She stepped out on the veranda just as he turned east on the track leading to the Canning Stock Route she watched them go down the track with Rogue running ahead and stopping frequently until they caught up. When they were near out of sight he reined in Gunner and turned to face the hotel. He lifted his hat and waved, she waved back not knowing if he was waving goodbye to her or maybe he meant it for Wiluna. Soon they were just a dot on the horizon headed toward the route and sure death, so like Alice before her she sat down and cried.

Maxine laid her hand on her shoulder and said. "Come on Kate it's over forget about him and get on with your life, he's not worth worrying about."

"I reckon you're right Maxine," she replied, but it hurts anyway."

She sat at her desk trying to get her mind on something that would relieve the worry about Warp out there in the hot Australian outback probably dieing from thirst. Two days had passed since she seen him ride away toward the Canning Stock Route, and Chung's words haunted her because she knew there was truth in them.

"Warp he die Kate, no hava water, water all gone, he die Kate, big bad birds eat him, Chung tell him he crazy lika Chinaman."

She glanced down at the wastebasket and noticed a wadded ball of paper lodged between the top of the wastebasket and the wall. She reached for it curious as to who discarded it because she never wadded paper up when she discarded it and she was the only one using the desk. She slowly unfolded and pressed out the wrinkles as best she could and began to read.

"Kate ye are on me mind, and bygol I be wrong for sure when I made promise after promise and broke them one after the other. I care for you Kate and always have, I jist let me past get get in th way and forgot what was important, but now I can see my mistakes and ask of your heart to forgive me. I ask fer yore hand in marriage Kate, well bygol I ain't no good at posting letters or love notes, I reckon what I'm trying to say is, I love you Kate, and it would warm me soul if you can see fit to spend the rest of yore life wit me and me bloody old dog Rogue. Think about it Kate and give me a signal of some kind before I head out for Halls Creek." I love ye, Warp.

She went limp as the color drained from her face, then she spied Maxine going down the hallway with an arm full of clean sheets and called to her. "Maxine come here quick."

When Maxine stopped and turned around but hesitated she yelled, "Drop the bloody sheets and come here."

Maxine came running noting the lack of color in her face and thought she was suffering from something since she had not risen to her feet.

She handed the note to her and said, "Read this quick and then I want you to go to Hobbs and give him a message that I want him to put on the wire, hurry up read it times a wasting."

Maxine hurriedly scanned over it and with a puzzled look on her face asked. "Where did you get this?"

"There at the wastebasket, Warp wrote it but must have got cold feet and threw it in the wastebasket, now I want you to tell Hobbs that this is my personal message to Warp.

"Warp, come back so we can plan our wedding, I'll have some apple cobbler waiting, now hurry I need you and this whole bloody territory needs you, you belong here, Love, Kate."

"Tell Hobbs to get it on the air as soon as he can, and tell him to ask help from all the territory especially the stations near the Canning Route, if any of their ringers spot Warp tell them to give him my message, now hurry Maxine before he sends out his next post."

Maxine hurried past the livery stable to a rundown white two-story building that had 'Hobbs funeral Home' hand painted in faded blue across the front. Hobbs had been in Wiluna about twenty years and for some unknown reason preferred to be known only by his last name Hobbs. He first set up a black smiths shop in a small shed between the livery stable and the undertakers business but soon became known as a jack of all trades, kind of man. He helped out at the livery stable and at the funeral home and it became natural for the business owners in Wiluna to call on Hobbs if they needed help.

So it came as no surprise when the Funeral Home owner died and after his will was probated Hobbs took his savings and purchased the funeral Home. He had watched the former owner do embalming and after he completed a short mail order course he qualified as an embalmer. He never gave up his blacks smith shop and divided his time between it and the Funeral Home depending on which of the two needed his attention at a given time. Then he added the wire service, which turned out to be a great plus for the territory. He could send and receive messages from the widely scattered towns plus most of the cattle stations including the Twisted Track. Young Lance, like most of the territory's youth got his education over the network because at that time there were no schools available except .the one in Wiluna which was to far away for youngsters on the stations.

She climbed the stairway to the second floor above the mortuary knowing that he would be there preparing his broadcast. The floor had six rooms he used five of them for his living quarters and the other one for his wire equipment. He had no family that anyone knew of, in fact no one knew where he came from which was not uncommon in the territory at that time, parts of Australia was a known haven for people of different backgrounds some of them shady.

He was studying some scribbled notes as Maxine walked in.

"Miz. Wampler at the hotel has a message she wants you to send out Mr. Hobbs, it's important it is."

He squinted at her through horn-rimmed glasses wondering what kind of message the hotel owner wanted to send. "If it be advertisement for th hotel I won't send it." He stated gruffly.

"No Mr. Hobbs it's a message she wants relayed to Warp" she proceeded to quote Kate's message as he scribbled it down. "And she said to tell you to ask all in the territory for help in getting the message to Warp."

He finally got it to his liking and added this. "And tell him Hobbs said he should heed this message and get his arse back to Waluna out o th bloody heat before it cooks what little brain he has left."

Maxine returned to the hotel and fifteen minutes later Hobbs sent the message out which caused much talk and excitement due to the well-known head stockman Warp from the Twisted Track.

"My word," One ringer remarked to his pals at a station north of the Twisted Track, "I reckon old Warp is on th run from that hotel owner in Wiluna, I reckon he ain't ready to marry up, she has a lot of bloody nerve trying to hunt him down."

"I reckon she might be doing him a favor," another remarked, "Hobbs said on th wire he was on th Canning Stock Route headed for Halls Creek, hell he'll die of thirst before he gets half way there."

"I wouldn't bet on that," another chimed in. "Warp is a very uncommon man and seeing that he is being chased by a woman I reckon he might make it."

"I reckon we might see him at th water hole on the Canning Route when we get out that way mustering next week if he makes it that far, th well between it and Wiluna went dry months ago. We can pass him th message but I reckon it's up to him we can't force him to go back"

"I wish a good looking woman like her with a hotel would start chasing me," another remarked, "I reckon she would catch me fer sure."

"From what I know about you chap she wouldn't have to be flash and own a hotel to get your attention cause you have been known to chase anything with a skirt on.'

Meanwhile Hobbs checked in on the wire twice daily without any news about Warp.

Six days later a wounded mother Kangaroo finally made it to the water hole she had been bitten by a dingo while defending her baby Roo and it set up infection. She went five days without water but now she was barely able to drink, after a few swallows she sought out shade from a nearby gum tree and slumped to the ground, the baby Roo popped out of her pouch and looked around warily before going to waters edge to drink. The well had flooded about three acres when it was first drilled and seldom went dry even in the driest seasons. All sorts of animals were around its banks quenching their thirst, while others after drinking their fill lay hidden in the underbrush waiting for prey like the wounded Roo and her baby to show up. Long legged birds were wading the edges looking for fish and frogs while overhead the trees were filled with birds, some were multicolored and seemed to be talking among themselves, while chirp, chirp, chirp, came from another tree as a mother bird stuffed worms down the throats of her young, and yet another flock of songbirds were scattered from tree to tree singing a melody of songs.

A hot arid desert like setting where life could not exist without the well giving up its life saving liquid, a place that refreshed the weary traveler whether human or animal and in some cases literally saved lives, a place where near death is watered and brought back to life much like a steady rain in a dry season saves a farmers corn crop from sheer ruin.

Yet a place of death also as carcasses were everywhere and the stench filled the hot air as vultures picked and pulled the meat leaving a pile of bones.

High in the tallest tree a Red Tailed Hawk set his eyes on the baby Roo as it sat near its sick mother unable to get back in her pouch, she was now on her belly and unable to move and had gave up on trying to keep the flies away from her wound just below her neck. Behind them a hungry Dingo lurked in the brush waiting his chance to take the baby Roo. He could see the mother Roo's life was slowly slipping away so he waited patiently and just as he prepared to lunge from the brush something disturbed a flock of birds overhead causing them to fly away making a lot of noise so he drew back and waited.

From high in the tree the Red Tailed Hawk loosened his grip on the tree limb and aimed straight as a bullet toward the baby Roo. At the same time the Dingo sprang out of the brush and pounced on the Roo picking it up by the back of its neck but before he could get away one of the hawk's sharp talons pierced his skin near his shoulder causing him to yep and drop the baby Roo. The hawk never touched the ground and quickly rose high above tree top level and flew out of sight.

The little Roo lay near its dieing mother with blood trickling from its neck completely confused and scared. The Dingo lunged again sinking his sharp teeth in its neck he stood there violently shaking the little Roo back and forth until life left its body.

The commotion had gotten other animals attention causing them to huddle with their own kind, they watched as the Dingo carried the little Roo away.

A mother kangaroo wounded but successful at protecting her baby from one Dingo only to face another one now lay dead as shadows of the vulture's already circling overhead would soon be picking her bones while out in the underbrush the Dingo bleeding from the hawks talon devours her baby as the cycle goes on around the water hole, life restored and life taken. The bleeding Dingo may suffer the same fate if infection sets up from where the hawk pierced him, but in the meantime he will remain true to his nature and hunt for more prey.

The disturbed birds return and take up their chatter in the same tree, the animal's return to normal, the air is filled with bees, mozzies, hornets, flies, dragonflies, all there in a tiny oasis that offers new life but at the same time is a trap for the weakest.

Three days later a group of cattle numbering about two dozen found their way to the water hole, they had wandered away from the Bonny Blue station just east of the Canning Stock Route owned by a Texan, by the name of Travis Yost. Travis, like Warp and Cal, fought the Germans in world War One. After the war ended he returned to America married the girl of his dreams and continued to work on his fathers ranch until one day one of the cowboys started telling him about Australia.

"It's a land of opportunity, he began, "land is up for grabs, thousands of acres and all you have to do is claim it Travis, just like your grandfather Tate Yost, staked out this land here in Texas."

Travis mentioned it to his wife Valerie, and she being a very optimistic and adventurous person by nature agreed they should consider going there. "We're still young Travis," she bubbled, "If it don't work out we can always come back here."

So one day he told his father. "Pa, I've been thinking about going to Australia for well over a year and can't get it off my mind, so I guess its best I go through with it."

His father not being a man to show emotion dropped his head and pondered before answering.

"Well Trav, a man has to do what he thinks is best in life cause we only have one shot at it, but I thought you understood the ranch is yours after I'm gone. I must tell you I'm disappointed to hear this because I wanted to keep the tradition going and keep this land in our family, but if you've made up your mind I better get in to town and get some things handled at the bank because you'll need money there in Australia, believe me no matter what you've heard nothing comes on a silver platter. I have saved a pretty good chunk in your name and I trust you to spend it wisely."

Undecided Travis and his wife Val, talked it over again and came to the conclusion that they had to give it a try, so now twenty-eight years and three kids later he runs a successful ranch or station in Australia. He named it Bonny Blue in remembrance of the Bonny Blue flag that Texas flew during the civil war, the war that claimed the life of his uncle. His dad's brother who fought on the confederate side.

The Bonny Blue station by horse back lay four hours east of the Canning Stock Route and Bonny Blue property joined the stock route property for several miles running north.

Travis knew Warp well and made it a point to his riders to keep an eye out for him.

One of the fellows rode out to the water hole daily to see if Warp might be there.

Meanwhile back in Wiluna Hobbs kept busy on the wire but wondered if Warp had already died.

Kate was getting to the point where she would go through the day without eating, Maxine and Chung became worried about her. "Warp he no good shun o a bun, crazy lika Chinaman, maka Kate sad."

"I know Chung I know, but he has his good side don't forget that." Maxine replied.

"He good man Maxie, but he stilla crazy lika Chinaman."

Everyone at the Twisted Track stayed in wait for Hobbs daily reports on the wire hoping for some good news about Warp but deep down no one thought it would be forth coming.

"I shoulda clobbered im that day he told me he was leaving," Thomas confided to Lance. "Th bloody Bugger has caused us a lot o pain he has and if he does come back bygol I mean to take im to task."

"Yeah I know pop," Lance answered, "I didn't realize how close I am to Warp until I don't see his face around here anymore, th Twisted Track ain't th same without him and old Rogue I reckon."

He poured the last few drops of water from the container and shared it with Rogue, the horses hadn't had water for more than ten hours and were foaming at the mouth.

"Its crook Rogue, this Canning Route is, like Chung said, th wells are dry, th next one up ahead is dry I reckon, it should come in sight directly. I be a bloody fool Rogue and bygol if we get there and it has water we'll freshen up a bit and head east to th Bonny Blue Station and hang out a few days, even if its dry th Station is four hours from th Canning Route we can make it anyway, old Gunner is losing strength and I might get off and walk meself."

"Trav Yost will befriend us Rogue, good man he is, he has worked hard on his land since coming from America twenty five or thirty years ago, he tried to hire me away from th Twisted Track bout ten years ago, offered me a better salary but like Thomas Kirk said. "You're like a brother to me Warp, I didn't tell him but he be like a brother to me to, and bygol that trumps a higher salary any day."

"Trav will furnish us enough supplies to get us back to Wiluna, yeah you be hearing right Rogue, I av made up me mind to swallow me pride and settle down wit Kate, she's a good woman she is and I love her I reckon"

Rogue looked up and wagged his tail in agreement. Warp smiled and said. "You old bugger you av out done me I thought I'd av to take you on old Gunner, but bygol ye keep plodding along."

The few trees around them were shedding parched leaves that crackled under the horse's hoofs but finally off in the distance he could see a group of trees that were green.

"There she be Rogue, and she has water bygol, see the greenery Rogue? Come on Gunner th waters waiting."

Soon they reached the green tree line about five hundred yards from waters edge, in spite of being on the verge of collapsing from the heat and lack of water the horses knew water was close by and picked up the pace. They traveled another hundred yards and went between two trees that had low hanging branches, about half way through Warp bent low and reached ahead and pushed one of the low hanging limbs aside to get under it without getting scratched up.

Then he saw it, but too late a very large hornets nest. Hundreds of hornets poured out covering man and beast, the packhorse bolted ahead just as Gunner reared wildly throwing Warp from the saddle, the tether rope that kept the packhorse in tow caused Gunner to lose his footing and he came crashing to the ground pinning Warp's legs underneath. Warp's face went ashen with pain and he knew his left leg and hip were shattered. The packhorse was still afoot unable to pull loose from the tether rope he was leaping in the air as far as the rope would allow, a blow from one of his hoofs had caught Rogue on top of his head and he lay bleeding from his mouth. A hunting knife was in Warp's reach in a sheath hung to the saddle, he took it and painfully reached and cut the rope freeing the packhorse. Gunner had made attempts to get up but had given up and lay there twitching and flailing his legs, He had a shattered leg and a gash on the side of his head with the eyeball hanging out from where his head hit one of the tree trunks.

A 303-25 rifle had slid from its scabbard and lay within Warp's reach, he bore the pain in his hip and leg that was now even more excruciating as he twisted his body so he could get a clear shot at Gunner's head, he aimed and pulled the trigger, gunner flailed his legs weakly quivered once and lay still, he turned his upper body the other direction to do the same favor for Rogue, but Rogue now lay still and flies had already covered his wound feeding off his blood. He could feel the tightness in his face and arms and knew they were swelling from the hornet stings. Overhead he noticed buzzards circling just above the treetops and realized it was hopeless, he knew he had gambled on beating the Cannon Stock Route and lost, a game with the highest of risks much like Russian roulette.

Tears came to his eyes and he could feel the remorse building inside pushing aside his fierce pride that had caused heartache to himself and others throughout the most of his life, he prayed earnestly for the first time in his life asking God for forgiveness,

"You av th power oer me soul master, and I know me mother is in your presence and I yearn to be wit her again, and be gentle wit Kate master, I av caused her pain and I pray you will heal her mind and some way let her understand that I was coming back to her, yes Bygol I was."

Then he thought about putting himself out of his misery knowing that he was going to die anyway, he pushed the rifle butt around on the ground and hooked the trigger lever over a jutting finger sized root that was protruding from the base of a tree, he lay flat on the ground and placed the rifle barrel to his neck just below the chin so the trajectory path would lead through and out the top of his head. But just as he started to jerk the rifle enough to trip the trigger everything went dark and he went into a coma.

Flies now covered his face and arms, the first to feed and then the vultures would take over.

The packhorse had trotted off out of range of the hornets and stood snorting and switching his tail trying to get some relief from the hornet stings that covered much of his body, but soon headed toward the water hole again.

The smaller animals shied away as he approached waters edge he waded out in the water causing a large bird to take flight across the water leaving the water rippling in the wake of its wings. He drank his fill and noticing the cool water soothed the hornet stings on his legs he moved into deeper water and stood there for the longest time. Warp's bedroll and the supply gear with what little supplies were left were still strapped to his back.

Across the water hole the group of cattle that now had grown to a dozen more, stood chewing their cuds, a pair of Doves pecked in the sparse grass along waters edge, colorful birds all nestled together were talking to each other, the chirp, chirp, sound that came from a tiny nest meant that a mother was feeding her babies, a peaceful setting as the song birds serenaded from tree to tree, but high in the tallest tree the Red Tail Hawk took it all in, waiting for his chance to swoop down and carry away his daily meal, while back in the brush the dingo lay in wait to claim another baby Roo or any other animal he could handle.

A place of peace and quiet, a place where dehydrated bodies are restored to live on, but also a place of death and dieing.

Off to the east two riders from the Bonny Blue station were headed that way mustering up cattle. As they drew close to the water hole one veered off to the south and the other north so as to circle the water hole and herd any cattle that they happened on around the water hole and meet on the other side.

The ringer that went south of the hole noticed vultures circling and beginning to land in a group of trees just a few hundred yards south, he decided to ride that way and check it out because their boss had told them to keep an eye out for Warp. He and his partner had been discussing it on the way out and both surmised that Warp would be found dead somewhere on the Canning Route.

"I reckon when they find Warp th buzzards will be picking his bones." His partner had said.

The ringer that went north circled his half of the water hole herding up a dozen
cattle on his way, he sat on his horse with an eye on the cattle waiting for his partner. He saw the packhorse now standing at waters edge.

Then he heard, "Yahoo Chap! Come here quick." Looking in that direction he could see the vultures circling and knew it must be something to do with Warp. He clucked to his horse and rode off in that direction.

His partner was already on the ground shooing the flies away, the buzzards had not yet made contact with the bodies but were still circling while others sat in trees at a distance waiting to see if the ringers were going to leave.

"Bloody mess it is," the ringer said as his partner rode up, "It be Warp, he pointed toward the hornet nest hanging low on the tree branch, "I reckon th hornets covered him and th animals, look at th swelling in his face."

They noticed the position of the rifle and one remarked. "He put his hoss Gunner out o his misery and looks like he was about to get some relief fer himself but died before he could trip th trigger. We av to take im wit us," the other one said, "His packhorse is back there at th water I'll go get him."

They tied a rope to Gunner's front legs and with the other end tied to his saddle horn the ringer gently coaxed his mount to back up pulling Gunner off Warp exposing a mangled leg with bone slivers sticking out through his skin, maggots had already covered his leg and the blood on the ground around it.

Being very careful not to disturb the hornets they took two soiled wet blankets from the packhorse, and used one to wrap his body then they draped him across the packhorse and secured him to the horse with rope. As they looked at the scene one remarked, "Poor old Rogue, he was faithful to th end, Warp thought a lot o the old bugger."

Without a word the other one rolled Rogue on the other blanket and wrapped him tight. They hefted him on the packhorse behind Warp and tied him down. "I reckon th buzzards will tend to Gunner," one remarked, "Well lets get a move on Chap, we'll circle th pond again and muster th stock and be off, we should be at th paddock before sunset I reckon."

They herded the small group of cattle along at a fast pace eager to get Warp and his dog to the paddock.

Travis was pleased at how the mustering had gone, the long hard days would soon come to an end and they could get back to the station and rest up a day or two. The head count had exceeded his estimation by a good margin and he felt good about that. As he sat on the fence and watched the ringers herd in a large group that they found further north he noticed their condition wasn't as bad as he expected from the dry hot season. He turned and looked west thinking it was about time the two ringers he sent in that direction to the water hole should be getting back.

'I hope they caught up with Warp out there and bring him in.' He thought, 'if he makes it to that well and goes on he's sure to die because I hear that well is the only wet one on th Route, he'll never get to Halls Creek alive.'

Then in the distance he picked up cattle headed that way as a dust cloud rose around and followed them. Soon they were within clear sight and he could make out the two ringers behind them, then he noticed another horse tethered to one of the ringers horse and noticed the load strapped to it resembled a body, he climbed down from the fence and started walking in their direction hoping that he was wrong about what he was thinking but afraid that he was right.

The oncoming herd was now one hundred yards away and Travis ordered two more ringers to take over and herd them in the paddocks. He walked to meet the other two ringers and now could see that there was a body wrapped in a blanket strapped to the back of the packhorse and he assumed the smaller bundle would be that of old Rogue.

They stopped and dismounted, "Yep, it be Warp and old Rogue," one of them remarked, "Bloody mess it is, he never made it to th water, stirred up a hornets nest about four hundred yards short of th water hole, I reckon it spooked th horses and his horse threw him off, then fell on top o his legs, one leg was all busted up."

"He put his horse out o his misery," the other one remarked, holding up the rifle. " And was about to do th same to himself, but he must have passed out from th heat and thirst and never woke up again, we had to pull th horse off im."

Travis eyes were fixed on the smaller bundle. "Yep that be his old dog Rogue," The other one said, we thought it be right that we bring him along Warp and him were close, not much we could do about his hoss though, th buzzards will take care of im I reckon."

"When do you think it happened?" Travis asked.

"Not long, th flies and maggots covered th wounds but buzzards sat in th trees waiting while others circled overhead."

Travis motioned to the driver of the old US Army surplus Dodge truck that had brought in supplies from the station two days earlier. "Hey Marcus, get ready to go back to th station, load everything up but save room for two dead bodies."

They untied the bundles from the packhorses and cradled them in their arms as they gentley placed them in the truck bed noticing the unmistakable smell of death.

"Bart you take over and I'll trust you to get the herd ready for shipment, I'll be at th station until I get ahold of Thomas Kirk and see how he wants to put Warp away, my guess is he'll want to bury him there on the Twisted Track, Warp and Thomas were like brothers they were, well lets get it rolling

Marcus we have to get these bodies in th freezer room at th station, it has been a godsend it has since I had it built and shelled out for that generator last year, don't have to worry about our food spoiling anymore, but never dreamed of th day that I would be carting dead bodies in there to keep for burial."

They arrived at the station late that night and hurried to get the bodies in the freezer room. Travis got on the wire to Hobbs in Wiluna, "Hobbs, this is Travis Yost at the Bonny Blue Station, with news about Warp, no it ain't good Hobbs, two of my ringers found him just short of th water hole on th Canning Route west of here, I have him and his old dog Rogue in my freezer room waiting to see if Thomas wants to bury them back at the Twisted Track. I could cart them to Wiluna in my old dodge truck but it would take a better part of two days and you know yourself th bodies wouldn't hang together that long in this heat."

"Yeah I know, I'll roust Thomas and see what he wants done about it." Hobbs replied.

"Tell him I can bury them out here in my family plot but I doubt if he will, he and Warp were close and I reckon he'll want to put him on the Twisted Track."

"I'll get moving and let you know what he says." Hobbs answered.

"Tom, this be Hobbs in Wiluna wit news about Warp."

He rubbed his sleepy eyes and replied, "Yeah Hobbs, is it good or bad?" hoping for good news but knew what the answer would be.

"No its not good Tom, they found him on th Canning Route near th water hole west of Travis Yost Bonny Blue station, Trav has him and his old dog Rogue iced down in his freezer room and said to tell you he could bury them on th Bonny Blue if you choose to."

Although he had expected such news and thought he was prepared for it, his body went limp at the thought of Warp dieing and never again to roam the Twisted Track He was overwhelmed with emotion, and for several seconds all was quiet, Hobbs thinking he had lost the connection said. "Tom, Tom, are ye there?"

"Yeah I be here Hobbs, and listen close I want you to get im to Wiluna and embalm and prepare im for burial here on th Twisted Track."

"Well Tom, th Royal Flying Doctor will be calling on a patient north of th Bonny Blue tomorrow so I'll give im th word to drop in at th Bonny Blue and pick up Warp, and what about th dog do you want im to come wit Warp?"

"Yep I do Hobbs, and I want im embalmed and laid in a decent box so I can place im near his master, bygol they was close and belong together."

"Now you do im up right Hobbs and total up th bill and I'll take care o it. I'll drive th old land rover in and after a short going away service there in Wiluna Lance will cart im back here to th Twisted Track in th supply utility and we'll lay im to rest."

Then he set about making arrangements for the funeral service at the Twisted Track. Mum suggested they place his casket on the veranda for at least a period of two hours before burial. "Warp he be well known and had a lot of friends." She said. "That way we can all set around and talk just like old times when Warp was with us, then you can read a verse from Psalms, say a few words from ye memories of Warp and then we can lay im to rest."

"No bygol, I not be up to that and I reckon th duty falls on Layton. He be faithful to Warp as his assistant he be up on Warp's ways as much as me and can quote th bible from lid to lid, and is bout th best wit words I ever run into."

He looked over at Lance who was taking it all in and said. "Lance, you give th word to Layton so he can brush up on th bible a bit, and tell im he can pick out a suit from me closet to wear, we be about th same size."

"And Seth is good wit th saw and hammer, tell im to use th heavy lumber from th supply house and nail together a vault for th casket to rest in, and tell im to fashion another one for old Rogue. And get th ringers busy digging a grave nine to ten feet long there in th corner o th family plot in line wit my my mum and pop. Warp he be a Scotsman he is, and bygol he belongs in that line."

Alice went to her room as soon as she heard about Warp's death and paced back and forth and at intervals lay on the bed weeping. She felt her life as she had lived it had brought nothing but shame to her and a family that she so dearly loved, she knew she would feel better about it if she could gather them up and confess but after weighing the consequences she realized that as being impossible.

Reba found that she held feelings for Warp that she couldn't explain and now that he was gone was sorry that she hadn't tried to get closer to him when he was living.

Tex Jr. showed his grief openly and felt as if a family member was checking out of his life, he wondered if he would ever become a cowboy now that Warp had died. Every day since Warp's leaving he had sat and watched the sunset just as he'd seen Warp do, he discovered how soothing and how natural it seemed for him to do the same things that Warp did, and he wondered if Warp had somehow passed his ways to him.

Then as the sun sank in the west he whispered. "There goes old Sol and like Warp she's gone but tomorrow morning she'll be back to light up the world once again just as Warp and his ways will be a constant companion in my life every day and his memories will have a special place in my heart."

The ringers got busy digging the grave, while Seth measured and sawed the heavy lumber for the vaults Cal came by and offered to help. "I'm pretty good at nailing things together if you need some help." He said.

"Oh my word, then grab a hammer I need yore help." Seth answered.

Alice watched from the veranda and thought how ironic it was that Cal was helping to build a vault for Warp and not knowing of her long ago affair with him that brought Reba into her life. 'Oh my God." She thought. 'I would surely die if he should find out because I love him with all my heart and losing him would be more that I can bear.'

The next day the Royal Flying Doctor picked up the bodies from the Bonny Blue Station and arrived in Wiluna just as Thomas left the Twisted Track, giving Hobbs ample time to embalm and get the bodies ready before he got there.

Hobbs led him to a small room where caskets of different colors and sizes lined three walls with one standing on end with scratches and dents where it had been damaged from shipment, leaving just enough room to display three open caskets in the remainder of the floor space. One of them a tan wood grain design was closed. He lifted the lid and said. "I put im in this one it's metal but th color design looks like wood, if you don't want it I can transfer im to any other one."

Thomas had stepped back when Hobbs raised the lid revealing Warp's face that was swollen and covered with bruised blood marks from the wasp stings. He stood there not wanting to get any closer but finally moved close enough to see that it was Warp, the only natural thing being his mustache and heavy bushy eyebrows.

Hobbs had chosen dark gray trousers with a matching vest instead of a coat, the vest blended in with a sky blue shirt highlighted by a red bowtie.

"No this one is flash, Hobbs, ye made th right choice, th color is fitting for Warp it is, but I don't care to look at his face so you can seal th casket and I'll explain to th folks that his face is all out o shape from th wasp stings."

"Well Thomas, I worked with im and did th best I could."

"I know ye did Hobbs, I know ye did, so don't you fret about it I'll make it right wit th mourners."

Hobbs handed him a brown paper bag that contained his clothing. "Ye can go through th pockets might be something that ye want to keep."

Thomas emptied the bag on the floor and momentarily turned away as the odor reached his nostrils. The pockets of his trousers yielded a few coins, a Barlow pocketknife, plus a well-worn wallet that contained a modest amount of money along with small folded papers that looked to be of no importance but he put them back in the wallet for further inspection later on. One shirt pocket contained a hard case that held his reading glasses, and from the other one he could see the corners of a faded blue silk woman's hankie tied together and perturbing from the pocket. Puzzled he untied it to see what it had hidden inside.

Something fell to the floor and rolled underneath one of the caskets, Hobbs retrieved it and handed it to him. "Well bygol Hobbs, what av we here?" Then he wondered whom the ring belonged to, 'I reckon that American nurse that jilted im back there in th war.' He thought.

He unfolded the papers that now reeked of a combination of foul odors. He moved to a small window that let light in to the small room and began to read, he first intended to read it out loud so Hobbs could hear but changed his mind and read in silence when it started with "Dearest William." When he finished he carefully refolded and placed it back in the hankie, laid the ring along side and retied the corners. He walked over to the casket and stood looking down at Warp finally he turned to Hobbs and said. "Here be his mother's ring and bygol it must be a treasure to im, and th papers are personal and not a comfort to him, but I reckon its best he take em wit im."

He reached and gently lifted Warp's huge hands that were clasped across his chest. He slipped the hankie underneath them and whispered. "Now I can see why ye left th Twisted Track ye be all tore up inside but was willing to give yoreself up for th sake of others, so long old chap, now ye av ye mother's ring and th papers th secret goes wit you, you can count on me bygol, I'll never utter it to a soul."

He turned to Hobbs who was standing out of hearing of his whispered words, and said, "Close th lid and seal it Hobbs, its best his friends not see im this way."

Hobbs closed the lid and sealed it, then opened a door to an adjoining room and Thomas recognized the droning sound of a generator outside behind it and knew that was the freezer room. "He'll stay fresher in here," Hobbs said. "And tomorrow I'll roll im out in th sanctuary." He pointed to a white wooden box and said. "His old dog sleeps here."

He lifted the lid and went on, "av a look Tom, he looks good his long hair covers th wasp stings."

He stood there looking down at old Rogue admiring the way Hobbs placed him in the box. He was on his belly with his nose half buried in his huge two front paws just like sleeping at his masters feet, a scene he had seen many times while sitting talking with Warp in the quarters and the times he and Rogue would come and sit on the veranda at the end of the day. The memories of Warp and Rogue caused him to sniffle but he held back the tears, finally he said. "Bygol ye did im up right ye did Hobbs he be sleeping but this un will be a long nap I reckon."

He turned to go but paused and laid his hand on Warp's casket. "Warp and Rogue will be missed at th Twisted Track Hobbs, Bygol they will, he was close to me, like me own brother, he was set in his ways but bygol," then his voice broke as tears started flowing and he made no attempt to hold them back.

Hobbs put his arm on his shoulder and guided him through the door and closed it behind them. "Best you get to th hotel and get some rest Tom."

"Ye be right Hobbs, me old bones are aching from th jarring I took in th old land rover I ain't th man I once was Hobbs, bygol I ain't and now that Warp and Rogue have turned in for a long sleep I reckon it will drag me down some more."

"One more thing Hobbs, I want you to get on the air and send out to all the territory this message,

"William 'Warp' Broderick" is at th Hobbs Funeral Home in Wiluna and there will be a service in his memory tomorrow morning at 10 A.M. in the sanctuary of the funeral home. After th service he will be on his last journey home to th Twisted Track, and after we say our goodbyes there we will lay im to rest jist as th sun sinks in th west."

"That way Hobbs, th ones that are to far away to get to Wiluna in time will have a head start and can make it to th Twisted Track by sundown."

Maxine checked him in at the hotel, he asked about Kate and was told she was in her room grieving over Warp. "She was fond of him Mr. Kirk, its crook that they never had a chance to get married and live out their lives together."

Chung passed by and said. "Miste Kick, Chung feela bad about Warp, he crazy lika Chinaman, but he good man." He hurried on down the hallway before Thomas could answer, muttering something about how the work was piling up on him. Just before he turned the corner he turned and called back. "Mr. Kick I no hava time but if you wanna ham an cabbage I maka fresh today, I no hava time but if you come to dining room I hava ham an cabbage."

He went to the empty dining room and sat down knowing that the hotel guests had already eaten and he was lucky that Chung had offered to feed him. Soon Chung bounced in with coffee pot in hand, "You wanna coffee Mr. Kick? Chung maka fresh."

"Yes Chung and give me a heaping plate o th ham and cabbage wit extra slab o ham."

"Chung hava cabbage, no hava ham, hava cabbage, ham all gone, you wanna cabbage, I no hava time, but Chung hava cabbage."

"Yeah Chung, ye old bugger bring me cabbage."

He ran toward the kitchen mumbling, "Chung no hava time, Chung hava to mucha work." Soon he reappeared with a heaping plate of hot steaming cabbage. 'Chung bringa cabbage, ham all gone, Chung hava ham tomorrow."

As he rushed away still mumbling Thomas smiled and realized he hadn't smiled since Warp left the Twisted Track.

Later that night Lance and Layton Bailey arrived and checked in the rooms that Thomas had reserved for them earlier.

Thomas awoke early the next morning and went to the dining room for breakfast, there he found Kate seated at a small table bent over a cup of coffee looking haggard and very unhappy. He walked over and she motioned for him to sit down. She had known he and his wife Amanda on a first name basis for many years.

"Well Tom, as you know it's never been a big secret about me and Warp and if it had been left up to me we would have been married, but you knew Warp better than I ever did and know that everything had to be done by his terms. I should have set my foot down and demanded he come to terms with me but I didn't and now I rue the day I met him.

Then he wrote that note but changed his mind and threw it in the wastebasket, I tried to get word to him to come back and we would start a life together but it never reached him." She pushed the coffee cup aside and buried her face in her arms on the table. "It's not right that it should end this way," she sobbed.

Thomas laid his hand on her shoulder and said. "I know Kate, he was a stubborn old bugger he was, and th way he went out o our lives is crook but life is that way, not always on th straight and narrow but going off in several directions, sumpin like th stock that wander off from th herd and have to be mustered in by th drovers. Warp's mind was laden wit bad memories that he could have managed wit help from th likes o you but he chose to keep em to he self."

"No blame can be placed on you Kate, you did all you could to bring em back from th Canning Route, and bygol, he would have if yore message had reached em, th note he left behind proves that, so get a hold on ye self Kate, and tomorrow we'll give em a proper send off, he deserves that he does, and I know Layton will do em proud he will."

More people arrived and checked in the hotel throughout the night and by eight the next morning the small sanctuary was already half full, some had traveled long distances just to pay last respects to a man they had long respected although some had never met him but felt they did from all the things they had heard about him the good and the bad, the good far outweighing the bad. As they chatted with the locals Hobbs rolled the casket out and noted the quiet that came over them as they stared at the long wood grain colored casket.

By nine A.M. all seats were taken except for two pews that were reserved for family or close friends. Hobbs removed a dusty cover from an age-old organ and an aging lady sat down and began to play. As she played softly deftly switching from one religious song to another they kept filing in filling all the seats, then Hobbs directed them to standing room along both walls and in back until the little place was filled.

Just before ten Kate came through the door, following behind her was Maxine, Thomas, Lance, Layton, Chung, Herbert the banker, Burgin the livery stable owner, and two other hotel workers.

Kate wore a long black dress with white lace around the collar and a black wide brimmed hat with gold colored threading design around the band. No one had ever seen her dressed like that, not even the locals and you could tell by the looks on their faces how much they admired her beauty and elegance. As the music drifted softly but sadly over the room they took their seats filling one of the reserved pews, Hobbs quietly directed some of the older standing mourners to the other reserved pew.

Layton sat down in a worn leather chair on the small platform and as the organ music continued he opened his bible and pretended to study the scripture he intended to use.

Thomas smiled as he watched him knowing he already knew the verses he intended to use without even opening the bible. He remembered all the times he had tried to stump him by quoting a verse from the bible, but Layton not only would have the right answer from where it came from in the bible, but would quote the verses preceding and following it.

'A genus he is when it comes to th bible,' he thought. ' He never went away to some fancy school he was born wit th knowledge. 'A natural he is bygol, he is that.'

On cue from Layton the organ player stopped playing. He rose and stood facing the mourners looking from one to the other individually as if searching out their thoughts.

Thomas noted how well he looked in his suit, 'th bugger wears it better than me,' he thought, 'I reckon I might make him a gift of it.' Then he wondered about his background because he had told Layton just as he had told all his hired hands that if they wanted to tell him anything about their life in the past they could, "But bygol I will never ask, because I av things in me past and its best they stay there, we all need each other here in this harsh land so its best we don't look back to old failures."

Layton had never revealed anything about his past, just went about doing everything that Warp ask him to do and done it well. Warp having a keen instinct for goodness and loyalty in men, and in spite of Layton bugging him with scripture, decided to ask him to be his assistant. Layton gladly accepted and as time went by Warp could always count on him. But verses from the bible never let up especially when he would get upset with the way things were going and do or say something to one of the ringers, then at the end of the day Layton would remind him of it and would always have a verse from the bible that fit the wrong that he had committed. It got to the point where Warp would ponder them and ask Layton to explain them in more detail and as time went on he actually looked forward to them and started reading the scriptures himself.

Finally Layton held the bible over his head and said. "In this great book of knowledge and truth there are many stories, parables, and verses that will guide us through our short stay here on earth if we will only seek them out."

"Words and deeds from Jesus are recorded here along with his disciples who helped him spread the word and record this great book. In it we can find scriptures and verses that will help us through our daily lives if we will only heed them. Verses for the sick, words for the down trodden, warnings to the wicked among us, and scriptures to lead us out of sin and into the forgiving hands of God."

"Scriptures and verses that will brighten the dark days of our stay here and lead us in the right direction, verses for all occasions, verses for each individual, and I cannot think of one more fitting to Warp than the one from Psalms 86 verse 3. "Be merciful unto me, O Lord for I cry unto thee daily."

"I reckon I was about as close to Warp as anyone out there in our daily lives on th Twisted Track, I made it a habit to quote scripture to him daily, he didn't like it at first but as time went on he took an interest and started reading scripture and quoting it to me. And this verse became his favorite, then one day he said."

"Layton this be my favorite verse and I ask it of me master every night jist before I close me eyes. Be merciful unto me, O Lord for I cry unto thee daily. Old Rogue hears it but I reckon th old bugger don't understand but th master does cause bygol, I can feel his presence."

"Warp just like me had to live with a past that held unpleasant memories and just like me when he finally gave up trying to solve them on his own and turned to our masters book of redemption he became a changed man, I reckon not that you could see or hear it from him because he still resembled the same old Warp, gruff and set in his ways, Warp's ways, that we all became familiar with. The last two months at th Twisted Track have been puzzling to all of us, he lost all interest in th station and everything around him and one morning rode away with little or no explanation except that he was going to Halls Creek over The Canning Stock Route."

"Now I believe he's in th presence of our Lord sitting along side th mother that he loved so dearly, and yes you might question that and rightly so because he never was a church goer and had his faults as all human beings do, but in spite of his checkered past, and just recently he had a bout with th yellowtail wine but he beat it. I reckon a mans past and lack of church going don't mean a lot to our master after we come to him and receive him in our hearts, Warp did that and out there on th Twisted Track rode close to God and talked with him daily. I reckon that's about all I have to say today but will pick up on it again tomorrow when we lay him to rest on th Twisted Track."

"Now the organist will play "Amazing Grace How Sweet Thou Name," and then Maxine and two of her friends from the hotel will sing one of Warp's favorite songs "The Dying Stockman. Then I'll close with a prayer and we'll cart him back to the Twisted Track and lay him to rest about sundown tomorrow' if any of you would like to attend Thomas has informed me he will put you up and feed you at the station, I'm sure Warp would be proud. One more thing I didn't mention his old dog Rogue there in the white box, a dog will never forsake his master so I reckon he's laying at Warp's feet in heaven."

Just before noon the caravan watched by a small crowd faded in the distance toward the Twisted Track with Warp in the lead, which seemed appropriate, immediately behind the utility bearing his body, the old Land rover driven by Thomas with passengers Kate, Maxine, Chung, and two other hotel workers chugged along as Kate's eyes were glued to the casket in back of the utility, they rode in silence except for Chung who kept muttering about all the work that he would find waiting for him at the hotel.

'Hotel no good wi outta Chung, Chung hard worker, maka hotel good for Kate, Kate good and pretty woman, but not happy, Warp maka Kate happy, now maka Kate sad, he good man but go horsey riding and no hava water, he crazy lika Chinaman.'

Mum had the ringers move a heavy strong table to the veranda, which she covered with her prettiest bedspread. One that she had spent many hours crocheting an Australian sunset in the center and long horned cattle around the sides that now hung touching the floor.

Long ago she remembered when she washed it and hung it out to dry Warp had came by and stood admiring it. "Good work you do wit th needle missus, like me mother used to do, bygol it is."

'I reckon this will be fitting to Warp. " She remarked to Alice and Reba, "It will look like the cattle are circling his casket."

Alice and Reba were busy working on several flower arrangements, Alice was still in her withdrawn mood, Mum and Reba both had tried to bring her out of it but had finally gave up.

"I reckon she might pull out of it herself," Mum whispered, "Sometimes its best to leave a woman and her troubles to herself." Reba smiled and agreed.

Hours later the caravan came in view and they watched as it slowly turned off the track and rolled to a stop at the veranda steps. Somber ringers stood watching with hats in hand and at a command from Thomas, they carefully removed the casket from the truck bed carried it up the steps and placed it on the covered table. The casket hid the center of the setting sun but the deep red from its glow that Mum had so painstakingly sewed in spread out from the casket to the edges of the table, and with the cattle below it was like Mum said. 'I reckon this will be fitting to Warp."

They placed the white box, containing Rogue on the floor at the foot of the casket.

Mum directed the flower arrangement as the men stood and watched, that done she put her arms around Alice and Reba, and they backed away from the casket. For several seconds not a sound could be heard until finally Alice turned her face to Mum's shoulder and began to sob and soon all three were crying as they consoled each other. Kate, Maxine, and the hotel group were now embraced shaking with grief as Chung stood to one side looking very uncomfortable. Some of the men stood rigid looking at the scene trying not to break but soon tears were visible on their faces as others turned away to hide them.

The overnight trek by the caravan had taken its toll on its travelers, Thomas, Lance, and Layton, broke away to nap and freshen up a bit, while Mum guided Kate and the hotel group to bedrooms. "I reckon you need a nap and after that you can freshen up and have a bite of tucker before we start the service." She said.

Chung refused any offers of a bed, instead he slumped down in one of the rockers near the casket and finally after much grumbling in his own language he dropped off to sleep.

In the meantime Travis Yost, and his wife Val, awoke from a nap at the hotel in Wiluna, bathed and went to the dining room to eat, but found the menu lacking due to Kate and the employees she took with her to the Twisted Track for Warp's funeral, leaving behind two cleaning girls and an aging lady that agreed to come in and do the cooking while they were gone.

"Not much to choose from." She said, "I reckon Chung is a master cook compared to what I can set before you, so please forgive me as you can see I be no master chef but its best you eat yore fill anyway to hold you until you get to th Twisted Track where Mum is sure to have tables laden with delicious tucker."

The long trip in the old dodge truck from the Bonny Blue station eating spam along the way had made any other kind of food look good to them, so they ate their fill and seemed to enjoy it, to the delight of the fill in cook. They arose and went out on the veranda to while away the time while waiting for Shane Daugherty, and his wife Isabel, to fly in from Queensland.

Travis met Shane at one of the annul races held in Wiluna many years ago and they had became fast friends keeping in touch over the wire. While on the wire talking about Warp right after the news went out about his death Shane told him he and his wife Isabel would fly in to Wiluna from Queensland for Warp's funeral. "I reckon we'll hitch a ride from there to th Twisted Track" He said.

"Tell you what Shane, Val and I will be leaving as soon as we get things in the truck, we had planned on going straight to th Twisted Track but instead I'll drive by Wiluna and wait for you there at the hotel."

"Well now Trav, that be fine by me but its crook for you to bypass th Twisted Track and go on to Wiluna."

"No trouble at all Shane just doing what's expected among friends."

"Well I reckon you can look for me and Isabel to drop out o th skies there in Wiluna tomorrow, I reckon its best I hang up and get out and get th plane gassed up and ready for th lift off about midmorning tomorrow, so long chap until tomorrow."

Shane was one of the so-called wild-bunch that came to Australia aboard the freighter with Warp. He and Warp had hung together and hired on to the same stations in their search for a better life. But whiskey, women, and song, marred their search as they roamed from station to station.

Once they went to the head stockman requesting time off to visit a town noted for its wild ways, a two days ride off to the east. When he refused they drew their pay and rode away never looking back, a habit that plagued them, always looking for greener pastures but never staying long enough to enjoy the surroundings.

They arrived in town and fell in to the regular routine, wine women and song whetted their appetite for adventure Shane became deeply involved in a poker game with three shady looking characters, Warp took a seat off to the side where he could observe the game sensing that trouble was sure to rear its ugly head.

Shane lost steadily and finally put the remainder of his pay in the pot. He held three kings but one of the players displayed three aces to win the pot. He challenged claiming that he had seen a card pass from one of the other players to the winner, Warp seen the same thing. Words were exchanged and a fight broke out, Shane knocked the winner to the floor and went to take the money, then the other two became involved, one pinned his arms behind his back as the other one came from the front brandishing a knife with six inch blade just as he lunged with the blade pointed toward Shane's heart Warp swung the chair he had been sitting on with all his might and caught the knife wielder square in the side of his head sending him to the floor where he lay groaning from pain. Shane and the other one wrestled and fought breaking the table to pieces, finally Shane pinned him to the floor and choked him until he begged for mercy. All the while Warp had watched and made sure the other one on the floor stayed there, now he walked over and pulled him to his feet expecting him to continue the fight but he slumped toward the door with the other two in tow, obliviously there was no fight left in them. Then he and

Shane picked up the money from the pot, which was scattered over the floor, paid the owner for the damage to the table and went on with their merry making.

But in more sobering times after the incident Shane began to realize he owed his life to Warp and they became closer to each other than ever before.

They rode out of town as usual broke and with a hangover, they worked at different stations on their way to Queensland a part of Australia they had heard was the place to be, still chasing dreams.

But one day Warp decided to give up on Queensland, "Shane I think it best I leave this vast land, I reckon I might work my way back to th coast and take a freighter to some other place."

"Where th hell you going Warp? Ye know yore self you won't feel at home around th hordes, this land is for th likes o you and me Warp, a land where we have never made any good memories to interfere wit our lives, but it holds promises for good uns that we can enjoy in our old age."

Warp hooked a finger in one end of his moustache and twirled it while pondering an answer.

"Well bygol Shane you might be right I reckon but I be hankering for a change of scenery." He reached out his hand and said. "Its best I say me goodbyes and move on afore you talk me out O it." They squeezed hands while looking in to each other's eyes, each knowing that what they were seeing was true friendship forged over years of trust and respect, but now might be coming to an end, they both felt like crying but before that could happen Warp turned his horse and rode south stopping just as he topped a knoll he turned lifted his hat and waved.

Shane waved back, then dried his eyes on his shirt sleeve sniffed a couple times, reined his horse around and rode on toward Queensland. He reached Queensland and found a job on a huge station three times the size in acerage of any station he had ever worked on in western Australia.

The land was a mixture of tableland greenery, some arid desert, then some rocky, mountainous, and dangerous, and unforgiving much like western Australia. Due to the owners pretty, innocent, and vibrant daughter he found his yearnings for greener pastures slowly fading from his thoughts.

After a short time of flirting and an even shorter time of courtship he asked her father Radford Easy, who went by the nickname "Big Easy" because of his huge muscled body for her hand in marriage.

Her father being a practical man wasted no time with speculation. "My word chap I reckon you must be smitten and it's alright by me but I must pass it on to her mother she be more a judge o men than me." He smiled and winked as he walked away.

The next day he approached Shane with a solemn look on his face, Shane's heart sank he just knew her mother had rejected him.

"Well chap, Myrtle wishes answers to three questions, and they are, number one, do you truly love Isabel? Number two, Will you stay on here wit us or close by here at the homestead? She's all we got and we would like to have her near us. Number three, this un is simple and is used in th ceremony but she would like to hear it coming from you personally, It's worded something like this, do you promise to stick wit her through thick and thin no matter what throughout all th days o yore lives? Now Myrtle said to tell you she wouldn't stand in th way if your answer is no to the number two question but I reckon the other two are very important to her and me also."

With a clear voice Shane answered, "Yes I love her with all my heart, and yes I promise to stay near and honor her the remaining days of my life. As for the second question, I reckon I want to stay here and help you wit th station it's th only place that feels like home since I left my home there in Dorchester England to fight th Germans in World War One."

Two weeks later he and Isabel were man and wife, living space was made for them from the sprawling homestead. He took on more responsibility and soon became a driving force to increase earnings by interbreeding cattle and increasing the work force.

One year later a son was born and they named him Caleb, at the age of eighteen Caleb went off to Melbourne for further education and while there met a girl from England who attended the same university. They fell in love and he brought her back home with him. Shane and Isabel approved of her but urged them to think it over before considering marriage.

"Marriage is not a game that you can get in and out of any time you feel like it." His grandmother Myrtle, had said, "It's a life time game that has to be played strictly by the rules."

They talked it over again and decided they would go ahead with their plans and get married.

Then later Caleb answered the call to duty in World War Two and was killed by a Japanese sniper leaving behind a grieving mother, father, his grandparents, a loving wife, and a baby girl that he never got to see.

Shane and Isabel lost all interest in the station for a time and Greta, Caleb's widow literally went to pieces then one day the silence of the homestead was shattered by a gunshot coming from her bedroom. Myrtle raced to the room and found her lying on the bed with blood trickling from her head and nose, a pistol lay near her head still smoking, the baby Brenda, lay in her crib crying.

The note read, "Please forgive me, I couldn't bear it anymore, I leave you Brenda, please take care of her. Love Greta."

The following months were torture and if not for the baby Brenda to occupy much of Isabel's time she would have had a nervous breakdown. Shane stayed busy with the work on the station and with time the baby became the apple of their eye.

Cattle and sheep production grew at a fast pace bringing great wealth to Isabel's parents.

When Brenda reached the age of eight Isabel's father called she and Shane to his office. He embraced them and asked them to sit down he looked at Isabel and said. "What I want to talk to you about is how hard it's been on me and your mother since Caleb left us and on top of that the way Greta took her leave, bless her soul, but thank God she left Brenda and she has become the light of our lives I reckon just when we thought darkness would never end. I have some plans here," he went on as he shuffled some papers on his desk, "These papers here gives you rightful ownership to the station and all its assets except for that spot of ground over by that stand of gum trees," he pointed toward a knoll through the office window. "The top o th knoll has about two acres of level land that we want to put a house on, and down at the bottom of the knoll will be a fence circling th knoll and consist of about ten total acres, just enough to putter around in. We want to live out the rest o our lives there if it be alright wit you, after you sign these papers agreeing to all this we never want a hand in running th station again, Shane is up to that, after all this station has increased two fold since he has been in charge. Any questions, or objections?" He asked.

Shane and Isabel stared at each other in astonishment, Isabel always knew that her parents plans were to leave the Station to her but she never dreamed it would be this soon, after all her parents were still robust and healthy, 'but I reckon they have decided they will be happy in a little house on the knoll.' She thought.

Her father waited for them to say something and when they didn't he said. "Well I reckon you will accept th station but maybe you don't want us living so close to you?"

That brought them to their feet and as they embraced him, Isabel said,

"Yes pa, we want you and mom close by for the rest of our lives, I'm embarrassed that you would even think such thoughts."

"Well then lets get these bloody papers signed and in order and that will get th Big Easy station out o my hair," he said. "And here I have plans for th house on th knoll, your mother wants you to look it over and see if there's anything you might add, she said you are good at th way a house should be laid out."

Over the years the station prospered even more under Shane's leadership, he had the wire service upgraded and is now in touch with all of Queensland and Western Australia. He took flying lessons and purchased a four-passenger airplane, which is an asset for any station in case of emergency.

Quite an accomplishment for a chap that worked his way to Australia aboard a freighter and wasted many years roaming the land before finally meeting Isabel, she was his salvation.

And about the same time Shane met Isabel, Warp hired on with Thomas Kirk at the Twisted Track, in comparison to Shane's success who married and had a happy family life there was no comparison, but he did settle down and in spite of his troubled mind worked hard and gained respect from the whole territory. In that respect I reckon the Twisted Track rescued his troubled mind from certain oblivion.

Shane looked down on the tiny runway at the Wiluna airport, and as he circled to line up for a landing his thoughts were about Warp.

Two years after he hired on at the station in Queensland a drifting rover came along looking for a job and he took him on. He told him he once worked at the Twisted Track station in Western Australia, "It was a well run station it was, and I worked under a good head stockman by th name o Warp, funny name I reckon and he had some strange ways but all in all he was a good man."

Shane couldn't believe what he was hearing. "Tell me," he said. "What did this chap Warp look like?" The rover grinned and said. "A long tall drink o water wit handlebar mustache and his long legs was bowed wide enough to chase a bull through."

Shane was elated to hear the news, because he never thought he would ever see or hear from him again. He quickly got in touch and they had met at the Wiluna races each year since then to hash over old times together.

From the hotel veranda Travis spotted the small plane and recognized it.

"That's Shane and Isabel, lets get moving Val we'll pick them up at the airport."

At the airport they noticed a third person with Shane and Isabel, it turned out to be their twelve-year old granddaughter Brenda.

"She wanted to come." Isabel remarked. "She remembers Warp from our yearly visits to the races in Wiluna."

After a minute of chatter Travis asked if they wanted to go to the hotel and freshen up a bit before the start on the long journey to the Twisted Track.

"No Trav, I reckon we don't have a lot of time I reckon it's best we get going we'll freshen up after we get there."

They piled in the old Dodge, Travis, Val, and Isabel, in the cab, Shane and Brenda rode in back, Travis had taken a seat from another old worn out rusting vehicle and bolted it to the truck bed.

"Not much flash to this transportation," He laughed, "But if we hang on I reckon it will get us there."

"I reckon it will Trav, so lets get her rolling." Shane answered as he boosted Brenda to the truck bed.

Back at the Twisted Track everyone sat on the veranda dressed in their Sunday best awaiting the funeral proceedings to begin. A short nap and Mum's table laden with good food had worked wonders with the weary tired bunch that arrived a short time before.

But one person was missing she went to her room and stayed there refusing to come and join the meal with the excuse she didn't feel well causing more worry to hover over her daughter Reba, who now realized that something was bothering her mother that needed correcting, she wanted to help but didn't know the problem and neither did anyone else except for Thomas, and he intended to hold fast to his pledge to Warp that he would never tell.

Reba went to her room again and asked if she could come in, " I need to talk to you momma."

"Yes come on in," she answered weakly, "I was just getting ready to dress and join you."

Reba noticed she had laid out her prettiest dress to wear and said. "Oh momma, I haven't seen you in that dress for a long time, I never could understand why you never wore it more, it always seemed it had to be a special occasion before you would wear it, you are so beautiful in that dress."

"Yes honey," she answered, "I have always held it back for special occasions and I consider Warp's funeral a very special occasion."

Puzzled by that answer Reba thought about asking her to explain it but changed her mind and rejoined the crowd on the veranda.

Thomas kept his eyes on the track leading to Wiluna and once remarked, "I reckon Trav and Val will be emerging shortly wit Shane and Isabel in tow, th news on th wire said Shane would set down at th Wiluna airport and Trav would cart them out here in his old dodge surplas truck. They be good friends wit Warp and I respect em coming to honor his going away."

One of the ringers grinned remembering all the tales Warp loved to tell about him and Shane roaming over Australia staying in one place just long enough to earn money to move on, and could hear his Scottish drawl "I reckon we wuz chasing dreams, and bygol he hit it big there in Queensland, and I reckon th one I caught when I settled here on th Twisted Track ain't as flash but it will stand above anything that's happened in me past life."

Tex jr. spoke up pointing toward Wiluna, "A patch of dust on th track, that must be them."

"Yep that's em chap," Thomas answered, "and jist in time for th beginning, Layton are ye ready?"

Layton looked surprised at the question.

"What I mean Layton are ye up on yore bible reading?" He grinned, "I would hate to see you forget th text and get things all twisted out o shape."

Layton grinned and replied, "Best you get that out o yore mind afore I quote some scripture describing yore sinful ways."

Everyone smiled knowing that the banter between the two had been an ongoing thing in the past and didn't expect it to stop anywhere in the near future.

Thomas was bent on enjoying the last jab so he said, "I count on ye to deliver a proper sermon, I do, and if ye fail I be wanting me suit back."

They watched as the old dodge approached and came to a halt near the steps, Mum and Thomas introduced them to Reba, Cal, and Tex, then Alice stepped out on the veranda looking beautiful in her dress, a true beauty everyone thought, as she was introduced to them, each noticed the sadness in her face and wondered why, Thomas noticed it too, the only difference is he knew the torture that troubled her mind.

When introduced to Tex Jr. Brenda smiled broadly and offered her hand, he hesitated momentarily but reached for her hand and as he felt the warmth of it and stared into her dark brown eyes he knew he was about to enter a world which up to this time had never entered his mind due to his whole body and soul being committed to becoming a cowboy. As he held her hand she returned the gaze and he knew as time went on he was bound to make room for her in his heart.

Both twelve years old nearing thirteen, neither ever having any serious thoughts about the opposite sex until this day, but now knew this was the beginning of something. They held the pose until they realized everyone was watching then stepped back in embarrassment.

As prearranged the guitar players joined by the accordion player and surrounded by the ringers played and sang two religious songs leading up to Layton's sermon. Layton eloquently expanded on the text that he used back in Wiluna the day before, and even added a self thought out parable to Warp's life, a half hour sermon that held the attention of all present, Thomas sat there thinking, 'I reckon Layton knows th bible and is th best when it comes to using words in a way that stirs yore soul but th old bugger went over th top today and bygol I reckon he can keep th suit.'

At the end of the sermon Layton asked if anyone had something they wanted to say.

"Mum suggested we honor him by just sitting around his casket and reminiscing about his life." He said, "So if you have something to say even it be funny just speak up from where you sit, Warp would want it that way."

Thomas hadn't intended to get involved afraid that his deep voice would break but now decided to say a few things. He told of the day he hired Warp and all the years he remained a faithful head stockman on the Twisted Track. "He not only be th best I ever see wit th stock, but he pointed me boy Lance in th right direction, and had a good start wit th chap Tex," he looked at Tex Jr. and said, "I reckon you be on th right track I begin to notice you av some o Warp's ways."

He noticed tears welling in the eyes of Lance and Tex Jr. and could feel the emotion in him self about to overflow so he ended by saying, "Warp will be missed here on th Twisted Track and throughout th whole territory, bygol he will, but I reckon he be riding herd for our master now." He started to say something else but knew is voice was trailing off to a whisper and tears were about to come, so he simply said, "Goodbye Warp we miss ye."

Then Shane added some amusing stories about the times he and Warp roamed over Australia without any sense of direction, which brought laughter to replace some of the sadness.

Mum followed with her remembrances of Old Rogue and his never dying faithfulness to Warp. She ended by saying, "They be jewels here in our lives, th both of them and I reckon th Twisted Track will never be th same again without them."

Seth told of the times he had witnessed Warp trying to save sick and wounded animals by sitting at their side all through the night doing what ever he could to ease their pain.

Then two other ringers voiced their thoughts of Warp.

Lance intended to say something but changed his mind because of the emotion that was building up inside listening to the others.

Layton asked if anyone else would like to say something and when no one responded he closed with a short prayer asking God to welcome Warp home, "and master set em free in a vast land like he grew accustomed to here in Australia, cause he likes to roam, he does."

Then the ringers placed the casket and the white box in the utility and they proceeded on to the little family plot, the mourners followed on foot.

Layton opened with another prayer then announced that the ringers would play and sing one of Warp's favorite songs.

"It's an old Scottish song that he would request the ringers to play and sing often, and he hummed it daily as he went about his work, I talked it over wit th ringers and we agreed it would be a fitting song to his memory, th title is, "Barbara Allen" and we would like all of you to join in especially th women."

The guitar players and the accordion player were now, joined by Seth who after many years practice had mastered the French harp. They began to play and sing and by the second verse most of the mourners joined in.

In scarlet town where I was born there was a fair maid dwellin'
Made every youth cry a well a day her name was Barbara Allen

Twas in the merry month of May when green buds they were swellin'
young Denny Grove on his death bed lay for want of Barbara Allen

He sent his man down to the town to the place where she was dwellin'
He said me master's sick he bids me call for you if you be Barbara Allen

So slowly, slowly she got up and slowly she went nigh him
And all she said when there she got was I think you're dyin'

Do you remember the other night you're at the public house drinkin'
you toasted health to all the girls except for Barbara Allen

Every one but Thomas had lent their voices and as he listened they were
in perfect harmony, and the musical instruments were in perfect unison, one
voice stood out from all the rest, that of Alice, she had turned toward the
setting sun and sang in a beautiful alto voice, that and the humming of the two
black ringers and Chung gave the rendition a haunting sound, even the horses
milling about the stockmen's quarters in the distance had all turned and stood
transfixed looking that way.
Thomas decided to lend his deep bass voice and found it blended in well
so he finished out the song.

He turned his head then toward the wall and death was near him drawin'
Adieu' my friends for I must die for slighting Barbara Allen

Then later as she walked o'er the moors she saw his corpse train comin'
Lay down lay down his corpse she said that I might gaze upon him

And the more she looked the more she wept until she burst out laughin'
And all his friends who were by her said hard hearted Barbara Allen

Oh mother go make my bed and make it long and make it narrow
For my true love has for me died today and I must die tomorrow

They buried Barbara in the old church yard and they buried Denny beside
her
And from his grave grew a red red rose and out of hers a briar

And they grew and grew at the old church yard till they could grow on no
higher
And at the top they ties a true lovers knot the red rose and the briar

A hush came over the little knoll when the song ended the women were
dabbing at their eyes with hankies as the men either looked away to hide the
tears or wiped them away on their shirtsleeves, but Alice was shaking with
grief as she faced the sunset, and everyone wondered why except for Thomas
and he wasn't about to reveal her secret. They lowered the casket down and

fitted it in the wooden vault, the white box was placed at the foot of the casket then heavy two-inch thick boards were placed across the vault to cover the casket.

Thomas and Mum stepped forward picked up a handful of dirt from the pile along side the grave and dropped it on the boards then two ringers started shoveling dirt into the grave.

The mourners drifted away and huddled watching the sunset, behind them sounds of the dirt thumping as each shovel full landed on the vault boards became muffled as the grave filled above ground level, the ringers smoothed it out forming a neat mound. The women placed the flowers on and around the mound. Up until this time Kate had been able to control her emotions but as she placed a wreath at the head of the grave she broke down and sobbed uncontrollably.

Reba and Cal were busy trying to console Alice while Mum and Maxine hugged and whispered to Kate.

Thomas said so everyone could hear, "Look at th sunset, shes gone, th timing is jist right.

They all turned and looked west to a glorious red sky. "Yep she's gone but she left th beauty behind, jist like Warp he be gone but bygol he leave a lot behind."

They slowly made their way back to the homestead.

Travis took a large canvas wrapped bundle from the old truck bed. He untied it to reveal Warp's saddle, rifle, and knife

"Here you are Tom and I'll get yore packhorse back to you, I'll load him up in th old truck and bring him back when we come to th races this fall, thought that would be better than bringing him in this hot weather."

"No, you keep em Trav, th Twisted Track has more horses than we need anyway, and I reckon you can find some use for em."

Thomas handed the rifle to Shane and said, "Here ye are chap I know ye be familiar wit this rifle since you gave it to Warp many years ago, he treasured th rifle simply because you made him a gift o it and he would be proud to know that you have it back."

Then he reached the knife to Lance and said, "You remember when you was a tot you would beg em fer this knife and he would tell you, "yeah chap th knife is yours but I'll hang on to it till you grow up enough to tote it around."

Lance took it from the scabbard and examined it thinking, 'I was hoping he'd offer me the knife, now I have something to remind me of Warp and th influence he had on my life.'

435

Thomas motioned for Tex Jr., "come here chap this saddle belongs to you, I know Warp would want you to av it."

Tex dropped to his knees and ran his hands over the well worn leather and was pleased beyond words but finally uttered, "Thank you, and I promise I'll take care of it," then using a phrase that he had heard Warp use many times, he added, "Yep bygol I will."

That brought grins to the ringer's faces, and one whispered to another, "That chap reminds me o Warp in more ways than one, I reckon he ain't from Warp's line but he be like him."

Mum ushered them to the table that was still laden with leftovers, they ate then went to the veranda where they talked late into the night before finally retiring for a nights sleep. At midmorning the next day they gathered outside to say goodbye to the Shane Daugherty, and Travis Yost families, and watched as the old truck bounced out of sight toward Wiluna.

Tex Jr. felt bad about not talking to Brenda more, he wanted to but for some reason could never muster up enough courage to start a conversation, but he took comfort in her last words just before Travis cranked up the old dodge, "I am so glad that I came and had the privilege of meeting you, maybe we can keep in contact over the wire."

Uncomfortable by the reaction from the others, their smiles and knowing looks between them was embarrassing to him but he managed to answer, "yes it's been a pleasure to me to and I look forward to your messages over the line."

Mum had talked Kate into Staying on another night. "You need to rest up some more." She said. "I reckon th hotel can do without you for one more day."

Maxine and the two other girls were delighted to spend another night but Chung protested, "Chung needa get back to hotel, hotel hava lotta work needa be done, Chung no hava time, Chung keepa hotel going, Chung nota happy away from hotel."

They all laughed, causing him to go into a rant, in his own language.

Thomas asked Mum if she would like to go with them and spend a couple days at the hotel. "You be deserving to get away for a few days," he insisted.

She readily agreed. "Well I reckon I'll go I can get some things I be needing while there."

Hearing this Chung said. "Hotel no hava good food whilea Chung gone and Chung no hava time to cook for you, to mucha work, no hava time to cook."

They piled in the old land rover early the next morning and headed toward Wiluna, and were surprised that Chung never fussed along the way but instead he hummed 'Barbara Allen' causing Maxine and the girls to join in with the words, that pleased him and he said, "Chung lika Barbee Ellen song, Chung sava money, send for pretty Chinese girl, we liva ina hotel, Kate say okay, Kate lika Chinese girl, she maka Kate happy again, Warp maka Kate sad, Warp good man but crazy lika Chinaman." Knowing that he was right about the way Warp's death had affected Kate they chose not to comment and pretended not to hear.

While in Wiluna Thomas settled up with Hobbs for Warp's funeral and picked out a stone from a catalogue for Warp's grave.

"What do you want engraved on it Tom?" Hobbs asked,

I want it to read like this Hobbs, "William 'Warp' Broderick, Born In Scotland 1900, and you know th date he died so have that scratched on it to. And he fought th Germans in World War One losing part O his leg, I reckon he deserves credit fer that, so put this on it, "World War One Combat Veteran, a good soldier he was. And add this, He gave his all in th war and later at th Twisted Track Station working for Thomas Kirk, Thomas loved em like a brother he did and bygol they was close as brothers."

"I reckon that will suffice fer his stone, now I want to pick out a smaller one fer old Rogue." And have this chiseled on it, His Old Dog Rogue, they be together for ever."

"That one will be planted at th foot o Warp's grave. I reckon that takes care o that. Now Hobbs, let me know when they come in and I'll have Lance bring th utility and cart them out to th Twisted Track, Layton and th ringers will plant them proper, Layton knows how to do things th right way and I reckon I'll be depending on him even more

Now that Warp has taken leave."

Hobbs had scribbled it down as he heard it but was puzzled at some of the wording, he scratched his head and with a puzzled look on his face asked. "Now Tom, it's best we go over this the way you worded it, don't sound right in spots."

"No Hobbs, I want it word fer word jist like I spoke it, so go ahead and post th order."

"Well let me get one thing straight Tom th part where you said, " He gave his all in th war and later at th Twisted Track where he worked for Thomas Kirk, Thomas loved em like a brother he did and bygol they was as close as brothers. Wouldn't it be better to change the last sentence to, "He and Thomas became as close as brothers, and that would get rid of some o the words including "Bygol."

"No Hobbs, Ye have it etched jist like I said it, me and Warp was close as brothers and we used th Scottish brogue between us and bygol it seems fitting that it be on his tombstone."

Two weeks later Lance and Reba were married in Wiluna, they were pleased with the large crowd that turned out which was more than expected. They spent three days at the hotel and laughingly called it their hotel Wiluna honeymoon.

The day before they were to return to the Twisted Track, Hobbs informed him the stones had arrived. "Okay Hobbs, we're leaving tomorrow I'll stop by and get them."

Back at the homestead unbeknownst to Lance, Thomas had met with Layton and notified him that he and Mum had talked it over and made up their minds to move to Broome a little ahead of schedule. "This be my last decision at th Twisted Track Layton, today I elevate you to operating manager oer th station now soon to be owned by Lance Kirk, Lance has a level head he does and bygol he deserves th likes o you to help him keep th Twisted Track going in th right direction. You and Lance can put yore heads together and work out yore salary, I leave that to em because bygol I think he might cough up more than I would so that's in yore favor."

Layton walked away on clouds of silver thinking, 'I reckon I be a lucky man, th bugger not only give me his best suit but now he makes me top man at th Twisted Track.' 'And that lad he be a good chap jist like his father and will be a fair man to work for.'

Lance and Reba returned from Wiluna happy and ready to embark on their journey through life together.

Layton directed the placement of the tombstones, when finished he stepped back to admire the etchings that stood out against the rich shiny gray background of the stone. He shaded his eyes from the bright sunshine and began to read.

William "Warp" Broderick
Born in Scotland in 1900
Died in Australia in 1954

World War One Combat Veteran
He gave his all in th war and later
At th Twisted Track Station working
For Thomas Kirk Thomas loved em as
A brother he did and bygol they was as
Close as brothers

Then he looked down at the stone laying flat at the foot of the grave with this simple engraving.
"His Old Dog Rogue they be together forever."

Thomas summoned Lance and Reba to his little office in back of the homestead, Mum was there waiting.
"I av some news fer ye newlyweds," He began. "Mum and me talked it over and we av decided to move away to Broome in sight o th next six months. I have th papers here that puts th Twisted Track in yore hands lock stock and barrel. From here on it be under yore direction, I divvied up th savings at th bank and kept enough to see me and Mum living comfortable fer th rest o our lives. I left you operating capital that will run out in due time if you don't manage it right, so it's up to you to build on that and keep th station going jist like me and me father before me. I av picked Layton to be yore right hand man and that be th last decision as owner o th station that I will make, Layton is willing to take it on but ye will have to jaw wit him and come to terms on his salary."
He pushed some papers across the desk and said, "Ye sign em and th bank will have th deed done up proper to show th new owner to be Lance Kirk."
Then he said to Reba,
"Ye be needing th company of yore mother and father and I urge you to talk to them about staying on here, I reckon they feel they are visitors and have overstayed th visit but bygol we want them here on th Twisted Track fer good, so it's best you find a job fer them to do around th station that will make them feel better about staying."
"My word," Mum butted in. "There's plenty for them to do now, but think about when all th little Kirk newcomers start sproutin' in th homestead, then you need all th help you can get." They smiled as she went on, "Me and Thomas will be close enough to come visit, but fer them they would be oceans away, and that's not good."
They signed the papers and Thomas reached for their hands, "I trust you

will keep th tradition going here on th Twisted Track, th tradition that Ward Kirk started, I be confident in me mind that you be up to th task, so now th Twisted Track is free o me hands and yore's to hold, now me and Mum can look forward to wetting our feet in th salt water fer th rest o our stay in our master's land."

Reba was at a loss for words so she didn't search for any but instead just said, "Thank You, Thank you."

As Lance held his hand and looked into his eyes he realized he was looking at a giant of a man when it came to fairness and common sense and only hoped he could measure up to the same standards.

"I'll do my best pop," He said firmly, "But your accomplishments may be out of my reach." Then he and Reba turned and walked away, Thomas sighed and said.

"Mum they make a pretty picture together they do, and bygol that be a sign o a happy life together."

"My word Thomas, they do and it reminds me of you and me and th way we started out together." He smiled leaned over and kissed her on the cheek. "And its lasted through th think and thin of it Mum and bygol that's what tallies up in th end."

"Reba honey, I don't won't you to think that I want to leave Australia to get away from you because that's not the reason, a very troubling thing has reared its head in my life and I feel I must go back to the states to rid it off my mind if that's possible. Then maybe we will return I know your father loves it here and I hate it he has to cater to my wishes but I see no other way."

"Momma what troubles you? Maybe I can help."

" Reba honey, I will tell you no more than I have told your father, I did something years ago that I should have explained to you and him but I simply cannot reveal it at least not now. Cal bless his heart seems to understand and is not demanding that I tell him, and even that bothers me to no end knowing how faithful he has been to me as a husband and to you as a father, he deserves a full explanation about my problem but as I said I will not for the sake of our family reveal it now."

The next month was a month of hectic activity on the station as Layton tried to catch up on work that had went undone due to Warp's death and the wedding. The ringers quickly found out that he was a fair man just as Warp had been before him but he expected a fair days work in return.

Lance and Reba were excited about owning the Twisted Track and looked forward to their life together.

Mum and Thomas whiled away their time packing for their move to Broome.

"My word Thomas." She said one day. "It makes no bloody sense to cart all this to Broome th house won't hold it."

He smiled and said. "I be knowing this all th time Mum but I reckon its best to leave it to you."

Cal and Alice made reservations for a flight to Illinois. "You'll get back to your old self again and we'll come back here Alice." Cal assured her.

"Yes Cal I'm sure I'll improve enough for us to return." She answered, but in her mind she didn't believe it.

Tex Jr. took orders from Layton in stride and performed his duties flawlessly in spite of being in a dream world about he and Brenda. On top of that Lance and Reba enrolled him in a correspondence school over the wire service, and after a hard days work on the station he would study and work on his lessons at night until sleep claimed him.

Kate took over more responsibility in running the hotel trying to rid herself of thoughts of Warp. Chung was happy that she was performing some of the duties that in the past had been expected from him, but still managed to find plenty to complain about.

To the northeast at the Bonny Blue Station Travis and Val were getting back to normal from the interruption in their daily schedule, and at the sprawling two million acre "Big Easy" Station in Queensland Shane Daugherty and his wife Isabel noticed a marked change in Brenda that could only lead them to one conclusion, she was smitten with Tex Jr. and could hardly wait between messages between them, they knew they were facing the day that they would lose their granddaughter.

"She's only thirteen now but how the years fly by." Isabel remarked. "She'll be gone before we realize it Shane."

"Yep you're right,' He answered. "But look at it this way, we have brought her up but we have no right to keep her against her will, so I reckon when she leaves she will be out o our minds." He spoke these words knowing that he dreaded the day when he would have to let her go.

One year later the homestead at the Twisted Track now had two new family members, twin boys one named Calvin after Reba's father and the other Thomas after Lance's father.

Mum and Thomas were settled in their new home in Broome but hurried to the homestead for a two weeks visit. Mum was so happy. "I be proud o you and th twins." She told them, "My word two at once should double th fun."

Thomas glanced at Lance and said. "Yep I reckon you av a good start on th tradition, th Kirk name still holds here on th Twisted Track."

Back in Illinois, Cal got a job at Motorola and Alice decided to take a refresher course in nursing. She hired on the staff of a large hospital and plunged into her work with hopes of some relief from her troubled mind, and it did wonders, the hurt was still there but not as before. They lived in a little rental apartment the first five years and saved enough money to buy a little cottage in Peoria on the edge of town. Black lung disease was making it even more difficult for Cal to breathe normal and Alice knew that somewhere in the near future it would take his breath away.

Three years later after periods of having to take off from work for weeks at a time due to his illness he retired from Motorola and after another year they talked it over and decided to go live out the rest of their lives in Australia. "We'll start preparing now," she said. "Lance and Reba will be here in two months for a two weeks visit, we can put the house on the market right after they leave."

"Yes,' he answered. "I don't know about you but I've never been able to get Australia out of my mind, a different kind of life it offers and makes me wish I had been born there in the first place."

"Yes Cal, I know what you mean I have the same feelings."

Thomas and Mum came to watch over the twins while Lance and Reba were away in the states and on their return were delighted to hear of Cal and Alice's plans to come back to Australia.

Lance voiced his opinion about living in the industrial sections of Illinois.

" I feel like I'm hemmed in here," he said. "I reckon I be used to the wide open spaces."

The last thing Reba said before they boarded the plane was, "I can't wait for you to get there and see the twins, so hurry up and get the house sold."

Three months later they landed in Perth and rode a supply truck to Wiluna where Lance picked them up in an updated land rover. Although they were familiar with the way the twins looked as Reba had sent many pictures as babies up until now, but were totally surprised at their size and their polite gentle ways. Surprised too at the height that Tex had grown to. He was now twenty-one years old, nearing twenty-two. "He looks like a bean pole reaching to th sky." Cal remarked.

"And that ain't all," Lance added. "He has a crush on a Shiela in Queensland he does, and I reckon she feels the same way toward him, so we all know what that will lead to. But in spite of it he's doing well he completed his schooling course with flying colors, and works hard on th station, he does, I reckon you can be proud and enjoy him before th Queensland Sheila snatches him away."

"Sounds like th Barton name will spread over Australia," Cal added, "His daddy would be proud of him."

Reba smiled broadly and the proud pleased look on her face meant only one thing she was content in the way her life was headed.

Alice revealed to them that their plans were to live in Perth, "I have inquired about a nursing job there," she said, "I will have to take another short course there to qualify to their standards and then I have already been offered a job at a large hospital in Perth."

"Now momma we expected you to stay here, we have made plans for that."

"Yes I thought you would honey, but I need to stay busy in my profession it has worked wonders for me mentally and I'm afraid of a relapse if I give it up."

Reba looked at Cal noting he looked even frailer than when she seen him in Illinois a short while ago. "But how about daddy he loves it here you know that."

"Yes honey, I know and we've talked that over also, Cal will divide his time between here and Perth and I'm sure Thomas and Mum will coax him to Broome to sit on the beach with them once in awhile. As for me once I get started on my job at the hospital I'll be all wrapped up in it. and time goes by at a fast pace. In my off time, I understand there are several during a year, one being for one whole month, so you can expect me to be here with you often."

She completed the course successfully and within a short time they found a little apartment in Perth and moved in before she started at the hospital.

The arrangement worked out well, Cal spent a lot of time at the station keeping busy at the things he liked to do, he missed Thomas not being there but true to what Alice had predicted Thomas and Mum would hail in from Broome to spend a week or two on the station often, and when leaving would convince Cal to come stay a while with them.

"Ye need to get some salt water on ye feet Cal," Thomas would say, "bygol ye do, so grab some duds and come along."

Two years later at the age of twenty-three Tex Jr. And Brenda, were united in marriage. It became a tug of war between their parents where they would live, Lance and Reba did all they could to persuade them to stay on the Twisted Track but in the end Shane and Isabel won the battle and they settled on the Big Easy station in Queensland.

Tex soon discovered that the Big Easy was operated on a much larger scale than the Twisted Track but he quickly adopted and soon had input of his own that Shane found very sound and helpful.

In their second year of marriage a son was born and they named him after William 'Warp' Broderick and soon he became known as Warp.

The deadly black lung disease continued to sap Cal's strength and finally a year after the birth of his grandson (at least he thought it was his grandson) he died with Alice hovering over him at the hospital in Perth.

Reba and Tex Jr. wanted him buried on the Twisted Track and she reluctantly went along with that after considering he didn't have any living relatives other than his brother in Illinois in the states anyway.

His brother and his wife came for the funeral and stayed two months with their time divided between her apartment in Perth and the homestead. She held up pretty well while they were there but soon fell into the depression rut after they returned to the states.

After some time off she returned to her job at the hospital and plunged into her work and became totally dedicated to the sick and dieing leaving little room for her past life to trouble her.

Two days before Tex Jr.'s twenty-fifth birthday Brenda gave birth to another baby, a boy and they named him Shane after his great grandfather.

Then five years later Shane and Isabel turned the station over to him and Brenda. "Th Big Easy is a big un she is chap, but I reckon you can handle th job, th way you go about getting things done remind me o Warp and th way he handled th job at th Twisted Track, I reckon some o it must have rubbed off on you."

Along about that time Thomas had a heart attack and spent some time in the hospital. A stroke had left him paralyzed in his left side from his waist down. Over the objections of Lance and Reba Mum insisted on caring for him at their home in Broome, but after about a year it became obvious that she wouldn't be able to go on seeing that her health was also failing.

Reba talked to her mother Alice about quitting the hospital and coming to the homestead to take care of Thomas there. Mum and Thomas had agreed to come back if she would take care of him. "They will pay you as much or more than your salary at the hospital momma, and as you know it won't cost you anything to stay here."

So she gave two weeks notice to the hospital and moved back to the homestead.

Over the next two years Mum's health deteriorated and surprisingly she died before Thomas.

Then after Thomas death Alice went to visit Tex Jr. in Queensland. She only intended to stay one month but at the urging of Shane and Isabel she spent three. She marveled at the way Tex Jr. was bringing his sons up, giving them lots of attention and advice just like Warp would do. Looking at them she thought, 'they christened one Shane after his great grandfather on his mother's side and the other one after William 'Warp' Broderick, if they only knew he is their real great grandfather on his father's side.'

As she watched the boy Warp, now seven years old, every thing about him fit Warp, long bowed legs massive shoulders, even his mannerisms were tailored after Warp. She could feel old melancholy creeping in so she tried to put it out of her mind.

Back at the Bonny Blue Station, Travis and Val, had just returned from Texas where they spent two months. His father had surgery for, prostate cancer while they were there and died three weeks later. Now his aging mother still back in Texas and refusing to come to Australia, he and Val were torn between staying in Australia or, giving it all up to return to Texas to be near his mother.

At the hotel Chung true to his word had sent for his pretty Chinese girl but not all the way to China.

Thomas had came to Wiluna while still living in Broome before his death to take care of some business and told him of one that had just arrived from China. "She be flash Chung, that she be, she work at th cleaners in Broome, bygol she be waiting fer th taking Chung."

Chung wasted no time, "Chung bringa pretty Chineese girl to hotel Kate, you be happy Kate, she maka Kate happy."

Kate took charge of the wedding making it a gala event to the delight of Chung his bride and the folks in Wiluna.

And just as Chung had predicted she did make Kate happy again with her gentle mannerisms and old world ways, she fit right in at the hotel and she and Kate became fast friends. She helped Chung with his chores but he still complained.

"To mucha work for Chung atta hotel Chung needa another Chinese girl, Chung send for another Chinese girl and maka Kate more happy, she do work and maka Chung happy." The only difference was he would smile and wink. Complaining was what he liked doing best but now it was different because he was having fun doing it.

Then two dry seasons in a row in Western Australia and problems that tend to pop up unexpected in families took spirits to a low but not for long as always a wet season followed bringing new life to the land and giving fresh hope to the its people.

Meanwhile back in Kentucky, the big brave lad still roamed the roadways in his oversized luxury car enjoying high profits from his drug operation. The Sheriff of Bell County thought he had him more than once but he always seemed to beat the rap one way or the other sometimes on a technicality that made no sense to anyone but the sitting judge.

Today he decides to drive over to Harlan County, at the town of Pineville he spots Julie's car at a service station. He watches as she pulls out in the road and turn toward home. He fell back just enough to keep her in sight and followed, when she turned into her driveway he thought about driving on but had a change of mind and followed, thinking that her husband Curt would be at the strip mine.

As she drove down the tree-lined driveway she happened to look in her rear view mirror and recognized his car. She picked up the pistol from the seat got out of the car and hurriedly went up the steps to the porch. She looked back to see him standing by the open door of his car. As she fumbled for her door key he started up the steps, seeing that she didn't have time to unlock the door and get in the house she whirled and aimed the pistol at him. "Stop right where you are and get out of here," She said.

Surprised at the pistol pointed at him he stopped but seemed not to be afraid. "Now come on sweetie," he said calmly, evidently the bravery was a result of a fix he had taken by mouth as he followed her from Pineville. "Lets you and me get up close and personal like we used to do."

"No," she shouted, " you go or so help me I'll blow your brains out."

Still not convinced of the danger he faced he started on up the steps, He took a small packet from his coat pocket that contained small white pills and said, "here now cool down and try one of these, I've been missing you sweetie, its been a long time, lets have a little fun."

He had stopped at the top of the steps but now took a step toward her she backed up against the door and as he lunged forward she squeezed the trigger hitting him in his left shoulder. That stopped him momentarily but he quickly recovered and wrenched the pistol from her hands. She could see the hate in his drug flushed face and knew he was about to kill her, she slumped to the floor and watched in horror as he aimed the pistol at her, she felt the stinging impact of two bullets as they tore through her body, she lay still thinking that would stop him but could see he was standing over her aiming at her head, she closed her eyes to ward off the scene knowing that she was going to die.

Then she was conscious of another car stopping in the driveway and heard two shots one from the yard and the other coming from her own gun in the hands of the big brave lad. She opened her eyes and seen Curt holding on to the car door his face was ashen and his eyes were on her but as she watched him release his hold on the car door and slump to the ground along side his car she knew his eyes weren't seeing her, now out of her sight she tried to raise up enough to see him but her pain was too great. Then she thought, 'he must be dieing, oh God please let him live.'

Big brave lad lay near her feet on the porch with blood now flowing freely from his shoulder where she had shot him but now blood was gushing from his neck from the bullet he took from Curt's pistol. He was moving and trying to reach the banister to pull himself up, he finally managed to pull up enough to swing his legs out over the steps, he slid down the steps one at a time on his rear, once on the ground he crawled to his car and with a lot of effort finally got behind the wheel and started the motor. From where Julie lay she could only see the top and windshield of his car, as she watched thinking that he was about to get away she seen him slump over the steering wheel and the horn began to blow, then she passed out.

Wayne 'Poor Boy' Burke, and Al Burkhart, were at the old farm place checking over some of the weed covered rusting strip-mining equipment.

'Dammit! Al, we have to get rid of some of this junk, no sense letting it sit here and rust away like this, I'll check around with some of the smaller operators and see if they might be able to use it. Some of them can't afford the newer equipment and I can let them have this at a fair price, so get your mechanics together and get it in operating condition again and we'll have a sale here on a weekend in the near future."

447

"Okay but we'll be needing a lot of new parts," Al answered.

"Yeah I know Al, but its best we get it done, shit if I just break even on it I'll be satisfied knowing that somebody is getting some use out of it instead of watching it rust away here in these damn weeds."

Then they heard three gunshots from the direction of Curt and Julie's place.

"Hey what the hell is that Al? Curt must be home today getting in a little target practice."

"Yeah might be." Al answered. "Probably teaching Julie, he worries about that drug dealer from Bell County and wants her to have her pistol with her at all times."

"Damn that bastard, tell me Al, how in hell he gets away with dealing dope all these years? Shit you and me or anybody else for that matter couldn't get away with that we'da been locked up years ago."

Then they heard two more gunshots almost simultaneously and shortly after a horn started blowing.

"Damn what the hells going on we better check it out Al."

They hopped in the jeep and drove the short cut road to Curt and Julie's place. There they found Curt on the ground beside his open car door with blood oozing from his ears and nose, his eyes were open but unseeing.

Al reached in and pulled the big brave lad away from the steering wheel and the horn stopped blowing, he pushed him over in the seat and noticed the blood still gushing from an artery in his neck. He could see him gasping for breath. 'he ain't got long ' he thought.

Then he looked toward the porch and his heart sank as he could see Julie's ashen face resting in Poor Boy's lap. He rushed up the steps and as he stood over her he thought she was dead but as Poor Boy rubbed her forehead she opened her eyes and asked.

"Is Curt alright? Check on Curt."

"Yeah Julie ain't nothing we can do for Curt but he saved you, here Al, hold her head off th floor while I get on th phone for an ambulance."

The ambulance arrived and rushed Julie to the hospital in Corbin and soon the driveway was filled with Sheriff's deputies going over the crime scene. After pictures were taken of the bodies of Curt and the big brave lad the ambulances took them to the morgue in Middlesboro.

Curt, as was previously planned by he and Julie, was buried beside his first wife.

A large crowd attended his funeral and he, being well known as a former highly respected law officer, police officers from all neighboring counties were there in a long line of fresh cleaned shiny police cars that reminded everyone of the bond that exists between law enforcement officers.

After a few hours in the Corbin hospital Julie was rushed to a hospital in Lexington where she underwent surgery for removal of a bullet that had torn through her rib cage and lodged in her back near her spine. The other bullet had went clean through her body damaging her digestive system causing loss of blood plus one kidney was completely destroyed. She went in and out of comas for days, sometimes for as long as twenty four hours at a time she knew nothing, but when she would finally come around she would fix her eyes on whoever was there, her children, or her friends Ann and Poor Boy, Burl and Laura, she would try to smile, but always it would end with a question, "Can you get Dale and his family here? I have to see him again before I die." Then tears would fill her eyes as she slipped back in the dark world of coma.

Dale had finally joined the army and seen duty in Vietnam. After returning to the states he met and married a girl from Louisville. He got a decent job bought a house on the outskirts of Louisville and proceeded to raise a family leaving behind his hippie way of life, a complete change except for one thing, he never mended fences with his mother. In spite of her and Curt begging and pleading on the phone to him he would not listen and as the years rolled by Curt could tell the worry from it was literally sapping her strength and robbing her of the happiness that she so much deserved.

One day Ann, Poor Boy, Burl and Laura, and Julie's children except for Dale were sitting around her bed watching and waiting to see if she would come out of the coma for just one more time. Finally her eyes fluttered open and they all stood in a group over her so she could see them all without trying to move her head, which was very difficult for her to do.

"Is Curt alright?" She whispered. A question she always asked even though she had been told of his death she simply wouldn't believe it and insisted he was in another room of the hospital recovering from his wounds.

No one answered her question so she whispered another familiar question, "Can you get Dale and his family here? I must see him before I die." Then she slipped back into a coma.

They stood and looked at each other as tears began to show in their eyes, calls had been made to Dale daily but he would not agree to visit her, passing it off with, "she's not in my life anymore, I don't need her and I'm sure she don't need me," and then he would hang up.

449

But today Poor Boy walked out and down the hallway to a pay phone with a solemn determined look on his face.

He dialed the phone and waited. "Heh this you Dale? Well listen to me boy and don't hang up because if you do so help me I'll show up on yore doorstep and drag yore ass all th way from Louisville to Lexington. Now listen by God and listen close as you already know yore mother is on her deathbed and asks for you every time she wakes up from a coma, no dammit you shut up and listen I'm the one that's doing the talking. I don't give a damn about what you think, you may be right about yore feelings toward her for the way she treated yore dad and me afterward but can't you see that's all in the past, yore mother's all together a different person now, and remember th letter yore dad wrote before he was killed there in Belgium. He told you in th letter to always honor and stick by yore mother and by god I'm here telling you that as of today I intend to see that you honor his wishes. So right now, right this minute you get yore self busy getting your family together to come see your momma, I'll give you till nine tomorrow morning to get to the hospital here in Lexington, and if you don't show by god I'll be there to get you."

He hung up the phone and walked back down the hallway and overheard some one say, "The language some people use over the phone, what's the world coming to."

That same night the doctor at the hospital stated that Julie was close to death. "I doubt if she'll live through the night," he said.

But at nine the next morning the Burke and Crawford families, her father Al Burkhart, and her children were all gathered in her room watching and wondering if she would wake from her coma just one more time.

Poor Boy looked at the clock at five past nine and thought, 'Well th damn ranting and raving I did didn't do anything to that damn stubborn mind of his so I guess she'll die without ever seeing him again.'

Then he looked up to see Dale along with his wife and two kids standing in the doorway. No one could say anything as they watched him stare at his mother. Finally he walked to her bedside fell to his knees and buried his face in her long black hair that covered one side of the pillow. Then his body shook with remorse and the muffled sounds of his voice said over and over, "I'm sorry Momma, I'm sorry, I truly am, I love you so much, please don't go away now because we have so much to catch up on, my wife and your grandchildren are here to see you so please momma don't go."

Sniffles could be heard in every part of the room and the nurse who had been standing in the doorway listening walked in and knelt down beside him reached for Julie's hand and said, "Wake up Julie your son and his family are here to see you."

Then Poor boy stepped forward and said loudly, "It's Dale Julie, it's Dale, come on wake up and look at yore grandkids, th girl looks just like you."

After several seconds her eyes fluttered open, Ann and Laura led Dale's wife and her children to the bedside, Dale got to his feet and stood beside them. As she stared up at them a smile started then slowly spread over her face clearly revealing the happiness she was experiencing.

"Momma this is my wife Donna, and here is our oldest Brad, we named him after daddy, and here is Julia, we call her Julie, she's named after you, and we have another one on the way, I'm sorry momma for the way I've acted all these years, believe me you were on my mind all along and I intended to come see you again but seems the longer I put it off it became harder to get myself to do it." Then he lost his composure and dropped to his knees again, he slid his arm under her head and as he stroked her forehead with his other hand the smile on her face blossomed with happiness as her eyes scanned the room resting on each individual as if saying 'goodbye I love you.'

Then her eyes opened wide as she gasped for air she shuttered twice and was gone.

Her other children joined Dale and his family at the bed, some kneeling over her and others embracing each other in sorrow. Finally the nurse pulled the curtain and asked them to leave the room.

Nine days from the date she was gunned down her funeral was held in the church followed by a graveside service on the knoll where they laid her to rest beside her first husband Brad Crawford. Sadness touched many in the large crowd which was somewhat of a mystery considering the life she had lived and the misdeeds she committed to her first husband and to her second Wayne 'Poor Boy' Burke, But the results are always constant once you make things right with God, love and respect from your fellow man will follow.

At the graveside service her father, Al Burkhart, stood near his wife's grave sobbing uncontrollably as he thought back on his past and blamed himself for the act he committed that brought her into a life that she had to live without a father for so many years.

Dale stayed at her graveside long after everyone else walked away grieving and expressing his love for her, knowing that the stubbornness that had consumed him and kept him from seeing her would now haunt him the rest of his life.

A few months later Al Burkhart, suffered kidney failure and had to go on dialysis, his son Jett, took him in his home where he could keep a close watch on him and drive him to the hospital three times weekly for the dialysis treatments.

One day Jett's wife called him at work and in a horrified voice told him his dad had committed suicide, "please hurry home," she pleaded.

Jett rushed to the bedroom to find blood and brains seeping from the side of his head where the bullet from a thirty eight-caliber pistol had exited from his head, he had carefully covered the pillow and most of the bed with a large piece of plastic to protect the bedding, then took a comfortable position on the bed and blew his brains out, cold and calculated and hard to understand to a sane person, but I'm sure the old saying 'driving me insane' holds true if you live most of your life filled with guilt and shame.

Jett and his family were devastated, a note on the table along side the bed stated.

"Jett I'm sorry it had to end this way, but as you know I fathered a daughter by another woman and your mother went to her grave never knowing about it, that and the fact that the daughter never knew real happiness in her life has worked on my mind to the point of driving me crazy, and facing sure painful death from kidney failure, plus being a burden on you and your family I decided this is the best way out, I pray that God will understand, pray for me Jett, and take this bit of advice, always be true to your wife and don't make the same mistake I did. I love you goodbye. Al."

They buried him on the knoll beside his wife just a few feet from a daughter that his wife never knew about. Years later, stories from locals abounded about sobbing sounds coming from the cemetery at night. "It's Al Burkhart," they would state, "He never got over the way he treated his wife."

The big brave lad's body lay in the morgue unclaimed for two weeks before County officials finally stepped in and made arrangements with a funeral home to give him a proper burial. He had left behind a large sum of money and property that the County would eventually lay claim to and used it for various projects that improved services for its people.

He had lived his life as a criminal never showing anything from his heart that resembled generosity or goodness, but now ironically, his ill-gotten wealth would benefit Bell-Counties people greatly.

Meanwhile across the mountains in Virginia the little mining town of St. Charles had lost even more of it's people as the larger mines closed they traveled to different parts of the country to find work and literally became scattered all over the United States.

The old Sycamore tree stood looking lonely and forlorn as the regulars slowly moved away to places like Dayton, Ohio, Chicago, Illinois, Detroit, Michigan and other far away places, and in nineteen eighty two the tree died and was cut down.

Could it be that since it was a living thing it had feelings just as we humans, and died from loneliness? Only God knows.

A small group planted another sycamore about twenty feet away in the nineteen eighties with a little ceremony in remembrance of the old tree. It has grown tall and proud since then but without the stature of the old one.

I stood under it in December of 2004 and as I strained my eyes to see things that have long been gone nothing would come in view. Finally I closed my eyes intending to stand there in remembrance to the way the town once was when all of a sudden the sights and memories came into view. It was like a summer day, a Saturday afternoon sometime in the nineteen forties. A group was gathered under the old tree dressed in their Saturday best which for many meant a clean pair of bib overalls, a fresh ironed starched dress shirt, white being the prevalent color, some wearing a suit coat usually some shade of blue, brown or black wing tipped dress slippers, topped off by a felt hat that sat on the head cocked to one side or the other and in different shades of gray.

The mayor Charlie Wheeler, the only one in the crowd dressed in a loose fitting suit and tie was getting a shoeshine from old Mainline as he kept up his steady chatter, "More pretty girls than one," "going back to Alabama."

There stands John wearing suspenders plus a belt, a long sleeved shirt with the sleeves pulled up slightly from the armbands that he wears just above his elbows. Some one once asked him, "John why do you wear suspenders and a belt?"

"To keep my britches up dummy," he answered. "Some one slipped up behind me and cut my suspenders there at the theater and my britches fell to my ankles, don't ever won't that to happen again."

One of them has just returned from an all nights fishing trip in Tennessee and is telling how many he caught, "One got away, Th thing was as big as my leg and this long," he spread his hands at least three feet. "Mighty big fish' Charlie the mayor remarked, "You must have been fishing in the Atlantic ocean."

Then old George 'Washington' Reynolds spoke up. "Ocean hell, I caught one that big right out of this creek last week."

"Aw come on George, you know you're lying ain't nothing but minnows in this creek and they'll all be gone before you know it from th poison water from th mines."

"By god if you don't believe me ask Black Gilley he seen th fish." George replied. "I caught it right up th creek there between here and Bonny Blue." Everyone laughs and George storms off up the street cussing a blue streak.

Then the sound of baseball cleats get my attention and I see Roy Ruthford, and Dame Pannell, go by on their way to the ballpark down the street to get in some practice for today's game. Black calls out. "Alright boys give it your best I have everything but th clothes on my back riding on th game today."

Across the street the little theater has opened and a line waits to buy tickets to see a double feature starring 'Wild Bill Elliot' known as 'The peaceable man' and another favorite singing cowboy 'Tex Ritter' both representing the good guys that meant so much to my generation but now is slowly but surely being replaced by things with no base at all to define between right and wrong to benefit our young generation.

Golden corn is poured into the heated popcorn machine and soon it bursts into a white buttered salt sprinkled delicacy, giving off an aroma that mixed with the odor from the poor sewer system along with the cigarette smoke and beer from the juke joints gave St. Charles a special smell. The long narrow cubbyhole of a place next to the theater is serving hot dogs as fast as they can put them together.

Bill, the Town police chief and one of his deputies Clint Hughes, have just took a young miner from Rogers café that has already had too much to drink and is causing a ruckus, they stand on the sidewalk trying to calm him down, but looks like he will wind up in the calaboose because Bill's patience is running thin.

The barber in Myers barbershop, wearing a sun visor cap peers out the open door at the scene as he strops his razor to shave a miner with a week old beard.

On the other side of the theater at Stallard's meat market, Butch Stallard, is busy cutting meat getting ready for his busiest day of the week.

Teenagers fill the stools and booths at Shoun's Drugs with just enough change in their pockets to buy and sip a coke before going to see the movie.

On up the street the noise from pool rooms one on each side of the street can be heard as soft spoken Gurney Tester, cuts my hair with others waiting, he knows them all by their first names, including mine.

The roller rink has been swept up clean from the night before and the shoes are all lined up ready to glide over the floor, some users are regulars and are a pleasure to watch as they swing and sway gracefully to the music as others skate wildly and stomp their feet trying to right themselves just before they collide into some one or worse yet crash into the retaining railing.

On up the street Evans and Sprinkle grocery, is busy filling orders to deliver to the surrounding coal camps.

On the other end of town just across the bridge Mutt Williams places of business on both sides of the street are busy. And next to them at Clyde Copeland Funeral Home, a body is being prepared for burial.

The ballpark is beginning to fill up and Black Gilley has a front row seat ready to root his team on. Next to the ballpark attendants at Smitty's Esso Station are busy gassing up and changing oil, some of the vehicles are cabs from a large fleet privately owned getting ready for a night of transporting the miners and family members back to the surrounding coal camps after the theater and juke joints close usually sometime after midnight.

Next to the Esso station a noisy steam engine pushes and bumps empty coal cars lining them up on tracks that lead to the mines.

On the depot platform a familiar figure sits with his legs hanging over the platform on the street side telling stories to the half dozen or so standing below him on the ground.

No matter that all sorts of other attractions are going on in the town, Dru Ely, 'the master story teller' always has an audience.

I stood there motionless with my eyes closed taking it all in while listening to a sad country tune coming out of the speakers mounted above the door to Rogers café. Then down the road toward Stone Creek I could hear another tune but it was different. I listen closely and recognize the group singing as 'The Chuck Wagon Gang' which only means one thing, Harden Stapleton is on his way to town to preach a sermon under the old sycamore tree. The sound gets louder, now I can see his car approaching the little bridge just past Mutt Williams place of business.

The speakers mounted on top of his car were pushing out the sounds of the chuck wagon gang with a vengeance drowning out the music from the jukebox. He parked near the tree and played another number before starting his sermon.

With my eyes still closed I listened afraid if I opened them the vision would be gone.

When he finished and played another number silence came over the town, I kept waiting to hear voices from some of the gang talking under the tree or the jukebox blaring from Rogers café, I waited thinking surely I would hear cheers from the ballpark but it was deathly quiet, then I realized the vision was gone and so were the smells and sounds, even the smell of popcorn had been wafted away.

I opened my eyes and slowly looked around at the spot where the old tree once stood and across the street at the bare empty lots where the theater, hot dog stand, Myers barber shop, and Stallard's meat market were once housed. And up a little ways from there the building that Shoun's drugs occupied for so long is now nothing but scattered ashes. Across the street from there the brick building that became a familiar landmark because it housed Jake's Place, a meeting place for about everyone during the nineteen forties is no more. And on up the street a number of buildings from that era have been torn down or abandoned over the years.

The old railroad depot down the other way where I so clearly saw Dru Ely just a few minutes ago was not there. It burned down years ago. Beyond their Smithy's ESSO station is history and across the bridge Mutt Williams business and Copeland funeral home no longer exist.

It's sad to look at all the empty lots where bustling places of business once flourished.

But sadder, that most of the people from that era have gone on.

I stood there in silence looking at a little building that has been erected near where the ESSO station once stood, housing their volunteer fire department with two men sitting on a bench out front whiling away the time. In a town that I could remember loaded with people walking on the sidewalks elbow to elbow on a Saturday, but now I only see two people and the empty feeling is overwhelming me.

No kind of business exists anywhere in town you can't even purchase a loaf of bread.

They do have a clinic that ministers to the few people that have hung on and stayed there over the years and a few that live in the ghostly coal camps that surround the town.

The last High School class graduated in 1970 and the building now serves as a Grammar school and as time goes on unless something drastic happens to bring life back to the town it cannot exist much longer either.

I got in my van and drove away waving to the two fellows at the fire department, at Stone Creek I took 421 the Harlan road to my old home place at dead mans curve one mile from the Kentucky state line. I parked got out and stood looking across the creek at the old place that has been repaired and renovated over the years all for the better but no longer looks the same. As I stood there I closed my eyes for a vision of my childhood growing up there but nothing appeared.

The only familiar thing that stirred my senses was the huge ice mass that clung to the rocky road bank above the road about fifty yards away and a cold biting wind from that direction that brought back memories of cold windy mornings. I had to face that same kind of wind wearing a thin jacket as I trudged to school two miles away.

I got back in my van and drove one mile up the mountain to the Kentucky line, I remembered Harve Roop had lived just across on the Kentucky side for as long as I could remember and wondered if he was still alive, to my surprise I seen him sitting astride an all terrain vehicle tooling around over his land. He stopped what he was doing and invited me in to his house.

"Harve, I don't have a lot of time," I protested.

"Ah never mind." He said. "We have to sit down and talk awhile."

We sat there for at least two hours going over old times we must have brought up a hundred names of folks that have gone on. Even though he was ninety-four years old at that time and has slowed down considerably his mind is as sharp as a tack and holds a storehouse of memories from his past.

I discovered I didn't need a vision while in his presence because his words and the pictures they painted took me back to another place and time in my life.

I finally got up to go. "Why don't you stay all night with us?" He said, as his wife nodded in agreement. "We still have a lot to talk about, we could talk all night."

I promised him I would come by again the next time I get up that way, and I intend to keep that promise if God lets me live and stay healthy enough to make the trip again.

I'm back at home here in Florida now seven hundred and sixty five miles and millions of memories away from my old home place in Lee County Virginia.

I sit among pictures hanging from the walls mostly of my dear wife that left me alone with nothing more than memories that linger and bring tears to my eyes daily. She died two days before Christmas nineteen ninety nine from alzheimers disease, a lingering slow death lasting twelve years and going through several phases each worse than the one before.

Two years before her death she no longer knew me and thought I was just some one assigned to take care of her. But at times she would remember my name, she preferred to call me Kirk. She would tearfully ask me if I thought Kirk would ever come back to her again. I could never convince her that I never left her in the first place I guess that has been the most heart-wrenching thing that has ever happened to me in my life.

Then about a year before she died she could no longer talk relieving me of the duty to answer that kind of question but in her eyes the confusion and agony stilled showed.

Now as I look back on my life, all of the older people that I have mentioned or wrote about from that era with the exception of Harve Roop are all gone even the most of my generation leaving me to wonder why I'm still here. Makes me wonder if the vision I experienced at St. Charles, Virginia will be my last. Could it be that my Lord let it pass before me just one more time then closed the door and said.

"My son its time you gave it up, you've hoed a long row but your harvest is small, now go and prepare yourself to leave it all behind."

I have no way of knowing God's mysterious ways but I do know I'm mighty tired and weary and long for a more peaceful setting.

I sit in old age and go over the, what ifs In my life and can see where I could have made a better decision a thousand times over that would have allowed me to leave behind a better legacy that would be more pleasing to my master. He dealt me a decent hand of cards and trusted me to play them in the right way but I came up short.

I look back at one of the pages where Warp said he was holding on to a card that he should have discarded long ago but for some reason held on to it. In my case I think I clung to more than one and now in old age it's too late to play or discard them.

And again I use the phrase, "Into each life some rain must fall" and I've had my share but I can't use that as an excuse for my poor harvest here on earth.

Now the year is 2005 and in far away Australia a land that one of my uncles spoke fond of after he spent some time there during World War Two, and it has been one of my yearnings ever since I heard him talk about it.

I'm sure the change the country has went through since the nineteen forties and fifties has been beneficial but at the same time erasing many long standing beliefs and customs of it's people. I suppose new towns and communities have spread across the vast land where only cattle and sheep once grazed and now offer a life style much like the glittering cities of Melbourne, Sydney, and Perth, where the affluent dine in the finest restaurants and sip the best world famous yellowtail wines. All in the name of progress which has only one correct explanation, a country must build and move with the times or else be left behind to struggle and be at the mercy of it's stronger neighbors.

But sadly that means some of the customs handed down from generation to generation will eventually erode away and become only a memory to some, and as their numbers dwindle and are replaced by future generations all will be forgotten and a rich history in time will be lost forever.

But some things remain a constant due to the demand for beef and mutton, some of the huge cattle and sheep stations continue to thrive and practice and preserve age-old traditions.

The Twisted Track hasn't changed that much, some equipment and living quarters updated for sure but basically the same as it has been from the day Ward Kirk claimed it back in the eighteen hundreds.

Ward, Thomas, Thomas father Weldon, and Lance now all rest on the knoll with their spouses beside them, Lance died from a massive heart attack soon followed by Reba, she suffered a slow painful death from skin cancer. Her mother Alice lived another three years after Reba's death as her demented mind faded she could no longer remember and grieve about the things from her past, but lived out the rest of her life on The Twisted Track where she would visit the little cemetery at least once a week reading the names on the tombstones as if trying to rediscover her past life, she died in her mid nineties.

They're all buried in the same row or as Thomas would put it, "In th same line."

The Kirk's and their spouses side by side, then comes Warp, and next to him Cal and Alice.

Another reserved row that up to now is still empty waits future family members.

Then a long row filled with former Twisted Track Ringers including Seth, Layton, and a dozen more including the two black ringers take up a part of the cemetery along the lower fence.

About a year after Layton was laid to rest, a bounty hunter posing as a law enforcement agent flew in and landed at the airport in Wiluna. He checked in at the hotel and spent the next day inquiring about a man by the name of Vince Palmer wanted for robbing a bank in Sydney in the nineteen fifties.

"I have traced him to a station in this area," He said, "The Twisted Track. Can you direct me there?"

"Sure I'll point you in that direction." Kate replied. "But it'll be a wasted trip because no Vince Palmer works at the Twisted Track and never has."

"Listen lady I'll let you in on something, I'm not a law officer, I'm a bounty hunter, and this man Palmer has a price on his head, a substantial amount of money put up by th bank and I intend to collect it. The case is old because it happened in the nineteen fifties, but the bank will still pay the ransom. Now if you'll give me a little information I'll see that it's worth your while."

"I'm sorry I told you there's never been a man by that name working on The Twisted Track so you're wasting your time."

"Now wait a minute lady he could have been using another name, have you ever heard the name Layton Bailey?"

She dropped her head and smiled, remembering Layton and the mystery that had surrounded him all the years he worked on The Twisted Track. Many had wondered about him but no one could ever come remotely close to his past life before he showed up in Wiluna well dressed and looking out of place.

She remembered the day he arrived in Wiluna and took a room at the hotel and stayed three weeks most of the time he stayed in his room out of sight except to go to the dining room for his meals.

One day he approached her and asked if there were any cattle stations near Wiluna, "I need to get a job," he said, "and I hear the stations are always on the look out for help."

She sized him up before answering, 'he looks more like a minister, professor, or maybe a banker,' she thought.' 'My word why would he be seeking a job on a cattle station?'

Looking at him dressed more like city folks she knew he wouldn't last long working at The Twisted Track but felt she should give him the information anyway.

"Yes there's a station north east of here called The Twisted Track," she replied, Thomas Kirk is the owner, it's a very well run successful station."

"How far out is it?" He asked.

"About a days ride on a supply truck which goes out that way once a month with supplies, you might ought to check down at the livery stable when the next one is due to go that way. My word, it will be a crook ride, hot and dusty."

"Oh that's no problem," he answered, "I need to get accustomed to this land and I can't think of a better way than seeing it from the bed of a supply truck."

He checked at the livery stable and found out the supply truck would be leaving for The Twisted track two days later. He went by the clothing store that stocked only work clothes but would special order dress clothing if you wanted it. He purchased two pairs of work trousers, two work shirts, boots, socks, under clothing, a lightweight jacket, leather vest, a heavy parka and a wide brimmed hat, ringer style. Back at the hotel he discarded the suit he was wearing plus all the other fancy duds, silk shirt, bow tie, Italian slippers, and fancy felt hat.

He sought out Chung and asked him if he would like the fancy clothes, Chung was delighted to take them off his hands and with a little alteration made them a perfect fit.

Then early one morning the day before he was supposed to ride the supply truck to the Twisted Track Kate seen him come down the hall from his room carrying the shiny black leather case that she had noticed when he checked in the hotel thinking it must contain his clothing and personal things.

She stared at him puzzled as to where he could be going. "Oh my word, you're leaving today? I thought you said the supply truck was supposed to leave tomorrow."

"Yes it is tomorrow I have a little business to take care of today." He answered.

She watched him walk out the door and down the veranda steps to the street noting the difference the work clothes made in his appearance.

'Must be going to the bank,' she thought, 'but it won't be open for at least another hour.'

At midmorning she seen him return minus the leather case and wondered if he left it along with its contents stashed away in the bank vault. As all this ran through her mind the bounty hunter became irritated that she hadn't answered his question and mumbled as he walked away,

"Well like I said the bounty is there for the taking and I'll share some of it with you if you know anything that will point me toward him, in the meantime I intend to find a way to get to The Twisted Track station,' by this time he was standing at the door of his room down the hallway he turned and looked back at her and called out, "Is there any place to land a plane at The Twisted Track?"

"No there isn't, Thomas Kirk won't allow planes to land on his station," She answered. "The only transportation is on the supply truck that goes out that way once a week."

She went to bed that night with Layton still on her mind. 'So he was a bank robber,' she thought, 'and that explains the leather carrying case that was probably stuffed with money,' 'now I wonder where he hid it because I asked the banker Herbert about him the day after he walked out of here with it, he said he had never been in the bank, and Warp told me he seen him arrive at The Twisted Track on the supply truck carrying nothing but a soiled paper bag containing a change of clothes.'

Then she thought about Thomas hiring him in spite of having doubts that he would stay for any length of time. But in the end it had worked out well he became a top hand and aide to Warp and after Warp's death went on to manage the station successfully right up until his death from a kick to his head from a fidgety horse as he was trying to re-shoe it.

She lay there till late thinking, 'If Layton hid the money and he must have, what were his plans? Maybe after retirement in his old age was he planning on going away to Broome, or Perth and live out the rest of his life in luxury?'

Then she smiled as she remembered him quoting the bible and leaving the impression that his background was that of a minister that perhaps had seen his church torn apart by a squabble among its members and decided to move on.

There had been a lot of talk among the locals over the years but his background much like Hobbs had remained a mystery.

She entered the dining room the next morning to find the bounty hunter fussing about the way Chung had fixed his breakfast. "I don't like my eggs on top of my steak." He scowled.

"Chung pila eggs on topa steak, Chung worka hard, Chung hava no time, you eata eggs lika Chung pila them on topa steak."

Then Chung headed toward the kitchen leaving behind a steady stream of Chinese language that no one understood but his pretty Chinese wife busy cleaning a nearby table and she looked embarrassed.

The bounty hunter scowled again but finally began to eat but not before raking the eggs from atop the steak.

Kate sat down across from him and asked. "The fellow you're looking for, Vince Palmer, the bank robber what name did you tell me he might be using?"

"I think it might be Layton Bailey, because a purchase of a leather carrying case was made at a department store near where the robbery took place in Sydney and he asked the sales clerk to write that name on the ID card attached to the case."

She smiled knowing now that Layton had to be the man he was looking for.

"Well I reckon I know where he is." She stated, "He's on The Twisted Track and has been there since some time in the 1950's, but I'm not looking for any of the bounty, you can enjoy that yourself, I want no part of that kind of money." As he wolfed down his breakfast he stared across the table at her but said nothing. When finished he hurriedly made his way to the livery stable to inquire about a ride on the supply truck.

Early the next morning he ordered his breakfast and again Chung sat the platter in front of him with the eggs piled on top of the steak.

"You eata steak wit eggs on top lika Chung fix, you eata and lika, Chung no hava time to jaw bone, Chung have mucha work to do."

He scowled again but raked the eggs to one side and proceeded to eat. Then he checked out of the hotel and rushed to the livery stable to get on the supply truck for the long ride to The Twisted Track.

Kate went to bed that night thinking about the bounty hunter and wondered how he would react when he arrived at The Twisted Track and found out Layton was there but was dead and buried in the station cemetery. She found it amusing that he was so eager to get there but would be highly disappointed and would return to the hotel with fire in his eyes.

Then she thought of the leather case again and wondered where Layton had hid it, could it be right here in town or further out on the track leading to The Twisted Track?

She had doubts if he ever spent any of it, he spent most of his time working on The Twisted Track coming to town occasionally to purchase a few things but not known as a big spender, his salary at The Twisted Track afforded him all he needed and with some left over, at his death Hobbs announced that Layton had entrusted him with his savings which amounted to a modest amount and had directed him to give it to the church in Wiluna.

As all this ran through her mind she thought of the bounty hunter again, smiled and dropped off to sleep.

He dropped to the ground from the bed of the supply truck, hot, sweaty, hungry, and in a bad mood.

Lance looked him up and down and wondered if he might be looking for a job, 'don't know if I would want this chap,' he thought, 'can't ever recall The Twisted Track turning anyone away without giving them a try, but this chap don't look very promising.'

"I blow in here from Sydney," he growled, "searching for a chap with th name Vincent Palmer, goes by Vince, but took on th name Layton Bailey some years ago, I hear he works here, can you tell me where he is? Best you point him out and let me do th talking."

Lance was taken aback by his gruff ways and wandered why he wanted to see Layton, and what is this other name Vince Palmer, what's that have to do with Layton?

"Well is he here?" he growled. "This ain't no social call, th chaps dangerous and has a price on his head."

Then Lance recoiled frustrated at his questions without any explanation, "Hold on chap, slow down and explain yore self, I can't make any bloody sense out of what you've told me about Layton, so start all over again."

"He robbed a bank in Sydney back in the nineteen fifties he did, and has been in hiding ever since, th bank put up a reward for his capture and I'm here to take him in and claim th reward. So lead me to him before I lose my bloody patience."

Lance pointed to the knoll and said. "See that fenced in plot there on th knoll? He's resting there, come on chap follow me."

As he walked along behind Lance he strained his eyes trying to see some one on the knoll but could not. But as they drew nearer he could make out the rows of tombstones and realized it must be the station cemetery.

He followed Lance through the gate and began to scan the names on the stones, Ward Kirk, Weldon Kirk, Thomas Kirk, William 'Warp' Broderick, Calvin Finley, then the line at the lower fence, Seth Rutherford, and next to him Layton Bailey.

"When did he die?' He asked, "and where is th money from th bank? He walked away from th bank with a lot of capital stashed in a leather case and no way did he spend it all while working on this bloody station, he must have hid it some where around here."

"He died about a year ago," Lance answered, "And th leather case stuffed with money I have no bloody idea where it is because this is th first I've heard about it and must admit I'm having trouble believing you after knowing Layton to be a faithful head stockman on th station for so many years and a religious man he was, Layton was an all around good chap."

"Oh my word, according to th records he did practice his religion back in Sydney but th records also show that he robbed th Sydney bank so th religion was nothing but a bloody cover."

"No that's not the right description of Layton," Lance replied. "Layton was a learned man and could quote scriptures from th bible as easy as saying th alphabet and he lived his life th way th bible teaches, he did, so I reckon he died a good man no matter how much bloody stuff you bring up from his past."

"Well have it yore way chap, but he did rob a bank and has been in hiding ever since, and now that I have finally found him that part is solved leaving me with th task of finding th money. Can you put me up a few days and furnish me some help to find that leather case? He must have stashed it away around here some place, I might have to do some digging to find it."

"No chap, you won't be digging up th soil on th Twisted Track, and I'll put you up for one night, tomorrow morning I have to go Wiluna to take care of some business at th bank, so rise early and I'll cart you back there."

He stormed in the hotel with fire in his eyes intending to confront Kate for the humiliation she caused him but changed his mind when he saw her sitting at her desk cool and collected and obliviously amused, so he decided to be as nice as his temper would let him because he was still very much interested in the black leather case and it's contents.

"Well my lady you sent me on a wild goose chase, you did, th bank robber was there just like you said, but to collect th reward I had to have him alive. I will lay up here for a few more days and see if I can get some help and find that leather case, If you can help in any way I'll see that you get a share of it."

"Oh no," she said, "Why should I tell you anything?" giving the impression that she knew something about it.

"You know you could get yourself in a fix if you're harboring a secret about th leather case so it's best you think about that before you decide to keep it from me." He turned and walked down the hall to his room.

She sat there smiling knowing his interest in the case and it's contents had nothing to do with it ever finding it's way back to the bank because he was itching to claim it and use it as his own.

He hung around for another three days asking questions from the locals, at the livery stable he was particularly interested if Layton had checked out a horse while carrying a leather case. The livery stable owner Burgin, after hearing how Kate had sent him to The Twisted Track thinking that Layton was there alive decided he would carry on and have some fun.

465

"What color was th case?" He asked. "Black." The bounty hunter replied.

Burgin spread his hands, "Was it about this size?" He asked. "And did it look like it was stuffed full and had a name tag dangling from it?"

"Yes it did." The bounty hunter said excitedly, "did you see him with it? Which way did he go from here? He must have hid it around here some place."

Burgin looked down at the ground and didn't answer. The bounty hunter shouted. "Well come on fella open up, did you see him with th case?"

"No chap, I reckon I never seen Layton lugging a case like that."

At the bank the next day he questioned Herbert but came up empty.

Midmorning the next day Kate sat on the hotel veranda as the plane roared overhead on its way back to Sydney carrying a greedy bounty hunter, humiliated and empty handed.

She sat there thinking. 'I reckon the leather case has my attention just like the bounty hunter but his interest in it is greed where mine is curiosity, I do wonder where Layton hid it, but I reckon no one will ever know.'

One year later Hobbs suffered a mild stroke luckily he had taken on a young man that had just completed his embalming course at Perth and came to Wiluna seeking experience in the funeral business with an eye toward having a business of his own.

He worked out well and to Hobbs amazement took over and managed the business like a professional, leaving him to piddle around with his wire service.

But within six months he suffered another stroke, this one more severe and laid him up in the Wiluna hospital. His condition worsened and over a two-week period loss of appetite and strength left him invulnerable to pneumonia that set up in both lungs and it became obvious that he would not survive.

Early one morning he weakly spoke to a nurse asking her to get the word to the hotel that he wished to see Kate. He tried to smile as Kate walked in his room remembering his friendship with her since coming to Wiluna.

She sat down by his bed noting the ashen color of his face and his labored breathing.

He reached a hand toward her and she gently took it in both of hers and said.

"Hobbs, I'm so sorry to see you laid up here like this and not feeling well but knowing you I reckon you'll be out of here in a day or two fit as a fiddle and back on the wire again."

In his eyes she could see he knew he didn't have long to live and had something he wanted to tell her. She leaned close and his weak voice came barely above a whisper. "Kate I want you to go to my place and," He hesitated as his breathing became more labored, "and go in th little room next to th freezer room where th caskets are, in one corner is one that was damaged in shipping, the casket company settled wit me but said they didn't want it shipped back to them, it stands on end in one corner against th wall."

"Tell th young man Ronald to open th lid and reach under a blanket to th foot and lift out a black leather case and I want you," He had to stop again from lack of air but finally went on. "I want you to take it to Herbert at th bank, when he opens it he will find a note on top of a pile of money, th note has instructions to send th money to th Sydney bank, Herbert knows all about how to do that. You see th money belongs to th Sydney bank, Layton walked away with it but had a change of heart after me and him had a talk, th moneys all there he never spent any of it. Layton worked at th Sydney bank and had access to th vault and th temptation finally got th best of him, he didn't use a gun to hold up th bank but I reckon he took th money so what's th difference?"

He paused again before he could go on, as she held his hand she could feel the coldness and wondered if he would live long enough to complete the story.

"I hid th case in th casket with th note, we thought about sending th money back but that would have made it easier to trace Layton so we decided to hold on to it until after one of us died then th one left behind could unload it before his death if he could see it coming, and I reckon it's time to give it up. I reckon I'm proud that I talked Layton out of it and he went on to be a good citizen out on th Twisted Track where he found th Lord or maybe the other way around th master found him, I av a checkered past Kate, ten years of my life I spent behind bars, after I pulled my time I wondered all over th land but finally put down here in Wiluna where I have made many friends and lived a good life."

"Layton meant a lot to me and I didn't want him to follow in my footsteps, go to prison and live in shame because he's my" She felt his hand go limp and seen his eyes close before he could finish the sentence.

They buried him in the Wiluna cemetery. He and the young embalmer Ronald had already made arrangements at the bank for him to take over the funeral home at his death. Young Ronald was visibly shaken by Hobbs death. A few days later he came in the hotel lobby carrying a bible and stood at Kate's desk. She asked him to sit down.

"I'm pretty busy this morning," he said. "But I need to tell you something about Hobbs and it won't take long, He had a good bit of savings stashed away in his living quarters that he entrusted to me in case of his death. His instructions were to divide the money between the Wiluna church and the school system, his wishes were that the donor remain anonymous but I believe it's better for the citizens to know of the goodness that dwelled in this mans heart, I turned it over to Herbert at the bank with instructions that he divide it and reveal the donor as Hobbs. He told me he changed his name to Hobbs when he came here because of his past, he said he thought it would be better to start all over again with a new name, his real name is Palmer, he said his father and mother died many years ago and are buried in Sydney.

He stood to go and handed her the bible "I found this bible hid away at the bottom of the casket under a blanket, it must have belonged to his mother and since you were one of his best friends I believe he would be pleased to know that I gave it to you." She thanked him for stopping by and sharing the goodness of Hobbs, "And this bible," She said. "I'll always treasure it."

As he walked away, her thoughts were, 'Hobbs could never have found a finer young man than him to keep the funeral home going here in Wiluna.'

Then she opened the bible to read the names, dates of birth, and death of the parents. Both died young.

Richard Palmer Sr. Born May 10 1890 Died April 14 1943 Florence 'Stapleton' Palmer Born December 28 1892 Died June 11 1947. Then the two names below which would be their children. Richard Palmer Jr. Born July 7 1916 Vincent Palmer Born October 20 1920.

She looked up at Maxine who had been standing watching.

"Now I know what Hobbs was trying to say just before he died Maxine, Layton was his brother."

"Layton Bailey was Hobbs brother?"

"Yes Maxine Richard Hobbs and Layton Bailey were names we knew them by, but their real names were Richard Palmer Jr. and Vincent Palmer and they were brothers."

Now its March 2005, the azaleas are in full bloom here in Brooksville Florida the orange trees are sprinkled with white buds that will soon be in full bloom spreading a distinct fragrance over the land that signifies new life to the trees after a cool dormant winter. Age-old rituals that restore hope among us mortals.

Yesterday I spent some time at the little village of Bay Port where the Weeki Wachee river flows into the Gulf Of Mexico just watching the boats as they made their way out in the gulf to deeper waters for a day of fishing. I used to take my wife there, roll her wheelchair on the fishing pier and watch her expressions as a great blue heron or a pelican walked the rails on the fishing pier mooching bait from the fishermen.

She could no longer talk and carry on a conversation so I would sit and watch her trying to get some idea of the things that go through a persons mind ravaged by deadly

Alzheimer's disease, Sometimes amusement would show in her eyes but only to be replaced by sadness moments later.

She died in 1999 and I continued to go there often to while the day away pretending that she, just like the outgoing boats would return at the setting of the sun. But now I don't go there very often because I feel her presence more when I'm here at home alone.

Yesterday as I watched the boats speeding out in the gulf leaving a wavy wake behind and finally drop out of sight I realized the wake that a boat leaves behind or the vapor trail from a jet plane being spread across the skies until it disappears is much like a loved ones legacy and memories that live on after they're gone, some of them warm close and amusing that will always cause us to smile but others sad and make us feel more like crying

I guess that's the way I feel today as I finish up this manuscript titled 'BackNtime'

I hate to give them up after being present in their journey through life but they're all gone leaving me sad and about to cry as I try to put a finish to something that has consumed me for the better part of two and one half years.

Sugar, Bud, Tex sr., Marty, Reba, Cam, Wayne 'Poor Boy' Burke, Julie, Ann, Curt Boyd, Brad Crawford, Burl and Laura, Doc, bless his soul, Larry Witt, The Lee County sheriff, the Harlan County sheriff, Thomas and Lance Kirk, Cal and Alice Finley, Kate, Chung, Maxine, Hobbs, Layton Bailey, Seth, Mum, Travis Yost, Shane Daugherty, Radford Easy, Herbert, Burgin, and Warp Broderick

They're all gone leaving behind images and memories that are a constant in my daily life. A lesson they taught me is, don't be too hasty to judge others because as the old saying goes, 'There's good in everyone' but I must admit I failed to find any good at all in The Big Brave Lad, Hoss, or The Bounty Hunter, maybe it was there, if so it was well hidden because as far as I know no one ever found it.

The Twisted Track is now headed by, Lance and Reba's son Thomas, keeping the Kirk tradition going. The other son Cal early on chose to go to

Melbourne to further his education and is now a successful lawyer in the city of Perth. He brings his family to The Twisted Track once a year to spend two weeks away from the city and show them a different way of life.

And as he walks among the tombstones on the knoll he secretly wishes he had not ever left because he was never cut out to live in a city, but he realizes he made his own bed at a young age and is now required to sleep in it, as the saying goes.

Travis Yost and his wife are both buried in Texas. They went back there to take care of his ailing mother and left the station in care of their children. None of them was up to the task of running the Bonny Blue station and as it is in any family witnessing a failing business they began to squabble as to how it should be run. And In the end Travis had to let it go, a life times dream that he and his wife had worked so hard for turned out to be a sad memory that followed them to their graves.

Two of their children came to live in Texas while the other two stayed in Australia now living In Perth.

Tex jr. and his wife Brenda handed over the Big Easy station in Queensland to their two sons and are now world travelers only spending two months out of the year in their private quarters at the Big Easy.

Their oldest William 'Warp' rules the station with an iron hand and is the spitting image of the William 'Warp' Broderick before him.

Herbert shipped the money laden leather case to the bank in Sydney with a letter explaining that Layton had died. The bank president wanted to send a reward to Kate she accepted but then assigned it over to the Wiluna school. She had no living relatives that she knew of so as she grew older she began to plan who would benefit from her estate after she died. The day after her funeral Herbert the banker summoned Chung and Maxine.

"Kate left a will," he said. "Her savings will be divided between the church and school here in Wiluna. She had a clear deed to the hotel and instructed me to do all the paper work and deed it over to you two. Her wishes are that you will operate and keep the hotel respectable just as she did for so many years."

Maxine and Chung were elated but as time went on they began to disagree as to how the hotel should be run, mostly Chung, he was never satisfied with any of Maxine's input.

Pretty soon the hotel became more like a boarding house. Then a newcomer to town with money to spare offered to buy them out, Maxine agreed to his offer but Chung held out for months before finally coming around to his terms.

Maxine stayed on for another year to help get the hotel back to respectability again.

Chung packed up his and his wife's few belongings and left town, they wound up in Perth where he bought into a laundry and later bought out his partner. After he and his wife died their two children, a boy and a girl took over the laundry and are still there, now with children of their own that will someday take over the business and keep Chung's tradition alive.

And with the passing of Herbert the banker, and Burgin the livery stable owner, Wiluna began to change, new faces and new names ushered in new ways, progressive? Maybe so maybe not depending on who you asked, the young sure, but the old never want to give up their ways to a new generation no matter how much easier it might make things in their lives.

The Canning Stock Route is still challenged by hearty souls driving expensive all terrain vehicles trying to get from one point to another so they can brag about it, but they often wind up with a broken vehicle or mired in a bog and come away distressed and beaten. The water hole is about the same as it was the day Warp died there, at one level the air is filled with dragon flies, hornets, and mozzie's, while higher up the buzzards are circling in watch for a dead carcass to feed on. Another flock of colorful birds perch in a tree talking amongst themselves just like the flocks before them. The songbirds are singing age-old tunes that have been handed down to them and they don't miss a note.

Chirp chirping comes from a dense patch of underbrush as a mother bird stuffs food into the little mouths of her babies.

A mother kangaroo scratches the dirt under a shade tree trying to make it a little cooler to lay on, her baby stares warily from her pouch. A dingo lurks back in the brush sizing up the group before him and will surely attack the weakest.

High in the tallest tree a red tail hawk's sharp eyes surveys the scene below him and finally rests on his prey. Near waters edge close to the chirp chirping a long slender snake slithers through the tall sparse grass ever closer to the mother bird feeding her babies, enough there to satisfy his need for food at least one week.

The red tail hawk releases his grip on the tree limb and dives down toward his daily meal. He lands with precision grasping his prey in sharp claws and in a flash rising to tree top level again.

Two long legged wading birds along with a half dozen ducks flap their wings and skim across the water disturbed by the hawk's sudden dive.

A dozen cattle, three steers, one bull, the rest cows with young calves stand in knee deep water unmoved by the hawk and are busy swishing their tails to keep the flies away.

The hawk has now climbed to a greater height and the snake dangles from his talons as he flies away to his habitat to enjoy his catch. The baby birds are spared to live another day and beyond if they're lucky, but the snake fell prey to the red tail hawk, just as it's always been around the water hole, death and birth comes daily the cycle never changes.

Off to the east two ringers from The Bonny Blue station ride toward the water hole looking for strays.

A man with the name Wesley Brewster, bought the station from Travis and made it into a successful operation again. And like so many before him he taught his oldest son how to manage a station and now in his old age he takes pride in watching his son manage the station in the way he taught him.

At the water hole the two ringers went different directions circled the hole and met on the other side just as the two ringers had done the day Warp died. They bunched the cattle together maybe two dozen and herded them east toward the Bonny Blue station paddock where the newborn calves will have the Bonny Blue brand burned to their hides with the same branding irons that Travis Yost used sixty years earlier.

Yes some things never change, like when the telephone rings in the middle of the night and you answer and hear a voice on the other end that you know must bear bad news about a loved one, just this morning I got word one of my aging aunts died in Virginia. That leaves me with four aunts and one uncle still living, I seen them all in 2004 my aunts are wobbly on their feet and basically worn out.

The day I called on my uncle I knocked on his door and heard him whistling as he came to the door, once inside I could smell the aroma of good food cooking, I followed him to the kitchen to see two steaming pots on the stove. He grabbed a towel and said, "Let me check on my cornbread in th oven, oh yeah it's about done, sit down there at the table and we'll have a bite to eat here shortly." I begged off because I had just had a meal at a restaurant.

We talked on and on about this and that and I was amazed how sharp his mind was at the age of ninety two but when I got up to go I remarked how well he looked. "Oh yeah," he said I guess I'm in pretty good shape to be one hundred two."

"Are you that old?" I asked, knowing that he was only ninety two I thought he might be kidding, but his answer was, "Yes sir one hundred and two and I'm still kicking."

Then I realized his mind had strayed a bit since the last time I saw him, but on my way to the car I could hear the rattling of pans coming from his kitchen as he whistled a happy tune. Then I thought, 'He's slipping a bit but at least he's happy.'

I should have added aging to death and dieing to 'some things never change' As I told you in the prologue at the beginning I am the oldest of thirteen children born in 1926, you do the math, at this writing all thirteen are still living, some like myself have had health problem's but are still hanging on. We have been blessed with medical advances that have taken place during our lifetime that add more years to our lives which is fine if we don't have to suffer, but that's one other thing to add to 'some things never change' because many are still suffering and dieing a slow death.

I woke up to a cold rainy morning and it has continued into the afternoon, the temperature hasn't reached 50 degrees all day, unusual for Florida, no sunshine and depressing which only adds to the way I feel about ending this and giving up all the characters I have walked with as they filled these pages with their past, their good sides as well as the bad. I feel that my life has been much like theirs and I can relate to them. As a soldier in World War Two among a carefree bunch of young warriors I along with others used some foul language much worse than Wayne 'Poor Boy' Burke became addicted to, but gave it up after the war. Now if some one should use a certain four-letter word in my house I would show them the door.

And like Warp I have been known to be stubborn, I have many flaws that I intend to keep to myself, and like Warp said "I've only told you jist a smidgeon about me self."

Well I reckon I'm glad that I'm down to a few more sentences and this journey will be over. But I'm already feeling pangs of loneliness that I know is bound to set in when I realize that Tex Sr., Doc 'bless his soul', Brad, Witt,

Hobbs, Layton. Chung, Kate, Warp, Poor Boy, Julie, Sugar, and all the rest are now fading memories that I would like to keep alive. The one that caused me the most anguish was Julie, I had my doubts about her but in the end she became the person I'd hoped she would.

And Wayne 'Poor Boy' Burke I prayed he would overcome his cussing habit but it never happened, could be that was the way it was supposed to work out because taking that away would have been taking from his character, and that ugly mutt of his 'Peanut' I became attached to him as if he were my own.

He invested in several orange groves in Central Florida in the 1970's and lost a lot of money when unusual cold weather killed all the trees. He replanted but in a few short years along came another freeze and he lost them again. He sold his land to developers as did many others and now what was once orange groves as far as you could see is covered with homes and businesses. But even with that set back he died a very wealthy man. His son Wayne Jr. owns a horse farm in the blue grass section near Lexington, Kentucky that he appropriately named "Poor Boy's Farm" in remembrance of his dad.

And Warp, I suffered with him through the nights as he poured down the yellowtail wine trying to relieve himself of the terrible pain of Alice showing up at the Twisted Track and to him the only solution had to be The Canning Stock Route. I tried to steer him away from that thought but to no avail, Warp and his ways could not be swayed.

Shortly after his death the ringers began to whisper among themselves, "Th lady Alice, she be nurse in World War One, and th chap Tex, he look and act like Warp, I reckon Warp is his mother's father he is, now I see why Warp went on th Yellowtail and ended it all out there on th Canning Route."

As time went on everyone on The Twisted Track knew about it including Reba and Tex Jr. and soon the word spread to Wiluna and beyond.

If anyone should have any doubts all they have to do is travel to the Big Easy station in Queensland and witness Tex son Warp, as he goes about his duties of running the Big Easy station. Six foot seven inches tall, long bowed legs that his large sheep dog walks through just like old Rogue did with Warp before him.

As one ringer put it, "My word, I reckon old Warp didn't die he jist rode off to Queensland."

Well it's still rainy, cold, and growing dark outside and as I finish this I'm becoming more depressed and feel like crying, so excuse me I reckon I'll do just that, so long Warp, Lance, Tex, Poor Boy, Julie, and all the rest, I'm gonna miss ye, and yore memories will always be near me heart.

Printed in the United States
61027LVS00003B/37